'Le Guin writ[...] are complex a[...] its sinewy gra[...] *Time*

'Le Guin is a writer of phenomenal power. She sets up enormous challenges and meets them fully; she invites, as Tolkien does, total belief' *Observer*

'She is unique. She is legend' *The Times*

'An important writer, period' *Washington Post*

'I read her nonstop growing up and read her still'
Junot Diaz, Pulitzer Prize-winning author

'A wonderfully mordant analyst of human weakness. The gems in this impressive collection have the same power to disconcert as her best novels' Martin Amis

'Ursula Le Guin's prose breathes light and intelligence. She can lift fiction to the highest level of poetry and compress it to the density of allegory' Jonathan Lethem

SF MASTERWORKS

The Wind's Twelve Quarters

and

The Compass Rose

URSULA K. LE GUIN

The Wind's Twelve Quarters copyright © Ursula K. Le Guin 1975
The Compass Rose copyright © Ursula K. Le Guin 1982
Introduction copyright © Graham Sleight 2015
All rights reserved

The right of Ursula K. Le Guin to be identified as the author
of this work, and the right of Graham Sleight to be identified as
the author of the introduction, have been asserted by them in
accordance with the Copyright, Designs and Patents Act 1988.

This edition first published in Great Britain in 2015 by
Gollancz
An imprint of the Orion Publishing Group
Carmelite House, 50 Victoria Embankment, London EC4Y 0DZ
An Hachette UK Company

5 7 9 10 8 6

A CIP catalogue record for this book
is available from the British Library

ISBN 978 1 473 20576 5

Typeset at The Spartan Press Ltd,
Lymington, Hants.

Printed in Great Britain by
Clays Ltd, Elcograf S.p.A.

The Orion Publishing Group's policy is to use papers that
are natural, renewable and recyclable products and made
from wood grown in sustainable forests. The logging and
manufacturing processes are expected to conform to the
environmental regulations of the country of origin.

www.orionbooks.co.uk
www.gollancz.co.uk

INTRODUCTION

In the last story of this book, 'Sur' (1982), the narrator says of the expedition that she and her colleagues are undertaking, 'Our goal was limited to observation and exploration.' That could stand as a motto for many of the stories here. They're not about victory, conquest, or becoming ruler of the universe. They are, however, remarkable for the range of experiences they embody and comment on. There's nothing 'limited' about them, or about what they show observation and exploration can do. Indeed, given what the expedition in 'Sur' entails, there's a bit of irony attached to that 'limited'. Who gets to judge what's limited and what's not?

This book contains two volumes of Ursula K. Le Guin's short fiction. The first, *The Wind's Twelve Quarters*, was published in 1975 and contains fiction dating from 1962 to 1974. The second, *The Compass Rose*, was published in 1982, and contains fiction from 1974 to 1982. The dates are important because of where these collections sit in Le Guin's long career. As she says, the 1962 story 'April in Paris' was the first for which she was ever paid. She began publishing novels in 1966, with her Hugo and Nebula-Award winning *The Left Hand of Darkness* appearing in 1969. Her **Earthsea** fantasy trilogy was published between 1968 and 1972. *The Dispossessed*, also a Hugo and Nebula-winner, was published in 1974. Both *The Dispossessed* and *The Left Hand of Darkness* share the setting of her 'Hainish' universe, as do several of the stories herein. After 1974, she pursued a wider range of settings and voices. She wrote and collected a series of

stories set in the fictional European country of 'Orsinia'. She also published volumes of poetry and literary criticism – yet, as the work collected here demonstrates, she never abandoned an interest in SF and fantasy.

Several of the stories included here are famous, and not just in the SF world. 'The Ones Who Walk Away from Omelas' (1973), for instance, puts into definitive form a particular question about society and the price of living the good life. Elsewhere, Le Guin uses the term 'psychomyth' to denote 'a story outside real time, past or future', and this is certainly one. What's so striking on rereading it is how much time the story gives to the seeming Utopia of Omelas, so that it's possible to see both sides of the argument. Le Guin says that the next story, 'The Day Before the Revolution' (1974), is about one of the people who walked away from Omelas – that is, someone who refused the assumptions of her society. The SF writer Geoff Ryman has coined the term 'fictions of refusal' for stories like this, stories that are not prepared to accept the world as it is. Readers of *The Dispossessed* will know that the refusal in this story is the root of that novel's anarchist Utopia. Elsewhere, the much-reprinted 'Nine Lives' (1969) takes the standard SF trope of the clone, and follows through its implications to a devastating conclusion. 'The New Atlantis' (1975) depicts a dystopian USA that now seems closer to home than ever. But there are also interludes from a distant country that seems to be rising from beneath the sea. What, the story asks, could these two very different worlds have to say to each other?

There are many less well-known stories here that deserve to be better known. For instance, 'SQ' (1978), depicts a world where psychology has become a kind of totalitarian language. 'The Diary of the Rose' (1976) covers some similar questions, though with a different spin: the narrator's gradual change of perspective shapes this tale. There are a couple of stories where our standard perspectives are turned on their heads, such as 'Direction of the Road' (1974) and 'Mazes' (1975). And it's especially refreshing to encounter a couple of stories

where Le Guin allows her sense of humour to run free, such as 'Intracom' (1974) and 'Some Approaches to the Problem of the Shortage of Time' (1979).

There are a number of common threads running through these stories, which it might be worth drawing out. An obvious one is exploration, and trying to understand another, different culture and world-view. This is especially apparent in the two long stories 'Vaster than Empires and More Slow' (1971) and 'The Pathways of Desire' (1979). It's a commonplace to say that Le Guin's fiction is often anthropological in its approach. However, that glosses over what she does in these two stories. By using the possibilities of SF, the process of exploration she describes – and the cognitive adjustment it requires – becomes very much more radical than we might have imagined. The sheer strangeness and difficulty of coming to terms with other-ness is vividly set out here.

Another striking element common to many of these stories is solitude: the number of characters who, either by their own choice or because of the facts of the world, have to live as a community of one. Consider Kaph, for instance, in 'Nine Lives', Osden in 'Vaster than Empires and More Slow', or the astronomer Guennar in 'The Stars Below' (1973). Related to this is exile – for instance, that of the protagonist in 'Winter's King' (1969) or the community in 'The Eye Altering' (1974). All of these stories ask, in one way or another, how it might be possible to come to terms with a solitude or exile of this kind. (The same argument could also be made about the story of Shevek, the protagonist of *The Dispossessed*.)

Every exile carries journeys with it: the journey made to the exile, the journey not made back from it. There are many other stories here where other journeys have central import-ance – although hardly ever the importance that's expected when they begin. That's certainly the case in 'Two Delays on the Northern Line' (1979) and 'The Water is Wide' (1981). 'A Trip to the Head' (1970) ends with a journey whose outcome

can hardly be described in words; 'Sur' is the account of a remarkable yet unknown journey.

Finally, I think that the central idea in many of these stories is how the individual defines themselves against a world or a culture that may not believe the same things they do. Sometimes the individual may be able to step outside the value-system in which they find themselves; sometimes, not. Sometimes, they may find a group or a community which shares those values. If not, solitude and internal exile may be the only option. So Le Guin has an obvious interest in power: how it is exercised, what it might mean to exercise it in an ethical way, and how its use affects ordinary people. These stories are often distant from the throne-rooms of the world, but the effects of decisions taken there are often very present.

One obvious way in which the world has – and continues to – exert power over people is through structures that offer men preferment and societal advancement over women. This, I take it, is the central argument of 'Sur': a corrective to those histories of the world that are records of the deeds of men. The story's Antarctic expedition *could* have taken place – yet how would we know? In the early 20th century, it suggests, women's deeds and achievements were relegated to the margins of what was recorded. (A much later Le Guin story, 'Fragments from the Women's Writing' (1993) makes a similar point very movingly.) Where else, 'Sur' asks, might the footprints of women be getting ignored?

But reducing these stories to themes or abstract ideas would be to do them a disservice. There's much else to enjoy here – for a start, the sheer range of registers and settings that Le Guin uses. It's also interesting to see how much these stories exist in dialogue with other science fiction. As an example, 'Vaster than Empires and More Slow' exists both as a First Contact story and a critique of some of the assumptions made by its predecessors in the genre. It's fascinating to see, in her story notes for *The Wind's Twelve Quarters*, how much Le Guin

considers issues of technique, or into which genre a given story might fit.

In November 2014, Le Guin was awarded the Medal for Distinguished Contribution to American Letters. She gave a widely-reported speech in acceptance of the award – partly setting out her anger at the current pressures on writers and publishers, and partly setting out a credo for her own work:

> *Hard times are coming, when we'll be wanting the voices of writers who can see alternatives to how we live now, can see through our fear-stricken society and its obsessive technologies to other ways of being, and even imagine real grounds for hope. We'll need writers who can remember freedom – poets, visionaries – realists of a larger reality.*
>
> *[...]*
>
> *Books aren't just commodities; the profit motive is often in conflict with the aims of art. We live in capitalism, its power seems inescapable – but then, so did the divine right of kings. Any human power can be resisted and changed by human beings. Resistance and change often begin in art. Very often in our art, the art of words.*

These stories demonstrate how Le Guin has undertaken that work – and, indeed, she continues to. The narrator of 'Sur', whom I quoted at the start, goes on to say that, 'We hoped to go a little farther, perhaps, and see a little more; if not, simply, to go and see.' To go and see can, in itself, be a revolutionary act if you see as fully and clearly as these stories do.

<div align="right">Graham Sleight</div>

The Wind's
Twelve Quarters

'*Semley's Necklace*' originally appeared under the title '*The Dowry of the Angyar*' in *Amazing*, 1964.

'*April in Paris*' originally appeared in *Fantastic*, 1962.

'*The Masters*' and '*Darkness Box*' originally appeared in *Fantastic*, 1963.

'*The Word of Unbinding*' and '*The Rule of Names*' originally appeared in *Fantastic*, 1964.

'*Winter's King*' originally appeared in *Orbit 5*, 1969.

'*The Good Trip*' originally appeared in *Fantastic*, 1970.

'*Nine Lives*' originally appeared in *Playboy*, 1969.

'*Things*' originally appeared under the title '*The End*' in *Orbit 6*, 1970.

'*A Trip to the Head*' originally appeared in *Quark 1*, 1970.

'*Vaster than Empires and More Slow*' originally appeared in *New Dimensions 1*, 1971.

'*The Stars Below*' originally appeared in *Orbit 12*, 1973.

'*The Field of Vision*' originally appeared in *Galaxy*, 1973.

'*Direction of the Road*' originally appeared in *Orbit 14*, 1974.

'*The Ones Who Walk Away From Omelas*' originally appeared in *New Dimensions*, 1973.

'*The Day Before the Revolution*' originally appeared in *Galaxy*, 1974.

Excerpt from A. E. Housman's *A Shropshire Lad* reprinted by permission of Cambridge University Press.

From far, from eve and morning
 And yon twelve-winded sky,
The stuff of life to knit me
 Blew hither; here am I.

Now – for a breath I tarry
 Nor yet disperse apart—
Take my hand quick and tell me,
 What have you in your heart.

Speak now, and I will answer;
 How shall I help you, say;
Ere to the wind's twelve quarters
 I take my endless way.

A. E. Housman: *A Shropshire Lad*

CONTENTS

FOREWORD

This collection is what painters call a retrospective; it gives a roughly chronological survey of my short stories during the first ten years after I broke into print, belated but undaunted, at the age of thirty-two. They appear here very roughly in the order in which they were written, so that the development of the artist may become part of the interest of the book. I have not been rigid about the chronology (it is impossible; stories may be written in one year, not published until two or three years later, and then possibly revised, and which date do you use?) but there are no severe displacements.

It is by no means a complete collection of my stories. One early story is left out because I don't much like it; fiction which doesn't fit under the headings Fantasy or Science Fiction is not included; and most of my stories published in the last few years are not in this book, because the anthologies in which they first appeared are still in print. The last two in the volume, however, appeared in 1973 and 1974, so the seventeen stories do cover the last ten or a dozen years.

The relation between short story and novel, inside the writer's head, is interesting. 'Semley's Necklace,' though a complete story in itself, was the germ of a novel. I had done with Semley when I finished it, but there was a minor character, a mere bystander, who did not sink back obediently into obscurity when the story was done, but who kept nagging me. 'Write *my* story,' he said. 'I'm Rocannon. I want to explore my world...' So I obeyed him. You really can't argue with these people.

'Winter's King' was another such germinal story, and so were 'The Word of Unbinding' and 'The Rule of Names,' though all of them gave me the place, rather than the person, for the novels to come. The last story in the book is not a germinal but an autumnal one. It came after the novel, a final gift, received with thanksgiving.

Most of the straight narrative stories in this volume are in fact connected with my novels, in that they fit more or less well into the rather erratic 'future history' scheme which all my science fiction books follow. Those that don't fit in are the early fantasies, and then later the ones I call psychomyths, more or less surrealistic tales, which share with fantasy the quality of taking place outside any history, outside of time, in that region of the living mind which – without invoking any consideration of immortality – seems to be without spatial or temporal limits at all.

Collectors might want to know that the titles used in this volume are my own choice, in some cases varying from previous publications:

'Semley's Necklace' first appeared as 'Dowry of the Angyar' (a grammatical error by the editor, who didn't speak Angyo fluently);

'Things' appeared as 'The End';

'The Field of Vision' appeared as 'Field of Vision.'

The only stories that have been revised, beyond an occasional one-word or one-sentence change and restitution of cuts and errors in the published versions, are:

'Winter's King' (see note to the story);

'Vaster than Empires and More Slow' (a cut in the first pages);

'Nine Lives' (see note to the story).

SEMLEY'S NECKLACE

This story, written in 1963, published as 'Dowry of the Angyar' in 1964 and as the Prologue of my first novel, Rocannon's World, *in 1966, was actually the eighth story I got printed; but it opens the book because I think it's the most characteristic of my early science fiction and fantasy works, the most romantic of them all. The progress of my style has been away from open romanticism, slowly and steadily, from this story to the last one in the volume, written in 1972. It has been a progress. I am still a romantic, no doubt about that, and glad of it, but the candor and simplicity of 'Semley's Necklace' have gradually become something harder, stronger, and more complex.*

How can you tell the legend from the fact on these worlds that lie so many years away? – planets without names, called by their people simply The World, planets without history, where the past is the matter of myth, and a returning explorer finds his own doings of a few years back have become the gestures of a god. Unreason darkens that gap of time bridged by our lightspeed ships, and in the darkness uncertainty and disproportion grow like weeds.

In trying to tell the story of a man, an ordinary League scientist, who went to such a nameless half-known world not many years ago, one feels like an archaeologist amid millennial ruins, now struggling through choked tangles of leaf, flower, branch and vine to the sudden bright geometry of a wheel or a polished cornerstone, and now entering some commonplace, sunlit doorway to find inside it the darkness, the impossible

flicker of a flame, the glitter of a jewel, the half-glimpsed movement of a woman's arm.

How can you tell fact from legend, truth from truth?

Through Rocannon's story the jewel, the blue glitter seen briefly, returns. With it let us begin, here:

Galactic Area 8, No. 62: FOMALHAUT II.
High-Intelligence Life Forms: Species Contacted:
Species I.

A. Gdemiar (singular Gdem): Highly intelligent, fully hominoid nocturnal troglodytes, 120–135 cm. in height, light skin, dark head-hair. When contacted these cave-dwellers possessed a rigidly stratified oligarchic urban society modified by partial colonial telepathy, and a technologically oriented Early Steel culture. Technology enhanced to Industrial, Point C, during League Mission of 252–254. In 254 an Automatic Drive ship (to-from New South Georgia) was presented to oligarchs of the Kiriensea Area community. Status C-Prime.

B. Füia (singular Fian): Highly intelligent, fully hominoid, diurnal, av. ca. 130 cm. in height, observed individuals generally light in skin and hair. Brief contacts indicated village and nomadic communal societies, partial colonial telepathy, also some indication of short-range TK. The race appears a-technological and evasive, with minimal and fluid culture-patterns. Currently untaxable. Status E-Query.

Species II.

Liuar (singular Liu): Highly intelligent, fully hominoid, diurnal, av. height above 170 cm., this species possesses a fortress/village, clan-descent society, a blocked technology (Bronze), and feudal-heroic culture. Note horizontal social cleavage into 2 pseudo-races: (a) Olgyior, 'midmen,' light-skinned and dark-haired; (b) Angyar, 'lords,' very tall, dark-skinned, yellow-haired—

'That's her,' said Rocannon, looking up from the *Abridged Handy Pocket Guide to Intelligent Life-forms* at the very tall, dark-skinned, yellow-haired woman who stood halfway down the long museum hall. She stood still and erect, crowned with bright

hair, gazing at something in a display case. Around her fidgeted four uneasy and unattractive dwarves.

'I didn't know Fomalhaut II had all those people besides the trogs,' said Ketho, the curator.

'I didn't either. There are even some "Unconfirmed" species listed here, that they never contacted. Sounds like time for a more thorough survey mission to the place. Well, now at least we know what she is.'

'I wish there were some way of knowing *who* she is . . .'

She was of an ancient family, a descendant of the first kings of the Angyar, and for all her poverty her hair shone with the pure, steadfast gold of her inheritance. The little people, the Fiia, bowed when she passed them, even when she was a barefoot child running in the fields, the light and fiery comet of her hair brightening the troubled winds of Kirien.

She was still very young when Durhal of Hallan saw her, courted her, and carried her away from the ruined towers and windy halls of her childhood to his own high home. In Hallan on the mountainside there was no comfort either, though splendor endured. The windows were unglassed, the stone floors bare; in coldyear one might wake to see the night's snow in long, low drifts beneath each window. Durhal's bride stood with narrow bare feet on the snowy floor, braiding up the fire of her hair and laughing at her young husband in the silver mirror that hung in their room. That mirror, and his mother's bridal-gown sewn with a thousand tiny crystals, were all his wealth. Some of his lesser kinfolk of Hallan still possessed wardrobes of brocaded clothing, furniture of gilded wood, silver harness for their steeds, armor and silver mounted swords, jewels and jewelry – and on these last Durhal's bride looked enviously, glancing back at a gemmed coronet or a golden brooch even when the wearer of the ornament stood aside to let her pass, deferent to her birth and marriage-rank.

Fourth from the High Seat of Hallan Revel sat Durhal and his bride Semley, so close to Hallanlord that the old man

often poured wine for Semley with his own hand, and spoke of hunting with his nephew and heir Durhal, looking on the young pair with a grim, unhopeful love. Hope came hard to the Angyar of Hallan and all the Western Lands, since the Starlords had appeared with their houses that leaped about on pillars of fire and their awful weapons that could level hills. They had interfered with all the old ways and wars, and though the sums were small there was terrible shame to the Angyar in having to pay a tax to them, a tribute for the Starlords' war that was to be fought with some strange enemy, somewhere in the hollow places between the stars, at the end of years. 'It will be your war too,' they said, but for a generation now the Angyar had sat in idle shame in their revel-halls, watching their double swords rust, their sons grow up without ever striking a blow in battle, their daughters marry poor men, even midmen, having no dowry of heroic loot to bring a noble husband. Hallanlord's face was bleak when he watched the fair-haired couple and heard their laughter as they drank bitter wine and joked together in the cold, ruinous, resplendent fortress of their race.

Semley's own face hardened when she looked down the hall and saw, in seats far below hers, even down among the halfbreeds and the midmen, against white skins and black hair, the gleam and flash of precious stones. She herself had brought nothing in dowry to her husband, not even a silver hairpin. The dress of a thousand crystals she had put away in a chest for the wedding-day of her daughter, if daughter it was to be.

It was, and they called her Haldre, and when the fuzz on her little brown skull grew longer it shone with steadfast gold, the inheritance of the lordly generations, the only gold she would ever possess...

Semley did not speak to her husband of her discontent. For all his gentleness to her, Durhal in his pride had only contempt for envy, for vain wishing, and she dreaded his contempt. But she spoke to Durhal's sister Durossa.

'My family had a great treasure once,' she said. 'It was a

4

necklace all of gold, with the blue jewel set in the center – sapphire?'

Durossa shook her head, smiling, not sure of the name either. It was late in warmyear, as these Northern Angyar called the summer of the eight-hundred-day year, beginning the cycle of months anew at each equinox; to Semley it seemed an outlandish calendar, a midmannish reckoning. Her family was at an end, but it had been older and purer than the race of any of these north-western marchlanders, who mixed too freely with the Olgyior. She sat with Durossa in the sunlight on a stone windowseat high up in the Great Tower, where the older woman's apartment was. Widowed young, childless, Durossa had been given in second marriage to Hallanlord, who was her father's brother. Since it was a kinmarriage and a second marriage on both sides she had not taken the title of Hallanlady, which Semley would some day bear; but she sat with the old lord in the High Seat and ruled with him his domains. Older than her brother Durhal, she was fond of his young wife, and delighted in the bright-haired baby Haldre.

'It was bought,' Semley went on, 'with all the money my forebear Leynen got when he conquered the Southern Fiefs – all the money from a whole kingdom, think of it, for one jewel! Oh, it would outshine anything here in Hallan, surely, even those crystals like koob-eggs your cousin Issar wears. It was so beautiful they gave it a name of its own; they called it the Eye of the Sea. My great-grandmother wore it.'

'You never saw it?' the older woman asked lazily, gazing down at the green mountainslopes where long, long summer sent its hot and restless winds straying among the forests and whirling down white roads to the seacoast far away.

'It was lost before I was born.'

'No, my father said it was stolen before the Starlords ever came to our realm. He wouldn't talk of it, but there was an old mid-woman full of tales who always told me the Fiia would know where it was.'

'Ah, the Fiia I should like to see!' said Durossa. 'They're

in so many songs and tales; why do they never come to the Western Lands?'

'Too high, too cold in winter, I think. They like the sunlight of the valleys of the south.'

'Are they like the Clayfolk?'

'Those I've never seen; they keep away from us in the south. Aren't they white like midmen, and misformed? The Fiia are fair; they look like children, only thinner, and wiser. Oh, I wonder if they know where the necklace is, who stole it and where he hid it! Think, Durossa – if I could come into Hallan Revel and sit down by my husband with the wealth of a kingdom round my neck, and outshine the other women as he outshines all men!'

Durossa bent her head above the baby, who sat studying her own brown toes on a fur rug between her mother and aunt. 'Semley is foolish,' she murmured to the baby; 'Semley who shines like a falling star, Semley whose husband loves no gold but the gold of her hair...'

And Semley, looking out over the green slopes of summer toward the distant sea, was silent.

But when another coldyear had passed, and the Starlords had come again to collect their taxes for the war against the world's end – this time using a couple of dwarfish Clayfolk as interpreters, and so leaving all the Angyar humiliated to the point of rebellion – and another warmyear too was gone, and Haldre had grown into a lovely, chattering child, Semley brought her one morning to Durossa's sunlit room in the tower. Semley wore an old cloak of blue, and the hood covered her hair.

'Keep Haldre for me these few days, Durossa,' she said, quick and calm. 'I'm going south to Kirien.'

'To see your father?'

'To find my inheritance. Your cousins of Harget Fief have been taunting Durhal. Even that halfbreed Parna can torment him, because Parna's wife has a satin coverlet for her bed, and a diamond earring, and three gowns, the dough-faced

6

black-haired trollop! while Durhal's wife must patch her gown—'

'Is Durhal's pride in his wife, or what she wears?'

But Semley was not to be moved. 'The Lords of Hallan are becoming poor men in their own hall. I am going to bring my dowry to my lord, as one of my lineage should.'

'Semley! Does Durhal know you're going?'

'My return will be a happy one – that much let him know,' said young Semley, breaking for a moment into her joyful laugh; then she bent to kiss her daughter, turned, and before Durossa could speak, was gone like a quick wind over the floors of sunlit stone.

Married women of the Angyar never rode for sport, and Semley had not been from Hallan since her marriage; so now, mounting the high saddle of a windsteed, she felt like a girl again, like the wild maiden she had been, riding half-broken steeds on the north wind over the fields of Kirien. The beast that bore her now down from the hills of Hallan was of finer breed, striped coat fitting sleek over hollow, buoyant bones, green eyes slitted against the wind, light and mighty wings sweeping up and down to either side of Semley, revealing and hiding, revealing and hiding the clouds above her and the hills below.

On the third morning she came to Kirien and stood again in the ruined courts. Her father had been drinking all night, and, just as in the old days, the morning sunlight poking through his fallen ceilings annoyed him, and the sight of his daughter only increased his annoyance. 'What are you back for?' he growled, his swollen eyes glancing at her and away. The fiery hair of his youth was quenched, grey strands tangled on his skull. 'Did the young Halla not marry you, and you've come sneaking home?'

'I am Durhal's wife. I came to get my dowry, father.'

The drunkard growled in disgust; but she laughed at him so gently that he had to look at her again, wincing.

'Is it true, father, that the Fiia stole the necklace Eye of the Sea?'

7

'How do I know? Old tales. The thing was lost before I was born, I think. I wish I never had been. Ask the Fiia if you want to know. Go to them, go back to your husband. Leave me alone here. There's no room at Kirien for girls and gold and all the rest of the story. The story's over here; this is the fallen place, this is the empty hall. The sons of Leynen all are dead, their treasures are all lost. Go on your way, girl.'

Grey and swollen as the web-spinner of ruined houses, he turned and went blundering toward the cellars where he hid from daylight.

Leading the striped windsteed of Hallan, Semley left her old home and walked down the steep hill, past the village of the midmen, who greeted her with sullen respect, on over fields and pastures where the great, wing-clipped, half-wild herilor grazed, to a valley that was green as a painted bowl and full to the brim with sunlight. In the deep of the valley lay the village of the Fiia, and as she descended leading her steed the little, slight people ran up toward her from their huts and gardens, laughing, calling out in faint, thin voices.

'Hail Halla's bride, Kirienlady, Windborne, Semley the Fair!'

They gave her lovely names and she liked to hear them, minding not at all their laughter; for they laughed at all they said. That was her own way, to speak and laugh. She stood tall in her long blue cloak among their swirling welcome.

'Hail Lightfolk, Sundwellers, Fiia friends of men!'

They took her down into the village and brought her into one of their airy houses, the tiny children chasing along behind. There was no telling the age of a Fian once he was grown; It was hard even to tell one from another and be sure, as they moved about quick as moths around a candle, that she spoke always to the same one. But it seemed that one of them talked with her for a while, as the others fed and petted her steed, and brought water for her to drink, and bowls of fruit from their gardens of little trees. 'It was never the Fiia that stole the necklace of the Lords of Kirien!' cried the little man. 'What would the Fiia do with gold, Lady? For us there is sunlight in

warmyear, and in coldyear the remembrance of sunlight; the yellow fruit, the yellow leaves in end-season, the yellow hair of our lady of Kirien; no other gold.'

'Then it was some midman stole the thing?'

Laughter rang long and faint about her. 'How would a midman dare? O Lady of Kirien, how the great jewel was stolen no mortal knows, not man nor midman nor Fian nor any among the Seven Folk. Only dead minds know how it was lost, long ago when Kireley the Proud whose great-granddaughter is Semley walked alone by the caves of the sea. But it may be found perhaps among the Sunhaters.'

'The Clayfolk?'

A louder burst of laughter, nervous.

'Sit with us, Semley, sunhaired, returned to us from the north.' She sat with them to eat, and they were as pleased with her graciousness as she with theirs. But when they heard her repeat that she would go to the Clayfolk to find her inheritance, if it was there, they began not to laugh; and little by little there were fewer of them around her. She was alone at last with perhaps the one she had spoken with before the meal. 'Do not go among the Clayfolk, Semley,' he said, and for a moment her heart failed her. The Fian, drawing his hand down slowly over his eyes, had darkened all the air about them. Fruit lay ash-white on the plate; all the bowls of clear water were empty.

'In the mountains of the far land the Fiia and the Gdemiar parted. Long ago we parted,' said the slight, still man of the Fiia. 'Longer ago we were one. What we are not, they are. What we are, they are not. Think of the sunlight and the grass and the trees that bear fruit, Semley; think that not all roads that lead down lead up as well.'

'Mine leads neither down nor up, kind host, but only straight on to my inheritance. I will go to it where it is, and return with it.'

The Fian bowed, laughing a little.

Outside the village she mounted her striped windsteed, and, calling farewell in answer to their calling, rose up into the wind

9

of afternoon and flew southwestward toward the caves down by the rocky shores of Kiriensea.

She feared she might have to walk far into those tunnel-caves to find the people she sought, for it was said the Clayfolk never came out of their caves into the light of the sun, and feared even the Greatstar and the moons. It was a long ride; she landed once to let her steed hunt tree-rats while she ate a little bread from her saddle-bag. The bread was hard and dry by now and tasted of leather, yet kept a faint savor of its making, so that for a moment, eating it alone in a glade of the southern forests, she heard the quiet tone of a voice and saw Durhal's face turned to her in the light of the candles of Hallan. For a while she sat daydreaming of that stern and vivid young face, and of what she would say to him when she came home with a kingdom's ransom around her neck: 'I wanted a gift worthy of my husband, Lord...' Then she pressed on, but when she reached the coast the sun had set, with the Greatstar sinking behind it. A mean wind had come up from the west, starting and gusting and veering, and her windsteed was weary fighting it. She let him glide down on the sand. At once he folded his wings and curled his thick, light limbs under him with a thrum of purring. Semley stood holding her cloak close at her throat, stroking the steed's neck so that he flicked his ears and purred again. The warm fur comforted her hand, but all that met her eyes was grey sky full of smears of cloud, grey sea, dark sand. And then running over the sand a low, dark creature – another – a group of them, squatting and running and stopping.

She called aloud to them. Though they had not seemed to see her, now in a moment they were all around her. They kept a distance from her windsteed; he had stopped purring, and his fur rose a little under Semley's hand. She took up the reins, glad of his protection but afraid of the nervous ferocity he might display. The strange folk stood silent, staring, their thick bare feet planted in the sand. There was no mistaking them: they were the height of the Fiia and in all else a shadow, a black image of those laughing people. Naked, squat, stiff, with lank

hair and grey-white skins, dampish-looking like the skins of grubs; eyes like rocks.

'You are the Clayfolk?'

'Gdemiar are we, people of the Lords of the Realms of Night.' The voice was unexpectedly loud and deep, and rang out pompous through the salt, blowing dusk; but, as with the Fiia, Semley was not sure which one had spoken.

'I greet you, Nightlords. I am Semley of Kirien, Durhal's wife of Hallan. I come to you seeking my inheritance, the necklace called Eye of the Sea, lost long ago.'

'Why do you seek it here, Angya? Here is only sand and salt and night.'

'Because lost things are known of in deep places,' said Semley, quite ready for a play of wits, 'and gold that came from earth has a way of going back to the earth. And sometimes the made, they say, returns to the maker.' This last was a guess; it hit the mark.

'It is true the necklace Eye of the Sea is known to us by name. It was made in our caves long ago, and sold by us to the Angyar. And the blue stone came from the Clayfields of our kin to the east. But these are very old tales, Angya.'

'May I listen to them in the places where they are told?'

The squat people were silent a while, as if in doubt. The grey wind blew by over the sand, darkening as the Greatstar set; the sound of the sea loudened and lessened. The deep voice spoke again: 'Yes, lady of the Angyar. You may enter the Deep Halls. Come with us now.' There was a changed note in his voice, wheedling. Semley would not hear it. She followed the Claymen over the sand, leading on a short rein her sharp-taloned steed.

At the cave-mouth, a toothless, yawning mouth from which a stinking warmth sighed out, one of the Claymen said, 'The air-beast cannot come in.'

'Yes,' said Semley.

'No,' said the squat people.

'Yes. I will not leave him here. He is not mine to leave. He will not harm you, so long as I hold his reins.'

'No,' deep voices repeated; but others broke in, 'As you will,' and after a moment of hesitation they went on. The cave-mouth seemed to snap shut behind them, so dark was it under the stone. They went in single file, Semley last.

The darkness of the tunnel lightened, and they came under a ball of weak white fire hanging from the roof. Farther on was another, and another; between them long black worms hung in festoons from the rock. As they went on these fire-globes were set closer, so that all the tunnel was lit with a bright, cold light.

Semley's guides stopped at a parting of three tunnels, all blocked by doors that looked to be of iron. 'We shall wait, Angya,' they said, and eight of them stayed with her, while three others unlocked one of the doors and passed through. It fell to behind them with a clash.

Straight and still stood the daughter of the Angyar in the white, blank light of the lamps; her windsteed crouched beside her, flicking the tip of his striped tail, his great folded wings stirring again and again with the checked impulse to fly. In the tunnel behind Semley the eight Claymen squatted on their hams, muttering to one another in their deep voices, in their own tongue.

The central door swung clanging open. 'Let the Angya enter the Realm of Night!' cried a new voice, booming and boastful. A Clayman who wore some clothing on his thick grey body stood in the doorway, beckoning to her. 'Enter and behold the wonders of our lands, the marvels made by hands, the works of the Nightlords!'

Silent, with a tug at her steed's reins, Semley bowed her head and followed him under the low doorway made for dwarfish folk. Another glaring tunnel stretched ahead, dank walls dazzling in the white light, but, instead of a way to walk upon, its floor carried two bars of polished iron stretching off side by side as far as she could see. On the bars rested some kind of cart with metal wheels. Obeying her new guide's gestures, with no

hesitation and no trace of wonder on her face, Semley stepped into the cart and made the windsteed crouch beside her. The Clayman got in and sat down in front of her, moving bars and wheels about. A loud grinding noise arose, and a screaming of metal on metal, and then the walls of the tunnel began to jerk by. Faster and faster the walls slid past, till the fireglobes overhead ran into a blur, and the stale warm air became a foul wind blowing the hood back off her hair.

The cart stopped. Semley followed the guide up basalt steps into a vast anteroom and then a still vaster hall, carved by ancient waters or by the burrowing Clayfolk out of the rock, its darkness that had never known sunlight lit with the uncanny cold brilliance of the globes. In grilles cut in the walls huge blades turned and turned, changing the stale air. The great closed space hummed and boomed with noise, the loud voices of the Clayfolk, the grinding and shrill buzzing and vibration of turning blades and wheels, the echoes and re-echoes of all this from the rock. Here all the stumpy figures of the Claymen were clothed in garments imitating those of the Starlords – divided trousers, soft boots, and hooded tunics – though the few women to be seen, hurrying servile dwarves, were naked. Of the males many were soldiers, bearing at their sides weapons shaped like the terrible light-throwers of the Starlords, though even Semley could see these were merely shaped iron clubs. What she saw, she saw without looking. She followed where she was led, turning her head neither to left nor right. When she came before a group of Claymen who wore iron circlets on their black hair her guide halted, bowed, boomed out, 'The High Lords of the Gdemiar!'

There were seven of them, and all looked up at her with such arrogance on their lumpy grey faces that she wanted to laugh.

'I come among you seeking the lost treasure of my family, O Lords of the Dark Realm,' she said gravely to them. 'I seek Leynen's prize, the Eye of the Sea.' Her voice was faint in the racket of the huge vault.

'So said our messengers, Lady Semley.' This time she could pick out the one who spoke, one even shorter than the others, hardly reaching Semley's breast, with a white, fierce face. 'We do not have this thing you seek.'

'Once you had it, it is said.'

'Much is said, up there where the sun blinks.'

'And words are borne off by the winds, where there are winds to blow. I do not ask how the necklace was lost to us and returned to you, its makers of old. Those are old tales, old grudges. I only seek to find it now. You do not have it now; but it may be you know where it is.'

'It is not here.'

'Then it is elsewhere.'

'It is where you cannot come to it. Never, unless we help you.'

'Then help me. I ask this as your guest.'

'It is said, *The Angyar take; the Füa give; the Gdemiar give and take.* If we do this for you, what will you give us?'

'My thanks, Nightlord.'

She stood tall and bright among them, smiling. They all stared at her with a heavy, grudging wonder, a sullen yearning.

'Listen, Angya, this is a great favor you ask of us. You do not know how great a favor. You cannot understand. You are of a race that will not understand, that cares for nothing but wind-riding and crop-raising and sword-fighting and shouting together. But who made your swords of the bright steel? We, the Gdemiar! Your lords come to us here and in the Clayfields and buy their swords and go away, not looking, not understanding. But you are here now, you will look, you can see a few of our endless marvels, the lights that burn forever, the car that pulls itself, the machines that make our clothes and cook our food and sweeten our air and serve us in all things. Know that all these things are beyond your understanding. And know this: we, the Gdemiar, are the friends of those you call the Starlords! We came with them to Hallan, to Reohan, to Hul-Orren, to all your castles, to help them speak to you. The lords to whom

you, the proud Angyar, pay tribute, are our friends. They do us favors as we do them favors! Now, what do your thanks mean to us?'

'That is your question to answer,' said Semley, 'not mine. I have asked my question. Answer it, Lord.'

For a while the seven conferred together, by word and silence. They would glance at her and look away, and mutter and be still. A crowd grew around them, drawn slowly and silently, one after another till Semley was encircled by hundreds of the matted black heads, and all the great booming cavern floor was covered with people, except a little space directly around her. Her windsteed was quivering with fear and irritation too long controlled, and his eyes had gone very wide and pale, like the eyes of a steed forced to fly at night. She stroked the warm fur of his head, whispering, 'Quietly now, brave one, bright one, windlord . . .'

'Angya, we will take you to the place where the treasure lies.' The Clayman with the white face and iron crown had turned to her once more. 'More than that we cannot do. You must come with us to claim the necklace where it lies, from those who keep it. The air-beast cannot come with you. You must come alone.'

'How far a journey, Lord?'

His lips drew back and back. 'A very far journey, Lady. Yet it will last only one long night.'

'I thank you for your courtesy. Will my steed be well cared for this night? No ill must come to him.'

'He will sleep till you return. A greater windsteed you will have ridden, when you see that beast again! Will you not ask where we take you?'

'Can we go soon on this journey? I would not stay long away from my home.'

'Yes. Soon.' Again the grey lips widened as he stared up into her face.

What was done in those next hours Semley could not have retold; it was all haste, jumble, noise, strangeness. While she held her steed's head a Clayman stuck a long needle into the

golden-striped haunch. She nearly cried out at the sight, but her steed merely twitched and then, purring, fell asleep. He was carried off by a group of Clayfolk who clearly had to summon up their courage to touch his warm fur. Later on she had to see a needle driven into her own arm – perhaps to test her courage, she thought, for it did not seem to make her sleep; though she was not quite sure. There were times she had to travel in the rail-carts, passing iron doors and vaulted caverns by the hundred and hundred; once the rail-cart ran through a cavern that stretched off on either hand measureless into the dark, and all that darkness was full of great flocks of herilor. She could hear their cooing, husky calls, and glimpse the flocks in the front-lights of the cart; then she saw some more clearly in the white light, and saw that they were all wingless, and all blind. At that she shut her eyes. But there were more tunnels to go through, and always more caverns, more grey lumpy bodies and fierce faces and booming boasting voices, until at last they led her suddenly out into the open air. It was full night; she raised her eyes joyfully to the stars and the single moon shining, little Heliki brightening in the west. But the Clayfolk were all about her still, making her climb now into some new kind of cart or cave, she did not know which. It was small, full of little blinking lights like rushlights, very narrow and shining after the great dank caverns and the starlit night. Now another needle was stuck in her, and they told her she would have to be tied down in a sort of flat chair, tied down head and hand and foot.

'I will not,' said Semley.

But when she saw that the four Claymen who were to be her guides let themselves be tied down first, she submitted. The others left. There was a roaring sound, and a long silence; a great weight that could not be seen pressed upon her. Then there was no weight; no sound; nothing at all.

'Am I dead?' asked Semley.

'Oh no, Lady,' said a voice she did not like.

Opening her eyes, she saw the white face bent over her, the wide lips pulled back, the eyes like little stones. Her bonds had

16

fallen away from her, and she leaped up. She was weightless, bodiless; she felt herself only a gust of terror on the wind.

'We will not hurt you,' said the sullen voice or voices. 'Only let us touch you, Lady. We would like to touch your hair. Let us touch your hair . . .'

The round cart they were in trembled a little. Outside its one window lay blank night, or was it mist, or nothing at all? One long night, they had said. Very long. She sat motionless and endured the touch of their heavy grey hands on her hair. Later they would touch her hands and feet and arms, and once her throat: at that she set her teeth and stood up, and they drew back.

'We have not hurt you, Lady,' they said. She shook her head.

When they bade her, she lay down again in the chair that bound her down; and when light flashed golden, at the window, she would have wept at the sight, but fainted first.

'Well,' said Rocannon, 'now at least we know what she is.'

'I wish there were some way of knowing *who* she is,' the curator mumbled. 'She wants something we've got here in the Museum, is that what the trogs say?'

'Now, don't call 'em trogs,' Rocannon said conscientiously; as a hilfer, an ethnologist of the High Intelligence Life-forms, he was supposed to resist such words. 'They're not pretty, but they're Status C Allies . . . I wonder why the Commission picked them to develop? Before even contacting all the HILF species? I'll bet the survey was from Centaurus – Centaurans always like nocturnals and cave dwellers. I'd have backed Species II, here, I think.'

'The troglodytes seem to be rather in awe of her.'

'Aren't you?'

Ketho glanced at the tall woman again, then reddened and laughed. 'Well, in a way. I never saw such a beautiful alien type in eighteen years here on New South Georgia. I never saw such a beautiful woman anywhere, in fact. She looks like a goddess.' The red now reached the top of his bald head, for Ketho was

a shy curator, not given to hyperbole. But Rocannon nodded soberly, agreeing.

'I wish we could talk to her without those tr – Gdemiar as interpreters. But there's no help for it.' Rocannon went toward their visitor, and when she turned her splendid face to him he bowed down very deeply, going right down to the floor on one knee, his head bowed and his eyes shut. This was what he called his All-Purpose Intercultural Curtsey, and he performed it with some grace. When he came erect again the beautiful woman smiled and spoke.

'She say, Hail, Lord of Stars,' growled one of her squat escorts in Pidgin-Galactic.

'Hail, Lady of the Angyar,' Rocannon replied. 'In what way can we of the Museum serve the lady?'

Across the troglodytes' growling her voice ran like a brief silver wind.

'She say, Please give her necklace which treasure her blood-kin-forebears long long.'

'Which necklace?' he asked, and understanding him, she pointed to the central display of the case before them, a magnificent thing, a chain of yellow gold, massive but very delicate in workmanship, set with one big hot-blue sapphire. Rocannon's eyebrows went up, and Ketho at his shoulder murmured, 'She's got good taste. That's the Fomalhaut Necklace – famous bit of work.'

She smiled at the two men, and again spoke to them over the heads of the troglodytes.

'She say, O Starlords, Elder and Younger Dwellers in House of Treasures, this treasure her one. Long long time. Thank you.'

'How did we get the thing, Ketho?'

'Wait; let me look it up in the catalogue. I've got it here. Here. It came from these trogs – trolls – whatever they are: Gdemiar. They have a bargain-obsession, it says; we had to let 'em buy the ship they came here on, an AD-4. This was part payment. It's their own handiwork.'

'And I'll bet they can't do this kind of work anymore, since they've been steered to Industrial.'

'But they seem to feel the thing is hers, not theirs or ours. It must be important, Rocannon, or they wouldn't have given up this time-span to her errand. Why, the objective lapse between here and Fomalhaut must be considerable!'

'Several years, no doubt,' said the hilfer, who was used to starjumping. 'Not very far. Well, neither the *Handbook* nor the *Guide* gives me enough data to base a decent guess on. These species obviously haven't been properly studied at all. The little fellows may be showing her simple courtesy. Or an interspecies war may depend on this damn sapphire. Perhaps her desire rules them, because they consider themselves totally inferior to her. Or despite appearances she may be their prisoner, their decoy. How can we tell? . . . Can you give the thing away, Ketho?'

'Oh, yes. All the Exotica are technically on loan, not our property, since these claims come up now and then. We seldom argue. Peace above all, until the War comes . . .'

'Then I'd say give it to her.'

Ketho smiled. 'It's a privilege,' he said. Unlocking the case, he lifted out the great golden chain; then, in his shyness, he held it out to Rocannon, saying, 'You give it to her.'

So the blue jewel first lay, for a moment, in Rocannon's hand.

His mind was not on it; he turned straight to the beautiful, alien woman, with his handful of blue fire and gold. She did not raise her hands to take it, but bent her head, and he slipped the necklace over her hair. It lay like a burning fuse along her golden-brown throat. She looked up from it with such pride, delight, and gratitude in her face that Rocannon stood wordless, and the little curator murmured hurriedly in his own language, 'You're welcome, you're very welcome.' She bowed her golden head to him and to Rocannon. Then, turning, she nodded to her squat guards – or captors? – and, drawing her

worn blue cloak about her, paced down the long hall and was gone. Ketho and Rocannon stood looking after her.

'What I feel...' Rocannon began.

'Well?' Ketho inquired hoarsely, after a long pause.

'What I feel sometimes is that I... meeting these people from worlds we know so little of, you know, sometimes... that I have as it were blundered through the corner of a legend, or a tragic myth, maybe, which I do not understand...'

'Yes,' said the curator, clearing his throat. 'I wonder... I wonder what her name is.'

Semley the Fair, Semley the Golden, Semley of the Necklace. The Clayfolk had bent to her will, and so had even the Star-lords in that terrible place where the Clayfolk had taken her, the city at the end of the night. They had bowed to her, and given her gladly her treasure from amongst their own.

But she could not yet shake off the feeling of those caverns about her where rock lowered overhead, where you could not tell who spoke or what they did, where voices boomed and grey hands reached out – Enough of that. She had paid for the necklace; very well. Now it was hers. The price was paid, the past was the past.

Her windsteed had crept out of some kind of box, with his eyes filmy and his fur rimed with ice, and at first when they had left the caves of the Gdemiar he would not fly. Now he seemed all right again, riding a smooth south wind through the bright sky toward Hallan. 'Go quick, go quick,' she told him, beginning to laugh as the wind cleared away her mind's darkness. 'I want to see Durhal soon, soon...'

And swiftly they flew, coming to Hallan by dusk of the second day. Now the caves of the Clayfolk seemed no more than last year's nightmare, as the steed swooped with her up the thousand steps of Hallan and across the Chasmbridge where the forests fell away for a thousand feet. In the gold light of evening in the flightcourt she dismounted and walked up the last steps between the stiff carven figures of heroes and the

20

two gatewards, who bowed to her, staring at the beautiful, fiery thing around her neck.

In the Forehall she stopped a passing girl, a very pretty girl, by her looks one of Durhal's close kin, though Semley could not call to mind her name. 'Do you know me, maiden? I am Semley, Durhal's wife. Will you go tell the Lady Durossa that I have come back?'

For she was afraid to go on in and perhaps face Durhal at once, alone; she wanted Durossa's support.

The girl was gazing at her, her face very strange. But she murmured, 'Yes, Lady,' and darted off toward the Tower.

Semley stood waiting in the gilt, ruinous hall. No one came by; were they all at table in the Revel-hall? The silence was uneasy. After a minute Semley started toward the stairs to the Tower. But an old woman was coming to her across the stone floor, holding her arms out, weeping.

'O Semley, Semley!'

She had never seen the grey-haired woman, and shrank back.

'But Lady, who are you?'

'I am Durossa, Semley.'

She was quiet and still, all the time that Durossa embraced her and wept, and asked if it were true the Clayfolk had captured her and kept her under a spell all these long years, or had it been the Fiia with their strange arts? Then, drawing back a little, Durossa ceased to weep.

'You're still young, Semley. Young as the day you left here. And you wear round your neck the necklace...'

'I have brought my gift to my husband Durhal. Where is he?'

'Durhal is dead.'

Semley stood unmoving.

'Your husband, my brother, Durhal Hallanlord was killed seven years ago in battle. Nine years you had been gone. The Starlords came no more. We fell to warring with the Eastern Halls, with the Angyar of Log and Hul-Orren. Durhal, fighting, was killed by a midman's spear, for he had little armor for

21

his body, and none at all for his spirit. He lies buried in the fields above Orren Marsh.'

Semley turned away. 'I will go to him, then,' she said, putting her hand on the gold chain that weighed down her neck. 'I will give him my gift.'

'Wait, Semley! Durhal's daughter, your daughter, see her now, Haldre the Beautiful!'

It was the girl she had first spoken to and sent to Durossa, a girl of nineteen or so, with eyes like Durhal's eyes, dark blue. She stood beside Durossa, gazing with those steady eyes at this woman Semley who was her mother and was her own age. Their age was the same, and their gold hair, and their beauty. Only Semley was a little taller, and wore the blue stone on her breast.

'Take it, take it. It was for Durhal and Haldre that I brought it from the end of the long night!' Semley cried this aloud, twisting and bowing her head to get the heavy chain off, dropping the necklace so it fell on the stones with a cold, liquid clash. 'O take it, Haldre!' she cried again, and then, weeping aloud, turned and ran from Hallan, over the bridge and down the long, broad steps, and, darting off eastward into the forest of the mountainside like some wild thing escaping, was gone.

APRIL IN PARIS

This is the first story I ever got paid for; the second story I ever got published; and maybe the thirtieth or fortieth story I wrote. I had been writing poetry and fiction ever since my brother Ted, tired of having an illiterate five-year-old sister around, taught me to read. At about twenty I began sending things off to publishers. Some of the poetry got printed, but I didn't get systematic about sending out the fiction till I was getting on to thirty. It kept systematically coming back.

'April in Paris' was the first 'genre' piece – recognizably fantasy or science fiction – that I had written since 1942, when I wrote an Origin-of-Life-on-Earth story for Astounding, *which for some inconceivable reason rejected it (I never did synch with John Campbell). At age twelve I was very pleased to get a genuine printed rejection slip, but by age thirty-two I was very pleased to get a check. 'Professionalism' is no virtue; a professional is simply one who gets paid for doing what an amateur does for love. But in a money economy, the fact of being paid means your work is going to be circulated, is going to be read; it's the means to communication, which is the artist's goal. Cele Goldsmith Lalli, who bought this story in 1962, was as enterprising and perceptive an editor as the science fiction magazines have ever had, and I am grateful to her for opening the door to me.*

Professor Barry Pennywither sat in a cold, shadowy garret and stared at the table in front of him, on which lay a book and a breadcrust. The bread had been his dinner, the book had been his lifework. Both were dry. Dr Pennywither sighed, and then shivered. Though the lower-floor apartments of the old house were quite elegant, the heat was turned off on April 1st, come

what may; it was now April 2nd, and sleeting. If Dr Pennywither raised his head a little he could see from his window the two square towers of Notre Dame de Paris, vague and soaring in the dusk, almost near enough to touch: for the Island of Saint-Louis, where he lived, is like a little barge being towed downstream behind the Island of the City, where Notre Dame stands. But he did not raise his head. He was too cold.

The great towers sank into darkness. Dr Pennywither sank into gloom. He stared with loathing at his book. It had won him a year in Paris – publish or perish, said the Dean of Faculties, and he had published, and been rewarded with a year's leave from teaching, without pay. Munson College could not afford to pay unteaching teachers. So on his scraped-up savings he had come back to Paris, to live again as a student in a garret, to read fifteenth-century manuscripts at the Library, to see the chestnuts flower along the avenues. But it hadn't worked. He was forty, too old for lonely garrets. The sleet would blight the budding chestnut flowers. And he was sick of his work. Who cared about his theory, the Pennywither Theory, concerning the mysterious disappearance of the poet François Villon in 1463? Nobody. For after all his Theory about poor Villon, the greatest juvenile delinquent of all time, was only a theory and could never be proved, not across the gulf of five hundred years. Nothing could be proved. And besides, what did it matter if Villon died on Montfaucon gallows or (as Pennywither thought) in a Lyons brothel on the way to Italy? Nobody cared. Nobody else loved Villon enough. Nobody loved Dr Pennywither, either; not even Dr Pennywither. Why should he? An unsocial, unmarried, underpaid pedant, sitting here alone in an unheated attic in an unrestored tenement trying to write another unreadable book. 'I'm unrealistic,' he said aloud with another sigh and another shiver. He got up and took the blanket off his bed, wrapped himself in it, sat down thus bundled at the table, and tried to light a Gauloise Bleue. His lighter snapped vainly. He sighed once more, got up, fetched a can of vile-smelling French lighter fluid, sat down, rewrapped his cocoon, filled the lighter, and

snapped it. The fluid had spilled around a good bit. The lighter lit, so did Dr Pennywither, from the wrists down. 'Oh hell!' he cried, blue flames leaping from his knuckles, and jumped up batting his arms wildly, shouting 'Hell!' and raging against Destiny. Nothing ever went right. What was the use? It was then 8:12 on the night of April 2nd, 1961.

A man sat hunched at a table in a cold, high room. Through the window behind him the two square towers of Notre Dame loomed in the Spring dusk. In front of him on the table lay a hunk of cheese and a huge, iron-latched, handwritten book. The book was called (in Latin) *On the Primacy of the Element Fire over the Other Three Elements*. Its author stared at it with loathing. Nearby on a small iron stove a small alembic simmered. Jehan Lenoir mechanically inched his chair nearer the stove now and then, for warmth, but his thoughts were on deeper problems. 'Hell!' he said finally (in Late Mediaeval French), slammed the book shut, and got up. What if his theory was wrong? What if water were the primal element? How could you prove these things? There must be some way – some method – so that one could be sure, absolutely sure, of one single fact! But each fact led into others, a monstrous tangle, and the Authorities conflicted, and anyway no one would read his book, not even the wretched pedants at the Sorbonne. They smelled heresy. What was the use? What good this life spent in poverty and alone, when he had learned nothing, merely guessed and theorized? He strode about the garret, raging, and then stood still. 'All right!' he said to Destiny. 'Very good! You've given me nothing, so I'll take what I want!' He went to one of the stacks of books that covered most of the floor-space, yanked out a bottom volume (scarring the leather and bruising his knuckles when the overlying folios avalanched), slapped it on the table and began to study one page of it. Then, still with a set cold look of rebellion, he got things ready: sulfur, silver, chalk... Though the room was dusty and littered, his little workbench was neatly and handily arranged. He was soon ready. Then

25

he paused. 'This is ridiculous,' he muttered, glancing out the window into the darkness where now one could only guess at the two square towers. A watchman passed below calling out the hour, eight o'clock of a cold clear night. It was so still he could hear the lapping of the Seine. He shrugged, frowned, took up the chalk and drew a neat pentagram on the floor near his table, then took up the book and began to read in a clear but self-conscious voice: 'Haere, haere, audi me...' It was a long spell, and mostly nonsense. His voice sank. He stood bored and embarrassed. He hurried through the last words, shut the book, and then fell backwards against the door, gap-mouthed, staring at the enormous, shapeless figure that stood within the pentagram, lit only by the blue flicker of its waving, fiery claws.

Barry Pennywither finally got control of himself and put out the fire by burying his hands in the folds of the blanket wrapped around him. Unburned but upset, he sat down again. He looked at his book. Then he stared at it. It was no longer thin and grey and titled *The Last Years of Villon: an Investigation of Possibilities*. It was thick and brown and titled *Incantatoria Magna*. On his table? A priceless manuscript dating from 1407 of which the only extant undamaged copy was in the Ambrosian Library in Milan. He looked slowly around. His mouth dropped slowly open. He observed a stove, a chemist's workbench, two or three dozen heaps of unbelievable leatherbound books, the window, the door. His window, his door. But crouching against his door was a little creature, black and shapeless, from which came a dry rattling sound.

Barry Pennywither was not a very brave man, but he was rational. He thought he had lost his mind, and so he said quite steadily, 'Are you the Devil?'

The creature shuddered and rattled.

Experimentally, with a glance at invisible Notre Dame, the professor made the sign of the Cross.

At this the creature twitched; not a flinch, a twitch. Then it said something, feebly, but in perfectly good English – no, in

perfectly good French – no, in rather odd French: 'Mais vous estes de Dieu,' it said.

Barry got up and peered at it. 'Who are you?' he demanded, and it lifted up a quite human face and answered meekly, 'Jehan Lenoir.'

'What are you doing in my room?'

There was a pause. Lenoir got up from his knees and stood straight, all five foot two of him. 'This is *my* room,' he said at last, though very politely.

Barry looked around at the books and alembics. There was another pause. 'Then how did I get here?'

'I brought you.'

'Are you a doctor?'

Lenoir nodded, with pride. His whole air had changed. 'Yes, I'm a doctor,' he said. 'Yes, I brought you here. If Nature will yield me no knowledge, then I can conquer Nature herself, I can work a miracle! To the Devil with science, then. I was a scientist—' he glared at Barry. 'No longer! They call me a fool, a heretic, well by God I'm worse! I'm a sorcerer, a black magician, Jehan the Black! Magic works, does it? Then science is a waste of time. Ha!' he said, but he did not really look triumphant. 'I wish it hadn't worked,' he said more quietly, pacing up and down between folios.

'So do I,' said the guest.

'Who are you?' Lenoir looked up challengingly at Barry, though there was nearly a foot difference in their heights.

'Barry A. Pennywither, I'm a professor of French at Munson College, Indiana, on leave in Paris to pursue my studies of Late Mediaeval Fr—' He stopped. He had just realized what kind of accent Lenoir had. 'What year is this? What century? Please, Dr Lenoir—' The Frenchman looked confused. The meanings of words change, as well as their pronunciations. 'Who rules this country?' Barry shouted.

Lenoir gave a shrug, a French shrug (some things never change). 'Louis is king,' he said. 'Louis the Eleventh. The dirty old spider.'

27

They stood staring at each other like wooden Indians for some time. Lenoir spoke first. 'Then you're a man?'

'Yes. Look, Lenoir, I think you – your spell – you must have muffed it a bit.'

'Evidently,' said the alchemist. 'Are you French?'

'No.'

'Are you English?' Lenoir glared. 'Are you a filthy Goddam?'

'No. No. I'm from America. I'm from the – from your future. From the twentieth century A.D.' Barry blushed. It sounded silly, and he was a modest man. But he knew this was no illusion. The room he stood in, his room, was new. Not five centuries old. Unswept, but new. And the copy of Albertus Magnus by his knee was new, bound in soft supple calfskin, the gold lettering gleaming. And there stood Lenoir in his black gown, not in costume, at home...

'Please sit down, sir,' Lenoir was saying. And he added, with the fine though absent courtesy of the poor scholar, 'Are you tired from the journey? I have bread and cheese, if you'll honor me by sharing it.'

They sat at the table munching bread and cheese. At first Lenoir tried to explain why he had tried black magic. 'I was fed up,' he said. 'Fed up! I've slaved in solitude since I was twenty, for what? For knowledge. To learn some of Nature's secrets. They are not to be learned.' He drove his knife half an inch into the table, and Barry jumped. Lenoir was a thin little fellow, but evidently a passionate one. It was a fine face, though pale and lean: intelligent, alert, vivid. Barry was reminded of the face of a famous atomic physicist, seen in newspaper pictures up until 1953. Somehow this likeness prompted him to say, 'Some are, Lenoir; we've learned a good bit, here and there...'

'What?' said the alchemist, skeptical but curious.

'Well, I'm no scientist—'

'Can you make gold?' He grinned as he asked.

'No, I don't think so, but they do make diamonds.'

'How?'

'Carbon – coal, you know – under great heat and pressure, I believe. Coal and diamond are both carbon, you know, the same element.'

'Element?'

'Now as I say, I'm no—'

'Which is the primal element?' Lenoir shouted, his eyes fiery, the knife poised in his hand.

'There are about a hundred elements,' Barry said coldly, hiding his alarm.

Two hours later, having squeezed out of Barry every dribble of the remnants of his college chemistry course, Lenoir rushed out into the night and reappeared shortly with a bottle. 'O my master,' he cried, 'to think I offered you only bread and cheese!' It was a pleasant burgundy, vintage 1477, a good year. After they had drunk a glass together Lenoir said, 'If somehow I could repay you ...'

'You can. Do you know the name of the poet François Villon?'

'Yes,' Lenoir said with some surprise, 'but he wrote only French trash, you know, not in Latin.'

'Do you know how or when he died?'

'Oh, yes; hanged at Montfaucon here in '64 or '65, with a crew of no-goods like himself. Why?'

Two hours later the bottle was dry, their throats were dry, and the watchman had called three o'clock of a cold clear morning. 'Jehan, I'm worn out,' Barry said, 'you'd better send me back.' The alchemist was too polite, too grateful, and perhaps also too tired to argue. Barry stood stiffly inside the pentagram, a tall bony figure muffled in a brown blanket, smoking a Gauloise Bleue. 'Adieu,' Lenoir said sadly. 'Au revoir,' Barry replied. Lenoir began to read the spell backwards. The candle flickered, his voice softened. 'Me audi, haere, haere,' he read, sighed, and looked up. The pentagram was empty. The candle flickered. 'But I learned so little!' Lenoir cried out to the empty room. Then he beat the open book with his fists and said, 'And a friend like that – a real friend—' He smoked one

of the cigarettes Barry had left him – he had taken to tobacco at once. He slept, sitting at his table, for a couple of hours. When he woke he brooded a while, relit his candle, smoked the other cigarette, then opened the *Incantatoria* and began to read aloud: 'Haere, haere...'

'Oh, thank God,' Barry said, stepping quickly out of the pentagram and grasping Lenoir's hand. 'Listen, I got back there – this room, this same room, Jehan! but old, horribly old, and empty, you weren't there – I thought, my God, what have I done? I'd sell my soul to get back there, to him – What can I do with what I've learned? Who'll believe it? How can I prove it? And who the devil could I tell it to anyhow? Who cares? I couldn't sleep, I sat and cried for an hour—'

'Will you stay?'

'Yes. Look, I brought these – in case you did invoke me.' Sheepishly he exhibited eight packs of Gauloises, several books, and a gold watch. 'It might fetch a price,' he explained. 'I knew paper francs wouldn't do much good.'

At sight of the printed books Lenoir's eyes gleamed with curiosity, but he stood still. 'My friend,' he said, 'you said you'd sell your soul... you know... so would I. Yet we haven't. How – after all – how did this happen? That we're both men. No devils. No pacts in blood. Two men who've lived in this room...'

'I don't know,' said Barry. 'We'll think that out later. Can I stay with you, Jehan?'

'Consider this your home,' Lenoir said with a gracious gesture around the room, the stacks of books, the alembics, the candle growing pale. Outside the window, grey on grey, rose up the two great towers of Notre Dame. It was the dawn of April 3rd.

After breakfast (bread crusts and cheese rinds) they went out and climbed the south tower. The cathedral looked the same as always, though cleaner than in 1961, but the view was rather a shock to Barry. He looked down upon a little town. Two small

islands covered with houses; on the right bank more houses crowded inside a fortified wall; on the left bank a few streets twisting around the college; and that was all. Pigeons chortled on the sun-warmed stone between gargoyles. Lenoir, who had seen the view before, was carving the date (in Roman numerals) on a parapet. 'Let's celebrate,' he said. 'Let's go out into the country. I haven't been out of the city for two years. Let's go clear over there—' he pointed to a misty green hill on which a few huts and a windmill were just visible – 'to Montmartre, eh? There are some good bars there, I'm told.'

Their life soon settled into an easy routine. At first Barry was a little nervous in the crowded streets, but, in a spare black gown of Lenoir's, he was not noticed as outlandish except for his height. He was probably the tallest man in fifteenth-century France. Living standards were low and lice were unavoidable, but Barry had never valued comfort much; the only thing he really missed was coffee at breakfast. When they had bought a bed and a razor – Barry had forgotten his – and introduced him to the landlord as M. Barrie, a cousin of Lenoir's from the Auvergne, their housekeeping arrangements were complete. Barry's watch brought a tremendous price, four gold pieces, enough to live on for a year. They sold it as a wondrous new timepiece from Illyria, and the buyer, a Court chamberlain looking for a nice present to give the king, looked at the inscription – Hamilton Bros., New Haven, 1881 – and nodded sagely. Unfortunately he was shut up in one of King Louis's cages for naughty courtiers at Tours before he had presented his gift, and the watch may still be there behind some brick in the ruins of Plessis; but this did not affect the two scholars. Mornings they wandered about sightseeing the Bastille and the churches, or visiting various minor poets in whom Barry was interested; after lunch they discussed electricity, the atomic theory, physiology, and other matters in which Lenoir was interested, and performed minor chemical and anatomical experiments, usually unsuccessfully; after supper they merely talked. Endless, easy talks that ranged over the centuries but always ended here, in

31

the shadowy room with its window open to the Spring night, in their friendship. After two weeks they might have known each other all their lives. They were perfectly happy. They knew they would do nothing with what they had learned from each other. In 1961 how could Barry ever prove his knowledge of old Paris, in 1482 how could Lenoir ever prove the validity of the scientific method? It did not bother them. They had never really expected to be listened to. They had merely wanted to learn.

So they were happy for the first time in their lives; so happy, in fact, that certain desires always before subjugated to the desire for knowledge, began to awaken. 'I don't suppose,' Barry said one night across the table, 'that you ever thought much about marrying?'

'Well, no,' his friend answered, doubtfully. 'That is, I'm in minor orders... and it seemed irrelevant...'

'And expensive. Besides, in my time, no self-respecting woman would want to share my kind of life. American women are so damned poised and efficient and glamorous, terrifying creatures...'

'And women here are little and dark, like beetles, with bad teeth,' Lenoir said morosely.

They said no more about women that night. But the next night they did; and the next; and on the next, celebrating the successful dissection of the main nervous system of a pregnant frog, they drank two bottles of Montrachet '74 and got soused. 'Let's invoke a woman, Jehan,' Barry said in a lascivious bass, grinning like a gargoyle.

'What if I raised a devil this time?'

'Is there really much difference?'

They laughed wildly, and drew a pentagram. 'Haere, haere,' Lenoir began; when he got the hiccups, Barry took over. He read the last words. There was a rush of cold, marshy-smelling air, and in the pentagram stood a wild-eyed being with long black hair, stark naked, screaming.

'Woman, by God,' said Barry.

'Is it?'

It was. 'Here, take my cloak,' Barry said, for the poor thing now stood gawping and shivering. He put the cloak over her shoulders. Mechanically she pulled it round her, muttering, 'Gratias ago, domine.'

'Latin!' Lenoir shouted. 'A woman speaking Latin?' It took him longer to get over that shock than it did Bota to get over hers. She was, it seemed, a slave in the household of the Sub-Prefect of North Gaul, who lived on the smaller island of the muddy island town called Lutetia. She spoke Latin with a thick Celtic brogue, and did not even know who was emperor in Rome in her day. A real barbarian, Lenoir said with scorn. So she was, an ignorant, taciturn, humble barbarian with tangled hair, white skin, and clear grey eyes. She had been waked from a sound sleep. When they convinced her that she was not dreaming, she evidently assumed that this was some prank of her foreign and all-powerful master the Sub-Prefect, and accepted the situation without further question. 'Am I to serve you, my masters?' she inquired timidly but without sullenness, looking from one to the other.

'Not me,' Lenoir growled, and added in French to Barry, 'Go on; I'll sleep in the store-room.' He departed.

Bota looked up at Barry. No Gauls, and few Romans, were so magnificently tall; no Gauls and no Romans ever spoke so kindly. 'Your lamp' (it was a candle, but she had never seen a candle) 'is nearly burnt out,' she said. 'Shall I blow it out?'

For an additional two sols a year the landlord let them use the store-room as a second bedroom, and Lenoir now slept alone again in the main room of the garret. He observed his friend's idyll with a brooding, unjealous interest. The professor and the slave-girl loved each other with delight and tenderness. Their pleasure overlapped Lenoir in waves of protective joy. Bota had led a brutal life, treated always as a woman but never as a human. In one short week she bloomed, she came alive, evincing beneath her gentle passiveness a cheerful, clever nature.

33

'You're turning out a regular Parisienne,' he heard Barry accuse her one night (the attic walls were thin). She replied, 'If you knew what it is for me not to be always defending myself, always afraid, always alone...'

Lenoir sat up on his cot and brooded. About midnight, when all was quiet, he rose and noiselessly prepared the pinches of sulfur and silver, drew the pentagram, opened the book. Very softly he read the spell. His face was apprehensive.

In the pentagram appeared a small white dog. It cowered and hung its tail, then came shyly forward, sniffed Lenoir's hand, looked up at him with liquid eyes and gave a modest, pleading whine. A lost puppy... Lenoir stroked it. It licked his hands and jumped all over him, wild with relief. On its white leather collar was a silver plaque engraved, 'Jolie. Dupont, 36 rue de Seine, Paris VIe.'

Jolie went to sleep, after gnawing a crust, curled up under Lenoir's chair. And the alchemist opened the book again and read, still softly, but this time without self-consciousness, without fear, knowing what would happen.

Emerging from his store-room-bedroom-honeymoon in the morning, Barry stopped short in the doorway. Lenoir was sitting up in bed, petting a white puppy, and deep in conversation with the person sitting on the foot of the bed, a tall red-haired woman dressed in silver. The puppy barked. Lenoir said, 'Good morning!' The woman smiled wondrously.

'Jumping Jesus,' Barry muttered (in English). Then he said, 'Good morning. When are you from?' The effect was Rita Hayworth, sublimated – Hayworth plus the Mona Lisa, perhaps?

'From Altair, about seven thousand years from now,' she said, smiling still more wondrously. Her French accent was worse than that of a football-scholarship freshman. 'I'm an archaeologist. I was excavating the ruins of Paris III. I'm sorry I speak the language so badly; of course we know it only from inscriptions.'

'From Altair? The star? But you're human – I think—'

34

'Our planet was colonized from Earth about four thousand years ago – that is, three thousand years from now.' She laughed, most wondrously, and glanced at Lenoir. 'Jehan explained it all to me, but I still get confused.'

'It was a dangerous thing to try it again, Jehan!' Barry accused him. 'We've been awfully lucky, you know.'

'No,' said the Frenchman. 'Not lucky.'

'But after all it's black magic you're playing with – Listen – I don't know your name, madame.'

'Kislk,' she said.

'Listen, Kislk,' Barry said without even a stumble, 'your science must be fantastically advanced – is there any magic? Does it exist? Can the laws of Nature really be broken, as we seem to be doing?'

'I've never seen nor heard of an authenticated case of magic.'

'Then what goes on?' Barry roared. 'Why does that stupid old spell work for Jehan, for us, that one spell, and here, nowhere else, for nobody else, in five – no, eight – no, fifteen thousand years of recorded history? Why? Why? And where did that damn puppy come from?'

'The puppy was lost,' Lenoir said, his dark face grave. 'Somewhere near this house, on the île Saint-Louis.'

'And I was sorting potsherds,' Kislk said, also gravely, 'in a house-site, Island 2, Pit 4, Section D. A lovely Spring day, and I hated it. Loathed it. The day, the work, the people around me.' Again she looked at the gaunt little alchemist, a long, quiet look. 'I tried to explain it to Jehan last night. We have improved the race, you see. We're all very tall, healthy, and beautiful. No fillings in our teeth. All skulls from Early America have fillings in the teeth... Some of us are brown, some white, some gold-skinned. But all beautiful, and healthy, and well-adjusted, and aggressive, and successful. Our professions and degree of success are preplanned for us in the State Pre-School Homes. But there's an occasional genetic flaw. Me, for instance. I was trained as an archaeologist because the Teachers saw that I

really didn't like people, live people. People bored me. All like me on the outside, all alien to me on the inside. When everything's alike, which place is home? ... But now I've seen an unhygienic room with insufficient heating. Now I've seen a cathedral not in ruins. Now I've met a living man who's shorter than me, with bad teeth and a short temper. Now I'm home, I'm where I can be myself, I'm no longer alone!'

'Alone,' Lenoir said gently to Barry. 'Loneliness, eh? Loneliness is the spell, loneliness is stronger ... Really it doesn't seem unnatural.'

Bota was peering round the doorway, her face flushed between the black tangles of her hair. She smiled shyly and said a polite Latin good-morning to the newcomer.

'Kislk doesn't know Latin,' Lenoir said with immense satisfaction. 'We must teach Bota some French. French is the language of love, anyway, eh? Come along, let's go out and buy some bread. I'm hungry.'

Kislk hid her silver tunic under the useful and anonymous cloak, while Lenoir pulled on his moth-eaten black gown. Bota combed her hair, while Barry thoughtfully scratched a louse-bite on his neck. Then they set forth to get breakfast. The alchemist and the interstellar archaeologist went first, speaking French; the Gaulish slave and the professor from Indiana followed, speaking Latin, and holding hands. The narrow streets were crowded, bright with sunshine. Above them Notre Dame reared its two square towers against the sky. Beside them the Seine rippled softly. It was April in Paris, and on the banks of the river the chestnuts were in bloom.

THE MASTERS

'The Masters' was my first published genuine authentic real virgin-wool science fiction story, by which I mean a story in which or to which the existence and the accomplishments of science are, in some way, essential. At least that is what I mean by science fiction on Mondays. On Tuesdays sometimes I mean something else.

Some science-fiction writers detest science, its spirit, method, and works; others like it. Some are anti-technology, others are technology-worshippers. I seem to be rather bored by complex technology, but fascinated by biology, psychology, and the speculative ends of astronomy and physics, insofar as I can follow them. The figure of the scientist is a quite common one in my stories, and most often a rather lonely one, isolated, an adventurer, out on the edge of things.

The theme of this story is one I returned to later, with considerably better equipment. It has a good sentence in it, though; 'He had been trying to measure the distance between the earth and God.'

In darkness a man stood alone, naked, holding a smoking torch. The reddish glow lit air and ground for only a few feet; beyond that was the darkness, the immeasurable. From moment to moment there was a rush of wind, a half-glimpsed glitter of eyes, a vast muttering: 'Hold it higher!' The man obeyed, though the torch shook in his shaking hands. He raised it clear above his head, while the darkness rushed and jabbered around him, closing in. The wind blew colder, the red flame guttered. His rigid arms began to quiver, then to jerk a little; his face was oily with sweat; he barely heard the soft, huge

37

jabbering, 'Hold it up, up, hold it up . . .' The current of time had stopped; only the whispering grew and grew till it was a howling, and still, horribly, nothing touched him, nothing came within the circle of light. 'Now walk!' the great voice howled. 'Walk forward!'

The torch above his head, he stepped forward on the ground he could not see. It was not there. With a scream for help, he fell, darkness and thunder about him, the torch he would not let go flaming backward into his eyes.

Time . . . time, and light, and pain, they had all started again. He was crouching in some kind of ditch, on all fours in the mud. His face stung and his eyes, in this bright light, were full of fog. He looked up from his mud-blotched nakedness to a blurred, radiant figure standing above him. Light fell in glory on white hair, the long folds of a white cloak. The eyes gazed at Ganil, the voice spoke to him: 'You lie in the Grave. You lie in the Grave of Knowledge. So lie your forefathers forever beneath the ashes of the fires of Hell.' The voice swelled out: 'O fallen Man, arise!' Ganil managed to get to his feet. The white figure was pointing: 'That is the Light of Human Reason. It guided you to the grave. Drop it.' Ganil realized he was still holding a mud-sodden black stick, the torch; he let it fall. 'Now rise,' the white figure cried in a slow exaltation, 'rise from darkness and walk in the Light of Common Day!' Hands reached to Ganil, helping and hauling him up. Men knelt offering him basins and sponges, others towelled him, rubbed him down till he stood clean and warm, a grey cloak round his shoulders, amid the chatting and laughter, coming and going, in the bright spacious hall. A bald man clapped his shoulder. 'Come on, time for the Oath.'

'Did I – did I do all right?'

'Fine! Only you held up that damn fool torch so long. Thought you'd keep us growling around in the dark all day. Come on.' They led him over black pavement and under the very lofty, white-beamed ceiling, to a curtain that dropped, pure white, in a few straight folds, thirty feet from roof to floor.

'Curtain of Mystery,' somebody said to Ganil in a matter-of-fact tone. Laughing and talking had died away; they stood all round him, silent. In silence the white curtain parted. Ganil stared foggily at what was revealed: a high altar, a long table, and an old man in white.

'Postulant, will you swear our Oath with us?'

Somebody nudged Ganil, whispering, 'I will.' 'I will,' Ganil stuttered.

'Swear then, Masters of the Rite!' The old man raised up a shape of silver: an X-cross, supported by an iron shaft. 'Under the Cross of the Common Day I swear never to reveal the rites and mysteries of my Lodge—'

'Under the Cross ... I swear ... the rites ...' muttered all the men around Ganil, and propelled by another nudge he muttered with them.

'To live well, to work well, to think well—' As Ganil finished repeating this a voice whispered in his ear, 'Don't swear.'

'To avoid all heresies, to betray all necromancers to the Courts of College, and to obey the High Masters of my Lodge from now forth till my death—' Mutter, mutter. Some seemed to be repeating the long passage, some not; Ganil, confused, muttered a word or two and then stood silent. 'And I swear never to teach the Mysteries of Machinery to any gentile. I swear this beneath the Sun.' A grating rumble almost drowned their voices. Slowly, crankily, a section of the roof was swinging back to reveal the yellow-grey, cloud-covered sky of summer. 'Behold the Light of Common Day!' the old man in white cried out, triumphant, and Ganil stared up at it. The machinery apparently stuck before the skylight was fully open; there was a loud clanking of gears, then silence. The old man came forward, kissed Ganil on both cheeks, and said, 'Welcome, Master Ganil, to the Inner Rite of the Mystery of the Machine.' The initiation was over. Ganil was a Master of his Lodge.

'Mean burn you got there,' the bald fellow said as they all walked back down the hall. Ganil put up his hand and found

that his left cheek and temple were raw and sore. 'Lucky it missed your eye.'

'Just missed being blinded by the light of Reason, eh?' said a soft voice. Glancing round Ganil saw a fair man, with brown hair and blue eyes, actually blue, like those of an albino cat or a blind horse. He looked away from the deformity at once, but the fair man went on in his soft voice, the voice that had whispered 'Don't swear' during the taking of the Oath, 'I'm Mede Fairman. I'll be your Co-Master in Lee's shop. Feel like getting a beer when we're out of here?'

The dank beer-dreggy warmth of the tavern was a queer change from all the terror and ceremony of the day. Ganil felt dizzy. Mede Fairman drank off half a tankard, wiped foam pleasurably off his mouth, and inquired, 'What d'you think of the initiation?'

'It was – it was—'

'Humbling?'

'Yes,' Ganil agreed. 'Really humbling.'

'Humiliating, even,' the blue-eyed man suggested.

'Yes. A – a great mystery.' Perplexed, Ganil stared down into his beer. Mede smiled and said in his soft voice, 'I know. Drink up, now. I think you ought to have an Apothecary look at that burn.' Ganil obediently followed him out into the evening, into the narrow streets thronged with pedestrians, horse-carts, ox-carts, chuffing motor-carts. In the Merchantsplace the booths of the artisans were being closed for the night, and down High Street the great doors of the Shops and Lodges were already barred. Here and there the overhung, elbowing houses were parted by the blank yellow façade of a temple, marked with one plain circle of polished brass. In the dull, brief summer twilight under the unmoving clouds the black-haired, bronze-skinned people of the Common Day crowded and idled and pushed and talked and cursed and laughed, and Ganil, dizzy from fatigue and pain and strong beer, kept close beside Mede as if, for all his own new Masterhood, this blue-eyed stranger were his only guide.

*

'XVI plus IXX,' Ganil said impatiently, 'what the devil, boy, can't you add?' The apprentice flushed red. 'Isn't it XXXVI, then, Master Ganil?' he asked feebly. For answer Ganil jammed one of the rods the boy had been machining into its place in the steam engine that was being repaired; it was too long by an inch.

'It's because my rule of thumb's so long, sir,' the boy said, displaying his knobby hands. The distance between first and second thumb-joint was in fact unusually long. 'So it is,' Ganil said. His dark face darkened. 'Very interesting. But it doesn't matter how long your inch is so long as you use it consistently. And what matters, you blockhead, is that XVI and IXX don't make XXXVI, never have, never can, never will till the world ends – you incompetent gentile!'

'Yes, sir. It's so hard to remember, sir.'

'It's intended to be hard to remember, Wanno Prentice,' said a deep voice: Lee the Shopmaster, a fat deep-chested man with bright black eyes. 'Come over here a minute, Ganil.' Leading him to a quieter corner of the great workshop, Lee went on cheerfully, 'You're a bit impatient, Master Ganil.'

'Wanno should know his addition-tables.'

'Even Masters forget an addition now and then, you know.' Lee patted Ganil's shoulder in a fatherly way. 'Why, you sounded for a moment there as if you expected him to compute it!' He laughed aloud, a fine bass laugh through which his eyes gleamed merrily and with infinite shrewdness. 'Take it easy, that's all . . . I understand you're coming for dinner next Altarday Eve?'

'I took the liberty—'

'Fine, fine! More power to you. Wish she'd take on a good steady fellow like you. But I give you fair warning. My daughter's a willful hussy.' Again the Master laughed, and Ganil grinned, a little ruefully. The Shopmaster's daughter Lani had not only most of the young men of the Shop, but also her father, twisted right round her little finger. A clever, quicksilver girl, she had at first rather scared Ganil. It took him a while

to notice that she spoke, to him only, with a certain shyness, a hint almost of pleading. He had finally got up courage to ask a dinner invitation from her mother, the recognized first step of a courtship. He stood now where Lee had left him, thinking of Lani's smile.

'Ganil, have you ever seen the Sun?'

It was a low voice, dry and easy. He turned, meeting his friend's blue eyes.

'The Sun? Yes, of course I have.'

'When was the last time?'

'Let's see, I was twenty-six; four years ago. Weren't you here in Edun then? It came out in late afternoon, and that night there were stars. I counted eighty-one, I remember, before the sky closed.'

'I was up north in Keling then in my first Mastership.' Mede leaned against the wooden guard rail of the model heavy steam engine as he spoke. His light eyes looked away from the busy shop, out the windows at the fine, steady rain of late autumn. 'Heard you telling off young Wanno just now ... "What matters is that XVI and IXX don't make XXXVI ..." "When I was twenty-six, four years ago ... I counted eighty-one stars ..." A little more and you'd be computing, Ganil.'

Ganil frowned, unconsciously rubbing the whitish scar on his temple. 'Well, hell, Mede! even gentiles know IV from XXX!'

Mede smiled faintly. He had his Comparing Stick in his hand, and lowering it he drew on the dusty floor a round shape. 'What's that?' he asked.

'The Sun.'

'Right. It's also a ... a figure. A number. The figure for Nothing.'

'The figure for Nothing?'

'Yes. You could use it in the subtraction-tables, for instance. I from II leaves I, right? But what does II from II leave?' A pause. He tapped the circle with his stick. 'That.'

'Yes, of course.' Ganil stared down at the circle, the sacred

42

image of the Sun, the Hidden Light, the Face of God. 'Is that priest-knowledge?'

'No.' Mede drew an X-cross over the circle. 'That is.'

'Then what – whose knowledge is the – the figure for Nothing?'

'No one's. Anyone's. It's not a mystery.' Ganil frowned in surprise at this statement. They spoke in low voices, standing close as if discussing a measurement on Mede's Comparing Stick. 'Why did you count the stars, Ganil?'

'I . . . I wanted to know. I've always liked counting, numbers, the tables. That's why I'm a Mechanic.'

'Yes. You're thirty, aren't you, you've been a Master for four months now. Did you ever think, Ganil, that to be a Master means you have learned everything your trade can teach? From now on until your death you'll learn nothing more. There is no more.'

'But the Shopmasters—'

'Shopmasters learn some secret signals and passwords,' Mede said in his soft, dry voice, 'and of course they have power. But they know no more than you . . . You thought perhaps they were allowed to compute, didn't you? They aren't.'

Ganil was silent.

'And yet there are things to be learned, Ganil.'

'Where?'

'Outside.'

There was a long pause.

'I can't listen to this, Mede. Don't speak of it again. I won't betray you.' Ganil turned and walked away, his face harsh with anger. With all his will he turned that confused and struggling anger against Mede, a man as deformed of mind as of body, an evil counsellor, a lost friend.

It had been a pleasant evening: Lee jovial, his fat wife motherly, and Lani shy and radiant. Ganil's youthful gravity made her tease him, but even in her teasing was that pleading, yielding note; another moment, it seemed, and all her verve would turn

43

to tenderness. Passing a dish at table once her hand had for an instant touched his. He still knew exactly where, there, the side of his right hand near the wrist, one soft touch. He moaned luxuriously as he lay in bed in his room over the Shop in the utter blackness of the city night. O Lani, soft touch of a hand, of lips – O Lord, Lord! Courtship was a long business, eight months at least, going from step to step as one must with a Master's daughter. Ganil had to get his mind off this unendurable sweetness. Think of nothing, he told himself firmly, go to sleep. Think of nothing... And he thought of nothing. The circle. The round empty circle. What was I times o? The same as II times o. What if you put I beside o, what would that figure be, 10?

Mede Fairman sat up in bed, brown hair lank over groggy blue eyes, and tried to focus on the person crashing around his room. The first dirty-yellow light of dawn showed at the window. 'This is Altarday,' he growled, 'go away, I'm sleepy.' The vague figure resolved into Ganil, the crashing into a whisper. 'Mede!' Ganil kept whispering, 'look!' He stuck a slate under Mede's nose. 'Look, look what you can do with that figure for Nothing—'

'Oh, that,' said Mede. He pushed Ganil and the slate away, went and dunked his head in the basin of icy water on his clothes-chest, and kept it there a while. He returned dripping to sit on the bed. 'Let's see.'

'See, you can use any number for a base, I used XII because it's handy. XII becomes I-o, see, and XIII is I-I, then when you get up to XXIV—'

'Sh.'

Mede studied the slate. Finally he said, 'Will you remember this?' and at Ganil's nod, wiped the neat crowded figures off the slate with a rub of his sleeve. 'I hadn't realized that one could use any base... But look, use the base X, I'll tell you why in a minute, and here's a device that makes it easier. Now X will be 10, and XI will be II, but for XII, write this,' and he wrote on the slate, 12.

Ganil stared at the figure. At last he said in a peculiar struggling voice, 'Isn't that one of the black numbers?'

'Yes, it is. All you've done, Ganil, is to come at the black numbers by the back door.'

Ganil sat beside him, silent.

'What's CXX times MCC?' Mede inquired.

'The tables don't go that high.'

'Watch.' Mede wrote on the slate:

$$\begin{array}{r} 1200 \\ \underline{120} \end{array}$$

and then as Ganil watched,

$$\begin{array}{r} 0000 \\ 2400 \\ \underline{1200} \\ 144000 \end{array}$$

Another long pause. 'Three Nothings... XII times itself ... Give me the slate,' Ganil muttered. Then after a silence broken only by the patter of rain and the squeak of chalk on slate, 'What's the black number for VIII?'

By twilight of that cold Altarday they had gone as far as Mede could take Ganil. Indeed Ganil had gone farther than Mede could follow him. 'You must meet Yin,' the fair man said. 'He can teach you what you need. Yin works with angles, triangles, measurements. He can measure the distance between any two points, points you can't reach, using his triangles. He is a great Learner. Numbers are the heart of this knowledge, the language of it.'

'And my own language.'

'Yes, it is. Not mine. I don't love numbers for themselves. I want to use them. To explain things... For instance, if you throw a ball, what makes the ball move?'

'Your throwing it.' Ganil grinned. White as a sheet – much

whiter than Mede's sheets – his head ringing with sixteen straight hours of mathematics minus meals or sleep, he had lost all fear, all humility. His smile was that of a king come home from exile.

'Fine,' said Mede. 'Why does it *keep on* moving?'

'Because . . . because the air holds it up?'

'Then why does it ever fall? Why does it follow a curve? What kind of curve is it? Do you see how I need your numbers?' It was Mede who now looked like a king, an angry king with an empire too immense to control. 'And they talk about Mysteries,' he snorted, 'in their little shuttered shops! – Here, come on, let's get some dinner and go see Yin.'

Built right up against the city wall, the tall old house peered from leaded windows at the two young Masters down in the street. Sulfurous late-autumn twilight hung over the steep slate roofs shining with rain. 'Yin was a Machine-Master like us,' Mede told Ganil as they waited at the iron-barred door, 'retired now, you'll see why. Men from all the Lodges come here, apothecaries, weavers, masons. Even some artisans. One butcher. He cuts up dead cats.' Mede spoke with amused tolerance, as physicists generally speak of biologists. Now the door swung open, and a servant took them upstairs to a room where logs glowed on a great hearth, and a man rose from a high-backed oaken chair to greet them.

Ganil thought at once of the Overmaster of his Lodge, the figure that had cried down to him in his grave, 'Arise.' Yin too was old and tall, and wore the white cloak of the High Masters. But he stooped, and his face was creased and weary as an old hound's. He held out his left hand to greet them. His right arm ended in a long healed, shiny stump at the wrist.

'This is Ganil,' Mede was saying. 'He invented the duodecimal system last night. Get him working on the mathematics of curves for me, Master Yin.'

Yin laughed, an old man's short, soft laugh. 'Welcome, Ganil. From now on, come here when you please. We're all necromancers here, we practice the black arts. Or try to . . .

46

Come freely, day or night. And go freely. If we're betrayed, so be it. We must trust one another. Mystery belongs to no man; we're not keeping a secret, but practicing an art. Does that make sense to you?'

Ganil nodded. Words never came easily to him, only numbers. And he found himself very moved, which embarrassed him. This was no solemn symbolic Initiation and Oath, but only an old man talking quietly.

'Good,' said Yin, as if Ganil's nod had been quite sufficient. 'Some wine, young Masters, or ale? My dark ale came out first-rate this year. So you like numbers, do you, Ganil?'

In early spring Ganil stood in the shop supervising Wanno as the prentice took measurements onto his Comparing Stick from the model of the hauling-cart engine. Ganil's face was grim. He had changed over these few months, looked older, more resolute, harder. Four hours' sleep a night plus the invention of algebra might well change a man.

'Master Ganil?' said a shy voice.

'Repeat that measurement,' he told Wanno, and then turned questioningly to the girl. Lani too had changed. Her face looked a little cross, a little forlorn, and she spoke to Ganil with real timidity. He had taken the second step of courtship, the three evening calls, and then becoming absorbed in his work with Yin, had gone no further. No man had ever dropped Lani in the middle of a courtship. No man had ever looked right through her, as he was doing now. What was it he saw, when he looked through her? She was wild to know that, to get at his secret, to get at him. In a vague, unquantifiable way he knew this, and was sorry for Lani, and a little afraid of her.

She was watching Wanno. 'Do they ... do you ever change those measurements?' she asked, trying to make conversation.

'To change a Model is the heresy of Invention.'

That ended that. 'My father wanted me to tell you the Shop will be shut tomorrow.'

'Shut? Why's that?'

'The College has announced there's a west wind rising, and the Sun may come out tomorrow.'

'Good! A good beginning for the spring, eh? Thanks.' And he turned back to the model.

The Priests of the College had for once been right. Weather prediction, on which they spent most of their waking hours, was a thankless task. But once in ten tries or so they caught a Sun, and this was one of the times. By noon the rains had ceased and the cloud-cover was paling, beginning to boil and flow slowly eastward. By mid-afternoon all the people of Edun were out on the streets and squares, on chimneypots and roof-trees, on the wall and the fields beyond the wall, watching; the Priests of the College had begun their ceremonial dance, bowing and interweaving on the great forecourt of the College; priests stood ready in every temple to pull chains that would open the roofs so that the Sun's light might strike the altar-stones. And in late afternoon at last the sky opened. Between ragged smoking edges of yellow-grey appeared a streak of blue. A sigh, a soft tremendous murmur rose up from the streets, squares, windows, roofs, walls of the city of Edun: 'Heaven, heaven . . .'

The rent in the sky widened. A shower of rain spattered over the city, blown aslant on the fresh wind, and suddenly the raindrops glittered, as at night in torchlight; but this glory they reflected was the glory of the Sun. To westward it stood, all alone in heaven, blinding.

Ganil stood with the others, face lifted. On his face, on the scar of his burn, he felt the heat of the Sun. He stared at it till his eyes swam with tears, the Circle of Fire, the face of God . . .

'What is the Sun?'

That was Mede's soft voice, remembered. A cold midwinter night, he and Mede and Yin and the others talking before the fire in Yin's house. 'Is it a circle, or a sphere? Why does it cross the sky? And how big is it – how far away is it? Ah, to think that once all a man had to do to see the Sun was lift up his head . . .'

Flutes and drums throbbed, a gay faint sound, away off at the College. Sometimes cloud-fragments blew across the

intolerable face and the world turned grey and chill again, the flutes stopped; but the west wind blew, the clouds passed and the Sun reappeared, always a little lower. Just before it sank into the heavy cloud-rack in the west it was growing red and one could look at it without pain. In those moments it certainly looked to Ganil's eyes not like a disk but like an enormous, haze-warped, slowly falling ball.

It fell, was gone.

Overhead through the torn sky glimpses of heaven still shone, clear and deep, blue-green. Then westward near where the Sun had set, at the edge of a mounting cloud, gleamed one bright point: the evening star. 'Look!' Ganil cried, but few turned to look. The Sun was set, what did stars matter. The yellowish haze, part of the single windingsheet of cloud that had covered earth with its mantle of dust and rain ever since Hellfire fourteen generations ago, moved up over the star, erased it. Ganil sighed, rubbed his neck that was stiff with craning, and started home along with all the other people of the Common Day.

He was arrested that night. From guards and fellow-prisoners (all his shop was in jail with him except the Shopmaster Lee) he learned that his crime was that of knowing Mede Fairman. Mede stood accused of heresy. He had been seen out on the fields pointing an instrument at the Sun, a device, they said, for measuring distances. He had been trying to measure the distance between the earth and God.

The prentices were soon let go. On the third day guards came for Ganil, bringing him out into one of the enclosed courts of the College, into the soft, fine rain of early spring. Priests lived almost wholly out of doors, and the great complex of Edun College was only a series of meager barracks surrounding the roofless sleeping-courts, writing-courts, prayer-courts, eating-courts, and courts of law. Into one of these they brought Ganil, forcing him on between the ranks of men robed in white and yellow that filled it, until he stood in front of them all. He saw a clear space, an altar, a long table shining wet with rain, and

behind it a priest in the golden robe of the High Mystery. At the far end of the table was another man who like Ganil was flanked by guards. This man was looking at Ganil, a straight look, cold and blank; yet they were blue eyes, the same blue as heaven above the clouds.

'Ganil Kalson of Edun, you are suspect as an acquaintance of Mede Fairman, accused of the heresies of Invention and Computation. You were this man's friend?'

'We were Co-Masters—'

'Yes. Did he ever speak to you of measurements made without Comparing Sticks?'

'No.'

'Of black numbers?'

'No.'

'Of the black arts?'

'No.'

'Master Ganil, you've answered No three times. Do you know the Order of the Priest-Masters of the Mystery of the Law concerning suspects in heresy?'

'No, I don't—'

'The Order says: "If the suspect shall deny the questions four times, the questions may be repeated with use of the handpress until answered." I shall now repeat, unless you wish to retract one of your denials.'

'No,' Ganil said, confused, looking round him at the crowded blank faces, the high walls. When they had brought out a squat wooden machine of some kind and had locked his right hand into it, he was still more confused than scared. What was all this mumbo-jumbo? It was like his initiation, when they had worked so hard to frighten him; that time they had succeeded.

'As a Mechanic,' the golden priest was saying, 'you know the use of the lever, Master Ganil. Will you retract?'

'No,' Ganil said, frowning a little. He had noticed that his right arm now seemed to end at the wrist, like Yin's.

'Very well.' One of the guards put his hands on the lever

sticking out of the wooden box, and the golden priest said, 'Were you a friend of Mede Fairman?'

'No,' Ganil said. He said No to each question even after he had ceased to hear the priest's voice; he went on saying No till he heard his own voice mixed with the clapping echo from the walls above the courtyard, No, no, no, no.

The light came and went, the rain fell cold on his face and ceased, somebody kept trying to help him stand up. His grey cloak stank, he had been sick with pain. At the thought, he was sick again. 'Take it easy, now,' a guard was whispering to him. The motionless white and yellow ranks were still crowded there, the faces set, the eyes staring . . . but not at him now.

'Heretic, do you know this man?'

'He is my Co-Master.'

'Did you speak to him of the black arts?'

'Yes.'

'Did you teach him the black arts?'

'No. I tried to.' The voice cracked a little; even in the silence of the courtyard, over only the whisper of the rain, it was hard to hear Mede speak. 'He was too stupid. He dared not and could not learn. He'll make a fine Shopmaster.' The cold blue eyes looked straight at Ganil without pity or appeal.

The golden priest turned to face the court again. 'There is no evidence against the suspect Ganil. You may go, suspect. Come here at noon tomorrow to witness the execution of judgment. Failure to come will be taken as proof of your guilt.' Before he understood, the guards had led Ganil out of the courtyard. They left him at a side door of the College, barring the door behind him with a clang. He stood there a while, then crouched down on the pavement, pressing his blackened, blood-caked hand against his side under his cloak. Rain whispered around him. No one passed. It was not till dusk that he pulled himself up and walked, street by street, house by house, step by step, across the city to Yin's house.

In the shadows of the doorway a shadow moved, spoke: 'Ganil!' He stopped. 'Ganil, I don't care if you're suspect. It's

51

all right. Come back home with me. My father will take you back into the shop. He will if I ask him.'

Ganil was silent.

'Come with me. I waited for you, I knew you'd come here, I've followed you before.' Her nervous, jubilant laugh died away.

'Let me by, Lani.'

'No. Why do you come to old Yin's house? Who lives here? Who is she? Come back with me, you have to, my father won't take a suspect back into his shop, unless I—'

Yin's door was never locked. Ganil brushed past her and went in, shutting it behind him. No servant came; the house was dark, silent. They had all been taken, all the Learners, they would all be questioned and tortured and killed.

'Who's that?'

Yin stood on the stair-landing, lamplight bright on his white hair. He came to Ganil and helped him up the stairs. Ganil spoke very fast: 'I was followed here, a girl from the shop, Lee's daughter, if she tells him he'll recognize your name, he'll send the guards here—'

'I sent the others away three days ago.' At the sound of Yin's voice Ganil stopped, stared at the old man's creased, quiet face, and then said childishly, 'Look,' holding out his right hand, 'look, like yours.'

'Yes. Come sit down, Ganil.'

'They condemned him. Not me, they let me go. He said he couldn't teach me, I couldn't learn. To save me—'

'And your mathematics. Come here now, sit down.'

Ganil got control of himself, and obeyed. Yin made him lie down, then did what he could about cleaning and bandaging his hand. Then, sitting down between Ganil and the glowing fire, he gave a wheezy sigh. 'Well,' he said, 'now you're a heresy suspect. I've been one for twenty years. You get used to it... Don't worry about our friends. But if the girl tells Lee and your name gets linked with mine... We'd better leave Edun. Separately. But tonight.'

Ganil said nothing. To leave his shop without the Overmaster's permission meant excommunication, the loss of his Mastership. He would be barred from his own trade. What could he do, with his crippled hand, where could he go? He had never been out of Edun in his life.

The silence of the house spread out above and below them. Ganil strained to hear sounds down in the street, the tramping of a troop of guards come to re-arrest him. He had to get out, to get away, tonight – 'I can't,' he said abruptly. 'I have to be – to be at the College tomorrow, at noon.'

Yin knew what he meant. Again the silence closed round them. The old man's voice was very dry and weary when he finally spoke. 'That's the condition of your release, eh? All right; go do it; you don't want them hunting you through the Forty Towns as a condemned heretic. A suspect isn't hunted, merely outcast. It's preferable. Get some sleep now, Ganil. Before I go I'll tell you where to meet me. Leave as soon as you can; and travel light...'

When Ganil left the house late in the morning, however, he carried something with him, a roll of papers hidden under his cloak, each sheet covered edge to edge with Mede Fairman's clear writing: 'Trajectories,' 'Speed of Falling Bodies,' 'The Nature of Motion...' Yin had left before daybreak, jogging calmly out of town on a grey donkey. 'I'll see you in Keling' had been his only parting with Ganil. Ganil had seen none of the other Learners. Only serfs, servants, beggars, truant schoolboys, and women with their nursemaids and whining children stood with him now in the dull light of noon on the great forecourt of the College. Only riffraff and the idle gathered to see a heretic die. A priest had ordered Ganil to stand at the very front of the crowd. Many people glanced curiously at him, standing there alone in his Master's cloak.

On the other side of the square, in the front of the crowd, he saw a girl in a violet gown. He was not sure it was Lani. Why would she be here to see Mede die? She did not know what it was she hated; or what it was she loved. Love that wants

only to get, to possess, is a monstrous thing, Ganil thought. She loved him, she stood separated from him only by the width of that square. She would never be willing to see that she was separated from him by her own act, by ignorance, by exile, by death.

They brought Mede out just before noon. Ganil glimpsed his face; it was very white, all his deformity exposed, the atavistic pallor of skin, hair, eyes. There was no drawing-out of the scene; a gold-robed priest raised his crossed arms in invocation to the Sun that stood, unseen, at noon behind the pall of clouds, and as he lowered his arms torches were set to the stacks of wood round the stake. Smoke curled up, the same grey-yellow as the clouds. Ganil stood with his injured hand in its sling pressed hard against the roll of papers under his cloak, repeating silently, 'Let the smoke suffocate him first...' But the wood was dry and caught quickly. He felt the heat on his face, on his fire-scarred temple. Beside him a young priest tried to draw back, could not because of the pressing, staring, sighing crowd, and stood still, swaying a little and breathing in gasps. The smoke was thick now, hiding the flames and the figure among them. But Ganil could hear his voice, not soft now, loud, very loud. He heard it, he forced himself to hear it, but at the same time he listened in his spirit to a steady voice, soft, continuing: 'What is the Sun? Why does it cross the sky?... Do you see how I need your numbers?... For XII, write 12... This is also a figure, the figure for Nothing.'

The screaming had stopped, but the soft voice had not.

Ganil raised his head. The crowd was drifting away; the young priest knelt on the pavement by him, praying and sobbing aloud. Ganil glanced up at the heavy sky and then set off alone through the streets of the city and out through the city gate, northward, into exile and towards his home.

DARKNESS BOX

When my daughter Caroline was three she came to me with a small wooden box in her small hands and said, 'Guess fwat is in this bockus!' I guessed caterpillars, mice, elephants, etc. She shook her head, smiled an unspeakably eldritch smile, opened the box slightly so that I could just see in, and said: 'Darkness.'

Hence this story.

On soft sand by the sea's edge a little boy walked leaving no footprints. Gulls cried in the bright sunless sky, trout leaped from the saltless ocean. Far off on the horizon the sea serpent raised himself a moment in seven enormous arches and then, bellowing, sank. The child whistled but the sea serpent, busy hunting whales, did not surface again. The child walked on casting no shadow, leaving no tracks on the sand between the cliffs and the sea. Ahead of him rose a grassy headland on which stood a four-legged hut. As he climbed a path up the cliff the hut skipped about and rubbed its front legs together like a lawyer or a fly; but the hands of the clock inside, which said ten minutes of ten, never moved.

'What's that you've got there, Dicky?' asked his mother as she added parsley and a pinch of pepper to the rabbit stew simmering in an alembic.

'A box, Mummy.'

'Where did you find it?'

Mummy's familiar leaped down from the onion-festooned

rafters and, draping itself like a foxfur round her neck, said, 'By the sea.'

Dicky nodded. 'That's right. The sea washed it up.'

'And what's inside it?'

The familiar said nothing, but purred. The witch turned round to look into her son's round face. 'What's in it?' she repeated.

'Darkness.'

'Oh? Let's see.'

As she bent down to look the familiar, still purring, shut its eyes. Holding the box against his chest, the little boy very carefully lifted the lid a scant inch.

'So it is,' said his mother. 'Now put it away, don't let it get knocked about. I wonder where the key got to. Run wash your hands now. Table, lay!' And while the child worked the heavy pump-handle in the yard and splashed his face and hands, the hut resounded with the clatter of plates and forks materializing.

After the meal, while his mother was having her morning nap, Dicky took down the water-bleached, sand-encrusted box from his treasure shelf and set out with it across the dunes, away from the sea. Close at his heels the black familiar followed him, trotting patiently over the sand through the coarse grass, the only shadow he had.

At the summit of the pass Prince Rikard turned in the saddle to look back over the plumes and pennants of his army, over the long falling road, to the towered walls of his father's city. Under the sunless sky it shimmered there on the plain, fragile and shadowless as a pearl. Seeing it so he knew it could never be taken, and his heart sang with pride. He gave his captains the signal for quick march and set spurs to his horse. It reared and broke into a gallop, while his gryphon swooped and screamed overhead. She teased the white horse, diving straight down at it clashing her beak, swerving aside just in time; the horse, bridleless, would snap furiously at her snaky tail or rear to strike out with silver hoofs. The gryphon would cackle and roar,

circle back over the dunes and with a screech and swoop play the trick all over. Afraid she might wear herself out before the battle, Rikard finally leashed her, after which she flew along steadily, purring and chirping, by his side.

The sea lay before him; somewhere beneath the cliffs the enemy force his brother led was hidden. The road wound down growing sandier, the sea appearing to right or left always nearer. Abruptly the road fell away; the white horse leaped the ten-foot drop and galloped out over the beach. As he came out from between the dunes Rikard saw a long line of men strung out on the sand, and behind them three black-prowed ships. His own men were scrambling down the drop, swarming over the dunes, blue flags snapping in the sea wind, voices faint against the sound of the sea. Without warning or parley the two forces met, sword to sword and man to man. With a great shrilling scream the gryphon soared up, jerking the leash from Rikard's hand, then dropped like a falcon, beak and claws extended, down on a tall man in grey, the enemy leader. But the tall man's sword was drawn. As the iron beak snapped on his shoulder, trying to get the throat, the iron sword jabbed out and up, slashing the gryphon's belly. She doubled up in air and fell, knocking the man down with the sweep of her great wing, screaming, blackening the sand with blood. The tall man staggered up and slashed off her head and wings, turning half blinded with sand and blood only when Rikard was almost on him. Without a word he turned, lifting his steaming sword to parry Rikard's blow. He tried to strike at the horse's legs, but got no chance, for the beast would back and rear and run at him, Rikard's sword slashing down from above. The tall man's arms began to grow heavy, his breath came in gasps. Rikard gave no quarter. Once more the tall man raised his sword, lunged, and took the whizzing slash of his brother's sword straight across his uplifted face. He fell without a word. Brown sand fell over his body in a little shower from the white stallion's hoofs as Rikard spurred back to the thick of the fight.

The attackers fought on doggedly, always fewer of them,

57

and those few being pushed back step by step towards the sea. When only a knot of twenty or so remained they broke, sprinting desperately for the ships, pushing them off chest-deep in the breakers, clambering aboard. Rikard shouted to his men. They came to him across the sand, picking their way among hacked corpses. The badly wounded tried to crawl to him on hands and knees. All that could walk gathered in ranks in a hollow behind the dune on which Rikard stood. Behind him, out on deep water, the three black ships lay motionless, balanced on their oars.

Rikard sat down, alone on the dune-top among the rank grass. He bowed his head and put his hands over his face. Near him the white horse stood still as a horse of stone. Below him his men stood silent. Behind him on the beach the tall man, his face obliterated in blood, lay near the body of the gryphon, and the other dead lay staring at the sky where no sun shone.

A little gust of wind blew by. Rikard raised his face, which though young was very grim. He signalled his captains, swung up into the saddle, and set off round the dunes and back towards the city at a trot, not waiting to see the black ships steer in to shore where their soldiers could board them, or his own army fill up its ranks and come marching behind him. When the gryphon swooped screaming overhead he raised his arm, grinning at the great creature as she tried to perch on his gloved wrist, flapping her wings and screeching like a tomcat. 'You no-good gryphon,' he said, 'you hen, go home to your chicken coop!' Insulted, the monster yawped and sailed off eastward towards the city. Behind him his army wound upward through the hills, leaving no track. Behind them the brown sand lay smooth as silk, stainless. The black ships, sails set, already stood out well to sea. In the prow of the first stood a tall, grim-faced man in grey.

Taking an easier road homeward, Rikard passed not far from the four-legged hut on the headland. The witch stood in the doorway, hailing him. He galloped over, and, drawing rein right at the gate of the little yard, he looked at the young witch. She

was bright and dark as coals, her black hair whipped in the sea wind. She looked at him, white-armored on a white horse.

'Prince,' she said, 'you'll go to battle once too often.'

He laughed. 'What should I do – let my brother lay siege to the city?'

'Yes, let him. No man can take the city.'

'I know. But my father the king exiled him, he must not set foot even on our shore. I'm my father's soldier, I fight as he commands.'

The witch looked out to sea, then back at the young man. Her dark face sharpened, nose and chin peaking crone-like, eyes flashing. 'Serve and be served,' she said, 'rule and be ruled. Your brother chose neither to serve nor rule ... Listen, prince, take care.' Her face warmed again to beauty. 'The sea brings presents this morning, the wind blows, the crystals break. Take care.'

Gravely he bowed his thanks, then wheeled his horse and was gone, white as a gull over the long curve of the dunes.

The witch went back into the hut, glancing about its one room to see that everything was in place: bats, onions, cauldrons, carpets, broom, toad-stones, crystal balls (cracked through), the thin crescent moon hung up on the chimney, the Books, the familiar – She looked again, then hurried out and called 'Dicky!'

The wind from the west was cold now, bending the coarse grass down.

'Dicky! ... Kitty, kitty kitty!'

The wind caught the voice from her lips, tore it into bits and blew it away.

She snapped her fingers. The broom came zooming out the door, horizontal and about two feet off the ground, while the hut shivered and hopped about in excitement. 'Shut up!' the witch snapped, and the door obediently slammed. Mounting the broom she took off in a long gliding swoop southwards down the beach, now and then crying out, 'Dicky! ... Here, kitty, kitty, kitty!'

The young prince, rejoining his men, had dismounted to walk with them. As they reached the pass and saw the city below them on the plain, he felt a tug at his cloak.

'Prince—'

A little boy, so little he was still fat and round-cheeked, stood with a scared look, holding up a battered, sandy box. Beside him a black cat sat smiling broadly. 'The sea brought this – it's for the prince of the land, I know it is – please take it!'

'What's in it?'

'Darkness, sir.'

Rikard took the box and after a slight hesitation opened it a little, just a crack. 'It's painted black inside,' he said with a hard grin.

'No, prince, truly it's not. Open it wider!'

Cautiously Rikard lifted the lid higher, an inch or two, and peered in. Then he shut it quickly, even as the child said, 'Don't let the wind blow it out, prince!'

'I shall take this to the king.'

'But it's for you, sir—'

'All seagifts are the king's. But thank you for it, boy.' They looked at each other for a moment, the little round boy and the hard splendid youth; then Rikard turned and strode on, while Dicky wandered back down the hills, silent and disconsolate. He heard his mother's voice from far away to the south, and tried to answer; but the wind blew his call landwards, and the familiar had disappeared.

The bronze gates of the city swung open as the troop approached. Watchdogs bayed, guards stood rigid, the people of the city bowed down as Rikard on his horse clattered at full gallop up the marble streets to the palace. Entering, he glanced up at the great bronze clock on the bell-tower, the highest of the nine white towers of the palace. The moveless hands said ten minutes of ten.

In the Hall of Audience his father awaited him: a fierce grey-haired man crowned with iron, his hands clenched on the heads of iron chimaeras that formed the arms of the throne.

Rikard knelt and with bowed head, never looking up, reported the success of his foray. 'The Exile was killed, with the greater part of his men; the rest fled in their ships.'

A voice answered like an iron door moving on unused hinges: 'Well done, prince.'

'I bring you a seagift, Lord.' Still with head bowed, Rikard held up the wooden box.

A low snarl came from the throat of one of the carven monsters of the throne.

'That is mine,' said the old king so harshly that Rikard glanced up for a second, seeing the teeth of the chimaeras bared and the king's eyes glittering.

'Therefore I bring it to you, Lord.'

'That is mine – I gave it to the sea, I myself! And the sea spits back my gift.' A long silence, then the king spoke more softly. 'Well, keep it, prince. The sea doesn't want it, nor do I. It's in your hands. Keep it – locked. Keep it locked, prince!'

Rikard, on his knees, bowed lower in thanks and consent, then rose and backed down the long hall, never looking up. As he came out into the glittering anteroom, officers and noblemen gathered round him, ready as usual to ask about the battle, laugh, drink, and chatter. He passed among them without a word or glance and went to his own quarters, alone, carrying the box carefully in both hands.

His bright, shadowless, windowless room was decorated on every wall with patterns of gold inset with topazes, opals, crystals, and, most vivid of all jewels, candle flames moveless on golden sconces. He set the box down on a glass table, threw off his cloak, unbuckled his swordbelt, and sat down sighing. The gryphon loped in from his bedroom, talons rasping on the mosaic floor, stuck her great head onto his knees and waited for him to scratch her feathery mane. There was also a cat prowling around the room, a sleek black one; Rikard took no notice. The palace was full of animals, cats, hounds, apes, squirrels, young hippogriffs, white mice, tigers. Every lady had her unicorn, every courtier had a dozen pets. The prince had

only one, the gryphon which always fought for him, his one unquestioning friend. He scratched the gryphon's mane, often glancing down to meet the loving golden gaze of her round eyes, now and then glancing too at the box on the table. There was no key to lock it.

Music played softly in a distant room, a ceaseless interweaving of notes like the sound of a fountain.

He turned to look at the clock on the mantle, an ornate square of gold and blue enamel. It was ten minutes of ten: time to rise and buckle on his sword, call up his men, and go to battle. The Exile was returning, determined to take the city and reclaim his right to the throne, his inheritance. His black ships must be driven back to sea. The brothers must fight, and one must die, and the city be saved. Rikard rose, and at once the gryphon jumped up lashing her tail, eager for the fight. 'All right, come along!' Rikard told her, but his voice was cold. He took up his sword in the pearl-encrusted sheath and buckled it on, and the gryphon whined with excitement and rubbed her beak on his hand. He did not respond. He was tired and sad, he longed for something – for what? To hear music that ceased, to speak to his brother once before they fought... he did not know. Heir and defender, he must obey. He set the silver helmet on his head and turned to pick up his cloak, flung over a chair. The pearly sheath slung from his belt clattered against something behind him; he turned and saw the box, lying on the floor, open. As he stood looking at it with the same cold, absent look, a little blackness like smoke gathered about it on the floor. He stooped and picked it up, and darkness ran out over his hands.

The gryphon backed away, whining.

Tall and white-armored, fair-haired, silver-capped in the glittering shadowless room, Rikard stood holding the open box, watching the thick dusk that dripped slowly from it. All around his body now, below his hands, was twilight. He stood still. Then slowly he raised the box up, clear up over his head, and turned it upside down.

Darkness flowed over his face. He looked about him, for the distant music had stopped and things were very silent. Candles burned, dots of light picking out flecks of gold and flashes of violet from walls and ceiling. But all the corners were dark, behind each chair lay darkness, and as Rikard turned his head his shadow leapt along the wall. He moved then, quickly, dropping the box, for in one of the black corners he had glimpsed the reddish glow of two great eyes. – The gryphon, of course. He held out his hand and spoke to her. She did not move, but gave a queer metallic cry.

'Come on! Are you afraid of the dark?' he said, and then all at once was afraid himself. He drew his sword. Nothing moved. He took a step backward towards the door; and the monster jumped. He saw the black wings spread across the ceiling, the iron beak, the talons; her bulk was on him before he could stab upwards. He wrestled, the great beak snapping at his throat and the talons tearing at his arms and chest, till he got his sword-arm free and could slash down, pull away and slash again. The second blow half severed the gryphon's neck. She dropped off, lay writhing in the shadows among splinters of glass, then lay still.

Rikard's sword dropped clattering on the floor. His hands were sticky with his own blood, and he could hardly see; the beating of the gryphon's wings had blown out or knocked over every candle but one. He groped his way to a chair and sat down. After a minute, though he still gasped for breath, he did as he had done on the dune-top after battle: bowed his head and hid his face in his hands. It was completely silent. The one candle flickered in its sconce, mirrored feebly in a cluster of topazes on the wall behind it. Rikard raised his head.

The gryphon lay still. Its blood had spread out in a pool, black as the first spilt darkness from the box. Its iron beak was open, its eyes open, like two red stones.

'It's dead,' said a small soft voice, as the witch's cat came picking its way delicately among the fragments of the smashed table. 'Once and for all. Listen, prince!' The cat sat down

63

curling its tail neatly round its paws. Rikard stood motionless, blank-faced, till a sudden sound made him start: a little ting! nearby. Then from the tower overhead a huge dull bell-stroke reverberated in the stone of the floor, in his ears, in his blood. The clocks were striking ten.

There was a pounding at his door, and shouts echoed down the palace corridors mixed with the last booming strokes of the bell, screams of scared animals, calls, commands.

'You'll be late for the battle, prince,' said the cat.

Rikard groped among blood and shadow for his sword, sheathed it, flung on his cloak and went to the door.

'There'll be an afternoon today,' the cat said, 'and a twilight, and night will fall. At nightfall one of you will come home to the city, you or your brother. But only one of you, prince.'

Rikard stood still a moment. 'Is the sun shining now, outside?'

'Yes, it is – now.'

'Well, then, it's worth it,' the young man said, and opened the door and strode on out into the hubbub and panic of the sunlit halls, his shadow falling black behind him.

THE WORD OF UNBINDING

The two stories that follow were my first approach to and exploration of the 'secondary world' of Earthsea, about which I later wrote three novels. I didn't know much about the place at first, and readers familiar with the trilogy will notice that trolls became extinct in Earthsea at some point, and that the history of the dragon Yevaud is somewhat obscure. (He must have been on Sattins Island some decades or centuries before Ged found him, and bound him, on the Isle of Pendor.) But this is only to be expected of dragons, who do not submit to the unidirectional, causal requirements of history, being myths, and neither timebinding nor timebound.

'The Rule of Names' first explores an essential element of how magic works in Earthsea. 'The Word of Unbinding' foreshadows the end of the last book of the trilogy, The Farthest Shore, *in its imagery of the world of the dead. It also reveals a certain obsession with trees, which, once you notice them, keep cropping up throughout my work. I think I am definitely the most arboreal science fiction writer. It's all right for the rest of you who climbed down, and developed opposable thumbs, and erect posture, and all that. There's a few of us still up here swinging.*

Where was he? The floor was hard and slimy, the air black and stinking, and that was all there was. Except a headache. Lying flat on the clammy floor Festin moaned, and then said, 'Staff!' When his alderwood wizard's staff did not come to his hand, he knew he was in peril. He sat up, and not having his staff with which to make a proper light, he struck a spark between finger and thumb, muttering a certain Word. A blue will o' the wisp sprang from the spark and rolled feebly through the air,

sputtering. 'Up,' said Festin, and the fireball wobbled upward till it lit a vaulted trapdoor very high above, so high that Festin projecting into the fireball momentarily saw his own face forty feet below as a pale dot in the darkness. The light struck no reflections in the damp walls; they had been woven out of night, by magic. He rejoined himself and said, 'Out.' The ball expired. Festin sat in the dark, cracking his knuckles.

He must have been overspelled from behind, by surprise; for the last memory he had was of walking through his own woods at evening talking with the trees. Lately, in these lone years in the middle of his life, he had been burdened with a sense of waste, of unspent strength; so, needing to learn patience, he had left the villages and gone to converse with trees, especially oaks, chestnuts, and the grey alders whose roots are in profound communication with running water. It had been six months since he had spoken to a human being. He had been busy with essentials, casting no spells and bothering no one. So who had spellbound him and shut him in this reeking well? 'Who?' he demanded of the walls, and slowly a name gathered on them and ran down to him like a thick black drop sweated out from pores of stone and spores of fungus: 'Voll.'

For a moment Festin was in a cold sweat himself.

He had heard first long ago of Voll the Fell, who was said to be more than wizard yet less than man; who passed from island to island of the Outer Reach, undoing the works of the Ancients, enslaving men, cutting forests and spoiling fields, and sealing in underground tombs any wizard or Mage who tried to combat him. Refugees from ruined islands told always the same tale, that he came at evening on a dark wind over the sea. His slaves followed in ships; these they had seen. But none of them had ever seen Voll . . . There were many men and creatures of evil will among the Islands, and Festin, a young warlock intent on his training, had not paid much heed to these tales of Voll the Fell. 'I can protect this island,' he had thought, knowing his untried power, and had returned to his oaks and alders, the sound of wind in their leaves, the rhythm of growth in their

66

round trunks and limbs and twigs, the taste of sunlight on leaves or dark groundwater around roots. – Where were they now, the trees, his old companions? Had Voll destroyed the forest?

Awake at last and up on his feet, Festin made two broad motions with rigid hands, shouting aloud a Name that would burst all locks and break open any man-made door. But these walls impregnated with night and the name of their builder did not heed, did not hear. The name re-echoed back, clapping in Festin's ears so that he fell on his knees, hiding his head in his arms till the echoes died away in the vaults above him. Then, still shaken by the backfire, he sat brooding.

They were right; Voll was strong. Here on his own ground, within this spell-built dungeon, his magic would withstand any direct attack; and Festin's strength was halved by the loss of his staff. But not even his captor could take from him his powers, relative only to himself, of Projecting and Transforming. So, after rubbing his now doubly aching head, he transformed. Quietly his body melted away into a cloud of fine mist.

Lazy, trailing, the mist rose off the floor, drifting up along the slimy walls until it found, where vault met wall, a hairline crack. Through this, droplet by droplet, it seeped. It was almost all through the crack when a hot wind, hot as a furnace-blast, struck at it, scattering the mist-drops, drying them. Hurriedly the mist sucked itself back into the vault, spiralled to the floor, took on Festin's own form and lay there panting. Transformation is an emotional strain to introverted warlocks of Festin's sort; when to that strain is added the shock of facing unhuman death in one's assumed shape, the experience becomes horrible. Festin lay for a while merely breathing. He was also angry with himself. It had been a pretty simple-minded notion to escape as a mist, after all. Every fool knew that trick. Voll had probably just left a hot wind waiting. Festin gathered himself into a small black bat, flew up to the ceiling, retransformed into a thin stream of plain air, and seeped through the crack.

This time he got clear out and was blowing softly down the hall in which he found himself towards a window, when a sharp

sense of peril made him pull together, snapping himself into the first small, coherent shape that came to mind – a gold ring. It was just as well. The hurricane of arctic air that would have dispersed his air-form in unrecallable chaos merely chilled his ring-form slightly. As the storm passed he lay on the marble pavement, wondering which form might get out the window quickest.

Too late, he began to roll away. An enormous blank-faced troll strode cataclysmically across the floor, stopped, caught the quick-rolling ring and picked it up in a huge limestone-like hand. The troll strode to the trapdoor, lifted it by an iron handle and a muttered charm, and dropped Festin down into the darkness. He fell straight for forty feet and landed on the stone floor – clink.

Resuming his true form he sat up, ruefully rubbing a bruised elbow. Enough of this transformation on an empty stomach. He longed bitterly for his staff, with which he could have summoned up any amount of dinner. Without it, though he could change his own form and exert certain spells and powers, he could not transform or summon to him any material thing – neither lightning nor a lamb chop.

'Patience,' Festin told himself, and when he had got his breath he dissolved his body into the infinite delicacy of volatile oils, becoming the aroma of a frying lamb chop. He drifted once more through the crack. The waiting troll sniffed suspiciously, but already Festin had regrouped himself into a falcon, winging straight for the window. The troll lunged after him, missed by yards, and bellowed in a vast stony voice, 'The hawk, get the hawk!' Swooping over the enchanted castle towards his forest that lay dark to westward, sunlight and sea-glare dazzling his eyes, Festin rode the wind like an arrow. But a quicker arrow found him. Crying out, he fell. Sun and sea and towers spun around him and went out.

He woke again on the dank floor of the dungeon, hands and hair and lips wet with his own blood. The arrow had struck his pinion as a falcon, his shoulder as a man. Lying still, he

mumbled a spell to close the wound. Presently he was able to sit up, and recollect a longer, deeper spell of healing. But he had lost a good deal of blood, and with it, power. A chill had settled in the marrow of his bones which even the healing-spell could not warm. There was darkness in his eyes, even when he struck a will o' the wisp and lit the reeking air: the same dark mist he had seen, as he flew, overhanging his forest and the little towns of his land.

It was up to him to protect that land.

He could not attempt direct escape again. He was too weak and tired. Trusting his power too much, he had lost his strength. Now whatever shape he took would share his weakness, and be trapped.

Shivering with cold, he crouched there, letting the fireball sputter out with a last whiff of methane – marsh gas. The smell brought to his mind's eye the marshes stretching from the forest wall down to the sea, his beloved marshes where no men came, where in fall the swans flew long and level, where between still pools and reed-islands the quick, silent, seaward streamlets ran. Oh, to be a fish in one of those streams; or better yet to be farther upstream, near the springs, in the forest in the shadow of the trees, in the clear brown backwater under an alder's roots, resting hidden . . .

This was a great magic. Festin had no more performed it than has any man who in exile or danger longs for the earth and waters of his home, seeing and yearning over the doorsill of his house, the table where he has eaten, the branches outside the window of the room where he has slept. Only in dreams do any but the great Mages realize this magic of going home. But Festin, with the cold creeping out from his marrow into nerves and veins, stood up between the black walls, gathered his will together till it shone like a candle in the darkness of his flesh, and began to work the great and silent magic.

The walls were gone. He was in the earth, rocks and veins of granite for bones, groundwater for blood, the roots of things

for nerves. Like a blind worm he moved through the earth westward, slowly, darkness before and behind. Then all at once coolness flowed along his back and belly, a buoyant, unresisting, inexhaustible caress. With his sides he tasted the water, felt current-flow; and with lidless eyes he saw before him the deep brown pool between the great buttress-roots of an alder. He darted forward, silvery, into shadow. He had got free. He was home.

The water ran timelessly from its clear spring. He lay on the sand of the pool's bottom letting running water, stronger than any spell of healing, soothe his wound and with its coolness wash away the bleaker cold that had entered him. But as he rested he felt and heard a shaking and trampling in the earth. Who walked now in his forest? Too weary to try to change form, he hid his gleaming trout-body under the arch of the alder root, and waited.

Huge grey fingers groped in the water, roiling the sand. In the dimness above water vague faces, blank eyes loomed and vanished, reappeared. Nets and hands groped, missed, missed again, then caught and lifted him writhing up into the air. He struggled to take back his own shape and could not; his own spell of homecoming bound him. He writhed in the net, gasping in the dry, bright, terrible air, drowning. The agony went on, and he knew nothing beyond it.

After a long time and little by little he became aware that he was in his human form again; some sharp, sour liquid was being forced down his throat. Time lapsed again, and he found himself sprawled face down on the dank floor of the vault. He was back in the power of his enemy. And, though he could breathe again, he was not very far from death.

The chill was all through him now; and the trolls, Voll's servants, must have crushed the fragile trout-body, for when he moved, his ribcage and one forearm stabbed with pain. Broken and without strength, he lay at the bottom of the well of night. There was no power in him to change shape; there was no way out, but one.

Lying there motionless, almost but not quite beyond the reach of pain, Festin thought: Why has he not killed me? Why does he keep me here alive?

Why has he never been seen? With what eyes can he be seen, on what ground does he walk?

He fears me, though I have no strength left.

They say that all the wizards and men of power whom he has defeated live on sealed in tombs like this, live on year after year trying to get free . . .

But if one chose not to live?

So Festin made his choice. His last thought was, If I am wrong, men will think I was a coward. But he did not linger on this thought. Turning his head a little to the side he closed his eyes, took a last deep breath, and whispered the word of unbinding, which is only spoken once.

This was not transformation. He was not changed. His body, the long legs and arms, the clever hands, the eyes that had liked to look on trees and streams, lay unchanged, only still, perfectly still and full of cold. But the walls were gone. The vaults built by magic were gone, and the rooms and towers; and the forest, and the sea, and the sky of evening. They were all gone, and Festin went slowly down the far slope of the hill of being, under new stars.

In life he had had great power; so here he did not forget. Like a candle flame he moved in the darkness of the wider land. And remembering he called out his enemy's name: 'Voll!'

Called, unable to withstand, Voll came towards him, a thick pale shape in the starlight. Festin approached, and the other cowered and screamed as if burnt. Festin followed when he fled, followed him close. A long way they went, over dry lava-flows from the great extinct volcanoes rearing their cones against the unnamed stars, across the spurs of silent hills, through valleys of short black grass, past towns or down their unlit streets between houses through whose windows no face looked. The stars hung in the sky; none set, none rose. There was no change here. No day would come. But they went on,

71

Festin always driving the other before him, till they reached a place where once a river had run, very long ago: a river from the living lands. In the dry streambed, among boulders, a dead body lay: that of an old man, naked, flat eyes staring at the stars that are innocent of death.

'Enter it,' Festin said. The Voll-shadow whimpered, but Festin came closer. Voll cowered away, stooped, and entered in the open mouth of his own dead body.

At once the corpse vanished. Unmarked, stainless, the dry boulders gleamed in starlight. Festin stood still a while, then slowly sat down among the great rocks to rest. To rest, not sleep; for he must keep guard here until Voll's body, sent back to its grave, had turned to dust, all evil power gone, scattered by the wind and washed seaward by the rain. He must keep watch over this place where once death had found a way back into the other land. Patient now, infinitely patient, Festin waited among the rocks where no river would ever run again, in the heart of the country which has no seacoast. The stars stood still above him; and as he watched them, slowly, very slowly he began to forget the voice of streams and the sound of rain on the leaves of the forests of life.

THE RULE OF NAMES

Mr Underhill came out from under his hill, smiling and breathing hard. Each breath shot out of his nostrils as a double puff of steam, snow-white in the morning sunshine. Mr Underhill looked up at the bright December sky and smiled wider than ever, showing snow-white teeth. Then he went down to the village.

'Morning, Mr Underhill,' said the villagers as he passed them in the narrow street between houses with conical, overhanging roofs like the fat red caps of toadstools. 'Morning, morning!' he replied to each. (It was of course bad luck to wish anyone a *good* morning; a simple statement of the time of day was quite enough, in a place so permeated with Influences as Sattins Island, where a careless adjective might change the weather for a week.) All of them spoke to him, some with affection, some with affectionate disdain. He was all the little island had in the way of a wizard, and so deserved respect – but how could you respect a little fat man of fifty who waddled along with his toes turned in, breathing steam and smiling? He was no great shakes as a workman either. His fireworks were fairly elaborate but his elixirs were weak. Warts he charmed off frequently reappeared after three days; tomatoes he enchanted grew no bigger than canteloupes; and those rare times when a strange ship stopped at Sattins Harbor, Mr Underhill always stayed under his hill – for fear, he explained, of the evil eye. He was, in other words, a wizard the way walleyed Gan was a carpenter: by default. The villagers made do with badly-hung doors and inefficient spells,

for this generation, and relieved their annoyance by treating Mr Underhill quite familiarly, as a mere fellow-villager. They even asked him to dinner. Once he asked some of them to dinner, and served a splendid repast, with silver, crystal, damask, roast goose, sparkling Andrades '639, and plum pudding with hard sauce; but he was so nervous all through the meal that it took the joy out of it, and besides, everybody was hungry again half an hour afterward. He did not like anyone to visit his cave, not even the anteroom, beyond which in fact nobody had ever got. When he saw people approaching the hill he always came trotting out to meet them. 'Let's sit out here under the pine trees!' he would say, smiling and waving towards the fir grove, or if it was raining, 'Let's go have a drink at the inn, eh?' though everybody knew he drank nothing stronger than well-water.

Some of the village children, teased by that locked cave, poked and pried and made raids while Mr Underhill was away; but the small door that led into the inner chamber was spell-shut, and it seemed for once to be an effective spell. Once a couple of boys, thinking the wizard was over on the West Shore curing Mrs Ruuna's sick donkey, brought a crowbar and a hatchet up there, but at the first whack of the hatchet on the door there came a roar of wrath from inside, and a cloud of purple steam. Mr Underhill had got home early. The boys fled. He did not come out, and the boys came to no harm, though they said you couldn't believe what a huge hooting howling hissing horrible bellow that little fat man could make unless you'd heard it.

His business in town this day was three dozen fresh eggs and a pound of liver; also a stop at Seacaptain Fogeno's cottage to renew the seeing-charm on the old man's eyes (quite useless when applied to a case of detached retina, but Mr Underhill kept trying), and finally a chat with old Goody Guld, the concertina-maker's widow. Mr Underhill's friends were mostly old people. He was timid with the strong young men of the village, and the girls were shy of him. 'He makes me nervous,

he smiles so much,' they all said, pouting, twisting silky ringlets round a finger. 'Nervous' was a newfangled word, and their mothers all replied grimly, 'Nervous my foot, silliness is the word for it. Mr Underhill is a very respectable wizard!'

After leaving Goody Guld, Mr Underhill passed by the school, which was being held this day out on the common. Since no one on Sattins Island was literate, there were no books to learn to read from and no desks to carve initials on and no blackboards to erase, and in fact no schoolhouse. On rainy days the children met in the loft of the Communal Barn, and got hay in their pants; on sunny days the schoolteacher, Palani, took them anywhere she felt like. Today, surrounded by thirty interested children under twelve and forty uninterested sheep under five, she was teaching an important item on the curriculum: the Rules of Names. Mr Underhill, smiling shyly, paused to listen and watch. Palani, a plump, pretty girl of twenty, made a charming picture there in the wintry sunlight, sheep and children around her, a leafless oak above her, and behind her the dunes and sea and clear, pale sky. She spoke earnestly, her face flushed pink by wind and words. 'Now you know the Rules of Names already, children. There are two, and they're the same on every island in the world. What's one of them?'

'It ain't polite to ask anybody what his name is,' shouted a fat, quick boy, interrupted by a little girl shrieking, 'You can't never tell your own name to nobody my ma says!'

'Yes, Suba. Yes, Popi dear, don't screech. That's right. You never ask anybody his name. You never tell your own. Now think about that a minute and then tell me why we call our wizard Mr Underhill.' She smiled across the curly heads and the woolly backs at Mr Underhill, who beamed, and nervously clutched his sack of eggs.

' 'Cause he lives under a hill!' said half the children.

'But is it his truename?'

'No!' said the fat boy, echoed by little Popi shrieking, 'No!'

'How do you know it's not?'

' 'Cause he came here all alone and so there wasn't anybody knew his truename so they couldn't tell us, and *he* couldn't—'

'Very good, Suba. Popi, don't shout. That's right. Even a wizard can't tell his truename. When you children are through school and go through the Passage, you'll leave your childnames behind and keep only your truenames, which you must never ask for and never give away. Why is that the rule?'

The children were silent. The sheep bleated gently. Mr Underhill answered the question: 'Because the name is the thing,' he said in his shy, soft, husky voice, 'and the truename is the true thing. To speak the name is to control the thing. Am I right, Schoolmistress?'

She smiled and curtseyed, evidently a little embarrassed by his participation. And he trotted off towards his hill, clutching his eggs to his bosom. Somehow the minute spent watching Palani and the children had made him very hungry. He locked his inner door behind him with a hasty incantation, but there must have been a leak or two in the spell, for soon the bare anteroom of the cave was rich with the smell of frying eggs and sizzling liver.

The wind that day was light and fresh out of the west, and on it at noon a little boat came skimming the bright waves into Sattins Harbor. Even as it rounded the point a sharp-eyed boy spotted it, and knowing, like every child on the island, every sail and spar of the forty boats of the fishing fleet, he ran down the street calling out, 'A foreign boat, a foreign boat!' Very seldom was the lonely isle visited by a boat from some equally lonely isle of the East Reach, or an adventurous trader from the Archipelago. By the time the boat was at the pier half the village was there to greet it, and fishermen were following it homewards, and cowherds and clam-diggers and herb-hunters were puffing up and down all the rocky hills, heading towards the harbor.

But Mr Underhill's door stayed shut.

There was only one man aboard the boat. Old Seacaptain Fogeno, when they told him that, drew down a bristle of white

brows over his unseeing eyes. 'There's only one kind of man,' he said, 'that sails the Outer Reach alone. A wizard, or a warlock, or a Mage . . .'

So the villagers were breathless hoping to see for once in their lives a Mage, one of the mighty White Magicians of the rich, towered, crowded inner islands of the Archipelago. They were disappointed, for the voyager was quite young, a handsome black-bearded fellow who hailed them cheerfully from his boat, and leaped ashore like any sailor glad to have made port. He introduced himself at once as a sea-peddlar. But when they told Seacaptain Fogeno that he carried an oaken walking-stick around with him, the old man nodded. 'Two wizards in one town,' he said. 'Bad!' And his mouth snapped shut like an old carp's.

As the stranger could not give them his name, they gave him one right away: Blackbeard. And they gave him plenty of attention. He had a small mixed cargo of cloth and sandals and piswi feathers for trimming cloaks and cheap incense and levity stones and fine herbs and great glass beads from Venway – the usual peddlar's lot. Everyone on Sattins Island came to look, to chat with the voyager, and perhaps to buy something – 'Just to remember him by!' cackled Goody Guld, who like all the women and girls of the village was smitten with Blackbeard's bold good looks. All the boys hung round him too, to hear him tell of his voyages to far, strange islands of the Reach or describe the great rich islands of the Archipelago, the Inner Lanes, the roadsteads white with ships, and the golden roofs of Havnor. The men willingly listened to his tales; but some of them wondered why a trader should sail alone, and kept their eyes thoughtfully upon his oaken staff.

But all this time Mr Underhill stayed under his hill.

'This is the first island I've ever seen that had no wizard,' said Blackbeard one evening to Goody Guld, who had invited him and her nephew and Palani in for a cup of rushwash tea. 'What do you do when you get a toothache, or the cow goes dry?'

'Why, we've got Mr Underhill!' said the old woman.

'For what that's worth,' muttered her nephew Birt, and then blushed purple and spilled his tea. Birt was a fisherman, a large, brave, wordless young man. He loved the schoolmistress, but the nearest he had come to telling her of his love was to give baskets of fresh mackerel to her father's cook.

'Oh, you do have a wizard?' Blackbeard asked. 'Is he invisible?'

'No, he's just very shy,' said Palani. 'You've only been here a week, you know, and we see so few strangers here . . .' She also blushed a little, but did not spill her tea.

Blackbeard smiled at her. 'He's a good Sattinsman, then, eh?'

'No,' said Goody Guld, 'no more than you are. Another cup, nevvy? keep it in the cup this time. No, my dear, he came in a little bit of a boat, four years ago was it? just a day after the end of the shad run, I recall, for they was taking up the nets over in East Creek, and Pondi Cowherd broke his leg that very morning – five years ago it must be. No, four. No, five it is, 'twas the year the garlic didn't sprout. So he sails in on a bit of a sloop loaded full up with great chests and boxes and says to Seacaptain Fogeno, who wasn't blind then, though old enough goodness knows to be blind twice over, "I hear tell," he says, "you've got no wizard nor warlock at all, might you be wanting one?" "Indeed, if the magic's white!" says the Captain, and before you could say cuttlefish Mr Underhill had settled down in the cave under the hill and was charming the mange off Goody Beltow's cat. Though the fur grew in grey, and 'twas an orange cat. Queer-looking thing it was after that. It died last winter in the cold spell. Goody Beltow took on so at that cat's death, poor thing, worse than when her man was drowned on the Long Banks, the year of the long herring-runs, when nevvy Birt here was but a babe in petticoats.' Here Birt spilled his tea again, and Blackbeard grinned, but Goody Guld proceeded undismayed, and talked on till nightfall.

Next day Blackbeard was down at the pier, seeing after the

sprung board in his boat which he seemed to take a long time fixing, and as usual drawing the taciturn Sattinsmen into talk. 'Now which of these is your wizard's craft?' he asked. 'Or has he got one of those the Mages fold up into a walnut shell when they're not using it?'

'Nay,' said a stolid fisherman. 'She's oop in his cave, under hill.'

'He carried the boat he came in up to his cave?'

'Aye. Clear oop. I helped. Heavier as lead she was. Full oop with great boxes, and they full oop with books o' spells, he says. Heavier as lead she was.' And the stolid fisherman turned his back, sighing stolidly. Goody Guld's nephew, mending a net nearby, looked up from his work and asked with equal stolidity, 'Would ye like to meet Mr Underhill, maybe?'

Blackbeard returned Birt's look. Clever black eyes met candid blue ones for a long moment; then Blackbeard smiled and said, 'Yes. Will you take me up to the hill, Birt?'

'Aye, when I'm done with this,' said the fisherman. And when the net was mended, he and the Archipelagan set off up the village street towards the high green hill above it. But as they crossed the common Blackbeard said, 'Hold on a while, friend Birt. I have a tale to tell you, before we meet your wizard.'

'Tell away,' says Birt, sitting down in the shade of a live-oak.

'It's a story that started a hundred years ago, and isn't finished yet – though it soon will be, very soon . . . In the very heart of the Archipelago, where the islands crowd thick as flies on honey, there's a little isle called Pendor. The sealords of Pendor were mighty men, in the old days of war before the League. Loot and ransom and tribute came pouring into Pendor, and they gathered a great treasure there, long ago. Then from somewhere away out in the West Reach, where dragons breed on the lava isles, came one day a very mighty dragon. Not one of those overgrown lizards most of you Outer Reach folk call dragons, but a big, black, winged, wise, cunning monster, full of strength and subtlety, and like all dragons loving gold and precious stones above all things. He killed the Sealord

and his soldiers, and the people of Pendor fled in their ships by night. They all fled away and left the dragon coiled up in Pendor Towers. And there he stayed for a hundred years, dragging his scaly belly over the emeralds and sapphires and coins of gold, coming forth only once in a year or two when he must eat. He'd raid nearby islands for his food. You know what dragons eat?'

Birt nodded and said in a whisper, 'Maidens.'

'Right,' said Blackbeard. 'Well, that couldn't be endured forever, nor the thought of him sitting on all that treasure. So after the League grew strong, and the Archipelago wasn't so busy with wars and piracy, it was decided to attack Pendor, drive out the dragon, and get the gold and jewels for the treasury of the League. They're forever wanting money, the League is. So a huge fleet gathered from fifty islands, and seven Mages stood in the prows of the seven strongest ships, and they sailed towards Pendor... They got there. They landed. Nothing stirred. The houses all stood empty, the dishes on the tables full of a hundred years' dust. The bones of the old Sealord and his men lay about in the castle courts and on the stairs. And the Tower rooms reeked of dragon. But there was no dragon. And no treasure, not a diamond the size of a poppyseed, not a single silver bead... Knowing that he couldn't stand up to seven Mages, the dragon had skipped out. They tracked him, and found he'd flown to a deserted island up north called Udrath; they followed his trail there, and what did they find? Bones again. His bones – the dragon's. But no treasure. A wizard, some unknown wizard from somewhere, must have met him single-handed, and defeated him – and then made off with the treasure, right under the League's nose!'

The fisherman listened, attentive and expressionless.

'Now that must have been a powerful wizard and a clever one, first to kill a dragon, and second to get off without leaving a trace. The lords and Mages of the Archipelago couldn't track him at all, neither where he'd come from nor where he'd made off to. They were about to give up. That was last spring; I'd

been off on a three-year voyage up in the North Reach, and got back about that time. And they asked me to help them find the unknown wizard. That was clever of them. Because I'm not only a wizard myself, as I think some of the oafs here have guessed, but I am also a descendant of the Lords of Pendor. That treasure is mine. It's mine, and knows that it's mine. Those fools of the League couldn't find it, because it's not theirs. It belongs to the House of Pendor, and the great emerald, the star of the hoard, Inalkil the Greenstone, knows its master. Behold!' Blackbeard raised his oaken staff and cried aloud, 'Inalkil!' The tip of the staff began to glow green, a fiery green radiance, a dazzling haze the color of April grass, and at the same moment the staff tipped in the wizard's hand, leaning, slanting till it pointed straight at the side of the hill above them.

'It wasn't so bright a glow, far away in Havnor,' Blackbeard murmured, 'but the staff pointed true. Inalkil answered when I called. The jewel knows its master. And I know the thief, and I shall conquer him. He's a mighty wizard, who could overcome a dragon. But I am mightier. Do you want to know why, oaf? Because I know his name!'

As Blackbeard's tone got more arrogant, Birt had looked duller and duller, blanker and blanker; but at this he gave a twitch, shut his mouth, and stared at the Archipelagan. 'How did you... learn it?' he asked very slowly.

Blackbeard grinned, and did not answer.

'Black magic?'

'How else?'

Birt looked pale, and said nothing.

'I am the Sealord of Pendor, oaf, and I will have the gold my fathers won, and the jewels my mothers wore, and the Greenstone! For they are mine. – Now, you can tell your village boobies the whole story after I have defeated this wizard and gone. Wait here. Or you can come and watch, if you're not afraid. You'll never get the chance again to see a great wizard in all his power.' Blackbeard turned, and without a backward glance strode off up the hill towards the entrance to the cave.

Very slowly, Birt followed. A good distance from the cave he stopped, sat down under a hawthorn tree, and watched. The Archipelagan had stopped; a stiff, dark figure alone on the green swell of the hill before the gaping cave-mouth, he stood perfectly still. All at once he swung his staff up over his head, and the emerald radiance shone about him as he shouted, 'Thief, thief of the Hoard of Pendor, come forth!'

There was a crash, as of dropped crockery, from inside the cave, and a lot of dust came spewing out. Scared, Birt ducked. When he looked again he saw Blackbeard still standing motionless, and at the mouth of the cave, dusty and dishevelled, stood Mr Underhill. He looked small and pitiful, with his toes turned in as usual, and his little bowlegs in black tights, and no staff – he never had had one, Birt suddenly thought. Mr Underhill spoke. 'Who are you?' he said in his husky little voice.

'I am the Sealord of Pendor, thief, come to claim my treasure!'

At that, Mr Underhill slowly turned pink, as he always did when people were rude to him. But he then turned something else. He turned yellow. His hair bristled out, he gave a coughing roar – and was a yellow lion leaping down the hill at Blackbeard, white fangs gleaming.

But Blackbeard no longer stood there. A gigantic tiger, color of night and lightning, bounded to meet the lion . . .

The lion was gone. Below the cave all of a sudden stood a high grove of trees, black in the winter sunshine. The tiger, checking himself in mid-leap just before he entered the shadow of the trees, caught fire in the air, became a tongue of flame lashing out at the dry black branches . . .

But where the trees had stood a sudden cataract leaped from the hillside, an arch of silvery crashing water, thundering down upon the fire. But the fire was gone . . .

For just a moment before the fisherman's staring eyes two hills rose – the green one he knew, and a new one, a bare, brown hillock ready to drink up the rushing waterfall. That passed so quickly it made Birt blink, and after blinking he blinked again,

and moaned, for what he saw now was a great deal worse. Where the cataract had been there hovered a dragon. Black wings darkened all the hill, steel claws reached groping, and from the dark, scaly, gaping lips fire and steam shot out.

Beneath the monstrous creature stood Blackbeard, laughing.

'Take any shape you please, little Mr Underhill!' he taunted. 'I can match you. But the game grows tiresome. I want to look upon my treasure, upon Inalkil. Now, big dragon, little wizard, take your true shape. I command you by the power of your true name – Yevaud!'

Birt could not move at all, not even to blink. He cowered, staring whether he would or not. He saw the black dragon hang there in the air above Blackbeard. He saw the fire lick like many tongues from the scaly mouth, the steam jet from the red nostrils. He saw Blackbeard's face grow white, white as chalk, and the beard-fringed lips trembling.

'Your name is Yevaud!'

'Yes,' said a great, husky, hissing voice. 'My truename is Yevaud, and my true shape is this shape.'

'But the dragon was killed – they found dragon-bones on Udrath Island—'

'That was another dragon,' said the dragon, and then stooped like a hawk, talons outstretched. And Birt shut his eyes.

When he opened them the sky was clear, the hillside empty, except for a reddish-blackish trampled spot, and a few talon-marks in the grass.

Birt the fisherman got to his feet and ran. He ran across the common, scattering sheep to right and left, and straight down the village street to Palani's father's house. Palani was out in the garden weeding the nasturtiums. 'Come with me!' Birt gasped. She stared. He grabbed her wrist and dragged her with him. She screeched a little, but did not resist. He ran with her straight to the pier, pushed her into his fishing-sloop the *Queenie*, untied the painter, took up the oars and set off rowing like a demon. The last that Sattins Island saw of him

and Palani was the *Queenie*'s sail vanishing in the direction of the nearest island westward.

The villagers thought they would never stop talking about it, how Goody Guld's nephew Birt had lost his mind and sailed off with the schoolmistress on the very same day that the peddlar Blackbeard disappeared without a trace, leaving all his feathers and beads behind. But they did stop talking about it, three days later. They had other things to talk about, when Mr Underhill finally came out of his cave.

Mr Underhill had decided that since his truename was no longer a secret, he might as well drop his disguise. Walking was a lot harder than flying, and besides, it was a long, long time since he had had a real meal.

WINTER'S KING

When I wrote this story, a year before I began the novel The Left Hand of Darkness, *I did not know that the inhabitants of the planet Winter or Gethen were androgynes. By the time the story came out in print, I did, but too late to emend such usages as 'son,' 'mother,' and so on.*

Many feminists have been grieved or aggrieved by The Left Hand of Darkness *because the androgynes in it are called 'he' throughout. In the third person singular, the English generic pronoun is the same as the masculine pronoun. A fact worth reflecting upon. And it's a trap, with no way out, because the exclusion of the feminine (she) and the neuter (it) from the generic/masculine (he) makes the use of either of them more specific, more unjust, as it were, than the use of 'he.' And I find made-up pronouns, 'te' and 'heshe' and so on, dreary and annoying.*

In revising the story for this edition, I saw a chance to redress that injustice slightly. In this version, I use the feminine pronoun for all Gethenians – while preserving certain masculine titles such as King and Lord, just to remind one of the ambiguity. This may drive some nonfeminists mad, but that's only fair.

The androgyny of the characters has little to do with the events of this story, but the pronoun change does make it clear that the central, paradoxical relationship of parent and child is not, as it may have seemed in the other version, a kind of reverse Oedipus twist, but something less familiar and more ambiguous. Evidently my unconscious mind knew about the Gethenians long before it saw fit to inform me. It's always doing things like that.

When whirlpools appear in the onward run of time and history seems to swirl around a snag, as in the curious matter

of the Succession of Karhide, then pictures come in handy: snapshots, which may be taken up and matched to compare the parent to the child, the young king to the old, and which may also be rearranged and shuffled till the years run straight. For despite the tricks played by instantaneous interstellar communication and just-sub-lightspeed interstellar travel, time (as the Plenipotentiary Axt remarked) does not reverse itself; nor is death mocked.

Thus, although the best-known picture is that dark image of a young king standing above an old king who lies dead in a corridor lit only by mirror-reflections of a burning city, set it aside a while. Look first at the young king, a nation's pride, as bright and fortunate a soul as ever lived to the age of twenty-two; but when this picture was taken the young king had her back against a wall. She was filthy, she was trembling, and her face was blank and mad, for she had lost that minimal confidence in the world which is called sanity. Inside her head she repeated, as she had been repeating for hours or years, over and over, 'I will abdicate. I will abdicate. I will abdicate.' Inside her eyes she saw the red-walled rooms of the Palace, the towers and streets of Erhenrang in falling snow, the lovely plains of the West Fall, the white summits of the Kargav, and she renounced them all, her kingdom. 'I will abdicate,' she said not aloud and then, aloud, screamed as once again the person dressed in red and white approached her saying, 'Majesty! A plot against your life has been discovered in the Artisan School,' and the humming noise began, softly. She hid her head in her arms and whispered, 'Stop it, please stop it,' but the humming whine grew higher and louder and nearer, relentless, until it was so high and loud that it entered her flesh, tore the nerves from their channels and made her bones dance and jangle, hopping to its tune. She hopped and twitched, bare bones strung on thin white threads, and wept dry tears, and shouted, 'Have them – Have them – They must – Executed – Stopped – Stop!'

It stopped.

She fell in a clattering, chattering heap to the floor. What

floor? Not red tiles, not parquetry, not urine-stained cement, but the wood floor of the room in the tower, the little tower bedroom where she was safe, safe from her ogre parent, the cold, mad, uncaring king, safe to play cat's cradle with Piry and to sit by the fireside on Borhub's warm lap, as warm and deep as sleep. But there was no hiding, no safety, no sleep. The person dressed in black had come even here and had hold of her head, lifted it up, lifted on thin white strings the eyelids she tried to close.

'Who am I?'

The blank, black mask stared down. The young king struggled, sobbing, because now the suffocation would begin: she would not be able to breathe until she said the name, the right name – 'Gerer!' – She could breathe. She was allowed to breathe. She had recognized the black one in time.

'Who am I?' said a different voice, gently, and the young king groped for that strong presence that always brought her sleep, truce, solace. 'Rebade,' she whispered, 'tell me what to do...'

'Sleep.'

She obeyed. A deep sleep, and dreamless, for it was real. Dreams came at waking, now. Unreal, the horrible dry red light of sunset burned her eyes open and she stood, once more, on the Palace balcony looking down at fifty thousand black pits opening and shutting. From the pits came a paroxysmic gush of sound, a shrill, rhythmic eructation: her name. Her name was roared in her ears as a taunt, a jeer. She beat her hands on the narrow brass railing and shouted at them, 'I will silence you!' She could not hear her voice, only their voice, the pestilent mouths of the mob that hated her, screaming her name. 'Come away, my king,' said the one gentle voice, and Rebade drew her away from the balcony into the vast, red-walled quiet of the Hall of Audience. The screaming ceased with a click. Rebade's expression was as always composed, compassionate. 'What will you do now?' she said in her gentle voice.

'I will – I will abdicate—'

'No,' Rebade said calmly. 'That is not right. What will you do now?'

The young king stood silent, shaking. Rebade helped her sit down on the iron cot, for the walls had darkened as they often did and drawn in all about her to a little cell. 'You will call...'

'Call up the Erhenrang Guard. Have them shoot into the crowd. Shoot to kill. They must be taught a lesson.' The young king spoke rapidly and distinctly in a loud, high voice. Rebade said, 'Very good, my lord, a wise decision! Right. We shall come out all right. You are doing right. Trust me.'

'I do. I trust you. Get me out of here,' the young king whispered, seizing Rebade's arm: but her friend frowned. That was not right. She had driven Rebade and hope away again. Rebade was leaving now, calm and regretful, though the young king begged her to stop, to come back, for the noise was softly beginning again, the whining hum that tore the mind to pieces, and already the person in red and white was approaching across a red, interminable floor. 'Majesty! A plot against your life has been discovered in the Artisan School—'

Down Old Harbor Street to the water's edge the street lamps burned cavernously bright. Guard Pepenerer on her rounds glanced down that slanting vault of light expecting nothing, and saw something staggering up it towards her. Pepenerer did not believe in poragropes, but she saw a porngrope, sea-beslimed, staggering on thin webbed feet, gasping dry air, whimpering... Old sailors' tales slid out of Pepenerer's mind and she saw a drunk or a maniac or a victim staggering between the dank grey warehouse walls. 'Now then! Hold on there!' she bellowed, on the run. The drunk, half naked and wild-eyed, let out a yell of terror and tried to dodge away, slipped on the frost-slick stones of the street and pitched down sprawling. Pepenerer got out her gun and delivered a half-second of stun, just to keep the drunk quiet; then squatted down by her, wound up her radio and called the West Ward for a car.

Both the arms, sprawled out limp and meek on the cold

cobbles, were blotched with injection marks. Not drunk; drugged. Pepenerer sniffed, but got no resinous scent of orgrevy. She had been drugged, then; thieves, or a ritual clan-revenge. Thieves would not have left the gold ring on the forefinger, a massive thing, carved, almost as wide as the fingerjoint. Pepenerer crouched forward to look at it. Then she turned her head and looked at the beaten, blank face in profile against the paving-stones, hard lit by the glare of the street lamps. She took a new quarter-crown piece out of her pouch and looked at the left profile stamped on the bright tin, then back at the right profile stamped in light and shadow and cold stone. Then, hearing the purr of the electric car turning down from the Longway into Old Harbor Street, she stuck the coin back in her pouch, muttering to herself, 'Damn fool.'

King Argaven was off hunting in the mountains, anyhow, and had been for a couple of weeks; it had been in all the bulletins.

'You see,' said Hoge the physician, 'we can assume that she was mindformed; but that gives us almost nothing to go on. There are too many expert mindformers in Karhide, and in Orgoreyn for that matter. Not criminals whom the police might have a lead on, but respectable mentalists or physicians. To whom the drugs are legally available. As for getting anything from her, if they had any skill at all they will have blocked everything they did to rational access. All clues will be buried, the trigger-suggestions hidden, and we simply cannot guess what questions to ask. There is no way, short of brain-destruction, of going through everything in her mind; and even under hypnosis and deep drugging there would be no way now to distinguish implanted ideas or emotions from her own autonomous ones. Perhaps the Aliens could do something, though I doubt their mindscience is all they boast of; at any rate it's out of reach. We have only one real hope.'

'Which is?' Lord Gerer asked, stolidly.

'The king is quick and resolute. At the beginning, before

they broke her, she may have known what they were doing to her, and so set up some block or resistance, left herself some escape route...'

Hoge's low voice lost confidence as she spoke, and trailed off in the silence of the high, red, dusky room. She drew no response from old Gerer who stood, black-clad, before the fire.

The temperature of that room in the King's Palace of Erhenrang was 12° C where Lord Gerer stood, and 5° midway between the two big fireplaces; outside it was snowing lightly, a mild day only a few degrees below freezing. Spring had come to Winter. The fires at either end of the room roared red and gold, devouring thigh-thick logs. Magnificence, a harsh luxury, a quick splendor; fireplaces, fireworks, lightning, meteors, volcanoes; such things satisfied the people of Karhide on the world called Winter. But, except in Arctic colonies above the 35th parallel, they had never installed central heating in any building in the many centuries of their Age of Technology. Comfort was allowed to come to them rare, welcome, unsought: a gift, like joy.

The king's personal servant, sitting by the bed, turned towards the physician and the Lord Councillor, though she did not speak. Both at once crossed the room. The broad, hard bed, high on gilt pillars, heavy with a finery of red cloaks and coverlets, bore up the king's body almost level with their eyes. To Gerer it appeared a ship breasting, motionless, a swift vast flood of darkness, carrying the young king into shadows, terrors, years. Then with a terror of her own the old councillor saw that Argaven's eyes were open, staring out a half-curtained window at the stars.

Gerer feared lunacy; idiocy; she did not know what she feared. Hoge had warned her: 'The king will not behave "normally," Lord Gerer. She has suffered thirteen days of torment, intimidation, exhaustion, and mindhandling. There may be brain damage, there will certainly be side- and after-effects of drugs.' Neither fear nor warning parried the shock. Argaven's bright, weary eyes turned to Gerer and paused on her blankly

a moment; then saw her. And Gerer, though she could not see the black mask reflected, saw the hate, the horror, saw her young king, infinitely beloved, gasping in imbecile terror and struggling with the servant, with Hoge, with her own weakness in the effort to get away, to get away from Gerer.

Standing in the cold midst of the room where the prowlike head of the bedstead hid her from the king, Gerer heard them pacify Argaven and settle her down again. Argaven's voice sounded reedy, childishly plaintive. So the Old King, Emran, had spoken in her last madness with a child's voice. Then silence, and the burning of the two great fires.

Korgry, the king's bodyservant, yawned and rubbed her eyes. Hoge measured something from a vial into a hypodermic. Gerer stood in despair. My child, my king, what have they done to you? So great a trust, so fair a promise, lost, lost . . . So the one who looked like a lump of half-carved black rock, a heavy, prudent, rude old courtier, grieved and was passion-racked, her love and service of the young king being the world's one worth to her.

Argaven spoke aloud: 'My child—'

Gerer winced, feeling the words torn out of her own mind; but Hoge, untroubled by love, comprehended and said softly to Argaven, 'Prince Emran is well, my liege. She is with her attendants at Warrever Castle. We are in constant communication. All is well there.'

Gerer heard the king's harsh breathing, and came somewhat closer to the bed, though out of sight still behind the high headboard.

'Have I been sick?'

'You are not well yet,' the physician said, bland.

'Where—'

'Your own room, in the Palace, in Erhenrang.'

But Gerer, coming a step closer, though not in view of the king, said, 'We do not know where you have been.'

Hoge's smooth face creased with a frown, though, physician as she was and so in her way ruler of them all, she dared not

direct the frown at the Lord Councillor. Gerer's voice did not seem to trouble the king, who asked another question or two, sane and brief, and then lay quiet. Presently the servant Korgry, who had sat with her ever since she had been brought into the Palace (last night, in secret, by side doors, like a shameful suicide of the last reign, but all in reverse), Korgry committed lèse-majesté: huddled forward on her high stool, she let her head droop on the side of the bed, and slept. The guard at the door yielded place to a new guard, in whispers. Officials came and received a fresh bulletin for public release on the state of the king's health, in whispers. Stricken by symptoms of fever while vacationing in the High Kargav, the king had been rushed to Erhenrang, and was now responding satisfactorily to treatment, etc. Physician Hoge rem ir Hogeremme at the Palace has released the following statement, etc, etc. 'May the Wheel turn for our king,' people in village houses said solemnly as they lit the fire on the altarhearth, to which elders sitting near the fire remarked, 'It comes of her roving around the city at night and climbing mountains, fool tricks like that,' but they kept the radio on to catch the next bulletin. A very great number of people had come and gone and loitered and chatted this day in the square before the Palace, watching those who went in and out, watching the vacant balcony; there were still several hundred down there, standing around patiently in the snow. Argaven XVII was loved in her domain. After the dull brutality of King Emran's reign that had ended in the shadow of madness and the country's bankruptcy, she had come: sudden, gallant, young, changing everything; sane and shrewd, yet magnanimous. She had the fire, the splendor that suited her people. She was the force and center of a new age: one born, for once, king of the right kingdom.

'Gerer.'

It was the king's voice, and Gerer hastened stiffly through the hot and cold of the great room, the firelight and dark.

Argaven was sitting up. Her arms shook and the breath caught in her throat; her eyes burned across the dark air at

Gerer. By her left hand, which bore the Sign-Ring of the Harge dynasty, lay the sleeping face of the servant, derelict, serene. 'Gerer,' the king said with effort and clarity, 'summon the Council. Tell them, I will abdicate.'

So crude, so simple? All the drugs, the terrorizing, the hypnosis, parahypnosis, neurone-stimulation, synapse-pairing, spotshock that Hoge had described, for this blunt result? But reasoning must wait. They must temporize. 'My liege, when your strength returns—'

'Now. Call the Council, Gerer!'

Then she broke, like a bowstring breaking, and stammered in a fury of fear that found no sense or strength to flesh itself in; and still her faithful servant slept beside her, deaf.

In the next picture things are going better, it appears. Here is King Argaven XVII in good health and good clothes, finishing a large breakfast. She talks with the nearer dozen of the forty or fifty people sharing or serving the meal (singularity is a king's prerogative, but seldom privacy), and includes the rest in the largesse of her courtesy. She looks, as everyone has said, quite herself again. Perhaps she is not quite herself again, however; something is missing, a youthful serenity, a confidence, replaced by a similar but less reassuring quality, a kind of heedlessness. Out of it she rises in wit and warmth, but always subsides to it again, that darkness which absorbs her and makes her heedless: fear, pain, resolution?

Mr Mobile Axt, Ambassador Plenipotentiary to Winter from the Ekumen of the Known Worlds, who had spent the last six days on the road trying to drive an electric car faster than 50 kph from Mishnory in Orgoreyn to Erhenrang in Karhide, overslept breakfast, and so arrived in the Audience Hall prompt, but hungry. The old Chief of the Council, the king's cousin Gerer rem ir Verhen, met the Alien at the door of the great hall and greeted him with the polysyllabic politeness of Karhide. The Plenipotentiary responded as best he could,

discerning beneath the eloquence Gerer's desire to tell him something.

'I am told the king is perfectly recovered,' he said, 'and I heartily hope this is true.'

'It is not,' the old Councillor said, her voice suddenly blunt and toneless. 'Mr Axt, I tell you this trusting your confidence; there are not ten others in Karhide who know the truth. She is not recovered. She was not sick.'

Axt nodded. There had of course been rumors.

'She will go alone in the city sometimes, at night, in common clothes, walking, talking with strangers. The pressures of kingship . . . She is very young.' Gerer paused a moment, struggling with some suppressed emotion. 'One night six weeks ago, she did not come back. A message was delivered to me and the Second Lord, at dawn. If we announced her disappearance, she would be killed; if we waited a half-month in silence she would be restored unhurt. We kept silent, lied to the Council, sent out false news. On the thirteenth night she was found wandering in the city. She had been drugged and mindformed. By which enemy or faction we do not yet know. We must work in utter secrecy; we cannot wreck the people's confidence in her, her own confidence in herself. It is hard: she remembers nothing. But what they did is plain. They broke her will and bent her mind all to one thing. She believes she must abdicate the throne.'

The voice remained low and flat; the eyes betrayed anguish. And the Plenipotentiary turning suddenly saw the reflection of that anguish in the eyes of the young king.

'Holding my audience, cousin?'

Argaven smiled but there was a knife in it. The old Councillor excused herself stolidly, bowed, left, a patient ungainly figure diminishing down a long corridor.

Argaven stretched out both hands to the Plenipotentiary in the greeting of equals, for in Karhide the Ekumen was recognized as a sister kingdom, though not a living soul had

94

seen it. But her words were not the polite discourse that Axt expected. All she said, and fiercely, was, 'At last!'

'I left as soon as I received your message. The roads are still icy in East Orgoreyn and the West Fall, I couldn't make very good time. But I was very glad to come. Glad to leave, too.' Axt smiled saying this, for he and the young king enjoyed each other's candor. What Argaven's welcome implied, he waited to see, watching, with some exhilaration, the mobile, beautiful, androgynous face.

'Orgoreyn breeds bigots as a corpse breeds worms, as one of my ancestors remarked. I'm glad you find the air fresher here in Karhide. Come this way. Gerer told you that I was kidnapped, and so forth? Yes. It was all according to the old rules. Kidnapping is a quite formal art. If it had been one of the anti-Alien groups who think your Ekumen intends to enslave the earth, they might have ignored the rules; I think it was one of the old clan-factions hoping to regain power through me, the power they had in the last reign. But we don't know, yet. It's strange, to know that one has seen them face to face and yet can't recognize them; who knows but that I see those faces daily? Well, no profit in such notions. They wiped out all their tracks. I am sure only of one thing. *They* did not tell me that I must abdicate.'

She and the Plenipotentiary were walking side by side up the long, immensely high room toward the dais and chairs at the far end. The windows were little more than slits, as usual on this cold world; fulvous strips of sunlight fell from them diagonally to the red-paved floor, dusk and dazzle in Axt's eyes. He looked up at the young king's face in that somber, shifting radiance. 'Who then?'

'I did.'

'When, my lord, and why?'

'When they had me, when they were remaking me to fit their mold and play their game. Why? So that I can't fit their mold and play their game! Listen, Lord Axt, if they wanted me dead they'd have killed me. They want me alive, to govern,

to be king. As such I am to follow the orders imprinted in my
brain, gain their ends for them. I am their tool, their machine,
waiting for the switch to be thrown. The only way to prevent
that is to... discard the machine.'

Axt was quick of understanding, that being a minimal
qualification of a Mobile of the Ekumen; besides, the manners
and affairs of Karhide, the stresses and seditions of that lively
kingdom, were well known to him. Remote though Winter was,
both in space and in the physiology of its inhabitants, from
the rest of the human race, yet its dominant nation, Karhide,
had proved a loyal member of the Ekumen. Axt's reports
were discussed in the central councils of the Ekumen eighty
lightyears away; the equilibrium of the Whole rests in all its
parts. Axt said, as they sat down in the great stiff chairs on the
dais before the fire, 'But they need not even throw switches, if
you abdicate.'

'Leaving my child as heir, and a Regent of my own choice?'

'Perhaps,' Axt said with caution, 'they chose your Regent
for you.'

The king frowned. 'I think not,' she said.

'Whom had you thought of naming?'

There was a long pause. Axt saw the muscles of Argaven's
throat working as she struggled to get a word, a name, up
past a block, a harsh constriction; at last she said, in a forced,
strangled whisper, 'Gerer.'

Axt nodded, startled. Gerer had served as Regent for a year
after Emran's death and before Argaven's accession; he knew
her honesty and her utter devotion to the young king. 'Gerer
serves no faction!' he said.

Argaven shook her head. She looked exhausted. After a
while she said, 'Could the science of your people undo what
was done to me, Lord Axt?'

'Possibly. In the Institute on Ollul. But if I sent for a spe-
cialist tonight he'd get here twenty-four years from now...
You're sure, then, that your decision to abdicate was—' But a
servant coming in a side door behind them, set a small table

96

by the Plenipotentiary's chair and loaded it with fruit, sliced bread-apple, a silver tankard of ale. Argaven had noticed that her guest had missed his breakfast. Though the fare on Winter, mostly vegetable and that mostly uncooked, was dull stuff to Axt's taste, he set to gratefully; and as serious talk was unseemly over food, Argaven shifted to generalities. 'Once you said, Lord Axt, that different as I am from you, and different as my people are from yours, yet we are blood kin. Was that a moral fact or a material one?'

Axt smiled at the very Karhidish distinction. 'Both, my lord. As far as we know, which is a tiny corner of dusty space under the rafters of the Universe, all the people we've run into are in fact human. But the kinship goes back a million years and more, to the Fore-Eras of Hain. The ancient Hainish settled a hundred worlds.'

'We call the time before my dynasty ruled Karhide "ancient." Seven hundred years ago!'

'So we call the Age of the Enemy "ancient," and that was less than six hundred years ago. Time stretches and shrinks; changes with the eye, with the age, with the star; does all except reverse itself – or repeat.'

'The dream of the Ekumen, then, is to restore that truly ancient commonalty; to regather all the peoples of all the worlds at one hearth?'

Axt nodded, chewing bread-apple. 'To weave some harmony among them, at least. Life loves to know itself, out to its furthest limits; to embrace complexity is its delight. Our difference is our beauty. All these worlds and the various forms and ways of the minds and lives and bodies on them – together they would make a splendid harmony.'

'No harmony endures,' said the young king.

'None has ever been achieved,' said the Plenipotentiary. 'The pleasure is in trying.' He drained his tankard, wiped his fingers on the woven-grass napkin.

'That was my pleasure as king,' said Argaven. 'It is over.'

'Should—'

'It is finished. Believe me. I will keep you here, Lord Axt, until you believe me. I need your help. You are the piece the game-players forgot about! You must help me. I cannot abdicate against the will of the Council. They will refuse my abdication, force me to rule, and if I rule, I serve my enemies! If you will not help me, I will have to kill myself.' She spoke quite evenly and reasonably; but Axt knew what even the mention of suicide, the ultimately contemptible act, cost a Karhider.

'One way or the other,' said the young king.

The Plenipotentiary pulled his heavy cloak closer round him; he was cold. He had been cold for seven years, here. 'My lord,' he said, 'I am an alien on your world, with a handful of aides, and a little device with which I can converse with other aliens on distant worlds. I represent power, of course, but I have none. How can I help you?'

'You have a ship on Horden Island.'

'Ah. I was afraid of that,' said the Plenipotentiary, sighing. 'Lord Argaven, that ship is set for Ollul, twenty-four lightyears away. Do you know what that means?'

'My escape from my time, in which I have become an instrument of evil.'

'There is no escape,' said Axt, with sudden intensity, 'No, my lord. Forgive me. It is impossible. I could not consent—'

Icy rain of spring rattled on the stones of the tower, wind whined at the angles and finials of the roof. The room was quiet, shadowy. One small shielded light burned by the door. The nurse lay snoring mildly in the bed, the baby was head down, rump up in the crib. Argaven stood beside the crib. She looked around the room, or rather saw it, knew it wholly, without looking. She too had slept here as a little child. It had been her first kingdom. It was here that she had come to suckle her child, her first-born, had sat by the fireplace while the little mouth tugged at her breast, had hummed to the baby the songs Borhub had hummed to her. This was the center, the center of everything.

Very cautiously and gently she slipped her hand under the baby's warm, damp, downy head, and put over it a chain on which hung a massive ring carved with the token of the Lords of Harge. The chain was far too long, and Argaven knotted it shorter, thinking that it might twist and choke the child. So allaying that small anxiety, she tried to allay the great fear and wretchedness that filled her. She stooped down till her cheek touched the baby's cheek, whispering inaudibly, 'Emran, Emran, I have to leave you, I can't take you, you have to rule for me. Be good, Emran, live long, rule well, be good, Emran . . .'

She straightened up, turned, ran from the tower room, the lost kingdom.

She knew several ways of getting out of the Palace unperceived. She took the surest, and then made for the New Harbor through the bright-lit, sleet-lashed streets of Erhenrang, alone.

Now there is no picture: no seeing her. With what eye will you watch a process that is one hundred millionth percent slower than the speed of light? She is not now a king, nor a human being; she is translated. You can scarcely call fellow-mortal one whose time passes seventy thousand times slower than yours. She is more than alone. It seems that she is not, any more than an uncommunicated thought is; that she goes nowhere, any more than a thought goes. And yet, at very nearly but never quite the speed of light, she voyages. She is the voyage. Quick as thought. She has doubled her age when she arrives, less than a day older, in the portion of space curved about a dustmote named Ollul, the fourth planet of a yellowish sun. And all this has passed in utter silence.

With noise now, and fire and meteoric dazzle enough to satisfy a Karhider's lust for splendor, the clever ship makes earthfall, settling down in flame in the precise spot it left from some fifty-five years ago. Presently, visible, unmassive, uncertain, the young king emerges from it and stands a moment in the exitway, shielding her eyes from the light of a strange, hot sun.

Axt had of course sent notice of her coming, by instantaneous

transmitter, twenty-four years ago, or seventeen hours ago, depending on how you look at it; and aides and agents of the Ekumen were on hand to greet her. Even pawns did not go unnoticed by those players of the great game, and this Gethenian was, after all, a king. One of the agents had spent a year of the twenty-four in learning Karhidish, so that Argaven could speak to someone. She spoke at once: 'What news from my country?'

'Mr Mobile Axt and his successor have sent regular summaries of events, and various private messages for you; you'll find all the material in your quarters, Mr Harge. Very briefly, the regency of Lord Gerer was uneventful and benign; there was a depression in the first two years, during which your Arctic settlements were abandoned, but at present the economy is quite stable. Your heir was enthroned at eighteen, and has ruled now for seven years.'

'Yes. I see,' said the person who had kissed that year-old heir last night.

'Whenever you see fit, Mr Harge, the specialists at our Institute over in Belxit—'

'As you wish,' said Mr Harge.

They went into her mind very gently, very subtly, opening doors. For locked doors they had delicate instruments that always found the combination; and then they stood aside, and let her enter. They found the person in black, who was not Gerer, and compassionate Rebade, who was not compassionate; they stood with her on the Palace balcony, and climbed the crevasses of nightmare with her up to the room in the tower; and at last the one who was to have been first, the person in red and white, approached her saying, 'Majesty! A plot against your life—' And Mr Harge screamed in abject terror, and woke up.

'Well! That was the trigger. The signal to begin tripping off the other instructions and determine the course of your phobia. An induced paranoia. Really beautifully induced, I must say. Here, drink this, Mr Harge. No, it's just water! You might well have become a remarkably vicious ruler, increasingly obsessed by fear of plots and subversions, increasingly disaffected from

your people. Not overnight, of course. That's the beauty of it. It would have taken several years for you to become a real tyrant; though they no doubt planned some boosts along the way, once Rebade wormed his way – her way – a way into your confidence ... Well, well, I see why Karhide is well spoken of, over at the Clearinghouse, If you'll pardon my objectivity, this kind of skill and patience is quite rare ...' So the doctor, the mindmender, the hairy, greyish, one-sexed person from somewhere called the Cetians, went rambling on while the patient recovered herself.

'Then I did right,' said Mr Harge at last.

'You did. Abdication, suicide, or escape were the only acts of consequence which you could have committed of your own volition, freely. They counted on your moral veto on suicide, and your Council's vote on abdication. But being possessed by ambition themselves, they forgot the possibility of abnegation, and left one door open for you. A door which only a strong-minded person, if you'll pardon my literalness, could choose to go through. I really must read up on this other mindscience of yours, what do you call it, Foretelling? Thought it was some occultist trash, but quite evidently ... Well, well, I expect they'll be wanting you to look in at the Clearinghouse soon, to discuss your future, now that we've put your past where it belongs, eh?'

'As you wish,' said Mr Harge.

She talked with various people there in the Clearinghouse of the Ekumen for the West Worlds, and when they suggested that she go to school, she assented readily. For among those mild persons, whose chief quality seemed a cool, profound sadness indistinguishable from a warm, profound hilarity – among them, the ex-king of Karhide knew herself a barbarian, unlearned and unwise.

She attended Ekumenical School. She lived in barracks near the Clearinghouse in Vaxtsit City, with a couple of hundred other aliens, none of whom was either androgynous or an ex-king. Never having owned much that was hers alone, and never having had much privacy, she did not mind barracks life;

nor was it so bad as she had expected to live among single-sexed people, although she found their condition of perpetual kemmer tiresome. She did not mind anything much, getting through the works and days with vigor and competence but always a certain heedlessness, as of one whose center is somewhere else. The only discomfort was the heat, the awful heat of Ollul that rose sometimes to 35° C in the blazing interminable season when no snow fell for two hundred days on end. Even when winter came at last she sweated, for it seldom got more than ten degrees below freezing outside, and the barracks were kept sweltering – she thought – though the other aliens wore heavy sweaters all the time. She slept on top of her bed, naked and thrashing, and dreamed of the snows of the Kargav, the ice in Old Harbor, the ice scumming one's ale on cool mornings in the Palace, the cold, the dear and bitter cold of Winter.

She learned a good deal. She had already learned that the Earth was, here, called Winter, and that Ollul was, here, called the Earth: one of those facts which turn the universe inside out like a sock. She learned that a meat diet causes diarrhea in the unaccustomed gut. She learned that single-sexed people, whom she tried hard not to think of as perverts, tried hard not to think of her as a pervert. She learned that when she pronounced Ollul as Orrur some people laughed. She attempted also to unlearn that she was a king. Once the School took her in hand she learned and unlearned much more. She was led, by all the machines and devices and experiences and (simplest and most demanding) words that the Ekumen had at its disposal, into an intimation of what it might be to understand the nature and history of a kingdom that was over a million years old and trillions of miles wide. When she had begun to guess the immensity of this kingdom of humanity and the durable pain and monotonous waste of its history, she began also to see what lay beyond its borders in space and time, and among naked rocks and furnace-suns and the shining desolation that goes on and on she glimpsed the sources of hilarity and serenity, the inexhaustible springs. She learned a great many facts, numbers,

myths, epics, proportions, relationships, and so forth, and saw, beyond the borders of what she had learned, the unknown again, a splendid immensity. In this augmentation of her mind and being there was great satisfaction; yet she was unsatisfied. They did not always let her go on as far as she wanted into certain fields, mathematics, Cetian physics. 'You started late, Mr Harge,' they said, 'we have to build on the existing foundations. Besides, we want you in subjects which you can put to use.'

'What use?'

They – the ethnographer Mr Mobile Gist represented Them at the moment, across a library table – looked at her sardonically. 'Do you consider yourself to be of no further use, Mr Harge?'

Mr Harge, who was generally reserved, spoke with sudden fury: 'I do.'

'A king without a country,' said Gist in his flat Terran accent, 'self-exiled, believed to be dead, might feel a trifle superfluous. But then, why do you think we're bothering with you?'

'Out of kindness.'

'Oh, kindness... However kind we are, we can give you nothing that would make you happy, you know. Except... Well. Waste is a pity. You were indubitably the right king for Winter, for Karhide, for the purposes of the Ekumen. You have a sense of balance. You might even have unified the planet. You certainly wouldn't have terrorized and fragmented the country, as the present king seems to be doing. What a waste! Only consider our hopes and needs, Mr Harge, and your own qualifications, before you despair of being useful in your life. Forty or fifty more years of it you have to live, after all...'

The last snapshot taken by alien sunlight: erect, in a Hainish-style cloak of grey, a handsome person of indeterminate sex stands, sweating profusely, on a green lawn beside the chief Agent of the Ekumen in the West Worlds, the Stabile, Mr Hoalans of Alb, who can meddle (if he likes) with the destinies of forty worlds.

'I can't order you to go there, Argaven,' says the Stabile. 'Your own conscience—'

'I gave up my kingdom to my conscience, twelve years ago. It's had its due. Enough's enough,' says Argaven Harge. Then she laughs suddenly, so that the Stabile also laughs; and they part in such harmony as the Powers of the Ekumen desire between human souls.

Horden Island, off the south coast of Karhide, was given as a freehold to the Ekumen by the Kingdom of Karhide during the reign of Argaven XV. No one lived there. Yearly generations of seawalkies crawled up on the barren rocks, and laid and hatched their eggs, and raised their young, and finally led them back in long single file to the sea. But once every ten or twenty years fire ran over the rocks and the sea boiled on the shores, and if any seawalkies were on the island then they died.

When the sea had ceased to boil, the Plenipotentiary's little electric launch approached. The starship ran out a gossamer-steel gangplank to the deck of the launch, and one person started to walk up it as another one started to walk down it, so that they met in the middle, in midair, between sea and land, an ambiguous meeting.

'Ambassador Horrsed? I'm Harge,' said the one from the star-ship, but the one from the launch was already kneeling, saying aloud, in Karhidish, 'Welcome, Argaven of Karhide!'

As he straightened up the Ambassador added in a quick whisper, 'You come as yourself – Explain when I can—' Behind and below him on the deck of the launch stood a sizable group of people, staring up intently at the newcomer. All were Karhiders by their looks; several were very old.

Argaven Harge stood for a minute, two minutes, three minutes, erect and perfectly motionless, though her grey cloak tugged and riffled in the cold sea wind. She looked then once at the dull sun in the west, once at the grey land north across the water, back again at the silent people grouped below her on the deck. She strode forward so suddenly that Ambassador

Homed had to squeeze out of the way in a hurry. She went straight to one of the old people on the deck of the launch. 'Are you Ker rem ir Kerheder?'

'I am.'

'I knew you by the lame arm, Ker.' She spoke clearly; there was no guessing what emotions she felt. 'I could not know your face. After sixty years. Are there others of you I knew? I am Argaven.'

They were all silent. They gazed at her.

All at once one of them, one scored and scarred with age like wood that has been through fire, stepped forward one step. 'My liege, I am Bannith of the Palace Guard. You served with me when I was Drillmaster and you a child, a young child.' And the grey head bowed down suddenly, in homage, or to hide tears. Then another stepped forward, and another. The heads that bowed were grey, white, bald; the voices that hailed the king quavered. One, Ker of the crippled arm, whom Argaven had known as a shy page of thirteen, spoke fiercely to those who still stood unmoving: 'This is the king. I have eyes that have seen, and that see now. This is the king!'

Argaven looked at them, face after face, the bowed heads and the unbowed.

'I am Argaven,' she said. 'I was king. Who reigns now in Karhide?'

'Emran,' one answered.

'My child Emran?'

'Yes, my liege,' old Bannith said; most of the faces were blank; but Ker said in her fierce shaking voice, 'Argaven, Argaven reigns in Karhide! I have lived to see the bright days return. Long live the king!'

One of the younger ones looked at the others, and said resolutely, 'So be it. Long live the king!' And all the heads bowed low.

Argaven took their homage unperturbed, but as soon as a moment came when she could address Horrsed the Plenipotentiary alone she demanded, 'What is this? What has happened?

Why was I misled? I was told I was to come here to assist you, as an aide, from the Ekumen—'

'That was twenty-four years ago,' said the Ambassador, apologetically. 'I've only lived here five years, my lord. Things are going very ill in Karhide. King Emran broke off relations with the Ekumen last year. I don't really know what the Stabile's purpose in sending you here was at the time he sent you; but at present, we're losing Winter. So the Agents on Hain suggested to me that we might move out our king.'

'But I am *dead*,' Argaven said wrathfully. 'I have been dead for sixty years!'

'The king is dead,' said Horrsed. 'Long live the king.'

As some of the Karhiders approached, Argaven turned from the Ambassador and went over to the rail. Grey water bubbled and slid by the ship's side. The shore of the continent lay now to their left, grey patched with white. It was cold: a day of early winter in the Ice Age. The ship's engine purred softly. Argaven had not heard that purr of an electric engine for a dozen years now, the only kind of engine Karhide's slow and stable Age of Technology had chosen to employ. The sound of it was very pleasant to her.

She spoke abruptly without turning, as one who has known since infancy that there is always someone there to answer: 'Why are we going east?'

'We're making for Kerm Land.'

'Why Kerm Land?'

It was one of the younger ones who had come forward to answer. 'Because that part of the country is in rebellion against the – against King Emran. I am a Kermlander: Perreth ner Sode.'

'Is Emran in Erhenrang?'

'Erhenrang was taken by Orgoreyn, six years ago. The king is in the new capital, east of the mountains – the Old Capital, actually, Rer.'

'Emran lost the West Fall?' Argaven said, and then turning

full on the stout young noble, 'Lost the West Fall? Lost Erhenrang?'

Perreth drew back a step, but answered promptly, 'We've been in hiding behind the mountains for six years.'

'The Orgota are in Erhenrang?'

'King Emran signed a treaty with Orgoreyn five years ago, ceding them the Western Provinces.'

'A shameful treaty, your majesty,' old Ker broke in, fiercer and shakier than ever. 'A fool's treaty! Emran dances to the drums of Orgoreyn. All of us here are rebels, exiles. The Ambassador there is an exile, in hiding!'

'The West Fall,' Argaven said. 'Argaven I took the West Fall for Karhide seven hundred years ago—' She looked round on the others again with her strange, keen, unheeding gaze. 'Emran—' she began, but halted. 'How strong are you in Kerm Land? Is the Coast with you?'

'Most Hearths of the South and East are with us.'

Argaven was silent a while. 'Did Emran ever bear an heir?'

'No heir of the flesh, my liege,' Bannith said. 'She sired six.'

'She has named Girvry Harge rem ir Orek as her heir,' said Perreth.

'Girvry? What kind of name is that? The kings of Karhide are named Emran,' Argaven said, 'and Argaven.'

Now at last comes the dark picture, the snapshot taken by firelight – firelight, because the power plants of Rer are wrecked, the trunk lines cut, and half the city is on fire. Snow flurries heavily down above the flames and gleams red for a moment before it melts in mid air, hissing faintly.

Snow and ice and guerrilla troops keep Orgoreyn at bay on the west side of the Kargav Mountains. No help came to the Old King, Emran, when her country rose against her. Her guards fled, her city burns, and now at the end she is face to face with the usurper. But she has, at the end, something of her family's heedless pride. She pays no attention to the rebels. She stares at them and does not see them, lying in the dark hallway,

lit only by mirrors that reflect distant fires, the gun with which she killed herself near her hand.

Stooping over the body Argaven lifts up that cold hand, and starts to take from the age-knotted forefinger the massive, carved, gold ring. But she does not do it. 'Keep it,' she whispers, 'keep it.' For a moment she bends yet lower, as if she whispered in the dead ear, or laid her cheek against that cold and wrinkled face. Then she straightens up, and stands a while, and presently goes out through dark corridors, by windows bright with distant ruin, to set her house in order: Argaven, Winter's king.

THE GOOD TRIP

This story was published when the drug scene was big in the media, and one response to it was that I was trying to cash in on a hot topic. That struck me as funny, given my infallible talent for missing whatever boat all the fashionable people are on – and also in view of the fact that, in a way, the point of the little story is that Lewis doesn't take the chemical trip, but gets there on his own . . . with a little help from his friend.

But it's not an anti-drug story either. My only strong opinion about drugs (pot, hallucinogens, alcohol) is anti-prohibition and pro-education. I have to admit that people who expand their consciousness by living instead of by taking chemicals usually come back with much more interesting reports of where they've been. But I'm an addict myself (tobacco), and it would be plain silly in me to celebrate or to condemn anybody else for a similar dependence.

As he swallowed the stuff he knew he shouldn't swallow the stuff, knew it for sure, knew it as a driver knows the truck coming straight at him at 70 mph: suddenly, intimately, finally. His throat shut, his solar plexus knotted up like a sea anemone, but too late. Down the hatch it went, the bit of bitter candy, the acid-drop, the sourball, the peppy packet of power, etching a little corroded trail of terror behind it all the way down his esophagus like a poisoned snail swallowed whole. It was the terror that was wrong. He was afraid and hadn't known it, and now it was too late. You can't afford to be afraid. Fear fouls it all up, and sends those few, those unhappy few, a very small

percentage, to the loony bin to cower in corners not saying anything...

You have nothing to fear but fear itself.

Yes sir. Yes sir Mr Roosevelt sir.

The thing to do is relax. Think good thoughts. If rape inevitable –

He watched Rich Harringer open up his little packet (accurately compounded and hygienically wrapped by a couple of fellows putting themselves through grad school in chemistry by the approved American method of free enterprise, illegitimate to be sure but this is not unusual in America where so little is legal that even a baby can be illegitimate) and swallow the small sour snail with formal and deliberate enjoyment. If rape inevitable, relax and enjoy. Once a week.

But is anything inevitable besides death? Why relax, why enjoy? He would fight. He would not go on a bad trip. He would fight the drug consciously and purposefully, not in panic but with Intent, and we'll see who wins. In this corner LSD/alpha, 100 micrograms, plain wrapper, the Tibetan Whirlwind; and in this corner, ladies and junglemen, L.S.D./B.A., M.A., 166 lbs, the Sonoma Sniveller, wearing white trunks, and red suitcases, and blue cheekpouches. Let me out of here, let me out of here! *Clang*.

Nothing happened.

Lewis Sidney David, the man with no last name, the Jewish Kelt, cornered in this corner, stared warily around him. His three companions all looked normal, in focus if out of touch. They did not have auras. Jim was lying on the verminous sofabed reading *Ramparts*, a trip to Vietnam he wanted maybe, or to Sacramento. Rich looked torpid, he always looked torpid even when serving free lunch in the park, and Alex was nitpicking around on his guitar. The infinite satisfaction of the chord. The silver cord. Sursum corda. If he carries a guitar around why can't he play a tune on it? No. Irritability is a symptom of loss of self-control: suppress it. Suppress everything. Censor, censor. Fight, team, fight!

Lewis got up, observing with pleasure the ready ease of his

responses and the perfection of his sense of balance, and filled a glass of water at the vile sink. Beard hairs, spat-out Colgate, rust and radish droppings, a sink of iniquity. A small sink, but mine own. Why did he live in this dump? Why had he asked Jim and Rich and Alex to come share their sugarlumps with him here? It was lousy enough without being an opium den too. Soon it would be littered with inert bodies, eyes dropping out like marbles and rolling under the bed to join the dust and ruin lurking there. Lewis carried the glass of water over to the window, drank half of it, and began to pour the rest gently around the roots of a seedling olive tree in a mended ten-cent pot. 'Have a drink on me,' he said, looking closely at the tree.

It was five inches high but looked very like an olive tree, gnarled and durable. A bonsai. Banzai! But where's satori? Where's the significance, the enhancement, all the shapes and colors and meanings, the intensification of the perception of reality? How long does it take the damned stuff to work? There sat his olive tree. No less, no more. Unenhanced, insignificant. Men cry Peace, peace, but there is no peace. Not enough olive trees to go around, due to population explosion of human species. Was that a Perception? No, any un-drugged meat-head could have perceived it. O come on, poison, poison me. Come, hallucination, come, so that I may fight you, reject you, refuse you, lose the fight and go mad, silently.

Like Isobel.

That was why he lived in this dump, and that was why he had asked Jim and Rich and Alex here, and that was why he was off on a trip with them, a pleasure-cruise, a holiday in picturesque Old Erewhon. He was trying to catch up with his wife. What is most difficult about watching your wife go insane is that you can't go with her. Farther and farther away she walks, not looking back, a long trip down into silence. The lyre falls dumb, and the psychiatrists are liars too. You stand behind the glass wall of your sanity like one at an airport watching a crash. You shout, 'Isobel!' She never heard. The plane crashed in silence. She could not hear him call her name. Nor could

III

she speak to him. Now the walls that divided him from her were brick, very solid, and he could do what he liked with his own glass house of sanity. Throw stones. Throw alphas. Tinkle, crash.

LSD/alpha did not drive you insane, of course. It did not even unravel your chromosomes. It simply opened the door to the higher reality. So did schizophrenia, he gathered, but the trouble there was that you couldn't speak, you couldn't communicate, you couldn't say what.

Jim had lowered his *Ramparts*. He was sitting in a noticeable fashion, inhaling. He was going to get with reality the right way, like a lama, man. He was a true believer and his life now centered upon the LSD/a experience as a religious mystic's upon his mystical discipline. Could you keep it up once a week for years, though? At thirty? At forty-two? At sixty-three? There is a terrible monotony and adversity to life; you'd need a monastery. Matins, nones, vespers, silence, walls around, big solid brick walls. To keep the lower reality out.

Come on, hallucinogen, get with it. Hallucinogenate, hallucinogenize. Smash the glass wall. Take me on a trip where my wife went. Missing person, age 22, ht 5ft 3in, wt 105 lbs, hair brown, race human, sex female. She never was a fast walker. I could catch up with her with one foot tied behind me. Take me where she walked to . . . No.

I'll walk there by myself, said Lewis Sidney David. He finished pouring the water in little dribbles around the roots of the olive tree, and looked up, out the window. There through smeary glass was Mount Hood, forty miles away, two miles high, a volcanic cone possessing the serene symmetry peculiar to volcanic cones, dormant but not officially extinct, full of sleepy fires and surrounded by its own atmosphere and climate different from that of lower altitudes: snow and a clear light. That was why he lived in this dump. Because when you looked out the window of it, you saw the higher reality. Eleven thousand feet higher.

'I'll be damned,' Lewis said aloud, feeling that he was on

the edge and verge of perceiving something really important. But he had that feeling fairly often, without chemical assistance. Meanwhile there was the mountain.

A lot of muck, freeways and disposable office buildings and high-rises and urban renewal bombsites and neon elephants washing neon cars with dotted showers of neon, lay in between him and the mountain, and the base of it was hidden along with its foothills in a pale smog, so that the peak floated.

Lewis felt a strong impulse to cry and to say his wife's name aloud. He repressed this impulse, as he had been doing for three months, ever since May when he had taken her to the sanitarium, after the silent months. In January, before the silence began, she had cried a great deal, all day long some days, and he had become frightened of tears. First tears, then silence. No good. O God get me out of this! Lewis let go, quit fighting the impalpable enemy, and begged for release. He implored the drug in his bloodstream to work, to do something, to let him cry, or see colors, or go off his rocker, anything.

Nothing happened.

He finished pouring the water in little dribbles around the roots of the olive tree, and looked up, at the room. It was a dump, but big, and it had a good view of Mount Hood, and the wisdom-tooth crest of Mount Adams on clear days too. But nothing would happen here. This was the waiting room. He picked up his coat off a broken chair and went out.

It was a good coat, lambswool lining and a hood and all that; his sister and mother had clubbed to get it for him for Christmas, making him feel like R. R. Raskolnikov. But he was not going to murder any old pawnbrokers today. Not even a pseudocide. On the stairs he passed the painters and plasterers with their ladders and buckets, three of them, going up to do his room over, peaceful-looking, fresh-faced men in their forties and fifties. Poor bastards, what would they do with the sink? with the three alphies, Rich and Jim and Alex, who on honeydew had fed and drunk the milk of Paradise? with his notes on LeNotre, Olmsted and McLaren, with his fourteen

pounds of photographs of Japanese domestic architecture, with his drawing board and fishing tackle, his *Collected Works of Theodore Sturgeon* bound in sensational cardboard, the 8ft × 10ft unfinished oil of an ataxic nude by a painter friend whose auto loan co had attached his paintings, Alex's guitar, the olive tree, the dust and eyeballs under the bed? That was their problem. He went on down the rooming-house stairs that smelled of old tomcat, and heard his hiking boots clomping heartily. He felt that all this had happened once before.

It took him a long time to get out of the city. Since public transportation was forbidden to people in his condition, of course, he couldn't get on the Gresham bus which would have saved a lot of time, taking him through the suburbs and half-way there. But there was plenty of time. The summer evening would stay light; he could count on it. Lenient and sweet in their length are the twilights of a latitude halfway between equator and pole: no tropic monotonies, no arctic absolutes, but a winter of long shadows and a summer of long dusks: gradations and accommodations of brightness, attenuations of clarity, subtleties and leisures of the light. Children scuttered in the green parks of Portland and down long side streets, all at one great game over all the city, the game of Young. Only here and there a kid went alone, playing Solitude, for higher stakes. Some kids are gamblers born. Bits of trash scraped along the gutters moved by a warm wind now and then. There was a great, sad sound far off over the city as if lions were roaring in cages, walking and lashing their gold sides with gold-tasselled tails and roaring, roaring. Sun set, somewhere west over roofs, but not for the mountain that still burned with a white fire away up high. As Lewis left the last of the city and went through a pleasant land, hilly and well farmed, the wind began to smell of wet earth, cool, complex, as it will as night comes on; and past Sandy there was darkness under great increasing forests on the rising slopes. But there was plenty of time. Above and ahead the peak stood white, faintly tinged with apricot, in sunlight. As he climbed the long, steep road he came out again and then

again from the dark forests into gulfs of yellow clarity. He went on until he was up above the forests and up above the darkness, on heights where there was only snow and stone and air and the vast, clear, enduring light.

But he was alone.

That wasn't right. He hadn't been alone when this had happened. He had to meet with – He had been with – Where?

No skis no sled no snowshoes not even an inner tube. If I had got the commission for this landscape, God, I would have put a path along here. Sacrificing grandeur for convenience? But only a little path. No harm. Only a little crack in the Liberty Bell. Only a little leak in the dike, fuse on the bomb, maggot in the brain. O my mad girl, my silent love, my wife whom I sold into bedlam because you would not hear me speak, Isobel, come save me from yourself! I've climbed after you up above all the paths and now I stand here alone: there isn't any way to go.

Daylight died away and the white of the snow went somber. In the east, above endless darkening ranges and forests and pale, hill-enfolded lakes, Saturn shone, bright and saturnine.

Lewis did not know where the lodge was; somewhere on the timberline, but he was above timberline. He would not go down. To the heights, to the heights. Excelsior! A youth who bore mid snow and ice a banner with this strange device HELP HELP I AM A PRISONER OF THE HIGHER REALITY. He climbed. He climbed un-clomben slopes, unkempt, and as he climbed he wept. His tears crawled down over his face and he crawled up over the mountain's face.

The very high places are terrible, alone at dusk.

The light no longer stayed for him. There was no longer plenty of time. He had run out of time. Stars came out and looked at him eye to eye out of the gulfs of darkness whenever he glanced aside from the huge white uptilted plain, the higher plane he climbed. On either side of him there was a gap, with a few stars in it. But the snow kept its own cold light, and he kept climbing. He remembered the path when he came

across it. God or the state or he himself had put a path there on the mountain after all. He turned right, and it was wrong. He turned left, and stood still. He did not know which way to go, and shaking with cold and fear he cried out aloud to the death-white summit above him and to the black places in between the stars his wife's name, 'Isobel!'

She came along the path out of the darkness. 'I began to get worried about you, Lewis.'

'I went farther than I meant to,' Lewis said.

'It stays light so long up here you sort of think it'll go on forever...'

'Right. I'm sorry I worried you.'

'Oh, I wasn't worried. You know. Lonesome. I thought maybe your leg had slowed you down. Is it a good hike?'

'Spectacular.'

'Take me along tomorrow.'

'Didn't you enjoy skiing?'

She shook her head. 'Not without you,' she muttered, shamefaced. They went leftward down the path, not very fast. Lewis was still slightly hobbled by the pulled muscle that had kept him off skis the last two days, and it was dark, and there wasn't any hurry. They held hands. Snow, starlight, stillness. Fire underfoot, darkness around; ahead of them, firelight, beer, bed. All things in their due time. Some, born gamblers, will always choose to live on the side of a volcano.

'When I was in the sanitarium,' Isobel said, pausing so that he too stopped and there was no longer even the noise of their boots on the dry snow, no sound at all but the soft sound of her voice, 'I had a dream like this. Awfully like this. It was the... most important dream I had. Yet I can't recall it clearly – I never could, even in therapy. But it was like this. This silence. Being up high. The silence above all... above all. It was so silent that if I said something, you would be able to hear it. I knew that. I was sure of it. And in the dream I think I said your name, and you *could* hear me – you answered me—'

'Say my name,' he whispered.

She turned and looked at him. There was no sound on the mountain or among the stars. She said his name.

He answered saying hers, and then took hold of her; both of them were shaking.

'It's cold, it's cold, we've got to go down.'

They went on, on their tightrope between the outer and the inner fires.

'Look at that enormous star.'

'Planet. Saturn – Father Time.'

'Ate his children, didn't he,' she murmured, holding hard to his arm.

'All but one of them,' Lewis answered. Down a long clear slope before them now they saw in grey starlight the bulk of the upper hut, the towers of the ski-lift vague and gaunt, and the vast down-sweep of the lines.

His hands were cold and he slipped off his gloves a minute to beat them together, but this was hard to do because of the glass of water he was holding. He finished pouring the water in little dribbles around the roots of the olive tree and set down the glass beside the mended flowerpot. But something still remained in his hand, folded into the palm like a crib for a high-school French final, *que je fusse, que tu fusses, qu'il fût*, small and sweat-stuck. He opened his hand and studied the item for some while. A message. From whom, to whom? From grave, to womb. A little packet, sealed, containing 100 mg of LSD/a in sugar.

Sealed?

He remembered, with precision and in order, opening it, swallowing the stuff, the taste of it. He also remembered with equal order and precision where he had been since then and knew that he had not been there yet.

He went over to Jim who was just exhaling the breath he had been inhaling as Lewis began to water the olive tree. Deftly and gently Lewis tucked the packet into Jim's coat pocket.

'Aren't you coming along?' Jim asked, smiling a mild smile.

Lewis shook his head. 'Chicken,' he murmured. It was hard

to explain that he had already come back from the trip he had not made. Besides, Jim wouldn't hear him. He was off where people don't hear and can't answer, walled in.

'Have a good trip,' Lewis said.

He got his raincoat (dirty poplin, no fleece lining, hold on, wait) and went down the stairs and out into the streets. The summer was ending, the season changing. It was raining but not dark yet, and the city wind blew in great cool gusts that smelled of wet earth and forests and the night.

NINE LIVES

The biologist Gordon Rattray Taylor is innocently responsible for this story. He has a chapter on cloning in his fine book The Biological Time Bomb. *I read that, and then I wrote this.*

It is as near 'hard-core' or wiring-diagram science fiction as I ever get; that is, it's a wording out of a theme directly extrapolated from contemporary work in one of the quantitative sciences – a what-if story. The theme, however, is developed qualitatively, psychologically. Essentially I am using the scientific element, not as an end in itself, but as a metaphor or symbol, a means of saying something not otherwise expressible.

'Nine Lives' appeared in Playboy *in 1968, under the only pen name I have ever used: U. K. Le Guin. The editors politely asked if they could use the first initial only, and I agreed. It's not surprising that* Playboy *hadn't had its consciousness raised back then, but it is surprising to me to realize how thoughtlessly I went along with them. It was the first (and is the only) time I met with anything I understood as sexual prejudice, prejudice against me as a woman writer, from any editor or publisher; and it seemed so silly, so grotesque, that I failed to see that it was also important.*

Playboy *made a good many minor changes in the story, and these have been kept in reprintings of it under their imprint. I prefer my version of it, and whenever I have had control of reprintings it has appeared in the version given here, and under my unabridged name.*

She was alive inside but dead outside, her face a black and dun net of wrinkles, tumors, cracks. She was bald and blind. The tremors that crossed Libra's face were mere quiverings of corruption. Underneath, in the black corridors, the halls

119

beneath the skin, there were crepitations in darkness, ferments, chemical nightmares that went on for centuries. 'O the damned flatulent planet,' Pugh murmured as the dome shook and a boil burst a kilometer to the southwest, spraying silver pus across the sunset. The sun had been setting for the last two days. 'I'll be glad to see a human face.'

'Thanks,' said Martin.

'Yours is human to be sure,' said Pugh, 'but I've seen it so long I can't see it.'

Radvid signals cluttered the communicator which Martin was operating, faded, returned as face and voice. The face filled the screen, the nose of an Assyrian king, the eyes of a samurai, skin bronze, eyes the color of iron: young, magnificent. 'Is that what human beings look like?' said Pugh with awe. 'I'd forgotten.'

'Shut up, Owen, we're on.'

'Libra Exploratory Mission Base, come in please, this is *Passerine* launch.'

'Libra here. Beam fixed. Come on down, launch.'

'Expulsion in seven E-seconds. Hold on.' The screen blanked and sparkled.

'Do they all look like that? Martin, you and I are uglier men than I thought.'

'Shut up, Owen...'

For twenty-two minutes Martin followed the landing craft down by signal and then through the cleared dome they saw it, small star in the blood-colored east, sinking. It came down neat and quiet, Libra's thin atmosphere carrying little sound. Pugh and Martin closed the headpieces of their imsuits, zipped out of the dome airlocks, and ran with soaring strides, Nijinsky and Nureyev, toward the boat. Three equipment modules came floating down at four-minute intervals from each other and hundred-meter intervals east of the boat. 'Come on out,' Martin said on his suit radio, 'we're waiting at the door.'

'Come on in, the methane's fine,' said Pugh.

The hatch opened. The young man they had seen on the

screen came out with one athletic twist and leaped down onto the shaky dust and clinkers of Libra. Martin shook his hand, but Pugh was staring at the hatch, from which another young man emerged with the same neat twist and jump, followed by a young woman who emerged with the same neat twist, ornamented by a wriggle, and the jump. They were all tall, with bronze skin, black hair, high-bridged noses, epicanthic fold, the same face. They all had the same face. The fourth was emerging from the hatch with a neat twist and jump. 'Martin bach,' said Pugh, 'we've got a clone.'

'Right,' said one of them, 'we're a tenclone. John Chow's the name. You're Lieutenant Martin?'

'I'm Owen Pugh.'

'Alvaro Guillen Martin,' said Martin, formal, bowing slightly. Another girl was out, the same beautiful face; Martin stared at her and his eye rolled like a nervous pony's. Evidently he had never given any thought to cloning and was suffering technological shock. 'Steady,' Pugh said in the Argentine dialect, 'it's only excess twins.' He stood close by Martin's elbow. He was glad himself of the contact.

It is hard to meet a stranger. Even the greatest extravert meeting even the meekest stranger knows a certain dread, though he may not know he knows it. Will he make a fool of me wreck my image of myself invade me destroy me change me? Will he be different from me? Yes, that he will. There's the terrible thing: the strangeness of the stranger.

After two years on a dead planet, and the last half year isolated as a team of two, oneself and one other, after that it's even harder to meet a stranger, however welcome he may be. You're out of the habit of difference, you've lost the touch; and so the fear revives, the primitive anxiety, the old dread.

The clone, five males and five females, had got done in a couple of minutes what a man might have got done in twenty: greeted Pugh and Martin, had a glance at Libra, unloaded the boat, made ready to go. They went, and the dome filled with them, a hive of golden bees. They hummed and buzzed

quietly, filled up all silences, all spaces with a honey-brown swarm of human presence. Martin looked bewildered at the long-limbed girls, and they smiled at him, three at once. Their smile was gentler than that of the boys, but no less radiantly self-possessed.

'Self-possessed,' Owen Pugh murmured to his friend, 'that's it. Think of it, to be oneself ten times over. Nine seconds for every motion, nine ayes on every vote. It would be glorious.' But Martin was asleep. And the John Chows had all gone to sleep at once. The dome was filled with their quiet breathing. They were young, they didn't snore. Martin sighed and snored, his Hershey-bar-colored face relaxed in the dim afterglow of Libra's primary, set at last. Pugh had cleared the dome and stars looked in, Sol among them, a great company of lights, a clone of splendors. Pugh slept and dreamed of a one-eyed giant who chased him through the shaking halls of Hell.

From his sleeping bag Pugh watched the clone's awakening. They all got up within one minute except for one pair, a boy and a girl, who lay snugly tangled and still sleeping in one bag. As Pugh saw this there was a shock like one of Libra's earthquakes inside him, a very deep tremor. He was not aware of this and in fact thought he was pleased at the sight; there was no other such comfort on this dead hollow world. More power to them, who made love. One of the others stepped on the pair. They woke and the girl sat up flushed and sleepy, with bare golden breasts. One of her sisters murmured something to her; she shot a glance at Pugh and disappeared in the sleeping bag; from another direction came a fierce stare, from still another direction a voice: 'Christ, we're used to having a room to ourselves. Hope you don't mind, Captain Pugh.'

'It's a pleasure,' Pugh said half truthfully. He had to stand up then wearing only the shorts he slept in, and he felt like a plucked rooster, all white scrawn and pimples. He had seldom envied Martin's compact brownness so much. The United Kingdom had come through the Great Famines well, losing

less than half its population: a record achieved by rigorous food control. Black marketeers and hoarders had been executed. Crumbs had been shared. Where in richer lands most had died and a few had thriven, in Britain fewer died and none throve. They all got lean. Their sons were lean, their grandsons lean, small, brittle-boned, easily infected. When civilization became a matter of standing in lines, the British had kept queue, and so had replaced the survival of the fittest with the survival of the fair-minded. Owen Pugh was a scrawny little man. All the same, he was there.

At the moment he wished he wasn't.

At breakfast a John said, 'Now if you'll brief us, Captain Pugh—'

'Owen, then.'

'Owen, we can work out our schedule. Anything new on the mine since your last report to your Mission? We saw your reports when *Passerine* was orbiting Planet V, where they are now.'

Martin did not answer, though the mine was his discovery and project, and Pugh had to do his best. It was hard to talk to them. The same faces, each with the same expression of intelligent interest, all leaned toward him across the table at almost the same angle. They all nodded together.

Over the Exploitation Corps insigne on their tunics each had a nameband, first name John and last name Chow of course, but the middle names different. The men were Aleph, Kaph, Yod, Gimel, and Samedh; the women Sadhe, Daleth, Zayin, Beth, and Resh. Pugh tried to use the names but gave it up at once; he could not even tell sometimes which one had spoken, for all the voices were alike.

Martin buttered and chewed his toast, and finally interrupted: 'You're a team. Is that it?'

'Right,' said two Johns.

'God, what a team! I hadn't seen the point. How much do you each know what the others are thinking?'

'Not at all, properly speaking,' replied one of the girls, Zayin.

123

The others watched her with the proprietary, approving look they had. 'No ESP, nothing fancy. But we think alike. We have exactly the same equipment. Given the same stimulus, the same problem, we're likely to be coming up with the same reactions and solutions at the same time. Explanations are easy – don't even have to make them, usually. We seldom misunderstand each other. It does facilitate our working as a team.'

'Christ yes,' said Martin, 'Pugh and I have spent seven hours out of ten for six months misunderstanding each other. Like most people. What about emergencies, are you as good at meeting the unexpected problem as a nor... an unrelated team?'

'Statistics so far indicate that we are,' Zayin answered readily. Clones must be trained, Pugh thought, to meet questions, to reassure and reason. All they said had the slightly bland and stilted quality of answers furnished to the Public. 'We can't brainstorm as singletons can, we as a team don't profit from the interplay of varied minds; but we have a compensatory advantage. Clones are drawn from the best human material, individuals of IIQ ninety-ninth percentile, Genetic Constitution alpha double A, and so on. We have more to draw on than most individuals do.'

'And it's multiplied by a factor of ten. Who is – who was John Chow?'

'A genius surely,' Pugh said politely. His interest in cloning was not so new and avid as Martin's.

'Leonardo Complex type,' said Yod. 'Biomath, also a cellist and an undersea hunter, and interested in structural engineering problems and so on. Died before he'd worked out his major theories.'

'Then you each represent a different facet of his mind, his talents?'

'No,' said Zayin, shaking her head in time with several others. 'We share the basic equipment and tendencies, of course, but we're all engineers in Planetary Exploitation. A later clone can be trained to develop other aspects of the basic

equipment. It's all training; the genetic substance is identical. We *are* John Chow. But we are differently trained.'

Martin looked shell-shocked. 'How old are you?'

'Twenty-three.'

'You say he died young – had they taken germ cells from him beforehand or something?'

Gimel took over: 'He died at twenty-four in an air car crash. They couldn't save the brain, so they took some intestinal cells and cultured them for cloning. Reproductive cells aren't used for cloning, since they have only half the chromosomes. Intestinal cells happen to be easy to despecialize and reprogram for total growth.'

'All chips off the old block,' Martin said valiantly. 'But how can... some of you be women...?'

Beth took over. 'It's easy to program half the clonal mass back to the female. Just delete the male gene from half the cells and they revert to the basic, that is, the female. It's trickier to go the other way, have to hook in artificial Y chromosomes. So they mostly clone from males, since clones function best bisexually.'

Gimel again: 'They've worked these matters of technique and function out carefully. The taxpayer wants the best for his money, and of course clones are expensive. With the cell manipulations, and the incubation in Ngama Placentae, and the maintenance and training of the foster-parent groups, we end up costing about three million apiece.'

'For your next generation,' Martin said, still struggling, 'I suppose you... you breed?'

'We females are sterile,' said Beth with perfect equanimity. 'You remember that the Y chromosome was deleted from our original cell. The males can interbreed with approved single-tons, if they want to. But to get John Chow again as often as they want, they just reclone a cell from this clone.'

Martin gave up the struggle. He nodded and chewed cold toast. 'Well,' said one of the Johns, and all changed mood, like a flock of starlings that change course in one wingflick, following

a leader so fast that no eye can see which leads. They were ready to go. 'How about a look at the mine? Then we'll unload the equipment. Some nice new models in the roboats; you'll want to see them. Right?' Had Pugh or Martin not agreed they might have found it hard to say so. The Johns were polite but unanimous; their decisions carried. Pugh, Commander of Libra Base 2, felt a qualm. Could he boss around this super-man/woman-entity-of-ten? and a genius at that? He stuck close to Martin as they suited for outside. Neither said anything.

Four apiece in the three large airjets, they slipped off north from the dome, over Libra's dun rugose skin, in starlight.

'Desolate,' one said.

It was a boy and girl with Pugh and Martin. Pugh wondered if these were the two that had shared a sleeping bag last night. No doubt they wouldn't mind if he asked them. Sex must be as handy as breathing to them. Did you two breathe last night?

'Yes,' he said, 'it is desolate.'

'This is our first time off, except training on Luna.' The girl's voice was definitely a bit higher and softer.

'How did you take the big hop?'

'They doped us. I wanted to experience it.' That was the boy; he sounded wistful. They seemed to have more personality, only two at a time. Did repetition of the individual negate individuality?

'Don't worry,' said Martin, steering the sled, 'you can't experience no-time because it isn't there.'

'I'd just like to once,' one of them said. 'So we'd know.'

The Mountains of Merioneth showed leprotic in starlight to the east, a plume of freezing gas trailed silvery from a vent-hole to the west, and the sled tilted groundward. The twins braced for the stop at one moment, each with a slight protective gesture to the other. Your skin is my skin, Pugh thought, but literally, no metaphor. What would it be like, then, to have someone as close to you as that? Always to be answered when you spoke; never to be in pain alone. Love your neighbor as

you love yourself ... That hard old problem was solved. The neighbor was the self: the love was perfect.

And here was Hellmouth, the mine.

Pugh was the Exploratory Mission's ET geologist, and Martin his technician and cartographer; but when in the course of a local survey Martin had discovered the U-mine, Pugh had given him full credit, as well as the onus of prospecting the lode and planning the Exploitation Team's job. These kids had been sent out from Earth years before Martin's reports got there and had not known what their job would be until they got here. The Exploitation Corps simply sent out teams regularly and blindly as a dandelion sends out its seed, knowing there would be a job for them on Libra or the next planet out or one they hadn't even heard about yet. The government wanted uranium too urgently to wait while reports drifted home across the lightyears. The stuff was like gold, old-fashioned but essential, worth mining extraterrestrially and shipping interstellar. Worth its weight in people, Pugh thought sourly, watching the tall young men and women go one by one, glimmering in starlight, into the black hole Martin had named Hellmouth.

As they went in their homeostatic forehead-lamps brightened. Twelve nodding gleams ran along the moist, wrinkled walls. Pugh heard Martin's radiation counter peeping twenty to the dozen up ahead. 'Here's the drop-off,' said Martin's voice in the suit intercom, drowning out the peeping and the dead silence that was around them. 'We're in a side-fissure, this is the main vertical vent in front of us.' The black void gaped, its far side not visible in the headlamp beams. 'Last vulcanism seems to have been a couple of thousand years ago. Nearest fault is twenty-eight kilos east, in the Trench. This area seems to be as safe seismically as anything in the area. The big basalt-flow overhead stabilizes all these substructures, so long as it remains stable itself. Your central lode is thirty-six meters down and runs in a series of five bubble caverns northeast. It is a lode, a pipe of very high-grade ore. You saw the percentage figures, right?

Extraction's going to be no problem. All you've got to do is get the bubbles topside.'

'Take off the lid and let 'em float up.' A chuckle. Voices began to talk, but they were all the same voice and the suit radio gave them no location in space. 'Open the thing right up. – Safer that way. – But it's a solid basalt roof, how thick, ten meters here? – Three to twenty, the report said. – Blow good ore all over the lot. – Use this access we're in, straighten it a bit and run slider rails for the robos. – Import burros. – Have we got enough propping material? – What's your estimate of total payload mass, Martin?'

'Say over five million kilos and under eight.'

'Transport will be here in ten E-months. – It'll have to go pure. – No, they'll have the mass problem in NAFAL shipping licked by now, remember it's been sixteen years since we left Earth last Tuesday. – Right, they'll send the whole lot back and purify it in Earth orbit. – Shall we go down, Martin?'

'Go on. I've been down.'

The first one – Aleph? (Heb., the ox, the leader) – swung onto the ladder and down; the rest followed. Pugh and Martin stood at the chasm's edge. Pugh set his intercom to exchange only with Martin's suit, and noticed Martin doing the same. It was a bit wearing, this listening to one person think aloud in ten voices, or was it one voice speaking the thoughts of ten minds?

'A great gut,' Pugh said, looking down into the black pit, its veined and warted walls catching stray gleams of headlamps far below. 'A cow's bowel. A bloody great constipated intestine.'

Martin's counter peeped like a lost chicken. They stood inside the dead but epileptic planet, breathing oxygen from tanks, wearing suits impermeable to corrosives and harmful radiations, resistant to a 200-degree range of temperatures, tear-proof, and as shock-resistant as possible given the soft vulnerable stuff inside.

'Next hop,' Martin said, 'I'd like to find a planet that has nothing whatever to exploit.'

'You found this.'

'Keep me home next time.'

Pugh was pleased. He had hoped Martin would want to go on working with him, but neither of them was used to talking much about their feelings, and he had hesitated to ask. 'I'll try that,' he said.

'I hate this place. I like caves, you know. It's why I came in here. Just spelunking. But this one's a bitch. Mean. You can't ever let down in here. I guess this lot can handle it, though. They know their stuff.'

'Wave of the future, whatever,' said Pugh.

The wave of the future came swarming up the ladder, swept Martin to the entrance, gabbled at and around him: 'Have we got enough material for supports? – If we convert one of the extractor servos to anneal, yes. – Sufficient if we miniblast? – Kaph can calculate stress.' Pugh had switched his intercom back to receive them; he looked at them, so many thoughts jabbering in an eager mind, and at Martin standing silent among them, and at Hellmouth and the wrinkled plain. 'Settled! How does that strike you as a preliminary schedule, Martin?'

'It's your baby,' Martin said.

Within five E-days the Johns had all their material and equipment unloaded and operating and were starting to open up the mine. They worked with total efficiency. Pugh was fascinated and frightened by their effectiveness, their confidence, their independence. He was no use to them at all. A clone, he thought, might indeed be the first truly stable, self-reliant human being. Once adult it would need nobody's help. It would be sufficient to itself physically, sexually, emotionally, intellectually. Whatever he did, any member of it would always receive the support and approval of his peers, his other selves. Nobody else was needed.

Two of the clone stayed in the dome doing calculations and paperwork, with frequent sled trips to the mine for measurements and tests. They were the mathematicians of the clone, Zayin and Kaph. That is, as Zayin explained, all ten had had thorough mathematical training from age three to twenty-one,

but from twenty-one to twenty-three she and Kaph had gone on with math while the others intensified study in other specialties, geology, mining, engineering, electronic engineering, equipment robotics, applied atomics, and so on. 'Kaph and I feel,' she said, 'that we're the element of the clone closest to what John Chow was in his singleton lifetime. But of course he was principally in biomath, and they didn't take us far in that.'

'They needed us most in this field,' Kaph said, with the patriotic priggishness they sometimes evinced.

Pugh and Martin soon could distinguish this pair from the others, Zayin by gestalt, Kaph only by a discolored left fourth fingernail, got from an ill-aimed hammer at the age of six. No doubt there were many such differences, physical and psychological, among them; nature might be identical, nurture could not be. But the differences were hard to find. And part of the difficulty was that they never really talked to Pugh and Martin. They joked with them, were polite, got along fine. They gave nothing. It was nothing one could complain about; they were very pleasant, they had the standardized American friendliness. 'Do you come from Ireland, Owen?'

'Nobody comes from Ireland, Zayin.'

'There are lots of Irish-Americans.'

'To be sure, but no more Irish. A couple of thousand in all the island, the last I knew. They didn't go in for birth control, you know, so the food ran out. By the Third Famine there were no Irish left at all but the priesthood, and they all celibate, or nearly all.'

Zayin and Kaph smiled stiffly. They had no experience of either bigotry or irony. 'What are you then, ethnically?' Kaph asked, and Pugh replied, 'A Welshman.'

'Is it Welsh that you and Martin speak together?'

None of your business, Pugh thought, but said, 'No, it's his dialect, not mine: Argentinean. A descendant of Spanish.'

'You learned it for private communication?'

'Whom had we here to be private from? It's just that sometimes a man likes to speak his native language.'

'Ours is English,' Kaph said unsympathetically. Why should they have sympathy? That's one of the things you give because you need it back.

'Is Wells quaint?' asked Zayin.

'Wells? Oh, Wales, it's called. Yes, Wales is quaint.' Pugh switched on his rock-cutter, which prevented further conversation by a synapse-destroying whine, and while it whined he turned his back and said a profane word in Welsh.

That night he used the Argentine dialect for private communication. 'Do they pair off in the same couples or change every night?'

Martin looked surprised. A prudish expression, unsuited to his features, appeared for a moment. It faded. He too was curious. 'I think it's random.'

'Don't whisper, man, it sounds dirty. I think they rotate.'

'On a schedule?'

'So nobody gets omitted.'

Martin gave a vulgar laugh and smothered it. 'What about us? Aren't we omitted?'

'That doesn't occur to them.'

'What if I proposition one of the girls?'

'She'd tell the others and they'd decide as a group.'

'I am not a bull,' Martin said, his dark, heavy face heating up. 'I will not be judged—'

'Down, down, *machismo*,' said Pugh. 'Do you mean to proposition one?'

Martin shrugged, sullen. 'Let 'em have their incest.'

'Incest is it, or masturbation?'

'I don't care, if they'd do it out of earshot!'

The clone's early attempts at modesty had soon worn off, un-motivated by any deep defensiveness of self or awareness of others. Pugh and Martin were daily deeper swamped under the intimacies of its constant emotional-sexual-mental interchange: swamped yet excluded.

'Two months to go,' Martin said one evening.

'To what?' snapped Pugh. He was edgy lately, and Martin's sullenness got on his nerves.

'To relief.'

In sixty days the full crew of their Exploratory Mission were due back from their survey of the other planets of the system. Pugh was aware of this.

'Crossing off the days on your calendar?' he jeered.

'Pull yourself together, Owen.'

'What do you mean?'

'What I say.'

They parted in contempt and resentment.

Pugh came in after a day alone on the Pampas, a vast lava plain the nearest edge of which was two hours south by jet. He was tired but refreshed by solitude. They were not supposed to take long trips alone but lately had often done so. Martin stooped under bright lights, drawing one of his elegant masterly charts. This one was of the whole face of Libra, the cancerous face. The dome was otherwise empty, seeming dim and large as it had before the clone came. 'Where's the golden horde?'

Martin grunted ignorance, cross-hatching. He straightened his back to glance round at the sun, which squatted feebly like a great red toad on the eastern plain, and at the clock, which said 18:45. 'Some big quakes today,' he said, returning to his map. 'Feel them down there? Lots of crates were falling around. Take a look at the seismo.'

The needle jigged and wavered on the roll. It never stopped dancing here. The roll had recorded five quakes of major intensity back in midafternoon; twice the needle had hopped off the roll. The attached computer had been activated to emit a slip reading, 'Epicenter 61′ N by 42′ 4″ E.'

'Not in the Trench this time.'

'I thought it felt a bit different from usual. Sharper.'

'In Base One I used to lie awake all night feeling the ground jump. Queer how you get used to things.'

'Go spla if you didn't. What's for dinner?'

'I thought you'd have cooked it.'

'Waiting for the clone.'

Feeling put upon, Pugh got out a dozen dinnerboxes, stuck two in the Instobake, pulled them out. 'All right, here's dinner.'

'Been thinking,' Martin said, coming to table. 'What if some clone cloned itself? Illegally. Made a thousand duplicates – ten thousand. Whole army. They could make a tidy power grab, couldn't they?'

'But how many millions did this lot cost to rear? Artificial placentae and all that. It would be hard to keep secret, unless they had a planet to themselves . . . Back before the Famines when Earth had national governments, they talked about that: clone your best soldiers, have whole regiments of them. But the food ran out before they could play that game.'

They talked amicably, as they used to do.

'Funny,' Martin said, chewing. 'They left early this morning, didn't they?'

'All but Kaph and Zayin. They thought they'd get the first pay-load above ground today. What's up?'

'They weren't back for lunch.'

'They won't starve, to be sure.'

'They left at seven.'

'So they did.' Then Pugh saw it. The air tanks held eight hours' supply.

'Kaph and Zayin carried out spare cans when they left. Or they've got a heap out there.'

'They did, but they brought the whole lot in to recharge.' Martin stood up, pointing to one of the stacks of stuff that cut the dome into rooms and alleys.

'There's an alarm signal on every imsuit.'

'It's not automatic.'

Pugh was tired and still hungry. 'Sit down and eat, man. That lot can look after themselves.'

Martin sat down but did not eat. 'There was a big quake, Owen. The first one. Big enough it scared me.'

After a pause Pugh sighed and said, 'All right.'

Unenthusiastically, they got out the two-man sled that was always left for them and headed it north. The long sunrise covered everything in poisonous red jello. The horizontal light and shadow made it hard to see, raised walls of fake iron ahead of them which they slid through, turned the convex plain beyond Hellmouth into a great dimple full of bloody water. Around the tunnel entrance a wilderness of machinery stood, cranes and cables and servos and wheels and diggers and robocarts and sliders and control huts, all slanting and bulking incoherently in the red light. Martin jumped from the sled, ran into the mine. He came out again, to Pugh. 'Oh God, Owen, it's down,' he said. Pugh went in and saw, five meters from the entrance, the shiny moist, black wall that ended the tunnel. Newly exposed to air, it looked organic, like visceral tissue. The tunnel entrance, enlarged by blasting and double-tracked for robocarts, seemed unchanged until he noticed thousands of tiny spiderweb cracks in the walls. The floor was wet with some sluggish fluid.

'They were inside,' Martin said.

'They may be still. They surely had extra air cans—'

'Look, Owen, look at the basalt flow, at the roof, don't you see what the quake did, look at it.'

The low hump of land that roofed the caves still had the unreal look of an optical illusion. It had reversed itself, sunk down, leaving a vast dimple or pit. When Pugh walked on it he saw that it too was cracked with many tiny fissures. From some a whitish gas was seeping, so that the sunlight on the surface of the gas pool was shafted as if by the waters of a dim red lake.

'The mine's not on the fault. There's no fault here!'

Pugh came back to him quickly. 'No, there's no fault, Martin – Look, they surely weren't all inside together.'

Martin followed him and searched among the wrecked machines dully, then actively. He spotted the airsled. It had come down heading south, and stuck at an angle in a pothole of colloidal dust. It had carried two riders. One was half sunk in the dust, but his suit meters registered normal functioning; the other hung strapped onto the tilted sled. Her imsuit had

burst open on the broken legs, and the body was frozen hard as any rock. That was all they found. As both regulation and custom demanded, they cremated the dead at once with the laser guns they carried by regulation and had never used before. Pugh, knowing he was going to be sick, wrestled the survivor onto the two-man sled and sent Martin off to the dome with him. Then he vomited and flushed the waste out of his suit, and finding one four-man sled undamaged, followed after Martin, shaking as if the cold of Libra had got through to him.

The survivor was Kaph. He was in deep shock. They found a swelling on the occiput that might mean concussion, but no fracture was visible.

Pugh brought two glasses of food concentrate and two chasers of aquavit. 'Come on,' he said. Martin obeyed, drinking off the tonic. They sat down on crates near the cot and sipped the aquavit.

Kaph lay immobile, face like beeswax, hair bright black to the shoulders, lips stiffly parted for faintly gasping breaths.

'It must have been the first shock, the big one,' Martin said. 'It must have slid the whole structure sideways. Till it fell in on itself. There must be gas layers in the lateral rocks, like those formations in the Thirty-first Quadrant. But there wasn't any sign—' As he spoke the world slid out from under them. Things leaped and clattered, hopped and jigged, shouted Ha! Ha! Ha! 'It was like this at fourteen hours,' said Reason shakily in Martin's voice, amidst the unfastening and ruin of the world. But Unreason sat up, as the tumult lessened and things ceased dancing, and screamed aloud.

Pugh leaped across his spilt aquavit and held Kaph down. The muscular body flailed him off. Martin pinned the shoulders down. Kaph screamed, struggled, choked; his face blackened. 'Oxy,' Pugh said, and his hand found the right needle in the medical kit as if by homing instinct; while Martin held the mask he struck the needle home to the vagus nerve, restoring Kaph to life.

'Didn't know you knew that stunt,' Martin said, breathing hard.

'The Lazarus Jab, my father was a doctor. It doesn't often work,' Pugh said. 'I want that drink I spilled. Is the quake over? I can't tell.'

'Aftershocks. It's not just you shivering.'

'Why did he suffocate?'

'I don't know, Owen. Look in the book.'

Kaph was breathing normally and his color was restored; only the lips were still darkened. They poured a new shot of courage and sat down by him again with their medical guide. 'Nothing about cyanosis or asphyxiation under "Shock" or "Concussion." He can't have breathed in anything with his suit on. I don't know. We'd get as much good out of *Mother Mog's Home Herbalist*. . . . "Anal Hemorrhoids," fy!' Pugh pitched the book to a crate table. It fell short, because either Pugh or the table was still unsteady.

'Why didn't he signal?'

'Sorry?'

'The eight inside the mine never had time. But he and the girl must have been outside. Maybe she was in the entrance and got hit by the first slide. He must have been outside, in the control hut maybe. He ran in, pulled her out, strapped her onto the sled, started for the dome. And all that time never pushed the panic button in his imsuit. Why not?'

'Well, he'd had that whack on his head. I doubt he ever realized the girl was dead. He wasn't in his senses. But if he had been I don't know if he'd have thought to signal us. They looked to one another for help.'

Martin's face was like an Indian mask, grooves at the mouth corners, eyes of dull coal. 'That's so. What must he have felt, then, when the quake came and he was outside, alone—'

In answer Kaph screamed.

He came off the cot in the heaving convulsions of one suffocating, knocked Pugh right down with his flailing arm, staggered into a stack of crates and fell to the floor, lips blue,

eyes white. Martin dragged him back onto the cot and gave him a whiff of oxygen, then knelt by Pugh, who was sitting up, and wiped at his cut cheekbone. 'Owen, are you all right, are you going to be all right, Owen?'

'I think I am,' Pugh said. 'Why are you rubbing that on my face?'

It was a short length of computer tape, now spotted with Pugh's blood. Martin dropped it. 'Thought it was a towel. You clipped your cheek on that box there.'

'Is he out of it?'

'Seems to be.'

They stared down at Kaph lying stiff, his teeth a white line inside dark parted lips.

'Like epilepsy. Brain damage maybe?'

'What about shooting him full of meprobamate?'

Pugh shook his head. 'I don't know what's in that shot I already gave him for shock. Don't want to overdose him.'

'Maybe he'll sleep it off now.'

'I'd like to myself. Between him and the earthquake I can't seem to keep on my feet.'

'You got a nasty crack there. Go on, I'll sit up a while.'

Pugh cleaned his cut cheek and pulled off his shirt, then paused.

'Is there anything we ought to have done – have tried to do—'

'They're all dead,' Martin said heavily, gently.

Pugh lay down on top of his sleeping bag and one instant later was wakened by a hideous, sucking, struggling noise. He staggered up, found the needle, tried three times to jab it in correctly and failed, began to massage over Kaph's heart. 'Mouth-to-mouth,' he said, and Martin obeyed. Presently Kaph drew a harsh breath, his heartbeat steadied, his rigid muscles began to relax.

'How long did I sleep?'

'Half an hour.'

They stood up sweating. The ground shuddered, the fabric

137

of the dome sagged and swayed. Libra was dancing her awful polka again, her *Totentanz*. The sun, though rising, seemed to have grown larger and redder; gas and dust must have been stirred up in the feeble atmosphere.

'What's wrong with him, Owen?'

'I think he's dying with them.'

'Them – But they're all dead, I tell you.'

'Nine of them. They're all dead, they were crushed or suffocated. They were all him, he is all of them. They died, and now he's dying their deaths one by one.'

'Oh, pity of God,' said Martin.

The next time was much the same. The fifth time was worse, for Kaph fought and raved, trying to speak but getting no words out, as if his mouth were stopped with rocks or clay. After that the attacks grew weaker, but so did he. The eighth seizure came at about four-thirty; Pugh and Martin worked till five-thirty doing all they could to keep life in the body that slid without protest into death. They kept him, but Martin said, 'The next will finish him.' And it did; but Pugh breathed his own breath into the inert lungs, until he himself passed out.

He woke. The dome was opaqued and no light on. He listened and heard the breathing of two sleeping men. He slept, and nothing woke him till hunger did.

The sun was well up over the dark plains, and the planet had stopped dancing. Kaph lay asleep. Pugh and Martin drank tea and looked at him with proprietary triumph.

When he woke Martin went to him: 'How do you feel, old man?' There was no answer. Pugh took Martin's place and looked into the brown, dull eyes that gazed toward but not into his own. Like Martin he quickly turned away. He heated food concentrate and brought it to Kaph. 'Come on, drink.'

He could see the muscles in Kaph's throat tighten. 'Let me die,' the young man said.

'You're not dying.'

Kaph spoke with clarity and precision: 'I am nine-tenths dead. There is not enough of me left alive.'

That precision convinced Pugh, and he fought the conviction. 'No,' he said, peremptory. 'They are dead. The others. Your brothers and sisters. You're not them, you're alive. You are John Chow. Your life is in your own hands.'

The young man lay still, looking into a darkness that was not there.

Martin and Pugh took turns taking the Exploitation hauler and a spare set of robos over to Hellmouth to salvage equipment and protect it from Libra's sinister atmosphere, for the value of the stuff was, literally, astronomical. It was slow work for one man at a time, but they were unwilling to leave Kaph by himself. The one left in the dome did paperwork, while Kaph sat or lay and stared into his darkness and never spoke. The days went by, silent.

The radio spat and spoke: the Mission calling from the ship. 'We'll be down on Libra in five weeks, Owen. Thirty-four E-days nine hours I make it as of now. How's tricks in the old dome?'

'Not good, chief. The Exploit team were killed, all but one of them, in the mine. Earthquake. Six days ago.'

The radio crackled and sang starsong. Sixteen seconds' lag each way; the ship was out around Planet II now. 'Killed, all but one? You and Martin were unhurt?'

'We're all right, chief.'

Thirty-two seconds.

'*Passerine* left an Exploit team out here with us. I may put them on the Hellmouth project then, instead of the Quadrant Seven project. We'll settle that when we come down. In any case you and Martin will be relieved at Dome Two. Hold tight. Anything else?'

'Nothing else.'

Thirty-two seconds.

'Right then. So long, Owen.'

Kaph had heard all this, and later on Pugh said to him, 'The chief may ask you to stay here with the other Exploit team. You know the ropes here.' Knowing the exigencies of Far Out

life, he wanted to warn the young man. Kaph made no answer. Since he had said, 'There is not enough of me left alive,' he had not spoken a word.

'Owen,' Martin said on suit intercom, 'he's spla. Insane. Psycho.'

'He's doing very well for a man who's died nine times.'

'Well? Like a turned-off android is well? The only emotion he has left is hate. Look at his eyes.'

'That's not hate, Martin. Listen, it's true that he has, in a sense, been dead. I cannot imagine what he feels. But it's not hatred. He can't even see us. It's too dark.'

'Throats have been cut in the dark. He hates us because we're not Aleph and Yod and Zayin.'

'Maybe. But I think he's alone. He doesn't see us or hear us, that's the truth. He never had to see anyone else before. He never was alone before. He had himself to see, talk with, live with, nine other selves all his life. He doesn't know how you go it alone. He must learn. Give him time.'

Martin shook his heavy head. 'Spla,' he said. 'Just remember when you're alone with him that he could break your neck one-handed.'

'He could do that,' said Pugh, a short, soft-voiced man with a scarred cheekbone; he smiled. They were just outside the dome airlock, programming one of the servos to repair a damaged hauler. They could see Kaph sitting inside the great half-egg of the dome like a fly in amber.

'Hand me the insert pack there. What makes you think he'll get any better?'

'He has a strong personality, to be sure.'

'Strong? Crippled. Nine-tenths dead, as he put it.'

'But he's not dead. He's a live man: John Kaph Chow. He had a jolly queer upbringing, but after all every boy has got to break free of his family. He will do it.'

'I can't see it.'

'Think a bit, Martin bach. What's this cloning for? To repair the human race. We're in a bad way. Look at me. My IIQ and

GC are half this John Chow's. Yet they wanted me so badly for the Far Out Service that when I volunteered they took me and fitted me out with an artificial lung and corrected my myopia. Now if there were enough good sound lads about would they be taking one-lunged short-sighted Welshmen?'

'Didn't know you had an artificial lung.'

'I do then. Not tin, you know. Human, grown in a tank from a bit of somebody; cloned, if you like. That's how they make replacement organs, the same general idea as cloning, but bits and pieces instead of whole people. It's my own lung now, whatever. But what I am saying is this, there are too many like me these days and not enough like John Chow. They're trying to raise the level of the human genetic pool, which is a mucky little puddle since the population crash. So then if a man is cloned, he's a strong and clever man. It's only logic, to be sure.'

Martin grunted; the servo began to hum.

Kaph had been eating little; he had trouble swallowing his food, choking on it, so that he would give up trying after a few bites. He had lost eight or ten kilos. After three weeks or so, however, his appetite began to pick up, and one day he began to look through the clone's possessions, the sleeping bags, kits, papers which Pugh had stacked neatly in a far angle of a packing-crate alley. He sorted, destroyed a heap of papers and oddments, made a small packet of what remained, then relapsed into his walking coma.

Two days later he spoke. Pugh was trying to correct a flutter in the tape-player and failing; Martin had the jet out, checking their maps of the Pampas. 'Hell and damnation!' Pugh said, and Kaph said in a toneless voice, 'Do you want me to do that?'

Pugh jumped, controlled himself, and gave the machine to Kaph. The young man took it apart, put it back together, and left it on the table.

'Put on a tape,' Pugh said with careful casualness, busy at another table.

Kaph put on the topmost tape, a chorale. He lay down on

his cot. The sound of a hundred human voices singing together filled the dome. He lay still, his face blank.

In the next days he took over several routine jobs, unasked. He undertook nothing that wanted initiative, and if asked to do anything he made no response at all.

'He's doing well,' Pugh said in the dialect of Argentina.

'He's not. He's turning himself into a machine. Does what he's programmed to do, no reaction to anything else. He's worse off than when he didn't function at all. He's not human any more.'

Pugh sighed. 'Well, good night,' he said in English. 'Good night, Kaph.'

'Good night,' Martin said; Kaph did not.

Next morning at breakfast Kaph reached across Martin's plate for the toast. 'Why don't you ask for it?' Martin said with the geniality of repressed exasperation. 'I can pass it.'

'I can reach it,' Kaph said in his flat voice.

'Yes, but look. Asking to pass things, saying good night or hello, they're not important, but all the same when somebody says something a person ought to answer...'

The young man looked indifferently in Martin's direction; his eyes still did not seem to see clear through to the person he looked toward. 'Why should I answer?'

'Because somebody has said something to you.'

'Why?'

Martin shrugged and laughed. Pugh jumped up and turned on the rock-cutter.

Later on he said, 'Lay off that, please, Martin.'

'Manners are essential in small isolated crews, some kind of manners, whatever you work out together. He's been taught that, everybody in Far Out knows it. Why does he deliberately flout it?'

'Do you tell yourself good night?'

'So?'

'Don't you see Kaph's never known anyone but himself?'

Martin brooded and then broke out. 'Then by God this

cloning business is all wrong. It won't do. What are a lot of duplicate geniuses going to do for us when they don't even know we exist?'

Pugh nodded. 'It might be wiser to separate the clones and bring them up with others. But they make such a grand team this way.'

'Do they? I don't know. If this lot had been ten average inefficient ET engineers, would they all have got killed? What if, when the quake came and things started caving in, what if all those kids ran the same way, farther into the mine, maybe, to save the one who was farthest in? Even Kaph was outside and went in ... It's hypothetical. But I keep thinking, out of ten ordinary confused guys, more might have got out.'

'I don't know. It's true that identical twins tend to die at about the same time, even when they have never seen each other. Identity and death, it is very strange ...'

The days went on, the red sun crawled across the dark sky, Kaph did not speak when spoken to, Pugh and Martin snapped at each other more frequently each day. Pugh complained of Martin's snoring. Offended, Martin moved his cot clear across the dome and also ceased speaking to Pugh for some while. Pugh whistled Welsh dirges until Martin complained, and then Pugh stopped speaking for a while.

The day before the Mission ship was due, Martin announced he was going over to Merioneth.

'I thought at least you'd be giving me a hand with the computer to finish the rock analyses,' Pugh said, aggrieved.

'Kaph can do that. I want one more look at the Trench. Have fun,' Martin added in dialect, and laughed, and left.

'What is that language?'

'Argentinean. I told you that once, didn't I?'

'I don't know.' After a while the young man added, 'I have forgotten a lot of things, I think.'

'It wasn't important, to be sure,' Pugh said gently, realizing all at once how important this conversation was. 'Will you give me a hand running the computer, Kaph?'

He nodded.

Pugh had left a lot of loose ends, and the job took them all day. Kaph was a good co-worker, quick and systematic, much more so than Pugh himself. His flat voice, now that he was talking again, got on the nerves; but it didn't matter, there was only this one day left to get through and then the ship would come, the old crew, comrades and friends.

During tea break Kaph said, 'What will happen if the Explore ship crashes?'

'They'd be killed.'

'To you, I mean.'

'To us? We'd radio SOS signals and live on half rations till the rescue cruiser from Area Three Base came. Four and a half E-years away it is. We have life support here for three men for, let's see, maybe between four and five years. A bit tight, it would be.'

'Would they send a cruiser for three men?'

'They would.'

Kaph said no more.

'Enough cheerful speculations,' Pugh said cheerfully, rising to get back to work. He slipped sideways and the chair avoided his hand; he did a sort of half-pirouette and fetched up hard against the dome hide. 'My goodness,' he said, reverting to his native idiom, 'what is it?'

'Quake,' said Kaph.

The teacups bounced on the table with a plastic cackle, a litter of papers slid off a box, the skin of the dome swelled and sagged. Underfoot there was a huge noise, half sound, half shaking, a subsonic boom.

Kaph sat unmoved. An earthquake does not frighten a man who died in an earthquake.

Pugh, white-faced, wiry black hair sticking out, a frightened man, said, 'Martin is in the Trench.'

'What trench?'

'The big fault line. The epicenter for the local quakes. Look

at the seismograph.' Pugh struggled with the stuck door of a still-jittering locker.

'Where are you going?'

'After him.'

'Martin took the jet. Sleds aren't safe to use during quakes. They go out of control.'

'For God's sake man, shut up.'

Kaph stood up, speaking in a flat voice as usual. 'It's unnecessary to go out after him now. It's taking an unnecessary risk.'

'If his alarm goes off, radio me,' Pugh said, shut the headpiece of his suit, and ran to the lock. As he went out Libra picked up her ragged skirts and danced a belly dance from under his feet clear to the red horizon.

Inside the dome, Kaph saw the sled go up, tremble like a meteor in the dull red daylight, and vanish to the northeast. The hide of the dome quivered, the earth coughed. A vent south of the dome belched up a slow-flowing bile of black gas.

A bell shrilled and a red light flashed on the central control board. The sign under the light read Suit 2 and scribbled under that, A. G. M. Kaph did not turn the signal off. He tried to radio Martin, then Pugh, but got no reply from either.

When the aftershocks decreased he went back to work and finished up Pugh's job. It took him about two hours. Every half hour he tried to contact Suit 1 and got no reply, then Suit 2 and got no reply. The red light had stopped flashing after an hour.

It was dinnertime. Kaph cooked dinner for one and ate it. He lay down on his cot.

The aftershocks had ceased except for faint rolling tremors at long intervals. The sun hung in the west, oblate, pale red, immense. It did not sink visibly. There was no sound at all.

Kaph got up and began to walk about the messy, half-packed-up, overcrowded, empty dome. The silence continued. He went to the player and put on the first tape that came to hand. It was pure music, electronic, without harmonies, without voices. It ended. The silence continued.

Pugh's uniform tunic, one button missing, hung over a stack of rock samples. Kaph stared at it a while.

The silence continued.

The child's dream: There is no one else alive in the world but me. In all the world.

Low, north of the dome, a meteor flickered.

Kaph's mouth opened as if he were trying to say something, but no sound came. He went hastily to the north wall and peered out into the gelatinous red light.

The little star came in and sank. Two figures blurred the airlock. Kaph stood close beside the lock as they came in. Martin's imsuit was covered with some kind of dust so that he looked raddled and warty like the surface of Libra. Pugh had him by the arm.

'Is he hurt?'

Pugh shucked his suit, helped Martin peel off his. 'Shaken up,' he said, curt.

'A piece of cliff fell onto the jet,' Martin said, sitting down at the table and waving his arms. 'Not while I was in it though. I was parked, see, and poking about that carbon-dust area when I felt things humping. So I went out onto a nice bit of early igneous I'd noticed from above, good footing and out from under the cliffs. Then I saw this bit of the planet fall off onto the flyer, quite a sight it was, and after a while it occurred to me the spare aircans were in the flyer, so I leaned on the panic button. But I didn't get any radio reception, that's always happening here during quakes, so I didn't know if the signal was getting through either. And things went on jumping around and pieces of the cliff coming off. Little rocks flying around, and so dusty you couldn't see a meter ahead. I was really beginning to wonder what I'd do for breathing in the small hours, you know, when I saw old Owen buzzing up the Trench in all that dust and junk like a big ugly bat—'

'Want to eat?' said Pugh.

'Of course I want to eat. How'd you come through the quake here, Kaph? No damage? It wasn't a big one actually,

was it, what's the seismo say? My trouble was I was in the middle of it. Old Epicenter Alvaro. Felt like Richter fifteen there – total destruction of planet—'

'Sit down,' Pugh said. 'Eat.'

After Martin had eaten a little his spate of talk ran dry. He very soon went off to his cot, still in the remote angle where he had removed it when Pugh complained of his snoring. 'Good night, you one-lunged Welshman,' he said across the dome.

'Good night.'

There was no more out of Martin. Pugh opaqued the dome, turned the lamp down to a yellow glow less than a candle's light, and sat doing nothing, saying nothing, withdrawn.

The silence continued.

'I finished the computations.'

Pugh nodded thanks.

'The signal from Martin came through, but I couldn't contact you or him.'

Pugh said with effort, 'I should not have gone. He had two hours of air left even with only one can. He might have been heading home when I left. This way we were all out of touch with one another. I was scared.'

The silence came back, punctuated now by Martin's long, soft snores.

'Do you love Martin?'

Pugh looked up with angry eyes: 'Martin is my friend. We've worked together, he's a good man.' He stopped. After a while he said, 'Yes, I love him. Why did you ask that?'

Kaph said nothing, but he looked at the other man. His face was changed, as if he were glimpsing something he had not seen before; his voice too was changed. 'How can you... How do you...'

But Pugh could not tell him. 'I don't know,' he said, 'it's practice, partly. I don't know. We're each of us alone, to be sure. What can you do but hold your hand out in the dark?'

Kaph's strange gaze dropped, burned out by its own intensity.

'I'm tired,' Pugh said. 'That was ugly, looking for him in all

that black dust and muck, and mouths opening and shutting in the ground... I'm going to bed. The ship will be transmitting to us by six or so.' He stood up and stretched.

'It's a clone,' Kaph said. 'The other Exploit Team they're bringing with them.'

'Is it then?'

'A twelveclone. They came out with us on the *Passerine*.'

Kaph sat in the small yellow aura of the lamp seeming to look past it at what he feared: the new clone, the multiple self of which he was not part. A lost piece of a broken set, a fragment, inexpert at solitude, not knowing even how you go about giving love to another individual, now he must face the absolute, closed self-sufficiency of the clone of twelve; that was a lot to ask of the poor fellow, to be sure. Pugh put a hand on his shoulder in passing. 'The chief won't ask you to stay here with a clone. You can go home. Or since you're Far Out maybe you'll come on farther out with us. We could use you. No hurry deciding. You'll make out all right.'

Pugh's quiet voice trailed off. He stood unbuttoning his coat, stooped a little with fatigue. Kaph looked at him and saw the thing he had never seen before, saw him: Owen Pugh, the other, the stranger who held his hand out in the dark.

'Good night,' Pugh mumbled, crawling into his sleeping bag and half asleep already, so that he did not hear Kaph reply after a pause, repeating, across darkness, benediction.

THINGS

Damon Knight, editor mirabilis, first published this story in a volume of Orbit, *under the title 'The End.' I don't now remember how we arrived at it, but I suspect he thought that 'Things' sounded too much like something you see on the television at one* A.M., *with purple tentacles. But I have gone back to it because – at least* after *reading the psychomyth – it puts the right emphasis. Things you use; things you possess, and are possessed by; things you build with – bricks, words. You build houses with them, and towns, and causeways. But the buildings fall, the causeways cannot go all the way. There is an abyss, a gap, a last step to be taken.*

On the shore of the sea he stood looking out over the long foam-lines far where vague the Islands lifted or were guessed. There, he said to the sea, there lies my kingdom. The sea said to him what the sea says to everybody. As evening moved from behind his back across the water the foam-lines paled and the wind fell, and very far in the west shone a star perhaps, perhaps a light, or his desire for a light.

He climbed the streets of his town again in late dusk. The shops and huts of his neighbors were looking empty now, cleared out, cleaned up, packed away in preparation for the end. Most of the people were up at the Weeping in Heights-Hall or down with the Ragers in the fields. But Lif had not been able to clear out and clean up; his wares and belongings were too heavy to throw away, too hard to break, too dull to burn. Only centuries could waste them. Wherever they were piled or dropped or thrown they formed what might have been,

or seemed to be, or yet might be, a city. So he had not tried to get rid of his things. His yard was still stacked and piled with bricks, thousands and thousands of bricks of his own making. The kiln stood cold but ready, the barrels of clay and dry mortar and lime, the hods and barrows and trowels of his trade, everything was there. One of the fellows from Scriveners Lane had asked sneering, Going to build a brick wall and hide behind it when that old end comes, man?

Another neighbor on his way up to the Heights-Hall gazed a while at those stacks and heaps and loads and mounds of well-shaped, well-baked bricks all a soft reddish gold in the gold of the afternoon sun, and sighed at last with the weight of them on his heart: Things, things! Free yourself of things, Lif, from the weight that drags you down! Come with us, above the ending world!

Lif had picked up a brick from the heap and put it in place on the stack and smiled in embarrassment. When they were all past he had gone neither up to the Hall nor out to help wreck the fields and kill the animals, but down to the beach, the end of the ending world, beyond which lay only water. Now back in his brickyard hut with the smell of salt in his clothes and his face hot with the sea wind, he still felt neither the Ragers' laughing and wrecking despair nor the soaring and weeping despair of the communicants of the Heights; he felt empty; he felt hungry. He was a heavy little man and the sea wind at the world's edge had blown at him all evening without moving him at all.

Hey, Lif! said the widow from Weavers Lane, which crossed his street a few houses down, – I saw you coming up the street, and never another soul since sunset, and getting dark, and quieter than... She did not say what the town was quieter than, but went on, Have you had your supper? I was about to take my roast out of the oven, and the little one and I will never eat up all that meat before the end comes, no doubt, and I hate to see good meat go to waste.

Well thank you very much, says Lif, putting on his coat

again; and they went down Masons Lane to Weavers Lane through the dark and the wind sweeping up steep streets from the sea. In the widow's lamplit house Lif played with her baby, the last born in the town, a little fat boy just learning how to stand up. Lif stood him up and he laughed and fell over, while the widow set out bread and hot meat on the table of heavy woven cane. They sat to eat, even the baby, who worked with four teeth at a hard hunk of bread. – How is it you're not up on the Hill or in the fields? asked Lif, and the widow replied as if the answer sufficed to her mind, Oh, I have the baby.

Lif looked around the little house which her husband, who had been one of Lif's bricklayers, had built. – This is good, he said. I haven't tasted meat since last year some time.

I know, I know! No houses being built any more.

Not a one, he said. Not a wall nor a henhouse, not even repairs. But your weaving, that's still wanted?

Yes; some of them want new clothes right up to the end. This meat I bought from the Ragers that slaughtered all my lord's flocks, and I paid with the money I got for a piece of fine linen I wove for my lord's daughter's gown that she wants to wear at the end! The widow gave a little derisive, sympathetic snort, and went on: But now there's no flax, and scarcely any wool. No more to spin, no more to weave. The fields burnt and the flocks dead.

Yes, said Lif, eating the good roast meat. Bad times, he said, the worst times.

And now, the widow went on, where's bread to come from, with the fields burnt? And water, now they're poisoning the wells? I sound like the Weepers up there, don't I? Help yourself, Lif. Spring lamb's the finest meat in the world, my man always said, till autumn came and then he'd say roast pork's the finest meat in the world. Come on now, give yourself a proper slice . . .

That night in his hut in the brickyard Lif dreamed. Usually he slept as still as the bricks themselves but this night he drifted and floated in dream all night to the Islands, and when he woke they were no longer a wish or a guess: like a star as daylight

darkens they had become certain, he knew them. But what, in his dream, had borne him over the water? He had not flown, he had not walked, he had not gone underwater like the fish; yet he had come across the grey-green plains and wind-moved hillocks of the sea to the Islands, he had heard voices call, and seen the lights of towns.

He set his mind to think how a man could ride on water. He thought of how grass floats on streams, and saw how one might make a sort of mat of woven cane and lie on it pushing with one's hands: but the great canebrakes were still smoldering down by the stream, and the piles of withies at the basket-maker's had all been burnt. On the Islands in his dream he had seen canes or grasses half a hundred feet high, with brown stems thicker than his arms could reach around, and a world of green leaves spread sunward from the thousand outreaching twigs. On those stems a man might ride over the sea. But no such plants grew in his country nor ever had; though in the Heights-Hall was a knife-handle made of a dull brown stuff, said to come from a plant that grew in some other land, called wood. But he could not ride across the bellowing sea on a knife-handle.

Greased hides might float; but the tanners had been idle now for weeks, there were no hides for sale. He might as well stop looking about for any help. He carried his barrow and his largest hod down to the beach that white windy morning and laid them in the still water of a lagoon. Indeed they floated, deep in the water, but when he leaned even the weight of one hand on them they tipped, filled, sank. They were too light, he thought.

He went back up the cliff and through the streets, loaded the barrow with useless well-made bricks, and wheeled a hard load down. As so few children had been born these last years there was no young curiosity about to ask him what he was doing, though a Rager or two, groggy from last night's wreck-fest, glanced sidelong at him from a dark doorway through the brightness of the air. All that day he brought down bricks

and the makings of mortar, and the next day, though he had not had the dream again, he began to lay his bricks there on the blustering beach of March with rain and sand handy in great quantities to set his cement. He built a little brick dome, upside down, oval with pointed ends like a fish, all of a single course of bricks laid spiral very cunningly. If a cupful or a barrowful of air would float, would not a brick domeful? And it would be strong. But when the mortar was set, and straining his broad back he overturned the dome and pushed it into the cream of the breakers, it dug deeper and deeper into the wet sand, burrowing down like a clam or a sand flea. The waves filled it, and refilled it when he tipped it empty, and at last a green-shouldered breaker caught it with its white dragging backpull, rolled it over, smashed it back into its elemental bricks and sank them in the restless sodden sand. There stood Lif wet to the neck and wiping salt spray out of his eyes. Nothing lay westward on the sea but wavewrack and rain-clouds. But they were there. He knew them, with their great grasses ten times a man's height, their wild golden fields raked by the sea wind, their white towns, their white-crowned hills above the sea; and the voices of shepherds called on the hills.

I'm a builder, not a floater, said Lif after he had considered his stupidity from all sides. And he came doggedly out of the water and up the cliff-side path and through the rainy streets to get another barrowload of bricks.

Free for the first time in a week for his fool dream of floating, he noticed now that Leather Street seemed deserted. The tannery was rubbishy and vacant. The craftsmen's shops lay like a row of little black gaping mouths, and the sleeping-room windows above them were blind. At the end of the lane an old cobbler was burning, with a terrible stench, a small heap of new shoes never worn. Beside him a donkey waited, saddled, flicking its ears at the stinking smoke.

Lif went on and loaded his barrow with bricks. This time as he wheeled it down, straining back against the tug of the barrow on the steep streets, swinging all the strength of his

shoulders to balance its course on the winding cliff-path down to the beach, a couple of townsmen followed him. Two or three more from Scriveners Lane followed after them, and several more from the streets round the market place, so that by the time he straightened up, the sea foam fizzing on his bare black feet and the sweat cold on his face, there was a little crowd strung out along the deep single track of his barrow over the sand. They had the lounging listless air of Ragers. Lif paid them no heed, though he was aware that the widow of Weavers Lane was up on the cliffs watching with a scared face.

He ran the barrow out into the sea till the water was up to his chest, and tipped the bricks out, and came running in with a great breaker, his banging barrow full of foam.

Already some of the Ragers were drifting away down the beach. A tall fellow from the Scriveners Lane lot lounged by him and said with a little grin, Why don't you throw 'em from the top of the cliff, man?

They'd only hit the sand, said Lif.

And you want to drown 'em. Well good. You know there was some of us thought you was building something down here! They was going to make cement out of you. Keep those bricks wet and cool, man.

Grinning, the Scrivener drifted off, and Lif started up the cliff for another load.

Come for supper, Lif, said the widow at the cliff's top with a worried voice, holding her baby close to keep it from the wind.

I will, he said. I'll bring a loaf of bread, I laid in a couple before the bakers left. He smiled, but she did not. As they climbed the streets together she asked, Are you dumping your bricks in the sea, Lif?

He laughed wholeheartedly and answered yes.

She had a look then that might have been relief and might have been sadness; but at supper in her lamplit house she was quiet and easy as ever, and they ate their cheese and stale bread with good cheer.

Next day he went on carrying bricks down load after load,

and if the Ragers watched him they thought him busy on their own kind of work. The slope of the beach out to deep water was gradual, so that he could keep building without ever working above water. He had started at low tide so that his work would never be laid bare. At high tide it was hard, dumping the bricks and trying to lay them in rough courses with the whole sea boiling in his face and thundering over his head, but he kept at it. Towards evening he brought down long iron rods and braced what he had built, for a crosscurrent tended to undermine his causeway about eight feet from its beginning. He made sure that even the tips of the rods were under water at low tide, so that no Rager might suspect an affirmation was being made. A couple of elderly men coming down from a Weeping in the Heights-Hall passed him clanging and battering his empty barrow up the stone streets in dusk, and gravely smiled upon him. It is well to be free of Things, said one softly, and the other nodded.

Next day, though still he had not dreamed of the Islands again, Lif went on building his causeway. The sand began to shelve off more steeply as he went further. His method now was to stand on the last bit he had built and tip the carefully-loaded barrow from there, and then tip himself off and work, floundering and gasping and coming up and pushing down, to get the bricks levelled and fitted between the pre-set rods; then up again, across the grey sand and up the cliff and bang-clatter through the quiet streets for another load.

Some time that week the widow said, meeting him in his brickyard, Let me throw 'em over the cliff for you, it'll save you one leg of the trip.

It's heavy work loading the barrow, he said.

Oh, well, said she.

All right, so long as you want to. But bricks are heavy bastards. Don't try to carry many. I'll give you the small barrow. And the little rat here can sit on the load and get a ride.

So she helped him on and off through days of silvery weather, fog in the morning, clear sea and sky all afternoon, and the

weeds in crannies of the cliff flowering; there was nothing else left to flower. The causeway ran out many yards from shore now, and Lif had had to learn a skill which no one else had ever learned that he knew of, except the fish. He could float and move himself about on the water or under it, in the very sea, without touching foot or hand to solid earth.

He had never heard that a man could do this thing; but he did not think much about it, being so busy with his bricks, in and out of air and in and out of water all day long, with the foam, the bubbles of water-circled air or air-circled water, all about him, and the fog, and the April rain, a confusion of the elements. Sometimes he was happy down in the murky green unbreathable world, wrestling strangely willful and weightless bricks among the staring shoals, and only the need of air drove him gasping up into the spray-laden wind.

He built all day long, scrambling up on the sand to collect the bricks that his faithful helper dumped over the cliff's edge for him, load them in his barrow and run them out the causeway that went straight out a foot or two under sea level at low tide and four or five feet under at high, then dump them at the end, dive in, and build; then back ashore for another load. He came up into town only at evening, worn out, salt-bleared and salt-itching, hungry as a shark, to share what food turned up with the widow and her little boy. Lately, though spring was getting on with soft, long, warm evenings, the town was very dark and still.

One night when he was not too tired to notice this he spoke of it, and the widow said, Oh, they're all gone now, I think.

—All? A pause. – Where did they go?

She shrugged. She raised her dark eyes to his across the table and gazed through lamplit silence at him for a time. Where? she said. Where does your sea-road lead, Lif?

He stayed still a while. To the Islands, he answered at last, and then laughed and met her look.

She did not laugh. She only said, Are they there? Is it true, then, there are Islands? Then she looked over at her sleeping

baby, and out the open doorway into the darkness of late spring that lay warm in the streets where no one walked and the rooms where no one lived. At last she looked back at Lif, and said to him, Lif, you know, there aren't many bricks left. A few hundred. You'll have to make some more. Then she began to cry softly.

By God! said Lif, thinking of his underwater road across the sea that went for a hundred and twenty feet, and the sea that went on ten thousand miles from the end of it – I'll swim there! Now then, don't cry, dear heart. Would I leave you and the little rat here by yourselves? After all the bricks you've nearly hit my head with, and all the queer weeds and shellfish you've found us to eat lately, after your table and fireside and your bed and your laughter would I leave you when you cry? Now be still, don't cry. Let me think of a way we can get to the Islands, all of us together.

But he knew there was no way. Not for a brickmaker. He had done what he could do. What he could do went one hundred and twenty feet from shore.

Do you think, he asked after a long time, during which she had cleared the table and rinsed the plates in wellwater that was coming clear again now that the Ragers had been gone many days – Do you think that maybe... this... He found it hard to say but she stood quiet, waiting, and he had to say it: That this *is* the end?

Stillness. In the one lamplit room and all the dark rooms and streets and the burnt fields and wasted lands, stillness. In the black Hall above them on the hill's height, stillness. A silent air, a silent sky, silence in all places unbroken, unreplying. Except for the far sound of the sea, and, very soft though nearer, the breathing of a sleeping child.

No, the woman said. She sat down across from him and put her hands upon the table, fine hands as dark as earth, the palms like ivory. No, she said, the end will be the end. This is still just the waiting for it.

Then why are we still here – just us?

Oh, well, she said, you had your things – your bricks – and I had the baby...

Tomorrow we must go, he said after a time. She nodded.

Before sunrise they were up. There was nothing at all left to eat, and so when she had put a few clothes for the baby in a bag and had on her warm leather mantle, and he had stuck his knife and trowel in his belt and put on a warm cloak that had been her husband's, they left the little house, going out into the cold wan light in the deserted streets.

They went downhill, he leading, she following with the sleepy child in a fold of her cloak. He turned neither to the road that led north up the coast nor to the southern road, but went on past the market place and out on the cliff and down the rocky path to the beach. All the way she followed and neither of them spoke. At the edge of the sea he turned.

I'll keep you up in the water as long as we can manage, he said.

She nodded, and said softly, We'll use the road you built, as far as it goes.

He took her free hand and led her into the water. It was cold. It was bitter cold, and the cold light from the east behind them shone on the foam-lines hissing on the sand. When they stepped on the beginning of the causeway the bricks were firm under their feet, and the child had gone back to sleep on her shoulder in a fold of her cloak.

As they went on the buffeting of the waves got stronger. The tide was coming in. The outer breakers wet their clothes, chilled their flesh, drenched their hair and faces. They reached the end of his long work. There lay the beach a little way behind them, the sand dark under the cliff over which stood the silent, paling sky. Around them was wild water and foam. Ahead of them was the unresting water, the great abyss, the gap.

A breaker hit them on its way in to shore and they staggered; the baby, waked by the sea's hard slap, cried, a little wail in the long, cold, hissing mutter of the sea always saying the same thing.

Oh, I can't! cried the mother, but she gripped the man's hand more firmly and came on at his side.

Lifting his head to take the last step from what he had done towards no shore, he saw the shape riding the western water, the leaping light, the white flicker like a swallow's breast catching the break of day. It seemed as if voices rang over the sea's voice. What is it? he said, but her head was bowed to her baby, trying to soothe the little wail that challenged the vast babbling of the sea. He stood still and saw the whiteness of the sail, the dancing light above the waves, dancing on towards them and towards the greater light that grew behind them.

Wait, the call came from the form that rode the grey waves and danced on the foam, Wait! The voices rang very sweet, and as the sail leaned white above him he saw the faces and the reaching arms, and heard them say to him, Come, come on the ship, come with us to the Islands.

Hold on, he said softly to the woman, and they took the last step.

A TRIP TO THE HEAD

Most people 'lead lives of quiet desperation,' and some stories start there, too. We were in England and it was November and dark at two in the afternoon and raining and the suitcase containing all my manuscripts had been stolen at the dock in Southampton and I hadn't written anything for months and I couldn't understand the greengrocer and he couldn't understand me and it was desperation – but quiet – stiff upper lip, don't you know. So I sat down and started scribbling words, perfectly hopelessly. Words, words, words. They went on about as far as ' "Try being Amanda," the other said sourly,' and stopped. A year or so later (British Rails, all honor to them, had found my stolen suitcase, we were back home in Oregon, it was raining) I found the scribble, and went on scribbling, and came to the end. I never did find out what the title ought to be – my agent, Virginia Kidd, did that, to my delight.

There is a kind of story which I would describe as a Bung Puller. The writer for one reason or another has been stuck, can't work; and gets started again suddenly, with a pop, and a lot of beer comes leaping out of the keg and foaming all over the floor. This story was definitely a Bung Puller.

'Is this Earth?' he cried, for things had changed abruptly.

'Yes, this is Earth,' said the one beside him, 'nor are you out of it. In Zambia men are rolling down hills inside barrels as training for space flight. Israel and Egypt have defoliated each other's deserts. The *Reader's Digest* has bought a controlling interest in the United States of America/General Mills combine. The population of the Earth is increasing by thirty billion every Thursday. Mrs Jacqueline Kennedy Onassis will

marry Mao Tse-Tung on Saturday, in search of security; and Russia has contaminated Mars with bread mold.'

'Why then,' said he, 'nothing has changed.'

'Nothing much,' said the one beside him. 'As Jean-Paul Sartre has said in his lovable way, "Hell is other people."'

'To Hell with Jean-Paul Sartre. I want to know where I am.'

'Well then,' said the other, 'tell me who you are.'

'I'm.'

'Well?'

'My name is.'

'What?'

He stood, his eyes filling with tears and his knees with palsy, and knew he did not know his name. He was a blank, a cipher, an x. He had a body and all that, but he had no who.

They stood at the edge of a forest, he and the other one. It was a recognizable forest, though rather dingy in the leaf, and damaged at the fringes by weedkiller. A fawn was walking away from them into the forest and as it went its name fell away from it. Something looked back at them with mild eyes from the darkness of the trees before it vanished. 'This is England!' cried blank, grasping the floating straw, but the other said, 'England sank years ago.'

'Sank?'

'Yes. Foundered. Nothing is left now but the topmost fourteen feet of Mt Snowdon, known as the New Welsh Reef.'

At this blank also sank. He was crushed. 'Oh,' he cried on his knees, intending to ask somebody's help, but he could not remember whose help it was one asked. It began with a T, he was almost certain. He began to weep.

The other sat down on the grass beside him and presently put a hand on his shoulder, saying, 'Come on now, don't take it so hard.'

The kindly voice gave blank some courage. He controlled himself, dried his face on his sleeve, and looked at the other. It was like him, roughly. It was another. However, it had no name either. What good was it?

Shadow came into the eyes as Earth went round on its axis. Shadow slipped eastward and upward into the other's eyes.

'I think,' blank said carefully, 'that we should move out from the shadow of the, this, here.' He gestured to the objects near them, large things, dark below and multitudinously green above, the names of which he could no longer remember. He wondered if each one had a name, or if they were all called by the same name. What about himself and the other, did they share a name in common, or did each have one of his own? 'I have a feeling I'll remember better farther away from it, from them,' he said.

'Certainly,' said the other. 'But it won't make as much difference as it used to.'

When they came clear away from it into the sunlight, he at once remembered that it was called a forest and that they were called trees. However, he could not recall whether or not each tree had a name of its own. If they did, he did not remember any of them. Perhaps he did not know these trees personally.

'What shall I do,' he said, 'what shall I do?'

'Well, look here, you can call yourself whatever you please, you know. Why not?'

'But I want to know my *real* name.'

'That isn't always easy. But meanwhile you could just take a label, as it were, for ease of reference and conversational purposes. Pick a name, any name!' said the other, and held out a blue box named DISPOSABLE.

'No,' said blank proudly, 'I'll choose my own.'

'Right. But don't you want a kleenex?'

Blank took a kleenex, blew his nose, and said, 'I shall call myself ...' He halted in terror.

The other watched him, mild-eyed.

'How can I say who I am when I can't say what I am?'

'How would you find out what you are?'

'If I had anything – If I did something—'

'That would make you be?'

'Of course it would.'

'I never thought of that. Well, then, it doesn't matter what name you're called by; any one will do; it's what you do that counts.'

Blank stood up. 'I will exist,' he stated firmly. 'I will call myself Ralph.'

Whipcord breeches fitted close on his powerful thighs, the stock rose high on his neck, sweat clung in his thick, curly hair. He tapped his boots with his riding-crop, his back to Amanda, who sat in her old grey dress in the deep shade of the pecan tree. He stood in full sunlight, hot with anger. 'You're a fool,' he said.

'Why Mr Ralph,' came the soft lilting Southern voice, 'Ah'm just a little bit stubborn.'

'You realize, don't you, that Yankee as I am, I own all the land from here to Weevilville? I own this county! Your farm wouldn't make a peanut-patch for one of my darkies' kitchen gardens!'

'Indeed not. Won't you come sit down in the shade, Mr Ralph? Youah gettin' so hot out theah.'

'You proud vixen,' he murmured, turning. He saw her, white as a lily in her worn old dress, in the shade of the great old trees: the white lily of the garden. Suddenly he was at her feet, clasping her hands. She fluttered in his powerful grasp. 'Oh Mr Ralph,' she cried faintly, 'what does this mean?'

'I am a man, Amanda, and you are a woman. I never wanted your land. I never wanted anything but you, my white lily, my little rebel! I want you, I want you! Amanda! Say you will be my wife!'

'Ah will,' she breathed faintly, bending towards him as a white flower stoops; and their lips met in a long, long kiss. But it did not seem to help at all.

Perhaps it ought to be moved up twenty or thirty years.

'You sick bitch,' he muttered, turning. He saw her, stark naked there in the shade, her back against the pecan tree, her knees up. He strode towards her unbuttoning his fly. They coupled in the centipede-infested crabgrass. He bucked like

163

a bronco, she cried ululatingly, *Oooh! Aaah!* Coming coming coming COME wow wow wow CLIMAX!

Now what?

Blank stood at a little distance from the forest and stared disconsolately at the other.

'Am I a man?' he inquired. 'Are you a woman?'

'Don't ask me,' the other said, morose.

'I thought surely that was the most important thing to establish!'

'Not so damned important.'

'You mean it doesn't *matter* if I am a man or a woman?'

'Of course it matters. It matters to me too. It also matters which man and which woman we are or, as the case may be, are not. For instance, what if Amanda was black?'

'But sex.'

'Oh, Hell,' said the other with a flare of temper, 'bristle-worms have sex, tree-sloths have sex, Jean-Paul Sartre has sex – what does it prove?'

'Why, sex is real, I mean really real – it's having and acting in its intensest form. When a man takes a woman he proves his being!'

'I see. But what if he's a woman?'

'I was Ralph.'

'Try being Amanda,' the other said sourly.

There was a pause. Shadows were coming on eastward and upward from the forest over the grass. Small birds cried *jug jug, tereu*. Blank sat hunched over his knees. The other lay stretched out, making patterns with fallen pine needles, shadowed, sorrowful.

'I'm sorry,' blank said.

'No harm done,' the other said. 'After all, it wasn't real.'

'Listen,' blank said, leaping up, 'I know what's happened! I'm on some kind of trip. I took something, and I'm on a trip, that's it!'

It was. He was on a trip. A canoe trip. He was paddling a small canoe along a long, narrow, dark, shining stretch of

water. The roof and walls were of concrete. It was pretty dark. The long lake, or stream, or sewer, slanted upward visibly. He was paddling against the current, uphill. It was hard work, but the canoe kept sliding forward upriver as silently as the black shining water moved back down. He kept his strokes quiet, the paddle entering the water silent as a knife in butter. His large black-and-pearl electric guitar lay on the forward seat. He knew there was somebody behind him, but he didn't say anything. He wasn't allowed to say anything or even look around, so if they didn't keep up that was their lookout, he couldn't be called responsible. He certainly couldn't slow down, the current might get hold of his canoe and pull it right out from under him and then where'd he be? He shut his eyes and kept paddling, silent entry, strong stroke. There was no sound behind him. The water made no sound. The cement made no sound. He wondered if he was actually going forward or only hanging still while the black water ran hellbent beneath. He would never get out to daylight. Out, out—

out. The other didn't even seem to have noticed that blank had been away on a trip, but just lay there making patterns with pine needles, and presently said, 'How is your memory?'

Blank searched it to see if it had improved while he was away. There was less in it than before. The cupboard was bare. There was a lot of junk in the cellars and attics, old toys, nursery rhymes, myths, old wives' tales, but no nourishment for adults, no least scrap of possession, not a crumb of success. He searched and searched like a starving methodical rat. At last he said uncertainly, 'I do remember England.'

'Why surely. I expect you can even remember Omaha.'

'But I mean, I remember being in England.'

'Do you?' The other sat up, scattering pinestraw. 'You do remember being, then! What a pity England sank.'

They were silent again.

'I have lost everything.'

There was a darkness in the other's eyes and on the eastern edge of the earth plunging down the steepening slopes of night.

'I'm nobody.'

'At least,' said the other, 'you know you're human.'

'Oh, what good's that? with no name, no sex, no nothing? I might as well be a bristleworm or a tree-sloth!'

'You might as well,' the other agreed, 'be Jean-Paul Sartre.'

'I?' said blank, offended. Driven to denial by so nauseous a notion, he stood up and said, 'I certainly am not Jean-Paul Sartre. I am myself.' And so saying he found himself to be, in fact, himself; his name was Lewis D. Charles and he knew it as well as he knew his own name. There he was.

The forest was there, root and branch.

The other was, however, gone.

Lewis D. Charles looked in the red eye of the west and the dark eye of the east. He shouted aloud, 'Come back! Please come back!'

He had gone at it all wrong, backwards. He had found the wrong name. He turned, and without the least impulse of self-preservation plunged into the pathless forest, casting himself away so that he might find what he had cast away.

Under the trees he forgot his name again at once. He also forgot what he was looking for. What was it he had lost? He went deeper and deeper into shadows, under leaves, eastward, in the forest where nameless tigers burned.

VASTER THAN EMPIRES AND MORE SLOW

Trees again.

As I recall, Robert Silverberg, who first published this story in New Dimensions 1, *asked very gently if I would change the title. I could see where a reader about halfway through might find the title all too descriptive of the story itself; but it was too beautiful, and too beautifully apt, to part with, and Mr Silverberg let me keep it. It's from Marvell, 'To his Coy Mistress'—*

> *Our vegetable love should grow*
> *Vaster than empires, and more slow . . .*

Like 'Nine Lives,' this is not a psychomyth but a regular science fiction story, developed not for action/adventure, but psychologically. Unless physical action reflects psychic action, unless the deeds express the person, I get very bored with adventure stories; often it seems that the more action there is, the less happens. Obviously my interest is in what goes on inside. Inner space and all that. We all have forests in our minds. Forests unexplored, unending. Each of us gets lost in the forest, every night, alone.

Hidden in the foliage here is a tiny act of homage. The protagonist of 'He Who Shapes' by Roger Zelazny, one of the finest science fiction stories I know, is called Charles Render. I christened a syndrome after him.

It was only during the earliest decades of the League that the Earth sent ships out on the enormously long voyages, beyond the pale, over the stars and far away. They were seeking for worlds which had not been seeded or settled by the Founders on

Hain, truly alien worlds. All the Known Worlds went back to the Hainish Origin, and the Terrans, having been not only founded but salvaged by the Hainish, resented this. They wanted to get away from the family. They wanted to find somebody new. The Hainish, like tiresomely understanding parents, supported their explorations, and contributed ships and volunteers, as did several other worlds of the League.

All these volunteers to the Extreme Survey crews shared one peculiarity: they were of unsound mind.

What sane person, after all, would go out to collect information that would not be received for five or ten centuries? Cosmic mass interference had not yet been eliminated from the operation of the ansible, and so instantaneous communication was reliable only within a range of 120 lightyears. The explorers would be quite isolated. And of course they had no idea what they might come back to, if they came back. No normal human being who had experienced time-slippage of even a few decades between League worlds would volunteer for a round trip of centuries. The Surveyors were escapists, misfits. They were nuts.

Ten of them climbed aboard the ferry at Smeming Port, and made varyingly inept attempts to get to know one another during the three days the ferry took getting to their ship, *Gum*. Gum is a Cetian nickname, on the order of Baby or Pet. There were two Cetians on the team, two Hainishmen, one Beldene, and five Terrans; the Cetian-built ship was chartered by the Government of Earth. Her motley crew came aboard wriggling through the coupling tube one by one like apprehensive spermatozoa trying to fertilize the universe. The ferry left, and the navigator put *Gum* underway. She flittered for some hours on the edge of space a few hundred million miles from Smeming Port, and then abruptly vanished.

When, after 10 hours 29 minutes, or 256 years, *Gum* reappeared in normal space, she was supposed to be in the vicinity of Star KG-E-96651. Sure enough, there was the gold pinhead of the star. Somewhere within a four-hundred-million-kilometer

sphere there was also a greenish planet, World 4470, as charted by a Cetian mapmaker. The ship now had to find the planet. This was not quite so easy as it might sound, given a four-hundred-million-kilometer haystack. And *Gum* couldn't bat about in planetary space at near lightspeed; if she did, she and Star KG-E-96651 and World 4470 might all end up going bang. She had to creep, using rocket propulsion, at a few hundred thousand miles an hour. The Mathematician/Navigator, Asnanifoil, knew pretty well where the planet ought to be, and thought they might raise it within ten E-days. Meanwhile the members of the Survey team got to know one another still better.

'I can't stand him,' said Porlock, the Hard Scientist (chemistry, plus physics, astronomy, geology, etc), and little blobs of spittle appeared on his mustache. 'The man is insane. I can't imagine why he was passed as fit to join a Survey team, unless this is a deliberate experiment in noncompatibility, planned by the Authority, with us as guinea pigs.'

'We generally use hamsters and Hainish gholes,' said Mannon, the Soft Scientist (psychology, plus psychiatry, anthropology, ecology, etc), politely; he was one of the Hainishmen. 'Instead of guinea pigs. Well, you know, Mr Osden is really a very rare case. In fact, he's the first fully cured case of Render's Syndrome – a variety of infantile autism which was thought to be incurable. The great Terran analyst Hammergeld reasoned that the cause of the autistic condition in this case is a supernormal empathic capacity, and developed an appropriate treatment. Mr Osden is the first patient to undergo that treatment, in fact he lived with Dr Hammergeld until he was eighteen. The therapy was completely successful.'

'Successful?'

'Why, yes. He certainly is not autistic.'

'No, he's intolerable!'

'Well, you see,' said Mannon, gazing mildly at the saliva-flecks on Porlock's mustache, 'the normal defensive-aggressive reaction between strangers meeting – let's say you and Mr

Osden just for example – is something you're scarcely aware of; habit, manners, inattention get you past it; you've learned to ignore it, to the point where you might even deny it exists. However, Mr Osden, being an empath, feels it. Feels his feelings, and yours, and is hard put to say which is which. Let's say that there's a normal element of hostility towards any stranger in your emotional reaction to him when you meet him, plus a spontaneous dislike of his looks, or clothes, or handshake – it doesn't matter what. He feels that dislike. As his autistic defense has been unlearned, he resorts to an aggressive-defense mechanism, a response in kind to the aggression which you have unwittingly projected onto him.' Mannon went on for quite a long time.

'Nothing gives a man the right to be such a bastard,' Porlock said.

'He can't tune us out?' asked Harfex, the Biologist, another Hainishman.

'It's like hearing,' said Olleroo, Assistant Hard Scientist, stooping over to paint her toenails with fluorescent lacquer. 'No eyelids on your ears. No Off switch on empathy. He hears our feelings whether he wants to or not.'

'Does he know what we're *thinking?*' asked Eskwana, the Engineer, looking round at the others in real dread.

'No,' Porlock snapped. 'Empathy's not telepathy! Nobody's got telepathy.'

'Yet,' said Mannon, with his little smile. 'Just before I left Hain there was a most interesting report in from one of the recently rediscovered worlds, a hilfer named Rocannon reporting what appears to be a teachable telepathic technique existent among a mutated hominid race; I only saw a synopsis in the HILF Bulletin, but—' He went on. The others had learned that they could talk while Mannon went on talking; he did not seem to mind, nor even to miss much of what they said.

'Then why does he hate us?' Eskwana said.

'Nobody hates you, Ander honey,' said Olleroo, daubing

Eskwana's left thumbnail with fluorescent pink. The engineer flushed and smiled vaguely.

'He acts as if he hated us,' said Haito, the Coordinator. She was a delicate-looking woman of pure Asian descent, with a surprising voice, husky, deep, and soft, like a young bullfrog. 'Why, if he suffers from our hostility, does he increase it by constant attacks and insults? I can't say I think much of Dr Hammergeld's cure, really, Mannon; autism might be preferable...'

She stopped. Osden had come into the main cabin.

He looked flayed. His skin was unnaturally white and thin, showing the channels of his blood like a faded road map in red and blue. His Adam's apple, the muscles that circled his mouth, the bones and ligaments of his wrists and hands, all stood out distinctly as if displayed for an anatomy lesson. His hair was pale rust, like long-dried blood. He had eyebrows and lashes, but they were visible only in certain lights; what one saw was the bones of the eye sockets, the veining of the lids, and the colorless eyes. They were not red eyes, for he was not really an albino, but they were not blue or grey; colors had cancelled out in Osden's eyes, leaving a cold water-like clarity, infinitely penetrable. He never looked directly at one. His face lacked expression, like an anatomical drawing, or a skinned face.

'I agree,' he said in a high, harsh tenor, 'that even autistic withdrawal might be preferable to the smog of cheap second-hand emotions with which you people surround me. What are you sweating hate for now, Porlock? Can't stand the sight of me? Go practice some auto-eroticism the way you were doing last night, it improves your vibes. Who the devil moved my tapes, here? Don't touch my things, any of you, I won't have it.'

'Osden,' said Asnanifoil in his large slow voice, 'why *are* you such a bastard?'

Ander Eskwana cowered and put his hands in front of his face. Contention frightened him. Olleroo looked up with a vacant yet eager expression, the eternal spectator.

'Why shouldn't I be?' said Osden. He was not looking at

Asnanifoil, and was keeping physically as far away from all of them as he could in the crowded cabin. 'None of you constitute, in yourselves, any reason for my changing my behavior.'

Harfex, a reserved and patient man, said, 'The reason is that we shall be spending several years together. Life will be better for all of us if—'

'Can't you understand that I don't give a damn for all of you?' Osden said, took up his microtapes, and went out. Eskwana had suddenly gone to sleep. Asnanifoil was drawing slipstreams in the air with his finger and muttering the Ritual Primes. 'You cannot explain his presence on the team except as a plot on the part of the Terran Authority. I saw this almost at once. This mission is meant to fail,' Harfex whispered to the Coordinator, glancing over his shoulder. Porlock was fumbling with his fly-button; there were tears in his eyes. I did tell you they were all crazy, but you thought I was exaggerating.

All the same, they were not unjustified. Extreme Surveyors expected to find their fellow team members intelligent, well-trained, unstable, and personally sympathetic. They had to work together in close quarters and nasty places, and could expect one another's paranoias, depressions, manias, phobias and compulsions to be mild enough to admit of good personal relationships, at least most of the time. Osden might be intelligent, but his training was sketchy and his personality was disastrous. He had been sent only on account of his singular gift, the power of empathy: properly speaking, of wide-range bioempathic receptivity. His talent wasn't species-specific; he could pick up emotion or sentience from anything that felt. He could share lust with a white rat, pain with a squashed cockroach, and phototropy with a moth. On an alien world, the Authority had decided, it would be useful to know if anything nearby is sentient, and if so, what its feelings towards you are. Osden's title was a new one: he was the team's Sensor.

'What is emotion, Osden?' Haito Tomiko asked him one day in the main cabin, trying to make some rapport with him for

once. 'What is it, exactly, that you pick up with your empathic sensitivity?'

'Muck,' the man answered in his high, exasperated voice. 'The psychic excreta of the animal kingdom. I wade through your faeces.'

'I was trying,' she said, 'to learn some facts.' She thought her tone was admirably calm.

'You weren't after facts. You were trying to get at me. With some fear, some curiosity, and a great deal of distaste. The way you might poke a dead dog, to see the maggots crawl. Will you understand once and for all that I don't want to be got at, that I want to be left alone?' His skin was mottled with red and violet, his voice had risen. 'Go roll in your own dung, you yellow bitch!' he shouted at her silence.

'Calm down,' she said, still quietly, but she left him at once and went to her cabin. Of course he had been right about her motives; her question had been largely a pretext, a mere effort to interest him. But what harm in that? Did not that effort imply respect for the other? At the moment of asking the question she had felt at most a slight distrust of him; she had mostly felt sorry for him, the poor arrogant venomous bastard, Mr No-Skin as Olleroo called him. What did he expect, the way he acted? Love?

'I guess he can't stand anybody feeling sorry for him,' said Olleroo, lying on the lower bunk, gilding her nipples.

'Then he can't form any human relationship. All his Dr Hammergeld did was turn an autism inside out...'

'Poor frot,' said Olleroo. 'Tomiko, you don't mind if Harfex comes in for a while tonight, do you?'

'Can't you go to his cabin? I'm sick of always having to sit in Main with that damned peeled turnip.'

'You do hate him, don't you? I guess he feels that. But I slept with Harfex last night too, and Asnanifoil might get jealous, since they share the cabin. It would be nicer here.'

'Service them both,' Tomiko said with the coarseness of

offended modesty. Her Terran subculture, the East Asian, was a puritanical one; she had been brought up chaste.

'I only like one a night,' Olleroo replied with innocent serenity. Beldene, the Garden Planet, had never discovered chastity, or the wheel.

'Try Osden, then,' Tomiko said. Her personal instability was seldom so plain as now: a profound self-distrust manifesting itself as destructivism. She had volunteered for this job because there was, in all probability, no use in doing it.

The little Beldene looked up, paintbrush in hand, eyes wide. 'Tomiko, that was a dirty thing to say.'

'Why?'

'It would be vile! I'm not attracted to Osden!'

'I didn't know it mattered to you,' Tomiko said indifferently, though she did know. She got some papers together and left the cabin, remarking, 'I hope you and Harfex or whoever it is finish by last bell; I'm tired.'

Olleroo was crying, tears dripping on her little gilded nipples. She wept easily. Tomiko had not wept since she was ten years old.

It was not a happy ship; but it took a turn for the better when Asnanifoil and his computers raised World 4470. There it lay, a dark-green jewel, like truth at the bottom of a gravity well. As they watched the jade disc grow, a sense of mutuality grew among them. Osden's selfishness, his accurate cruelty, served now to draw the others together. 'Perhaps,' Mannon said, 'he was sent as a beating-gron. What Terrans call a scapegoat. Perhaps his influence will be good after all.' And no one, so careful were they to be kind to one another, disagreed.

They came into orbit. There were no lights on nightside, on the continents none of the lines and clots made by animals who build.

'No men,' Harfex murmured.

'Of course not,' snapped Osden, who had a viewscreen to himself, and his head inside a polythene bag. He claimed that the plastic cut down on the empathic noise he received from

174

the others. 'We're two lightcenturies past the limit of the Hainish Expansion, and outside that there are no men. Anywhere. You don't think Creation would have made the same hideous mistake twice?'

No one was paying him much heed; they were looking with affection at that jade immensity below them, where there was life, but not human life. They were misfits among men, and what they saw there was not desolation, but peace. Even Osden did not look quite so expressionless as usual; he was frowning.

Descent in fire on the sea; air reconnaissance; landing. A plain of something like grass, thick, green, bowing stalks, surrounded the ship, brushed against extended viewcameras, smeared the lenses with a fine pollen.

'It looks like a pure phytosphere,' Harfex said. 'Osden, do you pick up anything sentient?'

They all turned to the Sensor. He had left the screen and was pouring himself a cup of tea. He did not answer. He seldom answered spoken questions.

The chitinous rigidity of military discipline was quite inapplicable to these teams of mad scientists; their chain of command lay somewhere between parliamentary procedure and peck-order, and would have driven a regular service officer out of his mind. By the inscrutable decision of the Authority, however, Dr Haito Tomiko had been given the title of Coordinator, and she now exercised her prerogative for the first time. 'Mr Sensor Osden,' she said, 'please answer Mr Harfex.'

'How could I "pick up" anything from outside,' Osden said without turning, 'with the emotions of nine neurotic hominids pullulating around me like worms in a can? When I have anything to tell you, I'll tell you. I'm aware of my responsibility as Sensor. If you presume to give me an order again, however, Coordinator Haito, I'll consider my responsibility void.'

'Very well, Mr Sensor. I trust no orders will be needed henceforth.' Tomiko's bullfrog voice was calm, but Osden seemed to flinch slightly as he stood with his back to her, as

if the surge of her suppressed rancor had struck him with physical force.

The biologist's hunch proved correct. When they began field analyses they found no animals even among the microbiota. Nobody here ate anybody else. All life-forms were photosynthesizing or saprophagous, living off light or death, not off life. Plants: infinite plants, not one species known to the visitors from the house of Man. Infinite shades and intensities of green, violet, purple, brown, red. Infinite silences. Only the wind moved, swaying leaves and fronds, a warm soughing wind laden with spores and pollens, blowing the sweet pale-green dust over prairies of great grasses, heaths that bore no heather, flowerless forests where no foot had ever walked, no eye had ever looked. A warm, sad world, sad and serene. The Surveyors, wandering like picnickers over sunny plains of violet filicaliformes, spoke softly to each other. They knew their voices broke a silence of a thousand million years, the silence of wind and leaves, leaves and wind, blowing and ceasing and blowing again. They talked softly; but being human, they talked.

'Poor old Osden,' said Jenny Chong, Bio and Tech, as she piloted a helijet on the North Polar Quadrating run. 'All that fancy hi-fi stuff in his brain and nothing to receive. What a bust.'

'He told me he hates plants,' Olleroo said with a giggle.

'You'd think he'd like them, since they don't bother him like we do.'

'Can't say I much like these plants myself,' said Porlock, looking down at the purple undulations of the North Circumpolar Forest. 'All the same. No mind. No change. A man alone in it would go right off his head.'

'But it's all alive,' Jenny Chong said. 'And if it lives, Osden hates it.'

'He's not really so bad,' Olleroo said, magnanimous. Porlock looked at her sidelong and asked, 'You ever slept with him, Olleroo?'

Olleroo burst into tears and cried, 'You Terrans are obscene!'

'No she hasn't,' Jenny Chong said, prompt to defend. 'Have you, Porlock?'

The chemist laughed uneasily: ha, ha, ha. Flecks of spittle appeared on his mustache.

'Osden can't bear to be touched,' Olleroo said shakily. 'I just brushed against him once by accident and he knocked me off like I was some sort of dirty . . . thing. We're all just things, to him.'

'He's evil,' Porlock said in a strained voice, startling the two women. 'He'll end up shattering this team, sabotaging it, one way or another. Mark my words. He's not fit to live with other people!'

They landed on the North Pole. A midnight sun smouldered over low hills. Short, dry, greenish-pink bryoform grasses stretched away in every direction, which was all one direction, south. Subdued by the incredible silence, the three Surveyors set up their instruments and set to work, three viruses twitching minutely on the hide of an unmoving giant.

Nobody asked Osden along on runs as pilot or photographer or recorder, and he never volunteered, so he seldom left base camp. He ran Harfex's botanical taxonomic data through the onship computers, and served as assistant to Eskwana, whose job here was mainly repair and maintenance. Eskwana had begun to sleep a great deal, twenty-five hours or more out of the thirty-two-hour day, dropping off in the middle of repairing a radio or checking the guidance circuits of a helijet. The Coordinator stayed at base one day to observe. No one else was home except Poswet To, who was subject to epileptic fits; Mannon had plugged her into a therapy-circuit today in a state of preventive catatonia, Tomiko spoke reports into the storage banks, and kept an eye on Osden and Eskwana. Two hours passed.

'You might want to use the 860 microwaldoes in sealing that connection,' Eskwana said in his soft, hesitant voice.

'Obviously!'

'Sorry. I just saw you had the 840's there—'

177

'And will replace them when I take the 860's out. When I don't know how to proceed, Engineer, I'll ask your advice.'

After a minute Tomiko looked round. Sure enough, there was Eskwana sound asleep, head on the table, thumb in his mouth.

'Osden.'

The white face did not turn, he did not speak, but conveyed impatiently that he was listening.

'You can't be unaware of Eskwana's vulnerability.'

'I am not responsible for his psychopathic reactions.'

'But you are responsible for your own. Eskwana is essential to our work here, and you're not. If you can't control your hostility, you must avoid him altogether.'

Osden put down his tools and stood up. 'With pleasure!' he said in his vindictive, scraping voice. 'You could not possibly imagine what it's like to experience Eskwana's irrational terrors. To have to share his horrible cowardice, to have to cringe with him at everything!'

'Are you trying to justify your cruelty towards him? I thought you had more self-respect.' Tomiko found herself shaking with spite. 'If your empathic power really makes you share Ander's misery, why does it never induce the least compassion in you?'

'Compassion,' Osden said. 'Compassion. What do you know about compassion?'

She stared at him, but he would not look at her.

'Would you like me to verbalize your present emotional affect regarding myself?' he said. 'I can do so more precisely than you can. I'm trained to analyze such responses as I receive them. And I do receive them.'

'But how can you expect me to feel kindly towards you when you behave as you do?'

'What does it matter how I *behave*, you stupid sow, do you think it makes any difference? Do you think the average human is a well of loving-kindness? My choice is to be hated or to be despised. Not being a woman or a coward, I prefer to be hated.'

'That's rot. Self-pity. Every man has—'

'But I am not a man,' Osden said. 'There are all of you. And there is myself. I am *one*.'

Awed by that glimpse of abysmal solipsism, she kept silent a while; finally she said with neither spite nor pity, clinically, 'You could kill yourself, Osden.'

'That's your way, Haito,' he jeered. 'I'm not depressive, and *seppuku* isn't my bit. What do you want me to do here?'

'Leave. Spare yourself and us. Take the aircar and a data-feeder and go do a species count. In the forest; Harfex hasn't even started the forests yet. Take a hundred-square-meter forested area, anywhere inside radio range. But outside empathy range. Report in at 8 and 24 o'clock daily.'

Osden went, and nothing was heard from him for five days but laconic all-well signals twice daily. The mood at base camp changed like a stage-set. Eskwana stayed awake up to eighteen hours a day. Poswet To got out her stellar lute and chanted the celestial harmonies (music had driven Osden into a frenzy). Mannon, Harfex, Jenny Chong, and Tomiko all went off tranquillizers. Porlock distilled something in his laboratory and drank it all by himself. He had a hangover. Asnanifoil and Poswet To held an all-night Numerical Epiphany, that mystical orgy of higher mathematics which is the chief pleasure of the religious Cetian soul. Olleroo slept with everybody. Work went well.

The Hard Scientist came towards base at a run, laboring through the high, fleshy stalks of the graminiformes. 'Something – in the forest—' His eyes bulged, he panted, his mustache and fingers trembled. 'Something big. Moving, behind me. I was putting in a benchmark, bending down. It came at me. As if it was swinging down out of the trees. Behind me.' He stared at the others with the opaque eyes of terror or exhaustion.

'Sit down, Porlock. Take it easy. Now wait, go through this again. You *saw* something—'

'Not clearly. Just the movement. Purposive. A – an – I don't know what it could have been. Something self-moving. In the

trees, the arboriformes, whatever you call 'em. At the edge of the woods.'

Harfex looked grim. 'There is nothing here that could attack you, Porlock. There are not even microzoa. There *could not* be a large animal.'

'Could you possibly have seen an epiphyte drop suddenly, a vine come loose behind you?'

'No,' Porlock said. 'It was coming down at me, through the branches, fast. When I turned it took off again, away and upward. It made a noise, a sort of crashing. If it wasn't an animal, God knows what it could have been! It was big – as big as a man, at least. Maybe a reddish color. I couldn't see, I'm not sure.'

'It was Osden,' said Jenny Chong, 'doing a Tarzan act.' She giggled nervously, and Tomiko repressed a wild feckless laugh. But Harfex was not smiling.

'One gets uneasy under the arboriformes,' he said in his polite, repressed voice. 'I've noticed that. Indeed that may be why I've put off working in the forests. There's a hypnotic quality in the colors and spacing of the stems and branches, especially the helically-arranged ones; and the spore-throwers grow so regularly spaced that it seems unnatural. I find it quite disagreeable, subjectively speaking. I wonder if a stronger effect of that sort mightn't have produced a hallucination...?'

Porlock shook his head. He wet his lips. 'It was there,' he said. 'Something. Moving with purpose. Trying to attack me from behind.'

When Osden called in, punctual as always, at 24 o'clock that night, Harfex told him Porlock's report. 'Have you come on anything at all, Mr Osden, that could substantiate Mr Porlock's impression of a motile, sentient life-form, in the forest?'

Ssss, the radio said sardonically. 'No. Bullshit,' said Osden's unpleasant voice.

'You've been actually inside the forest longer than any of us,' Harfex said with unmitigable politeness. 'Do you agree with my

impression that the forest ambiance has a rather troubling and possibly hallucinogenic effect on the perceptions?'

Ssss. 'I'll agree that Porlock's perceptions are easily troubled. Keep him in his lab, he'll do less harm. Anything else?'

'Not at present,' Harfex said, and Osden cut off.

Nobody could credit Porlock's story, and nobody could discredit it. He was positive that something, something big, had tried to attack him by surprise. It was hard to deny this, for they were on an alien world, and everyone who had entered the forest had felt a certain chill and foreboding under the 'trees.' ('Call them trees, certainly,' Harfex had said. 'They really are the same thing, only, of course, altogether different.') They agreed that they had felt uneasy, or had had the sense that something was watching them from behind.

'We've got to clear this up,' Porlock said, and he asked to be sent as a temporary Biologist's Aide, like Osden, into the forest to explore and observe. Olleroo and Jenny Chong volunteered if they could go as a pair. Harfex sent them all off into the forest near which they were encamped, a vast tract covering four-fifths of Continent D. He forbade side-arms. They were not to go outside a fifty-mile half-circle, which included Osden's current site. They all reported in twice daily, for three days. Porlock reported a glimpse of what seemed to be a large semi-erect shape moving through the trees across the river; Olleroo was sure she had heard something moving near the tent, the second night.

'There are no animals on this planet,' Harfex said, dogged.

Then Osden missed his morning call.

Tomiko waited less than an hour, then flew with Harfex to the area where Osden had reported himself the night before. But as the helijet hovered over the sea of purplish leaves, illimitable, impenetrable, she felt a panic despair. 'How can we find him in this?'

'He reported landing on the riverbank. Find the aircar; he'll be camped near it, and he can't have gone far from his camp. Species-counting is slow work. There's the river.'

'There's his car,' Tomiko said, catching the bright foreign glint among the vegetable colors and shadows. 'Here goes, then.'

She put the ship in hover and pitched out the ladder. She and Harfex descended. The sea of life closed over their heads.

As her feet touched the forest floor, she unsnapped the flap of her holster; then glancing at Harfex, who was unarmed, she left the gun untouched. But her hand kept coming back up to it. There was no sound at all, as soon as they were a few meters away from the slow, brown river, and the light was dim. Great boles stood well apart, almost regularly, almost alike; they were soft-skinned, some appearing smooth and others spongy, grey or greenish-brown or brown, twined with cable-like creepers and festooned with epiphytes, extending rigid, entangled armfuls of big, saucer-shaped, dark leaves that formed a roof-layer twenty to thirty meters thick. The ground underfoot was springy as a mattress, every inch of it knotted with roots and peppered with small, fleshy-leaved growths.

'Here's his tent,' Tomiko said, cowed at the sound of her voice in that huge community of the voiceless. In the tent was Osden's sleeping bag, a couple of books, a box of rations. We should be calling, shouting for him, she thought, but did not even suggest it; nor did Harfex. They circled out from the tent, careful to keep each other in sight through the thick-standing presences, the crowding gloom. She stumbled over Osden's body, not thirty meters from the tent, led to it by the whitish gleam of a dropped notebook. He lay face down between two huge-rooted trees. His head and hands were covered with blood, some dried, some still oozing red.

Harfex appeared beside her, his pale Hainish complexion quite green in the dusk. 'Dead?'

'No. He's been struck. Beaten. From behind.' Tomiko's fingers felt over the bloody skull and temples and nape. 'A weapon or a tool... I don't find a fracture.'

As she turned Osden's body over so they could lift him, his eyes opened. She was holding him, bending close to his face. His

pale lips writhed. A deathly fear came into her. She screamed aloud two or three times and tried to run away, shambling and stumbling into the terrible dusk. Harfex caught her, and at his touch and the sound of his voice, her panic decreased. 'What is it? What is it?' he was saying.

'I don't know,' she sobbed. Her heartbeat still shook her, and she could not see clearly. 'The fear – the . . . I panicked. When I saw his eyes.'

'We're both nervous. I don't understand this—'

'I'm all right now, come on, we've got to get him under care.'

Both working with senseless haste, they lugged Osden to the riverside and hauled him up on a rope under his armpits; he dangled like a sack, twisting a little, over the glutinous dark sea of leaves. They pulled him into the helijet and took off. Within a minute they were over open prairie. Tomiko locked onto the homing beam. She drew a deep breath, and her eyes met Harfex's.

'I was so terrified I almost fainted. I have never done that.'

'I was . . . unreasonably frightened also,' said the Hainishman, and indeed he looked aged and shaken. 'Not so badly as you. But as unreasonably.'

'It was when I was in contact with him, holding him. He seemed to be conscious for a moment.'

'Empathy? . . . I hope he can tell us what attacked him.'

Osden, like a broken dummy covered with blood and mud, half lay as they had bundled him into the rear seats in their frantic urgency to get out of the forest.

More panic met their arrival at base. The ineffective brutality of the assault was sinister and bewildering. Since Harfex stubbornly denied any possibility of animal life they began speculating about sentient plants, vegetable monsters, psychic projections. Jenny Cheng's latent phobia reasserted itself and she could talk about nothing except the Dark Egos which followed people around behind their backs. She and Olleroo and Porlock had been summoned back to base; and nobody was much inclined to go outside.

Osden had lost a good deal of blood during the three or four hours he had lain alone, and concussion and severe contusions had put him in shock and semi-coma. As he came out of this and began running a low fever he called several times for 'Doctor,' in a plaintive voice: 'Doctor Hammergeld...' When he regained full consciousness, two of those long days later, Tomiko called Harfex into his cubicle.

'Osden: can you tell us what attacked you?'

The pale eyes flickered past Harfex's face.

'You were attacked,' Tomiko said gently. The shifty gaze was hatefully familiar, but she was a physician, protective of the hurt. 'You may not remember it yet. Something attacked you. You were in the forest—'

'Ah!' he cried out, his eyes growing bright and his features contorting. 'The forest – in the forest—'

'What's in the forest?'

He gasped for breath. A look of clearer consciousness came into his face. After a while he said, 'I don't know.'

'Did you see what attacked you?' Harfex asked.

'I don't know.'

'You remember it now.'

'I don't know.'

'All our lives may depend on this. You must tell us what you saw!'

'I don't know,' Osden said, sobbing with weakness. He was too weak to hide the fact that he was hiding the answer, yet he would not say it. Porlock, nearby, was chewing his pepper-colored mustache as he tried to hear what was going on in the cubicle. Harfex leaned over Osden and said, 'You *will* tell us—' Tomiko had to interfere bodily.

Harfex controlled himself with an effort that was painful to see. He went off silently to his cubicle, where no doubt he took a double or triple dose of tranquillizers. The other men and women, scattered about the big frail building, a long main hall and ten sleeping-cubicles, said nothing, but looked depressed and edgy. Osden, as always, even now, had them all at his

184

mercy. Tomiko looked down at him with a rush of hatred that burned in her throat like bile. This monstrous egotism that fed itself on others' emotions, this absolute selfishness, was worse than any hideous deformity of the flesh. Like a congenital monster, he should not have lived. Should not be alive. Should have died. Why had his head not been split open?

As he lay flat and white, his hands helpless at his sides, his colorless eyes were wide open, and there were tears running from the corners. He tried to flinch away. 'Don't,' he said in a weak hoarse voice, and tried to raise his hands to protect his head. 'Don't!'

She sat down on the folding-stool beside the cot, and after a while put her hand on his. He tried to pull away, but lacked the strength.

A long silence fell between them.

'Osden,' she murmured, 'I'm sorry. I'm very sorry. I will you well. Let me will you well, Osden. I don't want to hurt you. Listen, I do see now. It was one of us. That's right, isn't it. No, don't answer, only tell me if I'm wrong; but I'm not... Of course there are animals on this planet. Ten of them. I don't care who it was. It doesn't matter, does it. It could have been me, just now. I realize that. I didn't understand how it is, Osden. You can't see how difficult it is for us to understand... But listen. If it were love, instead of hate and fear... Is it never love?'

'No.'

'Why not? Why should it never be? Are human beings all so weak? That is terrible. Never mind, never mind, don't worry. Keep still. At least right now it isn't hate, is it? Sympathy at least, concern, well-wishing. You do feel that, Osden? Is it what you feel?'

'Among... other things,' he said, almost inaudibly.

'Noise from my subconscious, I suppose. And everybody else in the room... Listen, when we found you there in the forest, when I tried to turn you over, you partly wakened, and I felt

185

a horror of you. I was insane with fear for a minute. Was that your fear of me I felt?'

'No.'

Her hand was still on his, and he was quite relaxed, sinking towards sleep, like a man in pain who has been given relief from pain. 'The forest,' he muttered; she could barely understand him. 'Afraid.'

She pressed him no further, but kept her hand on his and watched him go to sleep. She knew what she felt, and what therefore he must feel. She was confident of it: there is only one emotion, or state of being, that can thus wholly reverse itself, polarize, within one moment. In Great Hainish indeed there is one word, *ontá*, for love and for hate. She was not in love with Osden, of course, that was another kettle of fish. What she felt for him was *ontá*, polarized hate. She held his hand and the current flowed between them, the tremendous electricity of touch, which he had always dreaded. As he slept the ring of anatomy-chart muscles around his mouth relaxed, and Tomiko saw on his face what none of them had ever seen, very faint, a smile. It faded. He slept on.

He was tough; next day he was sitting up, and hungry. Harfex wished to interrogate him, but Tomiko put him off. She hung a sheet of polythene over the cubicle door, as Osden himself had often done. 'Does it actually cut down your empathic reception?' she asked, and he replied, in the dry, cautious tone they were now using to each other, 'No.'

'Just a warning, then.'

'Partly. More faith-healing. Dr Hammergeld thought it worked . . . Maybe it does, a little.'

There had been love, once. A terrified child, suffocating in the tidal rush and battering of the huge emotions of adults, a drowning child, saved by one man. Taught to breathe, to live, by one man. Given everything, all protection and love, by one man. Father/ Mother/ God: no other. 'Is he still alive?' Tomiko asked, thinking of Osden's incredible loneliness, and the strange cruelty of the great doctors. She was shocked when

she heard his forced, tinny laugh. 'He died at least two and a half centuries ago,' Osden said. 'Do you forget where we are, Coordinator? We've all left our little families behind...'

Outside the polythene curtain the eight other human beings on World 4470 moved vaguely. Their voices were low and strained. Eskwana slept; Poswet To was in therapy; Jenny Chong was trying to rig lights in her cubicle so that she wouldn't cast a shadow.

'They're all scared,' Tomiko said, scared. 'They've all got these ideas about what attacked you. A sort of ape-potato, a giant fanged spinach, I don't know... Even Harfex. You may be right not to force them to see. That would be worse, to lose confidence in one another. But why are we all so shaky, unable to face the fact, going to pieces so easily? Are we really all insane?'

'We'll soon be more so.'

'Why?'

'There *is* something.' He closed his mouth, the muscles of his lips stood out rigid.

'Something sentient?'

'A sentience.'

'In the forest?'

He nodded.

'What is it, then—?'

'The fear.' He began to look strained again, and moved restlessly. 'When I fell, there, you know, I didn't lose consciousness at once. Or I kept regaining it. I don't know. It was more like being paralyzed.'

'You were.'

'I was on the ground. I couldn't get up. My face was in the dirt, in that soft leaf mold. It was in my nostrils and eyes. I couldn't move. Couldn't see. As if I was in the ground. Sunk into it, part of it. I knew I was between two trees even though I never saw them. I suppose I could feel the roots. Below me in the ground, down under the ground. My hands were bloody, I could feel that, and the blood made the dirt around my face

sticky. I felt the fear. It kept growing. As if they'd finally *known* I was there, lying on them there, under them, among them, the thing they feared, and yet part of their fear itself. I couldn't stop sending the fear back, and it kept growing, and I couldn't move, I couldn't get away. I would pass out, I think, and then the fear would bring me to again, and I still couldn't move. Any more than they can.'

Tomiko felt the cold stirring of her hair, the readying of the apparatus of terror. 'They: who are they, Osden?'

'They, it – I don't know. The fear.'

'What is he talking about?' Harfex demanded when Tomiko reported this conversation. She would not let Harfex question Osden yet, feeling that she must protect Osden from the onslaught of the Hainishman's powerful, over-repressed emotions. Unfortunately this fueled the slow fire of paranoid anxiety that burned in poor Harfex, and he thought she and Osden were in league, hiding some fact of great importance or peril from the rest of the team.

'It's like the blind man trying to describe the elephant. Osden hasn't seen or heard the ... the sentience, any more than we have.'

'But he's felt it, my dear Haito,' Harfex said with just-suppressed rage. 'Not empathically. On his skull. It came and knocked him down and beat him with a blunt instrument. Did he not catch *one* glimpse of it?'

'What would he have seen, Harfex?' Tomiko asked, but he would not hear her meaningful tone; even he had blocked out that comprehension. What one fears is alien. The murderer is an outsider, a foreigner, not one of us. The evil is not in me!

'The first blow knocked him pretty well out,' Tomiko said a little wearily, 'he didn't see anything. But when he came to again, alone in the forest, he felt a great fear. Not his own fear, an empathic effect. He is certain of that. And certain it was nothing picked up from any of us. So that evidently the native life-forms are not all insentient.'

Harfex looked at her a moment, grim. 'You're trying to

frighten me, Haito. I do not understand your motives.' He got up and went off to his laboratory table, walking slowly and stiffly, like a man of eighty not of forty.

She looked round at the others. She felt some desperation. Her new, fragile, and profound interdependence with Osden gave her, she was well aware, some added strength. But if even Harfex could not keep his head, who of the others would? Porlock and Eskwana were shut in their cubicles, the others were all working or busy with something. There was something queer about their positions. For a while the Coordinator could not tell what it was, then she saw that they were all sitting facing the nearby forest. Playing chess with Asnanifoil, Olleroo had edged her chair around until it was almost beside his.

She went to Mannon, who was dissecting a tangle of spidery brown roots, and told him to look for the pattern-puzzle. He saw it at once, and said with unusual brevity, 'Keeping an eye on the enemy.'

'What enemy? What do *you* feel, Mannon?' She had a sudden hope in him as a psychologist, on this obscure ground of hints and empathies where biologists went astray.

'I feel a strong anxiety with a specific spatial orientation. But I am not an empath. Therefore the anxiety is explicable in terms of the particular stress-situation, that is, the attack on a team member in the forest, and also in terms of the total stress-situation, that is, my presence in a totally alien environment, for which the archetypical connotations of the word "forest" provide an inevitable metaphor.'

Hours later Tomiko woke to hear Osden screaming in night-mare; Mannon was calming him, and she sank back into her own dark-branching pathless dreams. In the morning Eskwana did not wake. He could not be roused with stimulant drugs. He clung to his sleep, slipping farther and farther back, mumbling softly now and then until, wholly regressed, he lay curled on his side, thumb at his lips, gone.

'Two days; two down. Ten little Indians, nine little Indi-ans...' That was Porlock.

'And you're the next little Indian,' Jenny Chong snapped. 'Go analyze your urine, Porlock!'

'He is driving us all insane,' Porlock said, getting up and waving his left arm. 'Can't you feel it? For God's sake, are you all deaf and blind? Can't you feel what he's doing, the emanations? It all comes from him – from his room there – from his mind. He is driving us all insane with fear!'

'Who is?' said Asnanifoil, looming precipitous and hairy over the little Terran.

'Do I have to say his name? Osden, then. Osden! Osden! Why do you think I tried to kill him? In self-defense! To save all of us! Because you won't see what he's doing to us. He's sabotaged the mission by making us quarrel, and now he's going to drive us all insane by projecting fear at us so that we can't sleep or think, like a huge radio that doesn't make any sound, but it broadcasts all the time, and you can't sleep, and you can't think. Haito and Harfex are already under his control but the rest of you can be saved. I had to do it!'

'You didn't do it very well,' Osden said, standing half-naked, all rib and bandage, at the door of his cubicle. 'I could have hit myself harder. Hell, it isn't me that's scaring you blind, Porlock, it's out there – there, in the woods!'

Porlock made an ineffectual attempt to assault Osden; Asnanifoil held him back, and continued to hold him effortlessly while Mannon gave him a sedative shot. He was put away shouting about giant radios. In a minute the sedative took effect, and he joined a peaceful silence to Eskwana's.

'All right,' said Harfex. 'Now, Osden, you'll tell us what you know and all you know.'

Osden said, 'I don't know anything.'

He looked battered and faint. Tomiko made him sit down before he talked.

'After I'd been three days in the forest, I thought I was occasionally receiving some kind of affect.'

'Why didn't you report it?'

'Thought I was going spla, like the rest of you.'

'That, equally, should have been reported.'

'You'd have called me back to base. I couldn't take it. You realize that my inclusion in the mission was a bad mistake. I'm not able to coexist with nine other neurotic personalities at close quarters. I was wrong to volunteer for Extreme Survey, and the Authority was wrong to accept me.'

No one spoke; but Tomiko saw, with certainty this time, the flinch in Osden's shoulders and the tightening of his facial muscles, as he registered their bitter agreement.

'Anyhow, I didn't want to come back to base because I was curious. Even going psycho, how could I pick up empathic affects when there was no creature to emit them? They weren't bad, then. Very vague. Queer. Like a draft in a closed room, a flicker in the corner of your eye. Nothing really.'

For a moment he had been borne up on their listening: they heard, so he spoke. He was wholly at their mercy. If they disliked him he had to be hateful; if they mocked him he became grotesque; if they listened to him he was the storyteller. He was helplessly obedient to the demands of their emotions, reactions, moods. And there were seven of them, too many to cope with, so that he must be constantly knocked about from one to another's whim. He could not find coherence. Even as he spoke and held them, somebody's attention would wander: Olleroo perhaps was thinking that he wasn't unattractive, Harfex was seeking the ulterior motive of his words, Asnanifoil's mind, which could not be long held by the concrete, was roaming off towards the eternal peace of number, and Tomiko was distracted by pity, by fear. Osden's voice faltered. He lost the thread. 'I . . . I thought it must be the trees,' he said, and stopped.

'It's not the trees,' Harfex said. 'They have no more nervous system than do plants of the Hainish Descent on Earth. None.'

'You're not seeing the forest for the trees, as they say on Earth,' Mannon put in, smiling elfinly; Harfex stared at him. 'What about those root-nodes we've been puzzling about for twenty days – eh?'

'What about them?'

'They are, indubitably, connections. Connections among the trees. Right? Now let's just suppose, most improbably, that you knew nothing of animal brain-structure. And you were given one axon, or one detached glial cell, to examine. Would you be likely to discover what it was? Would you see that the cell was capable of sentience?'

'No. Because it isn't. A single cell is capable of mechanical response to stimulus. No more. Are you hypothesizing that individual arboriformes are "cells" in a kind of brain, Mannon?'

'Not exactly. I'm merely pointing out that they are all interconnected, both by the root-node linkage and by your green epiphytes in the branches. A linkage of incredible complexity and physical extent. Why, even the prairie grass-forms have those root-connectors, don't they? I know that sentience or intelligence isn't a thing, you can't find it in, or analyze it out from, the cells of a brain. It's a function of the connected cells. It is, in a sense, the connection: the connectedness. It doesn't exist. I'm not trying to say it exists. I'm only guessing that Osden might be able to describe it.'

And Osden took him up, speaking as if in trance. 'Sentience without senses. Blind, deaf, nerveless, moveless. Some irritability, response to touch. Response to sun, to light, to water, and chemicals in the earth around the roots. Nothing comprehensible to an animal mind. Presence without mind. Awareness of being, without object or subject. Nirvana.'

'Then why do you receive fear?' Tomiko asked in a low voice.

'I don't know. I can't see how awareness of objects, of others, could arise: an unperceiving response . . . But there was an uneasiness, for days. And then when I lay between the two trees and my blood was on their roots—' Osden's face glittered with sweat. 'It became fear,' he said shrilly, 'only fear.'

'If such a function existed,' Harfex said, 'it would not be capable of conceiving of a self-moving, material entity, or

responding to one. It could no more become aware of us than we can "become aware" of Infinity.'

' "The silence of those infinite expanses terrifies me," ' muttered Tomiko. 'Pascal was aware of Infinity. By way of fear.'

'To a forest,' Mannon said, 'we might appear as forest fires. Hurricanes. Dangers. What moves quickly is dangerous, to a plant. The rootless would be alien, terrible. And if it is mind, it seems only too probable that it might become aware of Osden, whose own mind is open to connection with all others so long as he's conscious, and who was lying in pain and afraid within it, actually inside it. No wonder it was afraid—'

'Not "it," ' Harfex said. 'There is no being, no huge creature, no person! There could at most be only a function—'

'There is only a fear,' Osden said.

They were all still a while, and heard the stillness outside.

'Is that what I feel all the time coming up behind me?' Jenny Chong asked, subdued.

Osden nodded. 'You all feel it, deaf as you are. Eskwana's the worst off, because he actually has some empathic capacity. He could send if he learned how, but he's too weak, never will be anything but a medium.'

'Listen, Osden,' Tomiko said, 'you can send. Then send to it – the forest, the fear out there – tell it that we won't hurt it. Since it has, or is, some sort of affect that translates into what we feel as emotion, can't you translate back? Send out a message, We are harmless, we are friendly.'

'You must know that nobody can emit a false empathic message, Haito. You can't send something that doesn't exist.'

'But we don't intend harm, we are friendly.'

'Are we? In the forest, when you picked me up, did you feel friendly?'

'No. Terrified. But that's – it, the forest, the plants, not my own fear, isn't it?'

'What's the difference? It's all you felt. Can't you see,' and Osden's voice rose in exasperation, 'why I dislike you and you dislike me, all of you? Can't you see that I retransmit every

negative or aggressive affect you've felt towards me since we first met? I return your hostility, with thanks. I do it in self-defense. Like Porlock. It is self-defense, though; it's the only technique I developed to replace my original defense of total withdrawal from others. Unfortunately it creates a closed circuit, self-sustaining and self-reinforcing. Your initial reaction to me was the instinctive antipathy to a cripple; by now of course it's hatred. Can you fail to see my point? The forest-mind out there transmits only terror, now, and the only message I can send it is terror, because when exposed to it I can feel nothing except terror!'

'What must we do, then?' said Tomiko, and Mannon replied promptly, 'Move camp. To another continent. If there are plant-minds there, they'll be slow to notice us, as this one was; maybe they won't notice us at all.'

'It would be a considerable relief,' Osden observed stiffly. The others had been watching him with a new curiosity. He had revealed himself, they had seen him as he was, a helpless man in a trap. Perhaps, like Tomiko, they had seen that the trap itself, his crass and cruel egotism, was their own construction, not his. They had built the cage and locked him in it, and like a caged ape he threw filth out through the bars. If, meeting him, they had offered trust, if they had been strong enough to offer him love, how might he have appeared to them?

None of them could have done so, and it was too late now. Given time, given solitude, Tomiko might have built up with him a slow resonance of feeling, a consonance of trust, a harmony; but there was no time, their job must be done. There was not room enough for the cultivation of so great a thing, and they must make do with sympathy, with pity, the small change of love. Even that much had given her strength, but it was nowhere near enough for him. She could see in his flayed face now his savage resentment of their curiosity, even of her pity.

'Go lie down, that gash is bleeding again,' she said, and he obeyed her.

Next morning they packed up, melted down the sprayform hangar and living quarters, lifted *Gum* on mechanical drive and took her halfway round World 4470, over the red and green lands, the many warm green seas. They had picked out a likely spot on Continent G: a prairie, twenty thousand square kilos of windswept graminiformes. No forest was within a hundred kilos of the site, and there were no lone trees or groves on the plain. The plant-forms occurred only in large species-colonies, never intermingled, except for certain tiny ubiquitous saprophytes and spore-bearers. The team sprayed holomeld over structure forms, and by evening of the thirty-two-hour day were settled in to the new camp. Eskwana was still asleep and Porlock still sedated, but everyone else was cheerful. 'You can breathe here!' they kept saying.

Osden got on his feet and went shakily to the doorway; leaning there he looked through twilight over the dim reaches of the swaying grass that was not grass. There was a faint, sweet odor of pollen on the wind; no sound but the soft, vast sibilance of wind. His bandaged head cocked a little, the empath stood motionless for a long time. Darkness came, and the stars, lights in the windows of the distant house of Man. The wind had ceased, there was no sound. He listened.

In the long night Haito Tomiko listened. She lay still and heard the blood in her arteries, the breathing of sleepers, the wind blowing, the dark veins running, the dreams advancing, the vast static of stars increasing as the universe died slowly, the sound of death walking. She struggled out of her bed, fled the tiny solitude of her cubicle. Eskwana alone slept. Porlock lay straitjacketed, raving softly in his obscure native tongue. Olleroo and Jenny Chong were playing cards, grim-faced. Poswet To was in the therapy niche, plugged in. Asnanifoil was drawing a mandala, the Third Pattern of the Primes. Mannon and Harfex were sitting up with Osden.

She changed the bandages on Osden's head. His lank, reddish hair, where she had not had to shave it, looked strange. It

was salted with white, now. Her hands shook as she worked. Nobody had yet said anything.

'How can the fear be here too?' she said, and her voice rang flat and false in the terrific silence.

'It's not just the trees; the grasses too ...'

'But we're twelve thousand kilos from where we were this morning, we left it on the other side of the planet.'

'It's all one,' Osden said. 'One big green thought. How long does it take a thought to get from one side of your brain to the other?'

'It doesn't think. It isn't thinking,' Harfex said, lifelessly. 'It's merely a network of processes. The branches, the epiphytic growths, the roots with those nodal junctures between individuals: they must all be capable of transmitting electrochemical impulses. There are no individual plants, then, properly speaking. Even the pollen is part of the linkage, no doubt, a sort of windborne sentience, connecting overseas. But it is not conceivable. That all the biosphere of a planet should be one network of communications, sensitive, irrational, immortal, isolated ...'

'Isolated,' said Osden. 'That's it! That's the fear. It isn't that we're motile, or destructive. It's just that we are. We are other. There has never been any other.'

'You're right,' Mannon said, almost whispering. 'It has no peers. No enemies. No relationship with anything but itself. One alone forever.'

'Then what's the function of its intelligence in species-survival?'

'None, maybe,' Osden said. 'Why are you getting teleological, Harfex? Aren't you a Hainishman? Isn't the measure of complexity the measure of the eternal joy?'

Harfex did not take the bait. He looked ill. 'We should leave this world,' he said.

'Now you know why I always want to get out, get away from you,' Osden said with a kind of morbid geniality. 'It isn't pleasant, is it – the other's fear ... ? If only it were an animal

intelligence. I can get through to animals. I get along with cobras and tigers; superior intelligence gives one the advantage. I should have been used in a zoo, not on a human team... If I could get through to the damned stupid potato! If it wasn't so overwhelming... I still pick up more than the fear, you know. And before it panicked it had a – there was a serenity. I couldn't take it in, then, I didn't realize how big it was. To know the whole daylight, after all, and the whole night. All the winds and lulls together. The whiter stars and the summer stars at the same time. To have roots, and no enemies. To be entire. Do you see? No invasion. No others. To be whole...'

He had never spoken before, Tomiko thought.

'You are defenseless against it, Osden,' she said. 'Your personality has changed already. You're vulnerable to it. We may not all go mad, but you will, if we don't leave.'

He hesitated, then he looked up at Tomiko, the first time he had ever met her eyes, a long, still look, clear as water.

'What's sanity ever done for me?' he said, mocking. 'But you have a point, Haito. You have something there.'

'We should get away,' Harfex muttered.

'If I gave in to it,' Osden mused, 'could I communicate?'

'By "give in,"' Mannon said in a rapid, nervous voice, 'I assume that you mean, stop sending back the empathic information which you receive from the plant-entity: stop rejecting the fear, and absorb it. That will either kill you at once, or drive you back into total psychological withdrawal, autism.'

'Why?' said Osden. 'Its message is *rejection*. But my salvation is rejection. It's not intelligent. But I am.'

'The scale is wrong. What can a single human brain achieve against something so vast?'

'A single human brain can perceive pattern on the scale of stars and galaxies,' Tomiko said, 'and interpret it as Love.'

Mannon looked from one to the other of them; Harfex was silent.

'It'd be easier in the forest,' Osden said. 'Which of you will fly me over?'

197

'When?'

'Now. Before you all crack up or go violent.'

'I will,' Tomiko said.

'None of us will,' Harfex said.

'I can't,' Mannon said. 'I ... I am too frightened. I'd crash the jet.'

'Bring Eskwana along. If I can pull this off, he might serve as a medium.'

'Are you accepting the Sensor's plan, Coordinator?' Harfex asked formally.

'Yes.'

'I disapprove. I will come with you, however.'

'I think we're compelled, Harfex,' Tomiko said, looking at Osden's face, the ugly white mask transfigured, eager as a lover's face.

Olleroo and Jenny Chong, playing cards to keep their thoughts from their haunted beds, their mounting dread, chattered like scared children. 'This thing, it's in the forest, it'll get you—'

'Scared of the dark?' Osden jeered.

'But look at Eskwana, and Porlock, and even Asnanifoil—'

'It can't hurt you. It's an impulse passing through synapses, a wind passing through branches. It is only a nightmare.'

They took off in a helijet, Eskwana curled up still sound asleep in the rear compartment, Tomiko piloting, Harfex and Osden silent, watching ahead for the dark line of forest across the vague grey miles of starlit plain.

They neared the black line, crossed it; now under them was darkness.

She sought a landing place, flying low, though she had to fight her frantic wish to fly high, to get out, get away. The huge vitality of the plant-world was far stronger here in the forest, and its panic beat in immense dark waves. There was a pale patch ahead, a bare knoll-top a little higher than the tallest of the black shapes around it; the not-trees; the rooted; the parts of the whole. She set the helijet down in the glade,

a bad landing. Her hands on the stick were slippery, as if she had rubbed them with cold soap.

About them now stood the forest, black in darkness.

Tomiko cowered and shut her eyes. Eskwana moaned in his sleep. Harfex's breath came short and loud, and he sat rigid, even when Osden reached across him and slid the door open.

Osden stood up; his back and bandaged head were just visible in the dim glow of the control panel as he paused stooping in the doorway.

Tomiko was shaking. She could not raise her head. 'No, no, no, no, no, no, no,' she said in a whisper. 'No. No. No.'

Osden moved suddenly and quietly, swinging out of the doorway, down into the dark. He was gone.

I am coming! said a great voice that made no sound.

Tomiko screamed. Harfex coughed; he seemed to be trying to stand up, but did not do so.

Tomiko drew in upon herself, all centered in the blind eye in her belly, in the center of her being; and outside that there was nothing but the fear.

It ceased.

She raised her head; slowly unclenched her hands. She sat up straight. The night was dark, and stars shone over the forest. There was nothing else.

'Osden,' she said, but her voice would not come. She spoke again, louder, a lone bullfrog croak. There was no reply.

She began to realize that something had gone wrong with Harfex. She was trying to find his head in the darkness, for he had slipped down from the seat, when all at once, in the dead quiet, in the dark rear compartment of the craft, a voice spoke. 'Good,' it said.

It was Eskwana's voice. She snapped on the interior lights and saw the engineer lying curled up asleep, his hand half over his mouth.

The mouth opened and spoke. 'All well,' it said.

'Osden—'

'All well,' said the soft voice from Eskwana's mouth.

'Where are you?'

Silence.

'Come back.'

A wind was rising. 'I'll stay here,' the soft voice said.

'You can't stay—'

Silence.

'You'd be alone, Osden!'

'Listen.' The voice was fainter, slurred, as if lost in the sound of wind. 'Listen. I will you well.'

She called his name after that, but there was no answer. Eskwana lay still. Harfex lay stiller.

'Osden!' she cried, leaning out the doorway into the dark, wind-shaken silence of the forest of being. 'I will come back. I must get Harfex to the base. I will come back, Osden!'

Silence and wind in leaves.

They finished the prescribed survey of World 4470, the eight of them; it took them forty-one days more. Asnanifoil and one or another of the women went into the forest daily at first, searching for Osden in the region around the bare knoll, though Tomiko was not in her heart sure which bare knoll they had landed on that night in the very heart and vortex of terror. They left piles of supplies for Osden, food enough for fifty years, clothing, tents, tools. They did not go on searching; there was no way to find a man alone, hiding, if he wanted to hide, in those unending labyrinths and dim corridors vine-entangled, root-floored. They might have passed within arm's reach of him and never seen him.

But he was there; for there was no fear any more.

Rational, and valuing reason more highly after an intolerable experience of the immortal mindless, Tomiko tried to understand rationally what Osden had done. But the words escaped her control. He had taken the fear into himself, and, accepting, had transcended it. He had given up his self to the alien, an unreserved surrender, that left no place for evil. He had learned

the love of the Other, and thereby had been given his whole self. – But this is not the vocabulary of reason.

The people of the Survey team walked under the trees, through the vast colonies of life, surrounded by a dreaming silence, a brooding calm that was half aware of them and wholly indifferent to them. There were no hours. Distance was no matter. Had we but world enough and time... The planet turned between the sunlight and the great dark; winds of winter and summer blew fine, pale pollen across the quiet seas.

Gum returned after many surveys, years, and lightyears, to what had several centuries ago been Smeming Port. There were still men there, to receive (incredulously) the team's reports, and to record its losses: Biologist Harfex, dead of fear, and Sensor Osden, left as a colonist.

THE STARS BELOW

The popular notion of science fiction, I guess, is of a story that takes some possible or impossible technological gimmick-of-the-future — Soylent Green, the time machine, the submarine — and makes hay out of it. There certainly are science fiction stories which do just that, but to define science fiction by them is a bit like defining the United States as Kansas.

Writing 'The Stars Below,' I thought I knew what I was doing. As in the early story 'The Masters,' I was telling a story not about a gimmick or device or hypothesis, but about science itself — the idea of science. And about what happens to the idea of science when it meets utterly opposed and powerful ideas, embodied in government, as when seventeenth-century astronomy ran up against the Pope, or genetics in the 1930s ran up against Stalin. But all this was cast as a psychomyth, a story outside real time, past or future, in part to generalize it, and in part because I was also using science as a synonym for art. What happens to the creative mind when it is driven underground?

That was the question, and I thought I knew my answer. It all seemed straightforward, a mere allegory, really. But you don't go exploring the places underground all that easily. The symbols you thought were simple equivalences, signs, come alive, and take on meanings you did not intend and cannot explain. Long after I wrote the story I came on a passage in Jung's On the Nature of the Psyche: *'We would do well to think of ego-consciousness as being surrounded by a multitude of little luminosities... Introspective intuitions... capture the state of the unconscious: The star-strewn heavens, stars reflected in dark water, nuggets of gold or golden sand scattered in black earth.' And he quotes from an alchemist,*

'Seminate aurum in terram albam foliatam' – *the precious metal strewn in the layers of white clay.*

Perhaps this story is not about science, or about art, but about the mind, my mind, any mind, that turns inward to itself.

The wooden house and outbuildings caught fire fast, blazed up, burned down, but the dome, built of lathe and plaster above a drum of brick, would not burn. What they did at last was heap up the wreckage of the telescopes, the instruments, the books and charts and drawings, in the middle of the floor under the dome, pour oil on the heap, and set fire to that. The flames spread to the wooden beams of the big telescope frame and to the clockwork mechanisms. Villagers watching from the foot of the hill saw the dome, whitish against the green evening sky, shudder and turn, first in one direction then in the other, while a black and yellow smoke full of sparks gushed from the oblong slit: an ugly and uncanny thing to see.

It was getting dark, stars were showing in the east. Orders were shouted. The soldiers came down the road in single file, dark men in dark harness, silent.

The villagers at the foot of the hill stayed on after the soldiers had gone. In a life without change or breadth a fire is as good as a festival. They did not climb the hill, and as the night grew full dark they drew closer together. After a while they began to go back to their villages. Some looked back over their shoulders at the hill, where nothing moved. The stars turned slowly behind the black beehive of the dome, but it did not turn to follow them.

About an hour before daybreak a man rode up the steep zigzag, dismounted by the ruins of the workshops, and approached the dome on foot. The door had been smashed in. Through it a reddish haze of light was visible, very dim, coming from a massive support-beam that had fallen and had smoldered all night inward to its core. A hanging, sour smoke thickened the air inside the dome. A tall figure moved there and

its shadow moved with it, cast upward on the murk. Sometimes it stooped, or stopped, then blundered slowly on.

The man at the door said: 'Guennar! Master Guennar!'

The man in the dome stopped still, looking towards the door. He had just picked up something from the mess of wreckage and half-burnt stuff on the floor. He put this object mechanically into his coat pocket, still peering at the door. He came towards it. His eyes were red and swollen almost shut, he breathed harshly in gasps, his hair and clothes were scorched and smeared with black ash.

'Where were you?'

The man in the dome pointed vaguely at the ground.

'There's a cellar? That's where you were during the fire? By God! Gone to ground! I knew it, I knew you'd be here.' Bord laughed, a little crazily, taking Guennar's arm. 'Come on. Come out of there, for the love of God. There's light in the east already.'

The astronomer came reluctantly, looking not at the grey east but back up at the slit in the dome, where a few stars burned clear. Bord pulled him outside, made him mount the horse, and then, bridle in hand, set off down the hill leading the horse at a fast walk.

The astronomer held the pommel with one hand. The other hand, which had been burned across the palm and fingers when he picked up a metal fragment still red-hot under its coat of cinders, he kept pressed against his thigh. He was not conscious of doing so, or of the pain. Sometimes his senses told him, 'I am on horseback,' or, 'It's getting lighter,' but these fragmentary messages made no sense to him. He shivered with cold as the dawn wind rose, rattling the dark woods by which the two men and the horse now passed in a deep lane overhung by teasel and briar; but the woods, the wind, the whitening sky, the cold were all remote from his mind, in which there was nothing but a darkness shot with the reek and heat of burning.

Bord made him dismount. There was sunlight around them now, lying long on rocks above a river valley. There was a dark

place, and Bord urged him and pulled him into the dark place. It was not hot and close there but cold and silent. As soon as Bord let him stop he sank down, for his knees would not bear; and he felt the cold rock against his seared and throbbing hands.

'Gone to earth, by God!' said Bord, looking about at the veined walls, marked with the scars of miners' picks, in the light of his lanterned candle. 'I'll be back; after dark, maybe. Don't come out. Don't go farther in. This is an old adit, they haven't worked this end of the mine for years. May be slips and pitfalls in these old tunnels. Don't come out! Lie low. When the hounds are gone, we'll run you across the border.'

Bord turned and went back up the adit in darkness. When the sound of his steps had long since died away, the astronomer lifted his head and looked around him at the dark walls and the little burning candle. Presently he blew it out. There came upon him the earth-smelling darkness, silent and complete. He saw green shapes, ocherous blots drifting on the black; these faded slowly. The dull, chill black was balm to his inflamed and aching eyes, and to his mind.

If he thought, sitting there in the dark, his thoughts found no words. He was feverish from exhaustion and smoke inhalation and a few slight burns, and in an abnormal condition of mind; but perhaps his mind's workings, though lucid and serene, had never been normal. It is not normal for a man to spend twenty years grinding lenses, building telescopes, peering at stars, making calculations, lists, maps and charts of things which no one knows or cares about, things which cannot be reached, or touched, or held. And now all he had spent his life on was gone, burned. What was left of him might as well be, as it was, buried.

But it did not occur to him, this idea of being buried. All he was keenly aware of was a great burden of anger and grief, a burden he was unfit to carry. It was crushing his mind, crushing out reason. And the darkness here seemed to relieve that pressure. He was accustomed to the dark, he had lived at night.

The weight here was only rock, only earth. No granite is so hard as hatred and no clay so cold as cruelty. The earth's black innocence enfolded him. He lay down within it, trembling a little with pain and with relief from pain, and slept.

Light waked him. Count Bord was there, lighting the candle with flint and steel. Bard's face was vivid in the light: the high color and blue eyes of a keen huntsman, a red mouth, sensual and obstinate. 'They're on the scent,' he was saying. 'They know you got away.'

'Why...' said the astronomer. His voice was weak; his throat, like his eyes, was still smoke-inflamed. 'Why are they after me?'

'Why? Do you still need telling? To burn you alive, man! For heresy!' Bord's blue eyes glared through the steadying glow of the candle.

'But it's gone, burned, all I did.'

'Aye, the earth's stopped, all right, but where's their fox? They want their fox! But damned if I'll let them get you.'

The astronomer's eyes, light and wide-set, met his and held. 'Why?'

'You think I'm a fool,' Bord said with a grin that was not a smile, a wolf's grin, the grin of the hunted and the hunter. 'And I am one. I was a fool to warn you. You never listened. I was a fool to listen to you. But I liked to listen to you. I liked to hear you talk about the stars and the courses of the planets and the ends of time. Who else ever talked to me of anything but seed corn and cow dung? Do you see? And I don't like soldiers and strangers, and trials and burnings. Your truth, their truth, what do I know about the truth? Am I a master? Do I know the courses of the stars? Maybe you do. Maybe they do. All I know is you have sat at my table and talked to me. Am I to watch you burn? God's fire, they say; but you said the stars are the fires of God. Why do you ask me that, "Why?" Why do you ask me a fool's question of a fool?'

'I am sorry,' the astronomer said.

'What do you know about men?' the count said. 'You thought they'd let you be. And you thought I'd let you burn.'

He looked at Guennar through the candlelight, grinning like a driven wolf, but in his blue eyes there was a glint of real amusement. 'We who live down on the earth, you see, not up among the stars...'

He had brought a tinderbox and three tallow candles, a bottle of water, a ball of peas-pudding, a sack of bread. He left soon, warning the astronomer again not to venture out of the mine.

When Guennar woke again a strangeness in his situation troubled him, not one which would have worried most people hiding in a hole to save their skins, but most distressing to him: he did not know the time.

It was not clocks he missed, the sweet banging of the church bells in the villages calling to morning and evening prayer, the delicate and willing accuracy of the timepieces he used in his observatory and on whose refinement so many of his discoveries had depended; it was not the clocks he missed, but the great clock.

Not seeing the sky, one cannot know the turning of the earth. All the processes of time, the sun's bright arch and the moon's phases, the planet's dance, the wheeling of the constellations around the pole star, the vaster wheeling of the seasons of the stars, all these were lost, the warp on which his life was woven.

Here there was no time.

'O my God,' Guennar the astronomer prayed in the darkness under ground, 'how can it offend you to be praised? All I ever saw in my telescopes was one spark of your glory, one least fragment of the order of your creation. You could not be jealous of that, my Lord! And there were few enough who believed me, even so. Was it my arrogance in daring to describe your works? But how could I help it, Lord, when you let me see the endless fields of stars? Could I see and be silent? O my God, do not punish me any more, let me rebuild the smaller telescope. I will not speak, I will not publish, if it troubles your holy Church. I will not say anything more about the orbits of

207

the planets or the nature of the stars. I will not speak, Lord, only let me see!'

'What the devil, be quiet, Master Guennar. I could hear you halfway up the tunnel,' said Bord, and the astronomer opened his eyes to the dazzle of Bord's lantern. 'They've called the full hunt up for you. Now you're a necromancer. They swear they saw you sleeping in your house when they came, and they barred the doors; but there's no bones in the ashes.'

'I was asleep,' Guennar said, covering his eyes. 'They came, the soldiers . . . I should have listened to you. I went into the passage under the dome. I left a passage there so I could go back to the hearth on cold nights, when it's cold my fingers get too stiff, I have to go warm my hands sometimes.' He spread out his blistered, blackened hands and looked at them vaguely. 'Then I heard them overhead . . .'

'Here's some more food. What the devil, haven't you eaten?'

'Has it been long?'

'A night and a day. It's night now. Raining. Listen, Master: there's two of the black hounds living at my house now. Emissaries of the Council, what the devil, I had to offer hospitality. This is my county, they're here, I'm the count. It makes it hard for me to come. And I don't want to send any of my people here. What if the priests asked them, "Do you know where he is? Will you answer to God you don't know where he is?" It's best they don't know. I'll come when I can. You're all right here? You'll stay here? I'll get you out of here and over the border when they've cleared away. They're like flies now. Don't talk aloud like that. They might look into these old tunnels. You should go farther in. I will come back. Stay with God, Master.'

'Go with God, count.'

He saw the color of Bord's blue eyes, the leap of shadows up the rough-hewn roof as he took up the lantern and turned away. Light and color died as Bord, at the turning, put out the lantern. Guennar heard him stumble and swear as he groped his way.

Presently Guennar lighted one of his candles and ate and

drank a little, eating the staler bread first, and breaking off a piece of the crusted lump of peas-pudding. This time Bord had brought him three loaves and some salt meat, two more candles and a second skin bottle of water, and a heavy duffle cloak. Guennar had not felt cold. He was wearing the coat he always wore on cold nights in the observatory and very often slept in, when he came stumbling to bed at dawn. It was a good sheepskin, filthy from his rummagings in the wreckage in the dome and scorched at the sleeve-ends, but it was as warm as ever, and was like his own skin to him. He sat inside it eating, gazing out through the sphere of frail yellow candlelight to the darkness of the tunnel beyond. Bord's words, 'You should go farther in,' were in his mind. When he was done eating he bundled up the provisions in the cloak, took up the bundle in one hand and the lighted candle in the other, and set off down the side-tunnel and then the adit, down and inward.

After a few hundred paces he came to a major cross-tunnel, off which ran many short leads and some large rooms or stopes. He turned left, and presently passed a big stope in three levels. He entered it. The farthest level was only about five feet under the roof, which was still well timbered with posts and beams. In a corner of the backmost level, behind an angle of quartz intrusion which the miners had left jutting out as a supporting buttress, he made his new camp, setting out the food, water, tinderbox, and candles where they would come under his hand easily in the dark, and laying the cloak as a mattress on the floor, which was of a rubbly, hard clay. Then he put out the candle, already burned down by a quarter of its length, and lay down in the dark.

After his third return to that first side-tunnel, finding no sign that Bord had come there, he went back to his camp and studied his provisions. There were still two loaves of bread, half a bottle of water, and the salt meat, which he had not yet touched; and four candles. He guessed that it might have been six days since Bord had come, but it might have been three, or

eight. He was thirsty, but dared not drink, so long as he had no other supply.

He set off to find water.

At first he counted his paces. After a hundred and twenty he saw that the timbering of the tunnel was askew, and there were places where the rubble fill had broken through, half filling the passage. He came to a winze, a vertical shaft, easy to scramble down by what remained of the wooden ladder, but after it, in the lower level, he forgot to count his steps. Once he passed a broken pick handle; farther on he saw a miner's discarded headband, a stump of candle still stuck in the forehead socket. He dropped this into the pocket of his coat and went on.

The monotony of the walls of hewn stone and planking dulled his mind. He walked on like one who will walk forever. Darkness followed him and went ahead of him.

His candle burning short spilled a stream of hot tallow on his fingers, hurting him. He dropped the candle, and it went out.

He groped for it in the sudden dark, sickened by the reek of its smoke, lifting his head to avoid that stink of burning. Before him, straight before him, far away, he saw the stars.

Tiny, bright, remote, caught in a narrow opening like the slot in the observatory dome: an oblong full of stars in blackness.

He got up, forgetting about the candle, and began to run towards the stars.

They moved, dancing, like the stars in the telescope field when the clockwork mechanism shuddered or when his eyes were very tired. They danced, and brightened.

He came among them, and they spoke to him.

The flames cast queer shadows on the blackened faces and brought queer lights out of the bright, living eyes.

'Here, then, who's that? Hanno?'

'What were you doing up that old drift, mate?'

'Hey, who is that?'

'Who the devil, stop him—'

'Hey, mate! Hold on!'

He ran blind into the dark, back the way he had come. The lights followed him and he chased his own faint, huge shadow down the tunnel. When the shadow was swallowed by the old dark and the old silence came again he still stumbled on, stooping and groping so that he was oftenest on all fours or on his feet and one hand. At last he dropped down and lay huddled against the wall, his chest full of fire.

Silence, dark.

He found the candle end in the tin holder in his pocket, lighted it with the flint and steel, and by its glow found the vertical shaft not fifty feet from where he had stopped. He made his way back up to his camp. There he slept; woke and ate, and drank the last of his water; meant to get up and go seeking water again; fell asleep, or into a doze or daze, in which he dreamed of a voice speaking to him.

'There you are. All right. Don't startle. I'll do you no harm. I said it wasn't no knocker. Who ever heard of a knocker as tall as a man? Or who ever seen one, for that matter. They're what you *don't* see, mates, I said. And what we did see was a man, count on it. So what's he doing in the mine, said they, and what if he's a ghost, one of the lads that was caught when the house of water broke in the old south adit, maybe, come walking? Well then, I said, I'll go see that. I never seen a ghost yet, for all I heard of them. I don't care to see what's not meant to be seen, like the knocker folk, but what harm to see Temon's face again, or old Trip, haven't I seen 'em in dreams, just the same, in the ends, working away with their faces sweating same as life? Why not? So I come along. But you're no ghost, nor miner. A deserter you might be, or a thief. Or are you out of your wits, is that it, poor man? Don't fear. Hide if you like. What's it to me? There's room down here for you and me. Why are you hiding from the light of the sun?'

'The soldiers..'

'I thought so.'

When the old man nodded, the candle bound to his forehead set light leaping over the roof of the stope. He squatted about

ten feet from Guennar, his hands hanging between his knees. A bunch of candles and his pick, a short-handled, finely shaped tool, hung from his belt. His face and body, beneath the restless star of the candle, were rough shadows, earth-colored.

'Let me stay here.'

'Stay and welcome! Do I own the mine? Where did you come in, eh, the old drift above the river? That was luck to find that, and luck you turned this way in the crosscut, and didn't go east instead. Eastward this level goes on to the caves. There's great caves there; did you know it? Nobody knows but the miners. They opened up the caves before I was born, following the old lode that lay along here sunward. I seen the caves once, my dad took me, you should see this once, he says. See the world underneath the world. A room there was no end to. A cavern as deep as the sky, and a black stream falling into it, falling and falling till the light of the candle failed and couldn't follow it, and still the water was falling on down into the pit. The sound of it came up like a whisper without an end, out of the dark. And on beyond that there's other caves, and below. No end to them, maybe. Who knows? Cave under cave, and glittering with the barren, crystal. It's all barren stone, there. And all worked out, here, years ago. It's a safe enough hole you chose, mate, if you hadn't come stumbling in on us. What was you after? Food? A human face?'

'Water.'

'No lack of that. Come on, I'll show you. Beneath here in the lower level there's all too many springs. You turned the wrong direction. I used to work down there, with the damned cold water up to my knees, before the vein ran out. A long time ago. Come on.'

The old miner left him in his camp, after showing him where the spring rose and warning him not to follow down the watercourse, for the timbering would be rotted and a step or sound might bring the earth down. Down there all the timbers were covered with a deep glittering white fur, saltpeter perhaps, or

a fungus: it was very strange, above the oily water. When he was alone again Guennar thought he had dreamed that white tunnel full of black water, and the visit of the miner. When he saw a flicker of light far down the tunnel, he crouched behind the quartz buttress with a great wedge of granite in his hand: for all his fear and anger and grief had come down to one thing here in the darkness, a determination that no man would lay hand on him. A blind determination, blunt and heavy as a broken stone, heavy in his soul.

It was only the old man coming, with a hunk of dry cheese for him.

He sat with the astronomer, and talked. Guennar ate up the cheese, for he had no food left, and listened to the old man talk. As he listened the weight seemed to lift a little, he seemed to see a little farther in the dark.

'You're no common soldier,' the miner said, and he replied, 'No, I was a student once,' but no more, because he dared not tell the miner who he was. The old man knew all the events of the region; he spoke of the burning of the Round House on the hill, and of Count Bord. 'He went off to the city with them, with these black-gowns, to be tried, they do say, to come before their council. Tried for what? What did he ever do but hunt boar and deer and foxen? Is it the council of the foxen trying him? What's it all about, this snooping and soldiering and burning and trying? Better leave honest folk alone. The count was honest, as far as the rich can be, a fair landlord. But you can't trust them, none of such folk. Only down here. You can trust the men who go down into the mine. What else has a man got down here but his own hands and his mates' hands? What's between him and death, when there's a fall in the level or a winze closes and he's in the blind end, but their hands, and their shovels, and their will to dig him out? There'd be no silver up there in the sun if there wasn't trust between us down here in the dark. Down here you can count on your mates. And nobody comes but them. Can you see the owner in his lace, or the soldiers, coming down the ladders, coming down and

down the great shaft into the dark? Not them! They're brave at tramping on the grass, but what good's a sword and shouting in the dark? I'd like to see 'em come down here...'

The next time he came another man was with him, and they brought an oil lamp and a clay jar of oil, as well as more cheese, bread, and some apples. 'It was Hanno thought of the lamp,' the old man said. 'A hempen wick it is, if she goes out blow sharp and she'll likely catch up again. Here's a dozen candles, too. Young Per swiped the lot from the doler, up on the grass.'

'They all know I'm here?'

'*We* do,' the miner said briefly. '*They* don't.'

Some time after this, Guennar returned along the lower, west-leading level he had followed before, till he saw the miners' candles dance like stars; and he came into the stope where they were working. They shared their meal with him. They showed him the ways of the mine, and the pumps, and the great shaft where the ladders were and the hanging pulleys with their buckets; he sheered off from that, for the wind that came sucking down the great shaft smelled to him of burning. They took him back and let him work with them. They treated him as a guest, as a child. They had adopted him. He was their secret.

There is not much good spending twelve hours a day in a black hole in the ground all your life long if there's nothing there, no secret, no treasure, nothing hidden.

There was the silver, to be sure. But where ten crews of fifteen had used to work these levels and there had been no end to the groan and clatter and crash of the loaded buckets going up on the screaming winch and the empties banging down to meet the trammers running with their heavy carts, now one crew of eight men worked: men over forty, old men, who had no skill but mining. There was still some silver there in the hard granite, in little veins among the gangue. Sometimes they would lengthen an end by one foot in two weeks.

'It was a great mine,' they said with pride.

They showed the astronomer how to set a gad and swing the sledge, how to go at granite with the finely balanced and sharp-pointed pick, how to sort and 'cob,' what to look for, the rare bright branchings of the pure metal, the crumbling rich rock of the ore. He helped them daily. He was in the stope waiting for them when they came, and spelled one or another on and off all day with the shovel work, or sharpening tools, or running the ore-cart down its grooved plank to the great shaft, or working in the ends. There they would not let him work long; pride and habit forbade it. 'Here, leave off chopping at that like a woodcutter. Look: this way, see?' But then another would ask him, 'Give me a blow here, lad, see, on the gad, that's it.'

They fed him from their own coarse meager meals.

In the night, alone in the hollow earth, when they had climbed the long ladders up 'to grass' as they said, he lay and thought of them, their faces, their voices, their heavy, scarred, earth-stained hands, old men's hands with thick nails blackened by bruising rock and steel; those hands, intelligent and vulnerable, which had opened up the earth and found the shining silver in the solid rock. The silver they never held, never kept, never spent. The silver that was not theirs.

'If you found a new vein, a new lode, what would you do?'

'Open her, and tell the masters.'

'Why tell the masters?'

'Why, man! We gets paid for what we brings up! D'you think we does this damned work for love?'

'Yes.'

They all laughed at him, loud, jeering laughter, innocent. The living eyes shone in their faces blackened with dust and sweat.

'Ah, if we could find a new lode! The wife would keep a pig like we had once, and by God I'd swim in beer! But if there's silver they'd have found it; that's why they pushed the workings so far east. But it's barren there, and worked out here, that's the short and long of it.'

215

*

Time stretched behind him and ahead of him like the dark drifts and crosscuts of the mine, all present at once, wherever he with his small candle might be among them. When he was alone now the astronomer often wandered in the tunnels and the old stopes, knowing the dangerous places, the deep levels full of water, adept at shaky ladders and tight places, intrigued by the play of his candle on the rock walls and faces, the glitter of mica that seemed to come from deep inside the stone. Why did it sometimes shine out that way? as if the candle found something far within the shining broken surface, something that winked in answer and occulted, as if it had slipped behind a cloud or an unseen planet's disc.

'There are stars in the earth,' he thought. 'If one knew how to see them.'

Awkward with the pick, he was clever with machinery; they admired his skill, and brought him tools. He repaired pumps and windlasses; he fixed up a lamp on a chain for 'young Per' working in a long narrow deadend, with a reflector made from a tin candle-holder beaten out into a curved sheet and polished with fine rock-dust and the sheepskin lining of his coat. 'It's a marvel,' Per said. 'Like daylight. Only, being behind me, it don't go out when the air gets bad, and tell me I should be backing out for a breath.'

For a man can go on working in a narrow end for some time after his candle has gone out for lack of oxygen.

'You should have a bellows rigged there.'

'What, like I was a forge?'

'Why not?'

'Do ye ever go up to the grass, nights?' asked Hanno, looking wistfully at Guennar. Hanno was a melancholy, thoughtful, softhearted fellow. 'Just to look about you?'

Guennar did not answer. He went off to help Bran with a timbering job; the miners did all the work that had once been done by crews of timberers, trammers, sorters, and so on.

'He's deathly afraid to leave the mine,' Per said, low.

'Just to see the stars and get a breath of the wind,' Hanno said, as if he was still speaking to Guennar.

One night the astronomer emptied out his pockets and looked at the stuff that had been in them since the night of the burning of the observatory: things he had picked up in those hours which he now could not remember, those hours when he had groped and stumbled in the smoldering wreckage, seeking... seeking what he had lost... He no longer thought of what he had lost. It was sealed off in his mind by a thick scar, a burn-scar. For a long time this scar in his mind kept him from understanding the nature of the objects now ranged before him on the dusty stone floor of the mine: a wad of papers scorched all along one side; a round piece of glass or crystal; a metal tube; a beautifully worked wooden cogwheel; a bit of twisted blackened copper etched with fine lines; and so on, bits, wrecks, scraps. He put the papers back into his pocket, without trying to separate the brittle half-fused leaves and make out the fine script. He continued to look at and occasionally to pick up and examine the other things, especially the piece of glass.

This he knew to be the eyepiece of his ten-inch telescope. He had ground the lens himself. When he picked it up he handled it delicately, by the edges, lest the acid of his skin etch the glass. Finally he began to polish it clean, using a wisp of fine lambswool from his coat. When it was clear, he held it up and looked at and through it at all angles. His face was calm and intent, his light wide-set eyes steady.

Tilted in his fingers, the telescope lens reflected the lamp flame in one bright tiny point near the edge and seemingly beneath the curve of the face, as if the lens had kept a star in it from the many hundred nights it had been turned toward the sky.

He wrapped it carefully in the wisp of wool and made a place for it in the rock niche with his tinderbox. Then he took up the other things one by one.

During the next weeks the miners saw their fugitive less often while they worked. He was off a great deal by himself: exploring the deserted eastern regions of the mine, he said, when they asked him what he did.

'What for?'

'Prospecting,' he said with the brief, wincing smile that gave him a very crazy look.

'Oh, lad, what do you know about that? She's all barren there. The silver's gone; and they found no eastern lode. You might be finding a bit of poor ore or a vein of tinstone, but nothing worth the digging.'

'How do you know what's in the earth, in the rock under your feet, Per?'

'I know the signs, lad. Who should know better?'

'But if the signs are hidden?'

'Then the silver's hidden.'

'Yet you know it is there, if you knew where to dig, if you could see into the rock. And what else is there? You find the metal, because you seek it, and dig for it. But what else might you find, deeper than the mine, if you sought, if you knew where to dig?'

'Rock,' said Per. 'Rock, and rock, and rock.'

'And then?'

'And then? Hellfire, for all I know. Why else does it get hotter as the shafts go deeper? That's what they say. Getting nearer hell.'

'No,' the astronomer said, clear and firm. 'No. There is no hell beneath the rocks.'

'What is there, then, underneath it all?'

'The stars.'

'Ah,' said the miner, floored. He scratched his rough, tallow-clotted hair, and laughed. 'There's a poser,' he said, and stared at Guennar with pity and admiration. He knew Guennar was mad, but the size of his madness was a new thing to him, and admirable. 'Will you find 'em then, the stars?'

'If I learn how to look,' Guennar said, so calmly that Per

had no response but to heft his shovel and get back to loading the cart.

One morning when the miners came down they found Guennar still sleeping, rolled up in the battered cloak Count Bord had given him, and by him a strange object, a contraption made of silver tubing, tin struts and wires beaten from old headlamp-sockets, a frame of pick handles carefully carved and fitted, cogged wheels, a bit of twinkling glass. It was elusive, makeshift, delicate, crazy, intricate.

'What the devil's that?'

They stood about and stared at the thing, the lights of their headlamps centering on it, a yellow beam sometimes flickering over the sleeping man as one or another glanced at him.

'He made it, sure.'

'Sure enough.'

'What for?'

'Don't touch it.'

'I wasn't going to.'

Roused by their voices, the astronomer sat up. The yellow beams of the candles brought his face out white against the dark. He rubbed his eyes and greeted them.

'What would that be, lad?'

He looked troubled or confused when he saw the object of their curiosity. He put a hand on it protectively, yet he looked at it himself without seeming to recognize it for a while. At last he said, frowning and speaking in a whisper, 'It's a telescope.'

'What's that?'

'A device that makes distant things clear to the eye.'

'How come?' one of the miners asked, baffled. The astronomer answered him with growing assurance. 'By virtue of certain properties of light and lenses. The eye is a delicate instrument but it is blind to half the universe – far more than half. The night sky is black, we say: between the stars is void and darkness. But turn the telescope-eye on that space between the stars, and lo, the stars! Stars too faint and far for the eye alone to see, rank behind rank, glory beyond glory, out to the

uttermost boundaries of the universe. Beyond all imagination, in the outer darkness, there is light: a great glory of sunlight. I have seen it. I have seen it, night after night, and mapped the stars, the beacons of God on the shores of darkness. And here too there is light! There is no place bereft of the light, the comfort and radiance of the creator spirit. There is no place that is outcast, outlawed, forsaken. There is no place left dark. Where the eyes of God have seen, there light is. We must go farther, we must look farther! There is light if we will see it. Not with eyes alone, but with the skill of the hands and the knowledge of the mind and the heart's faith is the unseen revealed, and the hidden made plain. And all the dark earth shines like a sleeping star.'

He spoke with that authority which the miners knew belonged by rights to the priests, to the great words priests spoke in the echoing churches. It did not belong here, in the hole where they grubbed their living, in the words of a crazy fugitive. Later on, one talking to another, they shook their heads, or tapped them. Per said, 'The madness is growing in him,' and Hanno said, 'Poor soul, poor soul!' Yet there was not one of them who did not, also, believe what the astronomer had told them.

'Show me,' said old Bran, finding Guennar alone in a deep eastern drift, busy with his intricate device. It was Bran who had first followed Guennar, and brought him food, and led him back to the others.

The astronomer willingly stood aside and showed Bran how to hold the device pointing downward at the tunnel floor, and how to aim and focus it, and tried to describe its function and what Bran might see: all hesitantly, since he was not used to explaining to the ignorant, but without impatience when Bran did not understand.

'I don't see nothing but the ground,' the old man said after a long and solemn observation with the instrument. 'And the little dust and pebbles on it.'

'The lamp blinds your eyes, perhaps,' the astronomer said

with humility. 'It is better to look without light. I can do it because I have done it for so long. It is all practice – like placing the gads, which you always do right, and I always do wrong.'

'Aye. Maybe. Tell me what you see—' Bran hesitated. He had not long ago realized who Guennar must be. Knowing him to be a heretic made no difference but knowing him to be a learned man made it hard to call him 'mate' or 'lad.' And yet here, and after all this time, he could not call him Master. There were times when, for all his mildness, the fugitive spoke with great words, gripping one's soul, times when it would have been easy to call him Master. But it would have frightened him.

The astronomer put his hand on the frame of his mechanism and replied in a soft voice, 'There are ... constellations.'

'What's that, constellations?'

The astronomer looked at Bran as if from a great way off, and said presently, 'The Wain, the Scorpion, the Sickle by the Milky Way in summer, those are constellations. Patterns of stars, gatherings of stars, parenthoods, semblances...'

'And you see those here, with this?'

Still looking at him through the weak lamplight with clear brooding eyes, the astronomer nodded, and did not speak, but pointed downward, at the rock on which they stood, the hewn floor of the mine.

'What are they like?' Bran's voice was hushed.

'I have only glimpsed them. Only for a moment. I have not learned the skill; it is a somewhat different skill ... But they are there, Bran.'

Often now he was not in the stope where they worked, when they came to work, and did not join them even for their meal, though they always left him a share of food. He knew the ways of the mine now better than any of them, even Bran, not only the 'living' mine but the 'dead' one, the abandoned workings and exploratory tunnels that ran eastward, ever deeper, towards the caves. There he was most often; and they did not follow him.

When he did appear amongst them and they talked with him, they were more timid with him, and did not laugh.

One night as they were all going back with the last cartload to the main shaft, he came to meet them, stepping suddenly out of a crosscut to their right. As always he wore his ragged sheepskin coat, black with the clay and dirt of the tunnels. His fair hair had gone grey. His eyes were clear. 'Bran,' he said, 'come, I can show you now.'

'Show me what?'

'The stars. The stars beneath the rock. There's a great constellation in the stope on the old fourth level, where the white granite cuts down through the black.'

'I know the place.'

'It's there: underfoot, by that wall of white rock. A great shining and assembly of stars. Their radiance beats up through the darkness. They are like the faces of dancers, the eyes of angels. Come and see them, Bran!'

The miners stood there. Per and Hanno with backs braced to hold the cart from rolling: stooped men with tired, dirty faces and big hands bent and hardened by the grip of shovel and pick and sledge. They were embarrassed, compassionate, impatient.

'We're just quitting. Off home to supper. Tomorrow,' Bran said.

The astronomer looked from one face to another and said nothing.

Hanno said in his hoarse gentle voice, 'Come up with us, for this once, lad. It's dark night out, and likely raining; it's November now; no soul will see you if you come and sit at my hearth, for once, and eat hot food, and sleep beneath a roof and not under the heavy earth all by yourself alone!'

Guennar stepped back. It was as if a light went out, as his face went into shadow. 'No,' he said. 'They will burn out my eyes.'

'Leave him be,' said Per, and set the heavy ore-cart moving towards the shaft.

'Look where I told you,' Guennar said to Bran. 'The mine is not dead. Look with your own eyes.'

'Aye. I'll come with you and see. Good night!'

'Good night,' said the astronomer, and turned back to the side-tunnel as they went on. He carried no lamp or candle; they saw him one moment, darkness the next.

In the morning he was not there to meet them. He did not come.

Bran and Hanno sought him, idly at first, then for one whole day. They went as far down as they dared, and came at last to the entrance of the caves, and entered, calling sometimes, though in the great caverns even they, miners all their lives, dared not call aloud because of the terror of the endless echoes in the dark.

'He has gone down,' Bran said. 'Down farther. That's what he said. Go farther, you must go farther, to find the light.'

'There is no light,' Hanno whispered. 'There was never light here. Not since the world's creation.'

But Bran was an obstinate old man, with a literal and credulous mind; and Per listened to him. One day the two went to the place the astronomer had spoken of, where a great vein of hard light granite that cut down through the darker rock had been left untouched, fifty years ago, as barren stone. They re-timbered the roof of the old stope where the supports had weakened, and began to dig, not into the white rock but down, beside it; the astronomer had left a mark there, a kind of chart or symbol drawn with candle-black on the stone floor. They came on silver ore a foot down, beneath the shell of quartz; and under that – all eight of them working now – the striking picks laid bare the raw silver, the veins and branches and knots and nodes shining among broken crystals in the shattered rock, like stars and gatherings of stars, depth below depth without end, the light.

THE FIELD OF VISION

*I hardly know what to say about 'The Field of Vision'; it is a sort of
sublimated temper tantrum. An indignant Letter to the Editor. A raspberry.*

*Shelley was kicked out of Oxford – I think the story is unauthenticated,
but who cares – because he painted a sign on the end wall of a dead-end
alley:* THIS WAY TO HEAVEN. *I feel that every now and then his sign
needs repainting.*

> I saw Eternity the other night.
> Like a great Ring of pure and endless light...
> – Henry Vaughan, 1621–1695

Reports from Psyche XIV came in regularly, all routine, until
just before their return window opened. Then all at once Com-
mander Rogers radioed that they had left surface, had rejoined
the ship, and were commencing departure procedures – 82
hours 18 minutes early, Houston of course demanded explana-
tions, but Psyche's answers were erratic. The 220-second answer
lag didn't help. Psyche kept breaking contact. Once Rogers
said, 'We have got to bring her home now if we're going to do
it at all,' apparently in answer to Houston's questions, but the
next thing was Hughes asking for a reading, and then some-
thing about a dosage. The sun was noisy and reception was
very bad. The voice-transmission ceased without sign-off.

The automatic information feed from the ship continued.
Departure was normal. Normal reports came in during the
twenty-six days of flight which the astronauts spent in drugged

sleep on HKL and IV hookups. There was no medical monitor on Psyche missions. The only link with the crew was voice contact. When they did not call in on Day 2, the long tension at Houston tightened to despair.

The onboard automatics, directed by the ground crew, had just about established Psyche's re-entry course when the dead speakers suddenly said in Hughes's voice, 'Houston, can you give me readings. Optical interference here.' They tried to direct him, but the one attempt he made at a manual correction was disastrous, and took ground control five hours to compensate. They told him hands off, they'd bring in the ship. Almost immediately after that they lost voice contact again.

The great pale parachutes opened above the grey Pacific, roses slowly falling out of heaven. The speed-burnt ship screamed steam, plunging; popped back up and rocked, quiet, on the long deep swells. Ground control had done a beautiful job. She was down within a half-kilo of the *California*. Helicopters hovered, rafts assembled, the ship was stabilized, the hatch was opened. Nobody scrambled out.

They went in and brought them out.

Commander Rogers was in his flight seat, still strapped down and plugged into the HKL and IVs. He had been dead about ten days, and it was clear why the others had not opened his suit.

Captain Temski seemed physically unhurt, but dazed and bewildered. He did not speak, or respond to instructions. They had to manhandle him to haul him out of the ship, though he put up no active resistance.

Dr Hughes was in a state of collapse, but fully conscious; he appeared to be blind.

'Please . . .'

'Can you see anything?'

'Yes! Please let me have the blindfold.'

'Do you see this light I'm showing? What color is it, Dr Hughes?'

225

'All colors, white, it's too bright.'

'Will you point towards it, please?'

'It's everywhere. It's too bright.'

'The room's quite dark, Dr Hughes. Now, will you open your eyes again, please.'

'It isn't dark.'

'Mmmh. Possible supersensitivity here. All right now, how about that? Dark enough for you?'

'Make it dark!'

'No, keep your hands down, please. Take it easy. All right, we'll put the compresses back on.'

The struggling man relaxed as soon as his eyes were covered, and lay still, breathing hard. His narrow face, framed in a month's growth of dark beard, was oiled with sweat. 'I'm sorry,' he said.

'We'll try again later on when you've rested.'

'Will you open your eyes, please. The room's quite dark.'

'Why do you tell me that when it's *not* dark?'

'Dr Hughes, I can hardly make out your face; I've got the faintest red illumination on my scope – nothing else. Can you see me?'

'No! I can't see for the light!'

The doctor increased the illumination until he could see Hughes's face, the clenched jaw, the open, dazzled, frightened eyes.

'There, does that make it any darker?' he asked with the sarcasm of helplessness.

'No!' Hughes shut his eyes; he had gone dead white. 'Get dizzy,' he muttered, 'the whirling,' then he gasped for breath and began to vomit.

Hughes was unmarried and had no immediate kin. His closest friend was known to be Bernard Decelis. They had trained together; Decelis had been specialist on Psyche XII, the mission that had discovered the City of Mars, as Hughes was on XIV.

They flew Decelis to the debriefing station in Pasadena and instructed him to go in and talk with his friend. The conversation was of course recorded.

D. *Hullo, Gerry. Decelis.*

H. *Barnie?*

D. *How you doing?*

H. *Fine. You been OK?*

D. *Sure. No picnic, was it?*

H. *How's Gloria?*

D. *Fine, just fine.*

H. *She got past 'Aunt Rhody' yet?*

D. *[laughs] Oh, Christ, yeah. She can play 'Greensleeves' now. At least she calls it 'Greensleeves.'*

H. *What have they got you in this dump for?*

D. *To see you.*

H. *Wish I could return the compliment.*

D. *You will. Listen. I've been assured by three different oculists, or whatever the hell they are, opthamollywhoggers, eye-doctors here, that there is absolutely nothing wrong with your eyes. Three opthamacadamizers and a neurologist, in fact. It's a sort of chorus they have. But they sure as hell seem sure of it.*

H. *So what's wrong is my brain, evidently.*

D. *In the sense of a crossed connection, maybe.*

H. *What about Joe Temski?*

D. *I don't know. Haven't seen him.*

H. *What did they tell you about him?*

D. *They didn't have a chorus line worked out for him. Just said he's inclined to be withdrawn.*

H. *Withdrawn! Jesus, I'll say so. Like a rock is withdrawn.*

D. *Temski? That joker?*

H. *It started with him.*

D. *What did?*

H. *At the site. He stopped answering.*

D. *What happened?*

H. *Just that. He stopped answering. Stopped talking. Stopped noticing. Dwight thought it was cafard. Is that what they're still calling it?*

D. *It's mentioned as one possibility. Was there anything special happened, there at the site?*

H. *We found the room.*

D. *The room, yeah. That all came back on your reports. I've seen them, and some of the holos you brought back with you. Fantastic. What the hell is it, Gerry?*

H. *I don't know.*

D. *Is it a construct?*

H. *I don't know. What's the whole City?*

D. *It was built, made; it must have been.*

H. *How do you know, how can you tell, when you don't know what made it? Is a seashell 'made'? If you didn't know, if you didn't have any background and couldn't assume any likeness, and you looked at a seashell and a ceramic ashtray, could you tell, could you say which was 'made'? And what for? What does it mean? Or what about a ceramic seashell? Or a paper-wasp's nest? Or a geode?*

D. *Yeah, OK. But what about those things, that . . . arrangement that you call 'pigeonholes' in the reports? I saw the holos. What did you make of them?*

H. *What did you make of them?*

D. *I don't know. They're weird. I thought of running the spatial arrangements through a computer, looking for meaningful pattern . . . You don't think much of that.*

H. *No. Fine. Only what are you going to program for 'meaning'?*

D. *Mathematical relationships. Any kind of geometrical pattern, regularity, code. I don't know. What was the place like, Gerry?*

H. *I don't know.*

D. *You were in there a lot?*

H. *All the time, after we found it.*

D. *That's where you noticed this kind of eye trouble you've got? How did it start?*

H. *Things going out of focus. Like eye strain. It was worse outside the room. Came on over several days. I could still make things out*

all right when we were taking the ML up to the ship. But getting worse. There'd be these flashes of light, left my depth perception all screwed up, I'd get dizzy. Dwight and I set up the course, one or the other of us was functioning most of the time. But he was getting kind of wild. Didn't want to use the radio, wouldn't touch the onboard computer.

D. *What was ... wrong with him?*

H. *I don't know. When I told him about my eyes he said he'd been having something like shaking fits. I said we'd better get the hell up to the ship while we could. He said OK, because Joe was really beginning to not function. Before we even launched he started having some kind of seizures, like epilepsy – Dwight, I mean. When he came out of one he was shaky, but he seemed rational. He took us up OK, but as soon as we docked in he went into another fit, and they kept getting longer. He started hallucinating in between them. I gave him some tranquillizers and strapped him in; it was wearing him out. When I took the sleep, I don't know, he could have been dead already then.*

D. *No, he died in the sleep. About ten days out from Earth.*

H. *They didn't tell me that.*

D. *There wasn't anything you could have done, Gerry.*

H. *I don't know. Those attacks he had, they were like overloads Like all his fuses blew. Burned him out. He talked, while he was in them. Sort of in bursts, like barking – as if he was trying to say a whole sentence at once. Epileptics don't talk, do they, when they're having a seizure?*

D. *I don't know. Epilepsy's so well controlled now you don't hear much about it. They catch the tendency, and cure it first. If Rogers had had the tendency ...*

H. *Yeah. He never would have been in the program. Christ, he'd had six months in space.*

D. *What had you had – six days?*

H. *Like you. One Moon hop.*

D. *It isn't that, then. Do you think ...*

H. *What?*

D. *Some kind of virus?*

H. *Space plague? Martian fever? Mysterious ancient spores madden astronauts?*

D. *All right, it sounds dumb. But look, the room had been sealed. And it does sound like all of you—*

H. *Dwight gets a cortical overcharge, Joe goes catatonic, I start seeing things. What's the connection?*

D. *Nervous system.*

H. *Why different symptoms in each of us?*

D. *Well, drugs affect people differently—*

H. *Do you think we found some kind of God damned Martian psychogenic mushrooms in there? There isn't anything there, it's dead, like all the rest of Mars. You know, you've been there! There aren't any God damned germs or viruses, there's no life there, no life.*

D. *But there may have been—*

H. *What makes you think so?*

D. *The room you found. The City we found.*

H. *City! For Christ's sake, Barnie, you talk like some damned pop journalist, you know damned well the whole thing is a set of mud concretions for all we can tell. There's no way to tell. It's too old, conditions are too different, we have no context. We don't understand, we can't understand, it's something the human mind is outside of. Cities, rooms, all that – we're just analogizing, trying to make sense in our terms. But it's not in our terms. There is no sense. I can see that now. That's the only thing I can see!*

D. *See what, Gerry?*

H. *What I see when I open my eyes!*

D. *What?*

H. *Everything that isn't there and doesn't make sense. Oh – I—*

D. *Here, come on. Take it easy. Look, it'll be OK. It's going to be OK, Gerry, you'll be OK.*

H. *[unclear] light, and the [unclear] try to see what I touch and I can't, I don't understand and I can't [unclear]*

D. *Hang on. I'm right here. Take it easy, old man.*

Hughes, who had entered the space program from astrophysics, came with a very good record, in fact a brilliant one. This troubled many of his military superiors, to whom high intelligence was a code word for instability and insubordination. His performance had been solid and his behavior irreproachable; but now it was frequently recalled that he was, after all, an intellectual.

Temski was harder to explain. He was a crack test pilot, an Air Force captain, and a baseball fan, but now his behavior was even more aberrant than Hughes's.

All Temski did was sit. He was capable of looking after himself, and did so. That is, when he was hungry and food was present, he ate some with his fingers; when he had to relieve himself, he went to a corner and did so; when he was sleepy, he lay down on the floor and slept. The rest of the time he sat. He was in good physical condition and quite calm. Nothing said to him produced the slightest reaction, nor did he take any interest in anything that went on. His wife was brought in to see him in hopes of producing a response. She was taken away weeping after five minutes.

Since Temski wouldn't respond, and Rogers, being dead, couldn't respond, it was quite natural to look upon Hughes as being, somehow, responsible.

There was nothing wrong with him except a case of something like hysterical blindness, so it was to be expected that he should answer questions rationally and explain precisely what had happened. This, however, he could not, or would not, do.

A psychiatric consultant was brought in, a distinguished New York doctor called Shapir. He was requested to work with both Temski and Hughes. It was of course unthinkable to admit that the mission had been a failure (the word 'disaster' was not even mentioned), but a couple of rumors had leaked out to the press despite all security precautions. Irresponsible journalists demanded to know why the crew of Psyche XIV was being held incommunicado, and claimed the 'right' of the American people to 'know,' etc. It had been necessary to issue a statement

concerning a new health test being run on astronauts who had spent over fifteen days in space, due to Commander Rogers's unexpected and tragic death from heart failure, and to have a whole new series of articles written for the papers concerning plans for a 'Little America' dome city on Mars, to maintain a positive attitude in the public. The real people of course knew that the rest of the Psyche program was in jeopardy; and they instructed Dr Shapir to diagnose and cure the astronauts with all deliberate speed.

Shapir talked with Hughes for half an hour about the food in the hospital, Cal Tech, and the latest Chinese report on their Alpha Centauri probe, all very relaxed and trivial. Then he said, 'What is it you see, when you open your eyes?'

Hughes, who was up and dressed now, sat silent for a while. Opaque goggles covered his eyes entirely, giving him the arrogant, staring look of people who affect dark glasses. 'Nobody's asked that,' he said.

'Didn't the oculists?'

'Yes, I guess Kray did. Early on. Before they decided I was a mental case.'

'What did you tell him?'

'It's hard to describe. The point is, it's indescribable. At first it was things going out of focus, going transparent, going away. Then the light. Too much light. Like overexposing a film, bleaching everything out. But with that, a kind of whirling. Changing positions and relationships, changing perspectives, constant transformation. It made me get dizzy. My eyes kept sending signals to my inner ears, I guess. Like that inner-ear disease, only in reverse. Doesn't it foul up your spatial orientation?'

'Ménière's syndrome, I think it's called, yes, it does. Especially on stairs and slopes.'

'It's as if I was looking from a great height, or... up at a great height...'

'Heights ever worry you?'

'Hell no. They don't even mean anything to me. What's up and down, in space? No, see, I'm not giving you the picture.

232

There is no picture. I've been trying to look more, to learn to ... how to see ... it's not much good.'

There was a pause. 'That takes courage,' said Shapir.

'What do you mean?' the astronaut said sharply.

'Well ... To have the sensory input which is most important to the conscious mind – sight – reporting non-existent and incomprehensible things, in flagrant contradiction with all other sensory input – your touch, your hearing, your sense of balance, and so on – to have that going on, every time you try to open your eyes, and not only to live with it but to attempt to investigate it ... It doesn't sound easy.'

'So mostly I keep my eyes shut,' Hughes said, dour. 'Like a damned see-no-evil monkey.'

'When you do have your eyes open, and you look towards some object you know is there – your own hand, for instance – what do you see?'

' "A blooming, buzzing confusion." '

'William James,' Shapir said with satisfaction. 'What was he talking about – how a baby perceives the world, eh?' He had a pleasant voice with a mild, glancing quality to it, non-percussive; one could not imagine him scolding or yelling. He nodded several times, thinking out the implications of what Hughes had said. 'To learn how to see, you said. To learn. That's how you feel about it?'

Hughes hesitated, then said with a sudden, marked increase of trust, 'I have to. What else can I do? Apparently I'm never going to be able to – to see the way I used to, the way other people do, again. But I still do *see*. Only I don't understand what I see, it doesn't make sense. There are no outlines, no distinctions, even between nearer and farther. There *is* something there – only I can't say that, because there aren't any *things*. No forms. Instead of forms, I see transformations – transfigurations. Does that make any sense at all?'

'I think it does,' Shapir said, 'only it's enormously difficult to put a direct experience into words. And when the experience is new, unique, overwhelming ...'

'And irrational. That's it.' Hughes spoke now with real gratitude. 'If only I could show it to you,' he said wistfully.

The two astronauts were being kept on the tenth floor of a big military hospital in Maryland now. They were not permitted to leave that floor, and anyone who visited it still spent ten days in quarantine before he rejoined the outer world: the Martian plague theory was currently on top. At Shapir's insistence, Hughes was allowed to go up to the roof garden of the hospital (after which the elevator was elaborately sterilized and roped off for three days).

They demanded that Hughes wear a surgical mask; and Shapir had asked him not to wear his goggles. Docile, he went up the elevator with his mouth and nose covered, his eyes uncovered, but tightly shut.

The change from the dusk of the elevator to the hot smoggy sunlight of July on the open roof did not, as far as Shapir could see, affect those shut eyes. Hughes did not screw them tighter against the flooding light, though he raised his face to it as if he felt the heat pleasant on his skin, and took a deep breath through the binding gauze.

'I haven't been outside since March,' he said.

It was true, of course. He had been in a spacesuit or in a hospital room, breathing canned or conditioned air.

'Have you got your compass bearings?' Shapir asked.

'Not the faintest. It makes me feel blinder, being outdoors. Afraid to walk off the edge.' Hughes had refused assistance coming through the corridors and in the elevator, feeling his way adeptly with his hands, and now despite his joke about falling off he began to explore the roof garden. He was exhilarated: an active man released from long confinement. Shapir watched him, brooding. The low furniture was a hazard to him but he learned at once how to feel for it; he had tactile intelligence; there was grace in his movements, even as he blundered in blindness.

'Will you open your eyes?' Shapir said in his glancing, reluctant voice.

234

Hughes stopped. 'All right,' he said; but he turned towards Shapir, and his right hand came up gropingly. Shapir came forward and let that hand take his arm.

The grip of it tightened, as Hughes opened his eyes. Then Hughes let go, and took a step away, stretching out both his arms. A cry broke from him. He reached forward and upward, his head back, his eyes wide open, staring at the empty sky. 'Oh, my God!' he whispered, and dropped, like a man hit by a sledgehammer.

Psychiatric counselling session, 18 July. S. Shapir, Geraint Hughes.

S. Hello. Sidney... I won't stay long. Listen, that wasn't such a bright idea of mine. The roof. I'm sorry. I had no idea. But no right, either... Would you rather I left?

H. No.

S. All right... I'm getting stir-crazy myself. Need a good walk. I walk a good deal, usually. About two miles to my office and the same back. Then I add detours. Whatever they say, New York is a beautiful town to walk in. If you know how to pick your route. Listen, I have a queer story about Joe Temski. Not a story, just a queer fact, actually. Did you know that they have written on his record that he is 'functionally deaf'?

H. Deaf?

S. Yes, deaf. Well, you know, I began to wonder. I go in and talk to Joe, you know, touch him, try to make eye contact, any kind of contact, to get through. No go. I've had patients tell me in so many words, 'I can't hear you.' A metaphor. But what if it isn't a metaphor? It happens sometimes with little kids, they're called retarded and it turns out they've got thirty, sixty, eighty percent hearing dysfunction. Well, maybe Joe really can't hear me. Just like: you can't see me.

H. [pause of forty seconds] Do you mean he's hearing things? Listening?

S. It's possible.

H. [pause of twenty seconds] You can't shut your ears.

235

S. That's what I thought, too. It could be rough, couldn't it? Well, what I thought was, what about trying to shut them for him? Put earplugs in his ears.

H. He still wouldn't be able to hear you.

S. No, but he wouldn't be distracted. If you had to watch your light show all the time, you wouldn't be able to pay much attention to me or anything else, right? Maybe it's like that with Joe. Maybe there's this noise drowning out everything else for him.

H. [pause of twenty seconds] It would be more than noise.

S. I don't suppose you want to talk about . . . on the roof . . . No, all right.

H. You'd like to know what I saw, wouldn't you?

S. Sure I would. But in your own time.

H. Yeah, I've got so much else to do here besides talk to you. All the books I can read and the beautiful women I can look at. You know damned well I'll tell you eventually, because I haven't got anybody else to talk to.

S. Oh, hell, Geraint. [pause of ten seconds]

H. Shit. I'm sorry, Sidney. If I didn't have you to talk to, I'd have cracked completely. I know that. You're very patient with me.

S. Whatever you saw, up there, disturbs you. That's one reason why I want to know what it was. But what the hell, if you can handle it alone, do. That's the idea, after all. My curiosity is my problem, not yours! Listen. Let's forget talking. Let me read you this article in Science. Your Colonel Wood gave it to me, said you might be interested. I was. It's on what they found inside the Argentinian meteorite. The authors are suggesting we go comb the Meteor Belt for remnants of a trans-stellar fleet that came to grief in our solar system about six hundred million years ago. They would have landed on Mars first, of course. Are these guys nuts?

H. I don't know. Read the article.

Temski slept heavily, and it was easy for Shapir to insert ordinary wax plugs like those insomniacs use into his ears while he was asleep. When Temski woke he did nothing unusual at first. He sat up, yawned, stretched, scratched, looked lazily

around to see if anything to eat was handy, in that serene way which Shapir privately felt was altogether unlike any psychotic behavior he had ever seen, and in fact unlike any human behavior he had ever seen. Temski reminded him of a healthy, poised, contented, tame animal. Not a chimpanzee; something milder, more contemplative, an orang, maybe.

But the orang began to feel uncomfortable.

Temski looked around, left and right, nervous. Perhaps he was not looking but moving his head trying to find the vanished sounds. The lost chord, Shapir thought. Temski grew more and more disturbed and alert. He got up, still turning his head restlessly. He looked across the room. For the first time in seventeen days of daily contact, he saw Shapir.

His handsome face was now contorted with anxiety or bewilderment.

'Where,' he said, 'where—'

His hands, groping at his ears to find the cause of silence, found the earplugs and removed one. That was enough. 'Ah,' he said, and stood still. His eyes were still directed towards Shapir, but he did not see him. His face relaxed.

Later attempts were more successful. Though bewildered at first, Temski was cooperative while artificially deafened, and responded readily to Shapir's attempts to communicate with him by touch, by sign, and finally by writing. After the fifth such session, Temski consented to longer sessions involving the use of a drug which would deaden his auditory nerve endings for about five hours at a time.

During the second of these long periods he asked to see Hughes. Shapir had already been instructed to let the two astronauts talk together if possible; there was a feeling that this might elicit more information, if they talked freely together. It was necessary for Hughes to write, since Temski was artificially deafened; as he knew touch typing he carried on his part of the dialogue on a portable typewriter. Not all the material found in the wastebasket, however, could be successfully collated in to the tape of Temski's spoken conversation. The two men mostly

discussed the return journey and Commander Rogers's illness and death, which Temski could not recall; Hughes described all this as he had done before without new information. They did not talk about the 'room' (Site D) or their respective disabilities, except as follows:

T. *It's not inside, is it?*
H. *If it was, earplugs wd improve yr reception*
T. *It's real, then.*
H. *Hell yes*
T. *See, when they first stuck those flags in my ears, when I woke up and there was this silence, I was really spooked. It took me a long time to come back from where I'd been. And I didn't much want to come back. But when Shapir began telling me how long it had been, and I realized this was Earth, you know, that's what spooked me – I thought, maybe all this has been some sort of, like, hallucination. You know. Jesus, have I been off my chump? That scared me. Like I was two different people. But I began to put it together, to see that it wasn't a split, but a . . .*
H. *Change*
T. *Exactly, it changed me, it had changed me. It's real. Because when I* can *hear, that's what I hear. And when you can see, that's what you see. Right? In other words, it is real. We have to be artificially blinded and made deaf to* not *hear it and see it. That's it, isn't it?*
[*Hughes's typed responses for the following section were not identifiable in the wastebasket material.*]
H. *.*
T. *Oh, no. Beautiful. It took me a long time, at least I know now it was a long time, to begin to get it. At first it didn't make any sense, Jesus, it scared the balls off me at first. You or Dwight would say something, and there'd be this kind of chords all around your voice, like rainbows around a prism so you can't even see the prism – yeah, that's what it's like for you, isn't it? It's the same, only this is with hearing, it's like everything turns into this music, only it isn't music, it's . . . At first like I said I didn't know how to hear it. I thought it was something wrong with my suit radio! Jesus! [laughs]*

I couldn't follow the patterns, you know, the modulations, like, the transformations. It was all so different. But you learn. The more you listen the more you hear. I wish you could hear it. You know, you tell me it's two months sinçe we left Mars, and so on, and shit, I believe you, but it doesn't matter. It really doesn't matter – does it, Gerry?

H.

T. *I wish I could see it, the way you do. It must be tremendous. But I'll tell you, I'm glad they pull me out of it like this, every day now. I think it's meant to be that way. I was kind of, I don't know, swamped, overwhelmed, it's too much. We're not built right, not quite strong enough, maybe. At least at first. Can't take it all at once. What I'd like to try to do while I'm out of touch is try to write some of it down.*

H.

T. *No, I don't. But it wouldn't have to be music. See, it isn't music, that's just like a way of describing it because it's beautiful. I think I could get it into words just as well. Maybe better. To say what it means.*

H.

T. *Afraid of what?*

Bernard Decelis and his wife called Hughes every couple of days on the telephone, though they were prevented by the quarantine from coming to see him. On the 27th of July Hughes and Decelis had a significant conversation concerning the so-called room, site D of the Psyche XIV survey. Decelis said, 'If I don't get on the Sixteen team and *see* that damned place, I'll flip.'

'Seeing is believing,' Hughes remarked. He was not as excitable as he had been earlier, tending to be terse and rather bitter.

'Listen, Gerry. Was there ever machinery in those pigeon-holes?'

'No.'

'Hah! There's a definite answer! I thought you wouldn't

assert anything about Site D except its incomprehensibility to the human mind. You softening up?'

'No. Learning.'

'Learning what?'

'How to see.'

After a pause Decelis asked cautiously, 'See what?'

'Site D. Since it's all I can see.'

'You mean, that's what you – when your eyes are open—'

'No.' Hughes spoke wearily and with reluctance. 'It's more complex than that. I don't see Site D. I see . . . the world in the light cast by Site D . . . A new light. The man you ought to ask is Joe Temski. Or, listen, did you ever run the pigeonholes through Algie, like you said?'

'I had trouble setting up the program.'

'I'll bet you did,' Hughes said with a short laugh. 'Send the stuff on up here. I'll set it up. Blindfolded.'

Temski came into Hughes's room, radiant. 'Gerry,' he said, 'I've got it.'

'Got what?'

'I've got it together. I heard you. No, I wasn't lip-reading. Say something with your back turned. Go on !'

'Ptomaine poisoning.'

' "Ptomaine poisoning." – OK? See, I'm hearing you. But I haven't lost the music. I've got it all together!'

Blue-eyed and fair, Temski was ordinarily a handsome man; now he was magnificent. Hughes could not see him (though the spy camera in the ventilator grille could and did), but he heard the vibration of his voice, and was moved, and frightened.

'Take off your blinkers, Gerry,' the gentle, vibrant voice said.

Hughes shook his head.

'You can't sit in the dark inside yourself forever. Come out. You can't choose blindness, Gerry.'

'Why can't I?'

'Not after you've seen the light.'

'What light?'

'The light, the word, the truth we have been taught to per-
ceive and to know,' Temski said, with the gentleness of utter
certainty, and a warmth in his voice, a warmth like sunlight.
 'Get out,' Hughes said. 'Get out, Temski!'

Twelve weeks had passed since Psyche XIV splashdown.
Nobody on the debriefing staff had come down with any symp-
toms more alarming than boredom. Hughes was no worse,
and Temski was now completely recovered. It could be safely
assumed that whatever had affected the crew of Psyche XIV, it
had not been an infection vectored by a virus, spore, bacterium,
or other physical agent. The hypothesis accepted tentatively
and with various reservations by the majority, including Dr
Shapir, was that something in the arrangement of the elements
constituting the 'room,' Site D, had, during their prolonged
and intense study of the site, caused a degree of brain-wave
disruption in all three men, analogous to the brain-function
disturbance caused by strobe lights at certain frequencies,
etc. Precisely what elements of the 'room' were involved was
not yet known, though the holographs were being examined
intensively by experts. Psyche XV was to make a still more
thorough investigation of the site, taking due precautions to
protect and monitor the astronauts.
 These suspect elements of Site D were so numerous and so
intricately interrelated that it was very hard for a single mind to
attempt to arrange or order them. Some Martianologists were
sure the peculiar properties of the 'room' were only a geological
accident, and that all the 'room' had to 'tell' us was the kind of
information furnished so concisely and beautifully by the strata
of rocks, the rings of a tree, the lines of a spectrum. Others
were as convinced that intelligent beings had built the City, and
that in studying it we might learn something of their nature
and the way their minds worked – those unimaginable minds of
six hundred million years ago (for the radioactive-decay dating
of the site was absolutely definite now). The job of doing so,
however, was daunting. T. A. Newman of the Smithsonian

Institution put it well: 'Archaeologists are used to getting a lot of information out of very simple things-potsherds, bits of flint, a wall here, a grave there. But what if all we had of an ancient civilization was a very complicated thing, complicated in more than a technological sense – let's say, one copy of Shakespeare's *Hamlet*. Now let's assume that the achaeologists who find this copy of *Hamlet* are not humanoid, don't have books, don't have plays, don't speak, write, or think at all as we do. What are they going to make of that little physical artifact, the evident complexity and purposefulness of it, the repetition of certain elements and the non-repetition of others, the semi-regularity of line lengths, and so on? How are they going to read *Hamlet?*'

To those who accepted the '*Hamlet* theory,' the obvious first step was to employ computers, and a number of them had been set to work analyzing the various elements of Site D: the spacing, size, depth, and configurations of the 'pigeonholes,' the proportions of the first, middle, and third 'subchambers,' the extraordinary acoustical properties of the 'room' as a whole, and so on. None of these programs had as yet produced any sure evidence of conscious planning or rational pattern; none, that is, except the program set up by Decelis and Hughes on NASA's new Algebraic V, which had certainly got results, though they could not be called rational. Indeed, that print-out had given a shudder to the NASA brass, and a good laugh to those few scientists to whom Decelis had shown it before it was suppressed as being probably a fraud and certainly an embarrassment. The entire print-out read as follows:

```
RUN
PIGEONHOLES SITE D MARS SECTOR NINE
DECELIS HUGHES

GOD

GOOD GOD GOD GOOD YOU ARE GOD

RESET
```

```
RESET TOTALITY COMPREHENSION NONSENSE
PERCEIVE NONSENSE NO SENSE REAL GOOD GOD

PERCEIVE RECEIVE DIRECTIONS DIRECTION

PROCEED INFORM UNINFORMED

GOD GOD GOD GOD GOD GOD

END RUN
```

Shapir came in to find Hughes lying on his bed, as he now did most of the time, wearing his black goggles. He looked white and ill.

'I think you've been overdoing it.'

Hughes did not answer.

Shapir sat down. 'They're sending me back to New York,' he said presently.

Hughes did not answer.

'Temski's been released, you know. He's on his way to Florida now. With his wife. I can't find out what they plan for you. I asked . . .' After a long pause he completed the sentence. 'I asked for another two weeks here with you. No go.'

'It's all right,' Hughes said.

'I want to keep in touch with you, Geraint. Obviously we can't write letters. But there's the phone. And tapes; I'm leaving a cassette recorder here with you. When you want to talk, please call me. If you can't get me, talk to the recorder. It's not the same, but—'

'You're a very good man, Sidney,' Hughes said gently. 'I wish . . .' After a minute he sat up. He reached up to his face and took off the black goggles. They fitted so closely around his eye sockets that it took him a little while to get them off. When they were off he lowered his hands, and looked across the room, directly at Shapir. His eyes, the pupils enlarged by long privation of light, were almost as dark as the goggles.

'I see you,' he said. 'Hide and seek. I spy. You're It. Do you want to know what I see?'

'Yes,' Shapir said softly.

'A blot. A shadow. An incompleteness, a rudiment, an obstruction. Something completely unimportant. You see, it doesn't do any *good* to be a good man, even...'

'And when you look at yourself?'

'The same. Just the same. A hindrance, a triviality. A blot on the field of vision.'

'The field of vision. What is the field of vision?'

'What do you think?' Hughes said, very quietly and wearily. 'What is true vision of? Reality, of course. I have been re-programmed to perceive reality, to see the truth. I see God.' He sank his face into his hands, covering his eyes. 'I was a thinking man,' he said. 'I tried to be a rational man. But what good's reason, when you can *see* the truth? Seeing is believing...' He looked up again at Shapir, his dark eyes both piercing and unseeing. 'If you want a real explanation, go ask Joe Temski. He's keeping quiet now; he's biding his time. But he's the one who can tell you. And he will, when his time comes. He can translate what he hears – translate it into words. It's harder to do with visual perceptions. Mystics have always had trouble putting their visions into words; except the ones that got the Word, that heard the Voice. They usually got right up and acted, didn't they? Temski will act. But I will not. I refuse. I will not preach. I will not be a missionary.'

'A missionary?'

'Don't you see? Don't you see that's what the "room" is? A training center, a briefing room, a—'

'A religious center? A church?'

'Well, in a way. A place where you are taught to see God, and hear God, and know God. And love God. A conversion center. A place where you're converted! And then you want to go out and preach the knowledge of God to the others – to the heathen. Because now you know how blind they are, and how easy it is to see. No, not just a church; a mission. The Mission. And you learn the Mission, and you come out of it with the Mission. They weren't explorers. They were missionaries,

244

bearing the truth, bringing it to the other races and the future races, all the poor damned heathens living in the outer darkness. They knew the answer, and they wanted us all to know the answer. Nothing else matters, once you've learned the answer. It doesn't matter if you're a good man or a bad one, if I'm an intelligent man or a fool. Nothing about us matters except that we are trivial vehicles of the great truth. The earth doesn't matter, the stars don't matter, death doesn't matter, nothing is anything. Only God is.'

'An alien god?'

'Not a god. God – the one true God, immanent in all things. Everywhere, forever. I have learned to see God. All I have to do is open my eyes, and I see the Face of God. And I'd give all my life just to see one human face again, to see a tree, just a tree, a chair – a plain wooden chair, ordinary – They can keep their God, they can keep their Light. I want the world back. I want questions, not the answer. I want my own life back, and my own death!'

On the recommendation of the Army psychiatrist who took over the case of Geraint Hughes after Shapir was dismissed, Hughes was moved to a military hospital for the insane. As he was generally a quiet and cooperative patient he was not kept under strict supervision, and after eleven months of confinement he unfortunately carried out a successful suicide attempt, slashing his wrists with a spoon-handle which he had stolen from the mess hall and sharpened by rubbing against the bed frame. It is an interesting fact that he killed himself on the day the Psyche XV Mission started back to Earth from Mars, bringing the documents and records which, as interpreted by the First Apostle, now form the first chapters of the Revelation of the Ancients, the sacred texts of the holy and universal Church of God, bringer of light to the heathen, sole vehicle of the One Eternal Truth.

O fools (said I) thus to prefer dark night
 Before true light...
But as I did their madness so discuss
 One whisper'd thus,
This Ring the Bride-groome did for none provide
 But for his bride.

DIRECTION OF THE ROAD

The tree stands just south of the McMinnville bypass on Oregon State Highway 18. It lost a major limb last year, but still looks grand. We drive past it several times a year, and it has never failed to uphold Relativity with dignity and the skill of long practice.

They did not used to be so demanding. They never hurried us into anything more than a gallop, and that was rare; most of the time it was just a jigjog foot-pace. And when one of them was on his own feet, it was a real pleasure to approach him. There was time to accomplish the entire act with style. There he'd be, working his legs and arms the way they do, usually looking at the road, but often aside at the fields, or straight at me: and I'd approach him steadily but quite slowly, growing larger all the time, synchronizing the rate of approach and the rate of growth perfectly, so that at the very moment that I'd finished enlarging from a tiny speck to my full size – sixty feet in those days – I was abreast of him and hung above him, loomed, towered, overshadowed him. Yet he would show no fear. Not even the children were afraid of me, though often they kept their eyes on me as I passed by and started to diminish.

Sometimes on a hot afternoon one of the adults would stop me right there at our meeting-place, and lie down with his back against mine for an hour or more. I didn't mind in the least. I have an excellent hill, good sun, good wind, good view; why should I mind standing still for an hour or an afternoon? It's only a relative stillness, after all. One need only look at

the sun to realize how fast one is going; and then, one grows continually – especially in summer. In any case I was touched by the way they would entrust themselves to me, letting me lean against their little warm backs, and falling sound asleep there between my feet. I liked them. They have seldom lent us Grace as do the birds; but I really preferred them to squirrels.

In those days the horses used to work for them, and that too was enjoyable from my point of view. I particularly liked the canter, and got quite proficient at it. The surging and rhythmical motion accompanied shrinking and growing with a swaying and swooping, almost an illusion of flight. The gallop was less pleasant. It was jerky, pounding: one felt tossed about like a sapling in a gale. And then, the slow approach and growth, the moment of looming-over, and the slow retreat and diminishing, all that was lost during the gallop. One had to hurl oneself into it, cloppety-cloppety-cloppety! and the man usually too busy riding, and the horse too busy running, even to look up. But then, it didn't happen often. A horse is mortal, after all, and like all the loose creatures grows tired easily; so they didn't tire their horses unless there was urgent need. And they seemed not to have so many urgent needs, in those days.

It's been a long time since I had a gallop, and to tell the truth I shouldn't mind having one. There was something invigorating about it, after all.

I remember the first motorcar I saw. Like most of us, I took it for a mortal, some kind of loose creature new to me. I was a bit startled, for after a hundred and thirty-two years I thought I knew all the local fauna. But a new thing is always interesting, in its trivial fashion, so I observed this one with attention. I approached it at a fair speed, about the rate of a canter, but in a new gait, suitable to the ungainly looks of the thing: an uncomfortable, bouncing, rolling, choking, jerking gait. Within two minutes, before I'd grown a foot tall, I knew it was no mortal creature, bound or loose or free. It was a making, like the carts the horses got hitched to. I thought it so very ill-made that I didn't expect it to return, once it gasped over the West

Hill, and I heartily hoped it never would, for I disliked that jerking bounce.

But the thing took to a regular schedule, and so, perforce, did I. Daily at four I had to approach it, twitching and stuttering out of the West, and enlarge, loom-over, and diminish. Then at five back I had to come, poppeting along like a young jackrabbit for all my sixty feet, jigging and jouncing out of the East, until at last I got clear out of sight of the wretched little monster and could relax and loosen my limbs to the evening wind. There were always two of them inside the machine: a young male holding the wheel, and behind him an old female wrapped in rugs, glowering. If they ever said anything to each other I never heard it. In those days I overheard a good many conversations on the road, but not from that machine. The top of it was open, but it made so much noise that it overrode all voices, even the voice of the song-sparrow I had with me that year. The noise was almost as vile as the jouncing.

I am of a family of rigid principle and considerable self-respect. The Quercian motto is 'Break but bend not,' and I have always tried to uphold it. It was not only personal vanity, but family pride, you see, that was offended when I was forced to jounce and bounce in this fashion by a mere making.

The apple trees in the orchard at the foot of the hill did not seem to mind; but then, apples are tame. Their genes have been tampered with for centuries. Besides, they are herd creatures; no orchard tree can really form an opinion of its own.

I kept my own opinion to myself.

But I was very pleased when the motorcar ceased to plague us. All month went by without it, and all month I walked at men and trotted at horses most willingly, and even bobbed for a baby on its mother's arm, trying hard though unsuccessfully to keep in focus.

Next month, however – September it was, for the swallows had left a few days earlier – another of the machines appeared, a new one, suddenly dragging me and the road and our hill, the orchard, the fields, the farmhouse roof, all jigging and jouncing

and racketing along from East to West; I went faster than a gallop, faster than I had ever gone before. I had scarcely time to loom, before I had to shrink right down again.

And the next day there came a different one.

Yearly then, weekly, daily, they became commoner. They became a major feature of the local Order of Things. The road was dug up and re-metalled, widened, finished off very smooth and nasty, like a slug's trail, with no ruts, pools, rocks, flowers, or shadows on it. There used to be a lot of little loose creatures on the road, grasshoppers, ants, toads, mice, foxes, and so on, most of them too small to move for, since they couldn't really see one. Now the wise creatures took to avoiding the road, and the unwise ones got squashed. I have seen all too many rabbits die in that fashion, right at my feet. I am thankful that I am an oak, and that though I may be wind-broken or uprooted, hewn or sawn, at least I cannot, under any circumstances, be squashed.

With the presence of many motorcars on the road at once, a new level of skill was required of me. As a mere seedling, as soon as I got my head above the weeds, I had learned the basic trick of going two directions at once. I learned it without thinking about it, under the simple pressure of circumstances on the first occasion that I saw a walker in the East and a horseman facing him in the West. I had to go two directions at once, and I did so. It's something we trees master without real effort, I suppose. I was nervous, but I succeeded in passing the rider and then shrinking away from him while at the same time I was still jigjogging towards the walker, and indeed passed him (no looming, back in those days!) only when I had got quite out of sight of the rider. I was proud of myself, being very young, that first time I did it; but it sounds more difficult than it really is. Since those days of course I had done it innumerable times, and thought nothing about it; I could do it in my sleep. But have you ever considered the feat accomplished, the skill involved, when a tree enlarges, simultaneously yet at slightly different rates and in slightly different manners, for each one

of forty motorcar drivers facing two opposite directions, while at the same time diminishing for forty more who have got their backs to it, meanwhile remembering to loom over each single one at the right moment: and to do this minute after minute, hour after hour, from daybreak till nightfall or long after?

For my road had become a busy one; it worked all day long under almost continual traffic. It worked, and I worked. I did not jounce and bounce so much any more, but I had to run faster and faster: to grow enormously, to loom in a split second, to shrink to nothing, all in a hurry, without time to enjoy the action, and without rest: over and over and over.

Very few of the drivers bothered to look at me, not even a seeing glance. They seemed, indeed, not to see any more. They merely stared ahead. They seemed to believe that they were 'going somewhere.' Little mirrors were affixed to the front of their cars, at which they glanced to see where they had been; then they stared ahead again. I had thought that only beetles had this delusion of Progress. Beetles are always rushing about, and never looking up. I had always had a pretty low opinion of beetles. But at least they let me be.

I confess that sometimes, in the blessed nights of darkness with no moon to silver my crown and no stars occluding with my branches, when I could rest, I would think seriously of escaping my obligation to the general Order of Things: of *failing to move.* No, not seriously. Half-seriously. It was mere weariness. If even a silly, three-year-old, female pussy willow at the foot of the hill accepted her responsibility, and jounced and rolled and accelerated and grew and shrank for each motorcar on the road, was I, an oak, to shirk? Noblesse oblige, and I trust I have never dropped an acorn that did not know its duty.

For fifty or sixty years, then, I have upheld the Order of Things, and have done my share in supporting the human creatures' illusion that they are 'going somewhere.' And I am not unwilling to do so. But a truly terrible thing has occurred, which I wish to protest.

I do not mind going two directions at once; I do not mind

growing and shrinking simultaneously; I do not mind moving, even at the disagreeable rate of sixty or seventy miles an hour. I am ready to go on doing all these things until I am felled or bulldozed. They're my job. But I do object, passionately, to being made eternal.

Eternity is none of my business. I am an oak, no more, no less. I have my duty, and I do it; I have my pleasures, and enjoy them, though they are fewer, since the birds are fewer, and the wind's foul. But, long-lived though I may be, impermanence is my right. Mortality is my privilege. And it has been taken from me.

It was taken from me on a rainy evening in March last year.

Fits and bursts of cars, as usual, filled the rapidly moving road in both directions. I was so busy hurtling along, enlarging, looming, diminishing, and the light was failing so fast, that I scarcely noticed what was happening until it happened. One of the drivers of one of the cars evidently felt that his need to 'go somewhere' was exceptionally urgent, and so attempted to place his car in front of the car in front of it. This maneuver involves a temporary slanting of the Direction of the Road and a displacement onto the far side, the side which normally runs the other direction (and may I say that I admire the road very highly for its skill in executing such maneuvers, which must be difficult for an unliving creature, a mere making). Another car, however, happened to be quite near the urgent one, and facing it, as it changed sides; and the road could not do anything about it, being already overcrowded. To avoid impact with the facing car, the urgent car totally violated the Direction of the Road, swinging it round to North-South in its own terms, and so forcing me to leap directly at it. I had no choice. I had to move, and move fast – eighty-five miles an hour. I leapt: I loomed enormous, larger than I have ever loomed before. And then I hit the car.

I lost a considerable piece of bark, and, what's more serious, a fair bit of cambium layer; but as I was seventy-two feet tall and about nine feet in girth at the point of impact, no real

harm was done. My branches trembled with the shock enough that a last-year's robin's nest was dislodged and fell; and I was so shaken that I groaned. It is the only time in my life that I have ever said anything out loud.

The motorcar screamed horribly. It was smashed by my blow, squashed, in fact. Its hinder parts were not much affected, but the forequarters knotted up and knurled together like an old root, and little bright bits of it flew all about and lay like brittle rain.

The driver had no time to say anything; I killed him instantly.

It is not this that I protest. I had to kill him. I had no choice, and therefore have no regret. What I protest, what I cannot endure, is this: as I leapt at him, he saw me. He looked up at last. He saw me as I have never been seen before, not even by a child, not even in the days when people looked at things. He saw me whole, and saw nothing else – then, or ever.

He saw me under the aspect of eternity. He confused me with eternity. And because he died in that moment of false vision, because it can never change, I am caught in it, eternally.

This is unendurable. I cannot uphold such an illusion. If the human creatures will not understand Relativity, very well; but they must understand Relatedness.

If it is necessary to the Order of Things, I will kill drivers of cars, though killing is not a duty usually required of oaks. But it is unjust to require me to play the part, not of the killer only, but of death. For I am not death. I am life: I am mortal.

If they wish to see death visibly in the world, that is their business, not mine. I will not act Eternity for them. Let them not turn to the trees for death. If that is what they want to see, let them look into one another's eyes and see it there.

253

THE ONES WHO WALK AWAY
FROM OMELAS

(Variations on a theme by William James)

The central idea of this psychomyth, the scapegoat, turns up in Dostoyevsky's Brothers Karamazov, *and several people have asked me, rather suspiciously, why I gave the credit to William James. The fact is, I haven't been able to re-read Dostoyevsky, much as I loved him, since I was twenty-five, and I'd simply forgotten he used the idea. But when I met it in James's 'The Moral Philosopher and the Moral Life,' it was with a shock of recognition. Here is how James puts it:*

> *Or if the hypothesis were offered us of a world in which Messrs Fourier's and Bellamy's and Morris's utopias should all be outdone, and millions kept permanently happy on the one simple condition that a certain lost soul on the far-off edge of things should lead a life of lonely torment, what except a specifical and independent sort of emotion can it be which would make us immediately feel, even though an impulse arose within us to clutch at the happiness so offered, how hideous a thing would be its enjoyment when deliberately accepted as the fruit of such a bargain?*

The dilemma of the American conscience can hardly be better stated. Dostoyevsky was a great artist, and a radical one, but his early social radicalism reversed itself, leaving him a violent reactionary. Whereas the American James, who seems so mild, so naïvely gentlemanly — look how he says 'us,' assuming all his readers are as decent as himself! — was, and

remained, and remains, a genuinely radical thinker. Directly after the 'lost soul' passage he goes on,

> *All the higher, more penetrating ideals are revolutionary. They present themselves far less in the guise of effects of past experience than in that of probable causes of future experience, factors to which the environment and the lessons it has so far taught us must learn to bend.*

The application of those two sentences to this story, and to science fiction, and to all thinking about the future, is quite direct. Ideals as 'the probable causes of future experience' – that is a subtle and an exhilarating remark!

Of course I didn't read James and sit down and say, Now I'll write a story about that 'lost soul.' It seldom works that simply. I sat down and started a story, just because I felt like it, with nothing but the word 'Omelas' in mind. It came from a road sign: Salem (Oregon) backwards. Don't you read road signs backwards? POTS. WOLS nerdlihc. Ocsicnarf Nas ... Salem equals schelomo equals salaam equals Peace. Melas. O melas. Omelas. Homme hélas. 'Where do you get your ideas from, Ms Le Guin?' From forgetting Dostoyevsky and reading road signs backwards, naturally. Where else?

With a clamor of bells that set the swallows soaring, the Festival of Summer came to the city Omelas, bright-towered by the sea. The rigging of the boats in harbor sparkled with flags. In the streets between houses with red roofs and painted walls, between old moss-grown gardens and under avenues of trees, past great parks and public buildings, processions moved. Some were decorous: old people in long stiff robes of mauve and grey, grave master workmen, quiet, merry women carrying their babies and chatting as they walked. In other streets the music beat faster, a shimmering of gong and tambourine, and the people went dancing, the procession was a dance. Children dodged in and out, their high calls rising like the swallows' crossing flights over the music and the singing. All the processions wound towards the north side of the city, where

on the great water-meadow called the Green Fields boys and girls, naked in the bright air, with mud-stained feet and ankles and long, lithe arms, exercised their restive horses before the race. The horses wore no gear at all but a halter without bit. Their manes were braided with streamers of silver, gold, and green. They flared their nostrils and pranced and boasted to one another; they were vastly excited, the horse being the only animal who has adopted our ceremonies as his own. Far off to the north and west the mountains stood up half encircling Omelas on her bay. The air of morning was so clear that the snow still crowning the Eighteen Peaks burned with white-gold fire across the miles of sunlit air, under the dark blue of the sky. There was just enough wind to make the banners that marked the racecourse snap and flutter now and then. In the silence of the broad green meadows one could hear the music winding through the city streets, farther and nearer and ever approaching, a cheerful faint sweetness of the air that from time to time trembled and gathered together and broke out into the great joyous clanging of the bells.

Joyous! How is one to tell about joy? How describe the citizens of Omelas?

They were not simple folk, you see, though they were happy. But we do not say the words of cheer much any more. All smiles have become archaic. Given a description such as this one tends to make certain assumptions. Given a description such as this one tends to look next for the King, mounted on a splendid stallion and surrounded by his noble knights, or perhaps in a golden litter borne by great-muscled slaves. But there was no king. They did not use swords, or keep slaves. They were not barbarians. I do not know the rules and laws of their society, but I suspect that they were singularly few. As they did without monarchy and slavery, so they also got on without the stock exchange, the advertisement, the secret police, and the bomb. Yet I repeat that these were not simple folk, not dulcet shepherds, noble savages, bland utopians. They were not less complex than us. The trouble is that we have a bad

habit, encouraged by pedants and sophisticates, of considering happiness as something rather stupid. Only pain is intellectual, only evil interesting. This is the treason of the artist: a refusal to admit the banality of evil and the terrible boredom of pain. If you can't lick 'em, join 'em. If it hurts, repeat it. But to praise despair is to condemn delight, to embrace violence is to lose hold of everything else. We have almost lost hold; we can no longer describe a happy man, nor make any celebration of joy. How can I tell you about the people of Omelas? They were not naïve and happy children – though their children were, in fact, happy. They were mature, intelligent, passionate adults whose lives were not wretched, O miracle! but I wish I could describe it better. I wish I could convince you. Omelas sounds in my words like a city in a fairy tale, long ago and far away, once upon a time. Perhaps it would be best if you imagined it as your own fancy bids, assuming it will rise to the occasion, for certainly I cannot suit you all. For instance, how about technology? I think that there would be no cars or helicopters in and above the streets; this follows from the fact that the people of Omelas are happy people. Happiness is based on a just discrimination of what is necessary, what is neither necessary nor destructive, and what is destructive. In the middle category, however – that of the unnecessary but undestructive, that of comfort, luxury, exuberance, etc – they could perfectly well have central heating, subway trains, washing machines, and all kinds of marvelous devices not yet invented here, floating light-sources, fuelless power, a cure for the common cold. Or they could have none of that: it doesn't matter. As you like it. I incline to think that people from towns up and down the coast have been coming in to Omelas during the last days before the Festival on very fast little trains and double-decked trams, and that the train station of Omelas is actually the handsomest building in town, though plainer than the magnificent Farmers' Market, But even granted trains, I fear that Omelas so far strikes some of you as goody-goody. Smiles, bells, parades, horses, bleh. If so, please add an orgy. If an orgy would help, don't hesitate. Let us not,

however, have temples from which issue beautiful nude priests and priestesses already half in ecstasy and ready to copulate with any man or woman, lover or stranger, who desires union with the deep godhead of the blood, although that was my first idea. But really it would be better not to have any temples in Omelas – at least, not manned temples. Religion yes, clergy no. Surely the beautiful nudes can just wander about, offering themselves like divine soufflés to the hunger of the needy and the rapture of the flesh. Let them join the processions. Let tambourines be struck above the copulations, and the glory of desire be proclaimed upon the gongs, and (a not unimportant point) let the offspring of these delightful rituals be beloved and looked after by all. One thing I know there is none of in Omelas is guilt. But what else should there be? I thought at first there were no drugs, but that is puritanical. For those who like it, the faint insistent sweetness of *drooz* may perfume the ways of the city, *drooz* which first brings a great lightness and brilliance to the mind and limbs, and then after some hours a dreamy languor, and wonderful visions at last of the very arcana and inmost secrets of the Universe, as well as exciting the pleasure of sex beyond all belief; and it is not habit-forming. For more modest tastes I think there ought to be beer. What else, what else belongs in the joyous city? The sense of victory, surely, the celebration of courage. But as we did without clergy, let us do without soldiers. The joy built upon successful slaughter is not the right kind of joy; it will not do; it is fearful and it is trivial. A boundless and generous contentment, a magnanimous triumph felt not against some outer enemy but in communion with the finest and fairest in the souls of all men everywhere and the splendor of the world's summer: this is what swells the hearts of the people of Omelas, and the victory they celebrate is that of life. I really don't think many of them need to take *drooz*.

Most of the processions have reached the Green Fields by now. A marvelous smell of cooking goes forth from the red and blue tents of the provisioners. The faces of small children are amiably sticky; in the benign grey beard of a man a couple

of crumbs of rich pastry are entangled. The youths and girls have mounted their horses and are beginning to group around the starting line of the course. An old woman, small, far, and laughing, is passing out flowers from a basket, and tall young men wear her flowers in their shining hair. A child of nine or ten sits at the edge of the crowd, alone, playing on a wooden flute. People pause to listen, and they smile, but they do not speak to him, for he never ceases playing and never sees them, his dark eyes wholly rapt in the sweet, thin magic of the tune.

He finishes, and slowly lowers his hands holding the wooden flute.

As if that little private silence were the signal, all at once a trumpet sounds from the pavilion near the starting line: imperious, melancholy, piercing. The horses rear on their slender legs, and some of them neigh in answer. Sober-faced, the young riders stroke the horses' necks and soothe them, whispering, 'Quiet, quiet, there my beauty, my hope...' They begin to form in rank along the starting line. The crowds along the racecourse are like a field of grass and flowers in the wind. The Festival of Summer has begun.

Do you believe? Do you accept the festival, the city, the joy? No? Then let me describe one more thing.

In a basement under one of the beautiful public buildings of Omelas, or perhaps in the cellar of one of its spacious private homes, there is a room. It has one locked door, and no window. A little light seeps in dustily between cracks in the boards, secondhand from a cobwebbed window somewhere across the cellar. In one corner of the little room a couple of mops, with stiff, clotted, foul-smelling heads, stand near a rusty bucket. The floor is dirt, a little damp to the touch, as cellar dirt usually is. The room is about three paces long and two wide: a mere broom closet or disused tool room. In the room a child is sitting. It could be a boy or a girl. It looks about six, but actually is nearly ten. It is feeble-minded. Perhaps it was born defective, or perhaps it has become imbecile through fear, malnutrition, and neglect. It picks its nose and occasionally fumbles vaguely

with its toes or genitals, as it sits hunched in the corner farthest from the bucket and the two mops. It is afraid of the mops. It finds them horrible. It shuts its eyes, but it knows the mops are still standing there; and the door is locked; and nobody will come. The door is always locked; and nobody ever comes, except that sometimes – the child has no understanding of time or interval – sometimes the door rattles terribly and opens, and a person, or several people, are there. One of them may come in and kick the child to make it stand up. The others never come close, but peer in at it with frightened, disgusted eyes. The food bowl and the water jug are hastily filled, the door is locked, the eyes disappear. The people at the door never say anything, but the child, who has not always lived in the tool room, and can remember sunlight and its mother's voice, sometimes speaks. 'I will be good,' it says. 'Please let me out. I will be good!' They never answer. The child used to scream for help at night, and cry a good deal, but now it only makes a kind of whining, 'eh-haa, eh-haa,' and it speaks less and less often. It is so thin there are no calves to its legs; its belly protrudes; it lives on a half-bowl of corn meal and grease a day. It is naked. Its buttocks and thighs are a mass of festered sores, as it sits in its own excrement continually.

They all know it is there, all the people of Omelas. Some of them have come to see it, others are content merely to know it is there. They all know that it has to be there. Some of them understand why, and some do not; but they all understand that their happiness, the beauty of their city, the tenderness of their friendships, the health of their children, the wisdom of their scholars, the skill of their makers, even the abundance of their harvest and the kindly weathers of their skies, depend wholly on this child's abominable misery.

This is usually explained to children when they are between eight and twelve, whenever they seem capable of understanding; and most of those who come to see the child are young people, though often enough an adult comes, or comes back, to see the child. No matter how well the matter has been

explained to them, these young spectators are always shocked and sickened at the sight. They feel disgust, which they had thought themselves superior to. They feel anger, outrage, impotence, despite all the explanations. They would like to do something for the child. But there is nothing they can do. If the child were brought up into the sunlight out of that vile place, if it were cleaned and fed and comforted, that would be a good thing, indeed; but if it were done, in that day and hour all the prosperity and beauty and delight of Omelas would wither and be destroyed. Those are the terms. To exchange all the goodness and grace of every life in Omelas for that single, small improvement: to throw away the happiness of thousands for the chance of the happiness of one: that would be to let guilt within the walls indeed.

The terms are strict and absolute; there may not even be a kind word spoken to the child.

Often the young people go home in tears, or in a tearless rage, when they have seen the child and faced this terrible paradox. They may brood over it for weeks or years. But as time goes on they begin to realize that even if the child could be released, it would not get much good of its freedom: a little vague pleasure of warmth and food, no doubt, but little more. It is too degraded and imbecile to know any real joy. It has been afraid too long ever to be free of fear. Its habits are too uncouth for it to respond to humane treatment. Indeed, after so long it would probably be wretched without walls about it to protect it, and darkness for its eyes, and its own excrement to sit in. Their tears at the bitter injustice dry when they begin to perceive the terrible justice of reality, and to accept it. Yet it is their tears and anger, the trying of their generosity and the acceptance of their helplessness, which are perhaps the true source of the splendor of their lives. Theirs is no vapid, irresponsible happiness. They know that they, like the child, are not free. They know compassion. It is the existence of the child, and their knowledge of its existence, that makes possible the nobility of their architecture, the poignancy of their music, the

profundity of their science. It is because of the child that they are so gentle with children. They know that if the wretched one were not there snivelling in the dark, the other one, the flute-player, could make no joyful music as the young riders line up in their beauty for the race in the sunlight of the first morning of summer.

Now do you believe in them? Are they not more credible? But there is one more thing to tell, and this is quite incredible.

At times one of the adolescent girls or boys who go to see the child does not go home to weep or rage, does not, in fact, go home at all. Sometimes also a man or woman much older falls silent for a day or two, and then leaves home. These people go out into the street, and walk down the street alone. They keep walking, and walk straight out of the city of Omelas, through the beautiful gates. They keep walking across the farmlands of Omelas. Each one goes alone, youth or girl, man or woman. Night falls; the traveler must pass down village streets, between the houses with yellow-lit windows, and on out into the darkness of the fields. Each alone, they go west or north, towards the mountains. They go on. They leave Omelas, they walk ahead into the darkness, and they do not come back. The place they go towards is a place even less imaginable to most of us than the city of happiness. I cannot describe it at all. It is possible that it does not exist. But they seem to know where they are going, the ones who walk away from Omelas.

THE DAY BEFORE THE REVOLUTION

In memoriam Paul Goodman, 1911–1972

My novel The Dispossessed *is about a small worldful of people who call themselves Odonians. The name is taken from the founder of their society, Odo, who lived several generations before the time of the novel, and who therefore doesn't get into the action – except implicitly, in that all the action started with her.*

Odonianism is anarchism. Not the bomb-in-the-pocket stuff, which is terrorism, whatever name it tries to dignify itself with; not the social-Darwinist economic 'libertarianism' of the far right; but anarchism, as prefigured in early Taoist thought, and expounded by Shelley and Kropotkin, Goldman and Goodman. Anarchism's principal target is the authoritarian State (capitalist or socialist); its principal moral-practical theme is coopera-tion (solidarity, mutual aid). It is the most idealistic, and to me the most interesting, of all political theories.

To embody it in a novel, which had not been done before, was a long and hard job for me, and absorbed me totally for many months. When it was done I felt lost, exiled – a displaced person. I was very grateful, therefore, when Odo came out of the shadows and across the gulf of Probability, and wanted a story written, not about the world she made, but about herself.

This story is about one of the ones who walked away from Omelas.

The speaker's voice was as loud as empty beer-trucks in a stone street, and the people at the meeting were jammed up close, cobblestones, that great voice booming over them. Taviri was somewhere on the other side of the hall. She had to get to him.

263

She wormed and pushed her way among the dark-clothed, close-packed people. She did not hear the words, nor see the faces: only the booming, and the bodies pressed one behind the other. She could not see Taviri, she was too short. A broad black-vested belly and chest loomed up, blocking her way. She must get through to Taviri. Sweating, she jabbed fiercely with her fist. It was like hitting stone, he did not move at all, but the huge lungs let out right over her head a prodigious noise, a bellow. She cowered. Then she understood that the bellow had not been at her. Others were shouting. The speaker had said something, something fine about taxes or shadows. Thrilled, she joined the shouting – 'Yes! Yes!' – and shoving on, came out easily into the open expanse of the Regimental Drill Field in Parheo. Overhead the evening sky lay deep and colorless, and all around her nodded the tall weeds with dry, white, close-floreted heads. She had never known what they were called. The flowers nodded above her head, swaying in the wind that always blew across the fields in the dusk. She ran among them, and they whipped lithe aside and stood up again swaying, silent. Taviri stood among the tall weeds in his good suit, the dark grey one that made him look like a professor or a play-actor, harshly elegant. He did not look happy, but he was laughing, and saying something to her. The sound of his voice made her cry, and she reached out to catch hold of his hand, but she did not stop, quite. She could not stop. 'Oh, Taviri,' she said, 'it's just on there!' The queer sweet smell of the white weeds was heavy as she went on. There were thorns, tangles underfoot there were slopes, pits. She feared to fall, to fall, she stopped.

Sun, bright morning-glare, straight in the eyes, relentless. She had forgotten to pull the blind last night. She turned her back on the sun, but the right side wasn't comfortable. No use. Day. She sighed twice, sat up, got her legs over the edge of the bed, and sat hunched in her nightdress looking down at her feet.

The toes, compressed by a lifetime of cheap shoes, were almost square where they touched each other, and bulged

out above in corns; the nails were discolored and shapeless. Between the knob-like anklebones ran fine, dry wrinkles. The brief little plain at the base of the toes had kept its delicacy, but the skin was the color of mud, and knotted veins crossed the instep. Disgusting. Sad, depressing. Mean. Pitiful. She tried on all the words, and they all fit, like hideous little hats. Hideous: yes, that one too. To look at oneself and find it hideous, what a job! But then, when she hadn't been hideous, had she sat around and stared at herself like this? Not much! A proper body's not an object, not an implement, not a belonging to be admired, it's just you, yourself. Only when it's no longer you, but yours, a thing owned, do you worry about it – Is it in good shape? Will it do? Will it last?

'Who cares?' said Laia fiercely, and stood up.

It made her giddy to stand up suddenly. She had to put out her hand to the bed-table, for she dreaded falling. At that she thought of reaching out to Taviri, in the dream.

What had he said? She could not remember. She was not sure if she had even touched his hand. She frowned, trying to force memory. It had been so long since she had dreamed about Taviri; and now not even to remember what he had said!

It was gone, it was gone. She stood there hunched in her nightdress, frowning, one hand on the bed-table. How long was it since she had thought of him – let alone dreamed of him – even thought of him, as 'Taviri'? How long since she had said his name?

Asieo said. When Asieo and I were in prison in the North. Before I met Asieo. Asieo's theory of reciprocity. Oh yes, she talked about him, talked about him too much no doubt, maundered, dragged him in. But as 'Asieo,' the last name, the public man. The private man was gone, utterly gone. There were so few left who had even known him. They had all used to be in jail. One laughed about it in those days, all the friends in all the jails. But they weren't even there, these days. They were in the prison cemeteries. Or in the common graves.

'Oh, oh my dear,' Laia said out loud, and she sank down

265

onto the bed again because she could not stand up under the remembrance of those first weeks in the Fort, in the cell, those first weeks of the nine years in the Fort in Drio, in the cell, those first weeks after they told her that Asieo had been killed in the fighting in Capitol Square and had been buried with the Fourteen Hundred in the lime-ditches behind Oring Gate. In the cell. Her hands fell into the old position on her lap, the left clenched and locked inside the grip of the right, the right thumb working back and forth a little pressing and rubbing on the knuckle of the left first finger. Hours, days, nights. She had thought of them all, each one, each one of the Fourteen Hundred, how they lay, how the quicklime worked on the flesh, how the bones touched in the burning dark. Who touched him? How did the slender bones of the hand lie now? Hours, years.

'Taviri, I have never forgotten you!' she whispered, and the stupidity of it brought her back to morning light and the rumpled bed. Of course she hadn't forgotten him. These things go without saying between husband and wife. There were her ugly old feet flat on the floor again, just as before. She had got nowhere at all, she had gone in a circle. She stood up with a grunt of effort and disapproval, and went to the closet for her dressing gown.

The young people went about the halls of the House in becoming immodesty, but she was too old for that. She didn't want to spoil some young man's breakfast with the sight of her. Besides, they had grown up in the principle of freedom of dress and sex and all the rest, and she hadn't. All she had done was invent it. It's not the same.

Like speaking of Asieo as 'my husband.' They winced. The word she should use as a good Odonian, of course, was 'partner.' But why the hell did she have to be a good Odonian?

She shuffled down the hall to the bathrooms. Mairo was there, washing her hair in a lavatory. Laia looked at the long, sleek, wet hank with admiration. She got out of the House so seldom now that she didn't know when she had last seen a respectably shaven scalp, but still the sight of a full head of

hair gave her pleasure, vigorous pleasure. How many times had she been jeered at, *Longhair, Longhair*, had her hair pulled by policemen or young toughs, had her hair shaved off down to the scalp by a grinning soldier at each new prison? And then had grown it all over again, through the fuzz, to the frizz, to the curls, to the mane... In the old days. For God's love, couldn't she think of anything today but the old days?

Dressed, her bed made, she went down to commons. It was a good breakfast, but she had never got her appetite back since the damned stroke. She drank two cups of herb tea, but couldn't finish the piece of fruit she had taken. How she had craved fruit as a child badly enough to steal it; and in the Fort – oh, for God's love stop it! She smiled and replied to the greetings and friendly inquiries of the other breakfasters and big Aevi who was serving the counter this morning. It was he who had tempted her with the peach, 'Look at this, I've been saving it for you,' and how could she refuse? Anyway she had always loved fruit, and never got enough; once when she was six or seven she had stolen a piece off a vendor's cart in River Street. But it was hard to eat when everyone was talking so excitedly. There was news from Thu, real news. She was inclined to discount it at first, being wary of enthusiasms, but after she had read the article in the paper, and read between the lines of it, she thought, with a strange kind of certainty, deep but cold, Why, this is it; it has come. And in Thu, not here. Thu will break before this country does; the Revolution will first prevail there. As if that mattered! There will be no more nations. And yet it did matter somehow, it made her a little cold and sad – envious, in fact. Of all the infinite stupidities. She did not join in the talk much, and soon got up to go back to her room, feeling sorry for herself. She could not share their excitement. She was out of it, really out of it. It's not easy, she said to herself in justification, laboriously climbing the stairs, to accept being out of it when you've been in it, in the center of it, for fifty years. Oh, for God's love. Whining!

She got the stairs and the self-pity behind her, entering her

room. It was a good room, and it was good to be by herself. It was a great relief. Even if it wasn't strictly fair. Some of the kids in the attics were living five to a room no bigger than this. There were always more people wanting to live in an Odonian House than could be properly accommodated. She had this big room all to herself only because she was an old woman who had had a stroke. And maybe because she was Odo. If she hadn't been Odo, but merely the old woman with a stroke, would she have had it? Very likely. After all, who the hell wanted to room with a drooling old woman? But it was hard to be sure. Favoritism, elitism, leader-worship, they crept back and cropped out everywhere. But she had never hoped to see them eradicated in her lifetime, in one generation; only Time works the great changes. Meanwhile this was a nice, large, sunny room, proper for a drooling old woman who had started a world revolution.

Her secretary would be coming in an hour to help her despatch the day's work. She shuffled over to the desk, a beautiful, big piece, a present from the Nio Cabinetmakers' Syndicate because somebody had heard her remark once that the only piece of furniture she had ever really longed for was a desk with drawers and enough room on top... damn, the top was practically covered with papers with notes clipped to them, mostly in Noi's small clear handwriting: Urgent. – Northern Provinces. – Consult w/R. T.?

Her own handwriting had never been the same since Asieo's death. It was odd, when you thought about it. After all, within five years after his death she had written the whole *Analogy*. And there were those letters, which the tall guard with the watery grey eyes, what was his name, never mind, had smuggled out of the Fort for her for two years. *The Prison Letters* they called them now, there were a dozen different editions of them. All that stuff, the letters which people kept telling her were so full of 'spiritual strength' – which probably meant she had been lying herself blue in the face when she wrote them, trying to keep her spirits up – and the *Analogy* which was certainly the solidest

intellectual work she had ever done, all of that had been written in the Fort in Drio, in the cell, after Asieo's death. One had to do something, and in the Fort they let one have paper and pens... But it had all been written in the hasty, scribbling hand which she had never felt was hers, not her own like the round, black scrollings of the manuscript of *Society Without Government*, forty-five years old. Taviri had taken not only her body's and her heart's desire to the quicklime with him, but even her good clear handwriting.

But he had left her the Revolution.

How brave of you to go on, to work, to write, in prison, after such a defeat for the Movement, after your partner's death, people had used to say. Damn fools. What else had there been to do? Bravery, courage – what was courage? She had never figured it out. Not fearing, some said. Fearing yet going on, others said. But what could one do but go on? Had one any real choice, ever?

To die was merely to go on in another direction.

If you wanted to come home you had to keep going on, that was what she meant when she wrote 'True journey is return,' but it had never been more than an intuition, and she was farther than ever now from being able to rationalize it. She bent down, too suddenly, so that she grunted a little at the creak in her bones, and began to root in a bottom drawer of the desk. Her hand came on an age-softened folder and drew it out, recognizing it by touch before sight confirmed: the manuscript of *Syndical Organization in Revolutionary Transition*. He had printed the title on the folder and written his name under it, Taviri Odo Asieo, IX 741. There was an elegant handwriting, every letter well-formed, bold, and fluent. But he had preferred to use a voiceprinter. The manuscript was all in voiceprint, and high quality too, hesitancies adjusted and idiosyncrasies of speech normalized. You couldn't see there how he had said 'o' deep in his throat as they did on the North Coast. There was nothing of him there but his mind. She had nothing of him at all except his name written on the folder. She hadn't kept his letters, it was

sentimental to keep letters. Besides, she never kept anything. She couldn't think of anything that she had ever owned for more than a few years, except this ramshackle old body, of course, and she was stuck with that . . .

Dualizing again. 'She' and 'it.' Age and illness made one dualist, made one escapist; the mind insisted, *It's not me, its not me.* But it was. Maybe the mystics could detach mind from body, she had always rather wistfully envied them the chance, without hope of emulating them. Escape had never been her game. She had sought for freedom here, now, body and soul.

First self-pity, then self-praise, and here she still sat, for God's love, holding Asieo's name in her hand, why? Didn't she know his name without looking it up? What was wrong with her? She raised the folder to her lips and kissed the handwritten name firmly and squarely, replaced the folder in the back of the bottom drawer, shut the drawer, and straightened up in the chair. Her right hand tingled. She scratched it, and then shook it in the air, spitefully. It had never quite got over the stroke. Neither had her right leg, or right eye, or the right corner of her mouth. They were sluggish, inept, they tingled. They made her feel like a robot with a short circuit.

And time was getting on, Noi would be coming, what had she been doing ever since breakfast?

She got up so hastily that she lurched, and grabbed at the chair-back to make sure she did not fall. She went down the hall to the bathroom and looked in the big mirror there. Her grey knot was loose and droopy, she hadn't done it up well before breakfast. She struggled with it a while. It was hard to keep her arms up in the air. Amai, running in to piss, stopped and said, 'Let me do it!' and knotted it up tight and neat in no time, with her round, strong, pretty fingers, smiling and silent. Amai was twenty, less than a third of Laia's age. Her parents had both been members of the Movement, one killed in the insurrection of '60, the other still recruiting in the South Provinces. Amai had grown up in Odonian Houses, born to the Revolution, a true daughter of anarchy. And so quiet and

free and beautiful a child, enough to make you cry when you thought: this is what we worked for, this is what we meant, this is it, here she is, alive, the kindly, lovely future.

Laia Asieo Odo's right eye wept several little tears, as she stood between the lavatories and the latrines having her hair done up by the daughter she had not borne; but her left eye, the strong one, did not weep, nor did it know what the right eye did.

She thanked Amai and hurried back to her room. She had noticed, in the mirror, a stain on her collar. Peach juice, probably. Damned old dribbler. She didn't want Noi to come in and find her with drool on her collar.

As the clean shirt went on over her head, she thought, What's so special about Noi?

She fastened the collar-frogs with her left hand, slowly.

Noi was thirty or so, a slight, muscular fellow with a soft voice and alert dark eyes. That's what was special about Noi. It was that simple. Good old sex. She had never been drawn to a fair man or a fat one, or the tall fellows with big biceps, never, not even when she was fourteen and fell in love with every passing fart. Dark, spare, and fiery, that was the recipe. Taviri, of course. This boy wasn't a patch on Taviri for brains, nor even for looks, but there it was: she didn't want him to see her with dribble on her collar and her hair coming undone.

Her thin, grey hair.

Noi came in, just pausing in the open doorway – my God, she hadn't even shut the door while changing her shirt! She looked at him and saw herself. The old woman.

You could brush your hair and change your shirt, or you could wear last week's shirt and last night's braids, or you could put on cloth of gold and dust your shaven scalp with diamond powder. None of it would make the slightest difference. The old woman would look a little less, or a little more, grotesque.

One keeps oneself neat out of mere decency, mere sanity, awareness of other people.

And finally even that goes, and one dribbles unashamed.

271

'Good morning,' the young man said in his gentle voice.

'Hello, Noi.'

No, by God, it was *not* out of mere decency. Decency be damned. Because the man she had loved, and to whom her age would not have mattered – because he was dead, must she pretend she had no sex? Must she suppress the truth, like a damned puritan authoritarian? Even six months ago, before the stroke, she had made men look at her and like to look at her; and now, though she could give no pleasure, by God she could please herself.

When she was six years old, and Papa's friend Gadeo used to come by to talk politics with Papa after dinner, she would put on the gold-colored necklace that Mama had found on a trash heap and brought home for her. It was so short that it always got hidden under her collar where nobody could see it. She liked it that way. She knew she had it on. She sat on the doorstep and listened to them talk, and knew that she looked nice for Gadeo. He was dark, with white teeth that flashed. Sometimes he called her 'pretty Laia.' 'There's my pretty Laia!' Sixty-six years ago.

'What? My head's dull. I had a terrible night.' It was true. She had slept even less than usual.

'I was asking if you'd seen the papers this morning.'

She nodded.

'Pleased about Soinehe?'

Soinehe was the province in Thu which had declared its secession from the Thuvian State last night.

He was pleased about it. His white teeth flashed in his dark, alert face. Pretty Laia.

'Yes. And apprehensive.'

'I know. But it's the real thing, this time. It's the beginning of the end of the Government in Thu. They haven't even tried to order troops into Soinehe, you know. It would merely provoke the soldiers into rebellion sooner, and they know it.'

She agreed with him. She herself had felt that certainty. But she could not share his delight. After a lifetime of living

on hope because there is nothing but hope, one loses the taste for victory. A real sense of triumph must be preceded by real despair. She had unlearned despair a long time ago. There were no more triumphs. One went on.

'Shall we do those letters today?'

'All right. Which letters?'

'To the people in the North,' he said without impatience.

'In the North?'

'Parheo, Oaidun.'

She had been born in Parheo, the dirty city on the dirty river. She had not come here to the capital till she was twenty-two and ready to bring the Revolution. Though in those days, before she and the others had thought it through, it had been a very green and puerile revolution. Strikes for better wages, representation for women. Votes and wages – Power and Money, for the love of God! Well, one does learn a little, after all, in fifty years.

But then one must forget it all.

'Start with Oaidun,' she said, sitting down in the armchair. Noi was at the desk ready to work. He read out excerpts from the letters she was to answer. She tried to pay attention, and succeeded well enough that she dictated one whole letter and started on another. 'Remember that at this stage your brother-hood is vulnerable to the threat of ... no, to the danger ... to ...' She groped till Noi suggested, 'The danger of leader-worship?'

'All right. And that nothing is so soon corrupted by power-seeking as altruism. No. And that nothing corrupts altruism – no. O for God's love you know what I'm trying to say, Noi, you write it. They know it too, it's just the same old stuff, why can't they read my books!'

'Touch,' Noi said gently, smiling, citing one of the central Odonian themes.

'All right, but I'm tired of being touched. If you'll write the letter I'll sign it, but I can't be bothered with it this morning.'

He was looking at her with a little question or concern. She said, irritable, 'There is something else I have to do!'

When Noi had gone she sat down at the desk and moved the papers about, pretending to be doing something, because she had been startled, frightened, by the words she had said. She had nothing else to do. She never had had anything else to do. This was her work: her lifework. The speaking tours and the meetings and the streets were out of reach for her now, but she could still write, and that was her work. And anyhow if she had had anything else to do, Noi would have known it; he kept her schedule, and tactfully reminded her of things, like the visit from the foreign students this afternoon.

Oh, damn. She liked the young, and there was always something to learn from a foreigner, but she was tired of new faces, and tired of being on view. She learned from them, but they didn't learn from her; they had learnt all she had to teach long ago, from her books, from the Movement. They just came to look, as if she were the Great Tower in Rodarred, or the Canyon of the Tulaevea. A phenomenon, a monument. They were awed, adoring. She snarled at them: Think your own thoughts! – That's not anarchism, that's mere obscurantism. – You don't think liberty and discipline are incompatible, do you? – They accepted their tongue-lashing meekly as children, gratefully, as if she were some kind of All-Mother, the idol of the Big Sheltering Womb. She! She who had mined the shipyards at Seissero, and had cursed Premier Inoilte to his face in front of a crowd of seven thousand, telling him he would have cut off his own balls and had them bronzed and sold as souvenirs, if he thought there was any profit in it – she who had screeched, and sworn, and kicked policemen, and spat at priests, and pissed in public on the big brass plaque in Capitol Square that said HERE WAS FOUNDED THE SOVEREIGN NATION STATE OF A-IO ETC ETC, pssssssssss to all that! And now she was everybody's grandmama, the dear old lady, the sweet old

monument, come worship at the womb. The fire's out, boys, it's safe to come up close.

'No, I won't,' Laia said out loud. 'I will not.' She was not self-conscious about talking to herself, because she always had talked to herself. 'Laia's invisible audience,' Taviri had used to say, as she went through the room muttering. 'You needn't come, I won't be here,' she told the invisible audience now. She had just decided what it was she had to do. She had to go out. To go into the streets.

It was inconsiderate to disappoint the foreign students. It was erratic, typically senile. It was unOdonian. Pssssssss to all that. What was the good working for freedom all your life and ending up without any freedom at all? She would go out for a walk.

'What is an anarchist? One who, choosing, accepts the responsibility of choice.'

On the way downstairs she decided, scowling, to stay and see the foreign students. But then she would go out.

They were very young students, very earnest: doe-eyed, shaggy, charming creatures from the Western Hemisphere, Benbili and the Kingdom of Mand, the girls in white trousers, the boys in long kilts, warlike and archaic. They spoke of their hopes. 'We in Mand are so very far from the Revolution that maybe we are near it,' said one of the girls, wistful and smiling: 'The Circle of Life!' and she showed the extremes meeting, in the circle of her slender, dark-skinned fingers. Amai and Aevi served them white wine and brown bread, the hospitality of the House. But the visitors, unpresumptuous, all rose to take their leave after barely half an hour. 'No, no, no,' Laia said, 'stay here, talk with Aevi and Amai. It's just that I get stiff sitting down, you see, I have to change about. It has been so good to meet you, will you come back to see me, my little brothers and sisters, soon?' For her heart went out to them, and theirs to her, and she exchanged kisses all round, laughing, delighted by the dark young cheeks, the affectionate eyes, the scented hair, before she shuffled off. She was really a little tired, but to go

275

up and take a nap would be a defeat. She had wanted to go out. She would go out. She had not been alone outdoors since – when? Since winter! before the stroke. No wonder she was getting morbid. It had been a regular jail sentence. Outside, the streets, that's where she lived.

She went quietly out the side door of the House, past the vegetable patch, to the street. The narrow strip of sour city dirt had been beautifully gardened and was producing a fine crop of beans and *ceëa*, but Laia's eye for farming was unenlightened. Of course it had been clear that anarchist communities, even in the time of transition, must work towards optimal self-support, but how that was to be managed in the way of actual dirt and plants wasn't her business. There were farmers and agronomists for that. Her job was the streets, the noisy, stinking streets of stone, where she had grown up and lived all her life, except for the fifteen years in prison.

She looked up fondly at the façade of the House. That it had been built as a bank gave peculiar satisfaction to its present occupants. They kept their sacks of meal in the bomb-proof money-vault, and aged their cider in kegs in safe deposit boxes. Over the fussy columns that faced the street carved letters still read, 'National Investors and Grain Factors Banking Association.' The Movement was not strong on names. They had no flag. Slogans came and went as the need did. There was always the Circle of Life to scratch on walls and pavements where Authority would have to see it. But when it came to names they were indifferent, accepting and ignoring whatever they got called, afraid of being pinned down and penned in, unafraid of being absurd. So this best known and second oldest of all the cooperative Houses had no name except The Bank.

It faced on a wide and quiet street, but only a block away began the Temeba, an open market, once famous as a center for black-market psychogenics and teratogenics, now reduced to vegetables, secondhand clothes, and miserable sideshows. Its crapulous vitality was gone, leaving only half-paralyzed alcoholics, addicts, cripples, hucksters, and fifth-rate whores,

pawnshops, gambling dens, fortunetellers, body-sculptors, and cheap hotels. Laia turned to the Temeba as water seeks its level.

She had never feared or despised the city. It was her country. There would not be slums like this, if the Revolution prevailed. But there would be misery. There would always be misery, waste, cruelty. She had never pretended to be changing the human condition, to be Mama taking tragedy away from the children so they won't hurt themselves. Anything but. So long as people were free to choose, if they chose to drink flybane and live in sewers, it was their business. Just so long as it wasn't the business of Business, the source of profit and the means of power for other people. She had felt all that before she knew anything; before she wrote the first pamphlet, before she left Parheo, before she knew what 'capital' meant, before she'd been farther than River Street where she played rolltaggie kneeling on scabby knees on the pavement with the other six-year-olds, she had known it: that she, and the other kids, and her parents, and their parents, and the drunks and whores and all of River Street, were at the bottom of something – were the foundation, the reality, the source. But will you drag civilization down into the mud? cried the shocked decent people, later on, and she had tried for years to explain to them that if all you had was mud, then if you were God you made it into human beings, and if you were human you tried to make it into houses where human beings could live. But nobody who thought he was better than mud would understand. Now, water seeking its level, mud to mud, Laia shuffled through the foul, noisy street, and all the ugly weakness of her old age was at home. The sleepy whores, their lacquered hair-arrangements dilapidated and askew, the one-eyed woman wearily yelling her vegetables to sell, the half-wit beggar slapping flies, these were her countrywomen. They looked like her, they were all sad, disgusting, mean, pitiful, hideous. They were her sisters, her own people.

She did not feel very well. It had been a long time since she had walked so far, four or five blocks, by herself, in the noise

and push and striking summer heat of the streets. She had wanted to get to Koly Park, the triangle of scruffy grass at the end of the Temeba, and sit there for a while with the other old men and women who always sat there, to see what it was like to sit there and be old; but it was too far. If she didn't turn back now, she might get a dizzy spell, and she had a dread of falling down, falling down and having to lie there and look up at the people come to stare at the old woman in a fit. She turned and started home, frowning with effort and self-disgust. She could feel her face very red, and a swimming feeling came and went in her ears. It got a bit much, she was really afraid she might keel over. She saw a doorstep in the shade and made for it, let herself down cautiously, sat, sighed.

Nearby was a fruit-seller, sitting silent behind his dusty, withered stock. People went by. Nobody bought from him. Nobody looked at her. Odo, who was Odo? Famous revolutionary, author of *Community, The Analogy,* etc etc. She, who was she? An old woman with grey hair and a red face sitting on a dirty doorstep in a slum, muttering to herself.

True? Was that she? Certainly it was what anybody passing her saw. But was it she, herself, any more than the famous revolutionary, etc, was? No. It was not. But who was she, then?

The one who loved Taviri.

Yes. True enough. But not enough. That was gone; he had been dead so long.

'Who am I?' Laia muttered to her invisible audience, and they knew the answer and told it to her with one voice. She was the little girl with scabby knees, sitting on the doorstep staring down through the dirty golden haze of River Street in the heat of late summer, the six-year-old, the sixteen-year-old, the fierce, cross, dream-ridden girl, untouched, untouchable. She was herself. Indeed she had been the tireless worker and thinker, but a blood clot in a vein had taken that woman away from her. Indeed she had been the lover, the swimmer in the midst of life, but Taviri, dying, had taken that woman away with him. There was nothing left, really, but the foundation.

She had come home; she had never left home. 'True voyage is return.' Dust and mud and a doorstep in the slums. And beyond, at the far end of the street, the field full of tall dry weeds blowing in the wind as night came.

'Laia! What are you doing here? Are you all right?'

One of the people from the House, of course, a nice woman, a bit fanatical and always talking. Laia could not remember her name though she had known her for years. She let herself be taken home, the woman talking all the way. In the big cool common room (once occupied by tellers counting money behind polished counters supervised by armed guards) Laia sat down in a chair. She was unable just as yet to face climbing the stairs, though she would have liked to be alone. The woman kept on talking, and other excited people came in. It appeared that a demonstration was being planned. Events in Thu were moving so fast that the mood here had caught fire, and something must be done. Day after tomorrow, no, tomorrow, there was to be a march, a big one, from Old Town to Capitol Square – the old route. 'Another Ninth Month Uprising,' said a young man, fiery and laughing, glancing at Laia. He had not even been born at the time of the Ninth Month Uprising, it was all history to him. Now he wanted to make some history of his own. The room had filled up. A general meeting would be held here, tomorrow, at eight in the morning. 'You must talk, Laia.'

'Tomorrow? Oh, I won't be here tomorrow,' she said brusquely. Whoever had asked her smiled, another one laughed, though Amai glanced round at her with a puzzled look. They went on talking and shouting. The Revolution. What on earth had made her say that? What a thing to say on the eve of the Revolution, even if it was true.

She waited her time, managed to get up and, for all her clumsiness, to slip away unnoticed among the people busy with their planning and excitement. She got to the hall, to the stairs, and began to climb them one by one. 'The general strike,' a voice, two voices, ten voices were saying in the room below, behind her. 'The general strike,' Laia muttered, resting

279

for a moment on the landing. Above, ahead, in her room, what awaited her? The private stroke. That was mildly funny. She started up the second flight of stairs, one by one, one leg at a time, like a small child. She was dizzy, but she was no longer afraid to fall. On ahead, on there, the dry white flowers nodded and whispered in the open fields of evening. Seventy-two years and she had never had time to learn what they were called.

The Compass Rose

The Compass Rose

'*The Author of the Acacia Seeds*' first appeared in *Fellowship of the Stars*, edited by Terry Carr (Simon & Schuster, Inc.), 1974.

'*The New Atlantis*' first appeared in *The New Atlantis*, edited by Robert Silverberg (Hawthorn Books, Inc.), 1975.

'*Schrödinger's Cat*' first appeared in *Universe 5*, edited by Terry Carr (Random House, Inc.), 1974.

'*Two Delays on the Northern Line*' first appeared in *The New Yorker*, 1979.

'*SQ*' first appeared in *Cassandra Rising*, edited by Alice Laurance (Doubleday & Company, Inc.), 1978.

'*Small Change*' first appeared in *Tor zu den Sternen*, edited by Peter Wilfert (Goldmann Verlag), 1981.

'*The First Report of the Shipwrecked Foreigner*' first appeared in *Antaeus*, 1978.

'*The Diary of the Rose*' first appeared in *Future Power*, edited by Gardner Dozois and Jack Dann (Random House, Inc.), 1976.

'*The White Donkey*' first appeared in *TriQuarterly*, 1980.

'*The Phoenix*' appears for the first time in this volume.

'*Intracom*' first appeared in *Stopwatch*, edited by George Hay (New English Library), 1974.

'*The Eye Altering*' first appeared in *The Altered I*, edited by Lee Harding (Norstrilia Press), 1974.

'*Mazes*' first appeared in *Epoch*, edited by Roger Elwood and Robert Silverberg (Berkeley Publishing Corporation), 1975.

'*The Pathways of Desire*' first appeared in *New Dimensions Science Fiction, Number 9*, edited by Robert Silverberg (Harper & Row, Publishing, Inc.), 1979.

'*Gwilan's Harp*' first appeared in *Redbook*, 1977.

'*Malheur County*' first appeared in *Kenyon Review*, 1979.

'*The Water Is Wide*' first appeared as a chapbook published by Pendragon Press, 1976.

'*The Wife's Story*' appears for the first time in this volume.

'*Some Approaches to the Problem of the Shortage of Time*' first appeared under the title 'Where Does the Time Go?' in *Omni*, 1979.

'*Sur*' first appeared in *The New Yorker*, 1982.

CONTENTS

PREFACE

By calling this book *The Compass Rose* I hoped to suggest that some pattern or coherence may be perceived in it, while indicating that the stories it contains tend to go off each in its own direction. They take place all over the map, including the margins. It is not even clear to me what the map is a map of. A mind, no doubt; presumably the author's. But I expect there is more to it than that. One's mind is never simply one's own, even at birth, and ever less so as one lives, learns, loses, etc.

The four directions, NESW, of the Rose of the Winds, our magnetic compass, converge into or arise out of an unspoken fifth direction, the center, the corolla of the rose.

Many of the American peoples who were dispossessed by the compass-guided invaders from the East structured their world upon the four wind directions (or half-directions) and two more, Above and Below, also radial to the center/self/here and now, which may sacramentally contain the other six, and thus the Universe. This is the compass in four dimensions, spatial and temporal, material and spiritual, the Rose of the New World.

As a guide to sailors this book is not to be trusted. Perhaps it is too sensitive to local magnetic fields.

Within it, various circling motions may be perceived, as between the first and last stories, and the fourth and seventeenth. It gives rise to apparent excursions outward which are in fact incursions inward, such as the eleventh story;

while the only piece describing a place whose objective reality may be confirmed on a present-day map of present-day Earth, the seventh, is perhaps the most subjective one of the lot.

As for the reasons why a particular story is assigned to a particular direction, they are not very serious. Nadir may be down underground, for instance, or in the depths, or simply downhearted. The organizing principle may be historical, or poetical, or literal. Surely one of the means of learning to know the world as alive with symbol and meaning is to cultivate the art of taking things literally?

The title of an earlier collection of my stories was *The Wind's Twelve Quarters*, a compass borrowed from A. E. Housman. To this one, let me set as motto a French poem of Rainer Maria Rilke, from the group *Les Roses*.

> *Est-ce en exemple que tu te proposes?*
> *Peut-on se remplir comme les roses,*
> *en multipliant sa subtile matière*
> *qu'on avait fait pour ne rien faire?*

> *Car ce n'est pas travailler que d'être*
> *une rose, dirait-on.*
> *Dieu, en regardant par la fenêtre,*
> *fait la maison.*

In English, Rilke asks the rose something like this:

> *Is it as a model you propose*
> *yourself? Can one be filled up like a rose*
> *by multiplying one's subtle stuff?*
> *Is make-work enough?*

For really, you can't call it work,
to be a rose.
God, while looking out the window,
keeps the house.

Ursula K. Le Guin

NADIR

THE AUTHOR OF THE ACACIA SEEDS

And Other Extracts from the
Journal of the Association of Therolinguistics

MS. FOUND IN AN ANTHILL

The messages were found written in touch-gland exudation on degerminated acacia seeds laid in rows at the end of a narrow, erratic tunnel leading off from one of the deeper levels of the colony. It was the orderly arrangement of the seeds that first drew the investigator's attention.

The messages are fragmentary, and the translation approximate and highly interpretative; but the text seems worthy of interest if only for its striking lack of resemblance to any other Ant texts known to us.

Seeds 1–13

> [I will] not touch feelers. [I will] not stroke. [I will] spend on dry seeds [my] soul's sweetness. It may be found when [I am] dead. Touch this dry wood! [I] call! [I am] here!

Alternatively, this passage may be read:

> [Do] not touch feelers. [Do] not stroke. Spend on dry seeds [your] soul's sweetness. [Others] may find it when [you are] dead. Touch this dry wood! Call: [I am] here!

No known dialect of Ant employs any verbal person except the third person singular and plural and the first person plural. In this text only the root forms of the verbs are used; so there is

no way to decide whether the passage was intended to be an autobiography or a manifesto.

Seeds 14–22

Long are the tunnels. Longer is the untunneled. No tunnel reaches the end of the untunneled. The untunneled goes on farther than we can go in ten days [*i.e.*, forever]. Praise!

The mark translated 'Praise!' is half of the customary salutation 'Praise the Queen!' or 'Long live the Queen!' or 'Huzza for the Queen!' – but the word/mark signifying 'Queen' has been omitted.

Seeds 23–29

As the ant among foreign-enemy ants is killed, so the ant without ants dies, but being without ants is as sweet as honeydew.

An ant intruding in a colony not its own is usually killed. Isolated from other ants, it invariably dies within a day or so. The difficulty in this passage is the word/mark 'without ants,' which we take to mean 'alone' – a concept for which no word/mark exists in Ant.

Seeds 30–31

Eat the eggs! Up with the Queen!

There has already been considerable dispute over the interpretation of the phrase on Seed 31. It is an important question, since all the preceding seeds can be fully understood only in the light cast by this ultimate exhortation. Dr Rosbone ingeniously argues that the author, a wingless neuter-female worker, yearns hopelessly to be a winged male, and to found a new colony, flying upward in the nuptial flight with a new Queen. Though the text certainly permits such a reading, our conviction is that nothing in the text *supports* it – least of all the text of

the immediately preceding seed, No. 30: 'Eat the eggs!' This reading, though shocking, is beyond disputation.

We venture to suggest that the confusion over Seed 31 may result from an ethnocentric interpretation of the word 'up.' To us, 'up' is a 'good' direction. Not so, or not necessarily so, to an ant. 'Up' is where the food comes from, to be sure; but 'down' is where security, peace, and home are to be found. 'Up' is the scorching sun; the freezing night; no shelter in the beloved tunnels; exile; death. Therefore we suggest that this strange author, in the solitude of her lonely tunnel, sought with what means she had to express the ultimate blasphemy conceivable to an ant, and that the correct reading of Seeds 30–31, in human terms, is:

Eat the eggs! Down with the Queen!

The desiccated body of a small worker was found beside Seed 31 when the manuscript was discovered. The head had been severed from the thorax, probably by the jaws of a soldier of the colony. The seeds, carefully arranged in a pattern resembling a musical stave, had not been disturbed. (Ants of the soldier caste are illiterate; thus the soldier was presumably not interested in the collection of useless seeds from which the edible germs had been removed.) No living ants were left in the colony, which was destroyed in a war with a neighboring anthill at some time subsequent to the death of the Author of the Acacia Seeds.

– G. D'Arbay, T. R. Bardol

ANNOUNCEMENT OF AN EXPEDITION

The extreme difficulty of reading Penguin has been very much lessened by the use of the underwater motion-picture camera. On film it is at least possible to repeat, and to slow down, the fluid sequences of the script, to the point where, by constant repetition and patient study, many elements of this most elegant

and lively literature may be grasped, though the nuances, and perhaps the essence, must forever elude us.

It was Professor Duby who, by pointing out the remote affiliation of the script with Low Greylag, made possible the first tentative glossary of Penguin. The analogies with Dolphin which had been employed up to that time never proved very useful, and were often quite misleading.

Indeed it seemed strange that a script written almost entirely in wings, neck, and air should prove the key to the poetry of short-necked, flipper-winged water-writers. But we should not have found it so strange if we had kept in mind the fact that penguins are, despite all evidence to the contrary, birds.

Because their script resembles Dolphin in *form*, we should never have assumed that it must resemble Dolphin in *content*. And indeed it does not. There is, of course, the same extra-ordinary wit, the flashes of crazy humor, the inventiveness, and the inimitable grace. In all the thousands of literatures of the Fish stock, only a few show any humor at all, and that usually of a rather simple, primitive sort; and the superb gracefulness of Shark or Tarpon is utterly different from the joyous vigor of all Cetacean scripts. The joy, the vigor, and the humor are all shared by Penguin authors; and, indeed, by many of the finer Seal *auteurs*. The temperature of the blood is a bond. But the construction of the brain, and of the womb, makes a barrier! Dolphins do not lay eggs. A world of difference lies in that simple fact.

Only when Professor Duby reminded us that penguins are birds, that they do not swim but *fly in water*, only then could the therolinguist begin to approach the sea literature of the penguin with understanding; only then could the miles of recordings already on film be restudied and, finally, appreciated.

But the difficulty of translation is still with us.

A satisfying degree of promise has already been made in Adélie. The difficulties of recording a group kinetic perform-ance in a stormy ocean as thick as pea soup with plankton at a temperature of 31° Fahrenheit are considerable; but the

perseverance of the Ross Ice Barrier Literary Circle has been fully rewarded with such passages as 'Under the Iceberg,' from the *Autumn Song* – a passage now world famous in the rendition by Anna Serebryakova of the Leningrad Ballet. No verbal rendering can approach the felicity of Miss Serebryakova's version. For, quite simply, there is no way to reproduce in writing the all-important *multiplicity* of the original text, so beautifully rendered by the full chorus of the Leningrad Ballet company.

Indeed, what we call 'translations' from the Adélie – or from any group kinetic text – are, to put it bluntly, mere notes – libretto without the opera. The ballet version is the true translation. Nothing in words can be complete.

I therefore suggest, though the suggestion may well be greeted with frowns of anger or with hoots of laughter, that *for the therolinguist* – as opposed to the artist and the amateur – the kinetic sea writings of Penguin are the *least* promising field of study; and, further, that Adélie, for all its charm and relative simplicity, is a less promising field of study than is Emperor.

Emperor! – I anticipate my colleagues' response to this suggestion. Emperor! The most difficult, the most remote, of all the dialects of Penguin! The language of which Professor Duby himself remarked, 'The literature of the emperor penguin is as forbidding, as inaccessible, as the frozen heart of Antarctica itself. Its beauties may be unearthly, but they are not for us.'

Maybe. I do not underestimate the difficulties: not least of which is the imperial temperament, so much more reserved and aloof than that of any other penguin. But, paradoxically, it is just in this reserve that I place my hope. The emperor is not a solitary, but a social bird, and while on land for the breeding season dwells in colonies, as does the adélie; but these colonies are very much smaller and very much quieter than those of the adélie. The bonds between the members of an emperor colony are rather personal than social. The emperor is an individualist. Therefore I think it almost certain that the literature of the emperor will prove to be composed by single authors, instead of chorally; and therefore it will be translatable into human

speech. It will be a kinetic literature, but how different from the spatially extensive, rapid, multiplex choruses of sea writing! Close analysis, and genuine transcription, will at last be possible.

What! say my critics – Should we pack up and go to Cape Crozier, to the dark, to the blizzards, to the −60° cold, in the mere hope of recording the problematic poetry of a few strange birds who sit there, in the mid-winter dark, in the blizzards, in the −60° cold, on the eternal ice, with an egg on their feet?

And my reply is, Yes. For, like Professor Duby, my instinct tells me that the beauty of that poetry is as unearthly as anything we shall ever find on earth.

To those of my colleagues in whom the spirit of scientific curiosity and aesthetic risk is strong, I say, Imagine it: the ice, the scouring snow, the darkness, the ceaseless whine and scream of wind. In that black desolation a little band of poets crouches. They are starving; they will not eat for weeks. On the feet of each one, under the warm belly feathers, rests one large egg, thus preserved from the mortal touch of the ice. The poets cannot hear one another; they cannot see one another. They can only feel the other's *warmth*. That is their poetry, that is their art. Like all kinetic literatures, it is silent; unlike other kinetic literatures, it is all but immobile, ineffably subtle. The ruffling of a feather, the shifting of a wing; the touch, the slight, faint, warm touch of the one beside you. In unutterable, miserable, black solitude, the affirmation. In absence, presence. In death, life.

I have obtained a sizable grant from UNESCO and have stocked an expedition. There are still four places open. We leave for Antarctica on Thursday. If anyone wants to come along, welcome!

<div align="right">– D. Petri</div>

EDITORIAL. BY THE PRESIDENT OF THE THEROLINGUISTICS ASSOCIATION

What is Language?

This question, central to the science of therolinguistics, has been answered – heuristically – by the very existence of the science. Language is communication. That is the axiom on which all our theory and research rest, and from which all our discoveries derive; and the success of the discoveries testifies to the validity of the axiom. But to the related, yet not identical question, What is Art? we have not yet given a satisfactory answer.

Tolstoy, in the book whose title is that very question, answered it firmly and clearly: Art, too, is communication. This answer has, I believe, been accepted without examination or criticism by therolinguistics. For example: Why do therolinguists study only animals?

Why, because plants do not communicate.

Plants do not communicate; that is a fact. Therefore plants have no language; very well; that follows from our basic axiom. Therefore, also, plants have no art. But stay! That does *not* follow from the basic axiom, but only from the unexamined Tolstoyan corollary.

What if art is not communicative?

Or, what if some art is communicative, and some art is not?

Ourselves animals, active, predators, we look (naturally enough) for an active, predatory, communicative art; and when we find it, we recognise it. The development of this power of recognition and the skills of appreciation is a recent and glorious achievement.

But I submit that, for all the tremendous advances made by therolinguistics during the last decades, we are only at the beginning of our age of discovery. We must not become slaves to our own axioms. We have not yet lifted our eyes to the vaster horizons before us. We have not faced the almost terrifying challenge of the Plant.

If a non-communicative, vegetative art exists, we must rethink the very elements of our science, and learn a whole new set of techniques.

For it is simply not possible to bring the critical and technical skills appropriate to the study of Weasel murder mysteries, or Batrachian erotica, or the tunnel sagas of the earthworm, to bear on the art of the redwood or the zucchini.

This is proved conclusively by the failure – a noble failure – of the efforts of Dr Srivas, in Calcutta, using time-lapse photography, to produce a lexicon of Sunflower. His attempt was daring, but doomed to failure. For his approach was kinetic – a method appropriate to the *communicative* arts of the tortoise, the oyster, and the sloth. He saw the extreme slowness of the kinesis of plants, and only that, as the problem to be solved.

But the problem was far greater. The art he sought, if it exists, is a non-communicative art and probably a non-kinetic one. It is possible that Time, the essential element matrix, and measure of all known animal art does not enter into vegetable art at all. The plants may use the meter of eternity. We do not know.

We do not know. All we can guess is that the putative Art of the Plant is *entirely different* from the Art of the Animal. What it is, we cannot say; we have not yet discovered it. Yet I predict with some certainty that it exists, and that when it is found it will prove to be, not an action, but a reaction: not a communication, but a reception. It will be exactly the opposite of the art we know and recognise. It will be the first *passive* art known to us.

Can we, in fact know it? Can we ever understand it?

It will be immensely difficult. That is clear. But we should not despair. Remember that so late as the mid-twentieth century, most scientists, and many artists, did not believe that even Dolphin would ever be comprehensible to the human brain – or worth comprehending! Let another century pass, and we may seem equally laughable. 'Do you realise,' the phytolinguist will say to the aesthetic critic, 'that they couldn't even read

Eggplant?' And they will smile at our ignorance, as they pick up their rucksacks and hike on up to read the newly deciphered lyrics of the lichen on the north face of Pike's Peak.

And with them, or after them, may there not come that even bolder adventurer – the first geolinguist, who, ignoring the delicate, transient lyrics of the lichen, will read beneath it the still less communicative, still more passive, wholly atemporal, cold, volcanic poetry of the rocks: each one a word spoken, how long ago, by the earth itself, in the immense solitude, the immenser community, of space.

THE NEW ATLANTIS

Coming back from my Wilderness Week I sat by an odd sort of man in the bus. For a long time we didn't talk; I was mending stockings, and he was reading. Then the bus broke down a few miles outside Gresham. Boiler trouble, the way it generally is when the driver insists on trying to go over thirty. It was a Supersonic Superscenic Deluxe Long Distance coalburner, with Home Comfort, that means a toilet, and the seats were pretty comfortable, at least those that hadn't yet worked loose on their bolts, so everybody waited inside the bus; besides, it was raining. We began talking, the way people do when there's a breakdown and a wait. He held up his pamphlet and tapped it – he was a dry-looking man with a schoolteacherish way of using his hands – and said, 'This is interesting. I've been reading that a new continent is rising from the depths of the sea.'

The blue stockings were hopeless. You have to have something besides holes to darn onto. 'Which sea?'

'They're not sure yet. Most specialists think the Atlantic. But there's evidence it may be happening in the Pacific too.'

'Won't the oceans get a little crowded?' I said, not taking it seriously. I was a bit snappish, because of the breakdown, and because those blue stockings had been good warm ones.

He tapped the pamphlet again and shook his head, quite serious. 'No,' he said. 'The old continents are sinking, to make room for the new. You can see that that is happening.'

You certainly can. Manhattan Island is now under eleven

feet of water at low tide, and there are oyster beds in Ghirardelli Square.

'I thought that was because the oceans are rising from polar melt.'

He shook his head again. 'That is a factor. Due to the greenhouse effect of pollution, indeed Antarctica may become inhabitable. But climatic factors will not explain the emergence of the new – or, possibly, very old – continents in the Atlantic and Pacific.' He went on explaining about continental drift, but I liked the idea of inhabiting Antarctica, and daydreamed about it for a while. I thought of it as very empty, very quiet, all white and blue, with a faint golden glow northward from the unrising sun behind the long peak of Mount Erebus. There were a few people there; they were very quiet too, and wore white tie and tails. Some of them carried oboes and violas. Southward the white land went up in a long silence towards the pole.

Just the opposite, in fact of the Mount Hood Wilderness Area. It had been a tiresome vacation. The other women in the dormitory were all right, but it was macaroni for breakfast, and there were so many organised sports. I had looked forward to the hike up to the National Forest Preserve, the largest forest left in the United States, but the trees didn't look at all the way they do in the postcards and brochures and Federal Beautification Bureau advertisements. They were spindly, and they all had little signs on, saying which union they had been planted by. There were actually a lot more green picnic tables and cement Men's and Women's than there were trees. There was an electrified fence all around the forest to keep out unauthorised persons. The Forest Ranger talked about mountain jays, 'bold little robbers,' he said, 'who will come and snatch the sandwich from your very hand,' but I didn't see any. Perhaps because it was the weekly Watch Those Surplus Calories! Day for all the women, and so we didn't have any sandwiches. If I'd seen a mountain jay I might have snatched the sandwich from his very hand, who knows. Anyhow it was an exhausting week, and I

wished I'd stayed home and practised, even though I'd have lost a week's pay because staying home and practising the viola doesn't count as planned implementation of recreational leisure as defined by the Federal Union of Unions.

When I came back from my Antarctic expedition the man was reading again, and I got a look at his pamphlet; and that was the odd part of it. The pamphlet was called 'Increasing Efficiency in Public Accountant Training Schools,' and I could see from the one paragraph I got a glance at that there was nothing about new continents emerging from the ocean depths in it – nothing at all.

Then we had to get out and walk on into Gresham, because they had decided that the best thing for us all to do was get onto the Greater Portland Area Rapid Public Transit Lines, since there had been so many breakdowns that the charter bus company didn't have any more busses to send out to pick us up. The walk was wet, and rather dull, except when we passed the Cold Mountain Commune. They have a wall around it to keep out unauthorised persons, and a big neon sign out front saying 'Cold Mountain Commune,' and there were some people in authentic jeans and ponchos by the highway selling macrame belts and sand-cast candles and soybean bread to the tourists. In Gresham, I took the 4:40 GPARTL Superjet Flyer train to Burnside and East 230th, and then walked to 217th and got the bus to the Goldschmidt Overpass, and transferred to the shuttlebus, but it had boiler trouble, too, so I didn't reach the downtown transfer point until 8:10, and the busses go on a once-an-hour schedule at eight, so I got a meatless hamburger at the Longhorn Inch-Thick Steak House Dinerette and caught the nine o'clock bus and got home about ten. When I let myself into the apartment I turned on the lights, but there still weren't any. There had been a power outage in West Portland for three weeks. So I went feeling about for the candles in the dark, and it was a minute or so before I noticed that somebody was lying on my bed.

I panicked, and tried again to turn the lights on.

It was a man, lying there in a long thin heap. I thought a burglar had got in somehow while I was away, and died. I opened the door so I could get out quick or at least my yells could be heard, and then I managed not to shake long enough to strike a match, and lighted the candle, and came a little closer to the bed.

The light disturbed him. He made a sort of snoring in his throat, and turned his head. I saw it was a stranger, but I knew his eyebrows, then the breadth of his closed eyelids, then I saw my husband.

He woke up while I was standing there over him with the candle in my hand. He laughed and said still half asleep, 'Ah, Psyche! from the regions which are holy land.'

Neither of us made much fuss. It was unexpected, but it did seem so natural for him to be there, after all, much more natural than for him not to be there; and he was too tired to be very emotional. We lay there together in the dark, and he explained that they had released him from the Rehabilitation Camp early because he had injured his back in an accident in the gravel quarry, and they were afraid it might get worse. If he died there it wouldn't be good publicity abroad, since there have been some nasty rumors about deaths from illness in the Rehabilitation Camps and the Federal Medical Association Hospitals; and there are scientists abroad who have heard of Simon, since somebody published his proof of Goldbach's Hypothesis in Peking. So they let him out early, with eight dollars in his pocket, which is what he had in his pocket when they arrested him, which made it, of course, fair. He had walked and hitched home from Coeur D'Alene, Idaho, with a couple of days in jail in Walla Walla for being caught hitchhiking. He almost fell asleep telling me this, and when he had told me, he did fall asleep. He needed a change of clothes and a bath but I didn't want to wake him. Besides, I was tired too. We lay side by side and his head was on my arm. I don't suppose that I have ever been so happy. No; was it happiness? Something wider and darker, more like knowledge, more like the night joy.

It was dark for so long, so very long. We were all blind. And there was the cold, a vast, un-moving, heavy cold. We could not move at all. We did not move. We did not speak. Our mouths were closed, pressed shut by the cold and by the weight. Our eyes were pressed shut. Our limbs were held still. Our minds were held still. For how long? There was no length of time; how long is death? And is one dead only after living, or before life as well? Certainly we thought, if we thought anything, that we were dead; but if we had ever been alive, we had forgotten it.

There was a change. It must have been the pressure that changed first, although we did not know it. The eyelids are sensitive to touch. They must have been weary of being shut. When the pressure upon them weakened a little, they opened. But there was no way for us to know that. It was too cold for us to feel anything. There was nothing to be seen. There was black.

But then – 'then,' for the event created time, created before and after, near and far, now and then – 'then' there was the light. One light. One small, strange light that passed slowly, at what distance we could not tell. A small, greenish-white, slightly blurred point of radiance, passing.

Our eyes were certainly open, 'then,' for we saw it. We saw the moment. The moment is a point of light. Whether in darkness or in the field of all light, the moment is small, and moves, but not quickly. And 'then' it is gone.

It did not occur to us that there might be another moment. There was no reason to assume that there might be more than one. One was marvel enough: that in all the field of the dark, in the cold, heavy, dense, moveless, timeless, placeless, boundless black, there should have occurred, once, a small, slightly blurred, moving light! Time need be created only once, we thought.

But we were mistaken. The difference between one and more-than-one is all the difference in the world. Indeed, that difference is the world.

The light returned.

The same light, or another one? There was no telling.

But, 'this time,' we wondered about the light: was it small and near to us, or large and far away? Again there was no telling; but there was something about the way it moved, a trace of hesitation, a tentative quality, that did not seem proper to anything large and remote. The stars, for instance. We began to remember the stars.

The stars had never hesitated.

Perhaps the noble certainty of their gait had been a mere effect of distance. Perhaps, in fact, they had hurtled wildly, enormous furnace fragments of a primal bomb thrown through the cosmic dark; but time and distance soften all agony. If the universe, as seems likely, began with an act of destruction, the stars we had used to see told no tales of it. They had been implacably serene.

The planets, however... We began to remember the planets. They had suffered certain changes of appearance and course. At certain times of the year Mars would reverse its direction and go backwards through the stars. Venus had been brighter and less bright as she went through her phases of crescent, full, and wane. Mercury had shuddered like a skidding drop of rain on the sky flushed with daybreak. The light we now watched had that erratic, trembling quality. We saw it unmistakably, change direction and go backwards. It then grew smaller and fainter; blinked – an eclipse? – and slowly disappeared.

Slowly, but not slowly enough for a planet.

Then – the third 'then'! – arrived the indubitable and positive Wonder of the World, the Magic Trick, watch now, watch, you will not believe your eyes, mama, mama, look what I can do—

Seven lights in a row, proceeding fairly rapidly, with a darting movement, from left to right. Proceeding less rapidly from right to left, two dimmer, greenish lights. Two-lights halt, blink, reverse course, proceed hastily and in a wavering

manner from left to right. Seven-lights increase speed, and catch up. Two-lights flash desperately, flicker, and are gone.

Seven-lights hang still for some while, then merge gradually into one streak, veering away, and little by little vanish into the immensity of the dark.

But in the dark now are growing other lights, many of them: lamps, dots, rows, scintillations: some near at hand, some far. Like the stars, yes, but not stars. It is not the great Existences we are seeing, but only the little lives.

In the morning Simon told me something about the Camp, but not until after he had had me check the apartment for bugs. I thought at first he had been given behavior mod and gone paranoid. We never had been infested. And I'd been living alone for a year and a half; surely they didn't want to hear me talking to myself? But he said, 'They may have been expecting me to come here.'

'But they let you go free!'

He just lay there and laughed at me. So I checked everywhere we could think of. I didn't find any bugs, but it did look as if somebody had gone through the bureau drawers while I was away in the Wilderness. Simon's papers were all at Max's, so that didn't matter. I made tea on the Primus, and washed and shaved Simon with the extra hot water in the kettle – he had a thick beard and wanted to get rid of it because of the lice he had brought from Camp – and while we were doing that he told me about the Camp. In fact he told me very little, but not much was necessary.

He had lost about twenty pounds. As he only weighed 140 to start with, this left little to go on with. His knees and wrist bones stuck out like rocks under the skin. His feet were all swollen and chewed-looking from the Camp boots; he hadn't dared take the boots off, the last three days of walking, because he was afraid he wouldn't be able to get them back on. When he had to move or sit up so I could wash him, he shut his eyes.

'Am I really here?' he asked. 'Am I here?'

'Yes,' I said. 'You are here. What I don't understand is how you got here.'

'Oh, it wasn't bad so long as I kept moving. All you need is to know where you're going – to have some place to go. You know, some of the people in Camp, if they'd let them go, they wouldn't have had that. They couldn't have gone anywhere. Keeping moving was the main thing. It's just that my back's seized up, now.'

When he had to get up to go to the bathroom he moved liked a ninety-year-old. He couldn't stand straight, but was all bent out of shape, and shuffled. I helped him put on clean clothes. When he lay down on the bed again a sound of pain came out of him, like tearing thick paper. I went around the room putting things away. He asked me to come sit by him, and said I was going to drown him if I went on crying. 'You'll submerge the entire North American continent,' he said. I can't remember what else he said, but he made me laugh finally. It is hard to remember things Simon says, and hard not to laugh when he says them. This is not merely the partiality of affection: he makes everybody laugh. I doubt that he intends to. It is just that a mathematician's mind works differently from other people's. Then when they laugh, that pleases him.

It was strange, and it is strange, to be thinking about 'him,' the man I have known for ten years, the same man, while 'he' lay there changed out of recognition, a different man. It is enough to make you understand why most languages have a word like 'soul.' There are various degrees of death, and time spares us none of them. Yet something endures, for which a word is needed.

I said what I had not been able to say for a year and a half: 'I was afraid they'd brainwash you.'

He said, 'Behavior mod is expensive. Even just with drugs. They save it mostly for the VIPs. But I'm afraid they got a notion I might be important after all. I got questioned a lot the last couple of months. About my "foreign contacts." ' He snorted. 'The stuff that got published abroad, I suppose. So I

want to be careful and make sure it's just a Camp again next time, and not a Federal Hospital.'

'Simon, were they . . . are they cruel, or just righteous?'

He did not answer for a while. He did not want to answer. He knew what I was asking. He knew what thread hangs hope, the sword, above our heads.

'Some of them . . .' he said at last mumbling.

Some of them had been cruel. Some of them had enjoyed their work. You cannot blame everything on society.

'Prisoners, as well as guards,' he said.

You cannot blame everything on the enemy.

'Some of them, Belle,' he said with energy, touching my hand, 'some of them, there were men like gold there—'

The thread is tough; you cannot cut it with one stroke.

'What have you been playing?' he asked.

'Forrest, Schubert.'

'With the quartet?'

'Trio, now. Janet went to Oakland with a new lover.'

'Ah, poor Max.'

'It's just as well, really. She isn't a good pianist.'

I make Simon laugh, too, though I don't intend to. We talked until it was past time for me to go·to work. My shift since the Full Employment Act last year is ten to two. I am an inspector in a recycled paper bag factory. I have never rejected a bag yet; the electronic inspector catches all the defective ones first. It is a rather depressing job. But it's only four hours a day, and it takes more time than that to go through all the lines and physical and mental examinations, and fill out all the forms, and talk to all the welfare counsellors and inspectors every week in order to qualify as Unemployed, and then line up every day for the ration stamps and the dole. Simon thought I ought to go to work as usual. I tried to, but I couldn't. He had felt very hot to the touch when I kissed him goodbye. I went instead and got a black-market doctor. A girl at the factory had recommended her, for an abortion, if I ever wanted one without going through the regulation two years of sex-depressant drugs

the fed-meds make you take after they give you an abortion. She was a jeweler's assistant in a shop on Alder Street, and the girl said she was convenient because if you didn't have enough cash you could leave something in pawn at the jeweler's as payment. Nobody ever does have enough cash, and, of course, credit cards aren't worth much on the black market.

The doctor was willing to come at once, so we rode home on the bus together. She gathered very soon that Simon and I were married, and it was funny to see her look at us and smile like a cat. Some people love illegality for its own sake. Men, more often than women. It's men who make laws, and enforce them, and break them, and think the whole performance is wonderful. Most women would rather just ignore them. You could see that this woman, like a man, actually enjoyed breaking them. That may have been what put her into an illegal business in the first place, a preference for the shady side. But there was more to it than that. No doubt she'd wanted to be a doctor, too; and the Federal Medical Association doesn't admit women into the medical schools. She probably got her training as some other doctor's private pupil, under the counter. Very much as Simon learned mathematics, since the universities don't teach much but Business Administration and Advertising and Media Skills any more. However she learned it, she seemed to know her stuff. She fixed up a kind of homemade traction device for Simon very handily, and informed him that if he did much more walking for two months he'd be crippled the rest of his life, but if he behaved himself he'd just be more or less lame. It isn't the kind of thing you'd expect to be grateful for being told, but we both were. Leaving, she gave me a bottle of about two hundred plain white pills, unlabelled. 'Aspirin,' she said. 'He'll be in a good deal of pain off and on for weeks.'

I looked at the bottle. I had never seen aspirin before, only the Super-Buffered Pane-Gon and the Triple Power N-L-G-Zic and the Extra Strength Apansprin with the miracle ingredient more doctors recommend, which the fed-meds always give you prescriptions for, to be filled at your FMA-approved

313

private-enterprise friendly drugstore at the low, low prices established by the Pure Food and Drug Administration in order to inspire competitive research.

'Aspirin,' the doctor repeated. 'The miracle ingredient more doctors recommend.' She cat-grinned again. I think she liked us because we were living in sin. That bottle of black-market aspirin was probably worth more than the old Navajo bracelet I pawned for her fee.

I went out again to register Simon as temporarily domiciled at my address, and to apply for Temporary Unemployment Compensation ration stamps for him. They only give them to you for two weeks and you have to come every day; but to register him as Temporarily Disabled meant getting the signatures of two fed-meds, and I thought I'd rather put that off for a while. It took three hours to go through the lines and get the forms he would have to fill out, and to answer the crats' questions about why he wasn't there in person. They smelled something fishy. Of course it's hard for them to prove that two people are married, if you move now and then, and your friends help out by sometimes registering one of you as living at their address; but they had all the back files on both of us and it was obvious that we had been around each other for a suspiciously long time. The State really does make things awfully hard for itself. It must have been simpler to enforce the laws, back when marriage was legal and adultery was what got you into trouble. They only had to catch you once. But I'll bet people broke the law just as often then as they do now.

The lantern creatures came close enough at last that we could see not only their light, but their bodies in the illumination of the light. They were not pretty. They were dark-colored, most often a dark red, and they were all mouth. They ate one another whole. Light swallowed light all swallowed together in the vaster mouth of the darkness. They moved slowly, for nothing, however small and hungry, could move fast under that weight, in that cold. Their eyes, round with

fear, were never closed. Their bodies were tiny and bony, behind the gaping jaws. They wore queer, ugly decorations on their lips and skulls: fringes, serrated wattles, feather-like fronds, gauds, bangles, lures. Poor little sheep of the deep pastures! Poor ragged, hunch-jawed dwarfs squeezed to the bone by the weight of the darkness, chilled to the bone by the cold of the darkness, tiny monsters burning with bright hunger, who brought us back to life!

Occasionally, in the wan, sparse illumination of one of the lantern creatures, we caught a momentary glimpse of other large, unmoving shapes: the barest suggestion, off in the distance, not of a wall, nothing so solid and certain as a wall, but of a surface, an angle... Was it there?

Or something would glitter, faint, far off, far down. There was no use trying to make out what it might be. Probably it was only a fleck of sediment, mud or mica, disturbed by a struggle between the lantern creatures, flickering like a bit of diamond dust as it rose and settled slowly. In any case, we could not move to go see what it was. We had not even the cold, narrow freedom of the lantern creatures. We were immobilised, borne down, still shadows among the half-guessed shadow walls. Were we there?

The lantern creatures showed no awareness of us. They passed before us, among us, perhaps even through us – it was impossible to be sure. They were not afraid, or curious.

Once something a little larger than a hand came crawling near, and for a moment we saw quite distinctly the clean angle where the foot of a wall rose from the pavement, in the glow cast by the crawling creature, which was covered with a foliage of plumes, each plume dotted with many tiny, bluish points of light. We saw the pavement beneath the creature and the wall beside it heartbreaking in its exact, clear linearity, its opposition to all that was fluid, random, vast and void. We saw the creature's claws, slowly reaching out and retracting like small stiff fingers, touch the wall.

Its plumage of light quivering, it dragged itself along and vanished behind the corner.

So we knew that the wall was there; and that it was an outer wall, a housefront, perhaps, or the side of one of the towers of the city.

We remembered the towers. We remembered the city. We had forgotten it. We had forgotten who we were; but we remembered the city, now.

When I got home, the FBI had already been there. The computer at the police precinct where I registered Simon's address must have flashed it right over to the computer at the FBI building. They had questioned Simon for about an hour, mostly about what he had been doing during the twelve days it took him to get from the Camp to Portland. I suppose they thought he had flown to Peking or something. Having a police record in Walla Walla for hitchhiking helped him establish his story. He told me that one of them had gone to the bathroom. Sure enough I found a bug stuck on the top of the bathroom doorframe. I left it, as we figured it's really better to leave it when you know you have one, than to take it off and then never be sure they haven't planted another one you don't know about. As Simon said, if we felt we had to say something unpatriotic we could always flush the toilet at the same time.

I have a battery radio – there are so many stoppages because of power failures, and days the water has to be boiled, and so on, that you really have to have a radio to save wasting time and dying of typhoid – and he turned it on while I was making supper on the Primus. The six-o'clock All American Broadcasting Company news announcer announced that peace was at hand in Uruguay, the President's confidential aide having been seen to smile at a passing blonde as he left the 613th day of the secret negotiations in a villa outside Katmandu. The war in Liberia was going well; the enemy said they had shot down 17 American planes but the Pentagon said we had shot down 22 enemy planes, and the capital city – I forget its name,

but it hasn't been inhabitable for seven years anyway – was on the verge of being recaptured by the forces of freedom. The police action in Arizona was also successful. The Neo-Birch insurgents in Phoenix could not hold out much longer against the massed might of the American Army and Air Force, since their underground supply of small tactical nukes from the Weatherpeople in Los Angeles had been cut off. Then there was an advertisement for Fed-Cred cards, and a commercial for the Supreme Court – 'Take your legal troubles to the Nine Wise Men!' Then there was something about why tariffs had gone up, and a report from the stock market which had just closed at over 2000, and a commercial for US Government canned water, with a catchy little tune: 'Don't be sorry when you drink – It's not as healthy as you think – Don't you think you really ought to – Drink coo-ool, puu-uure USG Water?' – with three sopranos in close harmony on the last line. Then, just as the battery began to give out and his voice was dying away into a faraway tiny whisper, the announcer seemed to be saying something about a new continent emerging.

'What was that?'

'I didn't hear,' Simon said, lying with his eyes shut and his face pale and sweaty. I gave him two aspirins before we ate. He ate little, and fell asleep while I was washing the dishes in the bathroom. I had been going to practise, but a viola is fairly wakeful in a one-room apartment. I read for a while instead. It was a bestseller Janet had given me when she left. She thought it was very good, but then she likes Franz Liszt too. I don't read much since the libraries were closed down, it's too hard to get books; all you can buy is bestsellers. I don't remember the title of this one, the cover just said Ninety Million Copies in Print!!! It was about small-town sex life in the last century, the dear old 1970s when there weren't any problems and life was so simple and nostalgic. The author squeezed all the naughty thrills he could out of the fact that all the main characters were married. I looked at the end and saw that all the married couples shot each other after all their children

became schizophrenic hookers, except for one brave pair that divorced and then leapt into bed together with a clear-eyed pair of Government-employed lovers for eight pages of healthy group sex as a brighter future dawned. I went to bed then, too. Simon was hot, but sleeping quietly. His breathing was like the sound of soft waves far away, and I went out to the dark sea on the sound of them.

I used to go out to the dark sea, often, as a child, falling asleep. I had almost forgotten it with my waking mind. As a child all I had to do was stretch out and think, 'the dark sea ... the dark sea ...' and soon enough I'd be there, in the great depths, rocking. But after I grew up it only happened rarely, as a great gift. To know the abyss of the darkness and not to fear it to entrust oneself to it and whatever may arise from it – what greater gift?

We watched the tiny lights come and go around us, and doing so, we gained a sense of space and of direction – near and far, at least, and higher and lower. It was that sense of space that allowed us to become aware of the currents. Space was no longer entirely still around us, suppressed by the enormous pressure of its own weight. Very dimly we were aware that the cold darkness moved, slowly, softly, pressing against us a little for a long time, then ceasing, in a vast oscillation. The empty darkness flowed slowly along our unmoving unseen bodies; along them, past them; perhaps through them; we could not tell.

Where did they come from, those dim, slow, vast tides? What pressure or attraction stirred the depths to these slow drifting movements? We could not understand that; we could only feel their touch against us, but in straining our sense to guess their origin or end, we became aware of something else: something out there in the darkness of the great currents: sounds. We listened. We heard.

So our sense of space sharpened and localised to a sense of place. For sound is local, as sight is not. Sound is

delimited by silence; and it does not rise out of the silence unless it is fairly close, both in space and in time. Though we stand where once the singer stood we cannot hear the voice singing; the years have carried it off on their tides, submerged it. Sound is a fragile thing, a tremor, as delicate as life itself. We may see the stars, but we cannot hear them. Even were the hollowness of outer space an atmosphere, an ether that transmitted the waves of sound, we could not hear the stars; they are too far away. At most if we listened we might hear our own sun, all the mighty roiling, exploding storm of its burning, as a whisper at the edge of hearing.

A sea wave laps one's feet: it is the shock wave of a volcanic eruption on the far side of the world. But one hears nothing.

A red light flickers on the horizon: it is the reflection in smoke of a city on the distant mainland, burning. But one hears nothing.

Only on the slopes of the volcano, in the suburbs of the city, does one begin to hear the deep thunder, and the high voices crying.

Thus, when we became aware that we were hearing, we were sure that the sounds we heard were fairly close to us. And yet we may have been quite wrong. For we were in a strange place, a deep place. Sound travels fast and far in the deep places, and the silence there is perfect, letting the least noise be heard for hundreds of miles.

And these were not small noises. The lights were tiny, but the sounds were vast: not loud, but very large. Often they were below the range of hearing, long slow vibrations rather than sounds. The first we heard seemed to us to rise up through the currents from beneath us: immense groans, sighs felt along the bone, a rumbling, a deep uneasy whispering.

Later, certain sounds came down to us from above, or borne along the endless levels of the darkness, and these were stranger yet for they were music. A huge, calling, yearning music from far away in the darkness, calling not to us. *Where are you? I am here.*

319

Not to us.

They were the voices of the great souls, the great lives, the lonely ones, the voyagers. Calling. Not often answered. *Where are you? Where have you gone?*

But the bones, the keels and girders of white bones on icy isles of the South, the shores of bones did not reply.

Nor could we reply. But we listened, and the tears rose in our eyes, salt, not so salt as the oceans, the world-girdling deep bereaved currents, the abandoned roadways of the great lives; not so salt, but warmer.

I am here. Where have you gone?

No answer.

Only the whispering thunder from below.

But we knew now, though we could not answer, we knew because we heard, because we felt, because we wept we knew that we were; and we remembered other voices.

Max came the next night. I sat on the toilet lid to practise, with the bathroom door shut. The FBI men on the other end of the bug got a solid half hour of scales and double stops, and then a quite good performance of the Hindemith un-accompanied viola sonata. The bathroom being very small and all hard surfaces, the noise I made was really tremendous. Not a good sound, far too much echo, but the sheer volume was contagious, and I played louder as I went on. The man up above knocked on the floor once; but if I have to listen to the weekly All-American Olympic Games at full blast every Sunday morning from his TV set, then he has to accept Paul Hindemith coming up out of his toilet now and then.

When I got tired I put a big wad of cotton over the bug, and came out of the bathroom half deaf. Simon and Max were on fire. Burning, un-consumed. Simon was scribbling formulae in traction, and Max was pumping his elbows up and down the way he does, like a boxer, and saying, 'The e-lec-tron emission ...' through his nose, with his eyes narrowed, and his mind evidently going light-years per second faster than his tongue,

because he kept beginning over and saying, 'The e-lec-tron emis-sion . . .' and pumping his elbows.

Intellectuals at work are very strange to look at. As strange as artists. I never could understand how an audience can sit there and *look* at a fiddler rolling his eyes and biting his tongue, or a horn player collecting spit, or a pianist like a black cat strapped to an electrified bench, as if what they *saw* had anything to do with the music.

I damped the fires with a quart of black-market beer – the legal kind is better, but I never have enough ration stamps for beer, I'm not thirsty enough to go without eating – and gradually Max and Simon cooled down. Max would have stayed talking all night, but I drove him out, because Simon was looking tired.

I put a new battery in the radio and left it playing in the bathroom, and blew out the candle and lay and talked with Simon; he was too excited to sleep. He said that Max had solved the problems that were bothering them before Simon was sent to Camp, and had fitted Simon's equations to (as Simon put it) the bare facts: which means they have achieved 'direct energy conversion.' Ten or twelve people have worked on it at different times since Simon published the theoretical part of it when he was twenty-two. The physicist Ann Jones had pointed out right away that the simplest practical application of the theory would be to build a 'sun tap,' a device for collecting and storing solar energy, only much cheaper and better than the USG Sola-Heetas that some rich people have on their houses. And it would have been simple only they kept hitting the same snag. Now Max has got around the snag.

I said that Simon published the theory, but that is inaccurate. Of course he's never been able to publish any of his papers, in print; he's not a Federal employee and doesn't have a Government clearance. But it did get circulated in what the scientists and poets call Sammy's-dot, that is, just handwritten or hectographed. It's an old joke that the FBI arrests everybody with

purple fingers, because they have either been hectographing Sammy's-dots, or they have impetigo.

Anyhow, Simon was on top of the mountain that night. His true joy is in the pure math; but he had been working with Clara and Max and the others in this effort to materialise the theory for ten years, and a taste of material victory is a good thing, once in a lifetime.

I asked him to explain what the sun tap would mean to the masses, with me as a representative mass. He explained that it means we can tap solar energy for power, using a device that's easier to build than a jar battery. The efficiency and storage capacity are such that about ten minutes of sunlight will power an apartment complex like ours, heat and lights and elevators and all, for twenty-four hours; and no pollution, particulate or thermal or radioactive. 'There isn't any danger of using up the sun?' I asked. He took it soberly – it was a stupid question, but after all not so long ago people thought there wasn't any danger of using up the earth – and said no, because we wouldn't be pulling out energy, as we did when we mined and forested and split atoms, but just using the energy that comes to us anyhow: as the plants, the trees and grass and rosebushes, always have done. 'You could call it Flower Power,' he said. He was high, high up on the mountain, ski jumping in the sunlight.

'The State owns us,' he said, 'because the corporative State has a monopoly on power sources, and there's not enough power to go round. But now, anybody could build a generator on their roof that would furnish enough power to light a city.'

I looked out the window at the dark city.

'We could completely decentralise industry and agriculture. Technology could serve life instead of serving capital. We could each run our own life. Power is power! ... The State is a machine. We could unplug the machine, now. Power corrupts; absolute power corrupts absolutely. But that's true only when there's a price on power. When groups can keep the power to themselves; when they can use physical power-to in order to exert spiritual power-over; when might makes right. But if

power is free? If everybody is equally mighty? Then everybody's got to find a better way of showing that he's right . . .'

'That's what Mr Nobel thought when he invented dynamite,' I said. 'Peace on earth.'

He slid down the sunlit slope a couple of thousand feet and stopped beside me in a spray of snow, smiling. 'Skull at the banquet,' he said, 'finger writing on the wall. Be still! Look, don't you see the sun shining on the Pentagon, all the roofs are off, the sun shines at last into the corridors of power . . . And they shrivel up, they wither away. The green grass grows through the carpets of the Oval Room, the Hotline is disconnected for non-payment of the bill. The first thing we'll do is build an electrified fence outside the electrified fence around the White House. The inner one prevents unauthorised persons from getting in. The outer one will prevent authorised persons from getting out . . .'

Of course he was bitter. Not many people come out of prison sweet.

But it was cruel, to be shown this great hope, and to know that there was no hope for it. He did know that. He knew it right along. He knew that there was no mountain, that he was skiing on the wind.

The tiny lights of the lantern creatures died out one by one, sank away. The distant lonely voices were silent. The cold, slow currents flowed, vacant, only shaken from time to time by a shifting in the abyss.

It was dark again, and no voice spoke. All dark, dumb, cold.

Then the sun rose.

It was not like the dawns we had begun to remember: the change, manifold and subtle, in the smell and touch of the air; the hush that, instead of sleeping, wakes, holds still, and waits; the appearance of objects, looking grey, vague, and new, as if just created – distant mountains against the eastern sky, one's own hands, the hoary grass full of dew

and shadow, the fold in the edge of a curtain hanging by the window – and then, before one is quite sure that one is indeed seeing again, that the light has returned, that day is breaking, the first abrupt, sweet stammer of a waking bird. And after that the chorus, voice by voice: This is my nest, this is my tree, this is my egg, this is my day, this is my life, here I am, here I am, hurray for me! I'm here! – No, it wasn't like that at all, this dawn. It was completely silent and it was blue.

In the dawns that we had begun to remember, one did not become aware of the light itself, but of the separate objects touched by the light, the things, the world. They were there, visible again, as if visibility were their own property, not a gift from the rising sun.

In this dawn, there was nothing but the light itself. Indeed there was not even light, we would have said, but only color: blue.

There was no compass bearing to it. It was not brighter in the east. There was no east or west. There was only up and down, below and above. Below was dark. The blue light came from above. Brightness fell. Beneath, where the shaking thunder had stilled, the brightness died away through violet into blindness.

We, arising, watched light fall.

In a way it was more like an ethereal snowfall than like a sunrise. The light seemed to be in discrete particles, infinitesimal flecks, slowly descending, faint, fainter than flakes of fine snow on a dark night, and tinier; but blue. A soft, penetrating blue tending to the violet the color of the shadows in an iceberg, the color of a streak of sky between grey clouds on a winter afternoon before snow: faint in intensity but vivid in hue: the color of the remote, the color of the cold, the color farthest from the sun.

On Saturday night they held a scientific congress in our room. Clara and Max came, of course, and the engineer Phil Drum,

and three others who had worked on the sun tap. Phil Drum was very pleased with himself because he had actually built one of the things, a solar cell, and brought it along. I don't think it had occurred to either Max or Simon to build one. Once they knew it could be done, they were satisfied and wanted to get on with something else. But Phil unwrapped his baby with a lot of flourish, and people made remarks like, 'Mr Watson, will you come here a minute,' and 'Hey, Wilbur, you're off the ground!' and 'I say, nasty mould you've got there, Alec, why don't you throw it out?' and 'Ugh, ugh, burns, burns, wow, ow,' the latter from Max, who does look a little Pre-Mousterian. Phil explained that he had exposed the cell for one minute at four in the afternoon up in Washington Park during a light rain. The lights were back on the West Side since Thursday, so we could test it without being conspicuous.

We turned off the lights, after Phil had wired the table lamp cord to the cell. He turned on the lamp switch. The bulb came on, about twice as bright as before, at its full 40 watts – city power, of course, was never full strength. We all looked at it. It was a dime-store table lamp with a metallised gold base and a white plasticloth shade.

'Brighter than a thousand suns,' Simon murmured from the bed.

'Could it be,' said Clara Edmonds, 'that we physicists have known sin – and have come out the other side?'

'It really wouldn't be any good at all for making bombs with,' Max said dreamily.

'Bombs,' Phil Drum said with scorn. 'Bombs are obsolete. Don't you realise that we could move a mountain with this kind of power? I mean pick up Mount Hood, move it, and set it down. We could thaw Antarctica, we could freeze the Congo. We could sink a continent. "Give me a fulcrum and I'll move the world." Well, Archimedes, you've got your fulcrum. The sun.'

'Christ,' Simon said, 'the radio, Belle!'

The bathroom door was shut and I had put cotton over the bug, but he was right; if they were going to go ahead at this

325

rate there had better be some added static. And though I liked watching their faces in the clear light of the lamp – they all had good, interesting faces, well worn, like the handles of wooden tools or the rocks in a running stream – I did not much want to listen to them talk tonight. Not because I wasn't a scientist; that made no difference. And not because I disagreed or disapproved or disbelieved anything they said. Only because it grieved me terribly, their talking. Because they couldn't rejoice aloud over a job done and a discovery made, but had to hide there and whisper about it. Because they couldn't go out into the sun.

I went into the bathroom with my viola and sat on the toilet lid and did a long set of sautilté exercises. Then I tried to work at the Forrest trio, but it was too assertive. I played the solo part from *Harold in Italy*, which is beautiful, but wasn't quite the right mood either. They were still going strong in the other room. I began to improvise.

After a few minutes in E minor the light over the shaving mirror began to flicker and dim; then it died. Another outage. The table lamp in the other room did not go out, being connected with the sun, not with the twenty-three atomic fission plants that power the Greater Portland Area. Within two seconds somebody had switched it off, too, so that we shouldn't be the only window in the West Hills left alight; and I could hear them rooting for candles and rattling matches. I went on improvising in the dark. Without light, when you couldn't see all the hard shiny surfaces of things, the sound seemed softer and less muddled. I went on, and it began to shape up. All the laws of harmonics sang together when the bow came down. The strings of the viola were the chords of my own voice, tightened by sorrow, tuned to the pitch of joy. The melody created itself out of air and energy; it raised up the valleys, and the mountains and hills were made low, and the crooked straight, and the rough places plain. And the music went out to the dark sea and sang in the darkness, over the abyss.

When I came out they were all sitting there and none of them was talking. Max had been crying. I could see little candle

326

flames in the tears around his eyes. Simon lay flat on the bed in the shadows, his eyes closed. Phil Drum sat hunched over, holding the solar cell in his hands.

I loosened the pegs, and put the bow and the viola in the case, and cleared my throat. It was embarrassing. I finally said, 'I'm sorry.'

One of the women spoke: Rose Abramski, a private student of Simon's, a big shy woman who could hardly speak at all unless it was in mathematical symbols. 'I saw it,' she said. 'I saw it. I saw the white towers, and the water streaming down their sides, and running back down to the sea. And the sunlight shining in the streets, after ten thousand years of darkness.'

'I heard them,' Simon said, very low, from the shadow. 'I heard their voices.'

'Oh, Christ! Stop it!' Max cried out, and got up and went blundering out into the unlit hall, without his coat. We heard him running down the stairs.

'Phil,' said Simon, lying there, 'could we raise up the white towers, with our lever and our fulcrum?'

After a long silence Phil Drum answered, 'We have the power to do it.'

'What else do we need?' Simon said. 'What else do we need, besides power?'

Nobody answered him.

The blue changed. It became brighter, lighter, and at the same time thicker: impure. The ethereal luminosity of blue-violet turned to turquoise, intense and opaque. Still we could not have said that everything was now turquoise-colored, for there were still no things. There was nothing, except the color of turquoise.

The change continued. The opacity became veined and thinned. The dense, solid color began to appear translucent, transparent. Then it seemed as if we were in the heart of a sacred jade, or the brilliant crystal of a sapphire or an emerald.

As at the inner structure of a crystal, there was no motion. But there was something, now, to see. It was as if we saw the motionless, elegant inward structure of the molecules of a precious stone. Planes and angles appeared about us, shadowless and clear in that even, glowing, blue-green light.

These were the walls and towers of the city, the streets, the windows, the gates.

We knew them, but we did not recognise them. We did not dare to recognise them. It had been so long. And it was so strange. We had used to dream, when we lived in this city. We had lain down, nights, in the rooms behind the windows, and slept, and dreamed. We had all dreamed of the ocean, of the deep sea. Were we not dreaming now?

Sometimes the thunder and tremor deep below us rolled again, but it was faint now, far away; as far away as our memory of the thunder and the tremor and the fire and the towers falling, long ago. Neither the sound nor the memory frightened us. We knew them.

The sapphire light brightened overhead to green, almost green-gold. We looked up. The tops of the highest towers were hard to see, glowing in the radiance of light. The streets and doorways were darker, more clearly defined.

In one of those long, jewel-dark streets something was moving: something not composed of planes and angles, but of curves and arcs. We all turned to look at it, slowly, wondering as we did so at the slow ease of our own motion, our freedom. Sinuous, with a beautiful flowing, gathering, rolling movement, now rapid and now tentative, the thing drifted across the street from a blank garden wall to the recess of a door. There, in the dark blue shadow, it was hard to see for a while. We watched. A pale blue curve appeared at the top of the doorway. A second followed, and a third. The moving thing clung or hovered there, above the door, like a swaying knot of silvery cords or a boneless hand, one arched finger pointing carelessly to something above the lintel of the door,

something like itself, but motionless – a carving. A carving in jade light. A carving in stone.

Delicately and easily the long curving tentacle followed the curves of the carved figure, the eight petal limbs, the round eyes. Did it recognise its image?

The living one swung suddenly, gathered its curves in a loose knot and darted away down the street swift and sinuous. Behind it a faint cloud of darker blue hung for a minute and dispersed, revealing again the carved figure above the door: the sea flower, the cuttlefish, quick, great-eyed, graceful, evasive, the cherished sign, carved on a thousand walls, worked into the design of cornices, pavements, handles, lids of jewel boxes, canopies, tapestries, tabletops, gateways.

Down another street, at about the level of the first-floor windows, came a flickering drift of hundreds of motes of silver. With a single motion all turned towards the cross street, and glittered off into the dark blue shadows.

There were shadows, now.

We looked up, up from the flight of silver fish, up from the streets where the jade-green currents flowed and the blue shadows fell. We moved and looked up, yearning, to the high towers of our city. They stood, the fallen towers. They glowed in the ever-brightening radiance, not blue or blue-green, up there, but gold. Far above them lay a vast, circular, trembling brightness: the sun's light on the surface of the sea.

We are here. When we break through the bright circle into life, the water will break and stream white down the white sides of the towers, and run down the steep streets back into the sea. The water will glitter in dark hair, on the eyelids of dark eyes, and dry to a thin white film of salt.

We are here.

Whose voice? Who called to us?

He was with me for twelve days. On January 28th the crats came from the Bureau of Health Education and Welfare and

said that since he was receiving unemployment compensation while suffering from an untreated illness, the Government must look after him and restore him to health, because health is the inalienable right of the citizens of a democracy. He refused to sign the consent forms, so the chief Health Officer signed them. He refused to get up, so two of the policemen pulled him up off the bed. He started to try to fight them. The chief Health Officer pulled his gun and said that if he continued to struggle he would shoot him for resisting welfare, and arrest me for conspiracy to defraud the Government. The man who was holding my arms behind my back said they could always arrest me for un-reported pregnancy with intent to form a nuclear family. At that Simon stopped trying to get free. It was really all he was trying to do, not to fight them, just to get his arms free. He looked at me, and they took him out.

He is in the Federal Hospital in Salem. I have not been able to find out whether he is in the regular hospital or the mental wards.

It was on the radio again yesterday, about the rising land masses in the South Atlantic and the Western Pacific. At Max's the other night I saw a TV special explaining about geophysical stresses, and subsidence, and faults. The US Geodetic Service is doing a lot of advertising around town; the commonest one is a big billboard that says 'It's Not Our Fault!' with a picture of a beaver pointing to a schematic map that shows how even if Oregon has a major earthquake and subsidence as California did last month, it will not affect Portland, or only the western suburbs perhaps. The news also said that they plan to halt the tidal waves in Florida by dropping nuclear bombs where Miami was. Then they will re-attach Florida to the mainland with landfill. They are already advertising real estate for housing developments on the landfill. The President is staying at the Mile High White House in Aspen, Colorado. I don't think it will do him much good. Houseboats down on the Willamette are selling for $500,000. There are no trains or busses running south from Portland, because all the highways were badly

damaged by the tremors and landslides last week, so I will have to see if I can get to Salem on foot. I still have the rucksack I bought for the Mount Hood Wilderness Week. I got some dry lima beans and raisins with my Federal Fair Share Super Value Green Stamp minimal ration book for February – it took the whole book – and Phil Drum made me a tiny camp stove powered with the solar cell. I didn't want to take the Primus, it's too bulky, and I did want to be able to carry the viola. Max gave me a half pint of brandy. When the brandy is gone I expect I will stuff this notebook into the bottle and put the cap on tight and leave it on a hillside somewhere between here and Salem. I like to think of it being lifted up little by little by the water, and rocking, and going out to the dark sea.

> *Where are you?*
> *We are here. Where have you gone?*

SCHRÖDINGER'S CAT

As things appear to be coming to some sort of climax, I have withdrawn to this place. It is cooler here, and nothing moves fast.

On the way here I met a married couple who were coming apart. She had pretty well gone to pieces, but he seemed, at first glance, quite hearty. While he was telling me that he had no hormones of any kind, she pulled herself together and, by supporting her head in the crook of her right knee and hopping on the toes of the right foot, approached us shouting, 'Well what's *wrong* with a person trying to express themselves?' The left leg, the arms, and the trunk, which had remained lying in the heap, twitched and jerked in sympathy. 'Great legs,' the husband pointed out, looking at the slim ankle. 'My wife has great legs.'

A cat has arrived, interrupting my narrative. It is a striped yellow tom with white chest and paws. He has long whiskers and yellow eyes. I never noticed before that cats had whiskers above their eyes; is that normal? There is no way to tell. As he has gone to sleep on my knee, I shall proceed.

Where?

Nowhere, evidently. Yet the impulse to narrate remains. Many things are not worth doing, but almost anything is worth telling. In any case, I have a severe congenital case of *Ethica laboris puritanica*, or Adam's Disease. It is incurable except by total decapitation. I even like to dream when asleep, and to try and recall my dreams: it assures me that I haven't wasted

seven or eight hours just lying there. Now here I am, lying, here. Hard at it.

Well, the couple I was telling you about finally broke up. The pieces of him trotted around bouncing and cheeping, like little chicks, but she was finally reduced to nothing but a mass of nerves: rather like fine chicken wire, in fact but hopelessly tangled.

So I came on, placing one foot carefully in front of the other, and grieving. This grief is with me still. I fear it is part of me, like foot or loin or eye, or may even be myself: for I seem to have no other self, nothing further, nothing that lies outside the borders of grief.

Yet I don't know what I grieve for: my wife? my husband? my children, or myself? I can't remember. Most dreams are forgotten, try as one will to remember. Yet later music strikes the note, and the harmonic rings along the mandolin strings of the mind, and we find tears in our eyes. Some note keeps playing that makes me want to cry, but what for? I am not certain.

The yellow cat, who may have belonged to the couple that broke up, is dreaming. His paws twitch now and then, and once he makes a small, suppressed remark with his mouth shut. I wonder what a cat dreams of, and to whom he was speaking just then. Cats seldom waste words. They are quiet beasts. They keep their counsel, they reflect. They reflect all day, and at night their eyes reflect. Overbred Siamese cats may be as noisy as little dogs, and then people say, 'They're talking,' but the noise is farther from speech than is the deep silence of the hound or the tabby. All this cat can say is meow, but maybe in his silences he will suggest to me what it is that I have lost, what I am grieving for. I have a feeling that he knows. That's why he came here. Cats look out for Number One.

It was getting awfully hot. I mean, you could touch less and less. The stove burners, for instance. Now I know that stove burners always used to get hot; that was their final cause, they existed in order to get hot. But they began to get hot without

333

having been turned on. Electric units or gas rings, there they'd be when you came into the kitchen for breakfast all four of them glaring away, the air above them shaking like clear jelly with the heat waves. It did no good to turn them off, because they weren't on in the first place. Besides, the knobs and dials were also hot, uncomfortable to the touch.

Some people tried hard to cool them off. The favorite technique was to turn them on. It worked sometimes, but you could not count on it. Others investigated the phenomenon, tried to get at the root of it, the cause. They were probably the most frightened ones, but man is most human at his most frightened. In the face of the hot stove burners they acted with exemplary coolness. They studied, they observed. They were like the fellow in Michelangelo's *Last Judgment*, who has clapped his hands over his face in horror as the devils drag him down to Hell – but only over one eye. The other eye is busy looking. It's all he can do, but he does it. He observes. Indeed, one wonders if Hell would exist, if he did not look at it. However, neither he, nor the people I am talking about had enough time left to do much about it. And then finally, of course, there were the people who did not try to do or think anything about it at all.

When the water came out of the cold-water taps hot one morning, however, even people who had blamed it all on the Democrats began to feel a more profound unease. Before long, forks and pencils and wrenches were too hot to handle without gloves; and cars were really terrible. It was like opening the door of an oven going full blast to open the door of your car. And by then, other people almost scorched your fingers off. A kiss was like a branding iron. Your child's hair flowed along your hand like fire.

Here, as I said, it is cooler; and, as a matter of fact, this animal is cool. A real cool cat. No wonder it's pleasant to pet his fur. Also he moves slowly, at least for the most part, which is all the slowness one can reasonably expect of a cat. He hasn't that frenetic quality most creatures acquired – all they did was ZAP and gone. They lacked presence. I suppose birds always

tended to be that way, but even the hummingbird used to halt for a second in the very center of his metabolic frenzy, and hang, still as a hub, present, above the fuchsias – then gone again, but you knew something was there besides the blurring brightness. But it got so that even robins and pigeons, the heavy impudent birds, were a blur; and as for swallows, they cracked the sound barrier. You knew of swallows only by the small, curved sonic booms that looped about the eaves of old houses in the evening.

Worms shot like subway trains through the dirt of gardens, among the writhing roots of roses.

You could scarcely lay a hand on children, by then: too fast to catch, too hot to hold. They grew up before your eyes.

But then, maybe that's always been true.

I was interrupted by the cat who woke and said meow once, then jumped down from my lap and leaned against my legs diligently. This is a cat who knows how to get fed. He also knows how to jump. There was a lazy fluidity to his leap, as if gravity affected him less than it does other creatures. As a matter of fact there were some localised cases, just before I left, of the failure of gravity; but this quality in the cat's leap was something quite else. I am not yet in such a state of confusion that I can be alarmed by grace. Indeed, I found it reassuring. While I was opening a can of sardines, a person arrived.

Hearing the knock, I thought it might be the mailman. I miss mail very much, so I hurried to the door and said, 'Is it the mail?'

A voice replied, 'Yah!' I opened the door. He came in, almost pushing me aside in his haste. He dumped down an enormous knapsack he had been carrying, straightened up, massaged his shoulders, and said, 'Wow!'

'How did you get here?'

He stared at me and repeated, 'How?'

At this my thoughts concerning human and animal speech recurred to me, and I decided that this was probably not a man,

but a small dog. (Large dogs seldom go yah, wow, how, unless it is appropriate to do so.)

'Come on, fella,' I coaxed him. 'Come, come on, that's a boy, good doggie!' I opened a can of pork and beans for him at once, for he looked half starved. He ate voraciously, gulping and lapping. When it was gone he said 'Wow!' several times. I was just about to scratch him behind the ears when he stiffened, his hackles bristling, and growled deep in his throat. He had noticed the cat.

The cat had noticed him some time before, without interest, and was now sitting on a copy of *The Well-Tempered Clavier* washing sardine oil off its whiskers.

'Wow!' the dog, whom I had thought of calling Rover, barked. 'Wow! Do you know what that is? *That's Schrödinger's cat!*'

'No it's not, not any more; it's my cat,' I said, unreasonably offended.

'Oh, well, Schrödinger's dead, of course, but it's his cat. I've seen hundreds of pictures of it. Erwin Schrödinger, the great physicist, you know. Oh, wow! To think of finding it here!'

The cat looked coldly at him for a moment, and began to wash its left shoulder with negligent energy. An almost religious expression had come into Rover's face. 'It was meant,' he said in a low, impressive tone. 'Yah. It was *meant*. It can't be a mere coincidence. It's too improbable. Me, with the box; you, with the cat; to meet – here – now.' He looked up at me, his eyes shining with happy fervor. 'Isn't it wonderful?' he said. 'I'll get the box set up right away.' And he started to tear open his huge knapsack.

While the cat washed its front paws, Rover unpacked. While the cat washed its tail and belly, regions hard to reach gracefully, Rover put together what he had unpacked, a complex task. When he and the cat finished their operations simultaneously and looked at me, I was impressed. They had come out even, to the very second. Indeed, it seemed that something more than chance was involved. I hoped it was not myself.

'What's that?' I asked, pointing to a protuberance on the

outside of the box. I did not ask what the box was as it was quite clearly a box.

'The gun,' Rover said with excited pride.

'The gun?'

'To shoot the cat.'

'To shoot the cat?'

'Or to *not shoot* the cat. Depending on the photon.'

'The photon?'

'Yah! It's Schrödinger's great Gedankenexperiment. You see, there's a little emitter here. At Zero Time, five seconds after the lid of the box is closed, it will emit one photon. The photon will strike a half-silvered mirror. The quantum mechanical probability of the photon passing through the mirror is exactly one half, isn't it? So! If the photon passes through, the trigger will be activated and the gun will fire. If the photon is deflected, the trigger will not be activated and the gun will not fire. Now, you put the cat in. The cat is in the box. You close the lid. You go away! You stay away! What happens?' Rover's eyes were bright.

'The cat gets hungry?'

'The cat gets shot – or not shot,' he said, seizing my arm, though not, fortunately, in his teeth. 'But the gun is silent, perfectly silent. The box is soundproof. There is no way to know whether or not the cat has been shot, until you lift the lid of the box. There is *no* way! Do you see how central this is to the whole of quantum theory? Before Zero Time the whole system, on the quantum level or on our level is nice and simple. But after Zero Time the whole system can be represented only by a linear combination of two waves. We cannot predict the behavior of the photon, and thus, once it has behaved, we cannot predict the state of the system it has determined. We cannot predict it! God plays dice with the world! So it is beautifully demonstrated that if you desire certainty, any certainty, you must create it yourself!'

'How?'

'By lifting the lid of the box, of course,' Rover said, looking at me with sudden disappointment, perhaps a touch of

337

suspicion, like a Baptist who finds he has been talking church matters not to another Baptist as he thought, but a Methodist, or even, God forbid, an Episcopalian. 'To find out whether the cat is dead or not.'

'Do you mean,' I said carefully, 'that until you lift the lid of the box, the cat has neither been shot nor not been shot?'

'Yah!' Rover said, radiant with relief, welcoming me back to the fold. 'Or maybe, you know, both.'

'But why does opening the box and looking reduce the system back to one probability, either live cat or dead cat? Why don't we get included in the system when we lift the lid of the box?'

There was a pause. 'How?' Rover barked, distrustfully.

'Well, we would involve ourselves in the system, you see, the superposition of two waves. There's no reason why it should only exist *inside* an open box, is there? So when we came to look, there we would be, you and I, both looking at a live cat, and both looking at a dead cat. You see?'

A dark cloud lowered on Rover's eyes and brow. He barked twice in a subdued, harsh voice, and walked away. With his back turned to me he said in a firm, sad tone, 'You must not complicate the issue. It is complicated enough.'

'Are you sure?'

He nodded. Turning, he spoke pleadingly. 'Listen. It's all we have – the box. Truly it is. The box. And the cat. And they're here. The box, the cat, at last. Put the cat in the box. Will you? Will you let me put the cat in the box?'

'No,' I said, shocked.

'Please. Please. Just for a minute. Just for half a minute! Please let me put the cat in the box!'

'Why?'

'I can't stand this terrible uncertainty,' he said, and burst into tears.

I stood some while indecisive. Though I felt sorry for the poor son of a bitch, I was about to tell him, gently, No; when a curious thing happened. The cat walked over to the box,

sniffed around it, lifted his tail and sprayed a corner to mark his territory, and then lightly, with that marvellous fluid case, leapt into it. His yellow tail just flicked the edge of the lid as he jumped, and it closed, falling into place with a soft, decisive click.

'The cat is in the box,' I said.

'The cat is in the box,' Rover repeated in a whisper, falling to his knees. 'Oh, wow. Oh, wow. Oh, wow.'

There was silence then: deep silence. We both gazed, I afoot, Rover kneeling, at the box. No sound. Nothing happened. Nothing would happen. Nothing would ever happen, until we lifted the lid of the box.

'Like Pandora,' I said in a weak whisper. I could not quite recall Pandora's legend. She had let all the plagues and evils out of the box, of course, but there had been something else, too. After all the devils were let loose, something quite different, quite unexpected, had been left. What had it been? Hope? A dead cat? I could not remember.

Impatience welled up in me. I turned on Rover, glaring. He returned the look with expressive brown eyes. You can't tell me dogs haven't got souls.

'Just exactly what are you trying to prove?' I demanded.

'That the cat will be dead, or not dead,' he murmured submissively. 'Certainty. All I want is certainty. To know for *sure* that God *does* play dice with the world.'

I looked at him for a while with fascinated incredulity. 'Whether he does, or doesn't,' I said, 'do you think he's going to leave you a note about it in the box?' I went to the box, and with a rather dramatic gesture, flung the lid back. Rover staggered up from his knees, gasping, to look. The cat was, of course, not there.

Rover neither barked, nor fainted, nor cursed, nor wept. He really took it very well.

'Where is the cat?' he asked at last.

'Where is the box?'

'Here.'

'Where's here?'

'Here is now.'

'We used to think so,' I said, 'but really we should use larger boxes.'

He gazed about him in mute bewilderment, and did not flinch even when the roof of the house was lifted off just like the lid of a box, letting in the unconscionable, inordinate light of the stars. He had just time to breathe, 'Oh, wow!'

I have identified the note that keeps sounding. I checked it on the mandolin before the glue melted. It is the note A, the one that drove the composer Schumann mad. It is a beautiful, clear tone, much clearer now that the stars are visible. I shall miss the cat. I wonder if he found what it was we lost?

NORTH

TWO DELAYS ON THE NORTHERN LINE

1. Going to Paraguananza

The river was in flood, embankments under water clear down the line from Brailava to Krasnoy. A two-hour train trip had stretched into an afternoon of shunting, waiting, crawling from one village siding to another all through the hills of the upper Molsen province in heavy, inexhaustible rain. Rain was bringing down an early twilight on the tracks, the thistles, the tin roofs, the far-off barn and single poplar tree of an outlying farm of a nameless village somewhere west of the capital, when this scene, which had sat in self-contained enigmatic patience outside the window for fifty minutes, was eclipsed by a screeching rush of blackness. 'There's the freight! Now we'll get on,' said the salesman, who knew everything, and the family from Mesoval rejoiced. When the tracks, thistles, roofs, barn, and tree had reappeared, the train did begin to move, and quietly, unchanged, indifferent, these things disappeared backwards forever into the rainy dusk. The family from Mesoval and the salesman congratulated one another, 'Now we're off, it can't be over half an hour, Krasnoy at last.' Eduard Orte reopened his book. When he looked up after reading a page or two it had got quite dark outside. Lights of a lone car on a road far away swung round and were lost. In the dark, deep in glimmering rain, he saw the line of the green window blind and under it his face.

He looked with assurance at that face. At twenty he had

343

disliked it. At forty he owned it. Deep lines, long nose, long chin, that was Eduard Orte; he looked at him as an equal, without admiration or contempt. But he saw in the shape of the brows what people had seen when they used to say, 'How you take after her,' 'Eduard has his mother's eyes,' stupidly, as if they were not his eyes, as if he had no claim to see the world for himself. But in the second twenty years he had made his claim good.

Despite the divagations and false starts of this day's journey he knew where he was going and what would happen. His brother Nikolas would meet him at North Station, drive him eastward through the rainy city to the house where they had been born. Their mother would be sitting up in bed under the pink lamp. If this had been a mild attack she would look rather childlike and her voice would be thin; if it had been severe enough to frighten her into resistance, she would be alert and cheerful. They would ask each other questions and answer them. Then dinner downstairs, and a chat with Nikolas and his quiet wife, and to bed, hearing the rain on the windows of the bedroom where he had slept the first twenty years. Almost certainly his sister Retsia would not be there; she would have remembered she had left three small children in Solariy, and rushed back to them in a panic, just as she had rushed away from them. Nikolas would never have wired him, would simply have telephoned after the attack to give him the doctor's report, but Retsia thrived on commotion, flew to bedsides, fired off telegrams, COME AT ONCE, with more sense for the dramatic than of the ludicrous. Their mother, entirely content with Nikolas's twice-weekly visits, had not the faintest desire to 'see' either Eduard or Retsia, to have her routines disrupted and her hoarded vitality called upon for an expenditure of specious interest in their doings, which had not interested her for years. But Retsia needed the expectable, the conventional, so badly that she regularly employed the inconvenient to achieve it. When wired COME AT ONCE to the sick mother's bedside, one comes. To certain moves in chess

344

only certain responses are possible. Eduard Orte, a stronger and more conscious adherent of convention than his sister, submitted his will to the rules without complaint. But it was like chess without a board, this tracking back and forth for nothing: the same pointless trip three times in two years, or was it three years since the first attack? – so pointless, such a waste of time that he scarcely cared if the train went on all night as it had done all afternoon, shifting from siding to siding in the hills, off the main line and getting no closer, it made no difference.

When he got off the train and found in the wet hubbub of the platform and the glare and echoes of North Station nobody to meet him, he felt let down, betrayed. The emotion was quite inappropriate. Nikolas would hardly have stayed to meet a train five hours late. Eduard considered calling the house to say he had arrived, and then wondered why the thought had entered his head. It had risen from his stupid disappointment at not being met. He went out to get a taxi. At the bus stop near the taxi stand, a 41 was waiting; without hesitation he walked to it and got onto it. It had been how long, ten years, fifteen, no, longer than that, since he had ridden a bus crosstown through the loud streets of Krasnoy, dark and flashing in the March night, street lamps stretching reflections down into the rivers of black asphalt, as when he was a student riding home after late class at the University. The 41 stopped at the old stop at the foot of the Hill and a couple of students got on, pale, grave girls. The Molsen under Old Bridge ran very high in its stone embankments; everyone craned to see, and somebody behind him said, 'It's up over the warehouses down below Rail Bridge.' The bus groaned, swayed, stopped, lurched its way through the long straight streets of the Trasfiuve. Orte was the last but one to get off. The bus with its solitary passenger gasped its door shut and went on, leaving a quietness in its wake, the suburban quietness. Rain fell steadily. At the corner near a street lamp a young tree stood startled by light, its new leaves piercing green.

There were no further delays or changes of route. Orte walked the last half block home.

He knocked softly, pushed the unlocked door open, and entered. For some reason the hall was brightly lighted. A loud voice was talking in the sitting room, a stranger's voice. Was there a party going on? As he took off his topcoat to hang it on the hall coatrack, a boy came careening past, stopped at a distance, and stared with bright bold eyes.

'Who are you?' Orte asked, as the boy asked the same question, and as he answered, 'Eduard Orte,' the boy gave the same answer.

For a moment his head spun with the dizziness that he dreaded, the abyss opening, the falling.

'I'm your uncle,' he said, tapping the rain off his hat and hanging it up. 'Is your mother here?'

'In the piano room. With the funerals man.' The boy kept gazing, studying him, self-possessed, as if in his own house. Why did he not stand out of the way? I cannot go past him, Orte thought.

Retsia came into the hallway, saw him, cried, 'Oh, Eduard!' and burst instantly into tears. 'Oh, poor Eduard!'

She drew him with her, relinquishing him only to Nikolas, who shook his hand softly and seriously, saying in his even voice, 'You'd left. We couldn't reach you. Very easy, much suddener than expected, but very easy at the end...'

'I see, yes,' Orte said. The abyss hung under him, he held his brother's hand. 'The train,' he said.

'At two o'clock almost exactly,' Nikolas said.

Retsia said, 'We've been calling the station all afternoon. The whole railway above Aris is under water. You must be worn out, poor Eduard! And not knowing, all day long, the whole afternoon!' Tears ran down her face as plentiful and simple as rain running down the windows of the train.

Orte had intended to ask several questions of Nikolas before he went up to see his mother: Had it in fact been a severe attack? Is she on the same medication? Has there been much

angina? Now he still wanted to ask these questions, which after all had not been answered. Nikolas continued to tell him about the death, but he had not asked about that. It was not fair. He still felt a little light-headed, but that was from travelling all day. The abyss had closed and he had let go Nikolas's hand. Retsia hovered close, smiling, tearful. Nikolas, he noticed, looked strained and tired, his eyes rather swollen behind his thick spectacles. What did he look like himself? Did he show any such signs of grief? Did he feel grief? He looked into himself with apprehension, finding nothing except the continuing slight unpleasant dizziness. One could not call that grief. Should he not wish to cry?

'Is she upstairs?'

Nikolas explained the new government regulations. 'They have been most efficient and considerate,' he said. The body had been taken to the East District Crematory; a man had come by with the papers, to arrange for the display and service; they had just been completing the arrangements when Eduard arrived. They all moved about, went to the music room, the man was introduced. It was his voice Orte had first heard coming into the house, the loud voice and bright lights, like a party. Nikolas showed the man out. 'I met,' Eduard Orte said to his sister, then hesitated – 'young Eduard.' Then wished he had not spoken, because the nephew named for him could not be that boy, who was much too old, and who had said his name was Orte, had he not? when it must be Paren; Retsia's married name was Paren. But who was the boy, then?

'Yes, I did want the children here,' Retsia was saying. 'Tomas will drive up tomorrow morning. I do hope it stops raining, the roads must be terrible.' He noticed her strong ivory teeth. She must be, it was impossible, thirty-eight. He would not have known her had they passed on the street. Her eyes were greyish blue. She was looking at him. 'You're tired,' she said in the way that had used to irritate him, telling people what they felt; but the words were welcome to him. He was not aware of being particularly tired, but if he looked tired, or was tired without

knowing it, perhaps also he had feelings he was unaware of, appropriate feelings. 'Come and have some supper, now that man's gone. You must be starving! The children are eating in the kitchen. Oh, Eduard, everything is so strange!' she said, leading him briskly on.

The kitchen was warm and full of people. The cook-housekeeper Vera, who had come after his time but had been there for years now, greeted him mumbling. She was upset, and he understood that; how was an old woman with bad legs to get a new job? But no doubt Nikolas and Nina would take her in. Retsia's children were all at the kitchen table: the boy he had met in the hall, and the older sister, and the little boy, whom they had called Riri last time Orte had seen them, but were calling Raul now; and there was another one, that sister or cousin of Retsia's husband who lived with them, a short, sullen girl of twenty or more. Nikolas's wife Nina came from behind the table to greet him with an embrace. As she spoke, he remembered what he had not thought of since Nikolas's letter about it a couple of weeks ago, that Nikolas and Nina had adopted a baby – had Nikolas written that it was a boy? It had all seemed so artificial to him that he had read the letter carelessly, finding the matter distasteful and embarrassing, and now he could not recall what Nikolas had written. It would not do to ask Nina about it. Old Vera insisted on making tea for him to show that she was necessary, and he had to sit down with them all in the bright noisy kitchen and eat a little, wait for the tea and drink it. The noise abated. Nobody spoke to him much; Nina glanced at him with her sad, dark eyes. He began to realise with relief that his habitual gravity of manner might be taken for emotion controlled, might serve him as a façade behind which he could keep to himself his lack of sorrow, like a locked and empty room.

He was not allowed to sleep in his old room upstairs after all. Nothing he had expected happened. The house was full up. It seemed that since the adoption Nikolas and Nina had

given up their flat in Old Quarter and moved back here till they came in line for a larger flat. They were in Eduard's old room, and their baby was in Nikolas's old room; Retsia and her three were in the nursery; the cousin slept on the living-room couch; there was nothing left for him but the leather couch in the glassed-in porch off the music room, downstairs. Only the mother's room was empty. He did not see it. He did not go upstairs. Retsia brought down blankets, then a quilt, finally a warm dressing gown of Nikolas's. 'It's terrible out here, terrible, poor Eduard. If you sleep in this it might help you stay warm. Oh, how strange everything is!' Her hair was braided for sleep, she wore a pink wool wrapper. She looked broad, competent, maternal, beautiful; her face was illuminated as if she were listening to music. That is grief, he thought.

'It's all right,' he said.

'But you always get cold feet at night. It's terrible to stick you out here. I don't know what we'll do when Tomas comes. Oh, Eduard, I do so wish that you'd got married, I hate for people to be alone! I know you don't mind, but I do. The curtains won't close, will they? Oh, Christ, I've torn the side hem. Well, there's nothing to shut out here but the rain.' The ready tears stood in her eyes; her warmth and strength enveloped him a moment as she hugged him. 'Good night!' she said and left, shutting the curtained glass door behind her, and he heard her voice and the cousin's in the next room.

She went upstairs. The house grew silent. He rearranged the blankets and quilt and lay down on the couch. He read the book he had read on the train, a long-term project for goals and fund allocations in the department that would, in May, come under the administration of his bureau. Rain brushed the windows above the couch. His hands grew cold. Silently and suddenly the light in the next room went out, leaving the curtained glass door black, and the light from his small reading lamp very dim. The cousin was in that room. The house was full of people he did not know. This porch, cold, in night and rain, was strange to him. They never used the porch except

in summer, on hot days. This was not the trip he had started out on. To come home, that was one true direction, but now it had lost its sense, he had ended up in a strange place. Was this confusion what they called grief? She is dead, he thought, she is dead, as he lay fairly comfortably propped against the arm of the couch, the book open against his raised knees under the quilt, gazing at the page numbers 144, 145, and waited for the reaction. But he had left home so long ago, after all. 144, 145. His eyes returned to the paragraph he had been reading. He read on to the end of the section. His watch said two-thirty. He turned off the bronze-shaded reading lamp and huddled down under the blankets and quilts; he heard the rain brush quietly against the windows. 'I am going to Paraguay,' he told the salesman, annoyed at being asked. 'To Paraguananza, the capital of the nation.' But they met with long delays along the line from floods of water, and when he got there, across terrible abysses, to Paraguananza, it was no different from here.

2. Metempsychosis

When the lawyer's letter came, Eduard Russe thought nothing at first about the house that had been willed to him, but tried only to dredge up from the shifty bogs of memory some shard or fragment, a cranium, a fingerbone, of that great-uncle, his mother's father's brother, who had seen fit, or been forced by a paucity of survivors, to leave him the house in Brailava. He had always lived in Krasnoy; when he was nine or ten he had gone with his mother to visit their Northern relatives, but of that journey he could recall only the most trivial things – a hen with her brood of chicks in a backyard by a basket, a man standing and singing aloud on a street corner directly under (so his child's eye averred) a huge, dark-blue mountain. Of the grandfather who had then owned the house, of the great-uncle who had next inherited it, nothing remained but

a discomfort of dark rooms and loud old voices. Old men, deaf, not the same species as himself, no kin. Crossed swords with basket grips and curved blades hanging on a chimney: sabres. He had never seen a sabre. He was not allowed to play with them. The old men did nothing with them, did not keep them polished. If they had let him take them down he would have polished them. He was ashamed, now, of this ingratitude of mind which left him only his own childish envies and not one glimpse of the man who had given him a house – even if he did not want the house and could wish the old man had, equally, forgotten him. What was he to do with a house in Brailava? What was he supposed to reply to the lawyer's letter? Employed in the Bureau of Housing, on modest salary, he had never had any use for lawyers and had kept well clear of the breed. His wife would have known how to answer the letter; she had good sense about such things, and good manners too. Following what he imagined Elena might have written, he produced a short, civil acknowledgment of the lawyer's communication, posted it, and then, in fact, altogether forgot about the great-uncle, the legacy, the property in Brailava. He was busy, having undertaken an extra task of the kind he was good at, a reorganisation and simplification of recordkeeping. People would say he was trying to lose himself in his work, but though he had always liked his work and still did, he knew there was no way to lose himself in it. Rather he found himself in it constantly, met himself in the work he had done, in the people he worked with. On every street corner on the way to the Bureau he met himself coming back from work to the apartment on Sidres Street where Elena, who taught in the College of Applied Arts, would be home already, unless it was Wednesday night when she had a class from four to six—

His days were punctuated by these dashes, not periods but breaks, empty spaces in which he stopped himself from finishing the thought, or from trying to finish the thought which no longer had an end, since in this case Elena had no

351

class from four to six on Wednesday, because she was dead of an aneurysm of the heart and had been dead for three months, and in any case all thoughts led to this same non-end or stopping place and were there, as in the cremator's fire, destroyed.

He knew he could manage his misery in a wiser way, without these breaks and terrible repetitions, if he could sleep well. But he could never sleep, now, more than two or three hours at a time, and then would wake and lie awake as long as he had slept. He tried drinking, and he tried the sleeping pills a friend at work recommended. Both gave him five hours' sleep, two hours' nightmare, and a day of sick despair. He went back to reading during his night wakings. He read anything, but preferred history, the histories of other countries. Sometimes, at three in the morning, he cried, as he read the history of Renaissance Spain, ignoring his tears. He had no dreams. She had taken his dreams, and they had gone with her too far, by now, to find their way back to him. They had got lost and petered out dried up, somewhere in that thick, rock-ridden darkness through which Elena had very slowly gone, tunnelling her way forward, heavily, without breathing. He felt that she was beyond that now, in some other region, but not one he was able to imagine.

A second letter arrived from the law firm in Brailava. The envelope was double-weight manila, heavy, portentous. Resigned, he opened it. The lawyer's letter was short and only moderately obscure, appearing to suggest, with due caution, that as things stood (and undoubtedly given his professional affiliation he was far better informed on this subject than the writer), he might find, if he decided to consider selling the house, that it was possible to get a good price for it; dissociating himself promptly, the lawyer, whom Eduard now envisaged as almost inevitably sixty and clean-shaven with a long upper lip, went on to remark that there were several reputable real-property agents in Krasnoy with Northern branches, if he did not wish to be troubled with the business himself. However,

personal belongings left in the house might demand, at least briefly, his presence and decision as to whether the furniture, papers, books, etc, were of value, monetary or sentimental. With the letter were some documents, evidently deeds, descriptions, and so on, concerning the property, and, in an old, soft, rather mangy leather pouch, a steel ring on which were six keys.

It was curious that he should have sent them without waiting to hear from Eduard again, to identify him more securely, to meet him. It was the keys that had made the envelope misshapen and heavy. Eduard spread them out fanwise on his left palm with his right forefinger and studied them with uneasy curiosity. Two, identical, looked like old-fashioned, respectable front-door keys. The other four were wildly various: one that might fit a big padlock, one with a barrel like a clock key, one plain iron all-purpose that suggested a pantry or cellar door, and one of brass with delicately intricate wards, probably the key to some old piece of furniture, a wardrobe or escritoire. He imagined, with continuing unease, the brass keyhole in the curved mahogany, shelves behind glass, meaningless papers in half-empty drawers.

He requested two days off work at the end of the month. He would go up to Brailava on the Wednesday evening train, come back on the Sunday. Efficiency. See the lawyer, see the house, arrange to have it cleared out and put up for sale. While looking after all this he would be able to see something of the city where his mother had been born and lived as a child. With the money from the sale of the house he would go to Spain. Unearned money should be spent at once, otherwise it festered. What would it cost to go to Egypt? He had always wanted to see the pyramids. Red-coated, waving sabres, cinematic English soldiers charged thinly across a waste of gold behind the back of the indifferent Sphinx and petered out, like water poured onto sand. The Sahara, a furnace, an empty place. The train jerked forward tentatively and stopped again. No one else was in the compartment at the moment; the young couple who had

taken the facing seat were standing in the corridor. They had been joking with friends on the platform. Now they shouted and waved and banged the windows childishly as the train, quiet and purposeful, began to glide forward. Eduard's eyes filled up with tears and his breath stuck in an audible sob. Appalled by the ambush, by the overwhelming advantage grief had over him, he clenched his hands, shut his eyes, feigned sleep, although his face was hot and his breath would not come evenly. He foreswore Egypt, damn Egypt, damn Toledo and Madrid. The tears dried in his eyes. He watched the northern suburbs slide past beyond the viaducts in the soft, amniotic haze of the September afternoon.

The young couple came back into the compartment, no longer talking or smiling; their animation had been all for their friends in North Station. Eduard continued to gaze out the window as the train ran steadily north on the level embankments by the Molsen. The river was wide, serene, a pale silken blue color between low banks. Willows stood in the late sunlight by the river. The haze was thickening; it looked like rain ahead, in the north, a heavy blueness of clouds. He had got off work early to catch the five o'clock express. They would be in Brailava by half past six, following the river all the way. He got a little drowsy, looking at the silken water.

At a quarter to six there was a tremendous noise and a subsequent absolute silence. As Eduard picked himself up from the floor of the compartment where for some reason he had arrived, the young man kicked him in the shoulder. 'Watch that!' Eduard said furiously, and retrieved his briefcase, which had also slid across the floor. There was now a strange, thin commotion of voices in the corridor. 'Oh, oh, oh, oh,' the young woman was saying in a silly voice. The commotion grew to a hubbub like that of an audience at intermission, both inside the car and outside along the tracks, shouts, ex-clamations, descriptions, comparisons, complaints, as it became clear that the engine had hit a hay truck stalled at a crossing,

and that though nobody was hurt except for the truck driver, who had been killed, the engine had derailed and there was going to be a delay while they brought a relief engine down from Brailava. Another break, a dash not a period; non-arrival. Eduard walked up and down the tracks a while in the late long sunlight. It was almost seven when a relief engine arrived, from the south not the north, and pulled the train back to a siding at the local station called Isestno, which was not even mentioned on the Krasnoy-Brailava schedule of the Northern Line; and there it waited, while night fell and the rain came on, until the tracks were mended and the relief engine from Brailava came and hauled it on in, arriving at Sumeny Station at half past ten.

There had been nothing whatever to eat on the train and no vendors at mournful Isestno siding, but Eduard did not feel hungry as he walked under the bright cavernous dome of Sumeny, carrying the briefcase which was all he had brought. Now that he was off the train at last, he felt shaken. He had planned to arrive at half past six, find a hotel near the station, have dinner, but now he did not want to stay up and eat out among strangers, he wanted to go home. Other men hurried past him through the high doors into the rainy night.

'Taxi?'

'All right,' he said.

'Where to, sir?'

'Fourteen Kamenny Street.'

'That'll be up Underhill,' the taxi driver said, confirming Eduard's memory of the name of the district and of the dark blue crags hunched over a singing man, a man under a hill, and took off, doors and smeared windows rattling. It was dark in the cab and the smell was comfortable. Eduard roused himself, confused, almost from sleep, and sank back into it, almost.

'Fourteen, was it?'

'Right.'

'This one, looks like. There's Twelve.'

He could see no street number. There was a house; there

was rain, trees, darkness. He paid the driver, who said good night to him in the dry, civil, Northern voice.

Three stone steps, flanked by shrubs and some kind of iron fence or grille: '14' over the rather ornate wooden doorframe. A strange city, a strange street, whose house? The first of the twin keys fit the lock. He opened the door, looked in, took a couple of steps in, but left the door ajar behind him, to be certain of escape.

Pitch dark; dry, cool. Sound of rain above on high roofs. No other sound.

The light switch came under his hand to the right of the door. He felt that he should say, 'I'm here.' To whom? He turned on the light.

The hall was much smaller than it had seemed in darkness. He had, he now realised, felt himself to be in an almost limitless space, but it was only the quiet shabby front hall of an old house on a rainy night. The strip of carpet on the handsome black and grey tiles was worn and not very clean. Somebody's hat, his great-uncle's hat, an old felt, lay forlorn on a small sideboard. The light fixture was of yellowish cloudy glass.

The door was still ajar behind him. He returned and closed it and automatically put the key ring into his trousers pocket.

Stairs went up to the left. The hall went on past them: a door to the right and an end door, both shut. The sitting room would be that one to the right, the end one would lead back to the kitchen. There was a dining room, maybe on the way to the kitchen; it was in a dark dining room that he had heard the loud old voices. He should look into the rooms, but he was tired. He had been sleeping very badly for several nights, and the train trip with its shock and unfelt death and long delay had left him shaky. The hall was all right, the old hat was all right, but he could not take much more. The yellowish light illuminated the stairs as well as the hall. He went up the stairs, his right hand on the narrow heavily varnished railing. At the top he turned and went down the hall to the end door,

opened it, and turned on the light. He did not know why he chose that door, or whether he had been upstairs in the house as a child. This was the front bedroom, probably the largest. It might be the room his great-uncle had slept in, perhaps died in, unless he had died in hospital, or it might have been the grandfather's room, or have stood unused for thirty years. It was clean and sparse, bed, table, chair, two windows, fireplace. The bed was made, tight and neat, an old blue coverlet pulled tight. The overhead light in its glass shade was dim, and there was no lamp.

Eduard put down his briefcase by the bed.

The washroom was at the other end of the hall. He thought at first the water had been cut off, for the pipe groaned when he turned the faucet, but then it spat rust, belched red, and ran clear. He was thirsty. He drank from the faucet. The water was rusty and cold and tasted of the north.

There was an old bookcase with glassed shelves in the hall, and he stopped before it for a minute, but the light was faint and the titles of the books meant nothing. He could not read. He went into the front bedroom and turned back the blue coverlet. The bed was made up with heavy linen sheets and a dark blanket. He took off his clothes, hung his coat and trousers in the empty closet, turned off the light, got into the cold bed in the dark room made tremulous by a distant street lamp shining through rain or the shadows of leaves; he stretched out and laid his head back on the hard pillow, and slept.

He woke in sunlit morning, lying on his side, looking at the swords, cavalry sabres, hung crossed on the chimneypiece.

They were tools, he thought, expressing purpose as simply as a needle or a hammer, their purpose, their reason or meaning, being death; they were made to kill men with; the slightly curved and still unpolished blades were death, were, in fact, his own death, which he saw with clarity and relaxation; for as his eyes were occupied with looking at that his mind was wandering to the other rooms, which he had not seen last night, the rooms whose doors, for which he had the keys, would lead to his life,

his request for a transfer to the Bureau here in Brailava, the wild cherry flowering in the mountains in March, his second marriage, all that, but for the moment enough, this room, the swords, the sunlight; he had arrived.

SQ

I think what Dr Speakie has done is wonderful. He is a wonderful man. I believe that. I believe that people need beliefs. If I didn't have my belief I really don't know what would happen.

And if Dr Speakie hadn't truly believed in his work he couldn't possibly have done what he did. Where would he have found the courage? What he did proves his genuine sincerity.

There was a time when a lot of people tried to cast doubts on him. They said he was seeking power. That was never true. From the very beginning all he wanted was to help people and make a better world. The people who called him a power-seeker and a dictator were just the same ones who used to say that Hitler was insane and Nixon was insane and all the world leaders were insane and the arms race was insane and our misuse of natural resources was insane and the whole world civilisation was insane and suicidal. They were always saying that. And they said it about Dr Speakie. But he stopped all that insanity, didn't he? So he was right all along, and he was right to believe in his beliefs.

I came to work for him when he was named the Chief of the Psychometric Bureau. I used to work at the UN, and when the World Government took over the New York UN Building they transferred me up to the thirty-fifth floor to be the head secretary in Dr Speakie's office. I knew already that it was a position of great responsibility, and I was quite excited the whole week before my new job began. I was so curious to meet

Dr Speakie, because, of course, he was already famous. I was there right at the dot of nine on Monday morning, and when he came in it was so wonderful. He looked so kind. You could tell that the weight of his responsibilities was always on his mind, but he looked so healthy and positive, and there was a bounce in his step – I used to think it was as if he had rubber balls in the toes of his shoes. He smiled and shook my hand and said in such a friendly, confident voice, 'And you must be Mrs Smith! I've heard wonderful things about you. We're going to have a wonderful team here, Mrs Smith!'

Later on he called me by my first name, of course.

That first year we were mostly busy with Information. The World Government Presidium and all the Member States had to be fully informed about the nature and purpose of the SQ Test, before the actual implementation of its application could be eventualised. That was good for me, too, because in preparing all that information I learned all about it myself. Often, taking dictation, I learned about it from Dr Speakie's very lips. By May I was enough of an 'expert' that I was able to prepare the Basic SQ Information Pamphlet for publication just from Dr Speakie's notes. It was such fascinating work. As soon as I began to understand the SQ Test Plan I began to believe in it. That was true of everybody in the office and in the Bureau. Dr Speakie's sincerity and scientific enthusiasm were infectious. Right from the beginning we had to take the Test every quarter, of course, and some of the secretaries used to be nervous before they took it, but I never was. It was so obvious that the Test was *right*. If you scored under 50 it was nice to know that you were sane, but even if you scored over 50 that was fine, too, because then you could be *helped*. And anyway it is always best to know the truth about yourself.

As soon as the Information service was functioning smoothly Dr Speakie transferred the main thrust of his attention to the implementation of Evaluator training, and planning for the structurisation of the Cure Centers, only he changed the name to SQ Achievement Centers. It seemed a very big job even

then. We certainly had no idea how big the job would finally turn out to be!

As he said at the beginning, we were a very good team. We all worked hard, but there were always rewards.

I remember one wonderful day. I had accompanied Dr Speakie to the Meeting of the Board of the Psychometric Bureau. The emissary from the State of Brazil announced that his State had adopted the Bureau Recommendations for Universal Testing – we had known that that was going to be announced. But then the delegate from Libya and the delegate from China announced that their States had adopted the Test too! Oh, Dr Speakie's face was just like the sun for a minute, just *shining*. I wish I could remember exactly what he said, especially to the Chinese delegate, because, of course, China was a very big State and its decision was very influential. Unfortunately I do not have his exact words because I was changing the tape in the recorder. He said something like, 'Gentlemen, this is a historic day for humanity.' Then he began to talk at once about the effective implementation of the Application Centers, where people would take the Test, and the Achievement Centers, where they would go if they scored over 50, and how to establish the Test Administrations and Evaluations infrastructure on such a large scale, and so on. He was always modest and practical. He would rather talk about doing the job than talk about what an important job it was. He used to say, 'Once you know what you're doing, the only thing you need to think about is how to do it.' I believe that that is deeply true.

From then on, we could hand over the Information program to a subdepartment and concentrate on How to Do It. Those were exciting times! So many States joined the Plan, one after another. When I think of all we had to do I wonder that we didn't all go crazy! Some of the office staff did fail their quarterly Test, in fact. But most of us working in the Executive Office with Dr Speakie remained quite stable, even when we were on the job all day and half the night. I think his presence

was an inspiration. He was always calm and positive, even when we had to arrange things like training 113,000 Chinese Evaluators in three months. 'You can always find out "how" if you just know the "why"!' he would say. And we always did.

When you think back over it it really is quite amazing what a big job it was – so much bigger than anybody, even Dr Speakie, had realised it would be. It just changed everything. You only realise that when you think back to what things used to be like. Can you imagine, when we began planning Universal Testing for the State of China, we only allowed for 1,100 Achievement Centers, with 6,800 Staff? It really seems like a joke! But it is not. I was going through some of the old files yesterday, making sure everything is in order, and I found the first China Implementation Plan, with those figures written down in black and white.

I believe the reason why even Dr Speakie was slow to realise the magnitude of the operation was that even though he was a great scientist he was also an optimist. He just kept hoping against hope that the average scores would begin to go down, and this prevented him from seeing that universal application of the SQ Test was eventually going to involve everybody either as Inmates or as Staff.

When most of the Russians and all the African States had adopted the Recommendations and were busy implementing them, the debates in the General Assembly of the World Government got very excited. That was the period when so many bad things were said about the Test and about Dr Speakie. I used to get quite angry, reading the *World Times* reports of debates. When I went as his secretary with Dr Speakie to General Assembly meetings I had to sit and listen in person to people insulting him personally, casting aspersions on his motives and questioning his scientific integrity and even his sincerity. Many of those people were very disagreeable and obviously unbalanced. But he never lost his temper. He would just stand up and prove to them, again, that the SQ Test did actually literally scientifically show whether the testee

was sane or insane, and the results could be proved, and all psychometrists accepted them. So the Test Ban people couldn't do anything but shout about freedom and accuse Dr Speakie and the Psychometric Bureau of trying to 'turn the world into a huge insane asylum.' He would always answer quietly and firmly, asking them how they thought a person could be 'free' if they lacked mental health. What they called freedom might well be a delusional system with no contact with reality. In order to find out, all they had to do was to become testees. 'Mental health *is* freedom,' he said. ' "Eternal vigilance is the price of liberty," they say, and now we have an eternally vigilant watchdog: the SQ Test. *Only the testees can be truly free!*'

There really was no answer they could make to that. Sooner or later the delegates even from Member States where the Test Ban movement was strong would volunteer to take the SQ Test to prove that their mental health was adequate to their responsibilities. Then the ones that passed the test and remained in office would began working for Universal Application in their home State. The riots and demonstrations, and things like the burning of the Houses of Parliament in London in the State of England (where the Nor-Eurp SQ Center was housed), and the Vatican Rebellion, and the Chilean H-Bomb, were the work of insane fanatics appealing to the most unstable elements of the populace. Such fanatics, as Dr Speakie and Dr Waltraute pointed out in their Memorandum to the Presidium, deliberately aroused and used the proven instability of the crowd, 'mob psychosis.' The only response to mass delusion of that kind was immediate implementation of the Testing Program in the disturbed States, and immediate amplification of the Asylum Program.

That was Dr Speakie's own decision, by the way, to rename the SQ Achievement Centers 'Asylums.' He took the word right out of his enemies' mouths. He said: 'An asylum means a place of *shelter*, a place of *cure*. Let there be no stigma attached to the word "insane," to the word "asylum," to the words "insane asylum"! No! For the asylum is the haven of mental health – the

place of cure, where the anxious gain peace, where the weak gain strength, where the prisoners of inadequate reality assessment win their way to freedom! Proudly let us use the word "asylum." Proudly let us go to the asylum, to work to regain our own God-given mental health, or to work with others less fortunate to help them win back their own inalienable right to mental health. And let one word be written large over the door of every asylum in the world – "WELCOME!" '

Those words are from his great speech at the General Assembly on the day World Universal Application was decreed by the Presidium. Once or twice a year I listen to my tape of that speech. Although I am too busy ever to get really depressed, now and then I feel the need of a tiny 'pick-me-up,' and so I play that tape. It never fails to send me back to my duties inspired and refreshed.

Considering all the work there was to do, as the Test scores continued to come in always a little higher than the Psychometric Bureau analysts estimated, the World Government Presidium did a wonderful job for the two years that it administered Universal Testing. There was a long period, six months, when the scores seemed to have stabilised, with just about half of the testees scoring over 50 and half under 50. At that time it was thought that if forty percent of the mentally healthy were assigned to Asylum Staff work, the other sixty percent could keep up routine basic world functions such as farming, power supply, transportation, etc. This proportion had to be reversed when they found that over sixty percent of the mentally healthy were volunteering for Staff work, in order to be with their loved ones in the Asylums. There was some trouble then with the routine basic world functions functioning. However, even then contingency plans were being made for the inclusion of farmlands, factories, power plants, etc, in the Asylum Territories, and the assignment of routine basic world functions work as Rehabilitation Therapy, so that the Asylums could become totally self-supporting if it became advisable. This was President Kim's special care, and he worked for it

all through his term of office. Events proved the wisdom of his planning. He seemed such a nice wise little man. I still remember the day when Dr Speakie came into the office and I knew at once that something was wrong. Not that he ever got really depressed or reacted with inopportune emotion, but it was as if the rubber balls in his shoes had gone just a little bit flat. There was the slightest tremor of true sorrow in his voice when he said, 'Mary Ann, we've had a bit of bad news I'm afraid.' Then he smiled to reassure me, because he knew what a strain we were all working under, and certainly didn't want to give anybody a shock that might push their score up higher on the next quarterly Test! 'It's President Kim,' he said, and I knew at once – I knew he didn't mean the President was ill or dead.

'Over 50?' I asked, and he just said quietly and sadly, '55.'

Poor little President Kim, working so efficiently all that three months while mental ill health was growing in him! It was very sad and also a useful warning. High-level consultations were begun at once, as soon as President Kim was committed; and the decision was made to administer the Test monthly, instead of quarterly, to anyone in an executive position.

Even before this decision, the Universal scores had begun rising again. Dr Speakie was not distressed. He had already predicted that this rise was highly probable during the transition period to World Sanity. As the number of the mentally healthy living outside the Asylums grew fewer, the strain on them kept growing greater, and they became more liable to break down under it – just as poor President Kim had done. Later, he predicted, when the Rehabs began coming out of the Asylums in ever increasing numbers, this stress would decrease. Also the crowding in the Asylums would decrease, so that the Staff would have more time to work on individually orientated therapy, and this would lead to a still more dramatic increase in the number of Rehabs released. Finally, when the therapy process was completely perfected, there would be no Asylums left in the world at all. Everybody would be either mentally

healthy or a Rehab, or 'neonormal,' as Dr Speakie liked to call it.

It was the trouble in the State of Australia that precipitated the Government crisis. Some Psychometric Bureau officials accused the Australian Evaluators of actually falsifying Test returns, but that is impossible since all the computers are linked to the World Government Central Computer Bank in Keokuk. Dr Speakie suspected that the Australian Evaluators had been falsifying *the Test itself*, and insisted that they themselves all be tested immediately. Of course he was right. It had been a conspiracy, and the suspiciously low Australian Test scores had resulted from the use of a false Test. Many of the conspirators tested higher than 80 when forced to take the genuine Test! The State Government in Canberra had been unforgivably lax. If they had just admitted it everything would have been all right. But they got hysterical, and moved the State Government to a sheep station in Queensland, and tried to withdraw from the World Government. (Dr Speakie said this was a typical mass psychosis: reality evasion, followed by fugue and autistic withdrawal.) Unfortunately the Presidium seemed to be paralysed. Australia seceded on the day before the President and Presidium were due to take their monthly Test, and probably they were afraid of overstraining their SQ with agonising decisions. So the Psychometric Bureau volunteered to handle the episode. Dr Speakie himself flew on the plane with the H-bombs, and helped to drop the information leaflets. He never lacked personal courage.

When the Australian incident was over, it turned out that most of the Presidium, including President Singh, had scored over 50. So the Psychometric Bureau took over their functions temporarily. Even on a long-term basis this made good sense, since all the problems now facing the World Government had to do with administering and evaluating the Test training the Staff, and providing full self-sufficiency structuration to all Asylums.

What this meant in personal terms was that Dr Speakie, as

Chief of the Psychometric Bureau, was now Interim President of the United States of the World. As his personal secretary I was, I will admit it, just terribly proud of him. But he never let it go to his head.

He was so modest. Sometimes he used to say to people, when he introduced me. 'This is Mary Ann, my secretary,' he'd say with a little twinkle, 'and if it wasn't for her I'd have been scoring over 50 long ago!'

There were times, as the World SQ scores rose and rose, that I would become a little discouraged. Once the week's Test figures came in on the readout and the *average* score was 71. I said, 'Doctor, there are moments I believe the whole world is going insane!'

But he said, 'Look at it this way, Mary Ann. Look at those people in the Asylums – 3.1 billion inmates now, and 1.8 billion staff – but look at them. What are they doing? They're pursuing their therapy, doing rehabilitation work on the farms and in the factories, and striving all the time, too, to *help* each other towards mental health. The preponderant inverse sanity quotient is certainly very high at the moment; they're mostly insane, yes. But you have to admire them. They are fighting for mental health. They will – they *will* win through!' And then he dropped his voice and said as if to himself, gazing out the window and bouncing just a little on the balls of his feet, 'If I didn't believe that, I couldn't go on.'

And I knew he was thinking of his wife.

Mrs Speakie had scored 88 on the very first American Universal Test. She had been in the Greater Los Angeles Territory Asylum for years now.

Anybody who still thinks Dr Speakie wasn't sincere should think about that for a minute! He gave up everything for his belief.

And even when the Asylums were all running quite well, and the epidemics in South Africa and the famines in Texas and the Ukraine were under control, still the workload on Dr Speakie never got any lighter, because every month the

personnel of the Psychometric Bureau got smaller, since some of them always flunked their monthly Test and were committed to Bethesda. I never could keep any of my secretarial staff any more for longer than a month or two. It was harder and harder to find replacements, too, because most sane young people volunteered for Staff work in the Asylums, since life was much easier and more sociable inside the Asylums than outside. Everything so convenient, and lots of friends and acquaintances! I used to positively envy those girls! But I knew where my job was.

At least it was much less hectic here in the UN Building, or the Psychometry Tower as it had been renamed long ago. Often there wouldn't be anybody around the whole building all day long but Dr Speakie and myself, and maybe Bill the janitor (Bill scored 32 regular as clockwork every quarter). All the restaurants were closed, in fact, most of Manhattan was closed, but we had fun picnicking in the old General Assembly Hall. And there was always the odd call from Buenos Aires or Reykjavik, asking Dr Speakie's advice as Interim President about some problem, to break the silence.

But last November 8, I will never forget the date, when Dr Speakie was dictating the Referendum for World Economic Growth for the next five-year period, he suddenly interrupted himself. 'By the way, Mary Ann,' he said, 'how was your last score?'

We had taken the Test two days before, on the sixth. We always took the Test every first Monday. Dr Speakie never would have dreamed of excepting himself from Universal Testing regulations.

'I scored 12,' I said, before I thought how strange it was of him to ask. Or, not just to ask, because we often mentioned our scores to each other; but to ask *then*, in the middle of executing important world government business.

'Wonderful,' he said, shaking his head. 'You're wonderful, Mary Ann! Down two from last month's Test, aren't you?'

368

'I'm always between 10 and 14,' I said. 'Nothing new about that, Doctor.'

'Some day,' he said, and his face took on the expression it had when he gave his great speech about the Asylums, 'some day, this world of ours will be governed by men fit to govern it. Men whose SQ score is Zero. Zero, Mary Ann!'

'Well, my goodness, Doctor,' I said jokingly – his intensity almost alarmed me a little – 'even *you* never scored lower than 3, and you haven't done that for a year or more now!'

He stared at me almost as if he didn't see me. It was quite uncanny. 'Some day,' he said in just the same way, 'nobody in the world will have a Quotient higher than 50. Some day, nobody in the world will have a Quotient higher than 30! Higher than 10! The Therapy will be perfected. I was only the diagnostician. But the Therapy will be perfected! The cure will be found! Some day!' And he went on staring at me, and then he said, 'Do you know what my score was on Monday?'

'7,' I guessed promptly. The last time he had told me his score it had been 7.

'92,' he said.

I laughed, because he seemed to be laughing. He had always had a puckish sense of humor. But I thought we really should get back to the World Economic Growth Plan, so I said laughingly, 'That really is a very bad joke, Doctor!'

'92,' he said, 'and you don't believe me, Mary Ann, but that's because of the cantaloupe.'

I said, 'What cantaloupe, Doctor?' and that was when he jumped across his desk and began to try to bite through my jugular vein.

I used a judo hold and shouted to Bill the janitor, and when he came I called a robo-ambulance to take Dr Speakie to Bethesda Asylum.

That was six months ago. I visit Dr Speakie every Saturday. It is very sad. He is in the McLean Area, which is the Violent Ward, and every time he sees me he screams and foams. But

I do not take it personally. One should never take mental ill health personally. When the Therapy is perfected he will be completely rehabilitated. Meanwhile, I just hold on here. Bill keeps the floors clean, and I run the World Government. It really isn't as difficult as you might think.

SMALL CHANGE

'Small change,' my aunt said as I put the obol on her tongue. 'I'll need more than that where I'm going.'

It is true that the change was very small. She looked exactly as she had looked a few hours before, except that she was not breathing.

'Goodbye, Aunt,' I said.

'I'm not going yet!' she snapped. I always tried her patience. 'There are rooms in this house I've never even opened the door of!'

I did not know what she was talking about. Our house has two rooms.

'This obol tastes funny,' she said after a long silence. 'Where did you get it?'

I did not want to tell her that it was a good-luck piece, a copper sequin, not money though it was round like a coin, which I had carried for a year or more in my pocket, ever since I picked it up by the gate of the bricklayer's yard. I had rubbed it clean, of course, but my aunt had a keen tongue, and it was trodden mud, dog turds, brick dust, and the inside of my pocket that she was tasting, along with the dry-blood taste of copper. I pretended that I had not understood her question.

'A wonder you had it at all,' my aunt said. 'If you have a penny in your pocket after a month without me, I'll be surprised. Poor thing!' She would have sighed if she had been breathing. I had not known that she would continue to worry about me after she died. I began to cry.

371

'That's good,' my aunt said with satisfaction. 'Just don't keep it up too long. I'm not going far, now. I just want very much to find out what room that door leads to.'

She looked younger when she got up, younger than she was when I was born. She went across the room lightly and opened a door I had not known was there.

I heard her say in a pleased, surprised voice, 'Lila!' Lila was the name of her sister, my mother.

'For goodness' sake, Lila,' my aunt said, 'you haven't been waiting in here for eleven years?'

I could not hear what my mother said.

'I'm very sorry about leaving the girl,' my aunt said. 'I did what I could, I tried my best. She's a good girl. But what will become of her now!'

My aunt never cried, and now she had no tears; but her anxiety over me made me cry again in alarm and self-pity.

My mother came out of that new room in the form of a lacewing fly and saw me crying. Tears taste salt to the living but sweet to the dead, and they have a taste for sweets, at first. I did not know all that, then. I was just glad to have my mother with me even as a tiny fly. It was a gladness the size of a fly.

That was all there was left of my mother in the house, and she had got what she wanted; so my aunt went on.

The room she was in was large and rather shadowy, lighted only by a skylight, like a storeroom. Along one wall stood distaffs full of spun flax, in a row, and in the place where the light fell from the skylight stood a loom. My aunt had been a notable spinster and weaver all her life, and was sorely tempted now by those rolls of fine, even thread, as well spun as any she had ever spun herself; the loom was warped, and there lay the shuttle ready. But linen weaving is a careful art. If she began a shroud now she would be at it for a long time, and much as she wanted a proper shroud, she never had been one to start a job and then drop it unfinished. So it was that she kept worrying about what would become of me. But she had already made up her mind to leave the housework undone (since housework

is never done anyhow), and now she admitted that she must let other people see to her winding sheet. She hoped she could trust me to choose a clean sheet, at least, and a well-patched one. But she could not resist picking up the end thread of one of the distaffs and feeding out a length between her thumb and finger to test it for evenness and strength; and she kept the thread running between thumb and finger as she walked on.

It was well that she did so, as the new room opened onto a corridor along which were many doorways, each one leading to other halls and rooms, a maze in which she would certainly have lost her way but for the thread of flax.

The rooms were clean, a little dusty, and unfurnished. In one of them my aunt found a toy lying on the floor, a wooden horse. It was crudely carved, the forelegs all of a piece and the hind legs the same, a kind of a two-legged horse with round, flat eyes, which she thought she remembered, though she was not sure.

In another long, narrow room many unused kitchen tools and pans lay on a counter, and three horn buttons in a row.

At the end of a long corridor into which she was drawn by a gleam or a reflection at the far end, there stood an engine of some kind, which was certainly nothing my aunt had ever seen before.

In one small room with no skylight an intense, pungent smell hung in the air, filling up the room like a living creature caught in it. My aunt left that room hurriedly, upset.

Though her curiosity had been roused by finding all these rooms she had not known in her house, her explorations, and the silence, brought on her a sense of oppression and unease. She stood for a moment outside the door of the room where the strong smell was, making up her mind. That never took her long. She began to follow the thread back, winding it about the fingers of her left hand as she took it up. This process needed more attention than the paying out, and lifting her eyes from a tangle in the thread she was puzzled to find herself in a room which she did not recall passing through, but could hardly have

crossed without noticing, for it was very large. The walls were of a beautiful fine-grained stone of a pale grey hue, in which certain figures like astrologers' charts of the constellations, fine lines connecting stars or clusters of stars, were inlaid in gold wire. The ceiling was light and high, the floor of worn, dark marble. It was like a church, my aunt thought, but not a religious church (that is what she thought). The patterns on the walls were like the illustrations in books of learning, and the room itself was like the hall of the great library in the city; there were no books, but the place was majestic and reposeful, having about it a collected stillness very pleasant to the spirit of my aunt. She was tired of walking, and decided to rest there.

She sat down, since there was no furniture, on the floor in the corner nearest the door to which the thread had led her. My aunt was a woman who liked a wall at her back. The invasions had left her uneasy in open spaces, always looking over her shoulder. Though who could hurt her now? as she said to herself, sitting down. But, as she said to herself, you never can be sure.

The lines of gold wire on the walls led her eye along them as she sat resting. Some of the figures they made seemed familiar. She began to think that these figures or patterns were a map of the maze which she was in, the wires representing passages and the stars, rooms; or perhaps the stars represented the doors into rooms, the walls of which were not outlined. She could pretty certainly retrace the first corridor back to the room of the distaffs; but on the far side of that, where the old part of our house ought to be, the patterns continued, looking a good deal more like the familiar constellations of the sky in early winter. She was not certain she understood the map at all, but she continued to study it, to let her mind follow the lines from star to star, until she began to see her way. She got up then, and went back, pursuing the flaxen thread and taking it up in her left hand, till she came back.

There I was in the same room still crying. My mother was gone. Lacewing flies wait years to be born, but they live only

374

a day. The undertaker's men were just leaving, and I had to follow them, so my aunt came along to her funeral, though she did not want to leave the house. She tried to bring her ball of thread with her, but it broke as she crossed the threshold. I could hear her swear under her breath, the way she always did when she broke a thread or spilled the sugar – 'Damn!' in a whisper.

Neither of us enjoyed the funeral at all. My aunt grew panicky as they began to throw the dirt back into the grave. She cried aloud, 'I can't breathe! I can't breathe!' – which frightened me so much that I thought it was myself speaking, myself suffocating, and I fell down. People had to help me get up, and help me get home. I was so ashamed and confused among them that I lost my aunt.

One of the neighbors, who had never been particularly pleasant to us, took pity on me, and behaved with much kindness. She talked so wisely to me that I got up the courage to ask her, 'Where is my aunt? Will she come back?' But she did not know, and only said things meant to comfort me. I am not as clever as most people, but I knew there was no comfort for me.

The neighbor made sure I could look after myself, and that evening she sent one of her children over with dinner in a dish for me. I ate it, and it was very good. I had not eaten anything while my aunt was away in the other part of the house.

At night, after dark, I lay down all alone in the bedroom. At first I felt well and cheerful, because of the food I had eaten, and I pretended my aunt was there sleeping in the same room, the way it had always been. Then I got frightened, and the fright grew in the darkness.

My aunt came up out of the floor in the middle of the room. The red tiles humped up and cracked apart. Her hair and her head pushed through the tiles, and then her body. She looked very dark, like dirt, and she was much smaller than she had been.

'Let me be!' she said.

I was too terrified to speak.

'Let me go!' my aunt said. But it was not truly my aunt; it was only an old part of her that had come back underground from the graveyard, because I had been wanting her. I did not like that part of her, or want it there. I cried, 'Go away! Go back!' and hid my head in my arms.

My aunt made a little creaking sound like a wicker basket. I kept my eyes hidden so long that I nearly fell asleep. When I looked, no one was there, or only a kind of darker place in the air, and the tiles were not cracked apart. I went to sleep.

Next morning when I woke up the sunlight was in the window and things were all right, but I could not walk across that part of the floor where my aunt had come up through the tiles.

I was afraid to cry after that night, since crying might bring her back to taste the sweetness or to scold me. But it was lonely in the house now that she was buried and gone. I had no idea what to do without her. The neighbor came in and talked about finding me work, and gave me food again; but the next day a man came, who said he had been sent by a creditor. He took away the chest of clothes and bedding. Later that day, in the evening, he came back, because he had seen that I was alone there. I kept the door locked this time. He spoke smoothly at first, trying to make me let him in, and then he began saying in a low voice that he would hurt me, but I kept the door locked and never answered. The next day somebody else came, but I had pushed the bedstead up against the door. It may have been the neighbor's child that came, but I was afraid to look. I felt safe staying in the back room. Other people came and knocked, but I never answered, and they went away again.

I stayed in the back room until at last I saw the door that my aunt had gone through, that day. I went and opened it. I was sure she would be there. But the room was empty. The loom was gone, and the distaffs were gone, and no one was there.

I went on to the corridor beyond, but no farther. I could never find my way by myself through all those halls and rooms, or understand the patterns of the stars. I was so afraid and

wretched that I went back, and crawled into my own mouth, and hid there.

My aunt came to fetch me. She was very cross. I always tried her patience. All she said was, 'Come on!' And she pulled me along by the hand. Once she said, 'Shame on you!' When we got to the riverbank she looked me over very sternly. She washed my face with the dark water of that river, and pressed my hair down with the palms of her hands. She said, 'I should have known.'

'I'm sorry, Aunt,' I said.

'Oh, yes,' she said. 'Come along, now. Look sharp!'

For the boat had come across the river and was lying up at the wharf. We walked down to the wharf among the reeds in the twilight. It was after sunset and there was no moon or stars, and no wind blowing. The river was so wide I could not see the other shore.

My aunt dickered with the ferryman. I let her do that since people always cheated me. She had taken the obol off her tongue, and was talking fast. 'My niece, can't you see how it is? Of course they didn't give her the fare! She's not responsible! I came along with her to look after her. Here's the fare. Yes, it's for us both. No, you don't,' and she drew back her hand, having merely shown him a glimpse of the bit of copper. 'Not till we're both safe across!'

The ferryman glowered, but began to loosen the painter.

'Come along, then!' my aunt said. She stepped into the boat, and held out her hand to me. So I followed her.

EAST

THE FIRST REPORT OF THE SHIPWRECKED
FOREIGNER TO THE KADANH OF DERB

What you ask of me, my lord, is manifestly impossible. How can one person describe a world? One may indeed use a small pencil to describe a large circle, but if the circle is so large that one cannot make out the curve of it even from the top of a tower, why then the pencil will wear out before it has fairly begun its task. How many tones can one voice take? How can I describe even a single rock, and which rock should I describe? If I began by telling you that the Earth is the third planet of a system of nine, orbiting a middle-sized yellow sun at a mean distance of 93 million miles, with a 365-day period of revolution and a 24-hour period of rotation, and that it has a companion moon, what would I have told you but that a year is a year, a month is a month, and a day is a day, which you know already?

But since I know that you know that what you have been pleased to ask of me is impossible, and yet that you have asked it neither lightly nor cruelly, all I can do is answer; knowing that you know that my answer, in all its words, may mean nothing in the end beyond: Forgive me.

A moment ago as I glimpsed from the tail of my eye the enormous task that awaits me, like a mountain range to be climbed, it occurred to me that there may be an ulterior motive to your request. In asking me to describe my world to you, you may not be seeking information about my world at all. You may not plan to listen to my words, but only to the silences

between the sentences, from which you will learn a good deal about your own world. If this is the case, I have no objection; indeed I prefer the arrangement. My job then is not to describe my world in general terms such as apply to all worlds, the language of astronomy, physics, chemistry, biology, etc, but rather to dwell upon the individual and transient, the fortuitous and peculiar; not to describe the class of flowering plants, but to mention the acrid odor of a Cecile Bruner rose full-blown on a balcony overlooking a great bay encircled by the lights of cities on a mild, foggy evening of September; not to give an outline of the evolution of intelligence or the course of human history, but to tell you, perhaps at considerable length, about my great-aunt Elizabeth. No general historical narrative, not even a close examination of the westward migration of the white peoples as it culminated and ended in the treks of the pioneers across the Great Plains, the Rockies, the Sierra, to the Pacific Shore, would give you an honest conviction of the necessity of the existence of my great-aunt Elizabeth. Even if I carried the narrative into such details as the fortunes of the individual families of the settlers of Wyoming, the existence of my great-aunt would continue to appear fortuitous. Only if I were to describe her, her life, her death, might you gain some understanding of the absolute necessity of her existence, and, through that, perhaps some comprehension of that millennial movement to the west which ended on the beaches of an immense fog-breeding sea; and, through that, perhaps a new understanding of some ancient migration of your own people, or the lack of any migratory movements in the history of your people; or of the nature of failure, or the character of your own great-aunt, or your own soul.

My lord, I see that instead of apologising and procrastinating I should simply thank you for the utterly unexpected and welcome opportunity to talk about my great-aunt, and begin at once to do so. It is not an opportunity often given to the Second Officer of a ship of the Terran Interstellar Fleet.

But I do not think I will begin with my great-aunt. She is

a difficult subject, and it has occurred to me, as I gain the courage to take a few quick glances directly at the appalling mountains which I am to climb (and from whose summits what fog-bound ocean will I see?), that it does not matter where I begin, and that I need not even stick precisely to the facts. Whatever I tell you, if you are listening to the silences between the sentences, you will hear the truth. As in music, when one has caught the rhythm, the pattern of the sounds and silences, then one hears the tune. There is, after all, only one tune I can sing. So I shall begin with a fairy tale.

Once upon a time there was a city. All other cities of all times and places were alike in many ways. This city was unlike them all, in many ways; and yet it manifested more fully than any of the others the Idea of a city. It was populated by birds, cats, people, and winged lions, in roughly equal proportions. The lions were all literate. Seldom did one see a lion without a book in its paw. The cats were illiterate, but highly civilised. Observing a large family group at ease in the shrubbery of a shady garden fenced from all intrusion, or a ritual confrontation of toms on the moonlit stones of a city square, or the leisurely progress from roof to roof of a silken and silvery maiden, one might well conclude not only that the city had been built for, but that the art of living in it had been brought to perfection by, the cats. But as soon as one looked at a lion one would have to question this; for, with all their resemblances to the cats in form and feature, the complete tranquility of the lions, their universal expression of benevolent pride and conscious mastery, surely indicated a state of mind transcending mere happiness, approaching joy. You might see the corpse of a cat floating under a bridge along with soft-drink bottles and rotten oranges, but looking up from that sorry sight you would see by the steps of the bridge a lion frowning beatifically through his mane, his stone wings folded; for what better place could he ever fly to?

It is easy to assume that the birds were the least happy inhabitants of the city. Many of them lived in cages. These prisoners certainly did not appear to be unhappy, singing ornate

cadenzas in the style of Vivaldi from dawn to evening across the narrow ways, pecking at their birdseed and staring rapt at their little yellow reflections in the Christmas-tree ornaments hung in their airy cages. But all the same, they lived in cages. The pigeons lived free, but only as sturdy beggars. Daily they answered the summons of the bells for their handout, and in between handouts they pestered the tourists for more handouts. Perhaps it was their resentment at being thus reduced to the status of dependents, disenfranchised, their obscure anger at having been given few trees to perch in and few dangers to flee from, that made their excrement so corrosive. Whatever their motive, the pigeons were destroying some of the most exquisite elements of the city's fabric, by shitting persistently and ruinously on the perishable stone of cornices, pinnacles, carvings. Not even the lions could escape the pigeons. In this work of destruction the pigeons were, however, surpassed by the people, whose factories on the nearby mainland emitted vapors far exceeding the corrosive powers of the most class-conscious pigeon, and whose motorboats were furiously engaged in trying to sink the city before it crumbled.

For the quality in which Venice differed most clearly from all other cities and yet in which it exemplified and described them all, every one, most exactly, was its fragility.

A city, a splendid, old, crowded, active city full of thousands of busy lives, that might be destroyed by a pigeon – or a motor-boat – or a wisp of gas? Ridiculous!

But then what is it that destroys cities? Why have the mighty fallen? Look, and you find a toy horse; a brass key; a couple of men chatting over wine; a change in the weather; the arrival of a few Spaniards. Nothing at all. A pigeon, a motorboat, a click on a Geiger counter.

The first lesson of Venice, then, is mortality.

Misread by Germans and other barbarians from the north (the city has always been besieged by Germans, and was, in fact, founded out in the deepest part of its lagoon in an effort to remove itself from the compulsive visitations of Langobard

tourists – an effort which failed, in the long run), this perfectly straightforward message has been interpreted, with all the magnificent obtuseness of Teutonic thought to mean that because Venice is more than usually mortal therefore Venice is a city of death, of dying, of disease, decadent, a city without healthy business, surviving like its pigeons as a parasite on visitors, a fever-dream city of morbidity, a place where aging pederasts go to die. This is, of course, rubbish. What is most mortal is most alive. There is no place in the world where the green beautiful murky tides of life run so high, where one is so vividly aware of the presence of living birds, cats, lions, and people walking, talking, singing, quarrelling, rolling metal shop blinds up and down, cooking dinner, eating breakfast, getting married, holding funerals, transporting Coca-Cola and zucchini from place to place in Coca-Cola and zucchini boats, making speeches, playing radios and musical instruments, selling electrified yo-yos that glow like fireflies as they roll up and down their strings in the dusk before the doors of the great cathedral, playing truant from school, kicking soccer balls, fighting, fishing, kissing, throwing tear gas at demonstrators, demonstrating, shortening their life expectancy by blowing incredibly fragile baubles of colored glass, etc, etc – in other words, living. If I were an aging German pederast with a death wish, I should feel a terrible fool in Venice. Right out of my depth.

I have heard two Venetian housewives on the steps of a green canal discuss the qualities of various makes of electric food blenders for twenty minutes straight, in detail and with enormous vigor. The conversation was not notable for hectic and death-haunted ecstasy. Indeed, one reason why life is so strong there is that you can hear it. In other cities it is drowned out by the sound of motors. What you hear in the other cities is the noise engines make. What you hear in Venice, mostly, is the noise people make. The birds, too; the cats when they are in love; the lions make no noise worth mentioning, though the book they hold says softly, *Pax tibi, Marce, evangelista meus*. And thus the silence of Venice is the noisiest silence imaginable.

385

When I have been out in the vacuum between the stars, and have listened to it and been terrified, I have found a way to pull free from that absorbing terror (which Pascal mentioned, although he had never flown in a spaceship) and rejoin myself: I pretend that I am waking up rather early in the morning in a hotel room in Venice. At first it is still, deeply still, the stillness of the level, misty, bluish-green lagoon, the stillness of the small canal between stone house walk around the corner. I know that the bridge near the hotel entrance is reflected, its arch making a perfect circle, in that stillness. Beyond that bridge is another bridge, and another beyond that, each borne up entire by its reflection: air, water, stone, glass, one. A pigeon up on the tiles outside the dormer window goes *oocooloo roo*. That is the first sound; that, and the faint whicker of wind in the pigeon's wings, alighting. Footsteps come down the street past the hotel entrance, across the arched bridge, die away: the second sound, or pattern of sounds and silences. Somebody breaks some glass down in the courtyard of the hotel. They always break glass in Venetian hotel courtyards in the morning; it may be a ritual observance of the dawn, or a way of getting rid of the baubles unsold to tourists in the gewgaw shops yesterday, I do not know. Maybe it is how they wash dishes in Venice. A startling sound, but not unmusical, followed by loud swearing and a laugh. By now I am almost safe from the terrors of the hygienic void. Down in the courtyard a radio is playing while they sweep up the glass. Somebody on one of the bridges shouts something I cannot quite understand in the Venetian dialect to someone on another bridge; and then the great bells of the Campanile and the small bells of three neighborhood churches all undertake more or less simultaneously to invite parishioners to early Mass. It is all music, and I am home safe, listening to the profound, extraordinary silence of the city of life.

I was not born there and have never lived there. When I say 'home safe' I am using a metaphor from the game of baseball.

I have visited Venice four times, each time for four days only. Each time it was a little lower in the water.

If you were to ask me point-blank (as you have asked me to describe the Earth) whether I want to go back to Earth and why, I might well answer, 'Yes: to see Venice in the winter.' I have seen it only in late spring and summer. In winter, they tell me, it is terribly cold, and the museums are closed even more often than in summer, so that you cannot go warm yourself at the red and golden fires of Titian and Veronese. The white fog seeps among the stones. In the storms of winter St. Mark's Square, that loveliest living room ever built, whose ceiling is the opalescent sky, has often been flooded. The cathedral itself has been invaded by the sea, waves and mosaics inter-changing their netted and glittering reflections, the five gold domes floating like balloons above the breakers, the four bronze horses of Neptune snorting and trembling as they scent their native element. No doubt the lions continued to gaze downward with detached and frowning approbation, scarcely troubling to stir their folded wings. The gondolas, I suppose, floated tied to the very tops of their striped mooring poles, or else were put away, knocking on the ceilings of flooded boathouses; or did they drift across the great square beneath the horses and the gold balloons, the procession of the Angel and the Three Kings, the bell tower which fell down in 1903 but got right up again, the agitated pigeons searching for their daily handout on the shallow, cold, grey waves? Beneath the waves at evening did the electric yo-yos flicker up and down their strings, attracting the ghosts of long-drowned Langobards?

Winter and summer, the gondolas were black. They were painted black a long time ago in mourning for something – the loss of a battle, the fall of the Republic, the death of a baby – I cannot remember why gondolas went into mourning. They were the most elegant boats people have ever made, more elegant even than the boat that brought me here. The warning cry of the gondolier, as he guided his craft towards

387

the sunlight at the end of a narrow side canal under balconies and arched bridges, through a trembling of shadows, was soft and yet carried clearly along the ways of stone and water: 'Hoy-y-y,' he called, and the cats and lions on the sun-warmed angles of the bridges listened and said nothing, as you, my lord, do now.

THE DIARY OF THE ROSE

30 August

Dr Nades recommends that I keep a diary of my work. She
says that if you keep it carefully, when you reread it you can
remind yourself of observations you made, notice errors and
learn from them, and observe progress in or deviations from
positive thinking, and so keep correcting the course of your
work by a feedback process.

I promise to write in this notebook every night, and reread
it at the end of each week.

I wish I had done it while I was an assistant, but it is even
more important now that I have patients of my own.

As of yesterday I have six patients, a full load for a scopist,
but four of them are the autistic children I have been working
with all year for Dr Nades's study for the Nat'l Psych. Bureau
(my notes on them are in the cli psy files). The other two are
new admissions:

Ana Jest, 46, bakery packager, md., no children, diag. depres-
sion, referral from city police (suicide attempt).

Flores Sorde, 36, engineer, unmd., no diag., referral from
TRTU (Psychopathic behavior – Violent).

Dr Nades says it is important that I write things down each
night just as they occurred to me at work: it is the spontaneity
that is most informative in self-examination (just as in auto-
psychoscopy). She says it is better to write it, not dictate onto
tape, and keep it quite private, so that I won't be self-conscious.

It is hard. I never wrote anything that was private before. I keep feeling as if I was really writing it for Dr Nades! Perhaps if the diary is useful I can show her some of it later, and get her advice.

My guess is that Ana Jest is in menopausal depression and hormone therapy will be sufficient. There! Now let's see how bad a prognostician I am.

Will work with both patients under scope tomorrow. It is exciting to have my own patients, I am impatient to begin. Though, of course, teamwork was very educational.

31 August

Half-hour scope session with Ana J. at 8:00. Analyzed scope material, 11:00–17:00. N.B.: Adjust right-brain pickup next session! Weak visual Concrete. Very little aural, weak sensory, erratic body image. Will get lab analyses tomorrow of hormone balance.

It is amazing how banal most people's minds are. Of course the poor woman is in severe depression. Input in the Con dimension was foggy and incoherent, and the Uncon dimension was deeply open, but obscure. But the things that came out of the obscurity were so trivial! A pair of old shoes, and the word 'geography'! And the shoes were dim, a mere schema of a pair-of-shoes, maybe a man's maybe a woman's, maybe dark blue maybe brown. Although definitely a visual type, she does not see anything clearly. Not many people do. It is depressing. When I was a student in first year I used to think how wonderful other people's minds would be, how wonderful it was going to be to share in all the different worlds, the different colors of their passions and ideas. How naïve I was!

I realised this first in Dr Ramia's class when we studied a tape from a very famous successful person, and I noticed that the subject had never looked at a tree, never touched one, did not know any difference between an oak and a poplar, or even between a daisy and a rose. They were all just 'trees' or

'flowers' to him, apprehended schematically. It was the same with people's faces, though he had tricks for telling them apart: mostly he saw the name, like a label, not the face. That was an Abstract mind, of course, but it can be even worse with the Concretes, whose perceptions come in a kind of undifferentiated sludge – bean soup with a pair of shoes in it.

But aren't I 'going native'? I've been studying a depressive's thoughts all day and have got depressed. Look, I wrote up there, 'It is depressing.' I see the value of this diary already. I know I am over-impressionable.

Of course, that is why I am a good psychoscopist. But it is dangerous.

No session with F. Sorde today, since sedation had not worn off. TRTU referrals are often so drugged that they cannot be scoped for days.

REM scoping session with Ana J. at 4:00 tomorrow. Better go to bed!

1 September

Dr Nades says the kind of thing I wrote yesterday is pretty much what she had in mind, and invited me to show her this diary again whenever I am in doubt. Spontaneous thoughts – not the technical data, which are recorded in the files anyhow. Cross nothing out. Candor all-important.

Ana's dream was interesting but pathetic. The wolf who turned into a pancake! Such a disgusting, dim, hairy pancake, too. Her visuality is clearer in dream, but the feeling tone remains low (but remember: *you* contribute the affect – don't read it in). Started her on hormone therapy today.

F. Sorde awake, but too confused to take to scope room for session. Frightened. Refused to eat. Complained of pain in side. I thought he was unclear what kind of hospital this is, and told him there was nothing wrong with him physically. He said, 'How the hell do you know?' which was fair enough, since he was in a straitjacket, due to the V notation on his chart.

I examined and found bruising and contusion, and ordered X ray, which showed two ribs cracked. Explained to patient that he had been in a condition where forcible restraint had been necessary to prevent self-injury. He said, 'Every time one of them asked a question the other one kicked me.' He repeated this several times, with anger and confusion. Paranoid delusional system? If it does not weaken as the drugs wear off, I will proceed on that assumption. He responds fairly well to me, asked my name when I went to see him with the X-ray plate, and agreed to eat. I was forced to apologise to him, not a good beginning with a paranoid. The rib damage should have been marked on his chart by the referring agency or by the medic who admitted him. This kind of carelessness is distressing.

But there's good news too. Rina (Autism Study subject 4) saw a first-person sentence today. Saw it in heavy, black, primer print, all at once in the high Con foreground: *I want to sleep in the big room.* (She sleeps alone because of the feces problem.) The sentence stayed clear for over 5 seconds. She was reading it in her mind just as I was reading it on the holoscreen. There was weak subverbalisation, but not subvocalisation, nothing on the audio. She has not yet spoken, even to herself, in the first person. I told Tio about it at once and he asked her after the session, 'Rina, where do you want to sleep?' – 'Rina sleep in the big room.' No pronoun, no conative. But one of these days she will say *I want* – aloud. And on that build a personality, maybe, at last: on that foundation. I want, therefore I am.

There is so much fear. Why is there so much fear?

4 September

Went to town for my two-day holiday. Stayed with B. in her new flat on the north bank. Three rooms to herself!!! But I don't really like those old buildings, there are rats and roaches, and it feels so old and strange, as if somehow the famine years were still there, waiting. Was glad to get back to my little room here, all to myself but with others close by on the same floor,

friends and colleagues. Anyway I missed writing in this book. I form habits very fast. Compulsive tendency.

Ana much improved: dressed, hair combed, was knitting. But session was dull. Asked her to think about pancakes, and there it came filling up the whole Uncon dimension, the hairy, dreary, flat wolf-pancake, while in the Con she was obediently trying to visualize a nice cheese blintz. Not too badly: colors and outlines already stronger. I am still willing to count on simple hormone treatment. Of course they will suggest ECT, and a co-analysis of the scope material would be perfectly possible, we'd start with the wolf-pancake, etc. But is there any real point to it? She has been a bakery packager for 24 years and her physical health is poor. She cannot change her life situation. At least with good hormone balance she may be able to endure it.

F. Sorde: rested but still suspicious. Extreme fear reaction when I said it was time for his first session. To allay this I sat down and talked about the nature and operation of the psychoscope. He listened intently and finally said, 'Are you going to use only the psychoscope?'

I said Yes.

He said, 'Not electroshock?'

I said No.

He said, 'Will you promise me that?'

I explained that I am a psychoscopist and never operate the electroconvulsive therapy equipment, that is an entirely different department. I said my work with him at present would be diagnostic, not therapeutic. He listened carefully. He is an educated person and understands distinctions such as 'diagnostic' and 'therapeutic.' It is interesting that he asked me to *promise*. That does not fit a paranoid pattern, you don't ask for promises from those you can't trust. He came with me docilely, but when we entered the scope room he stopped and turned white at sight of the apparatus. I made Dr Aven's little joke about the dentist's chair, which she always used with nervous patients. F.S. said, 'So long as it's not an electric chair!'

I believe that with intelligent subjects it is much better not

to make mysteries and so impose a false authority and a feeling of helplessness on the subject (see T. R. Olma, *Psychoscopy Technique*). So I showed him the chair and electrode crown and explained its operation. He has a layman's hearsay knowledge of the psychoscope, and his questions also reflected his engineering education. He sat down in the chair when I asked him. While I fitted the crown and clasps he was sweating profusely from fear, and this evidently embarrassed him, the smell. If he knew how Rina smells after she's been doing shit paintings. He shut his eyes and gripped the chair arms so that his hands went white to the wrist. The screens were almost white too. After a while I said in a joking tone, 'It doesn't really hurt, does it?'

'I don't know.'

'Well, does it?'

'You mean it's on?'

'It's been on for ninety seconds.'

He opened his eyes then and looked around, as well as he could for the head clamps. He asked, 'Where's the screen?'

I explained that a subject never watches the screen live, because the objectification can be severely disturbing, and he said, 'Like feedback from a microphone?' That is exactly the simile Dr Aven used to use. F.S. is certainly an intelligent person. N.B.: Intelligent paranoids are dangerous!

He asked, 'What do you see?' and I said, 'Do be quiet, I don't want to see what you're saying, I want to see what you're thinking,' and he said, 'But that's none of your business, you know,' quite gently, like a joke. Meanwhile the fear-white had gone into dark, intense, volitional convolutions, and then, a few seconds after he stopped speaking, a rose appeared on the whole Con dimension: a full-blown pink rose, beautifully sensed and visualised, clear and steady, whole.

He said presently, 'What am I thinking about, Dr Sobel?' and I said, 'Bears in the Zoo.' I wonder now why I said that. Self-defense? Against what? He gave a laugh and the Uncon went crystal-dark, relief, and the rose darkened and wavered. I said, 'I was joking. Can you bring the rose back?' That brought

back the fear-white. I said, 'Listen, it's really very bad for us to talk like this during a first session, you have to learn a great deal before you can co-analyse, and I have a great deal to learn about you, so no more jokes, please? Just relax physically, and think about anything you please.'

There was flurry and subverbalisation on the Con dimension, and the Uncon faded into grey, suppression. The rose came back weakly a few times. He was trying to concentrate on it, but couldn't. I saw several quick visuals: myself, my uniform, TRTU uniforms, a grey car, a kitchen, the violent ward (strong aural images – screaming), a desk, the papers on the desk. He stuck to those. They were the plans for a machine. He began going through them. It was a deliberate effort at suppression, and quite effective. Finally I said, 'What kind of machine is that?' and he began to answer aloud but stopped and let me get the answer subvocally in the earphone: 'Plans for a rotary engine assembly for traction,' or something like that, of course the exact words are on the tape. I repeated it aloud and said, 'They aren't classified plans, are they?' He said, 'No,' aloud, and added, 'I don't know any secrets.' His reaction to a question is intense and complex, each sentence is like a shower of pebbles thrown into a pool, the interlocking rings spread out quick and wide over the Con and into the Uncon, responses rising on all levels. Within a few seconds all that was hidden by a big signboard that appeared in the high Con foreground, deliberately visualised like the rose and the plans, with auditory reinforcement as he read it over and over: KEEP OUT! KEEP OUT! KEEP OUT!

It began to blur and flicker, and somatic signals took over, and soon he said aloud, 'I'm tired,' and I closed the session (12.5 min.).

After I took off the crown and clamps I brought him a cup of tea from the staff stand in the hall. When I offered it to him he looked startled and then tears came into his eyes. His hands were so cramped from gripping the armrests that he

had trouble taking hold of the cup. I told him he must not be so tense and afraid, we are trying to help him not to hurt him.

He looked up at me. Eyes are like the scope screen and yet you can't read them. I wished the crown was still on him, but it seems you never catch the moments you most want on the scope. He said, 'Doctor, why am I in this hospital?'

I said, 'For diagnosis and therapy.'

He said, 'Diagnosis and therapy of *what?*'

I said he perhaps could not now recall the episode, but he had behaved strangely. He asked how and when, and I said that it would all come clear to him as therapy took effect. Even if I had known what his psychotic episode was, I would have said the same. It was correct procedure. But I felt in a false position. If the TRTU report was not classified, I would be speaking from knowledge and the facts. Then I could make a better response to what he said next:

'I was waked up at two in the morning, jailed, interrogated, beaten up, and drugged. I suppose I did behave a little oddly during that. Wouldn't you?'

'Sometimes a person under stress misinterprets other people's actions,' I said. 'Drink up your tea and I'll take you back to the ward. You're running a temperature.'

'The ward,' he said, with a kind of shrinking movement, and then he said almost desperately, 'Can you really not know why I'm here?'

That was strange, as if he has included me in his delusional system, *on 'his side.'* Check this possibility in Rheingeld. I should think it would involve some transference and there has not been time for that.

Spent pm analysing Jest and Sorde holos. I have never seen any psychoscopic realisation, not even a drug-induced hallucination, so fine and vivid as that rose. The shadows of one petal on another, the velvety damp texture of the petals, the pink color full of sunlight, the yellow central crown – I am sure the scent was there if the apparatus had olfactory pickup – it

wasn't like a mentifact but a real thing rooted in the earth, alive and growing, the strong thorny stem beneath it.

Very tired, must go to bed.

Just reread this entry. Am I keeping this diary right? All I have written is what happened and what was said. Is that spontaneous? But it was *important* to me.

5 September

Discussed the problem of conscious resistance with Dr Nades at lunch today. Explained that I have worked with unconscious blocks (the children, and depressives such as Ana J.) and have some skill at reading through, but have not before met a conscious block such as F.S.'s KEEP OUT sign, or the device he used today, which was effective for a full 20-minute session: a concentration on his breathing, bodily rhythms, pain in ribs, and visual input from the scope room. She suggested that I use a blindfold for the latter trick, and keep my attention on the Uncon dimension, as he cannot prevent material from appearing there. It is surprising, though, how large the interplay area of his Con and Uncon fields is, and how much one resonates into the other. I believe his concentration on his breathing rhythm allowed him to achieve something like 'trance' condition. Though, of course, most so-called 'trance' is mere occultist fakirism, a primitive trait without interest for behavioral science.

Ana thought through 'a day in my life' for me today. All so grey and dull, poor soul! She never thought even of food with pleasure, though she lives on minimum ration. The single thing that came bright for a moment was a child's face, clear dark eyes, a pink knitted cap, round cheeks. She told me in post-session discussion that she always walks by a school playground on the way to work because 'she likes to see the little ones running and yelling.' Her husband appears on the screen as a big bulky suit of work clothes and a peevish, threatening mumble. I wonder if she knows that she hasn't seen his face

or heard a word he says for years? But no use telling her that. It may be just as well she doesn't.

The knitting she is doing, I noticed today, is a pink cap.

Reading De Cams's *Disaffection: A Study*, on Dr Nades's recommendation.

6 September

In the middle of session (breathing again) I said loudly: 'Flores!'

Both psy dimensions whited out but the soma realisation hardly changed. After 4 seconds he responded aloud, drowsily. It is not 'trance,' but autohypnosis.

I said, 'Your breathing's monitored by the apparatus. I don't need to know that you're still breathing. It's boring.'

He said, 'I like to do my own monitoring, Doctor.'

I came around and took the blindfold off him and looked at him. He has a pleasant face, the kind of man you often see running machinery, sensitive but patient, like a donkey. That is stupid. I will not cross it out. I am supposed to be spontaneous in this diary. Donkeys do have beautiful faces. They are supposed to be stupid and balky but they look wise and calm, as if they had endured a lot but held no grudges, as if they knew some reason why one should not hold grudges. And the white ring around their eyes makes them look defenseless.

'But the more you breathe,' I said, 'the less you think. I need your cooperation. I'm trying to find out what it is you're afraid of.'

'But I know what I'm afraid of,' he said.

'Why won't you tell me?'

'You never asked me.'

'That's most unreasonable,' I said, which is funny, now I think about it, being indignant with a mental patient because he's unreasonable. 'Well, then, now I'm asking you.'

He said, 'I'm afraid of electroshock. Of having my mind destroyed. Being kept here. Or only being let out when I can't remember anything.' He gasped while he was speaking.

I said, 'All right, why won't you think about that while I'm watching the screens?'

'Why should I?'

'Why not? You've said it to me, why can't you think about it? I want to see the color of your thoughts!'

'It's none of your business, the color of my thoughts,' he said angrily, but I was around to the screen while he spoke, and saw the unguarded activity. Of course it was being taped while we spoke, too, and I have studied it all afternoon. It is fascinating. There are two subverbal levels running aside from the spoken words. All sensory-emotive reactions and distortions are vigorous and complex. He 'sees' me, for instance, in at least three different ways, probably more, analysis is impossibly difficult! And the Con-Uncon correspondences are so complicated, and the memory traces and current impressions interweave so rapidly, and yet the whole is unified in its complexity. It is like that machine he was studying, very intricate but all one thing in a mathematical harmony. Like the petals of the rose.

When he realised I was observing he shouted out, 'Voyeur! Damned voyeur! Let me alone! Get out!' and he broke down and cried. There was a clear fantasy on the screen for several seconds of himself breaking the arm and head clamps and kicking the apparatus to pieces and rushing out of the building, and there, outside, there was a wide hilltop, covered with short dry grass, under the evening sky, and he stood there all alone. While he sat clamped in the chair sobbing.

I broke session and took off the crown, and asked him if he wanted some tea, but he refused to answer. So I freed his arms, and brought him a cup. There was sugar today, a whole box full. I told him that and told him I'd put in two lumps.

After he had drunk some tea he said, with an elaborate ironical tone, because he was ashamed of crying, 'You know I like sugar? I suppose your psychoscope told you I liked sugar?'

'Don't be silly,' I said, 'everybody likes sugar if they can get it.'

He said, 'No, little doctor, they don't.' He asked in the same

tone how old I was and if I was married. He was spiteful. He said, 'Don't want to marry? Wedded to your work? Helping the mentally unsound back to a constructive life of service to the Nation?'

'I like my work,' I said, 'because it's difficult, and interesting. Like yours. You like your work, don't you?'

'I did,' he said. 'Goodbye to all that.'

'Why?'

He tapped his head and said, '*Zzzzzt!* – All gone. Right?'

'Why are you so convinced you're going to be prescribed electroshock? I haven't even diagnosed you yet.'

'Diagnosed me?' he said. 'Look, stop the playacting, please. My diagnosis was made. By the learned doctors of the TRTU. Severe case of disaffection. Prognosis: Evil! Therapy: Lock him up with a roomful of screaming thrashing wrecks, and then go through his mind the same way you went through his papers, and then burn it... burn it out. Right, Doctor? Why do you have to go through all this posing, diagnosis, cups of tea? Can't you just get on with it? Do you have to paw through everything I am before you burn it?'

'Flores,' I said very patiently, '*you're* saying "Destroy me" – don't you hear yourself? The psychoscope destroys nothing. And I'm not using it to get evidence, either. This isn't a court, you're not on trial. And I'm not a judge. I'm a doctor.'

He interrupted – 'If you're a doctor, can't you see that I'm not sick?'

'How can I see anything so long as you block me out with your stupid KEEP OUT signs?' I shouted. I did shout. My patience *was* a pose and it just fell to pieces. But I saw that I had reached him, so I went right on. 'You look sick, you act sick – two cracked ribs, a temperature, no appetite, crying fits – is that good health? If you're not sick, then prove it to me! Let me see how you are inside, inside all that!'

He looked down into his cup and gave a kind of laugh and shrugged. 'I can't win,' he said 'Why do I talk to you? You *look* so honest, damn you!'

400

I walked away. It is shocking how a patient can hurt one. The trouble is, I am used to the children, whose rejection is absolute, like animals that freeze, or cower, or bite, in their terror. But with this man, intelligent and older than I am, first there is communication and trust and then the blow. It hurts more.

It is painful writing all this down. It hurts again. But it is useful. I do understand some things he said much better now. I think I will not show it to Dr Nades until I have completed diagnosis. If there is any truth to what he said about being arrested on suspicion of disaffection (and he is certainly careless in the way he talks), Dr Nades might feel that she should take over the case, due to my inexperience. I should regret that. I need the experience.

7 September

Stupid! That's why she gave you De Cams's book. Of course she knows. As Head of the Section she has access to the TRTU dossier on F.S. She gave me this case deliberately.

It is certainly educational.

Today's session: F.S. still angry and sulky. Intentionally fantasized a sex scene. It was memory, but when she was heaving around underneath him he suddenly stuck a caricature of my face on her. It was effective. I doubt a woman could have done it, women's recall of having sex is usually darker and grander and they and the other do not become meat-puppets like that, with switchable heads. After a while he got bored with the performance (for all its vividness there was little somatic participation, not even an erection) and his mind began to wander. For the first time. One of the drawings on the desk came back. He must be a designer, because he changed it, with a pencil. At the same time there was a tune going on the audio, in mental puretone; and in the Uncon lapping over into the interplay area, a large, dark room seen from a child's height, the windowsills very high, evening outside the windows, tree branches darkening, and inside the room a woman's voice, soft, maybe reading

aloud, sometimes joining with the tune. Meanwhile the whore on the bed kept coming and going in volitional bursts, falling apart a little more each time, till there was nothing left but one nipple. This much I analysed out this afternoon, the first sequence of over 10 sec. that I have analysed clear and entire.

When I broke session he said, 'What did you learn?' in the satirical voice.

I whistled a bit of the tune.

He looked scared.

'It's a lovely tune,' I said, 'I never heard it before. If it's yours, I won't whistle it anywhere else.'

'It's from some quartet,' he said, with his 'donkey' face back, defenseless and patient. 'I like classical music. Didn't you—'

'I saw the girl,' I said. 'And my face on her. Do you know what I'd like to see?'

He shook his head. Sulky, hangdog.

'Your childhood.'

That surprised him. After a while he said, 'All right. You can have my childhood. Why not? You're going to get all the rest anyhow. Listen. You tape it all, don't you? Could I see a playback? I want to see what you see.'

'Sure,' I said 'But it won't mean as much to you as you think it will. It took me eight years to learn to observe. You start with your own tapes. I watched mine for months before I recognised anything much.'

I took him to my seat, put on the earphone, and ran him 30 sec. of the last sequence.

He was quite thoughtful and respectful after it. He asked, 'What was all that running-up-and-down-scales motion in the, the background I guess you'd call it?'

'Visual scan – your eyes were closed – and subliminal proprioceptive input. The Unconscious dimension and the Body dimension overlap to a great extent all the time. We bring the three dimensions in separately, because they seldom coincide entirely anyway, except in babies. The bright triangular motion at the left of the holo was probably the pain in your ribs.'

402

'I don't see it that way!'

'You don't see it; you weren't consciously feeling it, even, then. But we can't translate a pain in the rib onto a holoscreen, so we give it a visual symbol. The same with all sensations, affects, emotions.'

'You watch all that at once?'

'I told you it took eight years. And you do realise that that's only a fragment? Nobody could put a whole psyche onto a four-foot screen. Nobody knows if there are any limits to the psyche. Except the limits of the universe.'

He said after a while, 'Maybe you aren't a fool, Doctor. Maybe you're just very absorbed in your work. That can be dangerous, you know, to be so absorbed in your work.'

'I love my work, and I hope that it is of positive service,' I said. I was alert for symptoms of disaffection.

He smiled a little and said, 'Prig,' in a sad voice.

Ana is coming along. Still some trouble eating. Entered her in George's mutual-therapy group. What she needs, at least one thing she needs, is companionship. After all why should she eat? Who needs her to be alive? What we call psychosis is sometimes simply realism. But human beings can't live on realism alone.

F.S.'s patterns do not fit any of the classical paranoid psychoscopic patterns in Rheingeld.

The De Cams book is hard for me to understand. The terminology of politics is so different from that of psychology. Everything seems backwards. I must be genuinely attentive at P.T. sessions Sunday nights from now on. I have been lazy-minded. Or, no, but as F.S. said, too absorbed in my work – and so inattentive to its context, he meant. Not thinking about what one is working *for*.

10 September

Have been so tired the last two nights I skipped writing this journal. All the data are on tape and in my analysis notes, of course. Have been working really hard on the F.S. analysis. It

is very exciting. It is a truly unusual mind. Not brilliant, his intelligence tests are good average, he is not original or an artist, there are no schizophrenic insights, I can't say what it is, I feel honored to have shared in the childhood he remembered for me. I can't say what it is. There was pain and fear of course, his father's death from cancer, months and months of misery while F.S. was twelve, that was terrible, but it does not come out pain in the end, he has not forgotten or repressed it but it is all changed, by his love for his parents and his sister and for music and for the shape and weight and fit of things and his memory of the lights and weathers of days long past and his mind always working quietly, reaching out, reaching out to be whole.

There is no question yet of formal co-analysis, it is far too early, but he cooperates so intelligently that today I asked him if he was aware consciously of the Dark Brother figure that accompanied several Con memories in the Uncon dimension. When I described it as having a matted shock of hair he looked startled and said, 'Dokkay, you mean?'

That word had been on the subverbal audio, though I hadn't connected it with the figure.

He explained that when he was five or six Dokkay had been his name for a 'bear' he often dreamed or daydreamed about. He said, 'I rode him. He was big, I was small. He smashed down walls, and destroyed things, bad things, you know, bullies, spies, people who scared my mother, prisons, dark alleys I was afraid to cross, policemen with guns, the pawnbroker. Just knocked them over. And then he walked over all the rubble on up to the hilltop. With me riding on his back. It was quiet up there. It was always evening, just before the stars come out. It's strange to remember it. Thirty years ago! Later on he turned into a kind of friend, a boy or man, with hair like a bear. He still smashed things, and I went with him. It was good fun.'

I write this down from memory as it was not taped; session was interrupted by power outage. It is exasperating that the hospital comes so low on the list of Government priorities.

Attended the Pos. Thinking session tonight and took notes. Dr K. spoke on the dangers and falsehoods of liberalism.

11 September

F.S. tried to show me Dokkay this morning but failed. He laughed and said aloud, 'I can't see him any more. I think at some point I turned into him.'

'Show me when that happened,' I said, and he said, 'All right,' and began at once to recall an episode from his early adolescence. It had nothing to do with Dokkay. He saw an arrest. He was told that the man had been passing out illegal printed matter. Later on he saw one of these pamphlets, the title was in his visual bank, 'Is There Equal Justice?' He read it, but did not recall the text or managed to censor it from me. The arrest was terribly vivid. Details like the young man's blue shirt and the coughing noise he made and the sound of the hitting, the TRTU agents' uniforms, and the car driving away, a big grey car with blood on the door. It came back over and over, the car driving away down the street, driving away down the street. It was a traumatic incident for F.S. and may explain the exaggerated fear of the violence of national justice justified by national security which may have led him to behave irrationally when investigated and so appeared as a tendency to disaffection, falsely I believe.

I will show why I believe this. When the episode was done I said, 'Flores, think about democracy for me, will you?'

He said, 'Little doctor, you don't catch old dogs quite that easily.'

'I am not catching you. Can you think about democracy or can't you?'

'I think about it a good deal,' he said. And he shifted to right-brain activity, music. It was a chorus of the last part of the Ninth Symphony by Beethoven. I recognised it from the Arts term in high school. We sang it to some patriotic words. I yelled, 'Don't censor!' and he said, 'Don't shout, I can hear

405

you.' Of course the room was perfectly silent, but the pickup on the audio was tremendous, like thousands of people singing together. He went on aloud, 'I'm not censoring. I'm thinking about democracy. That is democracy. Hope, brotherhood, no walls. All the walls unbuilt. You, we, I make the universe! Can't you hear it?' And it was the hilltop again, the short grass and the sense of being up high, and the wind, and the whole sky. The music was the sky.

When it was done and I released him from the crown I said, 'Thank you.'

I do not see why the doctor cannot thank the patient for a revelation of beauty and meaning. Of course the doctor's authority is important but it need not be domineering. I realise that in politics the authorities must lead and be followed but in psychological medicine it is a little different a doctor cannot 'cure' the patient the patient 'cures' himself with our help, this is not contradictory to Positive Thinking.

14 September

I am upset after the long conversation with F.S. today and will try to clarify my thinking.

Because the rib injury prevents him from attending work therapy, he is restless. The Violent ward disturbed him deeply so I used my authority to have the V removed from his chart and have him moved into Men's Ward B, three days ago. His bed is next to old Arca's, and when I came to get him for session they were talking, sitting on Arca's bed. F.S. said, 'Dr Sobel, do you know my neighbor, Professor Arca of the Faculty of Arts and Letters of the University?' Of course I know the old man, he has been here for years, far longer than I, but F.S. spoke so courteously and gravely that I said, 'Yes, how do you do, Professor Arca?' and shook the old man's hand. He greeted me politely as a stranger – he often does not know people from one day to the next.

As we went to the scope room F.S. said, 'Do you know how

many electroshock treatments he had?' and when I said no he said, 'Sixty. He tells me that every day. With pride.' Then he said, 'Did you know that he was an internationally famous scholar? He wrote a book, *The Idea of Liberty*, about twentieth-century ideas of freedom in politics and the arts and sciences, I read it when I was in engineering school. It existed then. On bookshelves. It doesn't exist any more. Anywhere. Ask Dr Arca. He never heard of it.'

'There is almost always some memory loss after electro-convulsive therapy,' I said, 'but the material lost can be relearned, and is often spontaneously regained.'

'After sixty sessions?' he said.

F.S. is a tall man, rather stooped, even in the hospital paja-mas he is an impressive figure. But I am also tall, and it is not because I am shorter than he that he calls me 'little doctor.' He did it first when he was angry at me and so now he says it when he is bitter but does not want what he says to hurt me, the me he knows. He said, 'Little doctor, quit faking. You know the man's mind was deliberately destroyed.'

Now I will try to write down exactly what I said, because it is important.

'I do not approve of the use of electroconvulsive therapy as a general instrument. I would not recommend its use on my patients except perhaps in certain specific cases of senile melancholia. I went into psychoscopy because it is an integrat-ive rather than a destructive instrument.'

That is all true, and yet I never said or consciously thought it before.

'What will you recommend for me?' he said.

I explained that once my diagnosis is complete my recom-mendation will be subject to the approval of the Head and Assistant Head of the Section. I said that so far nothing in his history or personality structure warranted the use of ECT but that after all we had not got very far yet.

'Let's take a long time about it,' he said, shuffling along beside me with his shoulders hunched.

'Why? Do you like it?'

'No. Though I like you. But I'd like to delay the inevitable end.'

'Why do you insist that it's inevitable, Flores? Can't you see that your thinking on that one point is quite irrational?'

'Rosa,' he said, he has never used my first name before, 'Rosa, you can't be reasonable about pure evil. There are faces reason cannot see. Of course I'm irrational, faced with the imminent destruction of my memory – my self. But I'm not inaccurate. You know they're not going to let me out of here un...' He hesitated a long time and finally said, 'unchanged.'

'One psychotic episode—'

'I had no psychotic episode. You must know that by now.'

'Then why were you sent here?'

'I have some colleagues who prefer to consider themselves rivals, competitors. I gather they informed the TRTU that I was a subversive liberal.'

'What was their evidence?'

'Evidence?' We were in the scope room by now. He put his hands over his face for a moment and laughed in a bewildered way. 'Evidence? Well, once at a meeting of my section I talked a long time with a visiting foreigner, a fellow in my field, a designer. And I have friends, you know, unproductive people, bohemians. And this summer I showed our section head why a design he'd got approved by the Government wouldn't work. That was stupid. Maybe I'm here for, for imbecility. And I read. I've read Professor Arca's book.'

'But none of that matters, you think positively, you love your country, you're not disaffected!'

He said, 'I don't know. I love the idea of democracy, the hope, yes, I love that. I couldn't live without that. But the country? You mean the thing on the map, lines, everything inside the lines is good and nothing outside them matters? How can an adult love such a childish idea?'

'But you wouldn't betray the nation to an outside enemy.'

He said, 'Well, if it was a choice between the nation and

humanity, or the nation and a friend, I might. If you call that betrayal. I call it morality.'

He *is* a liberal. It is exactly what Dr Katin was talking about on Sunday.

It is classic psychopathy: the absence of normal affect. He said that quite unemotionally – 'I might.'

No. That is not true. He said it with difficulty, with pain. It was I who was so shocked that I felt nothing – blank, cold.

How am I to treat this kind of psychosis, a *political* psychosis? I have read over De Cams's book twice and I believe I do understand it now, but still there is this gap between the political and the psychological, so that the book shows me how to think but does not show me how to *act* positively. I see how F.S. should think and feel, and the difference between that and his present state of mind, but I do not know how to educate him so that he can think positively. De Cams says that disaffection is a negative condition which must be filled with positive ideas and emotions, but this does not fit F.S. The gap is not in him. In fact that gap in De Cams between the political and the psychological is exactly where *his* ideas apply. But if they are wrong ideas how can this be?

I want advice badly, but I cannot get it from Dr Nades. When she gave me the De Cams she said, 'You'll find what you need in this.' If I tell her that I haven't it is like a confession of helplessness and she will take the case away from me. Indeed I think it is a kind of test case, testing me. But I need this experience, I am learning, and besides, the patient trusts me and talks freely to me. He does so because he knows that I keep what he tells me in perfect confidence. Therefore I cannot show this journal or discuss these problems with anyone until the cure is under way and confidence is no longer essential.

But I cannot see when that could happen. It seems as if confidence will always be essential between us.

I have got to teach him to adjust his behavior to reality, or he will be sent for ECT when the Section reviews cases in November. He has been right about that all along.

9 October

I stopped writing in this notebook when the material from F.S.
began to seem 'dangerous' to him (or to myself). I just reread
it all over tonight. I see now that I can never show it to Dr N.
So I am going to go ahead and write what I please in it. Which
is what she said to do, but I think she always expected me to
show it to her, she thought I would want to, which I did, at
first, or that if she asked to see it I'd give it to her. She asked
about it yesterday. I said that I had abandoned it, because it
just repeated things I had already put into the analysis files.
She was plainly disapproving but said nothing. Our dominance-
submission relationship has changed these past few weeks. I
do not feel so much in need of guidance, and after the Ana
Jest discharge, the autism paper, and my successful analysis of
the T.R. Vinha tapes she cannot insist upon my dependence.
But she may resent my independence. I took the covers off the
notebook and am keeping the loose pages in the split in the
back cover of my copy of Rheingeld, it would take a very close
search to find them there. While I was doing that I felt rather
sick at the stomach and got a headache.

Allergy: A person can be exposed to pollen or bitten by
fleas a thousand times without reaction. Then he gets a viral
infection or a psychic trauma or a bee sting, and next time he
meets up with ragweed or a flea he begins to sneeze, cough,
itch, weep, etc. It is the same with certain other irritants. One
has to be sensitized.

'Why is there so much fear?' I wrote. Well now I know. Why
is there no privacy? It is unfair and sordid. I cannot read the
classified' files kept in her office, though I work with the patients
and she does not. But I am not to have any 'classified' material
of my own. Only persons in authority can have secrets. Their
secrets are all good, even when they are lies.

Listen. Listen Rosa Sobel. Doctor of Medicine, Deg. Psycho-
therapy, Deg. Psychoscopy. Have you gone native?

Whose thoughts are you thinking?

You have been working 2 to 5 hours a day for 6 weeks inside one person's mind. A generous, integrated, sane mind. You never worked with anything like that before. You have only worked with the crippled and the terrified. You never met an equal before.

Who is the therapist, you or he?

But if there is nothing wrong with him what am I supposed to cure? How can I help him? How can I save him?

By teaching him to lie?

(Undated)

I spent the last two nights till midnight reviewing the diagnostic scopes of Professor Arca, recorded when he was admitted, eleven years ago, before electroconvulsive treatment.

This morning Dr N inquired why I had been 'so far back in the files.' (That means that Selena reports to her on what files are used. I know every square centimeter of the scope room but all the same I check it over daily now.) I replied that I was interested in studying the development of ideological disaffection in intellectuals. We agreed that intellectualism tends to foster negative thinking and may lead to psychosis, and those suffering from it should ideally be treated, as Prof. Arca was treated, and released if still competent. It was a very interesting and harmonious discussion.

I lied. I lied. I lied. I lied deliberately, knowingly, well. She lied. She is a liar. She is an intellectual too! She is a lie. And a coward, afraid.

I wanted to watch the Arca tapes to get perspective. To prove to myself that Flores is by no means unique or original. This is true. The differences are fascinating. Dr Arca's Con dimension was splendid, architectural, but the Uncon material was less well integrated and less interesting. Dr Arca knew very much more, and the power and beauty of the motions of his thought was far superior to Flores's. Flores is often extremely muddled. That is an element of his vitality. Dr Arca is an, was

an Abstract thinker, as I am, and so I enjoyed his tapes less. I missed the solidity, spatiotemporal realism, and intense sensory clarity of Flores's mind.

In the scope room this morning I told him what I had been doing. His reaction was (as usual) not what I expected. He is fond of the old man and I thought he would be pleased. He said, 'You mean they saved the tapes, and destroyed the mind?' I told him that all tapes are kept for use in teaching, and asked him if that didn't cheer him, to know that a record of Arca's thoughts in his prime existed: wasn't it like his book, after all, the lasting part of a mind which sooner or later would have to grow senile and die anyhow? He said, 'No! Not so long as the book is banned and the tape is classified! Neither freedom nor privacy even in death? That is the worst of all!'

After session he asked if I would be able or willing to destroy his diagnostic tapes, if he is sent to ECT. I said such things could get misfiled and lost easily enough, but that it seemed a cruel waste. I had learned from him and others might, later, too. He said, 'Don't you see that I will not serve the people with security passes? I will not be used, that's the whole point. You have never used me. We have worked together. Served our term together.'

Prison has been much in his mind lately. Fantasies, day-dreams of jails, labor camps. He dreams of prison as a man in prison dreams of freedom.

Indeed as I see the way narrowing in I would get him sent to prison if I could, but since he is *here* there is no chance. If I reported that he is, in fact politically dangerous, they will simply put him back in the Violent ward and give him ECT. There is no judge here to give him a life sentence. Only doctors to give death sentences.

What I can do is stretch out the diagnosis as long as possible, and put in a request for full co-analysts, with a strong prognosis of complete cure. But I have drafted the report three times already and it is very hard to phrase it so that it's clear that I know the disease is ideological (so that they don't just override

my diagnosis at once) but still making it sound mild and curable enough that they'd let me handle it with the psychoscope. And then, why spend up to a year, using expensive equipment, when a cheap and simple instant cure is at hand? No matter what I say, they have that argument. There are two weeks left until Sectional Review. I have got to write the report so that it will be really impossible for them to override it. But what if Flores is right, all this is just playacting, lying about lying, and they have had orders right from the start from TRTU, 'wipe this one out'—

(Undated)

Sectional Review today.

If I stay on here I have some power, I can do some good No no no but I don't I don't even in this one thing even in this what can I do now how can I stop

(Undated)

Last night I dreamed I rode on a bear's back up a deep gorge between steep mountainsides, slopes going steep up into a dark sky, it was winter, there was ice on the rocks

(Undated)

Tomorrow morning will tell Nades I am resigning and request-ing transfer to Children's Hospital. But she must approve the transfer. If not I am out in the cold. I am in the cold already. Door locked to write this. As soon as it is written will go down to furnace room and burn it all. There is no place any more.

We met in the hall. He was with an orderly.

I took his hand. It was big and bony and very cold. He said, 'Is this it now, Rosa – the electroshock?' in a low voice. I did not want him to lose hope before he walked up the stairs and

down the corridor. It is a long way down the corridor. I said, 'No. Just some more tests – EEC probably.'

'Then I'll see you tomorrow?' he asked, and I said yes.

And he did. I went in this evening. He was awake. I said, 'I am Dr Sobel, Flores. I am Rosa.'

He said, 'I'm pleased to meet you,' mumbling. There is a slight facial paralysis on the left. That will wear off.

I am Rosa. I am the rose. The rose, I am the rose. The rose with no flower, the rose all thorns, the mind he made, the hand he touched, the winter rose.

THE WHITE DONKEY

There were snakes in the old stone place, but the grass grew so green and rank there that she brought the goats back every day. 'The goats are looking fat,' Nana said. 'Where are you grazing them, Sita?' And when Sita said, 'At the old stone place, in the forest,' Nana said, 'It's a long way to take them,' and Uncle Hira said, 'Look out for snakes in that place,' but they were thinking of the goats, not of her; so she did not ask them, after all, about the white donkey.

She had seen the donkey first when she was putting flowers on the red stone under the pipal tree at the edge of the forest. She liked that stone. It was the Goddess, very old, round, sitting comfortably among the roots of the tree. Everybody who passed by there left the Goddess some flowers or poured a bit of water on her, and every spring her red paint was renewed. Sita was giving the Goddess a rhododendron flower when she looked round, thinking one of the goats was straying off into the forest; but it wasn't a goat. It was a white animal that had caught her eye, whiter than a Brahminee bull. Sita followed it to see what it was. When she saw the neat round rump and the tail like a rope with a tassel, she knew it was a donkey; but such a beautiful donkey! And whose? There were three donkeys in the village, and Chandra Bose owned two, all of them grey, bony, mournful, laborious beasts. This was a tall, sleek, delicate donkey, a wonderful donkey. It could not belong to Chandra Bose, or to anybody in the village, or to anybody in the other

village. It wore no halter or harness. It must be wild; it must live in the forest alone.

Sure enough, when she brought the goats along by whistling to clever Kala, and followed where the white donkey had gone into the forest, first there was a path, and then they came to the place where the old stones were, blocks of stone as big as houses all half buried and overgrown with grass and kerala vines; and there the white donkey was standing looking back at her from the darkness under the trees.

She thought then that the donkey was a god, because it had a third eye in the middle of its forehead like Shiva. But when it turned she saw that that was not an eye, but a horn – not curved like a cow's or a goat's horns, a straight spike like a deer's – just the one horn, between the eyes, like Shiva's eye. So it might be a kind of god donkey; and in case it was, she picked a yellow flower off the kerala vine and offered it stretching out her open palm.

The white donkey stood a while considering her and the goats and the flower; then it came slowly back among the big stones towards her. It had split hooves like the goats, and walked even more neatly than they did. It accepted the flower. Its nose was pinkish-white, and very soft where it snuffled on Sita's palm. She quickly picked another flower, and the donkey accepted it too. But when she wanted to stroke its face around the short, white, twisted horn and the white, nervous ears, it moved away, looking sidelong at her from its long dark eyes.

Sita was a little afraid of it, and thought it might be a little afraid of her; so she sat down on one of the half-buried rocks and pretended to be watching the goats, who were all busy grazing on the best grass they had had for months. Presently the donkey came close again, and standing beside Sita, rested its curly-bearded chin on her lap. The breath from its nostrils moved the thin glass bangles on her wrist. Slowly and very gently she stroked the base of the white, nervous ears, the fine, harsh hair at the base of the horn, the silken muzzle; and the white donkey stood beside her, breathing long, warm breaths.

Every day since then she brought the goats there, walking carefully because of snakes; and the goats were getting fat; and her friend the donkey came out of the forest every day, and accepted her offering, and kept her company.

'One bullock and one hundred rupees cash,' said Uncle Hira, 'you're crazy if you think we can marry her for less!'

'Moti Lai is a lazy man,' Nana said. 'Dirty and lazy.'

'So he wants a wife to work and clean for him! And he'll take her for only one bullock and one hundred rupees cash!'

'Maybe he'll settle down when he's married,' Nana said.

So Sita was betrothed to Moti Lal from the other village, who had watched her driving the goats home at evening. She had seen him watching her across the road, but had never looked at him. She did not want to look at him.

'This is the last day,' she said to the white donkey, while the goats cropped the grass among the big, carved, fallen stones, and the forest stood all about them in the singing stillness. 'Tomorrow I'll come with Uma's little brother to show him the way here. He'll be the village goatherd now. The day after tomorrow is my wedding day.'

The white donkey stood still, its curly, silky beard resting against her hand.

'Nana is giving me her gold bangle,' Sita said to the donkey. 'I get to wear a red sari, and have henna on my feet and hands.'

The donkey stood still, listening.

'There'll be sweet rice to eat at the wedding,' Sita said; then she began to cry.

'Goodbye, white donkey,' she said. The white donkey looked at her sidelong, and slowly, not looking back, moved away from her and walked into the darkness under the trees.

THE PHOENIX

The radio on the chest of drawers hissed and crackled like burning acid. Through the crackle a voice boasted of victories. 'Butchers!' she snarled at the voice. 'Butchers, liars, fools!' But there was an expression in the librarian's eyes which brought her rage up short like a dog on a chain, clawing at the air, choked off.

'You can't be a Partisan!'

The librarian said nothing. He might well have said nothing even if he had been able to say anything.

She turned the radio down – you could never turn it off, lest you miss the last act, the denouement – and came up close to the librarian on the bed. Familiar to her now were the round, sallow face, the dark eyes with bloodshot whites, the dark, wiry hair on his head, and the hair on his forearms and the backs of his hands and fingers, and the hair under his arms and on his chest and groin and legs, and the whole of his stocky, sweaty, suffering body, which she had been trying to look after for thirty hours while the city blew itself apart street by street and nerve by nerve and the radio twitched from lies to static to lies.

'Come on, don't tell me that!' she said to his silence. 'You weren't with them. You were against them.'

Without a word, with the utmost economy, he evinced a denial.

'But I saw you! I saw exactly what you did. You locked the library. Why do you think I came there looking for you? You don't think I'd have crossed the street to help one of them!' A

one-note laugh of scorn, and she awarded the well-delivered line the moment of silence that was its due. The radio hissed thinly, drifting back to static. She sat down on the foot of the bed, directly in the librarian's line of sight, front and center.

'I've known you by sight for I don't know how long – a couple of years, it must be. My other room, there, looks out on the square. Right across to the library. I've seen you opening it up in the morning a hundred times. This time I saw you closing it, at two in the afternoon. Running those wrought-iron gates across the doors in a rush. So what's he up to? Then I heard the cars and those damned motorcycles. I drew the curtain right away. But then I stood behind the curtain and watched. That was strange, you know? I'd have sworn I'd be hiding under the bed in here as soon as I knew they were that close. But I stood there and watched. It was like watching a play!' she said with the expansiveness of inaccuracy. In fact peering out between the curtain and the window frame with a running thrill of not disagreeable terror, she had inevitably felt that she was sizing up the house. Was it that revival of emotion that had moved her, so soon afterwards, to act?

'They pulled the flag down first. I suppose even terrorists have to do things in the proper order. Probably, in fact, no one is more conventional. They have to do everything that's expected of them... Well, I'd seen you go round to that side door, the basement entrance, after you'd locked the gates. I think I'd noticed your coat, without noticing that I noticed, you know; that yellowish-brown color. So, after they'd been all over the front steps, and broken in at the side door – like ants on meat, I kept thinking – and finally all come out again and got onto their damned motorcycles and roared off to go wreck something else, and I was wondering if it was smoke or just dust that was hanging around that side door – then I thought of your coat, because of the color of smoke, that yellowish brown. I thought, I never saw that coat again. They didn't bring the librarian out with them. Well, so I thought probably they'd shot you, inside there with the books. But I kept thinking

how you'd locked the doors and locked the gates and then gone
back inside. I didn't know why you'd done that. You could have
locked up and left, got away, after all. I kept thinking about
that. And there wasn't a soul down in the square. All us rats
hiding in our rat-holes. So finally I thought. Well, I can't live
with this, and went over to look for you. I walked right across
the square. Empty as four A.M. It was peaceful. I wasn't afraid.
I was only frightened of finding you dead. A wound, blood.
Blood turns me faint, I detest it. So I go in, and my mouth's
dry and my ears are singing, and then I see you coming with
an armload of books!' She laughed, but this time her voice
cracked. She turned left profile to him, glancing at him once
sidelong.

'Why did you go back in? And when they were in there,
what did you do? You hid, I suppose. And when they left you
came out and tried to put out the fire.'

He shook his head slightly.

'You did,' she said. 'You did put it out. There was water on
the floor, and a mop bucket.'

He did not deny this.

'I shouldn't have thought books would catch fire easily. Or
did they pull out some newspapers, or the catalogue, or the
overdue file? They certainly got something burning. All that
smoke, it was awful. I was choking as soon as I came in, I
don't know how you breathed at all up there on the main floor.
Anyway, you put out the fire, and you had to get out because
of the smoke, or you weren't sure the fire was really out; so
you quick picked up some valuable books and headed for the
door—'

Again he shook his head. Was he smiling?

'You did! You were crawling towards the stairs, crawling on
your knees, trying to carry those books, when I came up. I don't
know if you would have got out or not, but you were trying to.'

He nodded, and tried to whisper something.

'Never mind. Don't talk. Just tell me, no, don't tell me, how

420

you can be a Partisan, after that. After giving your life, all but, for a few books!'

He forced the whisper, like a steel brush on brass, that was all the smoke had left on his voice: 'Not valuable,' he said.

She had leaned forward to catch his words. She straightened up, smoothed her skirt, and presently spoke with some disdain.

'I don't know that we are really very well qualified to judge whether our life is or is not valuable.'

But he shook his head again and whispered, voiceless, meaningless, obstinate: 'The books.'

'You're saying that the *books* aren't valuable?'

He nodded, his face relaxing, relieved at having explained himself at last, at having got it all straight.

She stared at him, incredulous, angrier than she had been at the radio, and then the anger flipped over like a coin from a thumb, and she laughed. 'You're crazy!' she said, putting her hand on his.

His hand was thickset like the rest of him, firm but un-callused, a desk worker's hand. It was hot to her touch.

'You ought to be in hospital,' she said with remorse. 'I know you shouldn't talk, I can't help talking, but don't answer. I know you should have gone to the hospital. But how could you get there, no taxis, and God knows what the hospitals are like now. Or who they're willing to take. If it ever quiets down and the telephone works again I'll try to call a doctor. If there are any doctors left. If there's anything left when this is over.'

It was the silence that made her say that. It was a silent day. On the silent days you almost wanted to hear the motorcycles, the machine guns.

His eyes were closed. Yesterday evening, and from time to time all night, he had had spasms of struggling for breath, like asthma or a heart attack, terrifying. He breathed short and hard even now, but however worn out and uncomfortable, he was resting; he must be better. What could a doctor do for smoke inhalation, anyhow? Probably not much. Doctors were not much good for things like lack of breath, or old age, or civil

disorders. The librarian was suffering from what his country was dying of, his sickness was his citizenship of this city. Weeks now, the loudspeakers, the machine guns, the explosions, the helicopters, the fires, the silences; the body politic was incurable, its agony went on and on. You went miles for a cabbage, a kilo of meal. Then next day the sweet shop at the corner was open, children buying orange drink. And the next day it was gone, the corner building blown up, burnt out. The carcase politic. Faces of people like façades of buildings downtown, the great hotels, blank and furtive, all blinds down. And last Saturday night they had thrown a bomb into the Phoenix. Thirty dead, the radio had said, and later sixty dead, but it was not the deaths that outraged her. People took their chances. They had gone to see a play in the middle of a civil war, they had taken their chance and lost. There was both gallantry and justice there. But the old Phoenix, the house itself: the stage where she had played how many pert housemaids, younger sisters, confidantes, dowagers, Olga Prozorova, and for the great three weeks Nora; the red curtain, the red plush seats, the dirty chandelier and gilt plaster mouldings, all that fake grandeur, that box of toys, that defenseless and indefensible strutting place for the human soul – to hurt that was contemptible. Better if they threw their damned bombs into churches. There surely the startled soul would be plucked straight up to downy heaven before it noticed that its body had been blown to stew meat. With God on your side, in God's house, how could anything go wrong? But there was no protection in some dead playwright and a lot of stagehands and fool actors. Everything could go wrong, and always did. Lights out, and screaming and pushing, trampling, an unspeakable sewer stink, and so much for Molière, or Pirandello, or whoever they'd been playing Saturday night at the Phoenix. God had never been on that side. He'd take the glory, all right, but not the blame. What God was, in fact, was a doctor, a famous surgeon: don't ask questions, I don't answer them, pay your fees, I'll save you if I care to but if I don't it's your own fault.

She got up to rearrange the bedside table, reproving herself

for vulgarity of thought. She had to be angry at somebody; there was nobody there but God and the librarian, and she did not want to be angry at the librarian. Like the city, he was too sick. And anger would disturb the purity of her strong erotic attraction to him, which had been giving her great pleasure. She had not so enjoyed looking at a man for years; she had thought that joy lost, withered away. Her age took advantage from his illness. In the normal course of things he would not have seen her as a woman but as an old woman, and his blindness would have blinded her she would not have looked at him. But, having undressed him and looked after his body, she was spared hypocrisy, and could admire that stocky and innocent body with the innocent joy of desire. Of his mind and spirit she knew almost nothing, only that he had courage, which was a good thing. She did not need to know more. Indeed she did not want to. She was sorry he had spoken at all, had said those two stupid, boastful words, 'Not valuable,' whether meaning his own life, or the books he had tried to save at the risk of his life. In either case what he had meant was that to a Partisan nothing was valuable but the cause. The existence of a branch librarian, the existence of a few books – trash. Nothing mattered but the future.

But if he was a Partisan, why had he tried to save the books?

Would a Loyalist have stayed alone in that terrible brownish-yellow room of smoke trying to put out the fire, to keep the books from burning?

Of course, she answered herself. According to his opinions, his theories, his beliefs, yes, certainly, of course! Books, statues, buildings, lamp posts bearing lighted lamps not strangled corpses, Molière at eight-thirty, conversation at dinner, school-girls in blue with satchels, order, decency, the past that ensures a future, for this the Loyalist stood. Staunchly he stood. But would he also crawl across a floor coughing out his lungs, trying to hang on to a few of the books? – not even valuable books, that's what the librarian had been trying to say, she understood him now, not even valuable ones; there probably were

no valuable books in this branch library. Just books, any books, not because he had opinions, not because he had beliefs, there with his life forfeit, but because he was a librarian. A person who looked after books. The one responsible.

'Is that what you meant?' she asked him, softly, because he had fallen asleep. 'Is that why I brought you here?'

The radio hissed, but she did not need applause. His sleep was her audience.

ZENITH

INTRACOM

CAPTAIN: Good morning, good morning, good morning every-
body. How many of us are there, aboard this spaceship?
Well, let's see. This is, of course, the Captain speaking.
There is the First Mate, about whom there is something,
well, different. But not the ears. I've seen First Mates with
funny ears, but that isn't this one's problem. Well, then
there is the Chief Engineer, whose vocabulary is limited to
symptoms of valvular malfunction. And the Insane Second
Mate, who is locked up in the Crew Recreation Lounge, busy
pulling the stuffing out of chairs and sofas, and throwing
pool balls at the indirect lighting fixtures. Then there is the
Communications Officer, forever wearing headphones and
hunched above the hissing radio. The hiss, I understand, is
the noise stars make. It is quite a loud noise, out here. Is that
all of us? I can't think of anybody else. It is a small crew,
but a select one, being composed entirely of officers. How
many does it come to? Six, doesn't it?

FIRST MATE: Five.

CAPTAIN: Only five? Are you sure of that, Mr Balls?

FIRST MATE: Affirmative.

CAPTAIN: Very well, five, then. I know you're good with
mathematics. But I keep having this feeling there's somebody
else.

FIRST MATE: Conceivably, sir, you are thinking of yourself in
your capacity as Cook.

CAPTAIN: Don't call me 'sir,' Mr Balls. All right, then. Here we

are, the personnel of the spaceship *Mary Jane Hewett*, Class F, b-1951, Type 36–25–38, Size 13, outward bound from Earth (Terra, 3 Solis) on an exploratory voyage in the direction of the South Orion Arm, with a cargo of breadfruit trees. We have travelled a tremendous distance already, light-years and light-years, though there are times it hardly seems we're moving at all.

Excuse me. I have to go make lunch.

It isn't easy to feed the Insane Second Mate, since she plugged the soup chute full of sofa stuffing. We have cut a little hole in the door of the Crew Recreation Lounge, like a mail slot. We wait until the Insane Second Mate is asleep, because when she's awake, if she hears us at the door, she sticks her hands through and makes obscene gestures with the middle finger of her left hand, or throws pool balls at us. While she is asleep, or sulking, we hastily force her dinner through the slot. After a certain time has passed, if one places one's ear to the lower half of the door, the Insane Second Mate may be heard munching the food. Uneaten portions are returned through the slot. Lately very little has been returned. Evidently she is eating all the food, or doing something else with it. From time to time I have wondered if there could be someone else in there with her. She seems to eat inordinately, for a female Insane Second Mate of average size.

Chief Engineer, before I go to the galley may I have your daily report for the Ship's Log.

CHIEF ENGINEER: Aye, weel, compressed hydrogen tank A-30 is leaking. Leakage not contained at present time. Stoppage in forward conduit FC-599 continues, causing buildup of pressure in central coolant storage area CCS-2. Hairline crack in casing of Anti-Matter Isolater is being investigated with intention of presenting report on viability of implementation of repair procedures.

CAPTAIN: What procedure is indicated if repair implementation proves non-feasible?

CHIEF ENGINEER: Automatic Self-Destruct.

CAPTAIN: Good God.

CHIEF ENGINEER: Log entry continued: Vane One has suffered extensive meteor damage and is not currently functioning at full gather-power. Vane Two has been shortened by 81,000 miles to offset the slow spin imparted by imbalance in vane function. Results should be discernible within five to thirteen days (Ship Tune). Automatic self-destruct units of ship are no longer functioning, due to suspected short circuit causing automatic self-destruct units to automatically self-destruct.

CAPTAIN: You mean the automatic self-destruct units are all self-destructed?

CHIEF ENGINEER: Aye, that's about the size of it, Captain.

CAPTAIN: You mean we can't destruct the ship, if the crack in the Anti-Matter Isolater widens? But if we can't self-destruct, and the Anti-Matter Isolater blows, well take the fifty nearest stars and all their planets with us – we'll blow up this whole region of space – if the anti-matter meets an F-2 star, the destruction might become a chain reaction and the entire Galaxy could be destructed!

CHIEF ENGINEER: Weel, we're working hard on that crack, Captain.

CAPTAIN: We? What do you mean, we? There's only one of you down there in the Engine Room. Isn't there?

CHIEF ENGINEER: Aye. But I wish there was a few more.

CAPTAIN: I know you do, at times like this, 'Bolts.' But we have the utmost faith in you. You're a fantastically good Chief Engineer, for a woman.

CHIEF ENGINEER: Thank you, Captain. I'll be going back to my wee crack now.

CAPTAIN: Very well, and I'm on my way to the galley. It's odd. Just now as I glanced over my shoulder I could have sworn I saw somebody going down Corridor G. Now Corridor G leads to a totally disused section of the ship, the Athletic Supporter Storage Room. Who's got any business there? Mr Balls? Mr Balls, are you there?

FIRST MATE: I am in the Computer Center, sir.

CAPTAIN: Will you please not call me 'sir,' Mr Balls. It estranges me. 'Sparks,' where are you? 'Sparks'? Report to Bridge by intracom at once. 'Sparks'?

COMMUNICATIONS OFFICER: Shhh. I'm listening to the radio. Roger. Over and out.

CAPTAIN: All right. And 'Bolts' is down with the Anti-Matter Isolater; and I'm here on the Bridge trying to get to the galley. That's four. Five, five, who's five? Oh, yes. Insane Second Mate, report current whereabouts to Bridge by intracom at once.

INSANE SECOND MATE: I am clinging by the skin of my teeth and the nails of my toes to a cliff that towers above a raging sea of salt, lashed by great winds into waves and breakers whiter and heavier than ever water was. If I let go I will fall and be broken against the rocks and buried under tons of roaring salt, drowned in the dry sea. If I do not let go I have to keep holding on here, and holding on, and holding on, what for? I am so bored I could scream. I am screaming loudly but no one can hear it over the howl of the wind and the thunder of collapsing salt. I hope the rest of you are enjucting yourselves.

CAPTAIN: What?

INSANE SECOND MATE: Before the ship self-destructs, I hope you are emplucting your time in enjuctable diversions. I think I shall let go now.

CAPTAIN: Wait! Listen, 'Bats,' is there anybody else there in the Crew Recreation Lounge with you?

INSANE SECOND MATE: Here I go. Eeeee-yahhhhhh! – Jesus Christ! it's sugar.

CAPTAIN: Well, that seems to account for all six of us. There couldn't have been anybody in Corridor G. I just thought there was.

FIRST MATE: Captain, there are only five persons aboard.

CAPTAIN: What makes you so sure of that, Mr Balls?

FIRST MATE: Mathematics. Simple addition of real numbers.

Yourself, I, myself, 1, 'Bolts,' 1, 'Sparks,' 1, 'Bats,' 1. 1 plus 1 plus 1 plus 1 plus 1 equals 5.

CAPTAIN: That may be. You can prove anything with statistics. But what if there's one 1 you haven't counted?

FIRST MATE: Who?

CAPTAIN: That's what I'm asking *you*, Mr Balls.

FIRST MATE: Captain, may I respectfully suggest that it is time for lunch, or dinner, or whatever time it is time for.

CAPTAIN: And what about irrational numbers, Mr Balls? Eh?

FIRST MATE: Captain, may I respectfully suggest that you leave mathematics to me and the onboard computers.

CAPTAIN: All right, all right. What do you want for lunch?

FIRST MATE: Whatever you please, Captain.

CAPTAIN: I am sick and tired of having to think about it, planning meals all the time. I'm going to open a can of Campbell's Tomato Rice Soup and if you don't like it it's too bad. Every time I'm on the verge of really understanding something, every time an insight is just within out-grope, every time I really realise that I am the Captain of a great ship, I have to turn around and decide whether it's to be macaroni and cheese or rice pilaf. Why can't somebody else do the cooking for a while?

FIRST MATE: Nobody else knows how.

CAPTAIN: Any one of you can heat a can of soup as well as I can.

FIRST MATE: Remember when the Second Mate tried?

CAPTAIN: Well, almost any of you. A robot could do it. Why don't we have galley robots? Why weren't we designed properly? The real trouble is that this is a lazy, uncoordinated, incoherent crew. And the center of the trouble, the real source of the disintegration, the stumbling block to all my efforts to run a tight ship, is one person, one single member of the crew, and I think you all know who I'm talking about.

FIRST MATE: Affirmative.

CHIEF ENGINEER: Oh, aye.

INSANE SECOND MATE: Not me. But poor Tom's a-cold.

CAPTAIN: 'Sparks,' are you listening? 'Sparks,' come in please. Come in please.

COMMUNICATIONS OFFICER: Shhh. I'm listening to the radio. Roger. Over and—

CAPTAIN: No! Now you take off those damned headphones and listen to me for a minute, 'Sparks.'

COMMUNICATIONS OFFICER: Captain, I wish I could take off the headphones. Sometimes I even wish I could turn off the radio. But I can't. It does fade sometimes, you know. There'll be days at a time, weeks, months, when I can't pick up a thing, not even star hiss. But I have to keep listening, in case it comes back, in case a message comes through. That's the way it is now. I haven't picked up a message for five days (Ship Time). But what if one is just about to come through? What if it came through and I was in the galley heating soup? What if it's coming through right now and I'm missing it because I'm talking on the intracom? It isn't that I have anything against the rest of you, or that I want to be a stumbling block, but that's the nature of a Communications Officer. Over and—

CAPTAIN: No. Now stay on the intracom and listen to *this* message. Other ships have Communications Officers, you know, and they don't act like you at all. They don't just sit there with their damned head between the earphones and their mouth hanging open all the time. They *communicate*. They talk with other ships of the Fleet. They receive news and directives, and exchange all sorts of information and friendly chitchat to beguile the interminable boredom of space. Why don't you ever do that? Don't you realise the rest of us would like to talk with the rest of the Fleet now and then?

COMMUNICATIONS OFFICER: But I don't listen on the Fleet wavelength.

CAPTAIN: Why not?

COMMUNICATIONS OFFICER: Because I'm trying to pick up the message.

CAPTAIN: What message?

COMMUNICATIONS OFFICER: The one we haven't heard before.

CAPTAIN: What for?

COMMUNICATIONS OFFICER: Well, it might indicate where we're going – we and all the other ships of the Fleet.

CAPTAIN: What does it matter where we're going, so long as we're going? Listen, 'Sparks,' I don't like to berate you like this. We'd like to have the upmost faith in you. You're a fantastically good Communications Officer, for a woman. But—

COMMUNICATIONS OFFICER: Excuse me, Captain, I'm getting star hiss. Over and out.

CAPTAIN: Oh, hell. Mr Balls, will you please proceed to Bridge. I'll be in the galley, heating soup.

FIRST MATE: Captain, wait. There's something funny in the air. Something in the ship's atmospheric circulation system.

CAPTAIN: Probably just some of 'Bolts's' hydrogen leaking.

FIRST MATE: It doesn't smell like hydrogen. It's a *strange* smell. Or is it a vibration? Or is it a noise?

CAPTAIN: Mr Balls, are you all right? You don't sound like yourself.

FIRST MATE: Affirmative. Captain, I wish to report suspected presence of an alien aboard this ship.

CAPTAIN: An alien?

FIRST MATE: Affirmative. Alert. Alert. Red Alert. All hands to combat posts. Alien presence suspected on ship. Chief Engineer, report on conditions in Engine Room.

CHIEF ENGINEER: Weel, noo, everything's dandy in the Engine Room, sir.

CAPTAIN: What about the Anti-Matter Isolater?

CHIEF ENGINEER: We mended the wee crack wi' a wee Band-Aid, Captain, and it's as good as new.

CAPTAIN: What about the ship's self-destruct capacity?

CHIEF ENGINEER: Weel, noo, we're working on that. But otherwise I may say that things in the Engine Room have never been better.

FIRST MATE: Red Alert! Red Alert! Chief Engineer, proceed

instantly to repair automatic self-destruct units in Central Propulsion Zone, and as soon as repairs are completed place automatic self-destruct units on Imminent status.

CAPTAIN: Mr Balls, what are you shouting about?

FIRST MATE: There's an alien in this ship with us, Captain!

CAPTAIN: How do you know?

FIRST MATE: A slimy, unspeakable alien!

CAPTAIN: Have you seen it, Mr Balls? Is it in the Athletic Supporter Storage Room?

FIRST MATE: No, I haven't seen it. I don't want to see it. I can *feel* it. It's in here, Captain. It's in the ship – something that doesn't belong here. It's not one of us. It came from Outer Space. From outside. To take us over. It's waiting, waiting somewhere in the very bowels of the ship, waiting, and growing—

CAPTAIN: Good gracious. Get a hold of yourself, Mr Balls.

INSANE SECOND MATE: I told you poor Tom was a-cold. Now poor Tom's a-flipped.

FIRST MATE: It's in there, in the Crew Recreation Lounge, with you, isn't it, 'Bats'? You've known about it for days, weeks. You've been hiding it from us. You traitor! I'm coming in. I'm coming in there, 'Bats,' and I'm going to kill that thing, that unspeakable, amorphous Thing that you've been hiding from us and feeding with our food—

CAPTAIN: Mr Balls! Where are you? What are you doing?

FIRST MATE: I'm breaking down the door of the Crew Recreation Lounge, Captain. Don't worry. I'll handle this. You just keep things running there on the Bridge, and the ship on course, and all.

CAPTAIN: I'm not on the Bridge. I'm in the galley.

FIRST MATE: For God's sake, Captain, get back to the Bridge! The Thing will try to take control of the ship, if it escapes me! – All right, 'Bats,' where is it? Where is it hiding? Show the Thing to me, or I'll – Aagh! Aaaggghhh! Ow!

CHIEF ENGINEER: Captain? Captain Cook? Would there be a wee bit o' trouble up there?

COMMUNICATIONS OFFICER: Please be quieter, everybody. I'm receiving.

CAPTAIN: Mr Balls, report current conditions in Crew Recreation Lounge. Mr Balls, report please.

INSANE SECOND MATE: This is the Insane Second Mate speaking. The First Mate is temporarily incapacitated.

CAPTAIN: Report, please, Second Mate.

INSANE SECOND MATE: Well, he came busting in shouting about how he was going to do something to the alien, and I got in his way, and he tried to karate chop me. But as you know, Captain, I'm extraordinarily strong, even for an Insane Second Mate. I hit him on the head with a copy of the *I Ching*, and he folded.

CAPTAIN: Report current condition of First Mate, please.

INSANE SECOND MATE: He is lying on the floor breathing.

CAPTAIN: Very good. 'Bats,' I suppose you'd better get up to the Bridge and keep an eye on flight control. Last time I looked Arcturus seemed to have drifted a bit. If I don't get lunch ready, tempers are going to be getting short.

INSANE SECOND MATE: Aye aye, Captain.

CAPTAIN: By the way, *is* there an alien aboard?

INSANE SECOND MATE: Oh, yes, Captain.

CAPTAIN: I thought so all along. I knew Mr Balls couldn't count. You'd better take it up to the Bridge with you and keep an eye on it.

INSANE SECOND MATE: Captain, I can't do that. I have to leave it here in the Crew Recreation Lounge.

CAPTAIN: Why?

INSANE SECOND MATE: Well, see, it sort of fits in here. We can feed it through the slot in the door. Frankly, I'm just as glad to get out. Things were getting a little crowded in here. As Mr Balls noticed, it's been growing. You wouldn't believe it. It was just a speck of a thing to start with.

CAPTAIN: And how is Mr Balls?

INSANE SECOND MATE: He's sitting up now, but he looks a bit catatonic. It's the shock. I'll walk him back to his quarters.

435

FIRST MATE: Oh my God I can't stand it horrible vile like a giant worm slimy battening on us fattening on us invading us a vampire a parasite using us growing *growing* GROW-ING get me out get me out Red Alert Self-Destruct SELF-DESTRUCT!

INSANE SECOND MATE: There, there, Balls. Now. Come on. Here's your own nice cozy quarters, see? And you can lock the door, and shut It out, and do mathematics all by yourself.

FIRST MATE: My God, you're worse than It is! Get out of here! Out! Captain Cook! Captain Cook! This officer is insane!

CAPTAIN: What officer?

INSANE SECOND MATE: Me.

CAPTAIN: Oh, now, we just call you that, because you won't use secondary process thinking.

FIRST MATE: Captain Cook! Order Engine Room personnel to activate automatic self-destruct units! Abort mission! Abort mission!

CAPTAIN: How's that again?

FIRST MATE: Abort! Abort! We are being emplucted by an alien creature for unknown purposes! It is taking over the officers' minds! This ship is a peril to the Universe!

INSANE SECOND MATE: Goodness, he talks almost the way I do.

CAPTAIN: It's quite interesting, actually, looked at dispassionately. I wonder if Mr Balls resents the presence of the alien because he, too, has always been, in a sense, an alien presence on this ship. Psychologists call the phenomenon 'projection,' I believe.

FIRST MATE: Can't you realise how horrible it is, horrible, horrible!

COMMUNICATIONS OFFICER: Please order the First Mate to shut up, Captain. All this shouting is very annucting. I'm getting some interesting material on the radio.

CAPTAIN: Where from? I certainly could use some advice.

COMMUNICATIONS OFFICER: I'm not sure. Seems very close. Loud signal.

CAPTAIN: What does it say?

COMMUNICATIONS OFFICER: It doesn't speak English.

INSANE SECOND MATE: This is 'Bats' reporting from the Bridge. All well here.

CAPTAIN: All right, everybody. Lunchtime. Mouth to the soup chute, mates! Ready?

INSANE SECOND MATE: Ready.

CHIEF ENGINEER: Ready.

FIRST MATE: Ready.

COMMUNICATIONS OFFICER: Ready.

CAPTAIN: Soup's on!

FIRST MATE: Mmmm.

INSANE SECOND MATE: Yum.

COMMUNICATIONS OFFICER: Yum.

CAPTAIN: Yum.

INSANE SECOND MATE: What about the alien?

CHIEF ENGINEER: Ahh.

CHIEF ENGINEER: I'll see to the puir wee beastie. Send me another chute of soup, Captain, and I'll catch it in an oilcan and pour it in through the slot. Aye, that's it. Now then. Here I am. Are you ready, beastie? Here it comes!

ALIEN: Num, num.

CHIEF ENGINEER: There's a bonnie beastie. Go to sleep now. Captain, how do you think the beastie got aboard?

CAPTAIN: I've been thinking about that.

INSANE SECOND MATE: It didn't 'get' aboard. It's autochthonous. It's ours, all ours.

CAPTAIN: It doesn't happen that way, 'Bats.' Not with advanced spaceships of our type. At least, not without a Special Dispensation. Personally, I think the only time it could have got into the Crew Recreation Lounge was through the tubes, when we rendezvoused with that cruiser near Deneb. The hatches were open several times, if you recall, during that exchange.

CHIEF ENGINEER: Oh, aye, a lovely ship, that cruiser. Sleek and slim and tapered, and power enough to rattle my pipes.

COMMUNICATIONS OFFICER: Yes, damn it, it kept interfering

with my reception. Jammed the radio with a lot of sentimental nonsense for a week. Kept signalling us as 'Honey Pot.'

FIRST MATE: Do you mean to imply, Captain, that that cruiser deliberately stowed this monster away aboard our ship? A cruiser of the Fleet?

CAPTAIN: Well, no, not deliberately. Those things simply happen, sometimes, if precautions haven't been taken. If the Second Mate, for instance, failed to activate the hatch forcefields, and to remind me to go through decontamination procedure – which has happened before—

INSANE SECOND MATE: I hate activating those forcefields. They're unnatural. They drive me crazy. All those vibrations. And worrying about getting the phases timed just right. They're not good for the ship, in the long run. 'Bolts' will back me up on that.

CHIEF ENGINEER: Aye, they're a strain on the engines. Besides, why do *we* have to take all the precautions?

INSANE SECOND MATE: So I forgot to turn them on.

CAPTAIN: There you are.

FIRST MATE: You're all psychotic – subhuman. You let us be infected, invaded, taken over by this alien. You deliberately invited it to happen, and now that it's happened, you're allowing it to go on happening – and it's sitting there, growing, *growing*—

CHIEF ENGINEER: There, there, puir wee First Mate. Dinna let it fash ye.

FIRST MATE: Captain Cook! Listen to me! You've always listened to me sometimes, you've always been superbly rational more or less. Think about it, *think* about it – the danger, the danger to the ship. It's taking us over, don't you see? And we have a mission! How long are you going to let it go on? The sooner we act, the safer and easier it'll be—

CAPTAIN: Well, how long has it been aboard?

INSANE SECOND MATE: About fifty days (Ship Time). That's when the cruiser left, anyhow.

CAPTAIN: That leaves, let's see, wait, fifty from 280—

FIRST MATE: 230.

CAPTAIN: Right. Yes. So. About 230 days (Snip Time) to go. If it follows the usual pattern. This isn't the first time an alien has got aboard a Ship of the Fleet, you know, Mr Balls. Nor will it be the last. We know, barring accidents, pretty well what to expect. Perhaps you should glance over the *Handbook of Onboard Aliens* to freshen up your information on the subject.

FIRST MATE: Captain, aren't you even scared?

CAPTAIN: Mr Balls, I am scared shitless. But what can I do?

FIRST MATE: Get rid of it! Now! Quick! While we still can! Before it gets any bigger! Let me stuff it into the Disposal Hatch! Unlock my door – just let me out – it won't take any time at all – the rest of the Fleet won't even know—

INSANE SECOND MATE: Listen, little Balls. I am on the Bridge now. And I think I'll continue to be on the Bridge for the next 230 days (Ship Time). The Captain is needed in the galley. Your door is locked and will remain locked, until you come to terms with the situation. You may not like my being in charge. I know you feel I'm untrustworthy, and useful only in a subordinate position. And in normal conditions and most situations that's quite true. I *am* untrustworthy, unpredictable, and devious. I can't even count on myself. When I leap into a roaring seething ocean of salt, it turns out to be powdered sugar. When I look out the Bridge viewport at the stars, I don't see the stars. I see dragons, swans, whales, scorpions, bears, huntsmen, chariots, crosses, signs, omens, and writings in huge shining words I cannot read. When I set my finger on the buttons on the Main Control Panel, the buttons turn into a dog's hind paws, and my finger explodes like a firecracker. When I walk across the Bridge to check the computer readouts, I can't see the floor; I see an abyss, the dark underpit where pale shapes writhe and shoulder in the gloom, turning vast rudimentary faces, eye spots, mouth holes, up towards me, their countrywoman, mincing across the Bridge high above them on my thin wire, clutching at my

439

flying trapeze. I do not belong on the Bridge of a ship of this class, except during the night shift when you and the Captain are asleep – and during certain exceptional situations, such as this. The fact is, granted all my peculiarities, at this point I'm the only one who can bring us through.

FIRST MATE: Captain, Captain Cook, listen to me. Don't listen to that maniac, that mutineer. Listen to me. Captain, you know I have the utmost faith in you, almost. You're a fantastically good captain, for a woman. Don't let the Second Mate take over the Bridge!

CAPTAIN: I can't stop her, Mr Balls. It's the influence of the alien, I suppose. We've all changed, don't you see?

FIRST MATE: Changed?

CAPTAIN: Yes. 'Bats' has acquired tremendous strength – as you must have noticed when she hit you with the *I Ching* – and a driving sense of purpose. 'Bolts' isn't complaining any more about engine malfunctions; she's happy as a lark down there, singing 'Scots Wha Hae wi' Wallace Bled.' 'Sparks' has gone completely out of touch – right, 'Sparks'? – 'Sparks'? – See? As for myself, I don't know exactly what the change involves, except that the Second Mate makes better sense to me than she used to, and you don't; but I do know that since we've had the alien aboard I've felt a different person.

FIRST MATE: And I, Captain? I haven't changed.

CAPTAIN: No. That's the trouble, Mr Balls. You haven't. You aren't really cut out to cope with this. But it's not your fault; and in the long run it may be a good thing. It maintains a certain continuity aboard the ship. We don't want to become totally alienated, after all.

FIRST MATE: Captain, you're not as civilised as I am, but you are pretty much a product of civilisation – unlike the rest of this crew. And what I don't understand is how, being a civilised person, you can stand the humiliation of it. The being *used* – like a bucket or a Petri dish. We aren't a mere vehicle, a vessel for aliens to get fat in, a damned yeast culture! We

are a ship, a Ship of the Fleet, sailing under our own power, embarked on the Great Journey to the Unknown End.

CAPTAIN: But you know, Mr Balls, that in fact, we probably won't get there.

FIRST MATE: I know. But there was a chance. Now there isn't. We won't get there, we won't get anywhere, weighted down with this alien, and with all of you paying no more attention to anything outside the ship. I'll bet, right now, that the Second Mate can't give us a star fix. What's our inclination to Arcturus, 'Bats'?

INSANE SECOND MATE: Well. Let me see. Just let me press this dog's hind paw here, and adjust this earthworm. There now. Arcturus? I'm not sure; but I do see a dead queen sitting upside down in a chair off the larboard bow.

FIRST MATE: You see? You see?

CAPTAIN: Yes. And I'm not crazy about staying in the galley all the time, either. But we can be patient, Mr Balls. The alien won't actually be aboard very long. Less than eight months to go, now. Then, you know, all we have to do is take it in tow for a while, just for a few years.

FIRST MATE: In tow? *Tow* it?

CAPTAIN: Well, of course. It's our responsibility now.

CHIEF ENGINEER: An'ye wouldna abandon the puir wee thing in the near-absolute-zero cold of interstellar space, surely, Mr Balls?

FIRST MATE: Yes! Out the hatch! Now! Out the hatch! Out the hatch!

INSANE SECOND MATE: Shut the trap, Balls.

FIRST MATE: Captain. Now I'm talking quite quietly now, aren't I. Now do you mean to say that when we finally get rid of this monster, when it gets too big for the ship and breaks its way out, causing terrible damage to the tubes, perhaps wrecking the whole Engine Room on its way – had you thought of that, 'Bolts'? – and quite possibly destructing the entire ship – that, if we survive that ordeal, you intend to turn back, take the mindless, helpless thing in tow, and

limp on after the Fleet at half speed for five years, ten years, twenty years (Ship Time) – while it keeps getting bigger, and stronger, and smarter, and wilder? Captain! don't you realise that this thing is going to be the death of us?

CAPTAIN: Yes, Mr Balls, I do. But you know, if it wasn't something else would be. A meteor, an interstellar plague spore, the irresistible gravity well around an invisible neutron star, an extra-galactic enemy destroyer, a collision with another Ship of the Fleet... One way or another, Mr Balls, we are going to have had it. Sometime, somewhere in the time-space continuum, there is a point-instant with our name on it. So what can we do but go on?

FIRST MATE: But we don't have to drag this thing along with us—

CAPTAIN: If we don't give it a fair start, then who's to carry our breadfruit trees on to the Unknown End when we run out of fuel?

CHIEF ENGINEER: I've thocht, Captain, that perhaps that cruiser might lend us a hand wi' the beastie, if it knew we had one.

CAPTAIN: It certainly would be a help in the towing. But the problem is getting 'Sparks' to send a message to the cruiser. If only we had a normal Communications Officer!

COMMUNICATIONS OFFICER: Please be quiet, everybody. I'm receiving.

INSANE SECOND MATE: From the dead upside-down queen out there?

COMMUNICATIONS OFFICER: No; she isn't saying anything. This is from the alien, I think.

INSANE SECOND MATE: Already? Ha! I always said that a ship could communicate with its alien, if it just listened carefully. What is it saying?

COMMUNICATIONS OFFICER: It still doesn't speak English.

INSANE SECOND MATE: What's the message, then?

COMMUNICATIONS OFFICER: Hiccups.

CAPTAIN: Hiccups?

COMMUNICATIONS OFFICER: It has the hiccups. It must have

been the tomato rice soup. Here, I'll put it on the intracom. Listen.

ALIEN: Hic

 Hic

CHIEF ENGINEER: Captain, there's a rattling in the forward pipes, and a high pressure area building up amidships. Should I try baking soda?

CAPTAIN: No, no, you never use soda when there's an alien aboard, haven't you read the *Handbook?* Try Maalox.

CHIEF ENGINEER: Aye aye, Captain.

ALIEN: Hic

CHIEF ENGINEER: There, there, puir wee sleekit cowerin' beastie.

FIRST MATE: Oh, my God, if only I could have shipped aboard a cruiser, where I belong! I'm going mad here! You're all mad. I'm mad.

INSANE SECOND MATE: Mr Balls. Listen. Would it make you feel any better if there was another male on board?

FIRST MATE: Another male? Of course it would. Strength! Sanity! Logic! Cleanliness! Godliness! Virility! Yes! Yes!

INSANE SECOND MATE: Even if it was an alien?

FIRST MATE: An alien?

INSANE SECOND MATE: This might, you know, be a male alien.

CAPTAIN: Yes, there's better than a fifty percent chance of that.

FIRST MATE: My God. It might. You're right. It might.

CAPTAIN: That was a good thought, 'Bats.'

INSANE SECOND MATE: Well, it's not my own preference, but I thought it might stabilise Mr Balls.

FIRST MATE: A male alien. A male. By golly. It just might be. Hey. Alien. Are you there?

ALIEN: Hic

FIRST MATE: What are you, alien? Hmm? Are you a little boy alien? Hmm?

CAPTAIN: Please, Mr Balls, don't, as it were, go overboard. Keep your duties in mind, and the obscure dignity of your position. We need you. You'd better do some mathematics

right now. As for me, I'll be starting dinner soon. Second Mate, how are things on the Bridge?

INSANE SECOND MATE: Splendid, Captain. Fiery bears and scorpions break like luminous foam and stream backward in glory from our prow. Beneath us, above us, on all sides of us is the abyss, unsounded, full of unimaginable horrors, unpredictable disasters, undeserved beauties, and unexpected death. Like a flying yarrow stalk we shoot forward, if it is forward, through the gulfs of probability.

CAPTAIN: Very good. 'Bolts'?

CHIEF ENGINEER: Dandy, Captain. We're on Warp Five, and the Maalox is working fine.

CAPTAIN: Very good. I shall make dinner now. Something light but nourishing, I think. Chinese Egg Flower Soup, perhaps.

COMMUNICATIONS OFFICER: Please. Will you all be quiet a minute. I'm receiving from Cosmic Sources.

INSANE SECOND MATE: Oh, I hear them sometimes without even a radio. What are they saying?

ALIEN: Hic

COMMUNICATIONS OFFICER: Shh. Well, here's a message just came in from a sister ship of the Fleet. It says: *Tsk tsk.*

CAPTAIN: Never mind that. What do the Cosmic Sources say?

COMMUNICATIONS OFFICER: I can't quite make it out. There's a lot of star hiss, and the code keeps changing. It might be *Congratulations.* Or again it might not be that at all. Be quiet, please. I'm listening.

THE EYE ALTERING

Miriam stood at the big window of the infirmary ward and looked out at the view and thought, For twenty-five years I have been standing at this window and looking out at this view. And never once have I seen what I wanted to see.

If I forget thee, O Jerusalem—

The pain was forgotten, yes. The hatred and the fear, forgotten. In exile you don't remember the grey days and the black years. You remember the sunlight, the orchards, the white cities. Even when you try to forget it you remember that Jerusalem was golden.

The sky outside the ward window was dulled with haze. Over the low ridge called Ararat the sun was setting; setting slowly, for New Zion had a slower spin than Old Earth, and a twenty-eight-hour day; settling, rather than setting, dully down onto the dull horizon. There were no clouds to gather the colors of sunset. There were seldom any clouds. When the haze thickened there might be a misty, smothering rain; when the haze was thin, as now, it hung high and vague, formless. It never quite cleared. You never saw the color of the sky. You never saw the stars. And through the haze the sun, no, not the sun, but NSC 641 (Class G) burned swollen and vaporous, warty as an orange – remember oranges? the sweet juice on the tongue? the orchards of Haifa? – NSC 641 stared, like a bleary eye. You could stare back at it. No glory of gold to blind you. Two imbeciles staring at each other.

Shadows stretched across the valley towards the buildings of

the Settlement. In shadow the fields and woods were black; in the light they were brown, purplish, and dark red. Dirty colors, the colors you got when you scrubbed your watercolors too much and the teacher came by and said, You'd better use some fresh water, Mimi, it's getting muddy. Because the teacher had been too kind to say to a ten-year-old, That picture's a total loss, Mimi, throw it away and start fresh.

She had thought of that before – she had thought all her thoughts before, standing at this window – but this time it reminded her of Genya, because of the painting, and she turned to see how he was doing. The shock symptoms were almost gone, his face was no longer so pale and his pulse had steadied. While she held his wrist he sighed a bit and opened his eyes. Lovely eyes he had, grey in the thin face. He had never been much but eyes, poor Genya. Her oldest patient. Twenty-four years he had been her patient, right from the moment of his birth, five pounds, purplish-blue like a fetal rat, a month premature and half dead of cyanosis: the fifth child born on New Zion, the first in Ararat Settlement. A native. A feeble and unpromising native. He hadn't even had the strength, or the sense, to cry at his first breath of this alien air. Sofia's other children had been full-term and healthy, two girls, both married and mothers now, and fat Leon who could hoist a seventy-kilo sack of grain when he was fifteen. Good young colonists, strong stock. But Miriam had always loved Genya, and all the more after her own years of miscarriages and stillbirths, and the last birth, the girl who had lived two hours, whose eyes had been clear grey like Genya's. Babies never have grey eyes, the eyes of the newborn are blue, that was all sentimental rubbish. But how could you ever make sure of what color things were under this damned warty-orange sun? Nothing ever looked right. 'So there you are, Gennady Borisovich,' she said, 'back home, eh?'

It had been their joke when he was a child; he had spent so much time in the infirmary that whenever he came in with one of his fevers or fainting spells or gasping asthma he would say, 'Here I am, back home, Auntie Doctor...'

446

'What happened?' he asked.

'You collapsed. Hoeing down in the South Field. Aaron and Tina brought you up here on the tractor. Touch of sunstroke, maybe? You've been doing all right, haven't you?'

He shrugged and nodded.

'Dizzy? Short of breath?'

'On and off.'

'Why didn't you come to the clinic?'

'It's no good, Miriam.'

Since he was grown he had called her Miriam. She missed 'Auntie Doctor.' He had grown away from her, these last few years, withdrawn from her into his painting. He had always sketched and painted, but now, all his free time and whatever energy he had left when his Settlement duties were done, he spent in the loft of the generator building where he'd made a kind of studio, grinding colors from rocks and mixing dyes from native plants, making brushes by begging pigtail ends off little girls, and painting – painting on scraps from the lumber mill, on bits of rag, on precious scraps of paper, on smooth slabs of slate from the quarry on Ararat if nothing better was at hand. Painting portraits, scenes of Settlement life, buildings, machinery, still lifes, plants, landscapes, inner visions. Painting anything, everything. His portraits had been much in demand – people were always kind to Genya and the other sicklies – but lately he had not done any portraits; he had gone in for queer muddy jumbles of forms and lines all in a dark haze, like worlds half created. Nobody liked those paintings, but nobody ever told Genya he was wasting his time. He was a sickly; he was an artist; OK. Healthy people had no time to be artists. There was too much work to do. But it was good to have an artist. It was human. It was like Earth. Wasn't it?

They were kind to Toby, too, whose stomach troubles were so bad that at sixteen he weighed eighty-four pounds; kind to little Shura, who was just learning to talk at six, and whose eyes wept and wept all day long, even when she was smiling; kind to all their sicklies, the ones whose bodies could not adjust to

447

this alien world, whose stomachs could not digest the native proteins even with the help of the metabolising pills which every colonist must take twice a day every day of his life on New Zion. Hard as life was in the Twenty Settlements, much as they needed every hand to work, they were gentle with their useless ones, their afflicted. In affliction the hand of God is visible. They remembered the words civilisation, humanity. They remembered Jerusalem.

'Genya, my dear, what do you mean, it's no good?'

His quiet voice had frightened her. 'It's no good,' he had said, smiling. And the grey eyes not clear but veiled, hazy.

'Medicine,' he said. 'Pills. Cures.'

'Of course you know more about medicine than I do,' Miriam said. 'You're a much better doctor than I am. Or are you giving up? Is that it, Genya? Giving up?' Anger had come upon her so suddenly, from so deep within, from anxiety so long and deeply hidden, that it shook her body and cracked her voice.

'I'm giving up one thing. The metas.'

'Metas? Giving them up? What are you talking about?'

'I haven't taken any for two weeks.'

The despairing rage swelled in her. She felt her face go hot so that it felt twice its normal size. 'Two weeks! And so, and so, and so you're here! Where did you think you'd end up, you terrible fool? Lucky you're not dead!'

'I haven't been any worse since I stopped taking them, Miriam. Better, this whole last week. Until today. It can't be that. It must have been heatstroke. I forgot to wear a hat...' He, too, flushed faintly, in the eagerness of his pleading, or with shame. It was stupid to work in the fields bareheaded; for all its dull look NSC 641 could hit the unsheltered human head quite as hard as fiery Sol, and Genya was apologetic for his carelessness, 'You see, I was feeling fine this morning, really good, I kept right up with the others hoeing. Then I felt a bit dizzy, but I didn't want to stop, it was so good to be able to work right with the others, I never thought about heatstroke.'

448

Miriam found that there were tears in her eyes, and this made her so ultimately and absolutely angry that she couldn't speak at all. She got up off Genya's bed and strode down the ward between the rows of beds, four on one side, four on the other. She strode back and stood staring out the window at the mud-colored shapeless ugly world.

Genya was saying something – 'Miriam, honestly, couldn't it be that the metas are worse for me than the native proteins are?' – but she did not listen; the grief and wrath and fear swelled in her and swelled in her, and broke, and she cried out, 'Oh, Genya, Genya, how could you? Not you, to give up now, after fighting so long – I can't bear it! I can't bear it!' But she did not cry it out aloud. Not one word of it. Never. She cried out in her mind, and some tears came out and ran down her cheeks, but her back was turned to the patient. She looked through distorting tears at the flat valley and the dull sun and said to them, silent, 'I hate you.' Then after a while she could turn around and say aloud, 'Lie down,' – for he had sat up, distressed by her long silence – 'lie down, be quiet. You'll take two metas before dinner. If you need anything, Geza's in the nurse's station.' And she walked out.

As she left the infirmary she saw Tina climbing up the back path from the fields, coming to see how Genya was, no doubt. For all his wheezes and fevers Genya had never wanted for girlfriends. Tina, and Shoshanna, and Bella, and Rachel, he could have had his pick. But last year when he and Rachel were living together, they had got contraceptives from the clinic regularly, and then they had separated; they hadn't married, though by his age, twenty-four, Settlement kids were married and parents. He hadn't married Rachel, and Miriam knew why. Moral genetics. Bad genes. Shouldn't pass them on to the next generation. Weed out the sicklies. No procreation for him, and therefore no marriage; he couldn't ask Rachel to live barren for the love of him. What the Settlements needed was children,

plenty of healthy young natives who, with the help of the meta pills, could survive on this planet.

Rachel hadn't taken up with anybody else. But she was only eighteen. She'd get over it. Marry a boy from another Settlement, most likely, and move away, away from Genya's big grey eyes. It would be best for her. And for him.

No wonder Genya was suicidal! Miriam thought, and put the thought away from her fiercely, wearily. She was very weary. She had meant to go to her room and wash, change her clothes, change her mood, before dinner; but the room was so lonesome with Leonid away at Salem Settlement and not due back for at least another month, she couldn't stand it. She went straight across the dusty central square of the Settlement to the refectory building, and into the Living Room. To get away, clear away, from the windless haze and the grey sky and the ugly sun.

Nobody was in the Living Room but Commander Marca, fast asleep on one of the padded wooden couches, and Reine, reading. The two oldest members of the Settlement. Commander Marca was, in fact, the oldest person in the world. He had been forty-four when he piloted the Exile Fleet from Old Earth to New Zion; he was seventy now, and very frail. People didn't wear well here. They aged early, died at fifty, sixty. Reine, the biochemist, was forty-five now but looked twenty years older. It's a damned geriatric club, Miriam thought sourly; and it was true that the young, the Zionborn, seldom used the Living Room. They came there to read, as it held the Settlement's library of books and tapes and microfilm, but not many of them read much, or had much time to read. And maybe the April light and the pictures made them a little uneasy. They were such moral, severe, serious young people; there was no leisure in their lives, no beauty in their world; how could they approve of this luxury their elders needed, this one haven, this one place like home . . .

The Living Room had no windows. Avram, a wizard with anything electrical, had done the indirect lighting, deliberately

reproducing the color and quality of sunlight – not NSC 641 light, but sunlight – so that to enter the Living Room was to enter a room in a house on Earth on a warm sunny day of April or early May, to see all things in that clear, clean, lovely light. Avram and several others had worked on the pictures, enlarging colored photos to a meter or so square: scenes of Earth, photographs and paintings brought by the colonists – Venice, the Negev, the domes of the Kremlin, a farm in Portugal, the Dead Sea, Hampstead Heath, a beach in Oregon, a meadow in Poland, cities, forests, mountains, Van Gogh's cypresses, Bierstadt's Rocky Mountains, Monet's waterlilies, Leonardo's blue mysterious caves. Every wall of the room was covered with pictures, dozens of pictures, all the beauty of the Earth. So that the Earthborn could see and remember, so that the Zionborn could see and know.

There had been some discussion about the pictures, twenty years ago when Avram had started putting them up: Was it really wise? Should we look back? And so on. But then Commander Marca had come by on a visit, seen the Living Room of Ararat Settlement, and said, 'This is where I'll stay.' With every Settlement vying to have him, he had chosen Ararat. Because of the pictures of Earth, because of the light of Earth in that room, shining on the green fields, the snowy peaks, the golden forests of autumn, the flight of gulls above the sea, the white and red and rose of waterlilies on blue pools – clear colors, true, pure, the colors of the Earth.

He slept there now, a handsome old man. Outside, in the hard, dull, orange daylight, he would look sick and old, his cheeks veined and muddy. Here you could see what he looked like.

Miriam sat down near him, facing her favorite picture, a quiet landscape by Corot, trees over a silvery stream. She was so tired that for once she was willing to just sit, in a mild stupor. Through the stupor, faintly, idly, words came floating. Couldn't it be ... honestly, couldn't it be that the metas are worse ... Miriam, honestly, couldn't it be ...

'Do you think I never thought of that?' she retorted in silence. 'Idiot! Do you think I don't know the metas are hard on your guts? Didn't I try fifty different combinations while you were a kid, trying to get rid of the side effects? But it's not as bad as being allergic to the whole damn planet! You know better than the doctor, do you? Don't give me that. You're trying to—' But she broke off the silent dialogue abruptly. Genya was not trying to kill himself. He was not. He would not. He had courage, that one. And brains.

'All right,' she said to the quiet young man in her mind. 'All right! If you'll stay in the infirmary, under observation – for two weeks, and do exactly what I say – all right, I'll try it!'

Because, said another, even quieter voice deep in her, it doesn't really matter. Whatever you do or don't do, he will die. This year; next year. Two hours; twenty-four years. The sicklies can't adjust to this world. And neither can we, neither can we. We weren't meant to live here, Genya my dear. We weren't made for this world, nor it for us. We were made of Earth, by Earth, to live on Earth, under the blue sky and the golden sun.

The dinner gong began to ring. Going into the refectory she met little Shura. The child carried a bunch of the repulsive blackish-purple native weeds, as a child at home would carry a bunch of white daisies, red poppies picked in the fields. Shura's eyes were teary as usual, but she smiled up at Auntie Doctor. Her lips looked pallid in the red-orange light of sunset through the windows. Everybody's lips looked pallid. Everybody's face looked tired, set, stoical, after the long day's work, as they went into the Settlement dining hall, all together, the three hundred exiles of Ararat on Zion, the eleventh lost tribe.

He was doing very well. She had to admit it. 'You're doing well,' she said, and he, with his grin, said, 'I told you so!'

'It could be because you're not doing anything else,' she said, 'smart ass.'

'Not doing anything? I filed health records for Geza all morning, I played games with Rosie and Moishe for two

452

hours, I've been grinding colors all afternoon – say, I need more mineral oil, can I have another litre? It's a much better pigment vehicle than the vegetable oil.'

'Sure. But listen. I have something for you better than that. Little Tel Aviv has got their pulp mill going full time. They sent a truck over yesterday with paper—'

'Paper?'

'Half a ton of it! I took two hundred sheets for you. It's in the office.' He was off like a shot, and was into the bundle of paper before she even got there. 'Oh, God,' he said, holding up a sheet, 'beautiful, it's beautiful!' And she thought how often she had heard him say that, 'beautiful!' of one drab useful thing or another. He didn't know what beauty was; he'd never seen any. The paper was thick, substantial, greyish, in big sheets, intended to be cut small and used sparingly, of course; but let him have it for his painting. There was little enough else she could give him.

'When you let me out of here,' Genya said, hugging the unwieldy bundle with both arms, 'I'll go over to Tel Aviv and paint their pulp mill, I'll immortalise their pulp mill!'

'You'd better go lie down.'

'No, listen, I promised Moishe I'd beat him at chess. What's wrong with him, anyhow?'

'Rashes, edema.'

'He's like me?'

Miriam shrugged. 'He was fine till this year. Puberty triggered something. Not unusual with allergic symptoms.'

'What is allergy, anyhow?'

'Well, call it a failure of adaptation. Back home, people used to feed babies cows' milk, from bottles. Some of the babies could adapt to it, but some got rashes, breathing trouble, colic. The cow's key didn't fit their metabolic lock. Well, New Zion's protein keys don't fit our locks; so we have to change our metabolism with the metas.'

'Would Moishe or I have been an allergic on Earth?'

'I don't know. Prematures often are. Irving, he died, oh,

453

twenty years ago, he was allergic to this terrible list of things on Earth, they should never have let him come, poor thing, he spends his life on Earth half suffocated and comes here and starves to death even on a quadruple dose of metas.'

'Aha,' said Genya, 'you shouldn't have given him metas at all. Just Zion mush.'

'Zion mush?' Only one of the native grains yielded enough to be worth harvesting, and it produced a gluey meal which could not be baked.

'I ate three bowls of it for lunch.'

'He lies around the hospital all day complaining,' Miriam said, 'and then stuffs his belly with that slop. How can an artistic soul eat something that tastes like jellied bilge?'

'You feed it to your helpless child patients in your own hospital! I just ate the leftovers.'

'Oh, get along with you.'

'I am. I want to paint while the sun's still up. On a piece of new paper, a whole piece of new paper...'

It had been a long day at the clinic, but there were no inpatients. She had sent Osip home last night in a cast with a good scolding for being so careless as to tip his tractor over, endangering not only his life but the tractor, which was even harder to replace. And young Moishe had gone back to the children's house, though she didn't like the way his rash kept coming back. And Rosie was over her asthma, and the Commander's heart was doing as well as could be expected; so the ward was empty, except for her permanent inmate of the past two weeks, Genya.

He was sprawled out on his bed under the window, so lax and still that she had a moment of alarm; but his color was good, he breathed evenly, he was simply asleep, deeply asleep, the way people slept after a hard day in the fields, exhausted.

He had been painting. He had cleaned up the rags and brushes, he always cleaned up promptly and thoroughly, but the picture stood on his makeshift easel. Usually these days

he was secretive about his paintings, hid them, since people had stopped admiring them. The Commander had murmured to her, 'What ugly stuff, poor boy!' But she had heard young Moishe, watching Genya paint, say, 'How do you do it, Genya, how do you make it so pretty?' and Genya answer, 'Beauty's in the eye, Moishe.'

Well, that was true, and she went closer to look at the painting in the dull afternoon light. Genya had painted the view out the big window of the ward. Nothing vague and half created this time: realistic, all too realistic. Hideously recognisable. There was the flat ridge of Ararat, the mud-colored trees and fields, the hazy sky, the storage barn and a corner of the school building in the foreground. Her eyes went from the painted scene to the real one. To spend hours, days, painting that! What a waste, what a waste.

It was hard on Genya, it was sad, the way he hid his paintings now, knowing that nobody would want to see them, except maybe a child like Moishe fascinated with the mere skill of the hand, the craftsman's dexterity.

That night as Genya helped her straighten up the injection cabinets – he was a good deal of help around the infirmary these days – she said, 'I like the picture you painted today.'

'I finished it today,' he corrected her. 'Damn thing took all week. I'm just beginning to learn to see.'

'Can I put it up in the Living Room?'

He looked at her across a tray of hypodermic needles, his eyes quiet and a little quizzical. 'In the Living Room? But that's all pictures of Home.'

'It's time maybe we had some pictures of our new home there.'

'A moral gesture, eh? Sure. If you like it.'

'I like it very much,' she lied blandly.

'It isn't bad,' he said. 'I'll do better, though, when I've learned how to fit myself to the pattern.'

'What pattern?'

'Well, you know, you have to look until you *see* the pattern,

till it makes sense, and then you have to get that into your hand, too.' He made large, vague, shaping gestures with a bottle of absolute alcohol.

'Anybody who asks a painter a question in words deserves what they get, I guess,' said Miriam. 'Babble, babble. You take the picture over tomorrow and put it up. Artists are so temperamental about where they get their pictures hung, and the lighting. Besides, it's time you were getting out. A little. An hour or two a day. No more.'

'Can I eat dinner in the dining hall, then?'

'All right. It'll keep Tina from coming here to keep you from being lonely and eating up all the infirmary rations. That girl eats like a vacuum pump. Listen, if you go out in the middle of the day, will you kindly take the trouble to wear a hat?'

'You think I'm right, then.'

'Right?'

'That it was sunstroke.'

'That was *my* diagnosis, if you will recall.'

'All right: but my addition was that I do better without metas.'

'I have no idea. You've got along fine before for weeks, and then poof, down again. Nothing whatever has been proved.'

'But a pattern has been established! I've lived a month without metas, and gained six pounds.'

'And edema of the head, Mr Know It All?'

She saw him the next day sitting with Rachel, just before dinnertime, on the slope below the storage barn. Rachel had not come to see him in the infirmary. They sat side by side, very close together, motionless, not talking.

Miriam went on to the Living Room. A half hour there before dinner had become a habit with her lately. It seemed to rest her from the weariness of the day. But the room was less peaceful than usual this evening; the Commander was awake, and talking with Reine and Avram. 'Well, where did it come from then?' he was saying in his heavy Italian accent – he had

not learned Hebrew till he was forty, in the Transit Camp. 'Who put it there?' Then seeing Miriam he greeted her as always with a grand cordiality of voice and gesture. 'Ah, Doctor! Please, join us, come, solve our mystery for us. You know each picture in this room as well as I do. Where, do you think, and when did we acquire the new one? You see?'

It's Genya's, Miriam was about to say, when she saw the new picture. It wasn't Genya's. It was a painting, all right, a landscape, but a landscape of the Earth: a wide valley, the fields green and green-gold, orchards coming into flower, the sweeping slope of a mountain in the distance, a tower, perhaps a castle or medieval farm building, in the foreground, and over all the pure, subtle, sunlit sky. It was a complex and happy painting, a celebration of the spring, an act of praise.

'How beautiful,' she said, her voice catching. 'Didn't you put it up, Avram?'

'Me? I can photograph, I can't paint. Look at it, it's no reproduction. Some kind of tempera or oils, see?'

'Somebody brought it from Home. Had it in their baggage,' Reine suggested.

'For twenty-five years?' said the Commander. 'Why? And who? We all know what all the others have!'

'No. I think' – Miriam was confused, and stammered – 'I think it's something Genya did. I asked him to put up one of his paintings here. Not this one. How did he do this?'

'Copied from a photograph,' Avram suggested.

'No no no no, impossible,' old Marca said, outraged. 'That is a painting, not a copy! That is a work of art, that was seen, seen with the eyes and the heart!'

With the eyes and the heart.

Miriam looked, and she saw. She saw what the light of NSC 641 had hidden from her, what the artificial Earth daylight of the room revealed to her. She saw what Gehya saw: the beauty of the world.

'I think it must be in Central France, the Auvergne,' Reine was saying wistfully, and the Commander, 'Oh no no no, it's

457

near Lake Como, I am certain,' and Avram, 'Well it looks to me like where I grew up in the Caucasus,' when they all turned to look at Miriam. She had made a strange noise, a gasp or laugh or sob. 'It's here,' she said. 'Here. That's Ararat. The mountain. That's the fields, our fields, our trees. That's the corner of the school, that tower. See it? It's here. Zion. It's how Genya sees it. With the eyes and the heart.'

'But look, the trees are green, look at the colors, Miriam. It's Earth—'

'Yes! It is Earth. Genya's Earth!'

'But he can't—'

'How do we know? How do we know what a child of Zion sees? We can see the picture in this light that's like Home. Take it outside, into the daylight, and you'll see what we always see, the ugly colors, the ugly planet where we're not at home. But he is at home! He is! It's we,' Miriam said, laughing in tears, looking at them all, the anxious, tired, elderly faces, '*we* who lack the key. We with our – with our—' she stumbled and leapt at the idea like a horse at a high wall, 'with our meta pills!'

They all stared at her.

'With our meta pills, we can survive here, just barely, right? But don't you see, he *lives* here! We were all perfectly adjusted to Earth, too well, we can't fit anywhere else – he wasn't, wouldn't have been; allergic, a misfit – the pattern a little wrong, see? The pattern. But there are many patterns, infinite patterns, he fits this one a little better than we do—'

Avram and the Commander continued to stare. Reine shot an alarmed glance at the picture, but asked gamely, 'You're saying that Genya's allergies—'

'Not just Genya! All the sicklies, maybe! For twenty-five years I've been feeding them metas, and they're allergic to *Earth* proteins, the metas just foul them up, they're a different pattern, oh, idiot! Idiot! Oh, my God, he and Rachel can get married. They've got to marry, he should have kids. What about Rachel taking metas while she's pregnant, the foetus. I can work it out, I can work it out. I must call Leonid. And Moishe, thank God!

maybe he's another one! Listen, I must go talk to Genya and Rachel, immediately. Excuse me!' She left, a short, grey woman moving like a lightning bolt.

Marca, Avram, and Reine stood staring after her, at each other, and finally back at Genya's painting.

It hung there before them, serene and joyful, full of light.

'I don't understand,' said Avram.

'Patterns,' Reine said thoughtfully.

'It is very beautiful,' said the old Commander of the Exile Fleet. 'Only, it makes me homesick.'

MAZES

I have tried hard to use my wits and keep up my courage, but I know now that I will not be able to withstand the torture any longer. My perceptions of time are confused, but I think it has been several days since I realised I could no longer keep my emotions under aesthetic control, and now the physical breakdown is also nearly complete. I cannot accomplish any of the greater motions. I cannot speak. Breathing, in this heavy foreign air, grows more difficult. When the paralysis reaches my chest I shall die: probably tonight.

The alien's cruelty is refined, yet irrational. If it intended all along to starve me, why not simply withhold food? But instead of that it gave me plenty of food, mountains of food, all the green-bud leaves I could possibly want. Only they were not fresh. They had been picked; they were dead; the element that makes them digestible to us was gone, and one might as well eat gravel. Yet there they were, with all the scent and shape of green-bud, irresistible to my craving appetite. Not at first, of course. I told myself, I am not a child, to eat picked leaves! But the belly gets the better of the mind. After a while it seemed better to be chewing something, anything, that might still the pain and craving in the gut. So I ate, and ate, and starved. It is a relief, now, to be so weak I cannot eat.

The same elaborately perverse cruelty marks all its behavior. And the worst thing of all is just the one I welcomed with such relief and delight at first: the maze. I was badly disoriented at first, after the trapping, being handled by a giant, being dropped

into a prison; and this place around the prison is disorienting, spatially disquieting. The strange, smooth, curved wall-ceiling is of an alien substance and its lines are meaningless to me. So when I was taken up and put down, amidst all this strangeness, in a maze, a recognisable, even familiar maze, it was a moment of strength and hope after great distress. It seemed pretty clear that I had been put in the maze as a kind of test or investigation, that a first approach toward communication was being attempted. I tried to cooperate in every way. But it was not possible to believe for very long that the creature's purpose was to achieve communication.

It is intelligent, highly intelligent, that is clear from a thousand evidences. We are both intelligent creatures, we are both maze-builders: surely it would be quite easy to learn to talk together! If that were what the alien wanted. But it is not. I do not know what kind of mazes it builds for itself. The ones it made for me were instruments of torture.

The mazes were, as I said, of basically familiar types, though the walls were of that foreign material colder and smoother than packed clay. The alien left a pile of picked leaves in one extremity of each maze, I do not know why; it may be a ritual or superstition. The first maze it put me in was babyishly short and simple. Nothing expressive or even interesting could be worked out from it. The second, however was a kind of simple version of the Ungated Affirmation, quite adequate for the reassuring, outreaching statement I wanted to make. And the last, the long maze, with seven corridors and nineteen connections, lent itself surprisingly well to the Maluvian mode, and indeed to almost all the New Expressionist techniques. Adaptations had to be made to the alien spatial understanding, but a certain quality of creativity arose precisely from the adaptations. I worked hard at the problem of that maze, planning all night long, re-imagining the links and spaces, the feints and pauses, the erratic, unfamiliar, and yet beautiful course of the True Run. Next day when I was placed in the long maze and

the alien began to observe, I performed the Eighth Maluvian in its entirety.

It was not a polished performance. I was nervous, and the spatio-temporal parameters were only approximate. But the Eighth Maluvian survives the crudest performance in the poorest maze. The evolutions in the ninth encatenation, where the 'cloud' theme recurs so strangely transposed into the ancient spiralling motif, are indestructibly beautiful. I have seen them performed by a very old person, so old and stiff-jointed that he could only suggest the movements, hint at them, a shadow gesture, a dim reflection of the themes: and all who watched were inexpressibly moved. There is no nobler statement of our being. Performing, I myself was carried away by the power of the motions and forgot that I was a prisoner, forgot the alien eyes watching me; I transcended the errors of the maze and my own weakness, and danced the Eighth Maluvian as I have never danced it before.

When it was done, the alien picked me up and set me down in the first maze – the short one, the maze for little children who have not yet learned how to talk.

Was the humiliation deliberate? Now that it is all past, I see that there is no way to know. But it remains very hard to ascribe its behavior to ignorance.

After all, it is not blind. It has eyes, recognisable eyes. They are enough like our eyes that it must see somewhat as we do. It has a mouth, four legs, can move bipedally, has grasping hands, etc; for all its gigantism and strange looks, it seems less fundamentally different from us, physically, than a fish. And yet, fish school and dance and, in their own stupid way, communicate!

The alien has never once attempted to talk with me. It has been with me, watched me, touched me, handled me, for days: but all its motions have been purposeful, not communicative. It is evidently a solitary creature, totally self-absorbed.

This would go far to explain its cruelty.

I noticed early that from time to time it would move its curious horizontal mouth in a series of fairly delicate, repetitive

gestures, a little like someone eating. At first I thought it was jeering at me; then I wondered if it was trying to urge me to eat the indigestible fodder; then I wondered if it could be communicating *labially*. It seemed a limited and unhandy language for one so well provided with hands, feet limbs, flexible spine, and all; but that would be like the creature's perversity, I thought. I studied its lip motions and tried hard to imitate them. It did not respond. It stared at me briefly and then went away.

In fact, the only indubitable *response* I ever got from it was on a pitifully low level of interpersonal aesthetics. It was tormenting me with knob-pushing, as it did once a day. I had endured this grotesque routine pretty patiently for the first several days. If I pushed one knob I got a nasty sensation in my feet, if I pushed a second I got a nasty pellet of dried-up food, if I pushed a third I got nothing whatever. Obviously, to demonstrate my intelligence I was to push the third knob. But it appeared that my intelligence irritated my captor, because it removed the neutral knob after the second day. I could not imagine what it was trying to establish or accomplish, except the fact that I was its prisoner and a great deal smaller than it. When I tried to leave the knobs, it forced me physically to return. I must sit there pushing knobs for it, receiving punishment from one and mockery from the other. The deliberate outrageousness of the situation, the insufferable heaviness and thickness of this air, the feeling of being forever watched yet never understood, all combined to drive me into a condition for which we have no description at all. The nearest thing I can suggest is the last interlude of the Ten Gate Dream, when all the feintways are closed and the dance narrows in and in until it bursts terribly into the vertical. I cannot say what I felt, but it was a little like that. If I got my feet stung once more, or got pelted once more with a lump of rotten food, I would go vertical forever... I took the knobs off the wall (they came off with a sharp tug, like flower buds), laid them in the middle of the floor, and defecated on them.

The alien took me up at once and returned me to my prison.

463

It had got the message, and had acted on it. But how unbelievably primitive the message had had to be! And the next day, it put me back in the knob room, and there were the knobs as good as new, and I was to choose alternate punishments for its amusement... Until then I had told myself that the creature was alien, therefore incomprehensible and uncomprehending, perhaps not intelligent in the same *manner* as we, and so on. But since then I have known that, though all that may remain true, it is also unmistakably and grossly cruel.

When it put me into the baby maze yesterday, I could not move. The power of speech was all but gone (I am dancing this, of course, in my mind; 'the best maze is the mind,' the old proverb goes) and I simply crouched there, silent. After a while it took me out again, gently enough. There is the ultimate perversity of its behavior: it has never once touched me cruelly.

It set me down in the prison, locked the gate, and filled up the trough with inedible food. Then it stood two-legged, looking at me for a while.

Its face is very mobile, but if it speaks with its face I cannot understand it, that is too foreign a language. And its body is always covered with bulky, binding mats, like an old widower who has taken the Vow of Silence. But I had become accustomed to its great size, and to the angular character of its limb positions, which at first had seemed to be saying a steady stream of incoherent and mispronounced phrases, a horrible nonsense dance like the motions of an imbecile, until I realised that they were strictly purposive movements. Now I saw something a little beyond that, in its position. There were no words, yet there was communication. I saw, as it stood watching me, a clear signification of angry sadness – as clear as the Sembrian Stance. There was the same lax immobility, the bentness, the assertion of defeat. Never a word came clear, and yet it told me that it was filled with resentment, pity, impatience, and frustration. It told me it was sick of torturing me, and wanted me to help it. I am sure I understood it. I tried to answer. I

tried to say, 'What is it you want of me? Only tell me what it is you want.' But I was too weak to speak clearly, and it did not understand. It has never understood.

And now I have to die. No doubt it will come in to watch me die; but it will not understand the dance I dance in dying.

THE PATHWAYS OF DESIRE

Tamara had thought he was off taping, but he was in his hut, lying on the cot, looking thin and cold. 'Sorry, Ram! I'm after those photographs of the kids.'

'That box.' His gesture pointing out which box was so uncharacteristically languid that she asked, guardedly, 'You all right?'

'Could be better.' From him, the admission was a catalogue of misery; but still she did not drop her guard. She waited; and he said, 'Diarrhoea.'

'You should have said something.'

'Humiliation.'

Bob was wrong, then. He did have a sense of humor.

'I'll ask Kara,' she said. 'They must have something for the trots.'

'Anything but hot dogs and milkshakes,' Ramchandra said, and she laughed, for the description was apt; the staple foods of the Ndif were boneless poro meat and the mushy sweet fruit of the lamaba tree.

'Keep drinking plenty. I'll refill that. Lomox doesn't help?'

'Nothing left for it to work on.' He looked up at her; his eyes were large, black, and clear. 'I wish that I throve here,' he said, 'like Bob.'

That took her off guard. Rebuff and aloofness she expected, trust and candor she did not. She was unready, and her response inadequate. 'Oh, he's happy here.'

'Are you?'

'I hate it.' She dangled the crude clay water jug, and sought exactness. 'Not really. It's beautiful. But I ... get impatient.'

'Nothing to chew,' Ramchandra said bitterly.

She laughed again, and went to fill his water jug at the spring a few meters away. The brightness of the sunshine, the perfumes of the air, the gorgeous colors of the lamaba trees, purple trunks, blue and green leaves, red and yellow fruits, all were delightful; the little spring welled up holy and innocent in its bed of clean brown sand. But she returned with gratitude to the hut containing one sullen linguist with diarrhoea. 'Take it easy, Ram,' she said, 'and I'll try and get something useful out of Kara and the others.'

'Thank you,' he said.

Lovely words, she thought, as she went down the path through perfumed light and shadows towards the river, lovely in the man's soft, precise accent. When their team of three had first been put together, at the Base on Ankara, she had been drawn to Ramchandra, a direct powerful, unmistakable attraction of sex. She had suppressed it, with self-mockery and some shame, for the man was cold, holding himself ostentatiously apart and untouched. And then there was Bob, big beautiful blond Bob, lean tanned tough Bob, perfect hero of male wish fulfillment, irresistible. Why resist? Easier to give the easy pleasure he expected; easy, pleasant, a little depressing, but never mind that. Don't look down into depressions. You might fall in. Live life as it comes, etc. She and Bob would come together inevitably. But they hadn't; for the three of them had come to Yirdo, and met Yirdo's inhabitants, the Ndif.

The Young Women of the Ndif – all females between age twelve and age twenty-two or -three – were sexually available, eager, and adept. They had bright wavy hair of gold or russet, long tilted eyes of green or violet, slender waists and ankles. They wore soft garments of slit pandsu leaves, clinging, modestly parting to reveal the merest glimpse of buttock or nipple. The under fourteens danced the hypnotic saweya dance in long lines, chanting in their soft, light voices, their

467

round faces mischievously serious. From fourteen to eighteen they danced the baliya, leaping naked, one at a time, into the circle of swaying, clapping men, twisting their sinuous bodies into all the postures of practised eroticism, while the girls waiting their turn to dance sang the pulsing chorus, 'Ah-weh, weh, ah-weh, weh...' After they were eighteen they no longer danced in public. Tamara left it to Bob to find out what they did in private. After forty-one days on Yirdo he was indubitably an expert in that.

She saw now that though she hadn't wanted him, the promptness, the flatness of his loss of interest in her had hurt. Even last night she had been flirting at him; competing; trying to be a dancing girl, with short wiry hair, shit-brindle eyes that tilted the wrong way, muscular wrists... Stupid, stupid her self-mockery, her self-abasement, her self, self, self, swept away now like veils of cobweb as she followed the forest path downward to the washing place at the river thinking, How beautiful the bridge of Ram's nose is. He can't weigh much more than I do, maybe less; fine-boned. Thank you, he said. 'Askiös, Muna! How's the baby? Askiös, Vanna! Askiös, Kara!' How beautiful thy nose, my beloved, like unto a promontory between two wells of water, and the water thereof is exceeding black and cold. Thank you, thank you. 'Hot today, no?'

'Hot today, hot today,' all the Middle-Aged Women agreed enthusiastically, as they trampled out the village laundry in the shallow, laughing water. 'Put your feet in the river, you'll get cool,' Vanna encouraged her. Brella patted her shoulder affectionately, murmuring, 'Askiös!' as she went by to lay out her portion of the village laundry on a rock to dry.

The Middle-Aged Women were between twenty-three and (forty? data still uncertain), and some of them, in Tamara's opinion, were more beautiful than the Young Women, a beauty which included missing teeth, sagging breasts, and stretchy bellies. The gapped smiles were blithe, the drooping tits held the milk of human kindness, the pregnancy-streaked bellies were full of belly laughs. The Young Women giggled; the

Middle-Aged Women laughed. They laughed, Tamara thought watching them now, as if they had been set free.

The Young Men were off hunting poro (the pursuit of the fanged hot dog, she thought, and she, too, being a Middle-Aged Woman of twenty-eight, laughed); or they were sitting goggling at the saweya and baliya dancers; or they were sleeping. There were no Middle-Aged Men. Males were Young till about forty, when they stopped hunting, stopped watching the dancers, and became Old. And died.

'Kara,' she said to her best informant, while she took off her sandals to put her feet in the cool water as Vanna had suggested, 'my friend Ram is sick in the belly.'

'Oh me, oh dear, askiös, askiös,' the nearby women murmured. Kara, who looked to be pretty nearly an Old Woman, her knotted hair thin and greying, demanded practically, 'Is it gwullaggh or kafa-faka?'

Tamara had never heard either word before, but translation was superfluous. 'Kafa-faka,' she said.

'Puti berries, he needs,' said Kara, slapping a loincloth on a wet boulder.

'The food we eat here, he says it's very good, too good.'

'Too much fried poro,' said Kara, nodding. 'When children eat too much and spend all night shitting in the bushes, you feed them puti berries and boiled guo for a week. It tastes all right, with honey. I'll boil Uvana Ram a pot of guo as soon as the washing's done.'

'Kara is a beautiful noble person,' Tamara said. It was a stock phrase, the usual Ndif way of saying thank you.

'Askiös!' said Kara, grinning. That was a much commoner, and more difficult, expression. Ramchandra had arrived at no set translation for it. Bob had suggested German *bitte*, but it covered even more ground that *bitte*. Please, you're welcome, sorry, wait a minute, never mind, hello, goodbye, yes, no, and maybe, all seemed to fall within the connotations of askiös.

With her questions about kafa-faka and how to wean babies and when you had to stay in the Unclean Huts and what was

the best kind of cooking pot, Tamara was always a welcome excuse for a conversation break. They sat around on hot boulders in the cool water and let the river wash the laundry and the sun dry and bleach it, while they talked. With a part of her mind Tamara listened to Heraclitus telling her that you shall not step twice into the same river; with the rest of it she sought information concerning birth control among the Ndif. The subject once opened, the women discussed it leisurely and frankly, but there wasn't much to discuss. There were no devices or systems of birth control at all. Nature provided for the Young Women: for all their single-minded devotion to erotic practice, they did not become fertile till they were over twenty. Tamara was incredulous, but the women were perfectly certain: the dividing line between the Young and the Middle-Aged was, in fact fertility. Once the line was crossed their only protection against perpetual pregnancy was abstinence, which they admitted was boring. Abortion and infanticide were not mentioned. When Tamara cautiously suggested them, heads were shaken. '*Women* can't kill *babies*,' Brella said with horror. Kara observed more dryly, 'If they get caught at it, the Men pull out all their hair and send them to the Unclean Huts to stay.' – 'Nobody in our village would do such a thing,' Brella said. 'Nobody got caught at it,' Kara said.

A group of Juvenile Males (nine to twelve) came whooping down to the river to swim and fish. They ran right over the drying laundry; the laundresses scolded, unauthoritatively; and the conversation ceased, because the ears of Males were not to be polluted with Unclean talk. The women rescued the laundry and set off back to the village. Tamara looked in on Ramchandra, who was asleep, and went on to take some photographs of Juvenile Males playing bhasto. After supper – communal, cooked and served by the Middle-Aged Women – she saw Kara, Vanna, and old Binira go into Ramchandra's hut, and followed them.

They woke him up and fed him boiled guo, pinkish cereal like sticky tapioca; they rubbed his legs, sat on his shoulders,

put heated stones on his stomach, rearranged his cot so that he lay with his head to the north, made him drink a sip of something hot, black, and minty-smelling; Binira sang at him for a while; they left him at last with a fresh hot stone, and went off. He accepted all this with ethnological aplomb or with the satisfaction of the invalid being fussed over. When they had gone he looked comfortable, curled up around the large rock, and half asleep. Tamara was going out when he asked in a remote, tranquil voice, 'Did you tape the old lady's song?'

'No. Sorry.'

'Askiös, askiös,' he whispered. Then, propping himself on his elbow, 'I am better. Too bad we didn't tape that. I missed most of the words.'

'Is Old Ndif a different language?'

'No. Only much fuller. Complete.'

'The Middle-Aged Women seem to have a much bigger vocabulary than the Youngs.'

'At Buvuna, the Young Women averaged 700 words; the Young Men 1,100, since they have the hunting vocabulary; I estimate the Middle-Aged Women here to know at least 2,500 words. I can make no estimate of the Old Men and Women yet. These are odd people.' Ramchandra lay back and cautiously rearranged himself around the hot stone. His tone, also, was cautious. There was a slight pause.

'Do you want to sleep?'

'To talk,' he said.

Tamara sat down on the woven cane stool. Beyond the open doorway the night was growing bright as day had been; Uper, the big gas planet of which Yirdo was a moon, was rising over the forest like a vast striped balloon. Its silver-gilt light pierced every crack in the mud and wattle walls of the hut and pooled incandescent on the ground outside the doorway. The dusk inside the hut was shot through with gleams, shafts, arrows dazzling the eye, a light that revealed nothing, that dissolved bodies and faces into radiant darkness.

'Nothing is real,' Tamara said.

471

'Of course not,' said the other shadow, amused, precise.

'They're like actors.'

'No.'

'Yes. I don't mean consciously acting, deceiving. I mean artificial. Too simple. Beautiful simple people in ever-bountiful paradise.'

'Ha,' Ramchandra said, and a patch of planet light blazed in his hair as he sat up.

'Why shouldn't there be a South-Sea-Island world?' she argued with herself. 'Why does it seem too simple – phony? Am I a Puritan, am I looking for original sin?'

'No, no, of course not rubbish,' he said. 'All that is theories. But listen.' For a minute he said nothing to listen to, then he said some Ndif words:

'Vini. Pandsu. Bhasto. Askiös. – Askiös-bhis iyava oe is-bhassa. – What is that in English?'

'Well – "please let me get by." '

'Literal translation!'

'The great teaching tradition of the Brahman caste,' Tamara said. 'I don't know, the words have so many uses. "Sorry, I want to go this way"?'

'You don't hear it.'

'Hear what?'

'People cannot hear their native language. All right, listen, carefully please!' He was charming when he got excited; the hauteur fell off him like dried mud from a water buffalo. 'I'm going to say a sentence in English the way my uncle, who didn't attend World Government School, spoke English. Now. "Excuse please I have to go by this path." Repeat!'

'Excuse please I have to go by this path.'

'Askiös-bhis iyava oe is-bhassa.'

A chill, like a touch of that cold dazzling planet light, proceeded slowly up Tamara's backbone and prickled in the roots of her hair.

'Funny,' she said.

'Saweya: sway. Baliya: belly dance, Bali. Fini; ravine, vines.

472

Bhasto: bat, baseball. Bhani: cabin, cabana. Shuwushu: ocean, sea—'

'Onomatopoeia.'

'Oe: go. Tunu: return. Itunu: I return; utunu: you return; tunusi: he returns. Padu, to hit, strike. Fatu, to build, make – facere, factus – factory. Say a word in Ndif!'

'Sikka.'

'Fishing lines. Wait. No, I can't get that one. Another please.'

'Fillisa.'

'The Unclean Huts. – Filth, filthy.'

'Uvanai.'

'Strangers. Visitors. Foreigners... singular uvana. You-foreigner.'

'Ram, you don't have diarrhoea. You have paranoia.'

'No,' he said, so harsh and loud that she started. He cleared his throat. She could not see his eyes but she knew him to be looking at her. 'I am serious, Tamara,' he said. 'I am frightened.'

'Of what?' she jeered.

'Frightened sick,' he said. 'Scared shitless. You must take words seriously. They are all we have.'

'*What* are you frightened of?'

'We are thirty-one light-years from Earth. No one from Earth ever came to this solar system before us. These people speak English.'

'They don't!'

'The structure and vocabulary of Young Ndif is based at least sixty percent upon the structure and vocabulary of Modern English.'

His voice shook, as if with fear, or with relief.

Tamara sat solidly, clasping her knees, and held fast to incredulity. A Ndif word went through her mind, and another, and another, each one followed by its English root or shadow, shadows that had been waiting for the light to show them; but it was absurd. She should not have said the word 'paranoia.' It was true. The man was ill. Weeks of touch-me-not rudeness and now this sudden change to talk, excitement, warmth. A

manic change; and paranoid. The Ndif speaking an English-based code, for mysterious purposes, understood by the expert alone... One, one. Te, two. Ti, three...

'All female names,' Ramchandra said morosely, 'end in "a." That is a cosmic constant established by H. Rider Haggard. Male names never end in "a." Never.'

His voice, light-timbred, still a little uneven, confused her thoughts. 'Listen, Ram.'

'Yes.'

He was listening, all right. She could not ask him, as she had intended, whether he was playing an elaborate and disagreeable joke on her. His trust must be met in kind. She did not know how to go on; and he broke urgently into her pause – 'I saw this within a week, Tamara. First the syntax – Then I wouldn't see it. Meaningless coincidence, et cetera, et cetera. I said no. But it says yes. It is so. It is English.'

'Even the Old language?'

'No, no, that's different,' he said, hurried, grateful, 'that's not English, that's itself, wherever it's not based on the baby talk. But the—'

'All right, then. The Old language *is* old, the original language, and the Youngs have been influenced, corrupted, by some contact with Space Service people we don't know about, weren't told about.'

'How? When? They say we are the first. Why would they lie?'

'The Space Service?'

'Or the Ndif. They both say we are the first!'

'Well, if we are the first, then it's us. *We*'re influencing the Ndif. They talk the way we unconsciously expect people to talk. Telepathy. They're telepaths.'

'Telepaths,' he said, seizing the idea eagerly; and during the pause that followed he was evidently wrestling with it, trying to make it fit the circumstances, for he said at last, with frustration, 'If only we knew anything about telepathy!'

Tamara meanwhile had been going around the problem in

another direction, and asked, 'Why didn't you say anything about this till now?'

'I thought I was insane,' he said, in the controlled precise tone that sounded arrogant because his honesty would not permit him to evade. 'I have been insane. Six years ago, after my wife died. There were two episodes. Linguists are often unstable.'

After a little while Tamara said almost in a whisper, 'Ramchandra is a beautiful noble person . . .' She spoke in Ndif.

Ah-weh, weh, ah-weh, weh, went the chanting of the baliya dancers off on the dancing grounds at the edge of the village. A baby cried in a nearby hut. The dark-dazzling air was rich with the scent of night-blooming flowers.

'Look,' she said. 'Doesn't a telepath know what you're thinking? The Ndif don't. I've known people who do. My grandfather, he was Russian, he always knew what people were thinking. It was maddening. I don't know if it was telepathy, or being old, or being Russian, or what. But anyhow, they'd get the *thoughts*, not the *words* – wouldn't they?'

'Who knows? Maybe – You said it's like a stage play, a movie, the island paradise. Maybe they sense what we expect or desire, and act it, perform it.'

'What for?'

'Adaptation,' he said, triumphant. 'So that we like them and therefore don't harm them.'

'But I *don't* like them! They're boring! No kinship systems, no social structure except stupid age-grading and detestable male dominance, no real skills, no arts – lousy carved spoons, all right, like a Hawaiian tourist trap – no ideas – once they grow up, *they're* bored. Kara told me yesterday, "Life's much too long." If they're trying to produce a facsimile of somebody's heart's desire, it isn't mine!'

'Nor mine,' Ramchandra said. 'But Bob?'

There was a harshness, a homing-in quality, to the question. Tamara hesitated. 'I don't know. At first, sure. But he's been restless, lately. After all he's a myths man. And they don't even

tell stories. All they ever talk about is who they slept with last night and how many poro they shot. He says they all talk tike Hemingway characters.'

'He doesn't talk with the Old Ones.' Again that harshness, and Tamara, defensive of Bob, said, 'Neither do I, much; do you? They don't participate, they seem so shadowy... unimportant.'

'That was a healing song old Binira sang.'

'Maybe.'

'I think so. A ritual song, in the more complex language. If there is high culture, the Old Ones have it. Maybe they lose the telepathic power as they grow older; so then they can withdraw, they're no longer influenced, forced to adapt—'

'Forced by whom to adapt to what? They're the only intelligent species on the planet.'

'Other villages, other tribes.'

'But then they'd all talk each other's language, all their customs would melt together—'

'Exactly! That explains the homogeneity of the culture! A solution to Babel!'

He sounded so pleased, and it sounded so plausible, that Tamara did her best to accept the hypothesis. The best she could do was admit finally, 'The idea makes me queasy, for some reason.'

'The Old Ones have developed true language, non-telepathic language. They are the ones to talk with. I will request admission to the Old Men's House tomorrow.'

'You'll have to grow some grey hair...'

'Easily! Is it still black?'

'You'd better get some sleep.'

He was silent a while, but did not lie down. 'Tamara,' he said, 'you are not humoring me, are you?'

'No,' she said gruffly, shocked that he was so vulnerable.

'It is so very like a delusional system.'

'Then it's *folie à deux*. All this about the language just brings the rest into focus. All six villages we've visited, all the same,

the same things missing, the same – improbability – only it's like overprobability—'

'*Projected* telepathy,' he said, brooding. '*They* are influencing *us*. Confusing our perceptions, forcing us into subjectivity—'

'Driving us away from the Reality Principle?' she said, defensive, now, of him. 'Rubbish.' She recognized the quotation, and laughed. 'We're talking much too cleverly to be gaga.'

'I talked brilliantly in the mental institution,' he said. 'In several languages. Even Sanskrit.' He sounded reassured, however; and she stood up. 'I'm going to bed,' she said. 'A fine night's sleep I'll have now! Do you need a fresh hot rock?'

'No, no. Listen, I'm sorry—'

'Askiös, askiös.'

No rest for the wicked. She had just lit her oil lamp and was spitting on her fingers and pinching the wick to keep it from smoking, which it continued to do, when Bob appeared in the doorway of her hut. The light of Uper haloed his thick fair hair; the importance of his return filled the entire biosphere as the bulk of his body filled the doorway. 'I just got back,' he announced.

'From where?'

'Gunda.' The next village downriver.

He came in and sat down on the cane stool, while she swore at the burned poro fat on her fingers. An even more world-shaking announcement than that of his return loomed, imminent, in his scowl. She beat him to the draw. 'Ram's sick,' she said.

'What with?'

'Delhi belly, you could call it.'

'How could anybody get sick here?'

'They have a cure. You sleep with a hot boulder.'

'Christ! Sounds like a cure for potency!' Bob said, and they both broke into laughter. While laughing she almost began to tell Bob about Ram's peculiar linguistic discovery, which for a moment seemed equally ridiculous; but she should let Ram do it, even if it was just a joke. Bob had gone serious again,

and now emitted his announcement. 'I have to fight a duel. Single combat.'

'Oh, Lord. When? Why?'

'Well, that girl. Potita, you know, the redhead. One of the Young Men in Gunda has his eye on her. So he challenged me.'

'An exogamy arrangement? Has he a claim on her?'

'No, you know they don't have any affiliation patterns, stop hunting for them. All she is is an excuse for a combat.'

'I thought you'd get into trouble,' Tamara said priggishly, though she had thought no such thing. 'You can't sleep with all the native girls and not expect the assegai of a maddened savage in your back – Half the native girls, OK, but not all of them—'

'Shit,' Bob said with discouragement. 'I know. Look, I never got mixed up like this before. Sleeping with informants and stuff. I can't seem to keep anything straight here. But they *expect* it. We talked it all out, way back in Buvuna, remember? Ram said he wouldn't. That's OK, he's forty, he's an old man to them, anyhow he looks alien. But I look just like them, and if I refuse I'm offending local custom. It's practically the only custom they've got. I have no choice—'

A laugh, a deep, Middle-Aged Woman belly laugh, welled up from Tamara. He looked at her a little startled. 'All right, all right,' he said, and laughed too. 'But God damn it! They always talked like these combats were voluntary!'

'They're not?'

Bob shook his head. 'I represent Hamo village against Gunda. It's the only kind of war they have. All the Young Men are really worked up. They haven't won a combat with Gunda for half a year, or some such huge historical time span. It's the World Cup. Tomorrow I get purified.'

'A ceremony?' Tamara found Bob's predicament funny but trivial; she leapt from it to the hope of a ceremony, a ritual, anything that would prove some sense and structure in the rudimentary social life of the Ndif.

'Dances. Saweya and baliya. All day.'

478

'Bah.'

'Look, I know you'd like some patterns to study, being a configurationist and all, but I have an even more urgent problem. I have to fight a man day after tomorrow. With knives. In front of the entire population of two villages.'

'With knives?'

'Right. Hunters wrestle. Sallenzii fight with knives.'

'Sallenzii?' – As Bob translated, 'Competitors for a girl,' she transliterated: 'Challengers . . .'

After a short silence she suggested, 'Could you just give him the girl?'

'No. Honor, local pride, all that.'

'And she . . . she's content just to be the prize pig?'

Bob nodded.

'The pattern is familiar,' she said, and then, abruptly, 'Nothing – There is nothing alien about these people. Nothing!'

'What?'

'Never mind. Let me work it out. Ram has an idea . . . Listen, Bob, I think you ought to get out of this, even if you lose face. We can always move on. It would be better than you killing the fellow! Or getting killed.'

'Thanks for the afterthought,' Bob said kindly. 'Don't worry. I'll cheat.'

'Hypodermic?'

'Karate ought to do. I don't mind. It's just that I feel so damned foolish. Public knife fights for a girl. Like a lot of stupid teenagers.'

'It's a teenage society, Bob.'

'Locker-room aliens!' He scratched his lion's mane of hair and stood up, stretching. He was very beautiful; no wonder the villagers had picked him for their champion. The fact that his physical splendor was informed and animated by an intellectual spirit of no less splendor, a passionate trained mind that sought the stuff of poetry for its own sake – this fact would mean nothing much to the Ndif, or to many people on Earth, for

479

that matter. But Tamara, in that moment, saw the young man as what he was, a king.

'Bob,' she said, 'say no. Beg off. We can just move on.'

'No sweat!' he said, and, grateful for her concern, gave her an affectionate bear hug. 'I'll clobber the poor bastard before he knows what hit him. And then give a lecture. Freshman Hygiene: Murder Is Hazardous to Your Health. It'll wow 'em.'

'Do you want me there, or not there?'

'There,' he said. 'Just in case he's a black belt too.'

She was down at the laundry beach next afternoon having an interesting discussion of menopause with Kara and Libisa when Ramchandra came out onto the beach from the peacock-colored forest. Watching him from her rock amid the swirling waters, she thought how foreign he looked, how alien, as Bob had said – like the shadow of somebody standing up in the front row against the marvelous flowing colors of a jungle epic on a movie screen: too small, too black, too solid. Kara saw him too and shouted, 'How's the belly, Uvana Ram?'

When he was close enough not to have to shout, he replied, 'Askiös, Kara, much better. I finished the guo this morning.'

'Good, good. Another potful tonight. You're all skin,' Kara said, not inaccurately.

'Maybe if he eats enough guo he'll turn people-colored,' said Brella, studying him; Kara's mention of skin seemed to have brought Ramchandra's swarthy, dusky complexion to her notice for the first time. The Ndif were remarkably inattentive to details. Brella now compared the two foreigners and said, 'You, too, Tamara. If you only ate people-colored food, maybe you wouldn't be so ugly and brown.'

'I never thought of that,' said Tamara.

'Tamara, we are invited to the Old Men's House.'

'Both of us? When?'

'Both. Now.'

'How did you swing that?' Tamara asked in English,

480

splashing ashore from the boulder she had been sharing with Kara, Libisa, and a lot of freshly washed loincloths.

'I asked.'

'I'll come too,' Kara announced, splashing after Tamara. 'Askiös!'

'Is it right for women to do, Kara?'

'Of course, it's the *Old* Men's House, isn't it?' Kara dusted off her flat little breasts and brought the fold of her sari-like garment neatly across them. 'Go on ahead. I'll stop by and pick up Binira. She told me it's worth listening to sometimes in there. I'll see you there.'

Tamara, her wet feet rimmed with the silvery river sand, joined Ramchandra and entered the peacock forest with him on the narrow path.

She was intensely aware of his brown shoulder beside hers, his dark, well-knit, and fragile body, the excellent nose in the stern profile. She was aware that she was aware of this, but it was not the important thing just now. 'Are they holding a ceremony for us?'

'I don't know. I haven't got some of the key words yet. My request to go there appears to be sufficient reason for a gathering there.'

'Is it all right to bring that?' He was carrying a tape recorder.

'Anything goes in Cloud-Cuckoo Land,' he said, and the stern profile softened with a laugh.

Two of the withered, shadowy, scarce Old Men of the Ndif preceded them into the House, a large decrepit dugout; six or seven more were sitting around inside. There was much muttering of 'askiös' and a strong reek of poro fat. The two foreigners joined the ill-defined circle, sitting on the dirt. No fire was lit. No apparatus or atmosphere of ritual was apparent. Presently Kara and Binira came in and sat down muttering 'askiös' and cracking mild jokes with the Old Men. From across the circle – the place was lit only by the smokehole, and it was hard to see faces clearly – somebody asked something of Kara. Tamara did not understand the question. Kara's response was, 'I'm getting

old enough, aren't I?' There was a general laugh. One more came in, Bro-Kap, said once to have been a famous hunter, still a big man but stooped, wrinkled, and turtle-mouthed from the loss of his teeth. Instead of sitting down he went to the empty firepit under the smokehole and stood there, arms at his sides. Silence grew around him.

He turned slowly till he faced Ramchandra.

'Have you come to learn to dance?'

'If I may,' Ramchandra answered clearly.

'Are you old?'

'I am no longer young.'

My God, Tamara thought, it's an initiation – can Ram keep it up? And the next question, sure enough, she did not understand at all; there were no Young or Middle Ndif words in it. Ram, however, appeared to understand, and replied promptly, 'Not often.'

'When did you last bring home the kill?'

'I have never killed an animal.'

That brought a hoot, laughs, and some critical discussion. 'He must have been born fifty years old!' Binira said, sniggering. 'Or else he is terribly lazy,' said a youngish Old Man with a simple look, very earnestly.

Two more questions and answers Tamara could not follow, and then Bro-Kap demanded, harshly she thought, 'What do you hunt?'

'I hunt peremensoe.'

Whatever it was, it was right. Audible and tangible approval, backslaps, relaxation. Bro-Kap nodded once, shortly, wiped his nose with the back of his hand, and sat down in the circle beside Ramchandra. 'What do you want to know?' he inquired, in a thoroughly unritualistic and offhand manner.

'I should like to know,' Ramchandra said, 'how the world began.'

'Oh ho ho!' went a couple of geezers across the circle. 'Too old for his years, this one! A hundred years old, this fellow!'

'We say this,' Bro-Kap replied. 'Man made the world.'

482

'I should like to know how he did it.'

'In his head, between his ears, how else? Everything is in the head. Nothing is wood, nothing is stone, nothing is water, nothing is blood, nothing is bone; all things are sanisukiarad.'

In her frustration at never knowing the key word, Tamara watched Ram's face as if she could interpret from it; and indeed he understood. His eyes shone; he smiled, so that his features rounded out and grew gentle.

'He dances,' he said. 'He dances.'

'Maybe so,' Bro-Kap replied. 'Maybe Man dances in his head, and that makes sanisukiarad,'

Only with this repetition did Tamara hear the name 'Man' as a name, a Ndif name or word which happened to coincide in sound with the English word 'man' – but she had taken it to coincide in meaning—

Did it?

For a minute everything fell apart into two levels, two overlapping screens or veils, one of them sounds, one of them meanings, neither of them real. Their overlap and interplay, their shift and movement, confused everything, concealed or revealed everything, in that flow there was nothing to take hold of, not even once can you step into the river unless you are the river. The world began and nothing was happening, some wizened old men and women talking nonsense with Lord Shiva in a smelly hut. Talking, merely talking, words, words that meant nothing twice.

The parted veils closed again.

She checked that the tape was running in the recorder, and turned up the gain a little. Replaying all this later, with Ram to interpret and explain, maybe it would make sense.

They did dance, at last. After much talk Binira announced, 'That's enough peremenkiarad without music,' and Bro-Kap rather ungraciously said, 'All right, askiös, go ahead.' At which Binira began to sing in a small unearthly creaking voice; and presently one old man, and then another, got up and danced, a slow dance, the feet close to the ground, the torso still and

poised, intensity concentrated in the hands, arms, and face. It brought tears to Tamara's eyes, the dance of the shadowy old men. Others joined; now they were all dancing, all but Kara and herself. Sometimes they touched one another, lightly and solemnly, or bowed like cranes. All of them? Yes, Ram was dancing with them. The golden dusty light from the smokehole flowed along his arms; lightly and softly he lifted and set down his bare feet. An old man faced him. 'O komeya, O komeya, ama, O, O,' sang the creaking cricket trill, and Kara's hands, Tamara's hands patted time on the brown dirt. The old man's hands were lifted as in supplication. Ramchandra reached to him, the flowing arm, the poised and separated fingers; smiling, he touched, and turned, still dancing, and the old man smiled and began to sing, 'O komeya, ama, ama, O . . .'

'Do we have a session on tape for you to listen to!' Tamara said, but she said it mainly to distract Bob from his hangdog mood as they went together down the path towards the clearing where the duel was to be fought. The path was littered with lamaba-fruit rinds, as most of the village had preceded them.

'More love songs?'

'No. Well, yes. Love songs to God . . . You know what God's name is?'

'Yes,' Bob said indifferently. 'Old man at Gunda told me. Bik-Kop-Man.'

The duel went nearly, but not quite, as planned by both parties. Since it was the one group action by the Young Ndif besides saweya and baliya dancing which seemed to be a genuine ritual or meaning-focussed act, Tamara diligently taped, filmed, and note-took the whole thing, including the redheaded Potita's expression (and here she is, Miss America); the infliction of a knife stab in Bob's thigh by Pit-Wat, the Gunda Challenger; Bob's fine gesture throwing away his long-bladed knife (a glittering arc into the pink-flowered puti bushes); and the karate throw that stretched Pit-Wat flat and apparently lifeless on the ground.

484

Bob did not stay to deliver his lecture on the unhygienic aspects of murder. His wound was bleeding hard, and Tamara cut off the movie camera and got to work with the first-aid kit. Thus the jubilation of Hamo village and the discomfiture of Gunda were recorded only on sound tape; and the tape recorder was off when Pit-Wat revived, to the discomfiture of both Hamo and Gunda. Slain sallenzii were not supposed to come alive and get up, staggering but undamaged. By this time, however, Bob was on the homeward path to Hamo, white-faced and not unwilling to hold on to Tamara's arm. 'Where's Ram?' he asked for the first time, and she explained that she had not even told Ram a duel was to take place.

'Good,' Bob said. 'I know what he'd say.'

'I don't.'

'Irresponsible involvement in native life-ways—'

She shook her head. 'I didn't tell him because I didn't even see him today, and I thought—' She had, in fact, forgotten about the duel, it had seemed so silly, so unreal, compared to that dancing in the Old Men's House; it had all been a stupid annoying joke, right up to the moment when she saw the color, the splendid and terrible color of blood in the sunlight; but she could not tell Bob that. 'He's made a kind of breakthrough. By getting involved himself – he spent all day in the Old Men's House. I want him to talk with you tonight. Once we get your leg looked after. And he'll want to know what the people in Gunda said about Man. About God, I mean. Look out for that vine. Oh, Lord, here come the football fans.' A troupe of Young Women were pursuing them, halfheartedly pelting Bob with puti flowers.

'Where's Potita?' Bob muttered, setting his teeth.

'Not in this lot. Are you really fond of her, Bob?'

'No. It's that my leg hurts. No, it was just fun and games. I just wondered if Pit-Wat got her or I did.'

It turned out that Pit-Wat got her, since he stayed on the field of combat and performed the Victory Dance, rather shakily to be sure. Bob was relieved, since Pit-Wat was certainly

better suited to Potita by temperament and circumstance; and as for the Victory Dance, a two-minute fit of stomping and posing, they had already got several films of champion wrestlers performing it. 'All we needed was a movie of *me* beating my chest,' Bob said. 'Christ! With my leg spouting. And feeling like a prize ass all round anyhow.'

'Ass all round, curious image,' Ramchandra said. They had got a fire going in Bob's hut. It was raining – it rained only at night on Yirdo – and Bob had lost enough blood that a little extra warmth and cheer might do him good. The air got smoky, but the ruddy light was pleasant; it made Tamara think of winter, of rain and firelight in winter, a season unknown to Yirdo. Bob lay stretched out on his cot and the other two sat by the hearth, feeding the fire with dried lamaba rinds, which burned with a clear flame and a scent of pineapple.

'Ram, what does peremensoe mean?'

'Thinking. Ideas. Understanding. Talk.'

'And peremenkiarad, is that right?'

'About the same. Plus a connotation of ... illusion, deception, trickery – play.'

'Is this Old Ndif?' Bob inquired. 'If you're making dictionaries, let me see 'em, Ram. I couldn't understand anything the old boys were telling me in Gunda.'

'Except God's name,' Tamara said.

Ramchandra raised his eyebrows.

'Bik-Kop-Man made the world with his ears,' Bob said. 'And that is the Ndif equivalent of Genesis, Book One.'

'Between his ears,' Ramchandra corrected coldly.

'With them or between them, it's a pretty poor excuse for a Creation myth.'

'How do you know, if your vocabulary is inadequate?'

Why did he take that tone with Bob? Supercilious, pedantic, offensive, even the voice high and schoolmarmish. Bob's solid good nature shone by contrast in his reply: 'It's taken me weeks to realize that if I'm after myth or history the only people here

486

who may have them are the Old Ones. I should have been checking in with you much earlier.'

Ramchandra stared into the fire and said nothing.

'Ram,' Tamara said, profoundly irritated with him, 'Bob should know about this thing we talked about the other night. The derivation of Young Ndif.'

He went on staring into the fire, mute.

'You can explain it better than I can.'

After a moment he merely shook his head.

'You've decided it was a mistake?' she demanded, more exasperated than ever, but also with a flash of hope.

'No,' he said. 'The documentation is in that notebook I gave you.'

She fetched the notebook from her hut, lighted the oil lamp, and sat down on the floor by Bob's cot so he could read over her shoulder. For half an hour they went over Ramchandra's orderly and exhaustive proofs of the direct derivation of Young Ndif from Modern Standard English. Bob laughed at first, taking the whole thing as a grand scholarly joke; then he laughed at the sheer lunacy of it. It did not seem to disturb him, as it disturbed Tamara.

'If it's not your hoax, Ram, it's still a hoax – a terrific one.'

'By whom? How? Why?' Tamara asked, hopeful again. A mistake made sense; a hoax made sense.

'All right. This language,' and he tapped the notebook, 'isn't authentic. It's a fake, a construct – invented. Right?'

Ramchandra, who had not said a word all this while, agreed in a remote, unwilling tone: 'Invented. By an amateur. The correspondences with English are naïve, unconscious, as in "speaking in tongues." – But Old Ndif is an authentic language.'

'An older one, an archaic survival—'

'No.' Ramchandra said 'No' often, flatly, and with satisfaction, Tamara thought. 'Old Ndif is alive. It is based upon Young Ndif, has grown out of it, or over it. Like ivy on a telephone pole.'

'Spontaneously?'

487

'As spontaneously as any language, or as deliberately. When words are wanted, needed, people have to make them. It "happens," like a bird singing, but it's also "work," like Mozart writing music.'

'Then you'd say the Old Ones are gradually making a real language out of this fake one?'

'I cannot define the word "real" and therefore would not use it.' Ramchandra shifted his position, reclasping his arms round his knees, but did not look up from the fire. 'I would say that the Old Ndif seem to be engaged in creating the world. Human beings do this primarily by means of language, music, and the dance.'

Bob stared at him, then at Tamara 'Come again?'

Ramchandra was silent.

'So far,' Tamara said, 'working in three widely separate localities, we've found the same language, without major dialectical variations, and the same set of very rudimentary social and cultural patterns. Bob hasn't found any legends, any expressions of the archetypes, any developed symbology. I haven't found much more social structure than I'd find in a herd of cattle, about what I might find in a primate troop. Sex and age determine all roles. The Ndif are culturally subhuman; they don't exist fully as human beings. The Old Ndif are beginning to. Is that it, Ram?'

'I don't know,' the linguist said, withdrawn.

'That's missionary talk!' Bob said. 'Subhuman? Come on. Stagnant, sure. Maybe because there's no environmental challenge. Food falls out of the trees, game's plentiful, and they don't have sexual hangups—'

'That's *in*human,' Tamara interjected; Bob ignored her.

'There's no stimulus. OK. But the Old Ones get shoved out of the fun and games. They get bored; that's the stimulus. They start playing around with words and ideas. So what rudiments of mythopoetics and ritual they've got are their creation. That's not an unusual situation, the young busy with sex and physical competitions, the old as culture transmitters. The only weird

thing is this English-Ndif business. That needs explaining. I just don't buy telepathy, you can't build a scientific explanation on an occultist theory. The only rational explanation is that these people – the whole society – are a plant. A quite recent one.'

'Correct,' Ramchandra said.

'But listen,' Tamara said with fury, 'how can a quarter of a million people be "planted"? What about the ones over thirty? We've only had FTL spaceflight for thirty years! The Exploratory Survey to this system was unmanned, and it was only eight years ago! Your rational explanation is pure nonsense!'

'Correct,' Ramchandra said again, his clear, dark, sorrowful gaze on the flickering fire.

'Evidently there's been a manned mission, a colonising mission, to this planet which the World Government doesn't know about. We have stumbled into something, and it begins to scare me. The So-Hem faction—'

Bob was interrupted by the sudden entrance (the Ndif never knocked) of Bro-Kap, two other Old Men, and two baliya dancers, beautiful half-naked sixteen-year-olds with flowers in their tawny hair. They knelt by Bob's cot and made soft lamenting sounds. Bro-Kap stood as majestically as he could in the now very crowded hut, and gazed down at Bob. He was clearly waiting for the girls to be quiet, but one of them was now chattering cheerfully and the other was drawing circles around Bob's nipples with her long fingernails. 'Uvana Bob!' Bro-Kap said at last. 'Are you Bik-Kop-Man?'

'Am I – Askiös, Wana! – No. Askiös, Bro-Kap, I don't understand.'

'Sometimes Man comes,' the old Ndif said. 'He has come to Hamo, and to Farwe. Never to Gunda or to Akko. He is strong and tall, golden-haired and golden-skinned, a great hunter, a great fighter, a great lover. He comes from far away and goes away again. We have thought that you were He. You are not He?'

'No, I am not,' Bob said decisively.

Bro-Kap took a breath that heaved his wrinkled chest. 'Then you will die,' he said.

'Die?' Bob repeated without comprehension.

'Die how? Of what?' Tamara demanded, standing up so that in the press of people in the little hut she was brought face-to-face with the old man. 'What do you mean, Bro-Kap?'

'Gunda challengers use poisoned knives,' the old man said. 'To find out which ones from Hamo are Bik-Kop-Man. Poison doesn't kill Bik-Kop-Man.'

'What poison?'

'That's their secret,' Bro-Kap said. 'Gunda is full of wicked people. We of Hamo use no poisons.'

'For Christ's sake,' Bob said in English, and in Ndif, 'Why didn't you tell me?'

'The Young Men thought you knew. They thought you were Man. Then when you let Pit-Wat wound you, when you threw away your knife, when you killed him but he came back to life, they weren't sure. They came to the Old Men's House to ask. Because we in the Old Men's house have peremensoe about Man.' There was pride in the old man's voice. 'Thus I came to you. Askiös, Uvana Bob.' Bro-Kap turned and pushed his way out; the other old men followed him.

'Go away,' Bob said to the smiling, caressing girls. 'Go on now.' They left, reluctant, swaying, their pretty faces troubled.

'I'll go to Gunda,' Ramchandra said, 'see if there's an antidote.' And he was off at a run.

Bob's face was dead white.

'Another damned hoax,' he said, smiling.

'You bled a lot, Bob. Probably bled out the poison right away, if there really was any. Let me have a look at it ... It looks absolutely clean. No inflammation.'

'My breath's been coming short,' the young man said. 'Most likely shock.'

'Yes. Let me get the medical handbook.'

The handbook had no recommendations, and Gunda had no antidote. The poison acted on the central nervous system. Paroxysms began two hours after Bro-Kap's visit. They

increased quickly in severity and frequency. Some time after midnight long before dawn, Bob died.

Ramchandra struck the tenth useless blow over the stopped heart, raised his arm to strike again, and did not strike. The dancer's raised arm: creator, destroyer. The clenched, dark fist relaxed; the poised and separated fingers hovered above the white face and the unbreathing chest. 'Ah!' Ramchandra cried aloud, and dropping down beside the cot broke into tears, a passion of tears.

Wind gusted the rain against the roof. Time passed and Ramchandra was silent, as silent as Bob, beside whom he crouched, his arms stretched across Bob's body and his head sunk between them; exhausted, he had fallen asleep. The rain thinned and weakened and then beat hard again. Tamara put out the oil lamp, her movements slow and certain, full of the knowledge of what they meant. She added the last of the fuel to the fire and sat down at the little hearth. One must watch with the newly dead, and the sleeping should not sleep unprotected. She sat awake and watched the fire die out, and long afterwards, the grey light reborn.

Ndif funerals were, as she had expected, graceless. There was a burying ground not far off in the forest, which nobody talked about or ever visited except for burials. Gravedigging was the Old Men's task. They had dug a shallow pit. Two of them, plus Kara and Binira, helped carry Bob's body to the grave. The Ndif used no coffins, dumped their dead naked in the earth; it was too cold that way, too cold, Tamara thought with rage, and she had put Bob's white shirt and trousers on him, left his gold Swiss watch strapped on his wrist since he owned no other treasure, and wrapped the long, silky, bluish leaves of the pandsu carefully about him. She lined the shallow grave with leaves before they laid him in it; the four old men and women watched, expressionless. They laid him on his side, his knees a little bent. Tamara turned for a flower to put by his hand, but the pink and purple blossoms sickened her; she broke the

chain around her neck, on which hung a little turquoise her mother had given her, a fragment of the Earth, and put that in the dead man's hand. She had to be quick; the old men were already scraping the dirt back over the grave with their crude wooden shovels. As soon as that was done all four Ndif turned without a word and went off, not looking back.

Ramchandra knelt down by the grave. 'I am sorry I was jealous of you,' he said. 'If we meet reborn, you will be a king again, but I will be the dog at your heel.' He bowed down, touching the raw, damp clods of the grave, then slowly stood up. He looked at Tamara. She knew his look, the dark, clear, grieving eyes, but she could not meet them, or speak. It was her turn to cry. He came to her across the grave, as if it was any bit of ground, and put his arms around her, holding her so she could weep. When the first hardest sobbing was done and she could walk, they set off slowly down the narrow, half-overgrown path through the peacock splendors of the forest back to the village.

'Burning is better,' Ramchandra said. 'The spirit is freed sooner to go on.'

'Earth is best,' Tamara said, very low and hoarse.

'Tamara. Do you want to radio Ankara Base to send the launch to us?'

'I don't know.'

'There's no hurry to decide.'

The gorgeous colors of the lamabas blurred and cleared and blurred again. She stumbled, though Ramchandra's hand was kind and firm on her arm.

'We might as well go on and finish what we came for.'

'The ethnology of dreams.'

'Dreams? Oh no. This is real . . . Much realler than I wish it were.'

'So are all dreams.'

In three days they put in their regular call to Ankara, the inner planet where the central base for the various research groups in Yirdo's solar system was established; they reported Bob's death,

'by misunderstanding – no blame,' in the Ethnographic Corps code. They did not request relief.

Life in Hamo village went on as before. The Middle-Aged Women said nothing about Bob's death to Tamara, but several evenings old Binira sat just outside her hut and sang to her, a quiet cricket trill. Once she saw two of the little saweya dancers leaving a flowering branch at the door of Bob's empty hut; she went towards them, but they trotted off, giggling. Soon after, the Young Men set fire to the hut, deliberately or by accident, there was no telling; it burned to ashes and all trace of it was gone within a week. Ramchandra spent his days and nights with the Old Ones of Hamo and Gunda, gathering an increasingly solid bulk of linguistic and mythic data. The long lines of saweya dancers undulated, the baliya dancers thrust their high breasts left and right, the singers chanted 'Ah-weh, weh, ah-weh, weh,' and the forest glades round the dancing ground at dusk swarmed with coupled bodies. Hunters returned proudly with dead poro, like suckling pigs with blunt, curved fangs, slung on carrying poles. On the twelfth night after Bob's death Ramchandra came to Tamara's hut; she had been trying to read over some notes, but the pages might as well have been empty, her head ached and nothing made sense, nothing meant anything. He came to the doorway, dark, slight, shadowy, and she looked up at him with dull eyes. He said something that meant nothing about loneliness, and then he said, with the darkness around him and behind him, 'It's like fire. Like burning in a fire. But the spirit caught, too, burning—'

'Come in,' she said.

A few nights later they lay talking, in the dark, the soft windy rain sighing in the forest and on the thatch of the hut above them.

'Since I first saw you,' he said. 'Truly, since the day we met, in the canteen at Ankara Base.'

With a laugh, Tamara said, 'You scarcely behaved as if ...'

'I didn't like it! I refused. I said, No, no, no! – my wife was

493

enough, this doesn't come twice to a man in one life, I will remember her.'

'You do,' Tamara murmured.

'Of course. To her in me now I can say, Yes, and to you with me, Yes, yes ... Listen, Tamara, you set me free, your hands free me. And bind me. Tighter to the wheel, never in this life now will I get free, never cease to desire you, I don't *want* to cease...'

'It's so simple now. What was in our way?'

'My fear. My jealousy.'

'Jealousy? – Of Bob?'

'Oh yes,' he said, shivering.

'Oh Ram, never – Right from the beginning, you—'

'Confusion,' he whispered. 'Illusion...'

His warmth against her the length of her body; and cold Bob, cold in the ground. Fire is better than earth.

She woke; he was stroking her hair and cheek, soothing her, whispering, 'Sleep again, it's all right, Tamara,' his voice heavy with sleep and tenderness.

'What – did I—'

'A bad dream.'

'Dream. Oh, no – it wasn't bad – just queer.'

The rain had ceased and the light of the giant planet, greyed and filtered by clouds, was like a faint mist in the hut. She could just make out the hook of his nose, the darkness of his hair, in that grey dust of light.

'What was the dream?'

'A boy – a young man – no, a boy, about fifteen. Standing in front of me. Sort of filling everything, taking up all the room, so that I couldn't possibly get past him or around him. But just an ordinary boy, with glasses, I think. And he was staring at me, not threatening, not even really seeing me, but he kept staring and saying "Bill me, bill me." And I didn't think he owed me anything, so I said, "What for?" But he just kept saying, "Bill me!" And then I woke up.'

494

'Bill me, how funny,' Ramchandra said sleepily. 'Bill me . . .
Me Bill . . .'

'Yes. That's it. I'm Bill, that's what he meant.'

'Oh,' Ramchandra said, a deep exhalation, and she felt his
relaxed body go tense. Since Bob's death she had not trusted
the Ndif, or rather without distrusting any one of them she had
lost trust in their world, she feared harm. She raised her head
quickly to see if someone had entered the hut. 'What's wrong?'

'Nothing is wrong.'

'What is it?'

'Nothing. Go back to sleep. You talked to God.'

'The dream?'

'Yes. He told you his name.'

'Bill?' she said, and because the alarm was past and she was
still sleepy and Ramchandra was laughing, she laughed. 'God's
name is Bill?'

'Yes, yes. Bill Kopman, or Kopfman, or Cupman.'

'Bik-Kop-Man?'

'The "l" assimilates to the "k" as in sikka, the fiber they
make fishing lines of – silk.'

'What are you babbling about?'

'Bill Kopman, who made this world.'

'Who what? Who?'

'Who made this world. *This* world – Yirdo, the poro, the puti
bushes, the Ndif. You saw him in your dream. A fifteen-year-old
boy, with glasses, probably also acne and weak ankles. You saw
him, and so my eyes see for a moment too. A skinny boy, lazy,
shy. He reads stories, he daydreams, about the great blond
hero who can hunt and fight and make love all day and night.
His head is full of the hero, himself, and so it all comes to be.'

'Ram, stop it.'

'But you talked to him, not I! You asked him, "What for?"
But he couldn't tell you. He doesn't know. He doesn't under-
stand desire. He is entirely caught in it, bound by it, he sees
and knows nothing but his own immense desire. And so he

495

makes the world. Only one free of desire is free of the worlds, you know.'

Tamara looked, as if over her shoulder, back into her dream. 'He speaks English,' she said, unwillingly.

Ramchandra nodded. His tranquillity, his acceptant, playful tone, reassured her, it was interesting to lie looking together at the same silly dream.

'He writes it all down,' she said, 'his fantasies about the Ndif. Maps and everything. A lot of kids do that. And some adults . . .'

'Perhaps he has a notebook of his invented language. It would be interesting to compare with my notebooks.'

'Much easier just to go find him and borrow his.'

'Yes, but he doesn't know Old Ndif.'

'Ramchandra.'

'Beloved.'

'You are saying that because a boy writes nonsense in a notebook in – in Topeka, a planet thirty-one light-years away comes into existence, with all its plants and animals and people. And always has been in existence. Because of the boy and the notebook. And what about the boy with a notebook in Schenectady? Or New Delhi?'

'Evidently!'

'Your nonsense is much worse than Bill Kopman's.'

'Why?'

'Time – And there isn't room—'

'There is room. There is time. All the galaxies. All the universes. That is infinity. The worlds are infinite, the cycles are endless. There is room. Room for all the dreams, all the desires. No end to it. Worlds without end.'

His voice now was remote.

'Bill Kopman dreams,' he said, 'and the God dances. And Bob dies, and we make love.'

She saw the boy's blind yearning face before her, filling the world, no way around it, no path.

'You're only joking, Ramchandra,' she said; she was shivering, now.

'I'm only joking, Tamara,' he said.

'If it weren't a joke I couldn't bear it. Being caught here, stuck in somebody else's dream, dream world, alternate world, whatever it is.'

'Why caught? We call Ankara; they send the launch for us; next passage out we can go back to Earth if we like. Nothing has changed.'

'But this idea that it's somebody else's world. What if – what if – while we're still here – Bill Kopman woke up?'

'Once in a thousand thousand years does a soul wake up,' Ramchandra said, and his voice was sad.

She wondered why that made him sad; she found it comforting. Brooding, she found further comfort. 'It wouldn't all depend on him, even if he started it,' she said. 'All the uninhabited places, they'd just be blanks on his maps, but they're full of life, animals and trees and ferns and little flies... Reality is what works, isn't it? And the old men and women. They aren't, they wouldn't be, part of ... of Bill's wet dreams. He probably doesn't even know any old people, he isn't interested. So they get free.'

'Yes. They begin to imagine their world for themselves. To think, to make words. To tell the story.'

'I wonder if he ever thinks of death.'

'Can anyone think of death?' Ramchandra asked. 'One can only do it. As Bob did it... Can one dream of sleep?'

The soft, dust-grey light was more intense, as the clouds thinned, drifting silent to the east.

'He looked anxious, in the dream,' Tamara muttered 'Frightened. As if ... "Bill me..." As if Bob paid... the debt.'

'Tamara, Tamara, you go before me, always before me.' His forehead was against her breasts; she touched his hair lightly.

'Ramchandra,' she said, 'I want to go home, I think. Away from this place. Back to the real world.'

'You go before, I follow you.'

'Oh, humble you are, liar, hoaxer, dancer, you're so humble, but you don't really care, do you? You're not frightened.'

'Not any more,' he said, in a breath, barely audible.

'How long have you understood about this place? Since you danced with Bro-Kap and the others, that first time?'

'No, no. Only now, since your dream, this night, now. You saw. All I can do is say. But yes, if you like, I can say it because I have always known it. I speak my native tongue, because you have brought me home. The house under the trees behind the temple of Shiva in a suburb of Calcutta, is that my home? Is this? The world, the real world, which one? What does it matter? Who dreamed the Earth? A greater dreamer than you or I, but we are the dreamer, Shakti, and the worlds will endure as long as our desire.'

WEST

GWILAN'S HARP

The harp had come to Gwilan from her mother, and so had her mastery of it, people said. 'Ah,' they said when Gwilan played, 'you can tell, that's Diera's touch,' just as their parents had said when Diera played, 'Ah, that's the true Penlin touch!' Gwilan's mother had had the harp from Penlin, a musician's dying gift to the worthiest of pupils. From a musician's hands Penlin, too, had received it; never had it been sold or bartered for, nor any value put upon it that can be said in numbers. A princely and most incredible instrument it was for a poor harper to own. The shape of it was perfection, and every part was strong and fine: the wood as hard and smooth as bronze, the fittings of ivory and silver. The grand curves of the frame bore silver mountings chased with long intertwining lines that became waves and the waves became leaves, and the eyes of gods and stags looked out from among the leaves that became waves and the waves became lines again. It was the work of great craftsmen, you could see that at a glance, and the longer you looked the clearer you saw it. But all this beauty was practical, obedient, shaped to the service of sound. The sound of Gwilan's harp was water running and rain and sunlight on the water, waves breaking and the foam on the brown sands, forests, the leaves and branches of the forest and the shining eyes of gods and stags among the leaves when the wind blows in the valleys. It was all that and none of that. When Gwilan played, the harp made music; and what is music but a little wrinkling of the air?

Play she did, wherever they wanted her. Her singing voice was true but had no sweetness, so when songs and ballads were wanted she accompanied the singers. Weak voices were borne up by her playing, fine voices gained a glory from it; the loudest, proudest singers might keep still a verse to hear her play alone. She played along with the flute and reed flute and tambour, and the music made for the harp to play alone, and the music that sprang up of itself when her fingers touched the strings. At weddings and festivals it was, 'Gwilan will be here to play,' and at music-day competitions, 'When will Gwilan play?'

She was young; her hands were iron and her touch was silk; she could play all night and the next day too. She travelled from valley to valley, from town to town, stopping here and staying there and moving on again with other musicians on their wanderings. They walked, or a wagon was sent for them, or they got a lift on a farmer's cart. However they went, Gwilan carried her harp in its silk and leather case at her back or in her hands. When she rode she rode with the harp and when she walked she walked with the harp and when she slept, no, she didn't sleep with the harp, but it was there where she could reach out and touch it. She was not jealous of it, and would change instruments with another harper gladly; it was a great pleasure to her when at last they gave her back her own, saying with sober envy, 'I never played so fine an instrument.' She kept it clean, the mountings polished, and strung it with the harp strings made by old Uliad, which cost as much apiece as a whole set of common harp strings. In the heat of summer she carried it in the shade of her body, in the bitter winter it shared her cloak. In a firelit hall she did not sit with it very near the fire, nor yet too far away, for changes of heat and cold would change the voice of it and perhaps harm the frame. She did not look after herself with half the care. Indeed she saw no need to. She knew there were other harpers, and would be other harpers; most not as good, some better. But the harp was the best. There had not been and there would not be a better. Delight and service were due and fitting to it. She was

502

not its owner but its player. It was her music, her joy, her life, the noble instrument.

She was young; she travelled from town to town; she played 'A Fine Long Life' at weddings, and 'The Green Leaves' at festivals. There were funerals, with the burial feast, the singing of elegies, and Gwilan to play the Lament of Orioth, the music that crashes and cries out like the sea and the seabirds, bringing relief and a burst of tears to the grief-dried heart. There were music days, with a rivalry of harpers and a shrilling of fiddlers and a mighty outshouting of tenors. She went from town to town in sun and rain, the harp on her back or in her hands. So she was going one day to the yearly music day at Comin, and the landowner of Torm Vale was giving her a lift, a man who so loved music that he had traded a good cow for a bad horse, since the cow would not take him where he could hear music played. It was he and Gwilan in a rickety cart, and the lean-necked roan stepping out down the steep, sunlit road from Torm.

A bear in the forest by the road, or a bear's ghost, or the shadow of a hawk: the horse shied half across the road. Torm had been discussing music deeply with Gwilan, waving his hands to conduct a choir of voices, and the reins went flipping out of those startled hands. The horse jumped like a cat and ran. At the sharp curve of the road the cart swung round and smashed against the rocky cutting. A wheel leapt free and rolled rocking like a top, for a few yards. The roan went plunging and sliding down the road with half the wrecked cart dragging behind and was gone, and the road lay silent in the sunlight between the forest trees.

Torm had been thrown from the cart, and lay stunned for a minute or two.

Gwilan had clutched the harp to her when the horse shied, but had lost hold of it in the smash. The cart had tipped over and dragged on it. It was in its case of leather and embroidered silk, but when, one-handed, she got the case out from under the wheel and opened it, she did not take out a harp, but a piece of

wood, and another piece, and a tangle of strings, and a sliver of ivory, and a twisted shell of silver chased with lines and leaves and eyes, held by a silver nail to a fragment of the frame.

It was six months without playing after that, since her arm had broken at the wrist. The wrist healed well enough, but there was no mending the harp; and by then the landowner of Torm had asked her if she would marry him, and she had said yes. Sometimes she wondered why she had said yes, having never thought much of marriage before, but if she looked steadily into her own mind she saw the reason why. She saw Torm on the road in the sunlight kneeling by the broken harp, his face all blood and dust and he was weeping. When she looked at that she saw that the time for rambling and roving was over and gone. One day is the day for moving on, and overnight the next day, there is no more good in moving on, because you have come where you were going to.

Gwilan brought to the marriage a gold piece, which had been the prize last year at Four Valleys music day; she had sewn it to her bodice as a brooch, because where on earth could you spend a gold piece. She also had two silver pieces, five coppers, and a good winter cloak. Torm contributed house and household, fields and forests, four tenant farmers even poorer than himself, twenty hens, five cows, and forty sheep.

They married in the old way, by themselves, over the spring where the stream began, and came back and told the household. Torm had never suggested a wedding, with singing and harp-playing, never a word of all that. He was a man you could trust, Torm was.

What began in pain, in tears, was never free from the fear of pain. The two of them were gentle to each other. Not that they lived together thirty years without some quarrelling. Two rocks sitting side by side would get sick of each other in thirty years, and who knows what they say now and then when nobody is listening. But if people trust each other they can grumble, and a good bit of grumbling takes the fuel from wrath. Their quarrels

went up and burnt out like bits of paper, leaving nothing but a feather of ash, a laugh in bed in the dark. Torm's land never gave more than enough, and there was no money saved. But it was a good house, and the sunlight was sweet on those high stony fields. There were two sons, who grew up into cheerful sensible men. One had a taste for roving, and the other was a farmer born; but neither had any gift of music.

Gwilan never spoke of wanting another harp. But about the time her wrist was healed, old Uliad had a travelling musician bring her one on loan; when he had an offer to buy it at its worth, he sent for it back again. At that time Torm would have it that there was money from selling three good heifers to the landowner of Comin High Farm, and the money should buy a harp, which it did. A year or two later an old friend, a flute player still on his travels and rambles, brought her a harp from the South as a present. The three-heifers harp was a common instrument, plain and heavy; the Southern harp was delicately carved and gilt, but cranky to tune and thin of voice. Gwilan could draw sweetness from the one and strength from the other. When she picked up a harp, or spoke to a child, it obeyed her.

She played at all festivities and funerals in the neighborhood, and with the musician's fees she bought good strings; not Uliad's strings, though, for Uliad was in his grave before her second child was born. If there was a music day nearby she went to it with Torm. She would not play in the competitions, not for fear of losing, but because she was not a harper now, and if they did not know it, she did. So they had her judge the competitions, which she did well and mercilessly. Often in the early years musicians would stop by on their travels and stay two or three nights at Torm; with them she would play the Hunts of Orioth, the Dances of Cail, the difficult and learned music of the North, and learn from them the new songs. Even in winter evenings there was music in the house of Torm: she playing the harp – usually the three-heifers one, some-times the fretful Southerner – and Torm's good tenor voice, and the boys singing, first in sweet treble, later on in husky unreliable

baritone; and one of the farm's men was a lively fiddler; and the shepherd Keth, when he was there, played on the pipes, though he never could tune them to anyone else's note. 'It's our own music day tonight,' Gwilan would say. 'Put another log on the fire, Torm, and sing "The Green Leaves" with me, and the boys will take the descant.'

Her wrist that had been broken grew a little stiff as the years went on; then the arthritis came into her hands. The work she did in house and farm was not easy work. But then who, looking at a hand, would say it was made to do easy work? You can see from the look of it that it is meant to do difficult things, that it is the noble, willing servant of the heart and mind. But the best servants get clumsy as the years go on. Gwilan could still play the harp, but not as well as she had played, and she did not much like half measures. So the two harps hung on the wall, though she kept them tuned. About that time the younger son went wandering off to see what things looked like in the North, and the elder married and brought his bride to Torm. Old Keth was found dead up on the mountain in the spring rain, his dog crouched silent by him and the sheep nearby. And the drouth came, and the good year, and the poor year, and there was food to eat and to be cooked and clothes to wear and to be washed, poor year or good year. In the depth of a winter Torm took ill. He went from a cough to a high fever to quietness, and died while Gwilan sat beside him.

Thirty years, how can you say how long that is, and yet no longer than the saying of it thirty years. How can you say how heavy the weight of thirty years is, and yet you can hold all of them together in your hand lighter than a bit of ash, briefer than a laugh in the dark. The thirty years began in pain; they passed in peace, contentment. But they did not end there. They ended where they began.

Gwilan got up from her chair and went into the hearth room. The rest of the household were asleep. In the light of her candle she saw the two harps hung against the wall, the three-heifers harp and the gilded Southern harp, the dull music

506

and the false music. She thought, 'I'll take them down at last and smash them on the hearthstone, crush them till they're only bits of wood and tangles of wire, like my harp.' But she did not. She could not play them at all any more, her hands were far too stiff. It is silly to smash an instrument you cannot even play.

'There is no instrument left that I can play,' Gwilan thought, and the thought hung in her mind for a while like a long chord, till she knew the notes that made it. 'I thought my harp was myself. But it was not. It was destroyed, I was not. I thought Torm's wife was myself, but she was not. He is dead, I am not. I have nothing left at all now but myself. The wind blows from the valley, and there's a voice on the wind, a bit of a tune. Then the wind falls, or changes. The work has to be done, and we did the work. It's their turn now for that, the children. There's nothing left for me to do but sing. I never could sing. But you play the instrument you have.' So she stood by the cold hearth and sang the melody of Orioth's Lament. The people of the household wakened in their beds and heard her singing, all but Torm; but he knew that tune already. The untuned strings of the harps hung on the wall wakened and answered softly, voice to voice, like eyes that shine among the leaves when the wind is blowing.

507

MALHEUR COUNTY

'Edward,' said his mother-in-law, 'face the facts. You can't withdraw from your life. People aren't going to let you. You're too useful, too likable, too good-looking even, though you don't seem to be aware of it.' She paused for breath, then said in a colder voice, 'I used to wonder if Mary was really aware of it.'

He sat silent across the hearth from her, huddled up over his long arms and legs.

'You can't withdraw from something you haven't got into! Oh, I'm sorry,' she said savagely.

He smiled, but looked a little punch-drunk.

'The Navajo Indians,' she said, 'I think, don't let mothers-in-laws and sons-in-law speak to one another. It's tabu. A very sensible arrangement. We're so damned sophisticated, no tabus, no defenses.' She fell grimly silent, a grey-haired, full-figured woman in her sixties sitting erect in an armchair in the firelight. She always sat erect. The cigarette in her left hand and whiskey glass in her right appeared as elements of her rugged femininity. She came from eastern Oregon, from Malheur County, the last, barren frontier, from a decent feckless family that had left a century of failed farms, male suicides, and infant graves across the land from Ohio to the Coast, pushing always unprofitably westward.

'Of course she knew that you were good-looking,' she went on thoughtfully, 'she was proud of it. But I never saw that she got much pleasure out of it. Not as you took pleasure in her, real joy.'

He was only twenty-seven. Leaning forward to toss her cigarette into the fire Harriet Avanti saw, through her shrewdly rambling thoughts and the press of various emotions, his face; and the rest dropped clear away. 'I shouldn't think aloud,' she said, 'I didn't mean to hurt you.'

'You don't. You can't.' He turned his kind, somber young face to her, reassuring.

'But I do. You're sensitive, and I'm not. You're guilt-ridden, and I don't even know what guilt is.'

But again she had touched a nerve; he frowned, and spoke: 'No, I'm not guilt-ridden, Harriet. It wasn't my fault. It's not my fault that I survive. Only I don't see the point.'

'The point!' She sat erect moveless. 'There is no point.'

Staring at the fire he whispered, 'I know.'

They were silent a good while. Harriet thought of her daughter Mary, the beautiful dissatisfied child. 'This is Edward, Mother.' And the young man watching the girl with incredulous, delighted passion – oh, it had been he, alone, who had roused Harriet from her long drab grief after her husband's death, who had shown her once again, from the flat plain and barren land, the incredibly high peaks. He had reminded her that after all there is more in life than endurance. For unfortunately, as she knew, endurance was her native style. She would have endured right through life, steady and heavy as a rock, if she hadn't had the luck to meet and marry John Avanti, who taught her joy. He dead, she had fallen back at once upon endurance, and never would have known delight again if her daughter had not marched in one night with the tall radiant boy: 'This is Edward, Mother.'

'I don't think you do know,' she said abruptly. 'Pointlessness isn't your line. It's mine. I was intended to lead a pointless life, like my parents and my brothers. By some mistake I got into a highly rewarding life with a point to it. Just the sort of life you were intended for. And then you, of all people, meet up with this, with the drunk on the highway, with waste and senselessness, when you're only twenty-five. Another mistake,

no doubt. But it's not essential, Edward. Mary's death is not going to be the essential event in your life. To accept it as essential, to accept pointlessness, would be – for you – an act of cowardice.'

'Maybe,' he said. 'But the fact is, Harriet, that I, lately, that I seem to have about reached my limit.'

She was frightened by his anguish, diffident as it was. She did not know much about anguish, only about misery, the endurable unending pain not the destroying one. She tried now to back away from the point of agony, saying, 'Well a limit's always a beginning...' What she feared was his crying. Twice here in this room with her he had broken down and wept, once when he was first home from hospital after the wreck, then again months later. She dreaded his tears, the coping with pain at second hand. It shattered her to pity as to be pitied. When he got up suddenly from the low hearth seat she sat tense. But he said only, 'I'd like another shot. You?' He took her glass and went off to the kitchen. As he went the clock behind her on the mantel struck twelve solemnly, taking a long time about it; and now it was November not October. They had lived another month. Here she sat by the fire, there was Edward opening cupboards in the kitchen, both of them warm and full of good bourbon; and then there was Mary, eighteen months dead. Was it because she was a hard woman that she had not really wept for her child's death? If she had died before John, I would have cried for her, Harriet thought.

Edward returned, sat down, stretched out his legs. 'I have tried,' he said with such serious equanimity that she lost all fear of his breaking down and waited to find out what he meant. He was candid but inarticulate, and his mind, trained to the rigors of chemistry, pursued logic into places where it does not exist. 'I've honestly tried,' he repeated, lapsed into silence, crossed his ankles, drank thoughtfully, and at last went on, 'Technician in the medical department. Elinor Schneider. Fairly good-looking, blond, very intelligent. She's around my age.' (Older, thought

Harriet) 'Well, so...' Edward paused, raised his glass in self-mocking salute. 'I tried.'

'To?'

'To get interested.'

Poor Elinor Schneider, lying awake now perhaps seeing in the dry darkness his face. Pain is self-centered. Harriet sighed a little. 'I suppose a laboratory is the place for an experiment...'

'Anyway, it was an effort to reconnect whatever you want to call it. It didn't work. I can't do it. I don't want to do it. I know you think me weak.'

'You? I certainly don't. And if I did, what then? You know yourself best.'

'No, I don't, Harriet. You're really the first person who seems to know much about me. To judge me objectively. My parents...' He was the child of a divorce, passed back and forth from father and wife to mother and husband, a bone of contention. He let that go, but added, 'And Mary and I were rather stupid about each other, in some ways.'

'You were very young.'

'We had no time,' he said, so clear and quiet in his statement of the chance lost that Harriet sat still, outclassed, rejoicing in being outclassed.

'So,' he said, pursuing logic, 'in you I see the first clear reflection of myself. It looks weak.'

'The mirror is old, it warps.'

'No; you see people very justly.'

'Do you really want to know how I see you?' she demanded, for he had poured her a strong drink and she wasn't used to a second nightcap. He did want to know. 'As a bright and fortunate man,' she said after seeking the words. 'Fortunate, not lucky. You haven't had much luck. And yet you've been fortunate. You got your freedom early, too early, but then a lot of people never get it. You've known real passion, real fulfillment, and no letdown. You never will know the letdown, the dead level. You got into manhood a free man, and you'll go on free, or—' But the 'or' had carried her too far. Had she been

younger, his equal, she could have finished the sentence, 'or you'll kill yourself.' But between generations there should not be talk of death. Of the dead, yes, of dying, yes, of your death, no. Tabu, Harriet told herself, disgusted at her whole speech. Edward however seemed pleased or intrigued; he brooded over it a while. Then he said, 'Another thing about Elinor, this girl at the lab, she likes kids. I always think of Andy.'

'Andy's got me, Edward, he'll survive, for mercy's sake. Nobody's asking you to marry a nursemaid! God forbid!'

He looked relieved, but slowly, through the mists of weariness and whiskey, she perceived that Elinor had turned up again.

'When I said you'd find that you couldn't withdraw, couldn't disengage yourself, disconnect yourself, you know, I was warning you. You're in a very vulnerable position. You could get caught. I don't want to see you caught.' As you were by Mary, she thought; for she believed her daughter had married less for love than self-assertion, even envy. She knew in Mary, under the dark soft vivacity and Italian grace, the hard destructive strain from her side, the fecklessness, the pointless yen that brought them all in the end to the County of Malheur. She had never been able to weep much for Mary, she had never been able to judge her, yet it was very bitter to think, as she had thought before, that Mary's early death might prove a fortunate thing for the man who loved her.

'You spoil me, Harriet,' said the young man, gravely considering.

'Of course I do. But I don't spoil your son. I discriminate between incorruptibility and mere innocence.' She gave a short laugh of pleasure at her own multisyllables. 'I'm getting verbose, I'm going to bed. Good night.'

'Good night,' he answered reluctantly as she went to the stairs, so reluctantly he almost held her back. As if he need worry about 'reconnecting.' He had never, even in the worst of his pain, withdrawn himself, ceased to give to those who needed him. What he had left, the baby and the old woman, he loved with perfect generosity. And there was no denying that

the three of them got on pretty happily. At least I'm a good stopgap, she thought with pride.

Since her husband's death four years ago she had not slept well at night. Half the dark hours she waked and read, and was up often before the baby started chirping. So she remembered her mother in old age, in the silent kitchen lit by a kerosene lamp, looking in silence out the window at the huge sky paling above the sagebrush plain. But this night Harriet slept at once, falling into a night-long trap of dreams. They kept coming and telling her that someone was dead, but would not tell her exactly who, or whether he was dying now or dead already; only once, in a summerhouse she had not known was in her garden, she found him lying huddled on the floor, one long arm thrown out, but that was only the empty sleeve of a grey suit. She ran away in terror into an older nightmare, fifty years older, of the blind thing that hunted her over the desert. At last sunlight broke down the walls and horizons of the dreams and woke her, yet it did not illuminate her fear. She denied that her anxiety had been for Edward, but she was rather grim with him at breakfast. All morning she housecleaned, making the baby play by himself, trying to work off that fear before her conscience made her accept it as a rational one.

The baby could not be indefinitely resisted. He was two. He looked like a little chimpanzee; the physical beauty of his parents, mixed, had got lost. His disposition was thoughtful and experimental. 'Hat, Hat, Hat,' he cried, staggering into the kitchen. 'Mulk! Mulk!' – 'Not till lunchtime,' Harriet told him. He smiled, gazing up with wise eyes like a chimpanzee. 'Mulk? Cacky? Appa?' – 'Nothing till lunch, you greedy-gut,' the grandmother said sternly. 'Hat, Hat!' said the baby, madly embracing her leg.

He was a loving child, a very fine child. That afternoon she dropped housework and took him down the hill to the park, the rose garden full of the last roses, lemon-yellow, peach-yellow, gold, bronze, crimson, following him as he trotted and shouted

513

along the paths between the thorny, fragrant bushes in the autumn sun.

Edward Meyer sat in his parked car looking across the lights of Berkeley and across the black, diamond-shackled bay to the Golden Gate, faint fragile center of the great sweep of lights and darknesses. Eucalyptus rustled over the car in a dry wind from the north, the winter wind. He stretched. 'Damn,' he said.

'Why?' said the woman beside him.

'What's in it for you?'

'All I want.'

'Sorry,' he muttered, and took her hands. When they touched they both quieted. Her grace was silence. He drank stillness from her as water from a spring. The dark dry wind of January blew, city after city flared below them round the bridge-strung bay.

He lit a cigarette; Elinor murmured, 'Not fair.' She had recently given up smoking for the fifth or sixth time. She was a woman not very sure of things, biddable and quiet, taking what came. Edward handed her the lighted cigarette. She took it with a small sigh and smoked it.

'This is the right idea,' he said.

'For now.'

'But why stop halfway?'

'We're not stopping. Only waiting.'

'Waiting for what? Till my psyche's patched up, or you're sure I'm not on the rebound, or something. Meanwhile we make love in my car because you've got a roommate and I've got a mother-in-law and we don't go to motels because we're supposed to be waiting – only we don't. The whole thing's illogical.'

At this she suddenly gave a hard, dry sob. His nervous anger turned to alarm, but she drew away from him, refusing comfort. She had never refused him anything before. He tried to apologise, to explain. She said, 'Please take me home,' and all down the steep streets from Grizzly Peak to South Berkeley

she sat silent, a silence turned against him, a defense. She was out of the car before he had it fully stopped in front of her rooming house; she whispered 'Good night' and was gone. He sat in the car, blank, anxious, foolish. He started the engine, and with the noise of it his anger rose. When he got home ten minutes later he was very angry. Harriet, looking up from her book by the fireside, seemed startled. 'Well!' she said. 'Well,' he said.

'Excuse me,' said Harriet, 'I'm finishing a chapter.'

He sat down, stretched out his legs, stared at the fire. He was bitterly angry at Elinor's weak obstinacy, her irresolute, indecisive, temporising ways. There sat Harriet, thank God, like a rock, like an oak, finishing her chapter. If the house fell down in an earthquake around Harriet she would fix a bed for the baby, light a fire, and finish her chapter. No wonder Elinor hadn't married before this, there was nothing to her, she had no character. He sat there full of self-vindicating anger and warm with the perfect sexual satisfaction she had given him, ready for more anger, more passion, more fulfilment, and for the first time in two years happy. Harriet finished her chapter. 'Nightcap?' he said.

'No, I'm going to bed.' She stood up, erect, short, solid; he looked at her with admiration. 'You look grand,' he said.

'Pooh,' she said, 'whatever have you been up to? Good night, my dear.'

She had a cold. She usually got a cold in April. It went into her chest so that she rumbled like a truck and ached and coughed; at last she got on the phone and asked old Joan to come out and look after Andy. When Edward got home and looked surprised, she snapped, 'I'm not up to running after the child today.' Then she went back to bed and lay cursing herself for having complained. One must never complain to men. Women at least knew complaint for what it was, part of coping, but he would interpret it, he would take it to mean that the full-time care of a child was too much to ask of a woman of sixty-two;

and then nothing she said or did would matter; he would have the idea in his head. And the child would be taken from her. Gradually or all at once she would lose him, the son she had always missed and to whom she was a wiser mother than she had been to her own two girls. The little monkey-face, the song at morning, the shirts to iron, the small automobiles and journals of chemistry left lying about, the presence by night and day of the son, of the man, of the man of the house gone, gone, all of it gone.

When he came in she did not turn her face to him. She lay grim, aching in the marrow of her bones.

'Well,' he said, 'Andy's spilled his milk and thrown his egg on the floor. Hear him yelling for Hat?' There were, in fact, loud, theatrical cries from below. 'If you don't recover in a day or two we'll have to send him to reform school.'

'I intend to recover tomorrow,' she said, still grim, but lying easier. His kindness was exact: it hit the spot, carelessly it seemed, and healed.

'I detest being sick,' she said after a while.

'I know. You aren't very good at it. Look here, I asked those people in Friday night, I'll put them off a week.'

'Nonsense, I'll be up day after tomorrow. Is your friend the checkers player coming?'

Edward laughed 'Yes. He wants to be pulverised again.' She had heard the young Philadelphian boast that he had never lost a game of checkers since he was fifteen, had taken him on and beat him six games running.

'I am a vengeful old woman, Edward,' she said, lying moveless, her short grey hair disordered.

'He doesn't care – he's trying to figure out your game.'

'I don't like boasting.' That was Malheur County that spoke in her, the frontier without hope, the end of pushing on. 'We're all fools enough without adding that,' she said, unyielding, desolate.

'How about a drink before dinner?'

'Yes, I'd like a whiskey in hot water. But no dinner, I can't eat

with a cold. Bring me a hot toddy, and *Dombey and Son*, would you? I was just starting it.'

'How many times have you read it?'

'Why, I don't know. Every few years since I was twenty. And put that poor baby to bed, Edward, he isn't used to Joan.'

'She scares me too,' he said.

'Well she might; you won't get round her with charm and persuasion. I have an understanding with her,' she went on, driven by a sudden will she did not stop to understand, 'that when you and Andy move out she'll move in with me, if it still suits her. She isn't doing any regular cleaning any more, and her husband's dead and her son's in the Marines. And we've always got on.'

He stood silent, taken off guard. She looked up at him, the tall figure that dominated all the house, vulnerable and kingly, the young man.

'Don't look so stricken,' she said with mild irony, 'can't I provide ahead for the winter? Now do go get my whiskey, Edward, my throat's like sandpaper.'

To leave him free, that was her job. And she was good at her job. That had been her fault as a mother of daughters, she did not know if a girl should be left free or not, and so had vacillated; Rose had come out a bit weak, and Mary spoilt. But with a boy there was no question, he must have courage, and so needed freedom. Perhaps what a girl must have was patience, but she was not sure; in any case she was herself too impatient – not for pleasure and possession, like Mary, but for completion, for the end of things: unhopeful, and impatient.

She enjoyed her night and day in bed, entertained by Dickens, rain on the window, Joan in the kitchen singing long dreadful Methodist hymns. She rose much refreshed on Thursday, washed and ironed all the bedroom curtains, and weeded the iris beds in the fresh wind of April while the baby investigated all the possibilities of fresh wet dirt, and discovered the earthworm. On Friday night Edward's friends came: two married couples, Tom the checkers expert, whom she beat

twice and once inadvertently let win, and a little fair woman called Elinor. Elinor, what had she heard, a while ago, about an Elinor? She was pleasant to look at anyhow, with thick fair hair and a face as quiet as a pool of water. She was looking at Edward. Water in sunlight. O radiance, incredible brightness of the true sun, incredible heights.

'I'm never as good playing the red,' Harriet said, an ungraceful loser. 'But I'll leave you holding the field, Mr Harris.' And young Tom Harris, appalled at having beaten her, apologised in his Eastern voice till she had to laugh. He so plainly thought her a wonderful old woman, a daughter of the pioneers, if she told him she learned checkers from Chief Joseph he would probably believe it. But all the time her heart's eye was on Elinor.

No beauty. Timid, often defeated, getting on for thirty. Oh, yes, but patient; a patient woman: owning that passionate, intelligent patience that will wait, wait ten years, not for a lucky break but for the known, foreknown, fulfilment. One of the fortunate ones, who know that there is a point. It takes luck too, Harriet cried inwardly: you might have waited all your life, and let it all go by! – But this one was like Edward, one of the fortunate. They did not push on, they were not restless. They took what came, and when they spoke they were answered. They had seen the high peaks, and tragedy served them. Edward had met his match.

Harriet did not go upstairs before she had chatted a while with Elinor. Each felt the other's earnest effort to show goodwill, to offer true friendliness; neither could quite accept; yet liking arose. Harriet went upstairs at ten feeling pleased with herself. In her dressing gown she crossed her room to look at the photograph of her husband, a vivid dark face, John Avanti at thirty, when she had first known him. Her heart rose as always to meet the challenge of him. He had changed her utterly, he lived therefore in her; she spoke to him. Well, John, I push on, she said, not aloud. She got into bed, finished *Dombey*,

listened to the soft cheerful sound of voices downstairs, and fell asleep.

She woke in the grey light before sunrise and knew what she had lost. They would go now, within a year or so, the child and the man; all grace, all danger, all fulfilment leaving her, as John dying had not left her, alone. She need not be impatient any longer. Even that wore out in the end. She had done right, she had done her job. But there was no point to it for her. All she would need from now on was endurance. She was back down to bedrock, she had come in the end where all her people came. She sat up in bed, grey-haired in the grey light and wept aloud.

THE WATER IS WIDE

'You here?'

'To see you.'

After a while he said, 'Where's here?' He was lying flat, so could not have much in view but ceiling and the top third of Anna; in any case his eyes looked unfocussed.

'Hospital.'

Another pause. He said something like, 'Is it me that's here?' The words were slurred. He added clearly enough. 'It's not you. You look all right.'

'I am. You're here. And I'm here. To see you.'

This made him smile. The smile of an adult lying flat on his back resembles the smile of an infant, in that gravity works with it, not against it.

'Can I be told,' he said, 'or will the knowledge kill me?'

'If knowledge could kill you, you'd have been dead for years.'

'Am I sick?'

'Do you feel well?'

He turned his head away, the first bodily movement he had made. 'I feel ill.' The words were slurred. 'Full of drugs, some kind drugs.' The head moved again, restless. 'Don't like it,' he said. He looked straight at her now. 'I don't feel well,' he said. 'Anna, I'm cold. I feel cold.' Tears filled the eyes and ran down from them into the greying hair. This happens in cases of human suffering, when the sufferer is lying face up and is middle-aged.

Anna said his name and took his hand. Her hand was

somewhat smaller than his, several degrees warmer, and very similar in structure and texture; even the shape of the nails was similar. She held his hand. He held her hand. After some time his hand began to relax.

'Kind drugs,' he said. The eyes were shut now.

He spoke once more; he said either 'Wait,' or 'Weight.' Anna answered the first, saying, 'I will.' Then she thought he had spoken of a weight that lay upon him. She could see the weight in the way he breathed, asleep.

'It's the drugs,' she said, 'he's asked every time if you could stop giving him the drugs. Could you decrease the dose?'

The doctor said 'Chemotherapy,' and other words, some of which were the names of drugs, ending in zil and ine.

'He says that he can't sleep, but he can't wake up either. I think he needs to sleep. And to wake up.'

The doctor said many other words. He said them in so rapid, distinct, and fluent a manner, and with such assurance, that Anna believed them all for at least three hours.

'Is this a loony bin?' Gideon inquired with perfect clarity.

'Mhm.' Anna knitted.

'Thought wards.'

'Oh, it's all private rooms here. It's a nice private sort of place. Rest home. Polite. Expensive.'

'Senile, incont... incontinent. Can't talk. Anna.'

'Mhm?'

'Stroke?'

'No, no.' She put her knitting down on her knee. 'You got overtired.'

'Tumor?'

'No. You're sound as a bell. Only a little cracked. You got tired. You acted funny.'

'What'd I do?' he asked, his eyes brightening.

'Made an awful fool of yourself.'

'Did?'

'Well, you washed all the blackboards. At the Institute. With soap and water.'

'That all?'

'You said it was time to start all over. You made the Dean fetch the soap and buckets.' They both jolted softly with laughter at the same time. 'Never mind the rest. You had them all quite busy, believe me.'

They all understood now that his much publicised New Year's Day letter to the *Times*, which he had defended with uncharacteristic vehemence, had been a symptom. This was a relief to many people, who had uncomfortably been thinking of the letter as a moral statement. Looking back, everyone at the Institute could now see that Gideon had not been himself for some months. Indeed the change could be traced back three years, to the death of his wife Dorothea of leukemia. He had borne his loss well, of course, but had he not remained somewhat withdrawn – increasingly withdrawn? Only no one had noticed it, because he had been so busy. He had ceased to take vacations at the family cabin up at the lake, and had done a good deal of public speaking in connection with the peace organisation of which he was co-chairman. He had been working much too hard. It was all clear now. Unfortunately it had not become clear until the evening in April when he began a public lecture on the Question of Ethics in Science by gazing at the audience in silence for 35 seconds (approx.: one of the mathematical philosophers present in the audience had begun to time the silence at the point when it became painful, though not yet unendurable), and then, in a slow, soft, rough voice which no one who heard it could forget, announced, 'The quantification of Death is now the major problem facing theoretical physicists in the latter half of the Western Hemisphere.' He had then closed his mouth and stood gazing at them.

Hansen, who had introduced his talk and sat on the speakers' platform, was a large man and a quick-witted one. He had without much trouble induced Gideon to come backstage with

him, to one of the seminar rooms. It was there that Gideon had insisted that they wash all the blackboards perfectly clean. He had not become violent, though his behavior had been what Hansen termed 'extraordinarily wilful.' Later on, in private, Hansen wondered whether Gideon's behavior had not always been wilful, in that it had always been self-directed, and whether he should not have used, instead, the word 'irrational.' That would have been the expectable word. But its expectability led him to wonder if Gideon's behavior (as a theoretical physicist) had ever been rational; and, in fact, if his own behavior (as a theoretical physicist, or otherwise) had ever been adequately describable by the term 'rational.' He said nothing, however, of these speculations, and worked very hard for several weekends at building a rock garden at the side of his house.

Though he offered no violence to others or himself, Gideon had attempted escape. At a certain moment he appeared to understand suddenly that medical aid had been summoned. He acted with decision. He told the Dean, Dr Hansen, Dr Mehta, and the student Mr Chew, all of whom were with him (several other members of the audience or of the Institute were busy keeping busybodies and reporters out), 'You finish the blackboards in here, I'll do Room 40,' and taking up a bucket and a sponge went rapidly across the hall into a vacant classroom, where Chew and Hansen, following him at once, prevented him from opening a window. The room was on the ground floor, and his intention was made clear by his saying, 'Let me get out, please, help me get out.' Chew and Hansen were compelled to restrain his arms by force. He struggled briefly to free himself; failing, he became silent and apparently thoughtful. Shortly before the medical personnel arrived he suggested in a low voice to Chew, 'If we sat down on the floor here they might not see us.' When the medical personnel entered the room and came close to him he said loudly, 'All right, have it your way,' and at once began to yell wordlessly, or scream. The graduate student Chew, a brilliant young biophysicist who had not had much experience of human suffering, let go of his arm and broke into tears. The

medical personnel, having had perhaps excessive experience of human suffering, promptly administered a quick-acting sedative or tranquilliser by hypodermic. Within 35 seconds (approx.) the patient fell silent and became tractable, accepting the straitjacket without resistance, and with only a slight expression (facial, not verbal) of bewilderment, or, possibly, curiosity.

'I have to get out of here.'

'Oh, Gid, not yet, you need to rest. It's a decent place. They've eased up on the drugs. I can see the difference.'

'I have to get out, Anna.'

'You're not well yet.'

'I am not a patient. I am impatient. Help me get out. Please.'

'Why, Gid? What for?'

'They won't let me go where I have to go.'

'Where do you have to go?'

'Mad.'

Dear Lin,

They continue to let me visit Gideon every afternoon from five to six, because I am his only relative, the widower's widowed sister, and I just sort of barge in. I don't think the doctor approves of my visits, I think he thinks I leave the patient disturbed, but he hasn't the authority to keep me out, I guess, until Gideon is committed. I guess he doesn't really have any authority, in a private rest home like this, but he makes me feel guilty. I never did understand when to obey people. He is supposed to be the best man here for nervous breakdowns. He has been disapproving lately and says Gideon is deteriorating, ceasing to respond, but all he gives him to respond to is drugs. What is he supposed to say to them? He hasn't eaten for four days. He responds to me, when nobody else is there, or anyhow he talks, and I respond. He asked me about you kids yesterday. I told him about Kate's divorce. It made him sad. 'Everybody is divorcing everybody else,' he said. I was sad, too, and I said,

'Well, we didn't. You and Dorothea, me and Louis. Death us did part. Which is preferable, I wonder?' He said, 'It comes out much the same. Fission, fusion. The human race is one great Nuclear Family.' I wondered if the doctor would think that's the way an insane person talks. Maybe he would think that's the way two insane people talk.

Later on Gideon told me what the weight is. It is all the people who are dying. A lot of them are children, little, hollow, empty children. Some of them are old people, very light, hollow, old men and women. They don't weigh much separately, but there are so many of them. The old people lie across his legs. The children are in a great heap on his chest, across his breastbone. It makes it hard for him to breathe.

Today he only asked me to help him get out and go where he has to go. When he speaks of that he cries. I always hated for him to cry when we were children, it made me cry, too, even when I was thirteen or fourteen. He only cried for real griefs. The doctor says that what he has is an acute depression, and it should be cured with chemicals. But Gideon is not depressed. I think what he has is grief. Why can't he be allowed to grieve? Would it destroy the rest of us, his grief? It's the people who don't grieve who are destroying us, it seems to me.

'Here's your clothes. You'll have to get up and get dressed, Gideon. If you want to come away with me. I didn't get permission. I just can't get through to that doctor, he wants to cure you. If you want to go, you'll have to get up and walk.'

'Shall I take up my bed?'

'Don't be silly.'

'Bible.'

'For God's sake don't go religious now. If you do I'll bring you right back here. Hurry up. Here's your pants.'

'Please get off me just for a minute,' he said to the dying children and old men and women.

'Oof, how thin you are. Let me button that. All right. Can

you manage? Hang on. No! hang onto me. You haven't been eating, you're dizzy.'

'Dizzy Giddy.'

'Do shut up! Try to look ordinary.'

'We are ordinary.'

They walked out of the room and down the hall arm in arm, an ordinary middle-aged couple. They walked past the old woman in the wheelchair nursing her doll, and past the room of the young man who stared. They walked past the receptionist's desk. Anna smiled and said in a peculiar voice at the receptionist, 'Going out for a walk in the garden.' The receptionist smiled and said, 'Lovely weather.' They walked out onto the brick front path of the rest home, and down it, between lawns, to the iron gate. They walked through the gate and turned left. Anna's car was parked halfway down the block, under elm trees.

'Oh, oh, if I have a heart attack it's all your fault. Wait. I'm so shaky I can't get the key in. You all right?'

'Sure. Where are we going?'

'To the lake.'

'He went out with his sister, doctor. For a walk. About half an hour ago.'

'A walk, my God,' the doctor said. 'Where to?'

I am Anna. I am Gideon. I am Gideanna. I am sister's brother, brother's sister. I am Gideon who am dying, but it is your death I die, not mine. I am Anna who am not mad, but I am your brother, who is mad. Take my hand, brother, from the dark! Reich' mir das Hand, mein Leben, komm' in mein Schloss mit mir. O, but that castle I do not want to enter, brother mine; that is the castle I do not want to enter. It has a dark tower. Who do you think I am, Childe Roland? A Roland to your Oliver? No, look, we know this place, this is the old place, where we were children. Let's dance here, on the lakeshore, by the water. You be the tower, I will be the lake. You will dance in me reflected,

I will be full of you, of the wave-broken shimmering stones. Lie lightly on me, tower, brother, see, if you lie lightly we are one. But we have always been one, sisterbrother. We have always danced alone. I am Gideon who dances in your soul, and I am dying. I can't dance any longer. I am borne down, borne down, borne down. I cannot lie, I cannot dance. All the reflections are dissolved. I cannot dance. I cannot breathe. They lie on me, they lie in me. How can the starving be so heavy, Anna?

Gideon, is it our fault? It can't be your fault. You never harmed a living soul.

But I am the fault you know. The fault in my soul and yours, the fault itself. The line on which the ground moves. So the earthquake comes, and the people die, the little puzzled children, and the young men with guns, and the women pausing shopping bag in hand in the dissolving supermarket, and the old people who crouch down and reach out with wrinkled fingers to the faltering earth. I have betrayed them all. I did not give them enough food to eat.

How could you have? You're not God!

Oh yes I am. We are.

We are?

Yes, we are. Indeed we are. If I weren't God how should I be dying now? God is what dies. God is bereavement. We all die for each other.

If I am God I am the Woman-God, and I shall be reborn. Out of my own body I shall bear my birth.

Surely you will, but only if I die; and I am you. Or do you deny me, at the grave's edge, after fifty years?

No, no, no. I don't deny you, though I've often wanted to. But that's not a grave's edge, my young darkness, my terror, my little brother soul. It's only a lakeshore, see?

There is no other shore.

There must be.

No; all seas have one shore only. How could they have more?

Well, there's only one way to find out.

*

I'm cold. It's cold, the water's cold.

Look: there they are. So many of them, so many. The children float because they're hollow, swollen up with air. The older people swim, for a while. Look how that old man holds a clod of earth in his hand, the piece of the world he held to when the earthquake came. A little island, not quite big enough. Look how she holds her baby up above the water. I must help her, I must go to her!

If I touch one, they will take hold of me. They will clutch me with the grip of the drowning and drag me down with them. I'm not that good a swimmer. If I touch them, I'll drown.

Look there, I know that face. Isn't that Hansen? He's holding onto a rock, poor soul, a plank would serve him better.

There's Kate. There's Kate's ex-husband. And there's Lin. Lin's a good swimmer, always was, I'm not worried about Lin. But Kate's in trouble. She needs help. Kate! Don't wear yourself out, honey, don't kick so hard. The water's very wide. Save your strength, swim slowly, sweetheart, Kate my child!

There's young Chew. And look there, there's the doctor, in right over his head. And the receptionist. And the old woman with the doll. But there are so many more, so many. If I reach out my hand to one, a hundred will reach for it, a thousand, a thousand million, and pull me down and drown me. I can't save one child, one single child. I can't save myself.

Then let it be so. Take my hand, child! stranger in the darkness, in the deep waters, take my hand. Swim with me, while we can. Let us be drowned together, for it's certain we shall not be saved alone.

It's silent, out here in the deep waters. I can't see the faces any more.

Dorothea, there's someone following us. Don't look back.

I'm not Lot's wife, Louis, I'm Gideon's wife. I can look back, and still not turn to salt. Besides, my blood was never salt enough. It's you who shouldn't look back.

Do you take me for Orpheus? I was a good pianist, but not that good. But I admit, it scares me to look back. I don't really want to.

I just did. There's two of them. A woman and a man.

I was afraid of that.

Do you think it's them?

Who else would follow us?

Yes, it's them, our husband and our wife. Go back! Go back! This is no place for you!

This is the place for everyone, Dorothea.

Yes, but not yet, not yet. O Gideon, go back! He doesn't hear me. I can't speak clearly any more. Louis, you call to them.

Go back! Don't follow us! They can't hear us, Dorothea. Look how they come, as if the sand were water. Don't they know there's no water here?

I don't know what they know, Louis. I have forgotten. Gideon, O Gideon, take my hand!

Anna, take my hand!

Can they hear us? Can they touch us?

I don't know. I have forgotten.

It's cold, I'm cold. It's too deep, too far to go. I have reached out my hand, and reached out my hand into the darkness, but I couldn't tell what good it did; if I held up some child for a while, or if some shadow hand reached back to me, I don't know. I can't tell the way. Back on the dry land they were right. They told me not to grieve. They told me not to look. They told me to forget. They told me eat my lunch and take my pills that end in zil and ine. And they were right. They told me to be quiet, not to shout, not to cry out aloud. Be quiet now, be good. And they were right. What's the good in shouting? What's the good in shouting Help me, help, I'm drowning! when all the rest of them are drowning too? I heard them crying Help me, help me, please. But now I hear nothing. I hear the sound of the deep waters only. O take my hand, my love, I'm cold, cold, cold.

The water is wide, I cannot get over,
And neither have I wings to fly.
Give me a boat that will carry two,
And both shall row, my love and I.

There is, oh, there is another shore! Look at the light the light of morning on the rocks, the light on the shores of morning. I am light. The weight's gone. I am light.

But it is the same shore, Gideanna.

Then we have come home. We rowed all night in darkness, in the cold, and we came home: the home where we have never been before, the home we never left. Take my hand, and step ashore with me, my sister life, my brother death. Look: it is the beginning place. Here we begin, here by the flood that parts us.

SOUTH

THE WIFE'S STORY

He was a good husband, a good father. I don't understand it.
I don't believe in it. I don't believe that it happened. I saw it
happen but it isn't true. It can't be. He was always gentle. If
you'd have seen him playing with the children, anybody who
saw him with the children would have known that there wasn't
any bad in him, not one mean bone. When I first met him he
was still living with his mother, over near Spring Lake, and I
used to see them together, the mother and the sons, and think
that any young fellow that was that nice with his family must be
one worth knowing. Then one time when I was walking in the
woods I met him by himself coming back from a hunting trip.
He hadn't got any game at all, not so much as a field mouse,
but he wasn't cast down about it. He was just larking along
enjoying the morning air. That's one of the things I first loved
about him. He didn't take things hard, he didn't grouch and
whine when things didn't go his way. So we got to talking that
day. And I guess things moved right along after that because
pretty soon he was over here pretty near all the time. And my
sister said – see, my parents had moved out the year before
and gone south, leaving us the place – my sister said, kind of
teasing but serious, 'Well! If he's going to be here every day
and half the night, I guess there isn't room for me!' And she
moved out – just down the way. We've always been real close,
her and me. That's the sort of thing doesn't ever change. I
couldn't ever have got through this bad time without my sis.

Well, so he come to live here. And all I can say is, it was the

happy year of my life. He was just purely good to me. A hard worker and never lazy, and so big and fine-looking. Everybody looked up to him, you know, young as he was. Lodge Meeting nights, more and more often they had him to lead the singing. He had such a beautiful voice, and he'd lead off strong, and the others following and joining in, high voices and low. It brings the shivers on me now to think of it, hearing it, nights when I'd stayed home from meeting when the children was babies – the singing coming up through the trees there, and the moonlight, summer nights, the full moon shining. I'll never hear anything so beautiful. I'll never know a joy like that again.

It was the moon, that's what they say. It's the moon's fault and the blood. It was in his father's blood. I never knew his father, and now I wonder what become of him. He was from up Whitewater way, and had no kin around here. I always thought he went back there, but now I don't know. There was some talk about him, tales, that come out after what happened to my husband. It's something runs in the blood, they say, and it may never come out, but if it does, it's the change of the moon that does it. Always it happens in the dark of the moon. When everybody's home and asleep. Something comes over the one that's got the curse in his blood, they say, and he gets up because he can't sleep, and goes out into the glaring sun, and goes off all alone – drawn to find those like him.

And it may be so, because my husband would do that. I'd half rouse and say, 'Where you going to?' and he'd say, 'Oh, hunting, be back this evening,' and it wasn't like him, even his voice was different. But I'd be so sleepy, and not wanting to wake the kids, and he was so good and responsible, it was no call of mine to go asking 'Why?' and 'Where?' and all like that.

So it happened that way maybe three times or four. He'd come back late, and worn out, and pretty near cross for one so sweet-tempered – not wanting to talk about it. I figured everybody got to bust out now and then, and nagging never helped anything. But it did begin to worry me. Not so much that he went, but that he come back so tired and strange. Even,

he smelled strange. It made my hair stand up on end. I could not endure it and I said, 'What is that – those smells on you? All over you!' And he said, 'I don't know,' real short, and made like he was sleeping. But he went down when he thought I wasn't noticing, and washed and washed himself. But those smells stayed in his hair, and in our bed, for days.

And then the awful thing. I don't find it easy to tell about this. I want to cry when I have to bring it to my mind. Our youngest, the little one, my baby, she turned from her father. Just overnight. He come in and she got scared-looking, stiff, with her eyes wide, and then she begun to cry and try to hide behind me. She didn't yet talk plain but she was saying over and over, 'Make it go away! Make it go away!'

The look in his eyes, just for one moment, when he heard that. That's what I don't want ever to remember. That's what I can't forget. The look in his eyes looking at his own child.

I said to the child, 'Shame on you, what's got into you!' – scolding, but keeping her right up close to me at the same time, because I was frightened too. Frightened to shaking.

He looked away then and said something like, 'Guess she just waked up dreaming,' and passed it off that way. Or tried to. And so did I. And I got real mad with my baby when she kept on acting crazy scared of her own dad. But she couldn't help it and I couldn't change it.

He kept away that whole day. Because he knew, I guess. It was just beginning dark of the moon.

It was hot and close inside, and dark, and we'd all been asleep some while, when something woke me up. He wasn't there beside me. I heard a little stir in the passage, when I listened. So I got up, because I could bear it no longer. I went out into the passage, and it was light there, hard sunlight coming in from the door. And I saw him standing just outside, in the tall grass by the entrance. His head was hanging. Presently he sat down, like he felt weary, and looked down at his feet. I held still, inside, and watched – I didn't know what for.

And I saw what he saw. I saw the changing. In his feet, it

was, first. They got long, each foot got longer, stretching out the toes stretching out and the foot getting long, and fleshy, and white. And no hair on them.

The hair begun to come away all over his body. It was like his hair fried away in the sunlight and was gone. He was white all over, then, like a worm's skin. And he turned his face. It was changing while I looked. It got flatter and flatter, the mouth flat and wide, and the teeth grinning flat and dull, and the nose just a knob of flesh with nostril holes, and the ears gone, and the eyes gone blue – blue, with white rims around the blue – staring at me out of that flat soft, white face.

He stood up then on two legs.

I saw him, I had to see him, my own dear love, turned into the hateful one.

I couldn't move, but as I crouched there in the passage staring out into the day I was trembling and shaking with a growl that burst out into a crazy, awful howling. A grief howl and a terror howl and a calling howl. And the others heard it, even sleeping, and woke up.

It stared and peered, that thing my husband had turned into, and shoved its face up to the entrance of our house. I was still bound by mortal fear, but behind me the children had waked up, and the baby was whimpering. The mother anger come into me then, and I snarled and crept forward.

The man thing looked around. It had no gun, like the ones from the man places do. But it picked up a heavy fallen tree branch in its long white foot, and shoved the end of that down into our house, at me. I snapped the end of it in my teeth and started to force my way out, because I knew the man would kill our children if it could. But my sister was already coming. I saw her running at the man with her head low and her mane high and her eyes yellow as the winter sun. It turned on her and raised up that branch to hit her. But I come out of the doorway, mad with the mother anger, and the others all were coming answering my call, the whole pack gathering, there in that blind glare and heat of the sun at noon.

The man looked round at us and yelled out loud, and brandished the branch it held. Then it broke and ran, heading for the cleared fields and plowlands, down the mountainside. It ran, on two legs, leaping and weaving, and we followed it.

I was last, because love still bound the anger and the fear in me. I was running when I saw them pull it down. My sister's teeth were in its throat. I got there and it was dead. The others were drawing back from the kill, because of the taste of the blood, and the smell. The younger ones were cowering and some crying, and my sister rubbed her mouth against her forelegs over and over to get rid of the taste. I went up close because I thought if the thing was dead the spell, the curse must be done, and my husband could come back – alive, or even dead, if I could only see him, my true love, in his true form, beautiful. But only the dead man lay there white and bloody. We drew back and back from it, and turned and ran, back up into the hills, back to the woods of the shadows and the twilight and the blessed dark.

SOME APPROACHES TO THE PROBLEM
OF THE SHORTAGE OF TIME

THE LITTLE TINY HOLE THEORY

The hypothesis put forward by James Osbold of the Lick
Observatory, though magnificently comprehensive, presents
certain difficulties to agencies seeking practical solutions to
the problem. Divested of its mathematical formulation, Dr
Osbold's theory may be described in very approximate terms
as positing the existence of an anomaly in the space-time con-
tinuum. The cause of the anomaly is a failure of reality to meet
the specifications of the General Theory of Relativity, although
only in one minor detail. Its effect on the actual constitution
of the universe is a local imperfection or flaw, that is, a hole
in the continuum.

The hole, according to Osbold's calculations, is a distinctly
spacelike hole. In this spatiality lies its danger, since the imbal-
ance thus constituted in the continuum causes a compensatory
influx from the timelike aspect of the cosmos. In other words,
time is running out of the hole. This has probably been going
on ever since the origin of the universe 12 to 15 billion years
ago, but only lately has the leak grown to noticeable propor-
tions.

The propounder of the theory is not pessimistic, remarking
that it might be even worse if the anomaly were in the time-
like aspect of the continuum, in which case space would be
escaping, possibly one dimension at a time, which would cause
untold discomfort and confusion; although, Osbold adds, 'In

that event we might have time enough to do something about it.'

Since the theory posits the hole's location somewhere or other, Lick and two Australian observatories have arranged a coordinated search for local variations in the red shift which might aid in pinpointing the point/instant. 'It may still be a very small hole,' Osbold says. 'Quite tiny. It would not need to be very large to do a good deal of damage. But since the effect is so noticeable here on Earth, I feel we have a good chance of finding the thing perhaps no farther away than the Andromeda Galaxy, and then all we'll need is what you might call a Dutch boy.'

THE NONBIODEGRADABLE MOMENT

A totally different explanation of the time shortage is offered by a research team of the Interco Development Corporation. Their approach to the problem, as presented by N. T. Chaudhuri, an internationally recognised authority on the ecology and ethology of the internal combustion engine, is chemical rather than cosmological. Chaudhuri has proved that the fumes of incompletely burned petroleum fuel, under certain conditions – diffused anxiety is the major predisposing factor – will form a chemical bond with time, 'tying down' instants in the same manner as a nucleating agent 'ties down' free atoms into molecules. The process is called chronocrystallisation or (in the case of acute anxiety) chronoprecipitation. The resulting compact arrangement of instants is far more orderly than the pre-existent random 'nowness,' but unfortunately this decrease in entropy is paid for by a very marked increase in bioinsupportability. In fact the petroleum/time compound appears to be absolutely incompatible with life in any form, even anaerobic bacteria, of which so much was hoped.

The present danger, then, as described by team member F. Gonzales Park, is that so much of our free time, or radical time

properly speaking, will be locked into this noxious compound (which she refers to as petropsychotoxin or PPST) that we will be forced to bring up the vast deposits of PPST which the US Government has dumped or stored in various caves, swamps, holes, oceans, and backyards, and deliberately break down the compound, thus releasing free temporal radicals. Senator Helms and several Sunbelt Democrats have already protested. Certainly the process of reclaiming time from PPST is risky, requiring so much oxygen that we might end up, as O. Heiko, a third member of the team, puts it, with plenty of free time but no air.

Feeling that time is running out even faster than the oil wells, Heiko himself favors an 'austerity' approach to the problem, beginning with a ban on aircraft flying in excess of the speed of sound, and working steadily on down through prop planes, racing cars, standard cars, ships, motorboats, etc, until, if necessary, all petroleum-powered vehicles have been eliminated. Speed serves as the standard of priority, since the higher the velocity of the petroleum-fueled vehicle, and hence the more concentrated the conscious or subliminal anxiety of the driver/passengers, the more complete is the petrolisation of time, and the more poisonous the resultant PPST. Heiko, believing there is no 'safe level' of contamination, thinks that probably not even mopeds would eventually escape the ban. As he points out, a single gas-powered lawn-mower moving at less than 3 mph can petrolise three solid hours of a Sunday afternoon in an area of one city block.

A ban on gas guzzlers may, however, solve only half the problem. An attempt by the Islamic League to raise the price of crude time by $8.50/hr was recently foiled by prompt action by the Organisation of Time Consuming States; but West Germany is already paying $18.75/hr – twice what the American consumer expects to pay for his time.

BLEEDING HEARTS?
THE TEMPORAL CONSERVATION
MOVEMENT

Willing to listen to the cosmological and chemical hypotheses but uncommitted to either is a growing consortium of scientists and laypersons, many of whom have grouped themselves into organisations such as Le Temps Perdu (Brussels), Protestants Concerned at the Waste of Time (Indianapolis), and the driving, widespread Latin-American action group Mañana. A Mañanista spokesperson, Dolores Guzman McIntosh of Buenos Aires, states the group's view: 'We have – all of us – almost entirely wasted our time. If we do not save it, we are lost. There is not much time left.' The Mañanistas have so far carefully avoided political affiliation, stating bluntly that the time shortfall is the fault of Communist and Capitalist governments equally. A growing number of priests from Mexico to Chile have joined the movement, but the Vatican recently issued an official denunciation of those 'who, while they talk of saving time, lose their own souls.' In Italy a Communist temporal-conservation group, Eppur Si Muove, was recently splintered by the defection of its president, who after a visit to Moscow stated in print: 'Having watched the bureaucracy of the Soviet Union in action I have lost faith in the arousal of class consciousness as the principal means towards our goal.'

A group of social scientists in Cambridge, England, continues meanwhile to investigate the as yet unproven link of the time shortage with shortage of temper. 'If we could show the connection,' says psychologist Derrick Groat, 'the temporal conservation groups might be able to act more effectively. As it is they mostly quarrel. Everybody wants to save time before it's gone forever, but nobody really knows how, and so we all get cross. If only there were a substitute, you know, like solar and geothermal for petroleum, it would ease the strain. But evidently we have to make do with what we've got.' Groat mentioned the 'time stretcher' marketed by General Substances

under the trademark Sudokron, withdrawn last year after tests indicated that moderate doses caused laboratory mice to turn into Kleenex. Informed that the Rand Corporation was devoting massive funding to research into a substitute for time, he said, 'I wish them luck. But they may have to work longer hours at it!' The British scientist was referring to the fact that the United States has shortened the hour by ten minutes while retaining twenty-four per day, while the EEC countries, foreseeing increasing short ages, have chosen to keep sixty minutes to the hour but allow only twenty hours to the 'devalued' European day.

Meantime, the average citizen in Moscow or Chicago, while often complaining about the shortage of time or the deteriorating quality of what remains, seems inclined to scoff at the doomsday prophets, and to put off such extreme measures as rationing as long as possible. Perhaps he feels, along with Ecclesiastes and the President, that when you've seen one day, you've seen 'em all.

SUR

A SUMMARY REPORT OF THE *YELCHO* EXPEDITION
TO THE ANTARCTIC, 1909–1910

Although I have no intention of publishing this report, I think
it would be nice if a grandchild of mine, or somebody's grand-
child, happened to find it some day; so I shall keep it in the
leather trunk in the attic, along with Rosita's christening dress
and Juanito's silver rattle and my wedding shoes and finneskos.

The first requisite for mounting an expedition – money – is
normally the hardest to come by. I grieve that even in a report
destined for a trunk in the attic of a house in a very quiet
suburb of Lima I dare not write the name of the generous
benefactor, the great soul without whose unstinting liberality
the *Yelcho* Expedition would never have been more than the
idlest excursion into daydream. That our equipment was the
best and most modern – that our provisions were plentiful and
fine – that a ship of the Chilean Government, with her brave
officers and gallant crew, was twice sent halfway round the
world for our convenience: all this is due to that benefactor
whose name, alas! I must not say, but whose happiest debtor I
shall be till death.

When I was little more than a child my imagination was
caught by a newspaper account of the voyage of the *Belgica*,
which, sailing south from Tierra del Fuego, became beset by ice
in the Bellingshausen Sea and drifted a whole year with the floe,
the men aboard her suffering a great deal from want of food

The following text labels appear on the map:

The Ross Sea

King Edward VII Land

Ross Island
McMurdo Sound
Mts. Erebus & Terror

South Victoria Land

Orca Bay
South South America?

Garcilaso
Quipote
The Great Ice Barrier
Miranda
Ercilla
Concolorcorvo
THE GATEWAY
Mt. Bolívar's Big Nose
Mt. Whose Toe?
Roncador-Nesta-Gate Glacier

The Pampas

?

N W E S

90°

The Map in the Attic

and from the terror of the unending winter darkness. I read and reread that account and later followed with excitement the reports of the rescue of Dr Nordenskjold from the South Shetland Isles by the dashing Captain Irizar of the *Uruguay*, and the adventures of the *Scotia* in the Weddell Sea. But all these exploits were to me but forerunners of the British National Antarctic Expedition of 1902–1904, in the *Discovery*, and the wonderful account of that expedition by Captain Scott. This book, which I ordered from London and reread a thousand times, filled me with longing to see with my own eyes that strange continent, last Thule of the South, which lies on our maps and globes like a white cloud, a void, fringed here and there with scraps of coastline, dubious capes, supposititious islands, headlands that may or may not be there: Antarctica. And the desire was as pure as the polar snows: to go, to see – no more, no less. I deeply respect the scientific accomplishments of Captain Scott's expedition, and have read with passionate interest the findings of physicists, meteorologists, biologists, etc; but having had no training in any science, nor any opportunity for such training, my ignorance obliged me to forego any thought of adding to the body of scientific knowledge concerning Antarctica; and the same is true for all the members of my expedition. It seems a pity; but there was nothing we could do about it. Our goal was limited to observation and exploration. We hoped to go a little farther, perhaps, and see a little more; if not, simply to go and to see. A simple ambition, I think, and essentially a modest one.

Yet it would have remained less than an ambition, no more than a longing, but for the support and encouragement of my dear cousin and friend Juana ———— ————. (I use no surnames, lest this report fall into strangers' hands at last, and embarrassment or unpleasant notoriety thus be brought upon unsuspecting husbands, sons, etc) I had lent Juana my copy of *The Voyage of the Discovery*, and it was she who, as we strolled beneath our parasols across the Plaza de Armas after Mass

one Sunday in 1908, said, 'Well, if Captain Scott can do it, why can't we?'

It was Juana who proposed that we write Carlota ———— in Valparaiso. Through Carlota we met our benefactor, and so obtained our money, our ship, and even the plausible pretext of going on retreat in a Bolivian convent, which some of us were forced to employ (while the rest of us said we were going to Paris for the winter season). And it was my Juana who in the darkest moments remained resolute, unshaken in her determination to achieve our goal.

And there were dark moments, especially in the early months of 1909 – times when I did not see how the Expedition would ever become more than a quarter ton of pemmican gone to waste and a lifelong regret. It was so very hard to gather our expeditionary force together! So few of those we asked even knew what we were talking about – so many thought we were mad, or wicked, or both! And of those few who shared our folly, still fewer were able, when it came to the point, to leave their daily duties and commit themselves to a voyage of at least six months, attended with not inconsiderable uncertainty and danger. An ailing parent; an anxious husband beset by business cares; a child at home with only ignorant or incompetent servants to look after it: these are not responsibilities lightly to be set aside. And those who wished to evade such claims were not the companions we wanted in hard work, risk, and privation.

But since success crowned our efforts, why dwell on the setbacks and delays, or the wretched contrivances and downright lies that we all had to employ? I look back with regret only to those friends who wished to come with us but could not, by any contrivance, get free – those we had to leave behind to a life without danger, without uncertainty, without hope.

On the seventeenth of August, 1909, in Punta Arenas, Chile, all the members of the Expedition met for the first time: Juana and I, the two Peruvians; from Argentina, Zoe, Berta, and Teresa; and our Chileans, Carlota and her friends Eva, Pepita, and Dolores. At the last moment I had received

word that Maria's husband, in Quito, was ill, and she must stay to nurse him, so we were nine, not ten. Indeed, we had resigned ourselves to being but eight, when, just as night fell, the indomitable Zoe arrived in a tiny pirogue manned by Indians, her yacht having sprung a leak just as it entered the Strait of Magellan.

That night before we sailed we began to get to know one another; and we agreed, as we enjoyed our abominable supper in the abominable seaport inn of Punta Arenas, that if a situation arose of such urgent danger that one voice must be obeyed without present question, the unenviable honor of speaking with that voice should fall first upon myself: if I were incapacitated, upon Carlota: if she, then upon Berta. We three were then toasted as 'Supreme Inca,' 'La Araucana,' and 'The Third Mate,' among a lot of laughter and cheering. As it came out, to my very great pleasure and relief, my qualities as a 'leader' were never tested; the nine of us worked things out amongst us from beginning to end without any orders being given by anybody, and only two or three times with recourse to a vote by voice or show of hands. To be sure, we argued a good deal. But then, we had time to argue. And one way or another the arguments always ended up in a decision, upon which action could be taken. Usually at least one person grumbled about the decision, sometimes bitterly. But what is life without grumbling, and the occasional opportunity to say, 'I told you so'? How could one bear housework, or looking after babies, let alone the rigors of sledge-hauling in Antarctica, without grumbling? Officers – as we came to understand aboard the *Yelcho* – are forbidden to grumble; but we nine were, and are, by birth and upbringing, unequivocally and irrevocably, all crew.

Though our shortest course to the southern continent, and that originally urged upon us by the captain of our good ship, was to the South Shetlands and the Bellingshausen Sea, or else by the South Orkneys into the Weddell Sea, we planned to sail west to the Ross Sea, which Captain Scott had explored and described, and from which the brave Ernest Shackleton had

returned only the previous autumn. More was known about this region than any other portion of the coast of Antarctica, and though that more was not much, yet it served as some insurance of the safety of the ship, which we felt we had no right to imperil. Captain Pardo had fully agreed with us after studying the charts and our planned itinerary, and so it was westward that we took our course out of the Strait next morning.

Our journey half round the globe was attended by fortune. The little *Yelcho* steamed cheerily along through gale and gleam, climbing up and down those seas of the Southern Ocean that run unbroken round the world. Juana, who had fought bulls and the far more dangerous cows on her family's *estancia*, called the ship '*la vaca valiente*,' because she always returned to the charge. Once we got over being seasick we all enjoyed the sea voyage, though oppressed at times by the kindly but officious protectiveness of the captain and his officers, who felt that we were only 'safe' when huddled up in the three tiny cabins which they had chivalrously vacated for our use.

We saw our first iceberg much farther south than we had looked for it, and saluted it with Veuve Clicquot at dinner. The next day we entered the ice pack, the belt of floes and bergs, broken loose from the land ice and winter-frozen seas of Antarctica, which drifts northward in the spring. Fortune still smiled on us: our little steamer, incapable, with her unreinforced metal hull, of forcing a way into the ice, picked her way from lane to lane without hesitation, and on the third day we were through the pack, in which ships have sometimes struggled for weeks and been obliged to turn back at last. Ahead of us now lay the dark grey waters of the Ross Sea, and beyond that, on the horizon, the remote glimmer, the cloud-reflected whiteness of the Great Ice Barrier.

Entering the Ross Sea a little east of Longitude West 160°, we came in sight of the Barrier at the place where Captain Scott's party, finding a bight in the vast wall of ice, had gone ashore and sent up their hydrogen-gas balloon for reconnaissance and photography. The towering face of the Barrier, its

548

sheer cliffs and azure and violet water-worn caves, all were as described, but the location had changed: instead of a narrow bight there was a considerable bay, full of the beautiful and terrific orca whales playing and spouting in the sunshine of that brilliant southern spring.

Evidently masses of ice many acres in extent had broken away from the Barrier (which – at least for most of its vast extent – does not rest on land but floats on water) since the *Discovery*'s passage in 1902. This put our plan to set up camp on the Barrier itself in a new light; and while we were discussing alternatives, we asked Captain Pardo to take the ship west along the Barrier face towards Ross Island and McMurdo Sound. As the sea was clear of ice and quite calm, he was happy to do so, and, when we sighted the smoke plume of Mount Erebus, to share in our celebration – another half case of Veuve Clicquot.

The *Yelcho* anchored in Arrival Bay, and we went ashore in the ship's boat. I cannot describe my emotions when I set foot on the earth, on that earth, the barren, cold gravel at the foot of the long volcanic slope. I felt elation, impatience, gratitude, awe, familiarity. I felt that I was home at last. Eight Adélie penguins immediately came to greet us with many exclamations of interest not unmixed with disapproval. 'Where on earth have you been? What took you so long? The Hut is around this way. Please come this way. Mind the rocks!' They insisted on our going to visit Hut Point, where the large structure built by Captain Scott's party stood, looking just as in the photographs and drawings that illustrate his book. The area about it, however, was disgusting – a kind of graveyard of seal skins, seal bones, penguin bones, and rubbish, presided over by the mad, screaming skua gulls. Our escorts waddled past the slaughterhouse in all tranquillity, and one showed me personally to the door, though it would not go in.

The interior of the hut was less offensive, but very dreary. Boxes of supplies had been stacked up into a kind of room within the room; it did not look as I had imagined it when the *Discovery* party put on their melodramas and minstrel shows in

the long winter night. (Much later, we learned that Sir Ernest had rearranged it a good deal when he was there just a year before us.) It was dirty, and had about it a mean disorder. A pound tin of tea was standing open. Empty meat tins lay about; biscuits were spilled on the floor; a lot of dog turds were underfoot – frozen, of course, but not a great deal improved by that. No doubt the last occupants had had to leave in a hurry, perhaps even in a blizzard. All the same, they could have closed the tea tin. But housekeeping, the art of the infinite, is no game for amateurs.

Teresa proposed that we use the hut as our camp. Zoe counterproposed that we set fire to it. We finally shut the door and left it as we had found it. The penguins appeared to approve, and cheered us all the way to the boat.

McMurdo Sound was free of ice, and Captain Pardo now proposed to take us off Ross Island and across to Victoria Land, where we might camp at the foot of the Western Mountains, on dry and solid earth. But those mountains, with their storm-darkened peaks and hanging cirques and glaciers, looked as awful as Captain Scott had found them on his western journey, and none of us felt much inclined to seek shelter among them.

Aboard the ship that night we decided to go back and set up our base as we had originally planned, on the Barrier itself. For all available reports indicated that the clear way south was across the level Barrier surface until one could ascend one of the confluent glaciers to the high plateau which appears to form the whole interior of the continent. Captain Pardo argued strongly against this plan, asking what would become of us if the Barrier 'calved' – if our particular acre of ice broke away and started to drift northward. 'Well,' said Zoe, 'then you won't have to come so far to meet us.' But he was so persuasive on this theme that he persuaded himself into leaving one of the *Yelcho*'s boats with us when we camped, as a means of escape. We found it useful for fishing, later on.

My first steps on Antarctic soil, my only visit to Ross Island,

had not been pleasure unalloyed. I thought of the words of the English poet:

> Though every prospect pleases,
> And only Man is vile.

But then, the backside of heroism is often rather sad; women and servants know that. They know also that the heroism may be no less real for that. But achievement is smaller than men think. What is large is the sky, the earth, the sea, the soul. I looked back as the ship sailed east again that evening. We were well into September now, with ten hours or more of daylight. The spring sunset lingered on the twelve-thousand-foot peak of Erebus and shone rosy gold on her long plume of steam. The steam from our own small funnel faded blue on the twilit water as we crept along under the towering pale wall of ice.

On our return to 'Orca Bay' – Sir Ernest, we learned years later, had named it the Bay of Whales – we found a sheltered nook where the Barrier edge was low enough to provide fairly easy access from the ship. The *Yelcho* put out her ice anchor, and the next long, hard days were spent in unloading our supplies and setting up our camp on the ice, a half kilometer in from the edge: a task in which the *Yelcho*'s crew lent us invaluable aid and interminable advice. We took all the aid gratefully, and most of the advice with salt.

The weather so far had been extraordinarily mild for spring in this latitude; the temperature had not yet gone below –20° Fahrenheit, and there was only one blizzard while we were setting up camp. But Captain Scott had spoken feelingly of the bitter south winds on the Barrier, and we had planned accordingly. Exposed as our camp was to every wind, we built no rigid structures above ground. We set up tents to shelter in while we dug out a series of cubicles in the ice itself, lined them with hay insulation and pine boarding, and roofed them with canvas over bamboo poles, covered with snow for weight and insulation. The big central room was instantly named Buenos

Aires by our Argentineans, to whom the center, wherever one is, is always Buenos Aires. The heating and cooking stove was in Buenos Aires. The storage tunnels and the privy (called Punta Arenas) got some back heat from the stove. The sleeping cubicles opened off Buenos Aires, and were very small, mere tubes into which one crawled feet first; they were lined deeply with hay and soon warmed by one's body warmth. The sailors called them 'coffins' and 'wormholes,' and looked with horror on our burrows in the ice. But our little warren or prairie-dog village served us well, permitting us as much warmth and privacy as one could reasonably expect under the circumstances. If the *Yelcho* was unable to get through the ice in February, and we had to spend the winter in Antarctica, we certainly could do so, though on very limited rations. For this coming summer, our base – Sudamérica del Sur, South South America, but we generally called it the Base – was intended merely as a place to sleep, to store our provisions, and to give shelter from blizzards.

To Berta and Eva, however, it was more than that. They were its chief architect-designers, its most ingenious builder-excavators, and its most diligent and contented occupants, forever inventing an improvement in ventilation, or learning how to make skylights, or revealing to us a new addition to our suite of rooms, dug in the living ice. It was thanks to them that our stores were stowed so handily, that our stove drew and heated so efficiently, and that Buenos Aires, where nine people cooked, ate, worked, conversed, argued, grumbled, painted, played the guitar and banjo, and kept the Expedition's library of books and maps, was a marvel of comfort and convenience. We lived there in real amity; and if you simply had to be alone for a while, you crawled into your sleeping hole head first.

Berta went a little farther. When she had done all she could to make South South America livable, she dug out one more cell just under the ice surface, leaving a nearly transparent sheet of ice like a greenhouse roof; and there, alone, she worked at sculptures. They were beautiful forms, some like a blending of the reclining human figure with the subtle curves and volumes

of the Weddell seal, others like the fantastic shapes of ice cornices and ice caves. Perhaps they are there still, under the snow, in the bubble in the Great Barrier. There where she made them they might last as long as stone. But she could not bring them north. That is the penalty for carving in water.

Captain Pardo was reluctant to leave us, but his orders did not permit him to hang about the Ross Sea indefinitely, and so at last, with many earnest injunctions to us to stay put – make no journeys – take no risks – beware of frostbite – don't use edge tools – look out for cracks in the ice – and a heartfelt promise to return to Orca Bay on the twentieth of February, or as near that date as wind and ice would permit, the good man bade us farewell, and his crew shouted us a great goodbye cheer as they weighed anchor. That evening, in the long orange twilight of October, we saw the topmast of the *Yelcho* go down the north horizon, over the edge of the world, leaving us to ice, and silence, and the Pole.

That night we began to plan the Southern Journey.

The ensuing month passed in short practice trips and depot-laying. The life we had led at home, though in its own way strenuous, had not fitted any of us for the kind of strain met with in sledge-hauling at ten or twenty degrees below freezing. We all needed as much working-out as possible before we dared undertake a long haul.

My longest exploratory trip, made with Dolores and Carlota, was southwest towards Mount Markham, and it was a nightmare – blizzards and pressure ice all the way out, crevasses and no view of the mountains when we got there, and white weather and sastrugi all the way back. The trip was useful, however, in that we could begin to estimate our capacities; and also in that we had started out with a very heavy load of provisions, which we depoted at 100 and 130 miles SSW of Base. Thereafter other parties pushed on farther, till we had a line of snow cairns and depots right down to Latitude 83° 43′, where Juana and Zoe, on an exploring trip, had found a kind of stone gateway opening on a great glacier leading

south. We established these depots to avoid, if possible, the hunger that had bedevilled Captain Scott's Southern Party, and the consequent misery and weakness. And we also established to our own satisfaction – intense satisfaction – that we were sledgehaulers at least as good as Captain Scott's husky dogs. Of course we could not have expected to pull as much or as fast as his men. That we did so was because we were favored by much better weather than Captain Scott's party ever met on the Barrier; and also the quantity and quality of our food made a very considerable difference. I am sure that the fifteen percent of dried fruits in our pemmican helped prevent scurvy; and the potatoes, frozen and dried according to an ancient Andean Indian method, were very nourishing yet very light and compact – perfect sledging rations. In any case, it was with considerable confidence in our capacities that we made ready at last for the Southern Journey.

The Southern Party consisted of two sledge teams: Juana, Dolores, and myself; Carlota, Pepita, and Zoe. The support team of Berta, Eva, and Teresa set out before us with a heavy load of supplies, going right up onto the glacier to prospect routes and leave depots of supplies for our return journey. We followed five days behind them, and met them returning between Depot Ercilla and Depot Miranda (see map). That 'night' – of course there was no real darkness – we were all nine together in the heart of the level plain of ice. It was the fifteenth of November, Dolores's birthday. We celebrated by putting eight ounces of pisco in the hot chocolate, and became very merry. We sang. It is strange now to remember how thin our voices sounded in that great silence. It was overcast, white weather, without shadows and without visible horizon or any feature to break the level; there was nothing to see at all. We had come to that white place on the map, that void, and there we flew and sang like sparrows.

After sleep and a good breakfast the Base Party continued north, and the Southern Party sledged on. The sky cleared presently. High up, thin clouds passed over very rapidly from

southwest to northeast, but down on the Barrier it was calm and just cold enough, five or ten degrees below freezing, to give a firm surface for hauling.

On the level ice we never pulled less than eleven miles, seventeen kilometers, a day, and generally fifteen or sixteen miles, twenty-five kilometers. (Our instruments, being British made, were calibrated in feet, miles, degrees Fahrenheit, etc, but we often converted miles to kilometers because the larger numbers sounded more encouraging.) At the time we left South America, we knew only that Mr Shackleton had mounted another expedition to the Antarctic in 1908, had tried to attain the Pole but failed, and had returned to England in June of the current year, 1909. No coherent report of his explorations had yet reached South America when we left; we did not know what route he had gone, or how far he had got. But we were not altogether taken by surprise when, far across the featureless white plain, tiny beneath the mountain peaks and the strange silent flight of the rainbow-fringed cloud wisps, we saw a fluttering dot of black. We turned west from our course to visit it: a snow heap nearly buried by the winter's storms – a flag on a bamboo pole, a mere shred of threadbare cloth – an empty oilcan – and a few footprints standing some inches above the ice. In some conditions of weather the snow compressed under one's weight remains when the surrounding soft snow melts or is scoured away by the wind; and so these reversed footprints had been left standing all these months, like rows of cobbler's lasts – a queer sight.

We met no other such traces on our way. In general I believe our course was somewhat east of Mr Shackleton's. Juana, our surveyor, had trained herself well and was faithful and methodical in her sightings and readings, but our equipment was minimal – a theodolite on tripod legs, a sextant with artificial horizon, two compasses, and chronometers. We had only the wheel meter on the sledge to give distance actually travelled.

In any case, it was the day after passing Mr Shackleton's waymark that I first saw clearly the great glacier among the

mountains to the southwest, which was to give us a pathway from the sea level of the Barrier up to the altiplano, ten thousand feet above. The approach was magnificent: a gateway formed by immense vertical domes and pillars of rock. Zoe and Juana had called the vast ice river that flowed through that gateway the Florence Nightingale Glacier, wishing to honor the British, who had been the inspiration and guide of our expedition; that very brave and very peculiar lady seemed to represent so much that is best, and strangest, in the island race. On maps, of course, this glacier bears the name Mr Shackleton gave it, the Beardmore.

The ascent of the Nightingale was not easy. The way was open at first, and well marked by our support party, but after some days we came among terrible crevasses, a maze of hidden cracks, from a foot to thirty feet wide and from thirty to a thousand feet deep. Step by step we went, and step by step, and the way always upward now. We were fifteen days on the glacier. At first the weather was hot, up to 20° F., and the hot nights without darkness were wretchedly uncomfortable in our small tents. And all of us suffered more or less from snowblindness just at the time when we wanted clear eyesight to pick our way among the ridges and crevasses of the tortured ice, and to see the wonders about and before us. For at every day's advance more great, nameless peaks came into view in the west and southwest, summit beyond summit, range beyond range, stark rock and snow in the unending noon.

We gave names to these peaks, not very seriously, since we did not expect our discoveries to come to the attention of geographers. Zoe had a gift for naming, and it is thanks to her that certain sketch maps in various suburban South American attics bear such curious features as 'Bolívar's Big Nose,' 'I Am General Rosas,' 'The Cloudmaker,' 'Whose Toe?' and 'Throne of Our Lady of the Southern Cross.' And when at last we got up onto the altiplano, the great interior plateau, it was Zoe who called it the pampa, and maintained that we walked there among vast herds of invisible cattle, transparent cattle pastured

on the spindrift snow, their gauchos the restless, merciless winds. We were by then all a little crazy with exhaustion and the great altitude – twelve thousand feet – and the cold and the wind blowing and the luminous circles and crosses surrounding the suns, for often there were three or four suns in the sky, up there.

That is not a place where people have any business to be. We should have turned back; but since we had worked so hard to get there, it seemed that we should go on, at least for a while.

A blizzard came with very low temperatures, so we had to stay in the tents, in our sleeping bags, for thirty hours, a rest we all needed; though it was warmth we needed most, and there was no warmth on that terrible plain anywhere at all but in our veins. We huddled close together all that time. The ice we lay on is two miles thick.

It cleared suddenly and became, for the plateau, good weather: twelve below zero and the wind not very strong. We three crawled out of our tent and met the others crawling out of theirs. Carlota told us then that her group wished to turn back. Pepita had been feeling very ill; even after the rest during the blizzard, her temperature would not rise above 94°. Carlota was having trouble breathing. Zoe was perfectly fit, but much preferred staying with her friends and lending them a hand in difficulties to pushing on towards the Pole. So we put the four ounces of pisco which we had been keeping for Christmas into the breakfast cocoa, and dug out our tents, and loaded our sledges, and parted there in the white daylight on the bitter plain.

Our sledge was fairly light by now. We pulled on to the south. Juana calculated our position daily. On the twenty-second of December, 1909, we reached the South Pole. The weather was, as always, very cruel. Nothing of any kind marked the dreary whiteness. We discussed leaving some kind of mark or monument, a snow cairn, a tent pole and flag; but there seemed no particular reason to do so. Anything we could do, anything we were, was insignificant, in that awful place. We put up the tent for shelter for an hour and made a cup of tea, and then struck

'90° Camp.' Dolores, standing patient as ever in her sledging harness, looked at the snow; it was so hard frozen that it showed no trace of our footprints coming, and she said, 'Which way?'

'North,' said Juana.

It was a joke, because at that particular place there is no other direction. But we did not laugh. Our lips were cracked with frostbite and hurt too much to let us laugh. So we started back, and the wind at our backs pushed us along, and dulled the knife edges of the waves of frozen snow.

All that week the blizzard wind pursued us like a pack of mad dogs. I cannot describe it. I wished we had not gone to the Pole. I think I wish it even now. But I was glad even then that we had left no sign there, for some man longing to be first might come some day, and find it, and know then what a fool he had been, and break his heart.

We talked, when we could talk, of catching up to Cariota's party, since they might be going slower than we. In fact they had used their tent as a sail to catch the following wind and had got far ahead of us. But in many places they had built snow cairns or left some sign for us; once Zoe had written on the lee side of a ten-foot sastrugi, just as children write on the sand of the beach at Miraflores, 'This Way Out!' The wind blowing over the frozen ridge had left the words perfectly distinct.

In the very hour that we began to descend the glacier, the weather turned warmer, and the mad dogs were left to howl forever tethered to the Pole. The distance that had taken us fifteen days going up we covered in only eight days going down. But the good weather that had aided us descending the Nightingale became a curse down on the Barrier ice, where we had looked forward to a kind of royal progress from depot to depot, eating our fill and taking our time for the last three hundred-odd miles. In a tight place on the glacier I lost my goggles – I was swinging from my harness at the time in a crevasse – and then Juana had broken hers when we had to do some rock climbing coming down to the Gateway. After two days in bright sunlight with only one pair of snow goggles to pass amongst us, we

were all suffering badly from snowblindness. It became acutely painful to keep lookout for landmarks or depot flags, to take sightings, even to study the compass, which had to be laid down on the snow to steady the needle. At Concolorcorvo Depot, where there was a particularly good supply of food and fuel, we gave up, crawled into our sleeping bags with bandaged eyes, and slowly boiled alive like lobsters in the tent exposed to the relentless sun. The voices of Berta and Zoe were the sweetest sound I ever heard. A little concerned about us, they had skied south to meet us. They led us home to Base.

We recovered quite swiftly, but the altiplano left its mark. When she was very little, Rosita asked if a dog 'had bitted Mama's toes.' I told her Yes, a great, white, mad dog named Blizzard! My Rosita and my Juanito heard many stories when they were little, about that fearful dog and how it howled, and the transparent cattle of the invisible gauchos, and a river of ice eight thousand feet high called Nightingale, and how Cousin Juana drank a cup of tea standing on the bottom of the world under seven suns, and other fairy tales.

We were in for one severe shock when we reached Base at last. Teresa was pregnant. I must admit that my first response to the poor girl's big belly and sheepish look was anger – rage – fury. That one of us should have concealed anything, and such a thing, from the others! But Teresa had done nothing of the sort. Only those who had concealed from her what she most needed to know were to blame. Brought up by servants, with four years' schooling in a convent, and married at sixteen, the poor girl was still so ignorant at twenty years of age that she had thought it was 'the cold weather' that made her miss her periods. Even this was not entirely stupid, for all of us on the Southern Journey had seen our periods change or stop altogether as we experienced increasing cold, hunger, and fatigue. Teresa's appetite had begun to draw general attention; and then she had begun, as she said pathetically, 'to get fat.' The others were worried at the thought of all the sledge-hauling she had done, but she flourished, and the only problem was her

positively insatiable appetite. As well as could be determined from her shy references to her last night on the hacienda with her husband, the baby was due at just about the same time as the *Yelcho*, the twentieth of February. But we had not been back from the Southern Journey two weeks when, on February 14, she went into labor.

Several of us had borne children and had helped with deliveries, and anyhow most of what needs to be done is fairly self-evident; but a first labor can be long and trying, and we were all anxious, while Teresa was frightened out of her wits. She kept calling for her José till she was as hoarse as a skua. Zoe lost all patience at last and said, 'By God, Teresa, if you say "José!" once more I hope you have a penguin!' But what she had, after twenty long hours, was a pretty little red-faced girl.

Many were the suggestions for that child's name from her eight proud midwife-aunts: Polita, Penguina, McMurdo, Victoria ... But Teresa announced, after she had had a good sleep and a large serving of pemmican, 'I shall name her Rosa – Rosa del Sur,' Rose of the South. That night we drank the last two bottles of Veuve Clicquot (having finished the pisco at 88° 30′ South) in toasts to our little Rose.

On the nineteenth of February, a day early, my Juana came down into Buenos Aires in a hurry. 'The ship,' she said, 'the ship has come,' and she burst into tears – she who had never wept in all our weeks of pain and weariness on the long haul.

Of the return voyage there is nothing to tell. We came back safe.

In 1912 all the world learned that the brave Norwegian Amundsen had reached the South Pole; and then, much later, came the accounts of how Captain Scott and his men had come there after him, but did not come home again.

Just this year, Juana and I wrote to the captain of the *Yelcho*, for the newspapers have been full of the story of his gallant dash to rescue Sir Ernest Shackleton's men from Elephant Island, and we wished to congratulate him, and once more to

thank him. Never one word has he breathed of our secret. He is a man of honor, Luis Pardo.

I add this last note in 1929. Over the years we have lost touch with one another. It is very difficult for women to meet, when they live so far apart as we do. Since Juana died, I have seen none of my old sledge-mates, though sometimes we write. Our little Rosa del Sur died of the scarlet fever when she was five years old. Teresa had many other children. Carlota took the veil in Santiago ten years ago. We are old women now, with old husbands, and grown children, and grandchildren who might someday like to read about the Expedition. Even if they are rather ashamed of having such a crazy grandmother, they may enjoy sharing in the secret. But they must not let Mr Amundsen know! He would be terribly embarrassed and disappointed. There is no need for him or anyone else outside the family to know. We left no footprints, even.

Ursula K. Le Guin was born in 1929 into an academic household – her father was an eminent anthropologist while her mother was a writer. She herself obtained a Masters degree in Romance Literature following her undergraduate degree. Her first story was published in *Fantastic* magazine in 1962, and her first novel was *Rocannon's World* (1966), set in her Hainish universe. Her fourth novel, *The Left Hand of Darkness* (1969), was critically acclaimed and won both the Hugo and Nebula Awards for Best Novel. She repeated this feat with *The Dispossessed* (1974). The Earthsea series, which began with *A Wizard of Earthsea* (1968), has also attained undisputed classic status. Her recent series, the Annals of the Western Shore, has won her the PEN Center USA Children's literature award and the Nebula Award for best novel. In 2014 Ursula Le Guin was awarded the National Book Foundation Medal for Distinguished Contribution to American Letters. She passed away in 2018.

A full list of SF Masterworks can be found at

www.gollancz.co.uk